TREADWELL
A Novel Of Alaska Territory

Book One of the Gastineau Channel Quartet

Also by Leonard W. Compton
(Stoney Compton)

Novels:
Russian Amerika (Baen Books)
Alaska Republik (Baen Books)
Whalesong (Pullo Pup Publishing)
Level Six (Pullo Pup Publishing)

Short Works:
Whalesong *(UNIVERSE 1)*
Messages *(Writers of the Future, Vol. IX)*
When the Ship Came *(Tomorrow, Speculative Fiction, Vol 12)*
Trappers *(Jim Baen's Universe)*
Deliverance (Pullo Pup Publishing)
Diplomatic Exchange (Pullo Pup Publishing)

LEONARD WAYNE COMPTON

TREADWELL
A Novel of Alaska Territory

Book One of the
Gastineau Channel Quartet

PULLO PUP PUBLISHING

An imprint of Wicked Cherub Productions

This novel is dedicated with gratitude to the
Residents of Gastineau Channel,
Past, Present, and Future

TREADWELL
A Novel of Alaska Territory
Book One of the Gastineau Channel Quartet

Leonard Wayne Compton

Copyright © Leonard W. Compton, 2011
Pullo Pup Publishing, Corpus Christi, Texas

This book is a work of fiction. The characters, incidents, and dialogue are drawn from the author's imagination and are not to be construed as real. In the depiction of actual historic persons, any resemblance to actual events is entirely coincidental and the product of the author's imagination.

TREADWELL, A NOVEL OF ALASKA TERRITORY, Copyright 2011 by Leonard W. Compton, dba Pullo Pup Publishing/ Wicked Cherub Productions. All rights reserved. No part of this book may be used or reproduced in any manner whatsoever without written permission except in the case of brief quotations embodied in critical articles and reviews. For information contact: stoney@stoneycompton.com.

Photos used are through the courtesy, and are property of the Alaska State Library, Historical Collections, the University of Washington Library – Special Collections, the Library of Congress, and the University of Alaska Fairbanks Archives. Information and listings are included after the author's biography.

For more photos and information go to http://www.facebook.com/treadwell.novel

ISBN-10 098374744X
ISBN-13 9780983747444

For My Lovely
Daughter,
Sarah Maisie
on the Anniversary of her
Birth 2012
I have always been
Proud of You!
I love You
"Da"

Prologue—Durango, Mexico, October 23, 1915 —
Saturday afternoon

For five hours the train sat baking in the desert sun. Although every window in the first class coach yawned open, the interior lay heavy with suffocating heat and resentment. Baroness Amanda Ganbor rolled her head listlessly, silently praying for the train to move out of this furnace called Mexico.

She wouldn't speak of it to her husband. He would only respond that if not for her they wouldn't be in this situation. She ignored his truculent presence and peeked at the young swell sitting at the opposite end of the coach.

Three days earlier at Tampico, in the cool of the evening, they had boarded the train. The dark, intense man with a thin scar across his left cheek had moved out of the station shadows ahead of them. Rather than board the coach first, he stood to one side, clicked his heels and bowed with the finest court manners she had seen since leaving Austria.

She rewarded him with a wide smile while staring deep into his eyes. Missing nothing, he stared back at her unwaveringly. The potency of the moment nearly became electric and her groin responded with the stirring sensation preceding sexual desire.

At that point Georg pushed her up the steps into the coach. "You forget, my dear, that you are on honeymoon, yes?" As he herded her the entire length of the coach she silently disagreed with him.

Georg's snore brought her back to the prickly present and she glanced over at him. He remained the hulking, spoiled youth she had married two years ago. His mouth hung open child-like under the heavy mustache. Pimples peeked from the shadows beneath his sweat-stained collar, and body odor misted swamp-like about him.

Amanda wrinkled her nose in familiar disgust and silently berated herself. When she first met Georg Fredrich Ganbor at the Spanish court she had seen only the land, wealth, and title his ancient father possessed. All three would become Georg's upon the baron's death.

Her childhood of nannies, tutors, and continental travel had honed her for what came next. The daughter of a member of the British diplomatic corps, she had little but her youth and beauty to offer a young man of Austrian nobility. He hadn't been astute enough to note her lack of virginity.

Both families looked askance at the marriage. After a lifetime of service to the crown, her father felt openly antagonistic toward the Austrian nobility. Baron Ganbor believed his son was marrying far beneath himself.

Her father, however, had been prescient to the point of asking her not to forget her heritage. "You're British born, my dear. When gadding about with your new husband, keep your eyes and ears open for dangers to your homeland. Do write often."

When war broke out last summer, Amanda had been amazed at her father's vision. She hadn't seen all that much since then, but she did write regularly, delineating her observations. She never mentioned her convictions that her marriage was a mistake and being married to a nobleman not at all what girls believe.

Two Mexicans in cheap linen suits, one grossly fat and the other a spare splinter of a man, also boarded in Tampico. For a time she puzzled about the pair before deciding they were businessmen or investors. The fat one ate constantly from a lidded wicker basket large enough for a good-sized dog to sleep in, while the other pulled fistfuls of paper from a calfskin valise, shook them in front of his masticating companion and harangued him in a thin whine.

Her Spanish was adequate enough to discern accusations of misplaced funds and poor investments, but she soon tired of their conversation and lost all interest in them or their problems. The fat man now complained of thirst and she hated him for reminding her. Shortly after their arrival at Durango with the dawn, the heavy green water bottle had squatted empty.

The handsome swell had inquired of the conductor about water replenishment, but was answered with an elaborate shrug. At that point both conductor and engineer disappeared. Amanda could feel sweat running down her ribcage under the smart dress purchased in Paris.

Paris! My God, what on earth had possessed her to demand a trip to the American continent? All she had seen of Mexico was squalor, poverty, dust, and heat. The granular patina on her dress rebuked her as thoroughly and silently as Georg's scowls.

Voices rose and boot leather scraped across the wooden platform outside. Amanda turned her head to see the conductor and engineer arguing with three other men. She elbowed Georg to mute his snoring and listened intently.

Two of the men wore uniforms. The off-white uniform was unknown to her, but the other belonged to the Imperial German Hussars. *How curious,* she thought.

The third man evidently served as stationmaster; he continually held a large pocket watch up in one hand, pointed at it with his other hand and complained about the train being off its schedule.

"Pray tell what is going on out there?"

Amanda's eyes swung back to look at the handsome passenger. His head craned over his hands on the windowsill. His long coat swung open far enough for her to see the butt of a holstered pistol strapped to his side. His accent rang of pure Oxford.

While the others watched silently, the German officer walked purposefully over to the man's window and peered up at him.

"And who might you be?" the officer asked with excellent English.

"M' name's Williams. I'm a journalist. And you?"

Their voices carried easily in the heat. Georg snored quietly beside her.

"A journalist for whom?" the officer asked.

Williams answered in flawless high-German, "For a newspaper you aren't likely to read, my good *Hauptmann.*" Amanda's eyes rounded in surprise. "Now who are you?" he finished in English.

"*Hauptmann* Rolf Heintzmann, Imperial Hussars. Seconded to General Carranza by order of General Ludendorf," he replied in English, coming to momentary attention.

Amanda glanced back to the Mexican officer. He certainly didn't look like a general. But then Williams didn't look like a journalist, either. With his cleanly hooked nose and sharp jaw he looked more the aristocrat than her husband. She looked back in time to see the *Hauptmann* smile grimly.

"You certainly don't speak German with an English accent," he said.

"What's happening here? What's the delay?" Williams demanded.

"Colonel Rojas," Heintzmann indicated the corpulent Mexican in army brown, "has been ordered by General Carranza to guard the railroad with his troop of cavalry." He spat on the ground. "Three days ago the last train to pass through was ambushed north of here, at Abasolo, by Villistas."

The *Hauptmann* slapped dust from his trousers and glanced at Williams. "The engineer and conductor request the colonel to embark his troops on the train to protect it. The colonel feels he needs orders from the general, but the telegraph lines to the north are out. The station master just wants to get the train moving."

Pancho Villa & staff

"A problem worthy of your General Staff," Williams said with a smile. "What do you think, *Hauptmann* Heintzmann? Should the colonel go with the train or stay here?"

Heintzmann stared into the distance and pulled off his spiked field helmet with one hand, wiped his forehead with the other. After carefully replacing the helmet he looked up at the journalist.

"The colonel and his troop have been here for some weeks. Revolutionary fervor in this area is abating at an alarming rate. The people no longer feel it necessary to treat us in the manner to which we have become accustomed."

Amanda smiled for the first time in hours.

"I think the colonel should put his troops on the train and go find Carrenza."

Both men glanced over at the Mexicans. Colonel Rojas pulled his shoulders back half an inch, causing his great stomach to protrude even further.

"Is this man part of your legation?" Rojas asked in Spanish.

"What did he say? Williams asked.

Heintzmann told him.

Williams grinned widely. "Tell him, yes. Tell him I feel he should board his men and seek out, ah, who is it you're fighting with?"

"Pancho Villa."

"Ah, yes. He should go to where General Carranza was last reported in an attempt to seek further orders. Failing that, he should seek out Pancho Villa and kill him." Williams' smile grew even wider. "If he can, of course."

"He cannot," Heintzmann said. The *Hauptmann* turned and walked back over to the Mexicans, speaking quickly in heavily accented Spanish.

Amanda found herself staring at Williams admiringly. *Georg*, she reflected, *merely waits for events to unfold. This man makes them happen.*

As Williams pulled his head back into the coach his eyes found hers. Once again the visceral electricity all but crackled between them. She saw desire and need in those blue eyes. He nodded to her.

Heintzmann returned, spoke to Williams. "Colonel Rojas thanks you for your opinion and is pleased to agree with you. We will all ride together as far as Chihuahua. The train will leave as soon as everyone is loaded."

"Thank God!" Williams said, echoing Amanda's thoughts.

Heintzmann disappeared for a time and then reappeared at the coach door carrying saddlebags reeking of horse sweat. He hesitated near her and Georg for a moment while he ostensibly fastened a loose flap. She felt his eyes on her and after a moment she looked up to catch his gaze.

He was brown as a Spaniard, which she found enticing. Beneath the Kaiser Wilhelm mustache bright white teeth suddenly appeared in a smile. His eyes danced at her as he spoke in English.

"Good afternoon, Madam. I thank God for providing such a lovely traveling companion."

She felt the flush come into her cheeks, smiled and nodded.

"You are too kind, sir."

Georg jerked awake, shifted his holstered revolvers fussily and changed his position on the thinly padded bench, groaning slightly. *Hauptmann* Heintzmann gave her a small salute and walked down the aisle to where Williams sat watching.

"How do you do it?" Georg asked heavily. "In the middle of a desert you can draw men like bees to a budding rose."

"It's certainly not due to *your* aroma."

He glanced away from her, through the windows on the other side of the coach to where a long line of ragged soldiers pushed emaciated nags and dark-eyed women carried babies toward cattle cars farther back on the train. The soldiers were identifiable as such only by virtue of the long rifles and bandoleers they bore.

Amanda looked away, wondering at the animosity she felt for the man beside her.

Williams and Heintzmann chatted and laughed. It took all of her will power to stay seated and not join them. Georg scratched idly at his stomach and continued watching the human drama outside the coach.

Library of Congress — The Mexican Army

Prior to their marriage his father told him a woman was like a good horse—an occasional slap would bring improved performance. On their wedding night, while they disrobed, he told her to fetch his smoking jacket. She responded she was busy just then and would help him in a moment.

His slap knocked her to the floor and spots swam before her eyes. As she rose she pulled her Spanish stiletto from its garter sheath and went for his face. The thick oak door of the bedroom saved his life.

A chattering group of women paraded past, breaking her reverie. From their rouged cheeks, painted lips, and bright clothing, Amanda knew them for prostitutes. Their bobbing, tight bodices gave ample testimony to the lack of foundation garments in Mexico.

The conductor stopped them, saying they needed to buy tickets. A large woman with over-hennaed hair pushed into him with her bosom.

"You think these men would fight without us? We are part of the revolution also!" She marched past him and went into one of the cattle cars with the rest of her group close behind. A knot of soldiers applauded and whistled; the conductor found business elsewhere.

Two sweaty men brought in a full bottle of water and wrestled it onto the heavy stand at the other end of the coach. Instantly Amanda jumped to her feet and hurried toward it. Williams stood and blocked the two Mexican businessmen, allowing Amanda and Georg to surge past, before stepping into line behind them.

Amanda drank two full cups before wiping her mouth and wryly deciding she had never before truly appreciated water. While Georg slurped she moved slowly past Williams, and murmured "Thank you," while staring at him boldly.

She knew she was shamelessly flirting, but what was the difference? She would probably never see him again. He *was* a very handsome and exciting man.

Twilight purpled the distant mountains and the village lay bereft of livestock when the train finally built up steam and lurched out of the small station. Colonel Rojas and two junior officers joined the other first class passengers under the three swinging compartment lamps. The heat dissipated, making the trip almost pleasant.

"*¡Adios, Durango!*" Colonel Rojas cried, holding up a bottle of clear liquid. He offered it to Williams. "*¿Senor?*" Georg and Amanda watched avidly.

"No, thank you, Colonel," he demurred.

"*¿Capitan?*" Rojas swung the bottle toward Heintzmann, who accepted.

"How can you drink that swill?" Williams asked in German.

"When in Rome, Herr Williams," he said in the same language, taking a long pull. "Where are you bound?"

Amanda felt her ears prick up. Williams hesitated and she thought about her own destination—San Francisco.

After banning Georg from the bridal chamber, she told him the marriage was off. He must begin courting her all over again. He agreed, but insisted they go about it quietly as he didn't wish his family to know. She demanded the grand tour and he acquiesced. Two days later word reached them that his father had died in his sleep and Georg was now truly a baron.

Not until they reached Istanbul at the edge of Asia did she allow him to consummate the marriage, and only then because she was deliciously besotted on sweet wine and hashish. Someone told her of the lovely little city of San Francisco in the American state of California, and she demanded they see it.

Williams glanced at Heintzmann and still in German, said, "To the Alaska Territory of the United States." He drew a metal flask from his valise. "Perhaps now that you have choked down that local product, you might like a drink of honest German schnapps?"

As Amanda watched Heintzmann take the flask and stare at it in astonishment, Georg said, "There is more to that journalist than meets the eye."

She sniffed but said nothing. Eavesdropping proved more entertaining than talking to her husband. Williams said something to the captain. Heintzmann drank deeply.

"He speaks high German with a Hessian accent," Georg continued, "and he appears to have noble blood. Perhaps at the next stop I will reveal myself to him."

"I'm sure he will find that greatly amusing."

He winced at her words and she found herself once more in that maddening middle ground between sympathy and loathing. There were so many women who would have made this boor a perfect wife; why had he asked her? Georg was a perfect copy of Baron Ganbor, more the pity.

Georg lapsed into silence and she heard Heintzmann's next comment clearly.

"I would wager you are less English than you appear. Thank you for the schnapps."

Williams smiled.

Colonel Rojas drank from his own bottle at an incredible rate. The two junior officers, a few seats behind Williams and Heintzmann, begged and cajoled until he joined them with his mesçal.

Heintzmann took another pull from the flask and handed it back. "Alaska. Isn't that near the North Pole?"

Williams laughed. "Not the part where I am bound." He took a drink.

Amanda wanted to put her lips to the flask, wanted to sip liquor that still held his breath. *I must stop this,* she thought, *or I shall torture myself to death.* She turned her gaze out the window.

Outside the rocking coach stars winked in brittle flirtation from the surprisingly cold, clear sky. *No moon*, she thought, *that's why it's so dark.* The conductor came through and shut most of the windows.

Rojas and his two officers slumped in their seats, their snores rolling off into the night. Williams and Heintzmann talked in tones low enough not to be overheard. The steady clatter of bogies on track created a lulling effect.

A loud report shattered her sleep along with the windowpane two seats away from them, and she screamed in alarm. Suddenly a volley of shots rang out and window glass fragmented along the entire length of the car. Colonel Rojas jerked to his feet, a huge revolver in his hand, and screamed, "¿Villistas?"

"¿Quien sabe?" one of the officers yelled back. The three Mexicans milled about, peering out windows as bullets snapped around their heads.

Hauptmann Heintzmann rose to a crouch and Williams threw himself to the floor, pistol in hand. "Get down, Rolf, they can see you!" he screamed.

As Heintzmann turned to respond, the window beside him shattered and his forehead exploded in a spray of gore. "Oh, my God," Amanda said, looking away and fighting the automatic urge to vomit. She felt faint.

She'd seen sudden death once before in Turkey. Two men had fought a knife duel on the far side of the square from where she watched. But this!

Georg reached across her, smashed out the only remaining window glass, and fired into the night with one of the two revolvers he owned.

I laughed at him for bringing those, she thought dully. He shoved one into her hands. Outside she saw horses and riders in the flashes of light.

"Here!" he hissed. "You're good at destroying men; make yourself useful!" The light at the other end of the coach winked out. She looked up to see Williams coolly smash the middle lamp with one shot from his pistol. She identified it as a Lugar and wondered from where that bit of knowledge had surfaced.

Amanda's heart thumped in her chest. She bit back her fear, acutely aware that one of those pieces of lead from the darkness could hit her as easily as the German officer. The coach stank of gunpowder and blood. Shots continued in a steady rain, hammering into the side of the car. The remaining lamp swinging wildly over the aisle felt like a spot light on a stage.

An angry bee buzzed past her head and she shrank down in the seat, trying to disappear. More glass shattered and shards nicked her cheek in passage. Frightened tears rolled down her face.

Yells, punctuated by the crack of rifles, rose above the din. The train rattled on mechanically, oblivious to mere flesh and blood.

Colonel Rojas fired his revolver at the riders. The other two officers fired steadily. The small businessman squirmed under the seats. His fat companion huddled wide-eyed on the floor, jammed between the benches, sobbing audibly, his face slick with tears.

The sight of them put steel into Amanda and she pushed up to peek out the window again. Muzzle blasts from long rifles illuminated the hard-charging horsemen for montage instants, freezing them into Kodak-like images that burned into the retina before vanishing into the night.

When another muzzle flash bit at the car Amanda aimed at its center and pulled the trigger. The pistol bucked in her hands and she thought she heard a scream of pain. Gunfire poured from the cars farther back on the train, making her hopeful.

One of the Mexican officers jerked back from the window, gurgling something to his friend, then fell dead in the aisle. The racket of battle shredded the night as the train thundered along. On the other side of the wall at her back, loud thumps sounded from the coach platform.

Suddenly the door swung open and gunshots cut down Colonel Rojas and his remaining officer. Williams was nowhere to be seen. Dead, thought Amanda, and promptly forgot him. A bearded revolutionary, bandoleers draped around him like lethal boas, pushed into the coach, a pistol in each hand.

Amanda shuddered and sank into her seat again, hiding behind Georg. Georg twisted and shot him point blank. The man stumbled backward and fell on the bench across the aisle from them. A hand holding a revolver snaked around the doorframe and fired.

Georg jolted back against her, blood spurting from his chest, and then fell forward. Ice enveloped her. The owner of the hand stepped into the car and grinned down at her husband. The man's eyes traveled up and saw her, widening in surprise.

"*¿Una senorita?*" he said.

She bit her lip and shot him in the face. He recoiled back and bounced off something to fall in the aisle. The something became another revolutionary who stared down at his companion in shock, then up to her gun barrel pointed at his face.

Perfect acceptance shone in his eyes. He knew he was dead. Amanda pulled the trigger. The hammer snapped down on a spent cartridge.

"Funny," Amanda said, calmly looking at him, "I don't remember firing that many times."

Confusion washed over his face for an instant before resolving into anger. He brought his revolver up with a snarl and leveled it at her head. She wondered if it would hurt to die.

"*¡Hola, amigo!*" someone shouted.

The weapon swung as the man looked around. Williams shot him between the eyes with a three-round burst. The man collapsed in the doorway.

Amanda stared at this magical man, her savior, who appeared from nowhere. She swallowed, her ears popped and the racket crashed back in on her.

She glanced down and found a pile of cartridges nesting in her lap. *Georg's last gift*. She opened the revolver's cylinder, dumped the spent casings and began thumbing in fresh rounds.

As she snapped the cylinder back into place something caught her eye. A rider was next to the coach, reaching for the windowsill next to her. She shot him out of the saddle.

"My pleasure, madam," Williams said dryly from behind one of the seats.

She realized she hadn't thanked him and blushed. It occurred to her San Francisco was still a great distance away. She hadn't known she would have to fight her way there.

The shooting faltered, and then stopped. A blue haze of gun smoke eddied in the coach before venting through broken windows. Glass, wood splinters, blood, and bodies littered the floor and benches.

Amanda put her hand on Georg's back. He lay quite still and she knew he was dead. She looked up at Williams, standing in the aisle.

Part of her wondered if this man was now going to be part of her life while another part recoiled in horror over the death of Georg and the others. At least the killing had stopped.

Williams ejected a clip from his pistol and snapped another into the butt. His left eye had developed a tic. Something scraped behind him and he whirled, the pistol an extension of his brain, seeking the noise.

"¡Se-, senor!" the fat man blurted and held out flabby, pink hands, palms up.

"Wait!" came a muffled cry in German from under the seats. "He doesn't understand your language, but I do." The small man's head appeared as he pulled himself into the aisle.

Williams hesitated, his pistol still pointed toward the men.

What's wrong with him? Amanda wondered.

"That's a pity," Williams said in German. He shot the small man through the head.

The fat man's eyes bugged in terror. "¡*No, senor!*"

"I can't leave you as a witness, even if you don't speak German," he said in that language. "I don't know what he told you. I just can't take the chance." He fired twice and the Mexican screamed and thrashed for a horribly long moment before growing silent.

Amanda held her revolver in both hands, resting it on the seat back in front of her. She carefully aimed at the center of Williams' back. He turned around and faced her, his pistol pointing up slightly.

If he brought the muzzle down toward her, she decided, she would kill him.

He dropped the pistol into the holster. His trigger finger pointed at Georg.

"I'm sorry about your friend," he said in German.

"Pardon?" She frowned up at him, not allowing the gun barrel to waver from his chest.

He repeated the statement in English.

"Thank you. He was my husband." She felt hot tears pop from the edge of her eyes and shook her head angrily. "Why did you shoot those men?"

"Perhaps we should have a chat," he said easily. "My name is Williams. Arnold Williams."

"Certainly, Mr. Williams," she said with a tight smile. "Have a seat." She jerked the barrel to her right, and then centered it on his chest again. "Over there."

San Francisco was *so* far away!

"What might I call you?" He carefully sat down.

"We'll skip the formalities," she said, feeling light-headed. "Just call me Amanda. Why did you shoot those men?"

"Obviously you don't speak German." His deliberate gaze fastened on her face.

"No," she said, trying not to shake.

"They thought the attack was my doing. They said they would kill me."

Georg had been right. There was much more to this man than met the eye. He had a secret he would murder to hide.

She felt sure he would murder her to eliminate his only witness, unless he thought it worth his while to keep her alive. Her heartbeat slowed toward normal and she tried to sort out her feelings. She imagined riding a tiger might be like this, exhilarating but deadly.

As he waited for her response she balanced her fear and fascination for this man. Austria held nothing for her until the war stopped. She didn't wish to return to her father's house and waste away in widow's weeds.

He thought her interesting but would kill her to protect himself. She knew more about him than he did her. His stated destination lay far beyond San Francisco. She was now alone, destitute, and very distant from England in so many ways.

I'll travel that far with him, she decided. Then I'll decide what to do next.

"I see," she said. "So where do we go from here?"

1 –Duncan Canal, Alaska Territory, October 24, 1915 — Sunday late afternoon

Captain Jim Plunkett felt proud of the *Lue*, his little twenty-four-foot gas boat. She counted as both his family and the sum of his worldly possessions.

His passenger sat quietly as the *Lue* motored down the narrow channel. Heavily forested fingers stretched out from Woodsky Island as if to pluck an unwary boat from Duncan Canal. Early rain had tapered off and southeast Alaska lay swathed in misty rainbows hiding the mountaintops.

Since building her at Juneau City back in '12, Plunkett had made his living chartering the *Lue* out to hunters, miners, and the occasional tourist. The large cabin offered bunk space for four and two more could sleep comfortably on the floor. The small galley proved adequate and the table running down the centerline could seat six in a pinch.

This charter seemed somewhat stranger than most.

"I demand complete secrecy, Captain," the big man with black hair and mustache told him two weeks ago. "You are to tell no one of the nature of this trip."

"Mr. Krause," he had replied. "Since I don't know anything about this charter, how could I tell anyone about it?"

He scratched his jaw through a salt-and-pepper beard as he thought about the man's odd manner. At fifty-one, Jim Plunkett had almost two decades in the Territory. During that time he had met some outlandish characters, but this fellow took the prize.

He stretched and glanced over his shoulder at his passenger. The man sat at the small chart table, face shaded by his wide-brimmed hat, fondling his revolver. They were supposed to be searching for a specific location on the shore and the fellow wasn't even looking out the damned window.

"Mr. Krause, I'm afraid we'll miss your landing while you're not watching. I don't know where we're going, you do."

"Illusion, merely illusion," the dark man said, not looking up from his weapon.

"Sir?"

"It doesn't matter, Captain. How much would it take to buy this boat?"

"Buy the *Lue*? Why, she's not for sale! I wouldn't sell her for love nor money!" he said indignantly.

"What if you didn't have a choice?" Krause asked quietly. His eyes gleamed up from his shadowed face.

Plunkett stiffened while a wave of fear washed through him. His mouth went dry. They were miles from the nearest town. The Olympic mine was a few miles away but at this time of year it might be deserted. Sometimes people just vanished in this part of the world. He didn't want to be one of them.

"I don't know what you mean," he said carefully.

"What I mean, Captain Plunkett, is you may sell her to me or I will simply take her." The revolver in his hand pointed at Plunkett's chest.

Stay calm, he told himself. *Give him what he wishes. The authorities can sort it all out later.*

"All right, since you put it that way. She's worth three-thousand-five-hundred dollars in any man's language. I won't sell her for a cent less." He stared down at the man and felt a surge of relief when the revolver thumped down on the chart table.

"I'll give you a draft for the full amount drawn on a bank in Seattle. You must promise me you'll go outside and not come back. A man can start a new life with thirty-five hundred dollars down in the States."

There was something almost hypnotic about the way his eyes pierced Plunkett's being as his words sought to chain the older man's mind.

"Do we have an agreement?" Edward Krause asked.

"Yah, you bet," Plunkett said instantly. This fellow must think him a fool!

"Stop the boat and drop anchor, Captain," Krause ordered.

Plunkett shut the throttle down but didn't switch off the battery. It might be easier to catch this thief if he had a dead battery. The throbbing engine went silent and the boat slowed, drifting with the incoming tide. He went out on deck and lowered the anchor carefully over the side.

The painted chain gave way to manila rope as the anchor disappeared into the dark water. Out of habit he counted the knots tied at fathom-lengths in the rope. At twenty-one-and-a-half, the anchor hit bottom. He set it, grunting a little with the effort, and went back into the cabin.

Krause pulled a sheet of paper from his inside breast pocket and handed it to Plunkett.

"Here's your draft. Now where are the boat papers?"

"You'll have to move, they're in the strong box."

"You tell me how to get them. After all, this boat is mine."

Krause's smile infuriated Plunkett. He thought longingly about the .38 Colt revolver waiting in the strong box with his papers. Well, the fellow had the drop on him anyway, better to make the best of it.

"Sure, good idea. Here's the key." His hand dropped inside his coat pocket.

The weapon suddenly pointed at him again.

"Make sure it's a small key, Captain Plunkett," Krause said, pulling the hammer back.

Slowly Plunkett pulled a key from his pocket and held it out to the man. *You'll pay for this, Mr. Krause,* he vowed silently. "The key, sir."

"Excellent. Now where is the box?"

"Under the chart table," he pointed toward the wall, "there's three small braces, see them? Now pull down on the center one."

A panel opened outward revealing a strong box built into the cabin wall. The brass keyhole caught the light, gleaming in the dim recess.

"Very ingenious, Captain. My hat is off to you." Krause quickly opened the small door and reached into the box.

When he pulled the .38 out he carefully examined it before looking up again.

"You weren't really going to try something, were you, Captain?" The words grated through the black mustache, muddy eyes bored into Plunkett.

"I'm not that big a fool, Mr. Krause. Now let me sign the papers over to you."

Krause sifted through the papers quickly and selected the boat documentation. He reached into the valise he brought with him and pulled out two sheets of paper. He put everything on the chart table, the blank paper on top of the others.

"Sign this as if it were the boat papers," he commanded.

"Why?"

"So I'll be able to compare the signatures. In fact, sign both of these sheets." Krause stood and moved to the other side of the cabin, one revolver in his belt, the other hanging from his hand.

The bastard didn't miss a trick, Plunkett reflected. He hadn't even considered sabotaging his own signature.

"All right." He sat down at the chart table and opened the ink well. He signed both sheets of paper and then the documentation. He replaced the pen and ink and stood.

"You'll see they are all the same. There is no deception here on my part."

"Of course not, Captain. Now let's get the skiff launched, we have a long way to go."

"We're going over to the mine?"

"No, not the mine. Petersburg. We are going to Petersburg, and you are doing the rowing."

A creeping fear kept him silent as he lowered the fourteen-foot skiff from its davits into the water. Hell, he couldn't row twenty-two miles. Doctor Eames had told him his heart couldn't take a lot of sustained stress.

"Slow down, Jim, or you'll make an early grave," echoed through his mind.

"I've agreed to everything you said. Why can't we take the *Lue* to Petersburg?"

"She's mine now, and I want to leave her here," Krause said gruffly. "Now get in the boat."

Plunkett carefully lowered himself into the skiff, his hands beginning to shake. This fellow had twenty years and fifteen pounds on him, why the hell couldn't **he** row?

Krause stepped down swiftly onto the rear bench and settled comfortably.

"You may proceed, Captain. Next stop is Petersburg, then we might go on to Fort Wrangell."

"Musta been in the army. No civilian calls it that." Plunkett took the first pull on the oars.

"I even made sergeant and went to fight Chinamen," Krause said. "Row a little faster, I need to be in Petersburg by ten tonight."

Captain Jim Plunkett quickened his exertions and felt invisible fingers tighten in his chest.

Maybe if I just pace myself. He began perspiring heavily as a light fog settled in his head.

The skiff moved away from the silently waiting *Lue* in the quiet, misty afternoon.

2 –Douglas, A.T., October 30, 1915 —
Saturday morning

Edward Krause, mingling with the crowd off the Juneau ferry in the cold, relentless rain, pulled his hat down over his eyes. The less attention he received today, the better. He patted down his dyed mustache, keeping his gaze on the ground as he trudged up the steps to the plank street connecting Douglas with Treadwell.

He pulled the slicker up to completely cover his dark wool suit. The steady thunder of the stamp mills rose to a tangible, physical presence the closer one got to Treadwell. Krause smiled. He'd worked at the Treadwell crusher four years ago. Then he'd gotten smart.

In those four years the mining complex had grown even larger. Now the company touted it as the largest low-grade gold mine in the whole world. At any rate, he couldn't remember the location of his destination.

"Excuse me, friend," he said to a passing miner. "Can you tell me how to get to the 700 Mill foreman's office?"

"Sure. See th' big water tower? Well, his office's jist below it one street," the miner said, staring hard at him.

"Thank you." Krause continued down the plank street into Treadwell. As he approached the office, his slouch disappeared and he pushed his hat back so his face was clearly visible. "The wolf assumes yet a different guise," he muttered to himself.

A medium-sized man wearing spectacles looked up from his high desk when the door opened.

"May I help you?"

"I need to see Foreman King."

"And you are?" Spectacles asked.

"Miller. I got a subpoena. This is a legal matter."

Spectacles stood up, suddenly much more polite. "One moment, Marshal. I'll go tell him you're here."

"You just do that," Krause said quietly to the room as Spectacles disappeared through a door boasting a leaded glass window.

A tall, sandy haired, slightly built, well-dressed man appeared immediately. Spectacles hung behind him like a caboose.

"I'm Foreman King, Marshal. What can I do for you?"

"Is William Christie here today? I need to see him."

"Why, I believe he should be down at the change house right now, getting ready for his shift. Check that, Morgan," he ordered over his shoulder.

"Yes, sir," Spectacles Morgan said, hurriedly opening a ledger. His finger moved down the page and stopped. "Yes, sir, you're correct. Bill Christie is on the next

shift."

"Would you please go ask him to come here?" King asked.

"Right away, sir." Morgan grabbed a slicker and pulled it on as he went out into the rain.

King stared at the big man.

"Are you new in the district? I thought I knew all the deputy marshals."

Krause nodded. "Name's Miller. They keep me moving around a lot. But I worked here at the Treadwell Crusher back in '11."

"Indeed?"

Morgan came through the door followed closely by a man in rough, heavy miner's clothing.

"You wanted to see me, Mr. King?"

"This gentleman does, Bill."

William Christie looked at Krause.

"What can I do for you?" His voice carried a soft Scottish burr.

Krause handed Christie an envelope.

"I have a summons for you to appear in court. You will have to accompany me to Juneau right away."

Bill Christie examined the document for a moment before handing it back to

Krause. He looked at King and shrugged.

"Guess I best go get it over with."

"I need you to sign this as proof of service," Krause said. He laid the summons on the edge of King's desk, and casually placed the envelope over the typewritten portion, leaving only a large blank area free for the signature. Christie signed his name.

"Christie, why don't you go change into your street clothes if you're going to appear in court," King suggested.

Christie nodded and left the office.

King studied Krause as if memorizing everything about him. "Will he be back in time to work part of his shift today?"

"Sure. This should only take about an hour and a half. I got a launch waiting down at the Douglas wharf."

"Well, Deputy Miller, I have work to attend to. Mr. Christie will be back in a moment. If you'll excuse me?"

"Thank you for your time, Foreman King," the big man said. He hooked a stool with his foot, pulled it away from the wall and sat down on it to wait for his man. Morgan resumed scratching at his ledger.

Minutes later the door opened and Christie stuck his head in.

"All right then, I'm ready to go."

They walked down the wide plank street built on pilings above the beach. Treadwell consisted of a complex of four gold mines sitting side-by-side on the edge of Douglas Island. The mines stretched for three and a half miles south from the town of Douglas. If one tallied all the people living on the island the number would be in excess of three thousand, making it the population center of Alaska Territory.

An ore train ground past on narrow gauge rails. The din of the stamp mills and the pounding rain made conversation difficult so the men didn't bother. Outside the Treadwell Club, domain of the bachelor miners with its extensive services and stores, stood two women sharing an umbrella.

"That's my sister-in-law!" Christie shouted, pointing.

Krause nodded, and averted his face as they neared the women.

"William!" the smaller of the two shouted, pronouncing the name as "Villiam."

"You're 'sposed to be at work. Where are you going?"

Without losing stride, he shouted back, "Juneau!" and waved in passing.

As they neared the wharf they saw the Island Ferry Company's new gas boat, **Gent**, chugging away toward Juneau. Krause nodded to a green-painted gas boat tied at the wharf.

"Down there."

As soon as they boarded, Krause started the engine and cast off thelines.

He put the boat in reverse, abruptly it jerked back and sideswiped another boat with two men on it.

"Watch where you're going, mister!" shouted one.

Ignoring them entirely, Krause piloted the boat out into Gastineau Channel. Christie sat on a bench in the small cabin and looked out the oval window.

"Pretty fast with women, aren't you, Billy?" Krause said accusingly.

"Wh-what are you talking about?" Christie looked at the big man, blinking rapidly.

"Took up with that widow so damn fast that the man she really deserved didn't have a chance to ask the time of day. You were Johnny-on-the-spot for fair." Krause glanced out the window and altered course slightly.

Christie's face went red. "My wife spent an entire year in mourning before she'd talk to any man. And I met her at the home of friends. This is quite infamous, Deputy Miller. And you may be sure I'll let Marshal Bishop know what I think of his staff!"

"Yeah," Krause said, ignoring the indignant outburst. "I figured it'd take her longer than that to get over John's death. That's why I didn't let her know how I felt for so long after I shot him. You and Celia have been married for three weeks now, isn't it?"

William Christie suddenly saw the cocked .32 revolver in the deputy's hand and gasped like a fish out of water.

"I hoped she'd change her mind. I just can't stand the thought of her with someone else—with you. Y'see, Billy, I'm a funny man that way. It always makes me angry when people get in the way of what I want." His voice dropped to a whisper as he stared into Christie's fear-wide eyes. "And I always get what I *want!*

A deafening explosion filled the closed cabin. The bullet smashed into William Christie's chest and he fell back against the bulkhead. Stunned and overcome by shock, he sagged down the smooth wood, unable to move.

Krause glanced out the window again before turning back to his victim.

"This isn't anything personal, I'd kill any man who had her."

Christie, struggled, tried to form a word.

Krause shot him again.

As the body rolled off the bench and hit the deck, Krause changed course and headed north up the channel past Juneau. Once in mid-channel, he tied the wheel down. Then he reached under the bench and dragged out three twenty-pound rocks crisscrossed with rope.

He tested the ropes before tying the rocks to the body. After the corpse was firmly anchored, Krause untied the wheel, made a slight course correction, and lit a cheroot. He stared out the window.

"The boys in the organization are going to give me old Ned for this one, Celia. The things I do for you," he said conversationally. "Now if you'll just give me a little more time than before, I'll have it all set up and we can be married. Well, maybe not get married right at first. We'd want to be sure of each other."

The boat slowly passed Juneau City on the mainland off the starboard side. Krause puffed on his cheroot and flicked ashes down on the dead, confused eyes of William Christie.

"Crab food, Billy. You just grew up to be crab food."

Al Sarby pushed into Foreman King's office.

"Hey, Morgan, there was a big guy lookin' for this office earlier on, did he find it?"

"Yes, he did. Marshal Miller had a summons for Bill Christie to appear in court in Juneau. Bill was supposed to be back to finish off his shift, but he hasn't shown up yet."

"Marshal Miller? Who's that?"

"The man you talked to, Al. The one asking directions."

"Miller, hell. That was Ed Krause. He worked here in the crusher back in '10 or '11. He ain't no marshal neither; he's some sort of socialist."

Morgan frowned at the miner for a moment.

"Maybe you should tell Foreman King about this, Al. Have a seat, I'll be right back."

3 —Portland, Oregon, November 4, 1915 —
Thursday morning

"Lepke, come in here, please." Superintendent Todd felt nearly paternal pride as his best operative walked across the busy bullpen toward him. Lepke's medium frame carried no extra weight, and the sandy-haired man's step resembled that of a cat.

"What is it, Superintendent Todd?" Lepke asked as the door shut behind him.

"Have a seat, August." Todd settled his beefy frame comfortably onto his protesting chair then leaned casually on the cluttered desk. For a moment he regarded the bright-eyed man, relishing what he had to say.

"The Bureau of Investigation just telephoned. Tompkins is down with influenza and probably won't be up and about for a few weeks."

Lepke's eyes showed mild interest. "That's unfortunate. Why did they phone us about it?"

"Because they've been asked to investigate a kidnapping up in Alaska. Now they've asked us to handle the work," Todd said with a grin. "Once again the Pinkerton Detective Agency pulls the federal fat out of the fire."

"Ah! Now understanding I am. I mean, I understand. Am I to investigate the incident?"

"Absolutely. After the job you did on that dynamite bombing, this should be a breeze. They've already identified the kidnapper and have a territory-wide manhunt going on right now. But this could be a bit complicated legally."

"Please explain."

"Officially, we are being retained by a consortium of organizations; the Juneau Masons, the Oddfellows, and the Treadwell Mining Company. They want us to produce the missing man, or bring his murderer to justice. But because this Krause fellow impersonated a U.S. Marshal, there were federal statutes violated during the kidnapping."

"Which is why the Bureau of Investigation was requested," Lepke said.

"Exactly. The Bureau said they would ask the marshal's office in Juneau to cooperate with us in every way, so there shouldn't be any problem. Go in and pay your respects when you arrive. You know the drill."

"I will do my best, Superintendent."

Todd grinned. This was the only man he'd ever met who had been recommended for the Medal of Honor. Over the past five years Lepke had proven to be a flawless operative.

"I know you will, August. By the way, your English is excellent. You've become fluent and accomplished."

Lepke blushed slightly. "I still make many mistakes. When I get excited or tired I slip into my old speech patterns. Thank you for noticing my progress."

"Sure. Go down to accounting and get your advance. I want you out of here tonight."

"Yes, sir. I'll send you a postal card."

"You just send reports twice a week and I'll be satisfied."

"Of course."

"Don't forget to pack your longjohns. I understand they have real winters up there."

Lepke grinned and waved as he left the office. Todd watched him walk across the bullpen.

I wish all my operatives were that diligent.

4 —Juneau City, A.T., November 6, 1915 —
Friday morning

"**Fiona, have you seen my button hook?**" The contralto voice drifted down the carpeted hall.

"Yes, Florence," came the slow answer. "I'm using it."

Florence Malone, completely dressed except for shoes, padded quickly to her sister's room and entered the open door without knocking. The cozy, floral-papered space lay ankle-deep with Fiona's clothing.

"Fiona Malone. I told you to ask before using my things! You never put them back where you find them. Besides, you have a button hook of your own."

"I've misplaced it. What do you want me to do, run down to Goldstein's and buy another before I get dressed?"

"You'd probably enjoy the stir you'd make doing it," Florence snapped. She stood in the door watching her sister finish buttoning her shoes. Fiona was beautiful, with long auburn hair, trim figure, and womanly bosom.

Both women wore stylish clothing. Florence's year in Seattle forever banished bustles and other silly accouterments of women's dress trying to hang on from the turn of the century. The modern styles didn't call for whalebone and wire assemblages. Now one could discern a woman's actual shape; she wasn't hidden by extra yards of cloth and convention.

Even so, a lady's skin didn't show above her elbows or below her neck. Modernity was to be appreciated, but it should not usurp morality. Dress was one thing, attitude quite another.

Fiona radiated an air about her that brought glances admiring from men and calculating from women. Florence felt like a small, gray vole next to an ermine when she went anywhere with her sister. Fiona suggested excitement, Florence realized, and she merely promised restraint.

Finishing the shoes, Fiona straightened up. She smiled and handed Florence the button hook. "There you are, dear sister. Thank you very much for allowing me to use your property."

"I don't mind you using my things. I just wish you would ask first and return them after," she said. Realizing she repeated herself, she returned to her bedroom. As she slipped her shoes on and began the tedious task of buttoning them, Fiona drifted through the door.

"Florence, where should I look for a position?"

"Position? Have you finally decided to do something other than be entertained by young men?"

"I've been graduated from high school for two years now. I want to do something exciting with my life. But where should I look?"

"Anywhere within walking distance. You don't want to have to take a ferry to

Douglas or Treadwell every day, do you?" Florence didn't look up from her task as she spoke.

"Oh, I don't know. That would be a good way to meet men," Fiona said lightly.

Florence quickly looked up, color rising in her cheeks.

"Why don't you marry Mr. Saunders? He has a good job at Mr. Behrends' bank; he likes you, and I think he has probably asked you to marry him, hasn't he?"

Now Fiona colored. "That's none of your business. I think Frank is a fine man. I just don't want to get married yet. There will be enough years of babies, laundry, and pipe smoke in the parlor. I needn't rush into it."

"It is not seemly in polite society to engage strange men in conversation at every opportunity. People are already watching you as if you were part of a moving picture. Father has mentioned to me more than once he regrets not remarrying after Mother's death. He feels we should have had a good woman's firm hand in our upbringing, and it's you he's worried about, not me!"

"Florence, you were an old woman the day you were born. I would surely have gone insane if there had been another like you around for the past six years. I'm doing just fine by myself, thank you."

"You needn't be rude. You are my little sister and I'm only giving you my opinion."

"You're two years older than I am, you do outrageous things, and you're still unmarried. Yet you constantly harp on me to marry Frank Saunders. At least I have a beau. Do you plan on being an old maid forever?"

"I believe we've had this discussion before, Fiona. I consider myself a modern woman and refuse to feel I am less a woman simply because I do not have a husband or even a beau. You make no secret of the fact you regard the suffragette movement as something humorous."

Fiona abruptly burst into laughter. "Oh, Florence, if you could only see yourself when you talk like that! You look like Father Reynolds when he's delivering a stemwinder!"

Florence snapped her mouth shut, pulled the final elastic loop over its button, stood, and exited the room with her chin held high.

"Don't go outside with your nose up like that," her sister called after her. "It's raining, you might drown."

Florence refused to be baited, kept her silence, and descended the carpeted stairway to the first floor. Mrs. Milivich stood in front of the kitchen stove cooking breakfast. The high-ceilinged room was redolent with the odors of fresh baked bread, frying bacon, Turkish coffee, and soap.

Mrs. Milivich defined ancient, so old she had ceased to age. The word "fossil" came to mind, but Florence refused to acknowledge it. Mrs. Milivich was small, exacting, diligent, and rooted firmly in the nineteenth century. She had been housekeeper for the Malones as long as Florence could remember.

Although uneasy about the amount of labor the old woman performed daily, Florence felt thankful for the woman's perpetual presence. If the Malones didn't employ a domestic, the running of the house would fall to Florence.

She didn't want to run a house. She wanted to make her own mark on society. In order to prove her equality in what was obviously a man's world, she shunned any task habitually associated with women.

For that very reason she had entered the profession of photography. Florence owned her own Crown Full Bellows, complete with tripod and portable dark room. For one glorious year she lived with Aunt Mary in Seattle while attending the University of Washington.

Her father's primary goal for financing her education was for her to obtain teaching credentials and then return to Juneau for a life-long bout with unruly students. She felt quite negative about the prospect, not that he had ever asked her opinion. Mrs. Milivich wasn't the only one in the house rooted in the nineteenth century.

Rather than concentrate on educational course work, Florence discovered the suffragette movement and photography instead. Soon after her father sent the tuition money for her second year, she returned home with her freshly purchased camera gear, and the resolve to become the first professional woman photographer in Alaska Territory.

Her father had been shocked and angry beyond words.

She tried to explain, but there seemed to be an entire vocabulary they didn't share. She knew he didn't understand, but that didn't mean he had to pull back from her. But he did.

He didn't explain the world to her any more. He just told her how it should be and what facets of it she should accept. His dogmatism elicited her rebellion.

She squared her jaw and stuck to her goal. Two of the Territory's most eminent photographers, Lloyd Winter and Percy Pond, hired her as a combined dark room technician and counter sales clerk. She held hope one day soon they would allow her to take some of the studio portraits for which the photographers were famous. Already she took views of the area, confident the partners would allow her to sell her work next to theirs.

But she hadn't spoken to them about it yet. Perhaps after she had accumulated a portfolio.

"Good morning, Florence," her father said.

"Oh. Good morning, Father," she said, turning to the kitchen table where he sat. "I didn't realize you were down yet."

"Y'were staring at Mrs. Milivich like she were a ghost or something. Do you feel all right?" Jack Malone pushed his chair back and stood with his arm extended. "Would you like a hand, daughter?"

"No, thank you, Father," she said with a chuckle. "I'm fine, I was just gathering wool. Please sit down and drink your coffee."

He eased back into his chair, but continued to watch her. She had caught up with her father in height, but not in girth. She wondered if her face would ever be that heavy and creased with lines. Was his hair turning gray?

"I'll be out this evening. You and Fiona have dinner without me."

"Yes, Father." She sat at the table in the same place she had taken every meal eaten in this house. The table remained bare where her mother's place used to be. Nobody ever sat there now.

Mrs. Milivich shuffled in and set a large platter of fried eggs, bacon, and ham in the center of the table. Jack Malone served himself and dug in with gusto. Florence didn't move. She sat and watched him with raised eyebrows.

In the midst of his second bite, his eyes found her face. He stopped chewing for a moment, before resuming with a dark scowl. As soon as his mouth became empty he looked toward the paneled stairs and bellowed, "Fiona!"

Florence heard her sister's footsteps as she hurried down the carpeted risers.

"I'm so sorry, Father, I misplaced my button hook," Fiona said breathlessly as she took her place.

Florence gave her a small scowl, then made the sign of the cross.

"In the name of the Father..." she slowed so the others could stay with her.

"...the Son, and the Holy Ghost," they intoned together. "Bless us, oh Lord, for these Thy gifts which we are about to receive from Thy bounty, through Christ our Lord, Amen." They crossed themselves again.

Jack began eating as fast as he could. "I've got an important engagement at eight-thirty," he mumbled through his food.

Fiona and Florence ate with decorum.

"I'm going to find a position today, Father," Fiona announced. "Possibly an even finer one than Florence has."

Florence frowned at her. "I didn't realize my position was all that fine."

"Well, you are the only woman I know who is both a technician and a clerk," Fiona said airily.

"But you haven't any education past high school. One doesn't just get handed important positions. You must work up to them or have studied for them." Florence broke off abruptly when she realized how stuffy she sounded.

Why do I do that with her all the time? she wondered. *She's a grown woman, let her make her own way, but she makes so many mistakes! She doesn't have her feet on the ground.*

"What sort of a position did you have in mind, Princess?" Jack asked.

"I don't know, Father. Something interesting that pays well, and where I can meet a lot of m-, ah, people."

"Well, you keep in mind that after the next election, we'll all no doubt be movin' to Washington City," he said grandly.

"What if the Democrats don't win?" Florence asked.

"We'll win," Jack said. "Wilson will easily win another term. The Republicans can't match his quality with a washed-up judge. And speaking of judges, this Territory is fed up with that pompous jurist as delegate. Between him and that damn prohibitionist, Snow, I don't know which is the bigger fool!"

"Father, I wasn't asking about Judge Wickersham or Representative Snow," Florence replied. "I was trying to point out that there is no guarantee as to how an election will turn out, and–"

"Duchess, you haven't been voting as long as I have. Leave the politicking to your old father. We'll live in Washington City after the next election."

"Father, I understand the political workings of our country. There's no way to predict the outcome of an election unless it is rigged. And I don't think you can rig that large an election." Florence clamped her jaw and lowered her head, too angry to respond further.

Jack ignored her.

"Will we have a grand house, Father?" Fiona asked.

"Of course we will, Princess. And we'll have one of those elegant automobiles to take us where we wish." He smiled widely at her, his eyes glinting.

Mrs. Milivich brought in the morning paper, which Jack eagerly grabbed. His attention shifted to the newsprint as he shook the paper out and began to read.

Florence took a few bites and realized her appetite had fled.

"First the *Lue* burns, an' now there's a fellow vanished from the Treadwell," Jack commented.

"I wish Uncle Jim would write us a letter," Florence said. Both she and Fiona had called the kindly bachelor "uncle" since they were children, even though they were not related by blood or law. Since reading about the loss of his boat in Hobart Bay the week before, they had anticipated word from him.

"I still don't know why would he would go to Seattle," Jack muttered. "There's nothin' for him there. He has friends who would help him here."

"Maybe he went down to buy a new boat?" Fiona suggested.

"With what? His boat wasn't insured."

"Well I just don't know, Father. You needn't be brisk with me!"

"Sorry, Princess. There's more to this than meets the eye. I'm worried about Jim."

"If you both will excuse me?" Florence left the table and moved quickly through the small, dark-paneled parlor into the front hall where her fox-trimmed coat hung. The coat always lifted her spirits. She had bought it herself.

Photographers needed good equipment, and a coat is part of one's equipage, she reasoned at the time. She never regretted the decision. She would be the first to admit the fox trim was not a necessity– but it did set the coat off to a turn, and it was irrefutable proof she made better wages than a mere clerk.

She felt armored as she carefully shut the front door. The steady rumble of distant stamp mills, the heartbeat of Gastineau Channel, carried easily through the cold rain. She walked down the graded gravel street toward the business district.

5 —Treadwell, A.T., November 8, 1915 —
Monday morning

"Every morning you get here, you right away peel potatoes enough to fill pans," Willie Ayamo said and pointed at six thirty-gallon pots. "Must be finished with by half way past nine. You understand me, nephew?"

Begay Santo nodded, never taking his eyes off his uncle's face. "Yes, I understand Uncle Willie."

"You call me Mr. Ayamo like all other workers!" he shouted. "Company don't like us to hire relatives. But we got different last names and I told your mother I would help."

"We appreciate your help, Un-, Mr. Ayamo. I will never forget your help as long as I breathe."

The old Filipino suddenly broke into a smile. "Much different here than cannery or college, no?"

"Much different, yes." Begay returned the smile.

"You work hard. That make company know I pick good men. It also help your sick mother."

"Should I start peeling now?"

"Yes!" the old man snapped. "Get to work. There is too much to do to stand around talking all day. When you done here, come find me. I give you more to do." The old man moved away on stiff legs.

"Yes, Mr. Ayamo." He settled down on the three-legged stool and began to quickly peel potatoes. Even though it was just past six in the morning he didn't think he could finish peeling enough spuds to fill those pots in three and a half hours.

But he would try as hard as he could. It took about ten potatoes to get into the rhythm his hands remembered from cannery work. The door opened and a young Filipino man came into the room carrying another three-legged stool. He sat down on it and went to work with a flourish.

"I thought I had to do all these by myself," Begay said with a smile.

"Mr. Ayamo likes to shake up new guys on their first day to make sure they'll do anything he says." The newcomer's dark eyes flashed up from his work for a moment. "Even if the new guy is his nephew."

They both laughed and Begay relaxed. He said his name and held out his hand.

"Frank Bagio, pleased to meet you, Begay." They shook. "You new to Alaska?"

"No," Begay said. "This is my third trip up. I worked in the canneries before."

"Oh! Got tired of being worked to death for nothing, huh?"

"That's for sure. I don't mind working hard, that's part of living. But if they

cheated me out of my pay one more time I was going to kill somebody."

"I never worked in a cannery, but I heard some pretty bad stories about it." Frank peeled so fast his knife nearly blurred.

"They bring you up from Seattle in sailing ships. They put you in the front or back of the ship, down in the holds, right next to the water. All the time you're going up and down with the motion of the water. Some guys got real sick."

"Could you go up on deck for air?"

"Only three times a day. They said they didn't want us to get in the crew's way."

"Three times a day must have helped."

"It was better than nothing," Begay agreed. "But they'd only give us ten minutes each time. Some of the men got so sick they couldn't get up the ladders by themselves and we'd have to help. Most of the time we used up the whole ten minutes just getting them up and then back down again."

"You must have been happy to get to Alaska, huh?"

"Yeah. But in some ways things got a lot worse." Begay tossed a potato in to a pot and picked up another one. "Look, I really don't want to talk about this right now. Tell me about this place."

"How long you been here?"

"I got in last night, came up on a fishing boat from Ketchikan."

"Oh," Frank said with a grin. "You really are fresh off the boat."

"C'mon," Begay said through his smile. "Tell me what it's like here."

"There's only about thirty Filipino residents along Gastineau Channel, and eighteen of them work at Treadwell. The rest work mostly at other mines, one or two have jobs in Douglas and Juneau. There's always a bunch brought up in the spring to work the canneries, and all but a few of them leave at the end of the season."

"How about Filipinas?" Begay asked.

Frank gave him a flat look. Humor fled from his face. "As far as I know the closest Filipina is in Seattle."

"No women at all?"

"Sure. There are white women, Indian women, and even one black woman. But not one Filipina."

Begay's hands stopped moving, the paring knife drooped, a half-peeled potato rolled across the floor. "I had such hopes for this place," he said huskily. "My mother wishes grandchildren. There are no jobs in the states. I thought I might find both here. Isn't this the population center of the territory?"

"Yes, it is. There's a lot of nothing out there. This is pretty much everything Alaska has to offer us. But don't you have a girl waiting in the Philippines?"

"Sure. We all do if our parents can arrange it, don't we?" Begay picked up the potato and finished peeling it. He threw it into the pot.

"Well, I do," Frank said. "So far I've sent over two hundred dollars back home. Nice and safe, just waiting for me."

"I had to borrow money to get here. For three years I've worked like a slave in the summers to get enough money to go to college," Begay said bitterly.

"Did you finish college?" Frank asked with admiration in his voice.

"No. I have one more year to go, *if* I bother."

"Why wouldn't you bother? To have an American education and go back to the Philippines with money in your pocket..."

"It's hard to explain, Frank. I wish I had spent the last three years in a mine just making money. College has shown me things I didn't know existed, as well as things I wish didn't exist."

"Huh?"

"Never mind. I don't know how to explain. I'm sorry, I shouldn't have said anything."

"You must have had something on your mind."

"Well, in college I had a lot of friends who weren't Filipinos," Begay said.

"I've heard it's pretty hard to get accepted by whites. I know it's almost impossible here."

"In the cities it's different. There are places where everyone goes. You don't have to be a certain color." He picked up another potato and continued peeling.

"How does that change you here? This isn't the city. This is Alaska where we're cheap labor and not good enough to vote," Frank said sharply.

"Knowing that isn't going to get me back to the Philippines," Begay said. "It just shows me I can live anywhere. I don't have to return to the Philippines to start my life. This is our life, Frank, we're living it now! What if we die here? Will we have ever really lived?"

6 —Douglas, A.T., November 11, 1915 —
Thursday afternoon

After a week went by Celia Christie knew her husband was dead. She moved around the small house silently, carefully, peering through the lace curtains. The thumping stamps provided a background chorus to her inner screaming agitation.

Edward, man of solicitude, paragon of understanding when she needed someone steadfast to listen, whose physical strength was matched by his mental acuity, had taken her new husband? Could this be?

But I've been through this once, she thought. *I've already been tested to prove my limits.* Despite her silent plea, the events mercilessly spiraled through her mind again like a motion picture. The stamps provided her organ music.

She and Johann, newly wed, spent their combined savings and emigrated to America from Germany. His sister and her husband wrote of the opportunities in this beautiful territory. They should come. They would see for themselves.

They moved to Petersburg, home of fishing fleets and shipyards. But America's wealth hinged on obscure doors in places like New York and Seattle. The price of fish dropped to the point where profits disappeared after the expense of fuel and labor.

After Johann's hours at the shipyard were reduced, their meager finances had been bolstered when Edward began taking meals with them. After two years of effort their first home in Alaska Territory had panned out to nothing. But Edward was a rarity; a friendly man who really listened.

After Johann went north and found work at Treadwell, it was Edward who helped her with the day-to-day problems of a woman in the family way. It was Edward who minded the two children while she gave birth to their little sister. He'd even helped her pack their belongings for the trip north after Johann found a house in Douglas.

Edward had continued writing to the family, keeping them informed of news in Petersburg.

When Johann died, she slipped perilously close to madness. She kept imagining his blood and brains shooting out over the waters of Oliver Inlet. He was only to be gone for three days, deer hunting.

The children held the insane grief at bay purely by the demands they put upon her. Being widowed at twenty-seven with three children in a land she hardly knew was almost more than she could bear. But her sister, Bertha, helped her fight the madness by being there every day.

Friends in Douglas and Treadwell helped. The continuing letters from Edward helped. She regained her equilibrium and forged ahead.

Bertha introduced her to William Christie.

A good man, Willy, a Scot; which gave her pause due to the events in Europe these days. But this was the new world, and a new life. She'd continued her correspondence with Edward until Willy expressed his displeasure.

After eleven months of courtship, they decided to marry. A woman soon to be married didn't exchange letters with a bachelor. It just wasn't done. She'd written a letter of explanation to Edward and that was that.

Three months ago Edward suddenly appeared. She and Bertha were just leaving for a picnic so he went along.

The day was uncharacteristically sunny, the food satisfying, and the conversation interesting. She told him she was marrying William Christie in two weeks.

"But he's not like us. He's an Englishman," Edward had said. But that was all he said.

So she became Mrs. William Christie. She had a husband, and her children had a father. Between the little store she operated out of the bottom floor of their house on Finn Hill and Willy's job with the Treadwell, things were looking pretty good.

Ten days ago Willy didn't come home from work on time. She'd waited, knowing him to be a considerate worker. She felt sure they were merely late finishing up in the amalgamation room at Treadwell.

There had been no emergency blast on the whistle signaling an injury or death. No litter had been borne to the hospital operated by the sisters of St. Ann. Nothing seemed amiss.

She'd fallen asleep. No alien sound disturbed her troubled slumber. At five in the morning her eyes had popped open; still no Willy.

At the bottom of the steps leading to their quarters, just inside the locked door, lay a letter:

"Dear Wife: Unforeseen circumstances force me to leave at once for Seattle. I will write you in the near future. Your loving husband."

The top of the page was torn and it was signed at the bottom in ink. The letter itself was typewritten. Where had Willy found a typewriter in the middle of the night?

Why hadn't he awakened her and explained this trip? A glance at his closet revealed his good suit and shoes. Would he take a long trip in his work clothes? She'd made a pot of coffee and waited another hour and a half thinking everything over carefully and fighting the growing unease.

Finally at 6:30 she could stand it no longer and went next door to Annali's. Torgid Pakkila was just leaving for his shift in the mine.

In moments Torgid was hurrying down to the marshal's office a block away. The marshal woke up Nick King and heard about the subpoena. The name of Edward Krause was spoken for the first time.

Why? Why would he do this to her? Strong, silent Edward. In all those hours of conversation in German, all those days of being nearby and helping her, all the times he had the opportunity to ask or tell her anything; he hadn't said one word about caring for her.

She had even expected those words from him. But they hadn't come. Some men are born to be bachelors. So she had gone on with her life.

Now he had ended her new happiness. Poor Willy, poor Willy. Her head was in constant pain.

The tears sprang unbidden at the sight, sound, smell, or touch of anything that reminded her of him. Thank God the children were at Bertha's. She was losing her mind to the stamp music. She had to get away from this place.

"Mrs. Christie, I'm sorry, but we need you to testify at the trial. There's still a lot of questions to be answered, ma'am. You'll have to stay for a while longer." The U.S. Marshal had been unbending.

She could still hear Willy's voice burr in her mind as she prepared the laudanum. The doctor said it would help her sleep.

7 –Ketchikan, A.T., November 11, 1915 —
Thursday night

Edward Krause stood in the shadows of the barroom in the Hotel Revilla. He'd been drinking all day, but was far from drunk. He was too frightened to get drunk.

For the first time in his life he thought he'd made a mistake. The disguise hadn't worked. People in Treadwell and Douglas had recognized him when he took Christie.

Damned sheep. They didn't understand life at all. So few understood the grand design of nature; kill or be killed. Eat or be eaten.

The organization had condemned his action and refused to help him hide from the authorities. Fine. He had never completely trusted that bunch in the first place.

He had prepared a bolt hole long ago. However, there was one drawback; he had to get to Seattle in order to go under cover. The whiskey numbed his anxiety and bolstered his spirits.

"Only the strong survive," he said, not realizing he spoke aloud.

"What's that, sir?" the bartender asked.

"I wasn't talking to you," he snapped, annoyed at his lapse.

The bartender backed away, his eyes hooded. Five men besides Krause enjoyed the hospitality of the establishment. Earlier there had been more, but the married ones had plodded out the door hours ago.

Mrs. Johnson, the hotel owner and wife of the bartender, edged into the room. She thought she was fooling Krause, but he knew she was watching him. They were all watching him.

So careful. He'd been so careful! He'd eluded the old, fat marshal at Juneau and made it all the way here without being recognized. Then five minutes after arriving, he'd run into Sam Jeffers.

"By Gott, Krause! I thought they'd got you in Juneau. I hear they was looking for you. I forget just why." The old man chewed his beard for a moment in consternation.

"Don't worry, Sam. That's all taken care of. It was all a big mistake."

"Yah? They had your description on the wireless. Yah, now I know. Kidnap, they say you did."

"Mistake, Sam. It was all a mistake. Everything is okay now. Don't worry."

"Me worry! Ha, ha. No. I just thought you should know." Then the old man had turned and limped away down Dock Street.

So he'd checked into the Revilla, gave his name as Moe, and refused to sign the register. Mrs. Johnson had watched him ever since. After spending most of the day in his room he relocated to the bar.

The whiskey felt good in his gut. But it couldn't quite drown the fear chewing there. The sheep had identified him. Astonishment filled him like molten lead.

Once in Seattle he could give them the slip. He had created many identities there to cover himself. The steamer sat at the dock, a block away.

At midnight they would pull the gangplank. The ship wouldn't stop for anything. In a day and a half he would be in Seattle. So close, but he couldn't touch it yet.

His eyes found the reflection of the clock in the mirror behind the bar. Eleven-forty. Nearly time to go. He laid a quarter on the smooth surface and waved his finger at the beefy bartender.

A jigger of whiskey appeared in front of him and the quarter disappeared with a mumbled, "Thank you, sir." Krause forced himself to sip the pungent amber. His suitcase sat at his feet, his left foot automatically monitoring the presence of the luggage.

The one thing he had brought with him from eight years in the U.S. Army was discipline. The sheep lacked it, even the ones who had been in the army themselves. He'd seen it time after time; a man would get out of the army and purposely destroy all the discipline he had gained under arms. Von Papen was right. These people deserved to lose everything they had. They were completely unworthy.

Von Papen. The German captain was not going to like this turn of events. Well, there were others in place who could do the kaisers work in America. After all, they granted him a free hand all those years ago.

He threw back the remainder of the liquor and picked up his bag. He went through the door and into the windy night. The rain had abated, damn the luck, and the crystalline air chilled him.

Bright electric lights illuminated the short city block to the dock, gangplank, and purser. Krause moved swiftly, his eyes sweeping from side to side, watching for pursuers. A second man stood next to the gangplank, talking to the boat officer.

Krause couldn't slow his step now. He was in full view of them, and he knew they watched him. They all watched him.

Behind him the bank clock began the laborious process of striking midnight. He strode up the slightly inclined plank and handed the purser a twenty dollar gold piece.

"Passage to Seattle," he said.

The man glanced at the coin then bent over the open ledger beside him.

"Name, please."

"O. E. Moe," Krause said with practiced weariness.

The man standing next to the purser stared hard at Krause. It took a lot of self-control not to hit the pop-eyed fool. The ship's whistle blasted into the night, which responded with a sudden heavy rain.

"Thank you, Mr. Moe. You're in cabin six."

Krause took the proffered key. "Thank you, purser." As he stepped into the main saloon a flood of exaltation rushed through him and he found it difficult not to laugh. Or cry.

8 —Juneau City, A.T., November 13, 1915 –
Saturday morning

Fiona Malone felt anxious. She had sought a position for almost two weeks and found nothing. Of course she hadn't gone down to any of the laundries, or checked at the hotels.

But then she didn't want a job washing clothes for miners or cleaning their rooms either. She wanted to meet more men, who, like her nice young banker, would buy her presents and leap to do her bidding. Florence had told her once that she could meet the best young men in town at any of a dozen church and social

functions.

But "the best" didn't intrigue her. She wanted a bit of mystery and perhaps a touch of danger in a man. Bank clerks proved boringly earnest and stable.

Perhaps she should go live with Aunt Mary in Seattle. Florence had, but her father had promised Washington City, so now would not be the time to leave.

She unconsciously assessed options available to her in this place.

Five thousand people lived on Gastineau Channel. Juneau City, nestling between salt water and the twin towering flanks of Mt. Roberts and Mt. Juneau, still enjoyed the building boom started in 1913. New concrete buildings seemed to pop up like mushrooms.

Juneau was the largest population center north of Vancouver. The only settlement farther north other than Indian and Eskimo villages was Fairbanks and it was just a small mining town. Oh yes, and the new tent city where a railroad was being built from tidewater to the Interior gold fields and Fairbanks. The newspaper said it was to be named Woodrow after the president, but everyone referred to it as Ship's Anchorage. Too far from Seattle to ever be very important, she decided.

The citizens of Juneau City enjoyed the comforts of ten miles of six-inch plank paving, two dozen grocery stores, five drug stores, three each furniture and hardware stores, three motion picture theaters, Mrs. Mathias' Palace Cigar Factory, and the Eagle Brewery and Soda Bottling Works.

Thirty automobiles clattered around the town, with a motor-stage operating regularly between Juneau City and Thane, three miles south on Gastineau Channel. A second operated between Juneau and the Perseverance mine, twelve miles back in the mountains. Juneau was home to the beautiful new Governor's Mansion, finished just last year. It sat in dignified gray splendor up on Dixon Street, overlooking the

Indian village as well as town.

Not much to offer a girl, she thought. Being a capital city wasn't all that wonderful either.

New lawmakers from all over the Territory came here last January for the second Territorial Legislature. Her father was never home while the legislature was in session. "Too many arms to twist," he would say with a twinkle in his eye.

By the first of March they were all gone again. The politicians reminded her of scavenger birds. They migrated in season, and picked at the carcass of the body politic until they had extracted the last possible favor before flying back to their nests to share... or not.

When she confided that thought to Florence, her sister had regarded her rather queerly. "That's very insightful, Fiona," she finally said. "Maybe there's hope for you yet." Fiona still wondered if she had been insulted or not.

Then, of course, there was the part of town where a woman didn't go unless she was loose. Fiona had seen some of those women. Some looked as plain as her sister. Others seemed exotic and Bohemian, and she wanted so much to ask them questions. She found herself enticingly close to that part of town now.

Fiona knew she had been "protected" from much unpleasantness thus far in her life. Between the Sisters of St. Ann, her domineering father, and the proper young men who came calling, she had only caught glimpses of the real world at the edges of her sheltered, boring existence.

A sharp wind blew in off the channel carrying coal smoke and she automatically grabbed her hat. The cold bit through her coat. She stopped idling and quickened her steps to one of the many cafes. A small pot of tea, and perhaps a confection, would suit her nicely.

She entered the small establishment and sat at a table for one. Two other women sat alone, and a few men lingered over late lunches. A cadaverously white, thin man sidled up to her.

"May I help you, ma'am?"

"I'd like a small pot of tea and a pastry."

His troubled eyes peered at her.

"Excuse me, ma'am, but you look familiar. Do I know you?"

"I don't believe so," she said graciously. "I am Fiona Malone."

His eyes widened and his skin actually seemed to pale further.

"Malone! You're Jack Malone's ki-, ah, daughter?"

"Yes!" She smiled prettily. "Do you know my father?"

He swallowed hard.

"Excuse me, Miss Malone. I'll see to your tea." He all but galloped from the room.

What a strange man, she thought. Then she noticed the other patrons looking at her. When she met their gaze they looked away or pretended they had been looking past her at the window.

This is too rude! She stood and picked up her coat.

"Change your mind about the tea, dearie?"

A heavy woman in a yellow print dress set a tray on the table. The tray contained a steaming pot of tea, a small plate of cookies and cakes, and two cups. Fiona's questioning look brought a smile that showed perfect ivory teeth.

"If you'll have tea with me, I'll treat," the woman said.

Fiona felt like a canary in a room full of cats. Excitement quickened in her breast. She replaced her coat and settled onto her chair.

The woman turned toward the back and barked, "Bones! Bring my chair!"

Instantly the cadaverous man rushed into the room pushing a heavy office chair on casters. The seat had been amply padded. The small wheels made no discernible sound.

He held the chair while she settled into it. Then he hurried away.

"I don't believe I know you," Fiona said.

"You're right, dearie. You don't." She cackled to herself as she poured tea into the cups. "Do you take sugar or cream, dearie?"

"Two lumps and a small bit of cream, please. Does that man work for you?"

The woman pushed the tea over to Fiona and then leaned back heavily.

"Must be getting old," she wheezed. "Can't even serve tea without losing my wind!"

"If you don't answer my very simple questions," Fiona said carefully, as though speaking to a child, "I shall get up and leave at once."

The woman looked up from her cup. Her eyes had a glint that, in combination with her small twisted smile, gave her fleshy features an ominous cast.

"You're the seed of Jack Malone, all right. Can't give a body two minutes to settle in before you're all over them with threats and orders."

Fiona felt her temper rise.

"I don't know why my father would be interested in you or your activities. That is entirely his affair, but-"

The woman interrupted with a bray of laughter.

"You're also as smart as your old man! You grab meaning and nuance out of thin air like a Marconi set. You'll do, Fiona, you'll do."

"I'll do what?"

"I am Maye Wattnem. I own this place."

Fiona glanced around.

"It's a nice little cafe."

"You're rather far down on Front Street aren't you?" Maye asked.

"What do you mean?"

"I didn't name this place the Line Cafe for nothing. There ain't no churches on Lower Front Street."

"Oh." Fiona suddenly understood why the other people in the room had examined her so carefully. She felt her cheeks warm.

"What a charming blush, dearie. What are you doing out on a day like this?"

"I've been looking for a position, for work. After being out in the rain and wind for hours I decided to have some tea."

"What sort of position did you have in mind?"

"I didn't realize I was this far south. I really should go."

"You're safe in here, dearie. Nobody messes with Maye Wattnem more than once, I assure you."

"How do you know my father?"

"We came to Juneau City on the same steamer twenty-five years ago," Maye wheezed. "Our paths cross every now and then. He probably wouldn't like it if he knew you were down here."

"No. I'm sure he wouldn't."

"This isn't the only place I own in town. I could use a nice looking girl like you."

"In what capacity?" Fiona asked quickly.

"The night manager in my hotel quit last night. I need a replacement by six tonight. Interested?"

"Which hotel is that?"

"The Division."

"*You* own the Division?"

"That's right, dearie. Do you want the job?"

"How do you know I'm the right person for the position?"

"I don't really, but you're Jack Malone's daughter and he's no fool. Besides, if you don't work out I can always sack you."

"What is the salary?"

"Fifteen dollars a week. After three months there'll be a raise if I like how you're doing. Fair enough?"

Sixty dollars a month! That was more than Florence made with her college and chemicals. All doubt vanished.

"Quite fair, Maye. I'll take the position." Fiona smiled and held out her hand. "You did say six, didn't you?"

9 —Seattle, Washington, November 14, 1915—
Early Sunday morning

Cold rain misted down past the arc lamps as Detective Captain Tennant watched the *SS Jefferson* tie up at the dock. Two of his men, dressed as longshoremen, idled next to the gangplank, two uniformed officers were posted at the dock entrance, and a plain-clothed detective stood at his side. Tennant wasn't taking any chances; the wireless from Juneau said the man was a kidnapper.

The purser appeared at the top of the gangplank and checked ticket stubs as the passengers disembarked. Two families carrying yawning children were first off the boat. A few drummers with their sample cases followed, their heavy-lidded eyes bloodshot and their steps careful in the deep shadows.

Then Tennant saw him. The fellow matched the description perfectly. Five foot, ten inches, dark hair and mustache, broad shouldered, and wearing a dark wool suit. The man did an excellent job of surveying the people on the dock without being obvious about it.

Tennant felt the familiar tightness in his chest as the man ambled nonchalantly down to the dock carrying a large briefcase. Ready for anything, he stepped forward.

"Mr. Edward Krause?"

Dark eyes reflected the arc lights. "No. I'm afraid you've mistaken me for someone else," the man said smoothly.

"What is your name, sir?"

"Moe. Oly E. Moe. Now if you'll excuse me..." He started to push past.

Tennant pulled out his badge and held it in front of Moe's eyes. "I'm sorry, Mr. Moe. But I'll have to ask you to wait here for a few minutes. You fit the general description we have, and until someone else walks down that plank who also fits it, you're our prime suspect." Tennant kept glancing at other passengers streaming off the boat.

Moe laughed easily. "This is a prank, isn't it? One of my friends put you up to this, didn't they?" He twisted his head around, looking for familiar faces.

Tennant felt a momentary twinge of doubt. This fellow is innocent, he thought, or else he's very, very good at subterfuge.

"I'm afraid this is quite serious. You'll have to wait here. And I'm afraid we'll have to ask you for your grip."

All traces of humor vanished from Moe's countenance.

"Now see here! What is it I've supposedly done?"

Tennant pulled the briefcase from Moe's hand and said, "We'll get to that in due time, sir."

More people eddied about on the dock, greetings were shouted, men hugged women, women hugged women, small, tired children cried for their beds. It was a typical ship's landfall. They occurred many times each day and night along the waterfront.

The stream of passengers thinned to a trickle, then stopped. Tennant glanced at his plain-clothes sergeant and nodded toward the purser. The man moved swiftly up the gangplank and spoke to the ship's officer. In moments he stood on the other side of Moe again.

"That's it, Captain. They're all off except crew."

"Mr. Moe, you are under arrest for kidnapping and suspicion of murder."

"That's absolutely preposterous! Who is the supposed victim?"

"We'll talk about it down at the station, sir. Now if you'll come along quietly we won't have to use the irons."

"Certainly," Moe said stiffly.

The two detectives disguised as longshoremen flanked the men. Tennant glanced back at them. "Burnett, make us a path to the mariah."

"Yes, sir!" The man pushed through the crowd at the gate and stood by the back door of a dark, enclosed Cadillac paddy wagon. The rain-slick sides boasted "Seattle Police Patrol" in white letters.

"Right in there, sir, out of the weather," Tennant said.

The prisoner climbed into the dark interior without a word. The Captain followed him in with the sick feeling in his gut that he had the wrong man.

10 —Seattle, Washington, November 18, 1915—
Thursday night

"All ashore that's going ashore! Last call!"

Pinkerton Operative August Lepke hurried up the dancing gangway as crewmen pulled the slack out of the webbed ropes. He thrust his ticket at the purser.

"I thought the boat left at seven."

"It does, sir," the purser purred as he punched the ticket. "Therefore we must haul in the gangway at six-fifty-five. Besides, according to my list, you're the last ticketed passenger to come aboard. You're in cabin nine."

His smirk measured his tolerance for landlubbers. "Haul it away!" he snapped to the longshoremen.

Beefy men in rough clothing pulled with authority and the heavy plank gangway lofted gracefully into the dark sky, random shafts of light flashed over it with a magical air.

Over the rumble of the ship's engines and the creak of ropes as the boom swung the gangway toward shore, an automobile horn could be heard. The horn suddenly became louder as a backfiring motor-taxi skidded onto the wharf. The driver honked frantically with one hand and steered with the other.

The auto screeched to a stop in front of the descending gangway. A man jumped out of the passenger side.

"I say there, is this the *S.S. Humboldt?*" he called importantly.

"That she is, sir," the purser answered.

"It's not sailing time yet! We have tickets for this boat and the schedule distinctly reads seven pee emma. It is only five of by my watch!" He shook the timepiece at the purser.

"You already have tickets?" the purser asked, glancing down at his list.

"The schedule is quite plain, my good man." He held the folded paper out so the purser might see for himself across the ten feet of space that dropped away into the humid darkness between ship and dock.

Lepke edged away from the purser and into the shadows on deck.

The purser cursed softly. "What are ya waitin' for?" he shouted at the longshoremen. "Get the damned plank over here."

"Ah, yes. That's more like it," the man said. He turned to the motor-taxi holding out a coin that reflected redly in the dim light on the dock. "You're a good wheelman," he said to the driver, dropping the coin into the outstretched hand.

He held the door as a handsome, dark-haired woman stepped from the back of the automobile. The driver scurried around, collected two large pieces of luggage, and was halfway up the gangway before it again touched down on the deck of the *Humboldt.*

The man and woman walked calmly up to the purser.

"Tickets, please," the purser said gruffly.

"Ah, yes. And how much are two first class berths to Juneau City?"

"Fifty dollars, American. I thought you said you already had tickets!"

"No, no. I said I had a schedule and you were ahead of it. Here you are, my good man."

Lepke stood in the shadows and watched the tall, slender man drop gold coins into the purser's outstretched hand. He carefully noted the hooked nose when the man's profile presented itself. A scar gleamed whitely on his left cheek as he turned to the woman.

"Just a moment, sir," the purser said. "I need your names for the passenger list, company policy."

"Quite. Mr. and Mrs. Arnold Williams."

The purser scratched at his ledger, slammed the book shut. "Cabin ten. Thank you, sir and madam. Now if you'll excuse me?" He turned to the dock. "Get that damned plank up, you apes! Be lively."

Mr. Williams chuckled as he unseeingly passed Lepke in the shadows. Mrs. Williams' eyes found him, however, and regarded him carefully as she passed.

She would make a good operative, Lepke mused.

The ship's whistle blew two short, sharp blasts. The longshoremen lifted great hawsers off bollards on the dock and dropped them into the dark, distant water. Deckhands pulled them in, hand over hand, and faked them down in a swirling pattern on the deck to maximize drying.

When Lepke looked at the dock again it had all but disappeared into the overall light and dark patterns of the nighttime Seattle waterfront. A damp breeze wafted across Puget Sound bearing salt and pine tar. He took a deep breath and went to find his cabin.

November 21, 1916— Sunday afternoon
Icy rain beat on the deck of the *SS Humboldt* as it steamed slowly up Gastineau Channel, three days out of Seattle. Lepke had never been this far north before. The fiords of the Alaskan panhandle were all new territory to him.

The mountains drop into the sea, he thought.

Low hanging clouds turned the scene into a Japanese woodcut.

He half expected to see a sampan drift past at any moment. In the few places where the ragged clouds offered a view, the snow line visibly inched down the mountains.

Collection: H.C. Barley — View of the 'Humboldt' with passengers and crew lining the deck.

A constant growing rumble pressed through the rain. He wondered at the noise for a moment, before remembering these were mining communities. The noise must be part of the mining or milling process.

Perhaps he could get a look at that sometime. The last time he ventured into a mining community there hadn't been time to play the tourist.

The rumble grew in intensity, taking on a life of its own, dominating all other sound. On the mainland side of the channel, the dusk glowed with the incandescence of hundreds of electric bulbs. But this wasn't Juneau City; it must be the newest mining community on the channel.

Thane Mine slid past on their starboard side. The main buildings appeared to be perched directly on top of each other as they ran up a 45-degree slope into the clouds. Around the base of the bustling operation crowded smaller buildings and rows of houses separated by wide plank streets.

The glow from the house windows looked warm and dry. Cozy. Everything a man might want from life.

"We could have had a little place like that," he muttered. An old familiar ache prodded thoughts of Alice from his mind. He'd gotten quite good at that over the past few years.

He saw people moving between the buildings. Only a very few stood still. Probably watching us go by, he thought. Off the ship's port side the long expanse

of Treadwell and Douglas gleamed bright on Douglas Island in the late afternoon gloom.

After the multitudinous miles of silent primeval forest since Seattle, interrupted only three times for stops at small, quiet fishing towns, all these electric lights and pounding mills proved a bit unnerving. Lepke felt part of a dream world.

His seven years as a Pinkerton operative had given him a sixth sense. It now told him someone stood behind him. Carefully he put his hand in his coat pocket and grasped the handle of the .455 Bulldog revolver. Then he nonchalantly turned around.

"It's lovely here!" Mrs. Williams exclaimed.

Lepke released the pistol but didn't take his hand out of his pocket. "It's also noisy, raining, and trying to snow." They both had to speak loudly to hear one another over the mill noise.

"Oh, but that makes no difference. This is such a lush and lovely place! So green."

"That's because of the rain."

"Are you always this pragmatic, Mr.–," she hesitated and smiled winningly. "Do you realize you're the only man on this ship I haven't been introduced to yet?"

Her accent was east coast finishing school, he decided. Even if she was trying to pass for British. Absolutely *striking* woman, though.

He hadn't seen her photograph in the Pinkerton files, he felt sure of that.

"Lepke, Mrs. Williams. August Lepke. I'm very pleased to make your acquaintance," he said, giving her a tight smile and the merest charade of a

handshake.

"But you already knew who I was. Did you ask about me?" Her eyes challenged his for a moment, then dropped, waiting for his answer.

"As you know, I saw you and your husband board." He tried to keep his eyes neutral when she looked up again.

"Ah, yes, my husband," she said in German.

"Do you speak my native tongue?" Lepke asked.

"Pardon?" Now her eyes held confusion.

"I was born in Germany and came to the United States as a youth. German is my first language."

"Your English is excellent! I had no idea you understood a word of **Deutche**."

She hesitated. "Please don't mention to Mr. Williams that I speak German. I'd rather he didn't know."

"Have you long been married?" he asked, puzzling over her request.

"No. Actually we've only been together since meeting in Mexico. Have you ever been to Mexico, Mr. Lepke?"

"No, Mrs. Williams, I haven't had the pleasure."

"Take my advice; don't bother." She smiled at him. They were so close in height that Lepke wasn't sure who was taller. He judged her weight at one hundred and ten pounds.

"Your wedding was not to your liking?" he asked blandly. He decided her eyes were indigo and her hair looked Spanish black. He concluded it wasn't a good idea to look too deeply into those dark eyes.

"They light off paper torpedoes at weddings down there. Very noisy, very smelly, and very unpleasant," she said with finality.

"You don't like loud noises?"

"Not in repetition, Mr. Lepke."

"Then this racket must—"

At that point the whistle on the *S.S. Humboldt* pierced through the rumbling from both sides of the channel. They put their hands over their ears. He knew the whistle would blast again.

He pulled open a door to the promenade deck with one hand and made a courtly flourish with the other. "After you, madam," he shouted.

She flashed past in a swirl of long skirts and the fragrance of gardenias. As he pulled the door shut the whistle again shrieked out the boat's presence. She stood in the softly lit passageway, her back against the flocked wallpaper.

"This is a very noisy place. I'm not sure how long I'm going to like it here."

"If you don't mind my asking," Lepke said. "Why aren't you with your husband?"

"I see such a lot of him. And I have a very keen interest in human nature." Her gaze measured his length. "Often I like what I see. Where will you be staying in Juneau City?"

"Why do you think I am stopping in Juneau? I could be going on to Skagway or Chilkoot Barracks."

"I asked the purser." Her eyes held him. For a brief moment he thought of moths and flames.

"Why do you wish to know?" he asked.

"We have no idea where to stay. I was sure a gentleman like yourself would stay only at the best house in town." Her smile was lop-sided, and her eyes mocked him. "Why else would I ask?"

"The Cain Hotel on Franklin Street is where I have a room reserved. Never before in my life have I visited this town. I can't give you knowledgeable advice on lodgings. Perhaps you should have asked the purser about that instead," he said stiffly.

Spots of color appeared high on her cheeks and her smile disappeared. "How does being disagreeable help you in your work, Mr. Lepke?"

His eyes narrowed slightly. Her chance remark had landed squarely on target. When the Pinkerton Detective Agency sent an operative out to investigate a crime, their task was called "a work."

She couldn't know he was an operative. But on the other hand, he wasn't trying to keep his occupation a secret, nor was he advertising it. Why was she being so forward?

"It doesn't help my work to be disagreeable, Mrs. Williams. Now, would you answer a question for me?"

She smiled. "Of course, sir. Turn about, fair play."

"You are a very handsome woman. Why are you in a dim passageway with a man you don't know instead of with your new husband?"

"You are very blunt, sir!" The color flowed back into her cheeks, but this time the smile did not evaporate. "Perhaps I am just a friendly person who happens to be a woman."

She turned and moved swiftly down the passageway. The boat whistle shrieked again as she turned a corner and was lost to his sight. He could hear men running on the deck as the *S.S. Humboldt* neared the Juneau City dock. The mills grumbled in the night.

11 — 600 Foot Level, Treadwell, A.T., November 22, 1915 — Monday early morning

Like a vast rock lung, Number Five West Drift Stope lay empty. Where men once wrestled pneumatic drills, blasted rock out of the solid mountain, and broke the ore into manageable pieces, relative silence reigned. The level languished bereft, mined out.

The miners bored deeper in the bowels of the earth pursuing the vein dipping below Gastineau Channel. The grade of ore seemed to descend along with the shafts. The company hoped for a better grade soon. They were, literally, banking on it.

Four mines, side-by-side on the northeast shore of Douglas Island, formed the Treadwell complex. The Treadwell was the largest of the four. Next was the 700 Mine, named for its width in feet. Beyond it lay the much wider Mexican Mine, and finally, three miles from Douglas, the Ready Bullion.

All four followed the wide vein of gold mixed liberally with worthless rock, most of it quartz. The Treadwell plummeted 2,300 feet beneath the earth. The "hanging wall" of igneous gabbro, acting much like a roof, formed a barrier between the miners and the salt-water-filled channel.

Fresh water from the mountains on Douglas Island seeped into all four of the mines. In 1911 the Ready Bullion exhibited signs of increased leakage. A twelve-foot-thick concrete wall was built, sealing off and protecting the other three mines should the Ready Bullion flood.

Adits, as the branching tunnels were called, united the other three mines far under ground. Stopes honeycombed the rock beneath the channel, large bays stripped of their wealth by the burrowing miners.

But, also as in a lung, the silence was not complete. The ever-present pounding heart of the stamp mills reducing ore to sand constantly reverberated down through the entire complex. There were other sounds of life in the mines; the creak and rattle of ore carts moving down to the miners, the sharp commands of the foremen telling the men which chunks of ore to break into smaller pieces, the grunts of the muckers bull-dozing the rock into the carts. Pry bars clinked and scraped across stone.

Teams of mules pulled the carts three hundred feet up the tracks to the ore bins where they were emptied, then rattled back down to be filled again. Electric lights illuminated the adits. The power lines hung on eight-by-eight braces that also supported the heavy air hoses for the pneumatic drills.

The tired cursing of exhausted miners, spending their best years encased in damp, cold rock, topped off the cacophony that marked the lifeblood of the Treadwell Mine. The stopes, the large bays where the vein was actually worked, from the surface down to the 1,750 foot level, had all been totally cleared of ore.

During excavation the miners left twenty-foot thick pillars of rock to support the roof of each stope. But those pillars held gold-bearing ore. Once the rest of the stope was cleaned out, the pillars were "bulldozed" also.

Management changed the policy after the 1,750 foot level was reached, but the miles of adits and stopes above that level still stood without support. It was not uncommon for one of those mined-out bays to measure two hundred feet high and two hundred feet in diameter.

The ore-bearing rock contained, among other elements, a certain amount of lime. When air from the surface came into contact with the exposed stopes and drifts, the lime slaked; absorbed moisture and crumbled. The 600-foot level contained more lime than in higher regions of the mine.

The lime had been crumbling and disintegrating for over five years. The constant pounding of the stamps; the daily blasting to loosen the next batch of ore; the shaking, noisy mechanical innards of the mine; and the ever-present dripping water had loosened the rock. A hemorrhage hung imminent.

Finally the high domed ceiling in Number Five West drift stope gave a deep groan that rasped up to a bellow as tons of rock suddenly cascaded down onto the floor of the bay. Had there been anyone at the 440-foot level, they suddenly would have been sitting atop the pile of rubble 160 feet lower.

Deeper in the mine, men froze as the air pressure suddenly increased, wondering if the whole mine is caving in or just one stope. Carbide lamps on work hats flickered; in the old days the air pressure would blow out their candle-lamps.

Stomachs knoted, sphincters clenched, and heart-accelerating adrenaline rushed through veins as men in mounting fear stared wide-eyed at the rock ceilings above them.

Finally a foreman spat and gruffly ordered the men back to work. This time they were lucky. They lost no friends in the cave-in. But it occured to more than a few that the cave-ins seem to be on the increase.

The top half of the mine subsided slightly, adjusting to the lessened support from below. The tide edged up the beach being created from the tailings, waste rock reduced to sand consistency and dumped at water's edge, and life at Treadwell continued.

12 —Juneau City, A.T., November 22, 1915—
Monday morning

Florence heard the bell on the shop door ring.

Will I never get this place cleaned? Putting down the hand broom, she absently patted her hair with one hand and worried at her dress with the other. Quietly she moved out of the back room to stand behind the counter in the shop.

A well-proportioned man, somewhat taller than herself, examined the views of Treadwell on display over one of the glass-fronted curio cases. Pushed by a gusting wind out of the southeast, rain drummed at the large shop windows. She didn't know if he was aware of her presence.

Something made her wait for a moment and just look at him. His pleasant, clean-shaven face was topped with sandy hair partially covered by a neat, gray derby. The rain-splattered overcoat, unbuttoned and open, revealed a three-piece suit that matched the hat. Water beaded on glossy black shoes.

When her gaze traveled back to his face she found him regarding her with warm, brown eyes. His slight smile brought a flush to her cheeks.

"May I help you, sir?" she asked formally.

"I would like five duplicates made of each of these photographs." He handed her two small photos of a hatless man. The subject stared out at the viewer from one, and presented a right profile in the other. Numbers marched across the bottom of each followed by "Seattle Police Dept."

"Have you ever seen this man before?" he asked.

Florence looked up into the customer's eyes for just a moment. They seemed lit up like those of a small boy holding up some loathsome object. *Innocent and prankster fighting for dominance,* she thought. She stared down at the likeness again.

She had seen eyes like those in the photograph before also. They had belonged to a murderer. She shook her head slowly.

"No. Never, Mr., ah..."

"Lepke, pleased to meet you, Miss...?"

"Malone. Florence Malone," she said primly. Her cheeks felt overly warm.

"His name is Edward Krause and we think he has murdered five men."

She jerked back from the photographs and they fell from her suddenly nerveless hands. For a moment she thought she might faint. She must have tottered, for his hand shot out and grasped her elbow firmly.

"Miss Malone, are you ill?" he asked gently.

"No," she said, still staring at the photographs on the floor. "That man is accused of killing someone I loved very much. The shock of realizing who he was just- just surprised me."

She looked up into his worried face. "If you'll release my arm, Mr. Lepke, I'll retrieve your photo-"

"No. That's quite all right, allow me, please." He bent quickly and snatched them off the floor. "Perhaps I should take them elsewhere?"

"No need to do that. We can make duplicates faster than any other shop."

"Oh. How soon can the duplicates be made?"

She took them from his hand.

"By tomorrow at noon."

The small brass bell tinkled as the shop door opened, pulling their attention toward it as if they were marionettes strung in tandem. An elegantly dressed couple hurried in out of the weather. Florence heard Mr. Lepke catch his breath slightly.

She glanced up at him again. Recognition lit in his eyes. She looked back to the couple.

The lady shook off a parasol. They had to be newcomers; anybody who had lived here more than a few days knew what worthless ornaments parasols were in Southeast Alaska. She would remember if she had seen the woman before; she was beautiful in a sharp-featured sort of way.

The woman looked up and saw Florence's customer and her eyes widened involuntarily before she caught herself.

"I say, this is beastly weather!" the man complained. Florence had to strain to keep from laughing. At an amateur play a few weeks earlier, she had heard the same line delivered with nearly the same theatric pomposity.

"I couldn't agree more, sir," Florence said, watching him as he glanced up from tapping his well-made umbrella on the shop floor. She knew better than to worry about the large puddle of water, for that spot never dried.

His eyes washed over her and Mr. Lepke without a glimmer of recognition.

Now this is interesting, she thought. Before the dripping man could intrude further, she added, "I'll be with you just as soon as I finish with my first customer, sir."

Both men spoke at once.

"Oh, of course!" the newcomer said.

"That's quite all right. I wanted to examine these views a moment," Lepke said smoothly. He stepped over to the counter and began leafing through the album of Treadwell views.

"Excellent." The man threw back his head and gave her a well-practiced smile. A long, narrow scar on his left cheek caught the light. "Now, miss, I understand this firm has the very latest views of the great Treadwell Mine?"

"Your understanding is quite correct, sir."

"May I see your catalogue?"

She wanted to tell him, no. Men like this always put her off. He was a caricature. But then caricatures existed because many people shared common traits.

Perhaps he spoke this way all the time. Eddie hadn't sounded like that, and he had lived in London all his life before coming to the University of Washington where they had met. She felt cross, she didn't have the time to think about Eddie now.

"I'm afraid you'll have to wait, it's being used by Mr.—"

"That's quite all right, Miss," Lepke interrupted. "I'm completely finished with it."

"Oh. Jolly good." The man stepped between Lepke and Florence and began examining the album. Florence saw Lepke and the woman exchange quick glances. The woman looked slightly flushed, but she *had* just come in from a cold rainy day.

The woman glanced around and saw Florence staring at her. Before she had time to think, Lepke broke in on her musings.

"I'll be in tomorrow for those duplicates. Good day." He lifted his hat and bolted through the door before she had time to respond.

"Peculiar man!" the woman exclaimed, looking at Florence expectantly.

So that was it, Florence thought. If I'll gossip about Mr. Lepke, I will have atoned for staring at her rudely. I also might learn how she knows Mr. Lepke.

Part of her wondered why she was so interested in total strangers. But her other side welcomed the novelty of tourists this late in the year. She would be seeing at least one of the men again. Both were rather nice-looking.

We'll trade, she decided.

"I thought him rather interesting," Florence said.

"Indeed?" The woman carefully looked her over.

Florence's faint uneasiness over her own perceived rudeness vanished. "Not that I know him, of course. I don't believe I've ever seen him before today."

"I believe he was aboard the *S.S. Humboldt* yesterday when we docked," the woman said casually.

"So you're all visitors! Where are you from?" Long ago Florence discovered that visitors liked to talk about how far they had traveled to get to Alaska Territory.

However, this one hesitated. She hadn't been ready for the question. She looked at the man still paging slowly through the Treadwell views.

"Arnold, where would you say we were from?"

Arnold was so intent on the photographs he didn't hear her.

"Sir!" the woman barked.

He jerked around as if he'd been slapped. His face darkened.

"Vas?" he snapped back, then caught himself. "Ah, what is it, dear?" The Lord Caricature accent had vanished in his confusion.

"This young woman just asked me where we were from. I really don't know how to answer that."

Arnold gave Florence an assessing look.

"Well, you see, miss, my wife and I have been traveling a great deal for the past year –"

"About five years for me," the woman interrupted.

"Yes, well," Arnold glared at his wife and then returned his attention to Florence. "We met in Mexico and were married there. However we are both British subjects so I suppose you could say we hail from England." The accent gained strength rapidly.

Arnold possessed aristocratic good looks. He was taller than Mr. Lepke, and also thinner. Florence's gaze moved to his hands as one rubbed the other. He had long "artistic" fingers as the saying went.

His dark hair framed a tanned traveler's face. Nobody had a chance to tan in Juneau City. Along with the dramatic scar down his left cheek, his eyes radiated a cold energy.

"How romantic, to meet and marry in a foreign country!" Florence said. "You must have had a whirlwind engagement."

"One could say that," the woman said dryly.

Florence found them fascinating. It wasn't every day visitors interested her to this degree. Rain rattled the windows.

"Then you're in the Territory as part of your world tour?" Florence realized she was behaving horribly, but she also knew a façade when she saw one. If they could play roles, so could she. Besides, it was only harmless entertainment.

"What is your name, miss?" the woman abruptly asked her.

"Florence Malone. And you are...?"

"Whomever I so choose." Her eyes flashed with malevolence. "You are a very impertinent girl, Florence Malone," she said, putting a slight twist in the word "girl" which raised Florence's hackles.

"Florence Malone, *assertive* woman, would appreciate knowing whom she is being condescended by –if *madam* would please identify one of her many roles," she said.

The door to Mr. Winter's studio opened with a snap. His large body filled three fourths of the doorframe. Florence hadn't known he was in today.

"Miss Malone, is there a problem out here?" he asked in a calm, amber voice.

"I am trying to determine that, Mr. Winter," she replied.

"There's no problem here, sir," the woman said. "I was merely having a chat with your shop girl."

At the term "girl" Florence felt her nostrils flare and bit her tongue to keep from flying at her.

"I see," Mr. Winter said. "For a moment there it sounded like an altercation of some sort." The door closed behind him.

The woman held out her hand, a smile played about her lips.

"I am Baroness Ganbor. Pleased to make your acquaintance, Florence Malone."

Florence shook her hand as if it were hot to the touch. The woman actually seemed friendly! "You're an English Baroness?" she asked slowly, trying to make the same mental turn.

"There you go again! You're hopelessly impertinent." This time a smile backed the words. "And I rather enjoy it."

"I was about to tell the baroness to get used to it," Florence said bluntly, returning the smile. "And I dislike being referred to as a 'shop girl.' I am both clerk and technician here at Winter and Pond, if you please."

"You're a suffragette, aren't you?" the baroness asked.

"I demand equality in my life, if that's what you mean. Did your mother really name you 'Baroness?'"

The baroness lost her composure long enough to emit a loud, "Hah!" Then she looked at Florence closely.

"You're not easy to make friends with, are you, Florence?" A hint of supplication tinted her tone. "No, I suppose not."

"Please answer the question," Florence said.

"My maiden name was Amanda Beckwourth Landes. My late husband was Baron Georg Ganbor. Georg was Austrian. He died in Mexico just before I met Mr. Williams." There was a definite twist on "Mister."

Mr. Arnold Williams stared at her, wide-eyed.

"I thought we had an agreement, Amanda, that we would be circumspect," he said with great vehemence.

"Well, Arnold, we agreed on so very many things," she replied tiredly. "If this had been the first broken confidence I would be distraught. But as you know, sir, it is merely *my* first."

Florence began to feel very uncomfortable.

"I'd like to conclude my business now, miss," he said. "I would like copies of the views indicated on this list. When may I pick them up?"

She almost told him they had copies already made up before she caught herself. "Tomorrow afternoon, Mr. Williams." *Circumspect about what?*

Amanda stepped up to her and whispered, "He's strange about my name." Then she straightened up and looked archly at Arnold. "Are we finished here, then, darling?" she asked.

"Quite!" he said with some heat, and walked toward the door.

Amanda looked down at her parasol with a frown. Florence followed her gaze.

"This was rather a waste of money, wasn't it?" Amanda asked in a forlorn tone.

Unthinkingly, Florence replied, "Quite."

The shop door slammed behind Mr. Williams and the two women erupted in giggles.

13 —Auk Village, A.T., November 23, 1915–
Tuesday morning

As Lepke walked down the plank street in the Indian village, his eyes were pulled to the snow-covered peaks across Gastineau Channel on Douglas Island. Large cumulus clouds drifted lazily, punctuating the cobalt blue sky, playing hide-and-seek with the sun.

The mountains reared magnificent with their snowy mantles and heavily wooded slopes. His gaze traveled to the towns of Douglas and Treadwell in the distance. Yesterday the stacks of the mining complex belched smoke into the pristine air, creating a haze that hung above the waters of the channel like a shroud. Today a brisk north wind moved the smelly fumes southward.

Much of the slopes around the towns had been cleared of trees to build the miles of pilings and plank streets connecting the hills to the water. Most of the trees within a half-mile of the mines that survived the building boom had fallen victim to chemical smoke and waste. Mercury and cyanide were used in the gold extraction process.

The hotel clerk told him locals still called snow "termination dust" even though it no longer heralded the end of the mining season. All the old placer miners had hired on to work hard rock, found other jobs, or else left the area decades ago.

The Auk People had settled in a location separated from Juneau by a ridge named for the industry newly located astride its spine— Telephone Hill. He decided the Indians had the better of the deal. The ridge shielded the village from some of the stamp mill racket and also from the prevailing southeasterly wind that usually brought bad weather.

The Auk People originally lived seventeen miles north of what became Juneau City. But despite Auke Bay's charms, the lure of jobs and civilization long ago drew the Indians closer to the big mines.

For over two centuries the Tlingits reigned as the most feared people on the North Pacific coast. The Russians tried in vain to subdue them, finally striking an edgy truce. The Americans ignored this proud people. After the U. S. Navy bombarded and destroyed Angoon over a misunderstood incident, the Tlingits pulled back.

Lepke had studied these people for a term paper in college. He owned a first edition of Aurel Krause's *Die Tlinkit Indianer*. He wondered if Aurel was related to the Edward Krause in his investigation. Who knew? There were all kinds in every family.

The few people he saw in the village ignored him or turned off onto one of the many long docks running across the mud flats to deeper water. The tide was out but the brisk wind kept the reek of exposed sewage bearable. Many small boats and canoes lay leashed to docks, stranded on the snow-covered mud, waiting for

Alaska State Library - Historical Collections

the afternoon high tide. He noticed daylight through the ribs of some boats that would continue to rot on the icy mud.

Two Indian men moved down the plank walk toward him. He observed how they ambled leisurely, chatting with one another. But they definitely intended to intercept him.

The younger one wore a rumpled hat and an old navy pea jacket boasting two buttons. His knees peeked through the ragged pants legs touching the tops of heavy, leather, work shoes. His hair hung unkempt and his sparse beard uneven.

Lepke noticed both men examined him carefully. The older man boasted a mustache flecked with gray, he wore a heavy shirt and a suit vest over it. The vest had seen better days. His Levi Strauss patented work pants seemed new, but the brown brogans visible beneath the cuffs bespoke years of use. His soiled hat had belonged to a junior naval officer in the distant past.

The men stopped in front of Lepke. The older man in the officer's cap nodded to him.

"You've been walking around here a lot. You looking for somebody in particular?" Tension arced between the three men. Lepke had encountered this before when dealing with neighbors of hunted men.

"In a way, I am." He pulled a pad from his jacket pocket and opened it to where a string divided the pages.

"I'm trying to find witnesses who may have seen a particular gas boat travel past on the 30th or 31st of October."

"Why?" the younger Indian asked.

"I think a man was murdered on that boat."

"The man who owns this boat, is he Indian?" the older man inquired.

"No. I think he's German by birth." Lepke felt the tension pop and disappear like a bubble.

The older man grinned, displaying good teeth under the salt-and-pepper moustache.

"It's not every day a white man asks me to help hang another white man." He nodded to the young man beside him. "This is my nephew, Jim Kisadis. I'm George Mak-we."

He held up the left side of his vest so Lepke could see the small metal badge pinned to the shirt. "I'm also an Indian policeman. Who are you?"

"August Lepke, Pinkerton operative. Pleased to meet you, Officer Mak-we." He shook the policeman's hand. "And you too, Jim."

Jim Kisadis gripped his hand strongly. "You really a Pinkerton man? Did you get tired of sittin' in the states shootin' strikers?"

Lepke frowned at the young man for a moment. He had never cared for the strikebreaking activities of the Pinkertons. More than once he felt he'd just changed armies.

As he saw it, the US Army was for the protection of the nation. The Pinkertons were an army for hire. So far he had successfully evaded strikebreaking work during his career. Still, this young man's rude question nettled him.

"Yes, I really am a Pinkerton operative. And I've never shot a striker in my life. Only Spaniards and rebels."

George Mak-we broke in before his nephew could speak again. "Well, I'm honored to meet one of Mr. Pinkerton's detectives. I will be happy to assist you in any way I can."

"Have you heard about the kidnapping of Mr. Christie from the Treadwell mine?"

Both men nodded.

"A group of individuals have hired the agency to locate Mr. Christie and bring his kidnapper to justice. The instrument of that justice I plan to be."

"So what are you doin' in the village?" Jim asked.

"I'm trying to record the movements of Edward Krause from October 23rd onward." He glanced down at his notebook. "I believe he was in this area with his boat the day of, or the day after, the kidnapping. That would be the 30th or the 31st. He owns a small boat, about 35 feet long, not rigged for fishing. It has a large cabin for such a small boat. The wheelhouse is located further toward the stern than is usual, and has oval windows."

"I've seen that boat," Jim said. "It's the one I always think is a government boat because it's painted green."

"Me too," George agreed.

"Did either of you see it on the 30th or after?"

"I'd have to check my log book at home," George said slowly. "But it seems to me I saw it right around the first of the month, right out there." He pointed at the channel. "It was headed north."

"I'm staying at the Cain Hotel, room six. If you remember anything more, or pin down the exact day and time you saw that boat, would you let me know?"

George Mak-we grinned widely. "For certain, Detective Lepke!"

Lepke shook hands with both men again and continued back toward Juneau City proper. As he walked he jotted down the essentials of the conversation. He hoped to see them again.

The sun brought a number of people out of doors. Winter days seemed brighter in Alaska than in Oregon. Maybe due to so many snow-covered mountains reflecting the sunshine.

Lepke described Krause's boat an even dozen times throughout the morning. Many knew the boat and some remembered seeing it during the time in question.

John Johnson, a cook in the Fairbanks Restaurant on Lower Front Street, lived north of the Indian village near Norway Point. He remembered seeing the boat anchored off Salmon Creek. He remembered because; "This fellow rowed in to the beach and put about five good-sized rocks in his skiff, and then rowed back out to his boat. Kinda curious, huh?"

Another fisherman was absolutely sure he had seen it the evening of November 2, dropping anchor across from the Salmon Creek powerhouse in upper Gastineau Channel.

"Could you see who was aboard?"

"Naw, the light was most gone. I could yust see one man on d' boat."

Leaving the fisherman, Lepke checked his watch and was surprised to see he had just five minutes to make his noon appointment at the Winter and Pond studio. He picked up his pace.

As he hurried along he thought about his brief, uncomfortable meeting with the U.S. Marshal and his deputies.

"We're going to make you a special deputy U. S. Marshal, Mr. Lepke," Marshal Bishop had said pompously.

"For what reason?"

"Well, the U.S. Attorney got word from the office in Seattle we couldn't have a member of a private agency working this investigation for the government. It's against regulations."

"So you're going to hire me as a federal agent in order to finish the work. Very neat. Does my office in Portland know about this?"

"Not officially. In fact, we want you to keep reporting to them. Just make sure we get carbon copies of everything you send."

"Done. I'll even show you what I've already sent."

"No need. Your office already provided a transcript of your file. You have a good mind for this kind of duty."

"It's just a big puzzle, Marshal. All you need to do is pick at it long enough and it will unravel."

"Just unravel enough rope to hang that son-of-a-bitch Krause. Jim Plunkett was a friend of mine. Put your left hand on the Bible and raise your right."

Bishop swore him in. August had suddenly felt a sense of duty that transcended even contractual arrangements. The added yoke of responsibility was something he recognized from his army days.

"You realize of course, this arrangement will end as soon as you've finished boxing Krause up," Bishop said.

"Of course." Lepke glanced across the room to where Deputy Marshal Clarke sat with a baleful look. "I want to assure both of you gentlemen I have no designs on either of your jobs."

Before Clarke could respond, Bishop said, "We really weren't worried, Mr. Lepke. You don't even know Judge Wickersham."

"Exactly," Lepke said. As he left he could hear them both laughing.

There was something about a politically appointed office, he reflected, that ruined good men.

The clock behind the counter chimed twelve when he walked into the photography and curio shop. A rather stout man wearing a boiled shirt and arm garters stood behind the counter.

"May I help you, sir?"

"Yes. I had arranged with a Miss Malone to make copies of two photographs. She said they would be ready by noon today."

"Ah, yes, you must be Mr. Lepke." The man smiled and extended his hand. "I am Lloyd Winter, one of the owners of this establishment. Terrible thing, this kidnapping business. I do hope you are able to bring the responsible party to justice."

Florence Malone emerged from the back room carrying a slim parcel wrapped in brown paper. She wore a coat and hat.

"Oh, Mr. Lepke! I was just going to leave this with Mr. Winter for you. I'm on my way to lunch."

"What is the charge?" Lepke asked Winter. As he handed the amount over, he glanced at Florence.

"I have not yet had my lunch. May I join you?"

She colored slightly and hesitated before answering.

"I don't see why not. There are definitely some establishments in this town to be avoided for one's health. A cheechako could use a guide. Besides, has there ever been a Pinkerton man who went bad?" She smiled and his heart picked up a beat.

"Just one," Lepke answered with a stern frown that evolved into a smile. "But we don't talk about him."

"I'll be back at one, Mr. Winter," she called brightly as they left the shop.

"Enjoy your lunch, Miss Malone. Nice meeting you, Mr. Lepke."

August Lepke smiled over his shoulder and waved. As they stepped into the sunshine he looked down at the handsome young woman beside him. He hadn't felt this good in a long time.

"We have a few choices. What kind of food do you eat?" she asked.

"I'll eat anything. You choose what you like."

"Very well. We'll go down to the White Lunch Café. They're new and trying to make a name for themselves."

As they sat down at the last available table, Lepke looked over at Florence and nodded his head at the full room. "They seem to be making a good reputation."

"Yes. That's why we're here."

"Do you dine out a great deal, Miss Malone?"

"Every weekday at lunch. I could walk home and eat, but then I would have to converse with my father or sister. I like to spend lunch by myself, or with someone interesting." She smiled at him and her eyes flashed.

He stared down at his hands, while casting about in his mind for a response.

The waiter bustled up to take their order.

"You order for me, surprise me with something good," he said.

"Two blue plate specials," she said to the waiter, who then hurried off.

"You live with your parents?" he asked lightly.

Her smile turned wistful. "Mother passed away when I was twelve. Father's still very loving but he's been different since she died."

"My mother died last year. I felt very, very bad about it. I hadn't seen her since I left Germany, sixteen years before."

"Oh. How sad," she said softly.

"I wrote to her at least once a month," he said quickly, "but I never had the necessary funds to make a trip back to the old country and see her."

"Did you leave a girl in the old country, too?" she asked.

"No." He stared into her eyes. "I haven't had much time for social relationships."

The waiter returned with their meal. Roast beef, potatoes, gravy, and steamed carrots. Lepke realized he was famished and dug in with knife and fork.

For a few minutes they ate in silence. Finally Florence took a sip of tea, and peered at him over the cup held with both hands. "Do you mean to tell me you've never paid court to a girl?"

"I didn't say that."

"So you've had time for at least one 'social relationship' in your life?"

"Do you have a beau?" he asked, staring into her eyes.

"Not really," she said matter-of-factly. "There are a few who have approached me with their romantic illusions, but they didn't stay very long."

"So you're not a romantic woman?" he asked with an air of detachment.

"I'm not sure," she said candidly. "Perhaps if I met a man who was looking for a partner instead of a domestic slave, I might become romantically inclined."

Lepke thoughtfully chewed his last bite of potato and swallowed. "Then you're not waiting for a rich man or someone with a title, like most pretty girls?"

She sipped her tea and carefully sat the cup on its saucer. "I don't consider myself a 'pretty girl,' Mr. Lepke. As for wealth or titles, well, my small experience has been that men with either tend to be even bigger boors than most."

"I can't argue with that," Lepke muttered.

"Does that mean there isn't a fiancée waiting for you back in the states?"

"No," he said, feeling uncomfortable, "there isn't."

"Was there ever someone in your life whom you loved?"

"My mother," he said, forcing a smile.

She threw back her head and laughed. "Well, one thing I can say for you, sir, you don't kiss and tell."

"No. I'm very discreet. My profession demands it."

"How long have you been a detective?"

"Five years. Prior to that I clerked at the Portland office for two years."

"And before that?"

"College."

"You have a college education?" she asked with surprise.

"Mostly," he admitted. "One more semester and I could put initials behind my name if I wished."

"Only one more semester to finish? Why did you stop?"

"College began to get oppressive, so I decided to quit for awhile and try something else."

"What made it oppressive? I found college interesting."

"You went to college, Miss Malone?"

"University of Washington, class of '16,'" she said with a twinkle in her eye.

"So why did you quit?" he asked with mock gravity.

"There was so much to do I couldn't find time to study. My grades reflected my lack of scholarship and the university terminated our contract. But the areas I did study more than made up for the academic nonsense I ignored."

This time Lepke laughed. "And which areas were those?"

"Photography and women's suffrage."

"Ah, you're a suffragette!"

"What's so amusing about that?"

"Well, it answers some of my questions—" He felt like biting his tongue. That sentence wasn't supposed to come out.

"And which questions are those, Mr. Lepke?" The sparkle danced back into her eyes.

He looked up at the clock on the wall. "Don't you have to be back at work at one pm?"

"That's not what you were questioning!"

"The only question I have for you at the moment is; will you have lunch with me again?"

"Depends on when," she said coyly.

"Well, I leave for Petersburg on Friday..." He relished the flash of disappointment that crossed her face. "...but I should be back in just a few days. Could I call on you then?"

He'd caught her off balance. He didn't think that would happen often.

After a moment of staring at him —he could almost see her thoughts darting about like mental swallows— she said, "That would be fine, Mr. Lepke. Thank you for lunching with me. I found it all very amusing."

THE DAILY ALASKA DISPATCH
Juneau, Alaska, Tuesday, November 23, 1915

SERBS BLOCK OPENING OF TURK PORT

HARRY STEEL HAS RESIGNED AS POSTMASTER

SUN GODDESS IS WORSHIPED BY JAPANESE

GREAT DOINGS WITH THE ELKS LAST NIGHT

MARKET PRICE OF RADIUM IS REDUCED SOME

GERMAN SPIES ARE BLAMED

FIND A GUN OF PLUNKETT KRAUSE BOAT
Evidence Also That Krause Was Leader
of Secret Organization in the North

REGULAR ARSENAL ABOARD HIS POWER BOAT IS FOUND
Evidence That Accused Used a Secret Code to Communicate With Others Of His Kind in Southeastern Alaska Towns—Other Notes.

A federal warrant charging Edward Krause with murder has been telegraphed to Seattle, and it is expected the necessary order for the extradition of Krause will be speedily made. The papers were mailed on the steamer Humboldt, to be placed in the hands of the Governor of Washington in case there is a legal fight made against extradition.
Believe Krause Guilty

Chief of Detectives Tennant, of the Seattle police force declares Krause guilty of three murders—William Christie, John Moe and James Plunkett. Krause was in the custody of the Seattle police for three days and nights, and is declared by Tennant to be the coolest prisoner ever in that jail. For three days and nights Krause faced Tennant in the detective's private office and rehashed and rehashed his story of the securing of the Christie and Plunkett signatures. These came to the customs house with the luggage of Krause when he was arrested. They were written on linen paper water-marked "Berkshire Bond," which is the identical make of paper upon which the note to Mrs. Christie, notifying her of her husband's kidnapping, and the note to the customs house with the forged signature of Captain Plunkett.

Chief Tennant will come north on an early steamer to assist the federal officers— (cont. on page 2)

14 —Juneau City, A.T., November 24, 1915—
Wednesday morning

"**Watch what yer doin' there, you ham-handed herring-choker!**" A half block away from the warehouse Jack Malone could hear Clancy out-shouting the Treadwell stamps. Jack walked off the plank street and into the huge open doors in time to see the short, barrel-chested Clancy staring with murder in his eyes up at a tall, wide-shouldered man.

"Clancy, I don't care if you sit at the right hand of God, but if you don't stop callin' me a herring-choker, I'm gonna break your nose," the tall man said softly.

"Shit! Whose goin' ta be breakin' me nose, Rankin? You? Perhaps ye got an English regiment in yer pocket? Now move them apple barrels around them crates of glass instead of through them, or I'll be breakin' a nose or two meself." The foreman snorted and hitched his pants a fraction higher under the prominent beer-belly. The pants immediately slid back.

Rankin took a deep breath and went back to his hand truck. The other workers ignored the two men and worked steadily.

"Top of the morning to you, Clancy. Morning, Rankin!" Jack said.

Rankin sniffed and moved his load of apples off through the warehouse. Jack stopped next to Clancy. "How's the warehousing business today?"

"I'm not crying in me beer, Jack. What brings you down here on a fine morning like this?" Clancy scratched at the stubble on his jaw and peered at Malone from beneath a raised bushy eyebrow.

"The party secretary asked me to go around and take up a collection from the faithful. We're coming up on an election year, y'know. The war chest needs more bills fer ballots, y'know what I mean?"

"Jasus, Jack! It ain't been but four months since I gave the party twenty dollars! Why d'ya keep hitting on me?"

"Think of it as an investment, Sean Clancy! D'ya want Chester God-damned Kingsley Snow ta win with this prohibition thing? You handle spirits for me and every other joint in town. What'll ya do without that custom?"

"I do an honest day's work for an honest wage, which is more than I can say for some! There'll always be freight on these docks, no matter what happens. And I don't talk politics with me customers. This town knows the Clancy Brothers Warehouse is dry, clean, and honest."

"Now how do ya mean 'dry'? I'm not saying there's anything wrong with your business, not at all. I'm saying there's a brighter future out there for ye if ye help protect our past. More'n that, you have promise, you could go far in the party. You could go far in the Territory."

"I'm as far into this Territory as I want to get. I like it here 'n—"

"Well then, look at it as insurance—"

"God damn it, Jack, I have insurance! You're gettin' pretty long in the tooth to be pullin' that Molly Maguire crap on me! This ain't Pennsylvania and I don't run no coal mine!"

"Sean! Calm yourself, man. Who bit your tit today? All I'm asking is that you

think about contributing a little something for the party and the wet vote. It's still a year off. No hurry."

"I'll tell ya what bit my tit! My worthless Goddamned brother is off drunk with his cigar girl again. We got a freighter unloading tonight, and me with no place to put the freight. Then you come in here acting like General Wolfe Tone with your damned hand out."

Clancy went red in the face. He gasped and sat down hard on a stack of flour sacks. "Shit. This fookin' place is gonna be the death of me yet," he sighed.

"Let me buy ya a pint when you're done, okay?" Jack asked tenderly. "You're workin' too hard, Sean. You should hire a couple more strong backs to help out around here."

"If Cullen would stop drinking up our profits or spending them on his fancy girl, I would. Ah, I wish he'd get drunk enough to catch a steamer south and not have the money to come back. Damn his worthless arse." He sighed again. "An' I'll be looking for that pint in an hour or two. Down at Armstrong's?"

"And where else would I be?" Jack slapped the shorter man heartily on the back and moved into the street. His smile slid into a grim line.

Now he had a mission for the morning. The police didn't bother with this part of Juneau unless called. The red light district flourished openly, fronted by bars, cigar stores, bathhouses, and gaming rooms. Jack Malone reigned as a law unto himself on Lower Front Street.

He pushed through the doors of the first bar he came to, stopped, and stood in the long, narrow space. His eyes traveled quickly from face to face around the room. Satisfied, he went up to the bar and nodded at the bartender.

"John, yer looking fit."

"Thanks, Jack. What can I get you?" The beefy man twisted on his huge mustache absently.

"I'd be ever so grateful to know the whereabouts of Cullen Clancy," he said in a low voice.

John grinned. "Hell, that's easy. He's upstairs with Lulu, dead drunk." His thumb jabbed the air over his shoulder.

Jack dropped a silver dollar on the bar.

"You're a good Democrat, John, and I appreciate it. I'd also appreciate it if ye'd go a bit deaf for the next half hour."

"You'll have to speak up," he said, his grin even wider, "my ears're botherin' me again." The silver dollar disappeared.

Jack slid into an empty chair at a table between two men in miner's clothing. Ralph and Silas, two corruptible lads indeed. They both looked at him and nodded.

"You boys look like you could use some extra income."

"Depends," said Silas, the smaller of the two.

"What'cha need, Jack?" Ralph said, his voice as bearish and shambling as its owner.

"I need moral support for a chastisement that's long over-due."

"Do we get, uh, do we gotta hurt somebody?" the smaller man asked quickly. A cold glow washed over the eyes in his fox-like face.

"Maybe. I'll tell you what's needed as soon as I assess the situation. But you'll do **only** what I tell you, got it?" Steel edged the words.

Silas sat back hooding the glow. "Sure, Jack. Whatever you say. How much ya willin' to spend on this chas, ches, what ya said?"

"A gold 1883 nickel for each of ye." He smiled, remembering New York when he was twenty-five and the new five-cent piece issued that year.

The mint in its infinite wisdom had placed the Roman numeral V swathed in olive leaves on the reverse, with the ubiquitous profile of Liberty as idealized by Mr. Morgan on the obverse. However, they neglected to put the word "cents" on the coin. Jack felt sure he was among the first to gild one and find a cigar store. All you did was walk in, pick up a five-cent cigar, and hand the storekeeper the coin.

If the man put it in his till and stared hard at you, you were only out a bit of gold leaf. But if providence smiled on you, the man gave you $4.95 in change without question. He eventually passed enough nickels to buy a ticket to Chicago, and keep himself fed for a week.

Within three months the mint had put out new coins with the word "CENTS" clearly visible under the olive leaves. Two years ago they'd changed the nickel again. This time they put an ugly Indian on one side and a buffalo on the other.

He'd never gone back to Tammany Hall. It would have taken a lifetime to gain power there. But he never forgot the lessons he learned in Tammany's lap.

"I ain't gittin' off m'ass fer a lousy nickel," Silas said contemptuously.

"Five dollars in gold, you fool. Fer each of ye," Jack snapped.

"When d'ya wanna' do this here thing, Jack?" Ralph asked, licking his lips.

Jack looked at the stairway, feeling young again.

"Right now, lads."

The narrow, musty hallway gained light by two windows on one side with facing doors on the other. This was a crib, one of about forty in this part of town. It cost the owners $10 per establishment each month to keep official interest at bay.

The threadbare carpet slightly softened their steps as they moved down to the fourth and last door. Another door at the end of the hall opened on an outside stairway leading down to one of the myriad docks lining the channel. A quick check revealed no boats tied to this one. Good.

Jack carefully turned the doorknob on room 4. It stopped after a quarter turn. He pressed back against the wall.

"Damn," he said softly. "That's a thirty-five-cent lock." He kicked the door inward with a crash. The three men rushed into the room.

Lulu, a small, skinny woman with wild, red-hennaed hair, jerked up from the bed. The dirty sheet fell away from her knobby breasts as she tried to focus on the men.

"What is it?" she shrilled. "I ain't done nothin'. Honest I ain't!"

Jack looked down at her with a sneer.

"'Honest you ain't' indeed!" he mimicked. "Get out of here before I squeeze yer head off."

The man on the bed hadn't moved nor made a sound. Suddenly he loosened a long snore and broke wind at the same time.

"Damn me if that ain't a Clancy for ya, blowin' hot air from both ends at once," Malone said.

Silas snickered. The room stank of unwashed bodies, stale sex, copious bowel

Thwaites 9482. Street Scene, Juneau, Capital of Alaska.

gas, and sour whisky.
Lulu grabbed her clothes and scurried between them. Silas pinched her butt as she squeezed past him.

"See ya later, Lulu!"

"Wake him up," Jack ordered.

"How?" Ralph asked. "He's drunker n' shit."

Jack pointed to the chamber pot in the corner.

"Then dump that on him."

Silas picked up the stoneware vessel and looked into it.

"Jesus, it's full of shit. That'll make a hell of a mess. I don't know as I'd wanna touch him after that."

The boy had more brains than he'd given him credit for, Jack mused.

"Never mind. I'll wake him!"

Cullen lay stretched out on the bed, limbs akimbo. Jack kicked him between the legs nearly as hard as he had kicked the door. The man jerked upright, his eyes wide, unseeing, his mouth making a silent, exaggerated "o."

Jack slapped him across the face and Cullen fell onto the floor, moaning.

"Get up, you worthless pea brain!" he grated. "I want a word with you."

Silas licked his lips. His arms trembled and his hands twitched.

"Help him up, boys," Jack said gently.

As he was lifted to his feet, Cullen began to choke.

"He's gonna upchuck!" Silas said. "Quick, Ralph, get him over the back rail."

The two men rushed the stunned man out through the hall and pushed him against the handrail on the dock stairs. He vomited into the water repeatedly until dry heaves wracked his body. Finally he slumped down on the small landing, his head resting against the center guard rail.

"Go get us a bucket of brine, Silas," Jack ordered. "Cullen needs a spot o' washin' up."

Cullen lay against the rail moaning until Silas dumped a bucket of seawater on him.

"Wha, whaddya want?" he whined. "Why yuh mad at me?"

"Take him back to the room. Too many ears out here."

They dropped him on the bed. He showed no inclination to move.

"Stand up, you worthless lout, or I'll tear off yer balls and give 'em to a Sassenach. There's plenty of 'em around and they're all wantin' fer a pair."

Cullen rolled over and groaned to his feet. He stared at Jack with red-veined eyes. His breath reeked and his nose dripped blood.

He had the same general build as his brother, but had gone completely to fat. He hadn't worked in over a year. It was common knowledge that years ago Sean had promised their dying mother he would take care of his little brother and it had turned into a habit. All Cullen did was live off the business the Clancy family owned.

Jack decided the habit would kill Sean if he kept it up. His friend needed some help.

"If you don't put in a twelve hour day beside your brother from here on out, you're gonna wish you had never seen this town, or met me."

"I feel that way already," Cullen replied sullenly.

"Then get out of town. Go to Seattle. Tonight."

"Tonight?" Cullen blinked owlishly and carefully rubbed his nose. "I don't got the money to do that."

"You've taken your last dime from yer brother's labors. There's a southbound freighter coming in tonight. I'll get ya a blue ticket. The boys here will make sure you don't miss your boat."

He handed Silas and Ralph each a coin.

"I'll have John bring something up for all of you. Make sure your guest here drinks with you, I don't want to see him around town any more."

"Don't you worry, Jack," Ralph said slowly. "He knows better'n ta try anything on us. Doncha, Cullen?"

"Hell, I **need** a drink!" Cullen said, gingerly rubbing his groin.

"You'll need an undertaker if you come back to Juneau City. Don't ever forget that," Jack said flatly. He turned on his heel and left the room. He had business downstairs.

15 —Treadwell, A.T., November 24, 1915— Wednesday morning

I should have shot her when I had the chance, thought the man who called himself Arnold Williams. A cloud of tobacco smoke filled the passenger cabin of the gas boat *Gent.* Just beneath the smoke lurked the heavy odors of wet wool, unwashed bodies, bowel gas, and diesel oil.

This mission was proving to be more difficult than he anticipated. Amanda turned out to be a complication of the first order. But for a time she had been a very provocative complication.

The week they spent in San Francisco still tormented him. All the delicious stories he had heard about English widows were in error when it came to this woman. She was positively brilliant at evading his sexual overtures.

At no time had she actually said "no." On the train in Mexico it had been obvious to him that all interest had departed from her marriage. Now that the man was dead, he miraculously regained a position of dominance in her mind. A position Williams doubted was ever fact in this life.

So he pushed it. "My lovely, either you share my bed or I will leave you on your own in Seattle."

"What do you mean?"

"You have an excellent grasp of the English language. What do you think I mean?"

"I think it means you're not as much of a man as you said you were. In Mexico you told me I could be of benefit to you with appearances alone. You gave me your word, sir, I would not be compromised in any other way."

His face flushed at the memory and he dug into his coat pocket for his packet of Fatima cigarettes. She had withdrawn, sullen and disagreeable since that night. He wished he had left her in Seattle. But she did provide excellent camouflage.

But *why* had she been on that train in Mexico? Was her husband in truth an *Austrian* count as she told the shop girl? He was positive she was British. He hadn't been able to ask her questions because he had already told her there must be no further revelations of his past.

He'd wondered at her smile when she'd answered, "That works in both directions, you know."

She wouldn't even tell him what her ultimate destination was to have been. Why hadn't the baron spoken to him once he realized Williams spoke German? He shook his head angrily.

Worse, he still didn't know if she spoke German or not. Enough of this! He had to concentrate on being an Englishman, on being Arnold Williams, correspondent for the *London Times.*

And somewhere on this channel was a man who would help him. Von Papen claimed he had paid a great deal for the man's cooperation. But no Mr. Moe had appeared when the *Humboldt* docked.

He glanced around the ferry cabin at the men in working clothes. They seemed a stolid lot, completely satisfied with working ten hours a day, seven days a week, for months and months.

Other than himself only two other men on the boat wore suits and overcoats. Both carried sample cases. They were drummers, another confusing Americanism to be dealt with. He made the mistake of letting the tall, horse-faced one catch his eye.

The man immediately elbowed his way through the clump of miners, transferring his sample case to his left hand he rubbed his right hand on the side of his pants and held it out.

"Good day, sir. Melton's my name, compression is my game." He grinned inanely through his unruly mustache at Williams while working his hand like a pump.

Arnold firmly pulled his hand free, and forced himself to be genial.

"Pleased, I'm sure. Williams. Press."

"Press? Tabloid or drill? Haw, haw."

He thought furiously for a moment before finding sense in the man's response.

"Tabloid. Newspaper, actually. The *Times*."

The man sobered instantly.

"You don't say! New York or Seattle?"

"London, old boy." He thickened his accent.

"Is that right?" Melton said.

"That's the second time you've intimated I'm not telling you the truth." he pointed out.

"Oh, my lands." The professional grin was back. "That's just the way we talk here in the colonies, you know." His attempted British accent proved a total disaster.

Williams allowed a small smile to crease his face. "Compression is a principle, how can you market that?"

"In hoses, drills, drill bits, and sharpening tools, all operated by air compression. Ingersoll-Rand has a complete line of mining equipment working hard in the Treadwell complex. I'm up from the Seattle office to show them the latest in modern couplers."

"Ingersoll. That's a German name, isn't it?"

"Now, Mr. Williams, just because your country is having some problems with the kaiser is no reason to go looking for bogeymen in America. We're an American company that goes back two generations. Rand certainly isn't a German name."

"Merely asking, my good man."

"There are a lot of Germans working in the mine here, as well as Englishmen, Serbs, Filipinos, Hungarians, and Turks. Hell, every country in Europe and half of Asia is represented in the Treadwell."

"And everyone gets along?" Williams asked.

"For the most part. I hear every now and then there's a knuckle sandwich delivered because someone's accent grates on a nerve, but that doesn't happen much."

"You seem to know a great deal about Treadwell for someone who doesn't live here."

"I make ninety per-cent of my commissions off this complex, so it's my job to know all about it."

"So you're telling me Americans aren't taking sides in the war?"

"C'mon, Mr. Williams. After the dirty Huns sank the *Lusitania*? There were American women and children on that ship! We'll never forget that."

There were also munitions destined for England on the ship, Williams thought. *Our agents discovered that before she left New York, but a British journalist wouldn't be privy to that information.*

"No. The *Lusitania* should never be forgotten, that's for certain," he said.

The pilot slipped the boat out of gear and throttled the engine back to an idle.

"Is this your first trip to Douglas Island, Mr. Williams?" Melton's voice rose automatically with the ambient noise level from the stamps.

"Yes, it is."

"Pray you're never over here when a Taku wind is blowing!"

"Is this 'Taku wind' like the snipe hunts school boys visit on newcomers?"

"Oh, no, sir! They're quite real. Y'see, on the other side of the Coastal Range are Yukon Territory and northern British Columbia. It gets down to fifty and sixty below zero there in the winter." His voice edged close to a shout.

"Well, the cold builds up in layers, like blankets on a bed, and when the air blankets get piled high enough, the top one flows down through the river valleys that lead to the ocean out here. A number of those rivers funnel into the Taku."

"Where's the Taku?" Williams asked.

"You came across Taku Inlet when you sailed into Juneau."

"We arrived after dark, and it was raining quite hard," Williams said.

"Well, it's a good-sized river for these parts. Only one bigger in southeast is the Stikine down by Wrangell."

"Ah, now I did see the mouth of that river. Very impressive. Not quite the Thames."

Melton laughed. "No, it's definitely not the Thames. The Yukon is bigger, but not any more treacherous. Anyway, when that cold arctic frost hits this warm, soggy, maritime soup, it creates very high winds." He gestured with his hands.

"They've blown houses down and ships aground. Men have been frozen to death in them, and children blown out to sea. The Taku winds are very real and not to be taken lightly. If they start blowing, stay indoors!"

All forward motion of the boat ceased. On the dock men shouted. Electric lights at Douglas and Treadwell beckoned through the swirling snow. The air reverberated with chaos from the stamp mills.

"Douglas City dock!" the bearded captain shouted. "All ashore that's going ashore!"

Williams nodded to Melton and stepped up over the high doorsill, elated to escape the man. Consideration of his next step needed work.

The snow dropped thickly past the lights. It was ten o'clock in the morning and gloomy as dusk. The constant crashing of the stamps and crushers created a physical presence shaking and encompassing the world. The dock rattled and popped under the men's boots. Face-stinging snow rode the hard wind. Dark, snow-shrouded warehouses anchored the wharf to the water.

He lowered his head, opened his umbrella and struck out for the town at the far end of the dock, wondering all the while how he would carry out his mission.

"So what's a British journalist doing in Alaska when there's a war to report?" Melton brayed into his ear. He had sidled up and kept pace, careful to stay under the umbrella.

Williams instantly resented the interruption to his thoughts. He wanted to shout at him, hit him. The man was an ass! But his rage died as quickly as it had risen, maybe this fool could be of use. He used the well-rehearsed lines for the first time.

"Well, we're publishing a series on the great gold mines of the world and the editors wanted me to come look at Treadwell, as well as the rest of the Juneau gold belt, first hand. Gold fuels the world, and the war, you know."

"Of course it does! Why, do you know this is the largest, most modern, low-grade gold mine in the *world*? They've pulled *seven* times what it cost to buy Alaska out of this complex."

"Then you don't think I'm a shirker for being here, old boy?" He forced a smile, remembering the meeting with Generals Ludendorf and von Falkenburg. A silent hero to the Fatherland, they called him.

"Heavens, no! The world needs to know about Treadwell. Of course it's pretty famous already. After all, you heard enough about it to come to Alaska from Europe."

Yes, Europe. Where massive amounts of life were spent on mere yards of muddy earth. Where this well-fed dolt in front of him wouldn't last a week. For a moment French prisoners again writhed under the spitting muzzles of the Spandaus before he suppressed the image.

"That's true," Williams said. "Whom should I petition to obtain a tour of the mines?"

It was the stamp mills, he decided. They sounded like a close barrage, one that would sweep over their position within moments. Part of his mind anticipated the impact of the shells.

Realizing the impossibility of the thought, he suddenly felt better. And the snowstorm muffled the sound somewhat. What would it be like on a clear day?

"You're in luck. I know the superintendent personally. I'll be happy to introduce you."

"Thank you, Mr. Melton, that's most considerate of you," he shouted. Now he did feel good!

"Sure, happy to do it." Melton's voice dropped an octave or two. "Uh, is there a chance you could mention the Ingersoll-Rand Company in your stories?"

"Certainly. And may I mention you by name also?" Williams hid his amusement by looking down at the snow-drifted planks in front of him. Melton soared close to rapture.

"Oh, gosh. Sure, I'd be honored. Here, let me give you my card!"

"Perhaps you should give me two or three," Williams said earnestly. "That way I can file one with my story when I send it in."

"Certainly, here." He held out the cards. "But why do you mail your stories when you could send them by wireless?"

Damn. I must be more careful! Williams thought. "Expense. They only want late developments, headline copy, sent by wireless," he said quickly.

"Oh. Yeah. Sure, that makes sense," Melton said dubiously. "Well, let me introduce you to Superintendent Bradley. He just took over a couple weeks ago."

Bending under the umbrella and shouting at one another like drunken conspirators, the men trudged along the snow-laden plank streets. The stamps roared out their broken language.

The snow underfoot became mushy gruel by the time they entered the more heavily traveled route. As they neared the Treadwell complex the stamps became louder. A sign over the door on a two-story building heralded St. Ann's Hospital.

Melton caught his glance.

"That's the only hospital on Douglas Island. This is the dividing line between Treadwell and Douglas."

Small groups of houses sat tucked between mine buildings, railroad tracks, fuel storage tanks, and other structures that Williams didn't recognize. They came to an open area where a rather impressive house sat surrounded by a fence and a normal-looking yard.

"That's where Mr. Bradley and his family live," Melton shouted. "But at this time of day he'll be at his office."

The street narrowed again. They walked under tracks built on pilings, between sheds and buildings adorned with signs proclaiming them to be electrical shops, fire equipment storage, warehouse #2, pump house #4. All were threaded together by railroad tracks that seemed to run in every direction. Small locomotives ground past, pulling cars filled with ore or waste rock.

"It's all rather confusing, isn't it?" Williams shouted.

"Not if you understand the process," Melton loudly replied. "You see it's all built to make the most efficient system possible. Each of the four mines has at

least one stamp mill where they reduce the ore to gravel and sand consistency." Melton was beginning to get hoarse.

"Let me see if I can figure it out," Williams said in his ear. "After the ore is crushed, they separate it somehow."

"Correct. They run it through the vanner rooms for that."

"Vanner rooms?"

"Long belts, about six feet wide and twenty feet long, that have a steady stream of water moving across them from one side to the other. The water carries away the waste rock and leaves the heavier elements that are collected at the end of the belts. The belts are constructed so they shake from side to side to aid in the separation."

"Ingenious!" Williams exclaimed. "So then they run the heavier ore into another refining process and move the waste elsewhere."

"Exactly. The waste is being used for land reclamation, which translates to 'dump it in the channel.'"

Williams laughed.

"But it is working," Melton continued. "Underneath these plank streets a beach is being formed. When they first started working this area, there was a very small tidal area."

"And that's why they built the whole thing on pilings to begin with," Williams said.

"Exactly."

Williams forgot his mission for a long moment admiring this incongruity, this gold mine. In the midst of virgin wilderness, deep in the guts of what was known as the "Inside Passage," lay a northern Pacific island holding this miracle of modern mining. To him it seemed totally out of context with the rest of the world.

But it existed. It was real. It was an economic, and therefore military, fact.

He would wage war for God, Kaiser, and Fatherland in this modern industrial complex set in the middle of nothing. If the Americans could do this, what wonders had they performed down in the states? Suddenly the size of the United States frightened him.

The somnolent threat to Germany inherent in this adolescent country loomed unmistakable. The future of the Fatherland hinged on men like himself. Could they do enough? Could they save their country?

For the first time in almost a year he thought of Millie, and his heart nearly burst. He prayed she wouldn't be caught in one of the zeppelin raids over Britain. But Cambridge lay a goodly distance from any military targets.

He knew it stupid to think of her now. But she suddenly seemed so immediate, so close. He could almost reach out and grasp her to him, pull her from his memory and bury his face in her hair once again.

"Are you okay, Mr. Williams?" Melton asked.

Williams snapped back to the present, and for the second time that night repressed the urge to strike the man.

"I'm fine," he hollered amiably. "Just doing a bit of wool gathering. How much farther to Mr. Bradley's office?"

"We're nearly there. I hope he isn't busy over in Juneau or something like that."

"You don't have an appointment?"

"No. I hate phoning ahead. It gives 'em a chance to dodge you completely. In my line of work you gotta surprise them, get the drop on them. It's like hunting deer. Do you do that in England?"

"No. But I know what you mean." Similar to making a surprise attack on an enemy fortification, he thought. But without weapons.

The concrete walls of the office building muffled the crashing of the stamps. Rich, hardwood paneling lined the room.

"Doesn't that steam heat feel good?" Melton said.

"Good morning, Mr. Melton," a thin, heavily mustached man said.

"Good morning, Francher. Good to see you again," he said jovially. "I'd like you to meet Mr. Williams. He's a journalist for the *London Times*. Francher here is secretary for Mr. Bradley."

"Do say?" Francher was impressed. "What brings you to Alaska Territory, Mr. Williams?"

"Your incredible mine, Mr. Francher. I'm doing a series of stories on mining around the world and the editor thought I'd best get a piece on this one."

"Is Barclay still the editor?" Francher asked blandly.

"Barclay? I think you have us mixed up with the *Post*, old man," Williams said stiffly.

Francher gave him a wry smile. "Just checking. You never know what you're going to get in the way of bunko men up here."

"I see." Williams felt a stab of coldness in his heart. Some of these fellows were sharper than he had supposed. It would be a mistake to underestimate these men.

"Yes, we'd like to see Mr. Bradley if he has the time."

"You should have called, Mr. Melton," he said through a grin. "Mr. Bradley is in San Francisco until after the first of the year."

"Damn. Just my luck. Whom would I talk to about the new couplings Ingersoll-Rand has developed?"

"Harris. He can place an order if you impress him sufficiently."

"Whom do I speak to about obtaining a tour of your complex?" Williams asked.

"Me. I'd be happy to show you around, but I'm pretty tied up today."

"Ah. Well, Mr. Francher, what I would really like is *carte blanche* to visit any portion of the mine as I wish."

"Sorry, I really can't allow that. It's far too easy to get seriously injured or killed around here," Francher said, knuckling his moustache. "But any time you wish to see something, just tell me or whoever is on shift in here, and we'll find you a knowledgeable guide. Fair enough?"

"Quite fair, quite fair. I really appreciate this. There's so very much I wish to see."

"You'll get the Cook's Tour. Have no doubt of that."

"Ah, there's no better claim than that," Williams said.

"Well, I need to catch the next boat back to town," Melton said forlornly. "Perhaps I can still make it out to the Ground Hog or Perseverance before the day is over."

"I'll go with you if we can take a different route back. You can tell me what we're passing," Williams said.

Melton brightened up at once. "Why, certainly. I would like that. Good day to you, Mr. Francher."

"Yes, thank you so very much for the courtesy," Williams said. "I'll see to it you get copies of every issue which mentions your mine."

"No need, Mr. Williams. The Treadwell library is a subscriber. Mr. Melton, I'll tell Mr. Bradley he missed you on this trip."

Williams fought back a wave of panic, wondering if the newspapers listed their reporters. He noticed the man stifled a smirk. Melton offered no further use to him in this office.

"Yes, let's be off."

The stamp mills enveloped them with their overpowering din. After the cozy paper-and-ink atmosphere of the office, the mine property suddenly reeked of hydraulic fluid, oil smoke, raw iron, and wet rock. Williams decided it would be a service to stop this mind-numbing noise. The sooner it went quiet at Treadwell, the sooner it would be quiet on the Western Front.

"That's the Treadwell Club," Melton said, pointing at a two-story structure.

"That's quite large for this country. What is it, exactly?"

"I'll show you."

Once inside, the noise abated to a dull thumping. Rather like a heart, Williams thought. Men passed them in the corridors at a steady rate. Melton importantly pointed out the barbershop, the billiards room, and the two bowling lanes as if responsible for their existence.

"There's also an auditorium that seats five hundred, a 15,000 volume library which subscribes to twenty-seven newspapers, including yours, and even a Turkish bath. Each miner has one dollar per month taken from his pay as dues. The families of the married workers have free access to the club."

A Filipino in a neat white uniform came up to them.

"Are you new members, gentlemen?"

"No," Melton said in dismissal. "I'm just showing this British journalist around Treadwell."

"If you are still here in the summer, we have complete tours of the mine for visitors off the boats."

Williams looked at the smaller man closely. This was the first non-white or non-Indian he had seen. Perhaps discontent lurked here that he could use after all.

"Thank you," Williams said. "But I believe I shall be gone from here by that time."

The man nodded and smiled warmly. "Very good. Enjoy your visit, sir." He

moved off down the corridor.

"You said there were Asians here," Williams said. "Are there a lot of them?"

"Oh sure. That was a Filipino boy. No women yet. Mostly young or middle-aged men who come over from the islands to build a grubstake to take back to the Philippines. These boys are rich compared to the folks back home, and they don't even make miner's wages."

"They're not miners?"

"Not many of them. Mostly they work in the kitchens and bunk houses doing whatever is needed."

"How do they feel about their jobs?" Williams asked in an offhand manner.

"Why, they like it just fine. Like I said, they're rich by Filipino standards."

"Is there a bar in this place?"

"Oh, no. No alcohol anywhere in Treadwell. We'd have to go into Douglas to have a glass of anything. Now that you mention it, I could use a beer myself."

"Well, like they say in London —the sun's over the yardarm somewhere in the empire."

"That's the spirit. Why don't we adjourn to the Douglas Grill and see what's cooking?"

Williams pulled his coat tight. "After you."

THE DOUGLAS ISLAND NEWS
Douglas, Alaska, Wednesday, November 24, 1915

The disappearance of Wm. Christie and the crimes of which Edward Krause is accused still occupy a large part of public attention. As far as Christie is concerned, absolutely nothing has been learned. From the day he left his work at Treadwell he has dropped out of sight as completely as if the earth opened up and swallowed him. Krause, who came to Treadwell and induced Christie to accompany him, presumably to Juneau, has been arrested at Seattle, turned loose, then re-arrested, and will probably be brought back to Juneau through extradition papers to answer the charge of murder. Krause still sticks to the story he acted for another in taking Christie to Juneau; that the other man was a stranger and on landing at Juneau, Christie and the stranger walked away and that was the last he saw of them. Besides laying the disappearance and possible murder of Christie upon the shoulders of Krause, local newspapers have not hesitated to add every imaginable form of crime; including three or four murders, robbery and anarchy. They have even gone so far as to declare that an anarchistic society existed at Petersburg, the bright little town at the head of Wrangell Narrows, of which society Krause was the moving spirit and head. In fact, these papers have shown an altogether vindictive spirit in the matter, inspired, perhaps in one case, by a rooted hatred for all peoples of German origin, and in both a play for sensational news. The introduction of so many suspicions, which in most cases are not at all well founded and in some instances positively foolish, and the positive manner in which they have been declared, has inflamed the minds of the people on both sides of the channel until there is even talk of lynching when the prisoner is brought North. If Edward Krause is to be found guilty, let him be punished, but it is surely not the province of a reputable newspaper to poison the minds of the people of this community against him that prejudice will usurp the place of justice.

16 —Juneau City, A.T., Thanksgiving Day, 1915—
Thursday early afternoon

"May I offer you some hors d'oeuvres, Mrs. Williams?" the waiter asked.

"No, I'll wait until my husband arrives," she said, giving him a grateful smile as he backed away.

The Gastineau Hotel put on a feast for its guests. Amanda stared in amazement at the variety of meats, side dishes, and pies streaming out of the kitchen. The Thanksgiving meal was well underway. The smell of roast venison made it difficult to wait much longer for Arnold's promised appearance. She assumed his name to be something much more Germanic. She'd thought a lot about the man who'd murdered two Mexicans.

She'd deliberately flirted with Williams to upset Georg. In his fatal provincial territorialism, her late husband had sequestered them at the far end of the car. If they had been at the other end, he would probably still be alive. And she'd be in San Francisco evading his pawing appetites.

A curious feeling had pecked at her since Georg's death. Yesterday, all alone in the hotel, she finally puzzled out just what it was.

Guilt.

The guilt became especially strong when she reflected on how relieved she felt to have him truly gone. Yes, it was guilt, she decided, about how wonderful and free she felt without him. He **had** died heroically! But of course his family wouldn't know unless she told them.

Why bother? They'd made it abundantly clear they saw her as a gold-digger and nothing more. Marriage into the Hapsburg dynasty had figured largely in the family plans for their son.

Georg's withered mother had informed Amanda in faultless high German that even when the baron died, she would personally receive nothing unless she bore a male heir. Now more than ever, her in-laws were nothing to her and would have nothing for her. Besides, they had more immediate things to worry about.

Yes, I'm glad he's gone.

But Williams turned out to be more than she had bargained for. Unlike all the other men in her life, he wasn't malleable. She couldn't penetrate the façade he presented to the world.

And it was a façade —British journalists did not awake from nightmares shrieking, "Kill them all!" in German. When angry or excited, his left eye developed a tic, and he exhibited total, iron-bar self control.

Amanda no longer entertained the illusion of control since the night on the boat when he told her he'd cut her throat if she didn't sleep with him within a week of their arrival. She now realized she had never been in control of this man. Fear scratched at her heart.

"May I sit next to you, ma'am?"

She started and looked up at the sweating horse-faced man in a heavy wool suit. She noticed Americans were not keen about bathing or masking their physical odors, and this one proved no exception. His ugliness could excite comment.

"I am expecting my husband at any moment."

"The English correspondent? Mr. Williams?" he asked eagerly, his eyes lighting up strangely.

"Why, yes," she said hesitantly. "Do you know Arnold?"

"Met him yesterday on the ferry over to Treadwell. Fine mind that man has."

"Yes," she said. "Isn't it?"

The man stood there waiting for her decision. He certainly looked disagreeable enough to turn away, but Americans had the strangest customs regarding persons to whom one hadn't been properly introduced.

"I'm sorry, sir. But you'll have to wait until my husband arrives and ask him."

He brayed out falsetto laughter. "Arnold said you wouldn't let a strange man sit down with you." He seemed delighted.

"I'm sorry, I don't understand," she said, wrinkling her brow with a frown.

"It's quite simple, my dear," Arnold said as he moved up behind her and put his hands on her shoulders. "I made a wager with Mr. Melton here that you would not allow him to sit at table with you until you were properly introduced."

She leaned her head back and gave him a dazzling smile. "Oh, you must be the British correspondent I've just heard about!"

He frowned down at her and quickly took a chair. "Very amusing, dear. This is Mr. Melton. He is a representative for the Ingersoll-Rand Company."

"Pleased to meet you, ma'am." His great horsy teeth flashed at her as he pulled his chair out and sat down.

"I am famished," Arnold said in a stage whisper. "How does one obtain drink around here?"

"One requests it," Amanda said, nettled at the two men. She held up her hand and two men in aprons rushed toward her.

The smaller man must be senior to the larger, she thought. For as soon as the heavier man saw him, he returned to his place along the wall.

"Yes, ma'am, how may I help you?" he asked unctuously, running a bent knuckle under his heavy blond mustache and smiling widely.

"We would like to order," Arnold said heavily.

"Very good, sir." The smile sagged.

"Do you have any German wines?"

"No, sir." The smile faded completely.

"Good!" Williams said in a jovial boom. "That means we can eat here."

Melton and the waiter both laughed. Amanda watched Arnold's face. His eyes didn't smile along with his lips.

She watched his mouth as he ordered. How his lips hesitated at the wrong places in his speech. How his tongue caressed the wet corners where his lips came together like miniature thighs, hesitating there in calculation of worthless decisions.

She would only be a dalliance to him. *What a sod he turned out to be after that first dashing and forceful episode in Mexico. It must have been the circumstances,* she decided.

She remembered how the fat, sweat-stinking bandito had looked when she clicked her empty pistol in front of his eyes. In one small moment, she had been close to death from two directions, first his, then hers. Thank God, **Arnold** shot him. His real name was probably Wolfgang or Hans.

He wouldn't tell her about himself. That irritated her, but she vowed not to let it show. The only time he spoke German was when startled, angry, or in the midst of nightmares.

Such an arrogant man!

Georg had been correct about Arnold's southern accent, however he could still be from any part of the German Empire. She needed to hear more before she could pin it down.

"Mrs. Williams, you should have seen how Superintendent Bradley's secretary took to your husband."

"Many people are taken by my husband, I'm sure," she said blandly.

Melton frowned at her. "Ma'am?"

"My wife is a bit of a character." Arnold lifted his nose slightly.

Melton decided to smile. "Yeah, she sure is. She's a real peach."

Amanda peered at him. "Pardon my asking, sir, but does that mean something good to eat, or something that's ripe?"

"In the Territory it means something of high value due to its rarity," he said simply.

Amanda took another look at Ingersoll, or Morton-Rand, or whatever his name was. His sincerity left her feeling surprisingly charmed. Even these uncultured Americans offered more than her "husband."

"Thank you, sir. What a very kind thing to say."

She felt Arnold trying to see through her skull again. His sharp eyes became scalpels that constantly cut at her mind. They hadn't been friends since Seattle; they became antagonists when she and the shop girl laughed at him.

She had also seen him murder two defenseless men. She knew if he even suspected her fear of him— he would kill her. She must find a safe way to leave him before his mandate of a week ended.

Contacting her father was out of the question. His instruction to keep her eyes and ears open to the Empire's enemies ceased being amusing when she met

Arnold. In her grew a half-formed intention to discover this man's secret.

No doubt existed in her mind that he was a German, though he claimed to be something entirely different and proved adept at the subterfuge. Why was he here? How could he advance the war by virtue of his presence in Alaska Territory?

He refused to give her more than five dollars at a time and wouldn't give her more money until she produced receipts for the full amount. *Such an ingenious bastard!*

If Arnold suspected she planned to leave, he would kill her. He thought she'd seen and heard too much in Mexico, even if she only heard enough to engender suspicion. She looked over at him.

He stared at her with eyes devoid of compassion, or life. She shivered and moved her gaze the table again. Whatever it took, she *had* to get away from him.

17 —Juneau City, A.T., Thanksgiving Day, 1915—
Thursday afternoon

Lepke didn't see Mrs. Williams when he walked into the dining room at the Gastineau Hotel. He stopped at the cigar stand and bought a good Havana. Only on very special occasions did he indulge in tobacco or alcohol, and never both at the same time.

He liked this American holiday of Thanksgiving. He had much for which to be thankful. When he first came to the United States he had only seventeen years and knew but a few words of English.

But he knew ambition, and possessed a good mind. An older immigrant told him he could profit from an enlistment in the army. At eighteen he fought Moros in the Philippines as an infantryman.

At nineteen he earned a battlefield promotion to sergeant and a recommendation for the Medal of Honor for heroism in the face of the enemy. He received a Silver Star and kept the stripes instead. Disenchanted at twenty-one with fighting revolutionaries, he didn't reenlist.

He'd entered the University of Oregon in 1904. Three years later he met Alice Hanley.

Abruptly his well-practiced mental switch tripped him out of the past, becoming aware that someone addressed him.

"If you will take a seat, sir, we will take your order." The maître d'hôtel lifted an eyebrow slightly, waiting for a response.

"Oh. Certainly. Is there any place in particular you would like me to sit?"

"Well," the maître d'hôtel softened the lines of his face without approaching a smile. "It would be easier to serve you if you filled out a table." He pointed to a table with three people.

"Glad to oblige," Lepke said with a nod. He removed his hat and coat as he moved between tables surrounded by diners.

Not until he sat down next to the woman did he realize two of his dinner partners were Mr. and Mrs. Williams.

"Good to see you, old boy," Williams muttered around a cigar.

"The stench of that thing is ruining my appetite!" Mrs. Williams said sharply.

Williams took the cigar from his mouth. A shutter fell across his eyes as he stabbed it out. He muttered quietly to himself, but Lepke still heard the faint, *"Scheisse!"*

Mrs. Williams looked at Lepke and smiled. "What a small world Alaska is. How nice to see you again, sir."

"Thank you, ma'am. I believe we haven't been properly introduced. Lepke is the name, August Lepke."

"I am Amanda Williams, and this is Mr. Williams."

The other man at the table stuck out his hand. "Melton's the name, compression is my game."

Lepke shook the man's hand and smiled, "Air, liquid, or solid?" He glanced around the table. "Pleased to meet you all."

The waiter appeared with a bottle of wine.

Melton blinked and his open jaw wavered for a moment before he said, "Ah, air actually."

The waiter offered the cork to Williams and poured a small glass for him. Williams nodded and the waiter sat glasses in front of everyone.

"None for me, thank you," Lepke said with a smile.

"Really now, old bean," Williams said. "It *is* Thanksgiving." He filled all four glasses.

Lepke quickly studied the menu while the others gave their orders. He opted for the roast of venison and mixed vegetables.

"I'm continually amazed at the variety of food available here," Amanda commented.

"All due to the Treadwell, missus," Melton said. "They have steamers that go all over the world buying exotic food and goods. And many of their prices are lower than in Seattle. The stores here in Juneau get ticked off because they can't compete with the Treadwell store."

"A toast!" Williams held his wine glass over the table. "To the Treadwell and the many comforts it provides."

Melton extended his glass. "Hear, hear!"

Lepke and Amanda lifted their wine slowly, almost in perfect time with each other, and the four glasses clinked over the well-appointed table setting. Lepke touched his lips to the glass before putting it back on the table.

"Did you even smell it, old boy?" Williams stared across the table at him, something dark and sinister moved deep in his eyes.

"It's an excellent wine, thank you."

"Most men look for excuses to imbibe, Mr. Lepke," Amanda said. "You're quite a rarity."

"I don't enjoy drinking to excess," he said. *Why all this attention?*

"Is there *anything* you do to excess?" she asked, giving him a slow smile. Then her knee moved against his and stayed there.

He pulled his leg slightly away from hers, feeling his face warm.

"Well, Mr. Lepke, answer the lady," Melton said, showing large teeth in an open-mouthed leer.

Her knee touched his again, before moving away.

"Actually, I'm a man of modest habits." The momentary pressure of her leg in combination with the scent of her perfume became disturbingly erotic. He knew the slightest movement of his knee would reestablish contact. The proximity of the woman pulled at him like a magnet. The heat in his cheeks intensified.

"I say, are you all right? You look flushed," Williams said with manufactured concern.

"Perhaps if we spoke of something else?" he said.

"I'm sure Mr. Lepke is more a man of *action* rather than words," Amanda said, favoring him with a dazzling smile.

The waiter returned bearing a large tray filled with steaming plates of food. Lepke hoped she wouldn't move her leg once they started eating. She didn't.

He felt hungry, but found it impossible to concentrate on his food. Part of him tried to analyze the situation, ignore the surface, and puzzle out hidden motives. Another part responded to the raw, animal magnetism of the lovely woman sitting next to him.

It troubled him that every time in the past he had encountered a woman this frank and open, she turned out to be a prostitute. He didn't want Amanda Williams to be a prostitute. He wanted to continue respecting her quick mind and go on wondering if she was perhaps the biggest flirt in his experience.

The first part of him felt positive she wanted something from him. Wanted something so badly she was willing to trade her body for it. August Wilhelm Lepke was a modest man.

Sharing his body with a woman meant a great deal to him. In fact he'd been a virgin before he met Alice. He felt sure he had been the only virgin sergeant in the U.S. Army.

Alice. There was much of Alice in Amanda. Perhaps more Alice than Amanda sat there giving him silent but urgent messages.

But he had finally dealt with Alice. He used anger to cauterize the old, aching wound. Abruptly he realized he no longer felt anything other than a lingering regret about her.

Was it just talking about her to Florence, or had Amanda here just pushed him over the edge? Amanda needed something. He needed something too, but not from just anybody.

The one sitting beside him was trying to use him to suit her means. It might prove pleasant to be used by her, but he never would be more to her than a lark. Women had used him quite enough.

"Excuse me." He stood up and pulled the napkin from around his throat, nodding at the table. "I really must leave now. Very nice seeing you both again."

He darted a glance at Amanda. Her eyebrows arched over a smile on her lips, but yearning lay in her perfect indigo eyes. He felt completely at a loss.

"I am pleased to have met you, Mr. Melton. Good day." He walked across the room as quickly as he could. Behind him he heard Williams say, "Now what brought *that* on?"

The restaurant was packed with people talking and eating. Utensils clinked

on china. The air hung heavy with savory aromas. Lepke's stomach demanded evidence of his nose's testimony.

Suspicion, lust, anger, and pain swirled through his mind.

"Are you leaving already?" the maître d'hôtel asked. His face actually lost its haughty aspect, however temporarily. "You certainly eat fast."

"Yes. Guess I don't feel well. How much do I owe you?"

"I'm afraid I'll have to charge you the full dinner price, ninety-five cents."

"That's fine. Here." Lepke thrust a crumpled bill into his hands. "Keep the change." He jammed his hat down on his head and pulled on the heavy overcoat as he walked through the lobby.

The wind carried the promise of more snow, but now pushed the clouds apart allowing the full harvest moon to shine through. The white streets lay deserted. Light beckoned from the windows of the hotels and restaurants, reflecting off the snow-covered planks.

Before entering the Line Cafe, he peered in and made certain there was nobody present he recognized. He went in and sat at a small table. A heavy-set woman moved over to him and held out a menu.

"Good evening, welcome to the Line Cafe. I'm Maye Wattnem and we're honored that you've joined us for Thanksgiving."

18 —Juneau City, A.T., November 26, 1915—
Friday afternoon

George Mak-we stopped at a store window and checked his reflection in the plate glass. *That's what I look like,* he thought. He continued on to the next building and pushed into the lobby of the Cain Hotel.

Two men stood on either side of the front desk. The clerk behind the desk looked up. His expression instantly shifted from inquiry to anger.

"Hey, you! Hey, chief!" he shouted. "Nothing in here for you. You go away!"

I knew it would be like this, George thought. *But I told Detective Lepke I would try.*

"Please let me say something to you," he said, holding open his coat to display his badge.

The clerk came out from behind the counter, his face dark, hands clenched into fists, and walked quickly across the room.

"Did you steal that?" he asked contemptuously.

"The marshal gave it to me when I became a policeman," George said firmly.

"Oh." The clerk stopped and looked at George inquiringly, taking in his appearance carefully for the first time. His frown returned but at a lesser degree.

"We don't allow Indians in here, uh, officer. It's a house rule and I can't do nothing about it." He stood unmoving and stared over George's shoulder, his face as firm as his stance.

"That's a double negative," George told the man kindly. "All I ask of you is to deliver this note to one of your guests. He asked me to get some information for him."

"Why would he want information from an Indian?" the clerk asked with a slight sneer as he took the envelope.

Lepke's voice cracked out from behind the clerk. "It really doesn't matter what the information is, sir. What really matters is that you convey the *sealed* note to the addressee, immediately!" Anger hummed in the air.

"And just who the hell are *you* to be giving me orders?" the clerk asked hotly.

"If I am not mistaken, I am the addressee," he said softly.

"Oh." The clerk looked down at the envelope George had thrust into his hands. "Are you Mr. Lepke?" he asked.

"Yes." He reached out and took the envelope. "Thank you."

"How do I know you're the right person?" he asked belligerently.

"He's the right man," George said.

The man whirled and stared angrily at him. "How do I know you—" He choked off the words. "Excuse me." He shouldered past Lepke and returned to his official position behind the front desk.

Lepke looked at George and frowned. "You're not allowed in the door?"

"No reason for me to be in here. They don't let Indians stay at this hotel, and they can't legally sell us alcohol."

"I'm sorry this happened. I didn't know," Lepke said.

"That's okay, I'm used to it. What they all forget is they wouldn't even be here if Kow-ee hadn't shown Juneau and Harris where to find the gold."

George turned and walked out into the morning sunshine. *Another storm brewing north along the Inside Passage, he decided. Better enjoy the warmth while they had it.* Lepke followed him out.

"Are all the hotels like that?"

"There's places where Indians can stay, but white men usually don't like to stay in 'em," George replied.

"I see. Are there places where they'll allow you to come in and talk to the guests?"

"Yeah, a few." George thought for a moment, and then looked up at the detective. "The Division is about the nicest place that will let Indians come in and sell trinkets and stuff polite-like. The tourists like it that way."

"Very well. This very day I shall move there," Lepke said flatly. "By the way, I am going to Ketchikan tonight to question the people who saw Krause before he boarded the *Jefferson*. Then I'll go to Seattle to join the *Humboldt* for the run back to Juneau. Krause will be on the boat, and he's mine for the entire trip. When I get back, I'll notify you."

"Just you and Krause, nobody else?" George felt stunned at the idea of it.

"They will have deputy traveling with him. But I am to have him all to myself for three days and two nights. At the end of that time about this murderer I will know a great deal." He seemed excited at the prospect.

"Sounds to me like you're going to be pretty busy, Detective Lepke," George said somberly.

"Oh, yes." He looked down at the envelope, then up at George again. "What did you find out?"

"That boat you were looking for, the *Celia*?" As soon as the words were out of George's mouth, Lepke narrowed his eyes.

"You mean Krause's boat is named *Celia*?"

"Yeah. Anyway, it went south down the channel on the 29th of October. It went north again on the afternoon of the 30th. The next morning it was gone, he'd gone south again in the night. I don't know if that helps you or not, but I told you I'd let you know."

"Thank you. It helps because I know its location during those times. Did you ask the Indians to the south, between Juneau and Thane?"

"That's the Taku People. I don't go down there much since my wife died. They're glad I don't."

Enough. This man doesn't need to know about my troubles, he thought.

"Oh." Lepke stood silent for a second or two, and then asked, "Well, could I go down there and get evidence better than you could?"

"No. The ones that would talk to you probably wouldn't tell you anything unless you gave 'em a bottle, and then you wouldn't be able to trust their words. You could trust the ones who wouldn't talk to you, but —" He held a hand palm up and shrugged.

"Would they talk to Officer George Mak-we?" Lepke persisted.

Damn it, I don't want to go down to the Taku village, he thought. *I don't have scars to atone for her loss. On the other hand, this might be important enough to hang a man. A white man at that. It would also make her family talk to me politely.*

"Yeah. I suppose they would talk to me, but it will not be a thing I can make happen quickly. I must be very formal, and that takes some time."

"Would it necessitate a few gifts also?" Lepke asked.

"No. If I bring a gift, that obligates the host to give me a gift more costly than mine. That in turn obligates me to give him a gift more costly than the one he gave me. Since I am related to those people by marriage, and my wife is now dead, I might not be able to get much information." He frowned at the acid of his fierce guilt when he thought of her.

"I'm sorry for your loss. I can't really understand it completely, as I have never been married. My mother died last year, but it had been many years since I last saw her . . ."

"Thank you, Detective Lepke. You are right; it is an ache which will ebb slowly but never completely."

"But I need to give you some money to seal our contract."

George opened his mouth to protest, Lepke held up his hand.

"No, wait. I am the one who wishes the information. So in essence I am hiring you to help me because you are uniquely qualified for the work." Lepke grinned at him.

"You're hiring me to be your assistant, is that what you're saying?" George asked. "Or am I just an informant?"

"You decide. I'll pay you five dollars a week. Agreed?" Lepke smiled and extended his hand.

"You got a deal, Detective. I gotta go now, there's some things I have to do." George shook Lepke's hand then turned to leave.

"In advance—that's how detectives get paid." Lepke held out a greenback. George took it.

"You'll be hearing from me," George said. He again turned to leave.

"Oh, Assistant Detective Mak-we, about Krause's boat."

George stopped and looked back, almost smiling. "Ai?"

"Christie's wife. Her name is Celia, too."

The ALASKA DAILY EMPIRE
Juneau, Alaska, Saturday, November 27, 1915

PLUNKETT WAS TO BE WELL PAID

KRAUSE TO COME NORTH MONDAY NIGHT

MEASURES AGAINST BRITAIN?

WEST POINT BEATS NAVY 14 - 0

KILLS SELF BECAUSE WAS "WAGE SLAVE"

FISHERMEN ARE DROWNED

SUPREME COURT PROBABLY KNOCKS OUT PROHIBITION

ALASKA WIRELESS TO BE EXTENDED

19 —Ketchikan, A.T., November 27, 1915—
Saturday noon

Scores of small wrinkles creased the face of the old Chinese man. Lepke thought he saw patterns in the webbed lines. The man must not have understood the question, so Lepke asked him again.

"Mr. Sing Lee, do you know this man?" He held the photograph before the blank gaze.

"Yes?"

"You know this man? What name do you know him by?"

"That Ed Klause," the old Chinese said distinctly, staring at him with bottomless black eyes.

"When did you last see him?"

"Twenty-six in November."

"Have you known him very long?"

"Since nineteen and eight."

"What time did he arrive here on the twenty-sixth?"

"Hour after midnight, 'bout." The old man's head nodded affirmation to his words.

"How are you so sure of the time?"

"It velly late, I on way to bed. He come in, wet down to skin. Demand his key. Velly unpleasant."

"Key to what?"

"Tlunk of clothes. He pay me to keep it for him."

"So he was very wet and unpleasant, and you noticed it was one o'clock in the morning on the 26th of November, 1915." He took a breath. "Right?"

"Yes?"

"How did he get here? Why was he wet?"

"He low small boat, he take it away next day."

"Where did he row from? Did he say?"

"He talk to nobody. I think he come from his cabin."

"Cabin! What cabin?"

"Ask Marshal Wick," Sing Lee said, smiling at Lepke in farewell.

The marshal had already sent all his information on Krause to Juneau and Seattle, but he was still willing to talk to a detective.

"Yeah, the last thing he told Sing Lee was to wake him in time to catch the steamer to Juneau the next morning. He was pretty surly."

"He's been in the territory since 1908?"

"Yeah. He's a damned socialist, even stood for the legislature here a couple of elections ago. He's always running between Wrangell, Petersburg, and Juneau. Lots of things he's said look different in light of what's happened."

"Different?"

"Yeah," Marshal Wick said slowly, hesitating for a blink. "There were two boys the Olympic mine hired as caretakers in the winter of '12. A Japanese kid and a white kid. They watched the place while it was shut down. Boats would bring fresh food out to them every month or so, and other folks would just drop in and visit."

Wick stopped, checked the toe of his boot and looked directly into Lepke's face.

"John Knudson's a logger. One of the boys had worked for him over the summer, made a lot of money, $500. John stopped by to see the boys, and they weren't there. The place was cold and we later discovered $70 in a wallet in a drawer, but no sign of the $500, or any other valuables. A bunch of us went out to look for them. Hell, in this country anything could have happened. They could have been stranded on a beach or something.

"We stopped by and asked Krause if he'd seen them. His cabin is about a mile from the mine and we know he used to have dinner with the boys occasionally. Sometimes he'd bring grub out from town for them."

Lepke wondered if Wick was aware his right eyebrow jiggled up and down when he was agitated.

"Yeah, we asked him and he said, 'I haven't seen them in quite a while,' then he went back to eating his grub like it was nothing to have missing neighbors." The marshal stopped and stared up at the low-hanging clouds.

"God damn, but I get tired of rain!" he said through clenched teeth.

Lepke waited for him to continue. Marshal Wick stared at the clouds.

"So what did he do then?"

"It's what he didn't do. He didn't help look for them."

Suddenly the marshal's eyes bored into Lepke again. "He knew we wouldn't find them. He wasn't about to waste his time trying to find someone who couldn't be found!" He breathed hard, trying to hold in his growing anger.

"We thought it was a bit strange of him at the time, but we all knew he was a radical of some sort anyway. Who knows what they will or won't do? Yeah, when we searched the cabin at the mine we found some bits of fuse."

"Fuse?"

"Yeah, they'd made a charge, a dynamite blasting charge. We thought that was sorta strange, too. They were just 'sposed to watch the mine while it was shut down. They weren't to be doing any blasting."

Wick rubbed his hand over his mouth and under his jaw before continuing.

"Then Krause said something that still haunts me. One of the fellows from Petersburg here—, we had guys from Wrangell looking, too—, kind of sniped at Krause 'cause he didn't seem concerned about the boys.

"Krause looked up at him with them shit-brown eyes of his, an' said, 'That Japanese kid is pretty careless with dynamite— he probably blew himself up,' then he just keeps eating."

"Does that ever happen around here? Is it common for someone to blow themselves up?"

"I've been in the territory for twenty-eight years, and I can count on one hand the number of men who've died that way. Not counting the big mines by Juneau, of course. Hell, they sent thirty-seven Treadwell men to glory back in '10 or '11, in one blast."

"How?" Lepke said, despite himself.

"An underground powder magazine went off during a shift change. They never could figure out why."

"So Krause suggested both boys had died because of their own blunders. Is that what you're saying?"

"That's how I heard it," Wick agreed.

"How far is the cabin from here?"

"Twenty miles, right about."

"Could a man row that far in a small boat?"

"Sure," Wick snorted. "If the wind and tide are right, you could do it in five hours. A lot of the boys who work at the mine in the summer will row in for a day or two and then go back out."

Lepke chewed his lip, thinking furiously. Krause and Plunkett had disappeared on the morning of the 24th. Krause arrived here "wet and surly" early on the 26th, and caught the northbound steamer that same morning. Then Krause kidnapped William Christie on the 30th and disappeared again until he was seen boarding the *Jefferson* in Ketchikan on his way to Seattle.

He nodded to the marshal. "Has anyone checked around Krause's cabin for Plunkett's gas boat?"

The marshal's eyes widened slightly. "No. We've been searching the Hobart Bay area. But we'll have Krause's place checked by tomorrow night!"

20—Juneau City, A.T., November 27, 1915—
Saturday night

Begay Santo and Frank Bagio edged through the door into Armstrong's Tavern. They hesitated as the bartender looked up at them.

"What'll it be, boys?" he said around the cigar in his mouth.

Begay glanced at Frank and then walked up to the bar.

"I'd like a beer."

"What kind?"

"San Miguel?" Frank said hopefully.

"Now that's a good beer. Had some once when I went around the world with the Great White Fleet, but we don't got any here. You'll have to choose from Rainier, Schlitz, Eagle, or Northern Star."

The two Filipinos looked at each other and shrugged.

"Whatever kind you drink will be fine," Begay said.

"Eagle it is." He set two bottles down in front of them, expertly popping off the caps and palming them. "That'll be ten cents," he said with a puff of cigar smoke.

They paid and looked around at the smoky room.

"There's a table, Begay. Let's sit down," Frank said.

A skinny woman slowly lurched down the stairs, pausing slightly on each step. Begay wondered if she were sick. Nobody else in the room paid her the slightest attention.

"Frank." When his friend looked at him, he nodded toward the stairs. "Do you think she's ill?"

Frank squinted for a moment then turned back to the table. "If she's ill it doesn't show. I think she's just drunk."

"Oh."

The woman noticed their brief attention and sauntered slowly over to their table. She peered down at them for a moment and pulled out a cigarette.

"Either one of you boys got some fire?" she asked in a wheezy voice.

"We don't smoke," Begay said apologetically.

"I'm sure you don't," she said heavily. "How about a match?"

"We don't have that either," Frank said flatly.

"God. They'll let anybody in here these days." She moved off between the tables of men.

"Are all the places here like this?" Begay asked.

"No. Some are worse. But there're lots more we can visit before we go back over to Treadwell. If you want to, that is."

"I wanted to look at women, but if they're all like that . . ."

"You're a long way from the Philippines, Begay. All of the guys feel the same way you do. That's why they don't come to places like this."

"Isn't it worse to just sit in the bunkhouse and play cards like we've been doing?"

"Not worse, just different."

"But all they talk about are the women they're going to marry when they go home again! What good is that going to do us?"

"At least we all understand each other. We all share the same pain of wanting what can't be had."

Begay took a long pull from his bottle and took in the room.

"Maybe this wasn't a good idea, Frank. Maybe we should go back before we feel any worse."

"I said I'd be your guide. If that's what you want to do, it's fine with me."

They drank up and pushed out into the chill night. Rain mixing with snow blew out of the southeast. The Treadwell stamps thumped across the channel, playing counterpoint to their circumstances.

"Let's walk around for awhile before we go back," Begay said.

"Sure." Frank pulled his coat collar around his ears and snugged down his fedora. "Where do you want to go?"

"This way." Begay moved down the plank street.

The two men walked north through Juneau City, finally rounding the point of a ridge.

"This trail goes out to Auke Bay as well as to the Auk village," Frank said.

"How far?"

"Which?"

"The Auk village."

"Oh, that's real close. You want to go down there?"

"Why not? Isn't it allowed?"

"Nobody's gonna stop you. But there's nothing there to do."

"You can say that about this whole country, Frank."

The plank street abruptly turned into a narrow boardwalk that stretched off into the night.

"Why don't we go back now?" Frank suggested.

Begay ignored him. "I don't see any village out there."

"The houses are back of the dock there, and some stretch up the hill. See the glow from the windows? We're almost in it."

Begay peered through the rain and wet snow, trying to make sense of the blackness.

Suddenly a figure rose up in front of him.

"What you fellows doin' down here? You lost 'r somethin'?"

Both Filipinos cried out in alarm. Begay could feel his heart thumping madly.

"W-we're just out on a walk."

"Kinda dark to be walkin' around down here, isn't it?"

"Sorry," Frank said. "We'll leave."

"You don't gotta leave. My name is Jim Kisadis. You help me get this coal to my mother's house, I'll give you each a cup of tea."

"Uh, sure." Begay said. "C'mon, Frank, let's give him a hand."

They hefted sacks of coal from a stack on the edge of the dock. They told Jim their names and waited for him to lead the way.

"This will be enough for tonight," Jim said. "There're no railings along here, so watch your step."

They followed Jim as closely as ore carts follow an engine. Closer to the house they could smell smoke and make out the plank building looming in the darkness. Jim opened the door of a shed and dropped his sack with a grunt.

"Just put them right on top. I'll get the other sacks in the morning. Let's go in and have tea."

He motioned them through the door ahead of him. Begay and Frank found themselves in a pleasant living room. Through an open door a woman with streaks of gray in her dark hair worked at a stove.

"Mother, this is Begay Santo and Frank Bagio. They were out walking and offered to help me carry the coal to the shed. I've invited them in for tea."

"Oh, how kind of you, gentlemen. Please, come in and sit at the table."

They moved self-consciously into the kitchen. "I am Irene Kisadis, Jim's mother. This is Ruth, my daughter."

A young woman sitting at the table looked up at them and smiled. Begay winced when he saw the scar from a burn along her right jaw line.

Both men said hello and sat down.

"Would you like some dried fish?" Ruth asked, pushing a wooden bowl of dark strips over to them.

"Oh, yes," Begay said. "We like fish very much." He stared at the young woman, wondering how she had received the scar.

"Do you live in Juneau?" she asked.

"No," Frank said. "We both live at Treadwell."

"So you came over to visit us," she declared with a smile. "How nice."

Her words unexpectedly thrilled Begay. He felt very much at home in this warm little house. "How long have you lived here?"

"My father built this house about thirty-five years ago," Irene said. "Both of my children were born here."

"Begay," Frank said softly behind him. "We should be going soon. It's getting late."

"In a while, Frank. In a while." He smiled at Ruth.

21 —Juneau City, A.T., November 29, 1915—
Monday morning

Amanda glanced up and down the street before pushing into the jeweler's shop. Overly warm and the air somewhat on the stale side, the shop boasted two glass-front display cases complete with an array of gold watches and an assortment of rings. She peered about in the dim shop and, deciding it was actually closed, turned to leave.

"Is there something I may help you with, ma'am?"

Amanda jumped in surprise and turned to see a man in his middle to late forties, somewhat stooped, but with a patient face.

"Are you Mr. Valentine?"

"No, no. I am his clerk, Lee Pulver. How may we help you today? A watch for a gentleman's birthday, perhaps?"

She turned at an angle to him and looked down at her hands. "Quite the opposite, I assure you, Mr. Pulver. I would like to sell you some of my jewelry."

"Oh. Yes, I see. Well, I am not authorized to do that sort of thing. If you'll just wait here I will fetch Mr. Valentine. Hmm?" He turned and took a small step before looking back. "Very nice meeting you, ma'am."

A door shut in the dimness at the back of the room and for a moment all remained silent. Then the door opened again and a taller figure stomped in. The door shut with a slam and the man moved into the light.

"I'm Emery Valentine. You got something you want to sell?" The tall, elderly man with deep-set eyes and walrus mustache all but glared at her.

"Yes. Ah, I'm a bit down on my luck and . . ."

"Save the story, lady. Just show me what you got, okay?"

His directness ignited a flare of anger she quickly dampened. Clenching her jaw, she pulled out the heirloom. "Here." She handed it to him.

He peered down at it, glanced up at her, then pulled a loupe from his waistcoat pocket and bent his head to study the piece carefully.

"It was my mother's," Amanda said to break the uncomfortable silence.

"Top-notch piece of work, miss. I couldn't give you more than twenty-five dollars for it."

She frowned. "Please, how much is that in pounds sterling?"

"Umm, about six and a half, I reckon."

"Six bloody pounds! That's highway robbery, sir! I know for a fact my father paid ten times that amount for this piece."

"Wouldn't surprise me a bit, miss. Like I said, it's a top-notch piece of work. If there was a market for something like this I could probably sell it for a couple of hundred dollars." He pushed it back into her hands. "But there isn't a market for this sort of thing any more. People around here want gold bands, pocket watches, and

stick pins. This is a working town, we don't have this sort of money."

"But I have nothing else . . ."

"I'm a business man, not a charity. That thing is worth twenty-five dollars to me, take it or leave it."

Anger flashed through her again. "You just stomp in here and," she glanced down at his feet and saw one leg ended in a wooden peg. ". . . and, oh my God, *that's* why you stomped."

Her face went scarlet and she turned and rushed from the shop. As the door swung shut, she heard Emery Valentine say, "Hell, lady, don't get all upset. I'm used to this thing."

Amanda felt the complete fool. She hurried down Front Street just to be moving. The hotel clerk said Mr. Valentine was strictly honest and would quote her the best price for valuables.

The brooch was her— how did these Americans put it— her ace in the hole. If this man would only give her six pounds for it—

The dog stepped from a doorway; she really didn't even see it before she tripped over the animal. Her arms flew outward in automatic search for support, the brooch snapped out of her grasp like a shot, and she fell headlong over the now-yipping dog.

"Damn!" she shrieked, turning her head as the slush-covered boardwalk flew up and hit her. For a moment the only thing her mind could settle on was how nice the cold moisture felt on the side of her face. Brilliant specks of light blossomed and faded like miniature Chinese rockets minus the disagreeable noise.

Strong hands picked her off the walk, "Here we are, ma'am." The hands supported her for an eternity until a chair pushed into the back of her legs and she sat. "There you go," the voice was so reassuring. "Don't just stand there, man! Get her some water or soda."

Amanda blinked and clenched her hand on a small void.

"My brooch!" Her voice sounded immediate and obnoxious to her. The side of her face stung and her temples began to ache. "Where's my brooch?"

A glass pushed into her hands. "Take a drink of this. It will clear your head."

She obediently swallowed a mouthful. "Oh! Ginger ale," she said distractedly.

"How do you feel?" She looked up into the face of a rather boyishly handsome man. His dark eyes and hair complemented the full, rosy cheeks that all radiated concern as he looked at her.

"I, I feel, where's my brooch?"

The man looked around. There was a small crowd, mostly men, circling them. "Did anybody see a brooch?"

"I saw something, Mr. Thane," an old man offered.

"What?" the man asked.

"I dunno what it was. It flew outta the lady's hand and went through the street planks over there." He pointed.

"Through the planks?" Amanda said. "How could it go through the planks?"

"Between them, he means," Mr. Thane said. "Are you new to Juneau?"

"Yes."

"Our streets are planks laid on pilings. The beach is down there." Suddenly he looked over at a youth who stood watching. "You, boy. Is the tide in or out down there?"

The boy ran to the side of the street, bent down, cupped his hands around his face and peered carefully. "Out, sir."

Mr. Thane grinned. "If you can fetch it for the lady I'll give you a five dollar gold piece."

"Yes, sir!" He sprinted toward the waterfront, a block away. Three other boys and a man followed in his wake.

"How very kind of you, sir," she said. "I am Amanda Ganbor. I'm sorry for making such a fuss, but the brooch was my mother's, and . . ."

"No explanations needed, Miss Ganbor. I'm Bartlett Thane, and I'm happy to assist you in any way I can."

"Your name seems very familiar to me. How can that be?"

"Well," he said looking down at his hands. *He preened,* she thought, *he actually preened.* "The Alaska-Gastineau Mine site has been named after me because I'm the manager." He grinned at her in accomplishment.

"Oh, yes. Of course. You must be an exceptionally busy man, yet here you are helping me."

"A gentleman always has time to help a damsel in distress," he said earnestly.

Amanda smiled in spite of herself. Two boys scuffled toward the small group, arguing loudly.

"Give it to me, I found it first!"

"Did not! If I hadn't pointed you'd still be lookin' fer it!"

The first boy began to pummel the larger.

"Here, here!" Thane shouted. "Let's sort this out like gentlemen." He pointed to the smaller boy. "You saw *what* first?"

"That jewel thing."

"Let's have a look," he said to the other boy.

"I found it first!" he cried.

Thane held his hand out, palm up. The boy frowned and handed over his treasure. Thane held it up for all to see.

"That's my brooch," Amanda said. "How can I ever repay you?"

"You just did," Thane said giving it to her. He turned to the boys and gave them each a coin. "Here's a two-and-a-half piece for each of you. Fair enough?"

The boys eyed each other for a moment, and nodded. "Thanks, Mister Thane." They ran off together.

"May I be of any further service to you, Miss Ganbor?"

Amanda glanced down at her dripping dress. "No, thank you, sir. You've done so much already I will be forever grateful. Now I must go."

"Very well." Thane helped her to her feet and tipped his hat as she walked away.

These Alaskans. From one extreme to the other.

22 —Ground Hog Mine, A.T., November 29, 1915—
Monday afternoon

Arnold Williams followed the man through the entrance and into the main shaft of the mine. The violent protest of ore being reduced to gravel receded as they walked deeper into the mountain.

"This is a much smaller operation than the Treadwell, you understand. But we still move a lot of ore out of here. We're part of the Perseverance-Alaska-Gastineau complex."

"What was your output for 1914, Mr. Bennett?" Williams asked. As the man importantly rattled off tonnage and percentages, Williams studied the slightly sloping shaft. Narrow gauge track ran down the middle of the tunnel. Barely enough room existed for a man to hug the hewn rock walls when the donkey engine whined past, pulling groaning iron carts filled with chunks of gold ore.

"So we're making a profit here, which is all the stockholders ask of us. 'Course we don't make the percentage of profit the Treadwell does, but then they got the biggest operation in the world."

Yes, thought Williams, *I'll get to them in due time.*

"And what is this, my good man?" They had entered a large bay, shaped like an inverted bowl. He pointed to a heavy rope hanging down from a box arrangement built high on one rock wall.

"In the Treadwell they're digging down, under the curve of the channel. Here, we're digging into a mountain and going up. So we get the benefit of gravity to move the ore out. That's the bottom of a finger chute. The ore is dumped into big chutes located in every shaft above this one. To move it from there to the crushers and stamp mills we use the train that just passed us." His hand waved around as he spoke.

"See how the rails run right under the opening? If you take a turn on that handle there, the cable pulls that big door up and the ore falls down into the carts. Pretty efficient, huh?"

Williams smiled. "Why, that's damned efficient."

"All of the mines of any size at all are extremely efficient. They have to be or they wouldn't be worth the expense of operating them."

"It looks pretty cut and dried to me, old boy. You dig a tunnel, break up the rocks, and extract the gold. All it takes is a lot of money to get the operation going, right?"

Bennett laughed. "First of all there's no guarantee the vein will hold a workable grade of ore long enough to make the mine pay."

"But there are gold mines all over this area. Don't you just dig where ever you like?"

Bennett laughed again. "No. You have to know where the gold is, or where you think it is. Visualize Douglas Island, then the mainland where Juneau and Thane sit. Okay, the gold ore starts on the island, dips under Gastineau Channel, then comes up through the mountains on the mainland." He paused and licked his lips.

"What we're doing here at the Ground Hog is gambling on that wide vein —think of it as a layer of butter between two slices of bent bread —extending through the mountains to this point, where we dig it out of the ground." His eyes lost their excited gleam and he refocused on Williams. "Did that make sense to you, sir?"

"Actually, yes. But this is called the Juneau Gold Belt. There are mines all along the mainland for a hundred miles or more. Is the vein *that* wide?"

"No. There are at least four veins in the district, and we hope this one is the richest. The problem of course, is the inconsistency of the ore grade."

"Sir?"

"The Treadwell complex enjoys a fairly good, but low, grade of ore. They make a profit of twenty-five cents per ton of ore milled. Mr. Thane's operation here isn't making much of a profit just yet, but then we just got the whole shootin' match up and running this year. So we're probably at the southern-most extent of the vein.

"The Treadwell people have started a small operation on the mainland, called the Alaska-Juneau mine. From what I've heard, the A-J has been showing a good grade of ore near the surface of Mt. Roberts. It's my guess the vein from Treadwell hugs the bottom of the channel and comes right up and through Mt. Roberts and peters out somewhere in Canada." His thumb jerked toward the Coastal Range.

"Perseverance seems to be doing okay back there. So the vein must extend right under the ice. We don't know how far north it goes."

"I see. You say the gold hugs the bottom of the channel?"

"Sure, everybody knows that."

"Yes. Well, what keeps the Treadwell from flooding?" Williams felt his pulse throb in his forehead under the wide-brimmed hat.

"The hanging wall," Bennett answered.

"Hanging wall? What is that?"

"They call it greenstone. It's a very dense waste rock that forms the layer nearest the surface in this area. They had to dig through it to get to the main vein twenty years ago."

"And it just holds the water away from the rest of the mine?"

"Pretty much, yeah. There's seepage of course, but that's to be expected."

Williams forced himself to ask casually, "What would happen if the wall broke, or was shattered in one location?"

"The Treadwell complex would flood, of course."

23 —Juneau City, A.T., November 30, 1915—
Tuesday morning

"**Father, I wish to invite someone to dinner on Christmas,**" **Florence said as she finished breakfast.**

"An' who might that be, Duchess?" Jack asked, taking another sip of coffee.

"A gentleman, whom I met at the gallery."

"A man? I thought you didn't like men!" Fiona exclaimed.

"Don't be absurd!" Florence said. "Just because I don't throw myself at every man I see doesn't mean I don't like men." Fiona was beginning to annoy her.

"Well, what's his name? Do I know him?" Jack Malone asked.

"He's new in town. He's a, ah, a detective," she said, wondering why she had hesitated.

"A detective now?" Jack grinned at her.

She felt her temper flare. First Fiona and now her father!

"Yes. A detective. He's investigating that Krause man."

Jack lost his smile. "Why, I heard they had a Pinkerton man nosing around about all that."

"That's right. He works for the Pinkerton Detective Agency in Portland."

"There's no way on God's green earth I'll have a Pinkerton man in me own house!" Jack roared.

Even Fiona jumped at his vehemence.

"Why, Father!" Florence said in shock. "You don't even know him!"

"I know his kind, right enough! They're the bullyboys what snuck inta the Mollies an' fingered the leaders. Red O'Bannion an' his missus were murdered in their beds by goons led by the Pinks. They hung seventeen of the boys that year, 'an you wanta invite one of 'em in for a bite!" His nostrils flared and his eyes rolled wildly. "What a month! First yer sister goes ta work fer Maye Wattnem down on the line, an' now this!

"Father!" Fiona said sharply. "I don't work on the line!"

"That happened forty years ago, Father," Florence said. "Those men were hung for murder. I know you're sentimental about the Irish working man, but . . ."

"Sentimental!" he roared. "Like all the *true* Irish, I have a steel-trap memory when it comes t' those who've wronged us. An' the Pinkertons have earned themselves a place in the deepest pits of hell for what they've done!"

"Father, you're no longer in the Fenians. Are you?"

"It's not like a lodge or gentleman's club," he said, obviously trying to get hold of himself. "It's part of the blood, a piece of the brain, as much of Jack Malone as me right hand. I'll be a Fenian only for as long as I'm drawin' breath. I'm sorry, Duchess, but I'll not have the man in me house."

"But, Father . . ."

"That's all for it. He's not welcome here." He glanced over at Fiona with a scowl. "An' I wish you'd get yerself a job in a better part o' town."

Florence glanced over at Fiona. She was also astonished. For the first time in many months she felt a strong bond with her sister. She looked back at her father.

"I'm going to have Christmas dinner with Mr. Lepke. If we can't dine here then we'll dine elsewhere," she said levelly.

"I can't stop ye. Would that I could," he said.

"Daddy!" Fiona said plaintively. "She's never even looked at any other man. Don't you realize . . ."

"I'll hear no more of this," Jack said as he stood up. "I'll be home for dinner." He turned and left the house.

Florence felt tears stinging the corners of her eyes. Her own father perpetuating an injustice like this!

"Flo, I'm sorry."

"Thank you, Fio, I appreciate your help." They hadn't called each other by their childhood nicknames for years. Florence stepped around the table and the sisters embraced.

24 —Northbound aboard the *S.S. Humboldt*, December 1, 1915— Wednesday afternoon

"I haven't killed anybody."

Lepke stared down at Edward Krause. After only ten minutes, this sullen, broad-shouldered man had gained the detective's animosity. Still, Lepke felt pleased about finishing his Ketchikan interviews in time to catch the *Humboldt* north from Seattle. The Seattle Police Department had agreed to cooperate fully with the agency on the work.

He took in the man's dark hair, dark eyes, and incongruous red mustache. Although the rest of his hair needed trimming, the mustache had been cut down to where it barely covered his upper lip.

"Why did you trim your moustache so closely, Mr. Krause?" Lepke asked.

"It kept getting in my soup. Who are you, anyway, asking me all these questions?"

"An interested party."

"Interested in what?"

"In the whereabouts of Captain Plunkett and William Christie."

"I have no idea."

"But you were the man last seen with both of them."

"You just haven't talked to the right people yet if you believe that."

"I believe you killed both of them, Mr. Krause."

"I didn't kill anybody. I just told you that."

"Yes, you did say that, however, I'm confused. I might believe you if you could clear up a few points for me."

Krause looked over at U.S. Deputy Marshal Sid Hooper, his escort to Alaska. "Do I have to talk to this mug?"

"As long as you got nothin' to hide, why not?" Hooper grinned at him.

Krause looked up at Lepke again. "What points are bothering you, mister?"

"How did you obtain the *Lue's* skiff you rowed to Ketchikan?"

"I didn't row the *Lue's* skiff into Ketchikan. I rowed there in my own dingy that I later sold to a man." Small beads of sweat formed on Krause's forehead.

"Mr. Sing Lee says you did. He says he saw the name painted on the bow. He further stated you were going to leave the boat tied to his dock until he told you to move it."

"That Chink can't even speak English, let alone read." Krause stared at the floor with heavy-lidded eyes, his speech slowing.

"He seems to make a very good profit for an illiterate man. Who bought your dingy?"

"I don't remember his name."

"How do you suppose Captain Plunkett's skiff got to Ketchikan?"

"He probably rowed it there after his boat burned. Didn't I see in the paper where he went on to Seattle after his boat burned in Hobart Bay?"

"Yes, a typed letter was received in Juneau telling that tale. And by an odd coincidence, the letter William Christie left for his wife was typed also."

"What's so odd about that?" Krause sounded sleepy.

"Neither man had ever typed before in his life, according to friends and family. Yet when they both disappear they leave typed letters behind. Don't you find that very odd?"

"Lots of people have typewriters these days. They're efficient," Krause muttered.

"Don't you own a typewriter?"

"My typewriter hasn't worked for almost three years. I was taking it to Seattle to have it repaired. Look, I've already been through all this with that damned police captain in Seattle. Can't a man get a little rest?"

"Why were you traveling under the name of O. E. Moe?"

"I had some business with him once. I heard the authorities were looking for me for giving those two fellows a ride from Douglas to Juneau. So I thought I'd use his name and go south until this Christie fellow shows up again and things get back to normal."

"O. E. Moe has been missing for two years. Yet you have more recent mail addressed to him in your luggage. You have his signature on at least three sheets of paper. Did you kill him, too?"

"I didn't kill anybody!" Krause repeated. He stared hard at Lepke for a long moment before dropping his gaze to the floor again.

"Mrs. Christie wants to talk to you," Lepke said quietly.

Krause's head snapped up, true discomfort registering in his eyes. "I don't want to talk to her. She would just get more upset."

"How long have you known her?"

"I used to take meals with her and her first husband when we all lived in Petersburg." His eyes flicked back and forth over Lepke's face. "That's a common thing bachelors do in Alaska after they get tired of their own cooking."

"But when her husband went to Juneau to find work, she and the children stayed behind," Lepke stated.

Krause remained silent and dropped his eyes.

"Did you continue taking meals at the house after her husband went north?"

"Sure. What of it?" His cheek muscles worked after he stopped talking.

"Why did you name your boat after her?"

"I didn't." He hesitated a moment before continuing slowly, "My mother's name was Celia. I named the boat after her." He stared fixedly at the rug and licked his lips.

"Another coincidence in your life. What happened to her first husband?"

"He was killed in a hunting accident over on Admiralty Island about two years ago," he said grudgingly.

"You weren't hunting with him, were you?"

"No, mister, I wasn't. He was hunting alone." He cleared his throat, then raised his manacled hands and wiped a drop of sweat from his nose.

"Don't you think it odd for one man to have so much coincidence in his life, Mr. Krause?"

"Coincidence, luck, fate, natural selection, they all play a part," Krause drawled.

"Natural selection, do you believe in that?"

"And Social Darwinism. Yes. I believe in them."

"I suppose you see yourself in a more elevated state than most of your fellow humans?" Lepke asked.

"In some ways. I'm a very modern man."

"Superior to most you meet?"

Krause held Lepke's eyes again. "Most," he agreed.

Lepke smiled grimly. The reek of sour sweat radiated from Krause. "Then how do you account for the fact you're in chains and I'm not? Doesn't that take a bit of wind out of your sails?"

"Like I said, mister, luck and fate are in there, too. Both of those can change."

"You don't seem very worried about these charges against you."

"Is that a question?"

"Observation. There's been a great deal of observation in this work."

"Whattya mean?"

"Let's go over your movements of the 30th of October."

"I already talked to the copperhead in Seattle about that."

"Then it should be fresh in your mind. What happened after you and Christie left the Treadwell?"

"It started before that," Krause said tiredly. "I was at the dock in Juneau and this fellow comes up and asks me to take him over to Douglas and back. I told him he could catch a ferry for fifteen cents. He said it was worth five dollars in gold to get over and back in jig time."

"He offered you five dollars to take him across the channel and back?"

"Your hearing seems to be okay."

"Did he tell you his name?"

"No."

"What did he want to do in Douglas?"

"He said he wanted to pick up a fellow and take him back to Juneau. He acted like it was a practical joke or something."

"Then what happened?"

"Well I took him over to Douglas. Once we got there, he asked me if I'd go get this Christie mug for him."

"He asked you to impersonate a federal officer?"

"I didn't tell anyone I was a federal marshal! They started calling me 'marshal,' and I decided to go along with it if it would help get Christie down to the dock for my passenger."

"What happened when you returned to the dock with Mr. Christie?"

"My passenger greeted him like they were long-lost brothers. I took 'em back to Juneau and let them off at the city dock. I haven't seen either one of them since."

"You took them straight back to Juneau, without stopping anywhere else?"

"That's what I just said, mister."

"That's very curious, Mr. Krause. I have three witnesses who will swear under oath your boat didn't go anywhere near the Juneau dock that day. All three accounts have your boat going directly up the channel and anchoring near Salmon Creek."

"I think you're full of crap, mister. I think you're lying in your teeth. This is one big frame job and I'm going to beat it."

"I *have* the witnesses. Each one of them has identified your green boat with the oval windows. You shouldn't have followed the federal boat design so closely when you built it if you were going to use it for criminal activities."

"I don't use it for criminal activities."

"What do you do for a living, Mr. Krause?"

"I'm a boatwright by trade."

"When did you last build a boat?"

"In 1914."

"You earned enough from building one boat to live on the proceeds for a year?"

"I'm frugal, and I invest my money."

"In what?"

"Real estate."

"Under your real name or under aliases?"

"I use pseudonyms mostly. Is there a law against that?"

"Only when you use a name that already has a different owner."

"I didn't use Oly Moe's name in any business deals."

Lepke looked down at his notebook.

"Under the name of Alfred Hartman you hired a legal firm in Victoria, British Columbia to foreclose on a piece of property owned by a Mr. Yamato. Mr. Yamato was a watchman at the Olympic mine on Woodsky Island when he disappeared. At the time of his disappearance you were in the vicinity and even refused to help search for him."

Krause stared at the deck.

"You didn't help because you knew he was already dead, didn't you?"

"That kid probably went back to Japan."

"Three years for him has his family searched!" Lepke stopped and forced himself to calm down. "Alfred Hartman has not been seen since 1913 when he went to Haines with you on your boat."

"Al went up into the Interior. Told me he was going to Fairbanks and then on to Livengood," Krause said heavily. "I used his name because he owed me money and left the mortgage on the Jap kid's land as collateral. Al didn't come back, so I get the land."

"Knowing you must be hard on a man. So many of them have gone on trips from which they did not return."

"Alaska's a tough place, mister. Only the strong survive."

"Especially if they prey on the weak and trusting, Mr. Krause. You are a rabid beast who strikes from behind. I'm sure if any of these men had been attacked openly, one of them would have surely killed you. You are a coward."

"Who are you, Goddamn it?" Krause hissed through clenched teeth. The short chain between the manacles clanked as it went tight between his straining hands. The chain around his waist held him firmly to the chair.

Deputy Marshal Hooper, sitting on the far side of the cabin, rose to his feet with a look of concern. Lepke waved his hand negligently and the man sank down again. Hooper glanced at his pocket watch. He looked exhausted.

"I'm a professional hunter of thieves, murderers, and liars, Mr. Krause," Lepke said. "And I think you fit all three categories."

"Good luck trying to produce any evidence, penny-head," Krause sneered.

"You might be good at what you do, Lepke replied, "but no man is perfect. Somewhere I'll find the one mistake you surely made. That mistake you will pay for with your life."

Krause stared at him. "Someone's gonna die, all right. But it might not be me."

Lepke ignored him as he stood. He looked over at the deputy. "I'm going to get some sleep. I'll be back in five or six hours."

As Hooper locked the cabin door behind him, Lepke felt a fierce conviction. This man was a murderer. He knew it in his bones.

25 —Taku Village, A.T., December 1, 1915—
Wednesday evening

Feeling nervous, George Mak-we unclenched his fists and trudged through new snow to the house of his dead wife's father. The Taku village tumbled along the shoreline of Gastineau Channel. George had seen maps of Juneau that labeled this area as "Taku Alley" by the cartographer.

Between Douglas and Treadwell lay a third village inhabited by both the Auk People and the Taku People called 'Tlingit Alley.' He didn't dwell on the labels of the whites, it would only make for anger to which he must not succumb. Anger was what made him drink, and look what that had led to.

Tasnit John owned a substantial house of heavy plank construction in the old manner. At an angle next to the house stood a story totem. It celebrated ownership of a story the clan had possessed for many years. Tasnit told the story very well, George had been fortunate enough to hear it twice from the old man's lips.

Flanking the door stood two carved posts depicting the clans related to Tasnit. George pushed firmly on the door. If it opened, he was as welcome as any other visitor. It moved inward on protesting hinges. The last time he had gone through this door Amalie had been alive.

A fire burned brightly in the center of the house. Smoke filled the top third of the structure before escaping through the smoke hole in the roof. The fire pit, dug into the sand and shored up with rocks, measured about eight by twelve feet. The floor built up around the fire pit extended five feet before rising another three feet to the next level.

In total, two tiered platforms surrounded the fire pit. Four people sat next to the fire talking or cooking. Nobody looked up at him; that would have been unmannerly.

He pushed the door shut behind him and carefully negotiated the two levels down to the fire, which provided the only illumination in the house. Boxes and bundles containing Tasnit John's wealth crowded the upper platforms.

Once all the levels in this house had teemed with people; children scampering about in bright-eyed games, cared for by older sisters; women doing household chores elbow-to-elbow, each dealing with her own family's needs.

The women had been daughters to Rebecca, the wife of Tasnit John. In the Tlingit culture a young man married into the family of his wife. The husband lived in the house of his father-in-law while gathering the necessary wealth to build his own house.

Rebecca belonged to the Raven phraety; therefore all of her sons-in-law belonged to the Eagle phraety. Her own sons learned the lessons of youth and manhood from her brother, Deets-nu Solomon. He performed the duties of an uncle and taught his nephews well, just as his uncle had taught him.

Tasnit John educated the two sons of his older sister while still in his teens, and had proven to be an inspiring teacher. Now in his early seventies, Tasnit John presided over a house empty of all but one daughter and her husband.

George had never lived in this house. Things changed when he was a young man. Traditions went through a period of stress unparalleled in the spoken and carved history of the Tlingit people. Young men could afford houses more quickly than their fathers had.

There was work for everybody. Compared to the previous generation, the men now in their twenties and thirties were wealthy. The fact their pay did not equal that of a white man made no difference. It was enough they were able to work at all.

When George married Amalie, he worked as a kitchen helper for the Ground Hog Mine in the Silverbow Basin, just up the Perseverance wagon road from Juneau. He built a small house in the Indian town that grew up at the edge of the mining property. They settled into married life.

George sat near the fire, remembering his foolish youth. A cup of water appeared in front of him. No one spoke to him as he drank and listened politely to the conversation that had not faltered at his entrance.

"My cousin tells me there are very few Taku kwáan at Tulseqah now. And he says the people-across-the-mountains are moving up into the land of the Tagish and trade now with the Jilkaat kwáan," Jee-nak said. He was thirty-seven, married to the oldest daughter of the house, Mary. George thought him lazy and self-important.

"When I was a boy there was a potlatch at Tulseqah," Tasnit said.

George had not heard the quaver in his voice before. He sneaked a look at his father-in-law and felt astonishment at how old the man appeared. The vital man of recent memory had withered alarmingly.

"I was only a child but I was given a Hudson Bay hatchet," he said, pausing to wheeze. "And two slaves were given away. Nobody is that rich any more. The world changes.

"Now there are those of our people who would only speak English, never go to potlatch, and become little white men. I do not think I like this change."

"Change is everywhere," George agreed, taking the opening. "Yesterday I was asked to help hang a white man."

The house fell silent as his words settled. A bowl of venison appeared in front of him and he picked up a piece and began to eat.

"They would have you tie the rope, or pull it?" Jee-nak asked in a tone of disbelief.

"Are they going to hang the man who sold you the whiskey that killed my daughter?" Rebecca asked sharply.

"No, Mother. I have been asked to gather evidence, news of what people saw, about this man," George said.

"A white man, you say?" Tasnit asked.

"Yes, Father. A man named Edward Krause. He has a boat . . ." As George described the boat and explained how he became involved in the work, he watched the faces of his dead wife's family.

Tasnit was interested in the story because it was something new for a bored old man to hear. Rebecca radiated hate and distrust for George. She hadn't heard a word he'd said since she spoke. Jee-nak listened carefully; he was an observant man when it came to the actions of others.

George knew if anyone could get information out of the Taku people, it was Jee-nak. Much enmity existed between them so he didn't dare ask directly for a favor. Mary sat and stared at George. As usual, he could not fathom what lay behind her face.

"When I was a young man I saw them hang a man here in Tsenta-ka-hini. He was an Indian that the white man said had robbed and killed a white woman. I do not think that was so, but they hanged him anyway." Tasnit lapsed back into silence.

George ignored the man's use of the old Tlingit name for Juneau City. Tasnit probably wasn't aware of the slip. His mind seemed to be wandering a great deal this day. Perhaps every day?

"So you have come to ask our help, or to pick treasures from our minds like a raven?" Mary asked in a flat voice.

"I ask your help. This man is dangerous, and Detective Lepke asks for our help to bring him to justice."

"Our help, or your help?" Mary asked.

"In asking my help he believes he is gaining the wisdom and knowledge of our people," George said evenly. "Would you have me advise him otherwise?"

"Does the detective offer a reward for this knowledge?" Jee-nak's eyes glistened bright with reflected fire.

"Only gratitude and honor." George tried to keep reproach out of his voice.

"Does he know you are without honor?" Rebecca's voice cut at him. "Does he know you killed my youngest daughter and will never have my gratitude? Does he know you will not come to Jesus?"

"I was drunk, I admit it," George said softly, making the others strain to hear him over the fire's crackle. "Amalie was drunker than I was, and knocked over the lamp when she fell down. At first I was too stupefied to realize what had happened."

The others stared at him, waiting for his words.

"Then it was too late," George said.

"You gave her hooch. You got her drunk. And you left her in a burning house to die!" Rebecca shrieked.

"The oil flowed under her! The whole room was in flames; she was in flames. She would have died even if I had pulled her out then," he said, staring down at the fire in the center of the room.

"I, I was too drunk to do anything except get out of the house myself," he whispered. "I haven't taken a drink since that day. I have educated myself and have made myself useful to my people."

"You killed my daughter and now you help the white man. You are not of the People any more. You won't even come to Jesus!" Rebecca stood and waddled quickly behind the house screen where she and Tasnit slept.

The fire cracked and hissed. Mary rose to her feet and followed her mother.

"I never saw them hang a white man," Tasnit said.

Jee-nak stared at George with new softness in his eyes. "I will ask our people if any saw this boat you spoke of. Come back in a week."

"Thank you, brother," George said, staring at the fire. The visit was over and all knew it. But one did not just run away after being granted a request. One sat and thought about it, and shared silence or conversation with others for a while.

He stared at the fire and thought about his dead wife.

26 —Northbound aboard the *S.S. Humboldt*, December 2, 1915— Thursday afternoon

"Why didn't you respond to the note the marshal left on your boat?" Lepke asked.

"I told you, I didn't find any note. The wind must have blown it away or something." Bags bulged under Krause's dark eyes. His fingers twitched for no external reason and his voice rasped hoarse. He had made mistakes in his story.

"And where did you last see Captain Plunkett?"

"He dropped me off at the Petersburg dock and sailed south."

"I suppose you have witnesses who will swear to that?"

"Sure do, three of 'em."

"What are their names?" Lepke asked quickly.

Krause's bloodshot eyes peered up at him. "Pete Sommers, Bob Bennett, and Horace Powell. They all live in Petersburg and all three were on the dock that day."

"What time did you get into Petersburg?"

"Late afternoon. About four-thirty, five o'clock."

"You're sure of the time?"

"Yes, I'm sure, 'cause I looked at my watch."

"Did they know you were coming in prior to that time? Were they there to meet you on purpose?"

"Naw, they just happened to be down on Bob's boat."

"They saw you from a distance?"

"They must have. Why, what difference does it make?"

"Were they waiting at the dock when the *Lue* pulled up?"

"Yeah, what of it?"

"How far away from your friend's boat was the *Lue* when it tied up?"

"Maybe a hundred feet." Krause yawned and stretched his chained hands out in front of him.

"So they saw *you* when the *Lue* was still out on the water, before it tied up at the dock?"

"Yeah. They even waved. What's the big deal?"

"Well, I find it rather incredible your friends could recognize you hundreds of feet away in darkness," Lepke said in a mocking tone.

Krause abruptly sat up straight in his chair. "Dark! I, ah, I must have been mistaken about the time. It was still light out. They saw me coming for about two or three hundred feet."

"You misread your watch?" Lepke gave him a tight smile.

"I must have," Krause returned with a smoldering glare. "Look, could you take these things off long enough for me to go to the head?"

Lepke glanced over at the deputy who was fast asleep. "Sure, let me get the key."

He walked over and picked the key off the table next to the snoring deputy. Krause avidly watched him approach, he held out his hands.

"No. First I'll undo the chain around your waist." Lepke stepped behind the man and opening the first lock, pulled the chain through the rings bolted into the back of the chair. He stepped back. "Stand up slowly and put your hands over your head."

Krause groaned as he stood. "My God, am I cramped up!"

"Hands over your head," Lepke repeated.

Krause was larger than Lepke. The big man leaned his head forward and put his wrists on his shoulders, letting the chain rest lightly across his back. Lepke took a firm grip on the chain and unlocked the right manacle.

Krause's right elbow suddenly came back and up sharply, aiming at Lepke's chest, but Lepke had already stepped to the side. He jerked back sharply on the chain which made Krause stumble backward over the chair.

"Damn!" Krause shouted as he hit the deck flat on his back.

Hooper jerked awake with an oath.

Lepke had his .455 Bulldog revolver pointed between Krause's eyes.

"You must think I'm stupid. You try anything like that again and I'll save them the expense of trying or hanging you." The weapon pointed steadily at the big man, without a quiver. "Do you understand me?"

"Yeah. Now can I go take a crap?"

"Mister," Hooper said from across the room. "Next time you let me know what's going on, okay?"

Lepke glanced over. The man held a large bore revolver in his hand.

"What the hell is that?"

"A Colt .44. And I'm brutal good with it."

"Next time I'll tell you," Lepke agreed. He looked down at Krause. "Get up and go to the head. Leave the door open."

"This is the longest damn boat trip I've ever been on," the deputy said sullenly. "When do we get to Juneau?"

"Tomorrow afternoon. I've still got lots of time to question him further."

"I don't know how he's putting up with all your questions," Hooper grumbled. "I'm gettin' damn sick of them!"

Lepke grinned. "Good. I must be wearing him down too."

"I'm coming out now," Krause said from the head. "Be careful with those damn guns."

Lepke chained him to the chair again and secured the manacles. He stepped back. The deputy holstered his large weapon.

"All right now, where were we?" Lepke said jovially. "Oh, yes. What time did you arrive in Petersburg?"

Both Krause and the deputy groaned.

THE ALASKA DAILY EMPIRE
Juneau, Alaska, Friday, December 3, 1915

HUGHES TO BE NAMED BY G.O.P.'S

GERMANS ORDERED TO LEAVE

MONASTIR CAPTURED BY TEUTONS

CHRISTIANIA IS FIRST STOP OF PEACE SHIP

KRAUSE IS PLACED IN U.S. JAIL

Edward Krause, man of many alleged murders and aliases, was locked up in the United States jail at 2:10 o'clock this afternoon. He was taken ashore from the steamship *Humboldt* at Thane, at 1:30 o'clock, handcuffed to Sidney J. Hooper, a guard, and whisked to Juneau in George Burford's automobile. The *Humboldt* put in at Thane at the request of United States Marshal H. A. Bishop, in order to give Krause no embarrassment at being taken ashore at Juneau or Douglas. As a result, a large crowd of curiosity seekers was cheated of an opportunity of seeing Krause.

Deputy Marshal James L. Clarke and William W. Casey, Jr., met the *Humboldt* with the Burford car and accompanied Krause and his guard to Juneau. The automobile burned up the mileage in reaching the jail, making the trip over the rough road from Thane in less than ten minutes.

27 —Juneau City, A.T., December 4, 1915—
Saturday afternoon

Fiona Malone watched the man track snow across the lobby of the Division Hotel. At least he owned luggage, expensive from the look of it. He pushed up against the desk and looked directly into her eyes.

"I would like a room, miss."

"Yes, sir. How long will you be staying with us?"

"Do you have a weekly rate?"

"Certainly. Six dollars and fifty cents a week or twenty dollars per month."

"Let's start with a week." He reached inside his coat and brought out a large wallet which he flipped open.

Fiona saw the badge flash for an instant before the man covered it with his hand. A law officer coming here? Should she let Maye know about it?

"May I have my key, miss?"

"Oh. Certainly, Mr.—," She glanced down at the register and found his name. "—Lepke. You're in room three." She turned to the pigeonholes and found his key. As she handed it to him she smiled and asked, "What business are you in, Mr. Lepke?"

"Well, I am an investigator."

"Did you know there is a Pinkerton man in town?" she said brightly.

"Where did you hear that?" he asked. His eyes cooled as his gaze slowly washed over her.

She blushed, feeling alarm.

"M-my sister told me. He's an acquaintance."

"Oh!" His manner became very friendly. "You must be Fiona Malone. Florence has spoken of you a number of times."

"She has? Why would she—," Fiona faltered as realization rushed through her. She felt her cheeks burning again. And she felt foolish. "You're the Pinkerton man, aren't you?"

"Yes, I am. August Lep—" He laughed awkwardly. "You have my name right there in front of you. I am very pleased to meet you, Miss Malone." He extended his hand and she reached out and shook it.

"Please call me Fiona," she said with a smile. Florence hadn't mentioned he was good looking. *How does she always get the best of everything?*

"There is one thing I would like to inquire about."

"What's that, Mr. Lepke?" She prepared her best coy smile in case the question was a personal one.

"Does this house have any rules about visitors?"

"Visitors! What kind of visitors?"

"That's just it. Are there rules against any particular type of visitor? Within the bounds of decency, of course."

"Ah, not to my knowledge, sir, Mr. Lepke." What a strange question.

"Excellent. I have a Tlingit assistant who will leave letters for me from time to time. If he should ever come in when I am here, please direct him to my room immediately," he said with authority.

"Tlingit? Like the Indians?"

"Yes."

"Oh. That will be fine, sir. I'll see to it the day staff are told." To her knowledge Maye didn't question who or what went into a guest's room as long as the guest was doing the inviting and the visits were quiet.

"Ah, that was a male assistant you said?" Fiona asked officially.

"Yes, George Mak-we, my assistant, is definitely a male," he said with a chuckle.

"Oh." She colored again. What was it about this man that had her continually blushing? Why was she suddenly so inept?

"Would you like me to show you to your room, Mr. Lepke?"

"No, thank you, Miss Malone. I'm sure I'll have no trouble finding it. Well, nice meeting you." He picked up his luggage and walked quickly up the stairway.

"Please call me Fiona," she whispered. But he was gone. Florence's detective.

Her eyes stayed on the stairs where he had disappeared. She was seeing the young men who had called on her or shown romantic interest. All four of them seemed as bland as granny's soup.

She wanted to meet a man who had some mystery to him, and was handsome, of course. Someone who thought her beautiful and clever, and knew she belonged someplace more exciting than Alaska Territory.

She fussed at straightening up the desk but there was little in disarray. Sometimes this job could be so boring! Twelve rooms and only three guests. Maye said early December was very slow in the hotel business.

Well, at least she had a job. The front door opened again and a thick-set man wearing a dark overcoat and fur hat trudged across the room toward her. His dark, brown beard held rapidly melting snow.

He smiled widely at her and pulled off his hat.

"The name is Pete Sommers, and I'd like a room."

Fiona gave him a business smile. This man was far from handsome but he certainly radiated danger. He also radiated body odor.

"Yes, sir. Our rates are a dollar fifty a day. Would you please sign the register?"

"Sure." He hunched over, picked up the pen and signed his name laboriously. "Let's just take it a day at a time, pretty lady." He dug into a pocket and pulled out two greasy bills.

"Very well. Let me get your change." She turned away toward the small office.

"No. You go buy yourself something pretty at the store and see how many people don't notice 'cause they're looking at you. May I have my key?"

"I really can't accept this, Mr. Sommers."

"I insist," he said flatly. My key please."

"Very well. Thank you. Here you are, room seven."

"Aren't you going to show me where it's at?"

"No, sir. You'll find it at the end of the hall on the second floor." She had already fallen for that one once.

"You got spunk. I like that." He grinned at her again and strode off toward the stairs.

She watched him out of sight. I'll wager he would call me Fiona, she thought ruefully. The door opened again.

A well-dressed, rather handsome woman came up to the desk. She glanced over her shoulder once, and fixed Fiona with an intense stare.

"My name is Amanda Landes Ganbor. I desperately need your help."

"What can I do for you?"

"I need a place to stay where I will be safe."

"The Division Hotel is quite safe, Miss Ganbor," Fiona said.

"There is a man I must be free of. He, he would harm me if he could find me."

Fiona let her hand drop to the shelf hidden under the desk top, she pulled out the double-barreled shotgun so the woman could see it.

"Nobody is going to harm you in this house," she said flatly.

Amanda Ganbor smiled her relief. "Oh, you have no idea how wonderful that makes me feel." Her eyes widened. "What is your name?"

"Fiona Malone. I'm the night clerk."

"Are there a terribly lot of Malones in Juneau or are you related to Florence?"

"Florence? She's my sister. We're quite different."

"But just as able, I'm sure. Fiona, I have a slight problem."

"What? I said you'd be safe here."

"I only have five American dollars."

"That will pay for a week," she lied.

"But that is all the money I have, for food, lodging, incidentals . . ." she hesitated and put something on the desk. "And I have this brooch."

Fiona glanced at the jewelry.

"But you're in danger?"

"Yes. I'm afraid I am."

"Perhaps I should telephone Miss Wattnem and ask her to come down and talk to you. She's the owner."

"A woman owns this establishment?"

Fiona nodded through her smile and picked up the phone and cranked the handle twice. "Operator? Yes, I'd like two-three please. Thank you. Bones? This is Fiona. I need to talk to Maye . . ."

28 —Juneau City, A.T., December 5, 1915—
Sunday afternoon

"Krause, you got a visitor."

Ed Krause rolled over on his bunk and peered at the cell door. The corpulent form of his lawyer, Kazis Krauczunas, slipped through the opening and took the only chair in the cell.

Neither man said anything until the turnkey locked the door and shuffled off down the hall.

"Nick King was here yesterday," Krause said in a listless tone. "Only said two words; 'that's him,' before he left again."

"The problem, you see," Kazis wheezed, "is that damned detective."

"That notebook-scribbling, righteous son-of-a-bitch!" Krause spat.

"He's a very good detective. Too good. He has found witnesses you didn't even realize were near you or your actions." Kazis looked around at the spare cell, and lowered his voice.

"Why Christie? There was nothing the man had on him or obtainable with his signature that was worth killing him. We've talked about this before. These fools all believe in a different creed than we do. They don't understand the law of the jungle . . ."

"It was personal. Besides, I only saw him until I delivered him to the man who paid me, *remember?*" Krause hissed.

"Of course. What about the holdings you have secured? Are you going to sign them over to the organization?"

"We're going to beat this inquisition, aren't we?" Krause asked.

"Of course, my friend, of course." The heavy man's face clicked into a professional grin, before slackening again. He began to sweat.

"They just think they're in control. We all know what an all-encompassing illusion that can be. They cannot hang you for murder if they cannot produce a body. It's as simple as that. Their own laws work against them, ties their hands, and aids anarchy at every turn."

"That's wonderful," Krause snapped. "But you say this detective is putting an awful lot of words together; we need to deal with him once and for all. And soon!"

"Not so fast, my dear fellow," Kazis soothed. "First we let him gather what information he can, then we take steps to eliminate the most incriminating informants."

"Eliminate the God-damned detective," Krause said flatly. "As long as he's alive, I'm in danger."

"Not to worry. I've already got Pete Sommers here from Petersburg."

"That's the stuff. Get the whole organization up here. Tell 'em to get that damned detective first!"

"You still might have to do time. I don't think I can get you off clean."

"As long as the detective is dead, I can do anything. I want him dead and I don't even know his name! Get me his name!"

"Of course, Ed, of course. That will be an easy thing to find out. I'll tell you tomorrow."

"Bring me some cheroots tomorrow. And tell Pete this for me . . ."

Kazis leaned forward and listened attentively.

29 —Juneau City, A.T., December 6, 1915—
Monday late morning

August Lepke noticed how Florence Malone's eyes lit up when he walked into Winter and Pond's shop. He brushed snow off his shoulders. It made him feel so good to mirror her smile.

"When did you get back to town?" she asked.

"Friday afternoon on the *Humboldt*."

Her smiled dimmed abruptly. "The paper said Ed Krause was on that boat."

"He was. And he answered questions all the way from Ketchikan."

"Did he say anything about Unc —, ah, Jim Plunkett?"

"He told a lot of lies," August said with a sigh. "Miss Malone, I'm certain both Mr. Christie and Captain Plunkett are dead. I'm sorry, but there's no use deluding yourself about it."

She stared at him with anguished round eyes; her lower lip trembled.

"He'll hang, won't he?"

"Yes. He'll hang. I promise you."

"Good." She glanced up at the clock. "It's almost time for lunch. Would you care to have a bite with me?"

He smiled broadly. "I'd be honored."

She gestured at the curio-filled shop. "Look around, I'll be out in a few minutes." She disappeared into the back.

He wandered between the glass-fronted cases. Bentwood boxes, willow baskets, beaded blankets, bows and arrows, carved rattles and paddles, painted trays, and miniature totems all waiting for the discerning shopper. Some of the pieces were quite handsome. *The place looks like an ethnographic museum,* he mused.

Photographs covered the walls, many in ornate frames that cost more than the photograph itself. The partners had been everywhere in Alaska. There were views of Indian villages, canneries, mine shafts, waterfalls, boats, bears, and children.

"Rather an eclectic collection, wouldn't you say?" Florence said, emerging from the back room with her coat.

"Well put," August said. "Is any of this your work?"

"No. I need to add to my body of work before I show it to anyone."

"Why is that?" August held the door for her.

"Why is what?" She pulled the door shut tightly and locked it.

"Why must you add to it before showing anyone?" They moved quickly down the snowy street.

"Because one's competence depends on the body of work, not just one or two pieces." She pulled her fox skin collar up around her ears.

"I would just like to see your photography, not pass judgment on your competence."

"Thank you, Mr. Lepke. I'll consider your request. Now let's quickly find someplace to have lunch before I freeze solid."

"How about the Alaskan Hotel?"

Her eyes flashed from the fur collar.

"That's one of the most expensive places in town!" "Please, allow me to treat you to lunch?"

Her step slowed as she considered. "I'm not sure that would be proper, Mr. Lepke."

"Why not? The place is a public eating establishment. What wouldn't be proper about it?"

"Having lunch with you isn't the problem. But allowing you to pay for my lunch might be construed by some."

"Miss Malone, if you won't tell, neither shall I."

She laughed. "Done, Mr. Lepke. Now let's hurry."

The Alaskan Hotel proved plush even by Portland standards. Mahogany wainscoting ran around the walls below massively framed paintings. Lepke thought the paintings were only copies of European originals, but wasn't sure. Three massive chandeliers hung from the high ceiling and provided soft illumination.

"May I help you, sir?" The glacial maître d'hôtel, wearing a three-piece suit complete with frock coat, stood at attention before them.

"We would like a table for lunch," Lepke said.

"Do you have a reservation, sir?"

Lepke glanced over the man's shoulder. Diners filled about half the tables in the long room.

"No. Do I need one?" Lepke took Florence's arm, pulled gently to turn her to leave.

The maître d'hôtel caught both actions, warmly smiled, and quickly said, "No, of course not. Not for lunch. This way, please." He turned and led them to a table equidistant between other diners. A waiter dressed almost as elegantly as the maître d'hôtel materialized with two menus.

Once the waiter had departed with their orders for tea and coffee, Florence looked up at August.

"This place is rather stuffy, isn't it?"

"The food is excellent," he said with a smile.

She looked at her menu again. "And expensive."

"Please. Order what you wish. The Agency grants me an expense account for most of my meals, and they pay me a decent wage besides. It is not inconvenient to do this once in a while."

"Very well. I'll pretend I'm dining with one of the Mellons and consider price no object."

"Good. Who are the Mellons?"

"One of the richest banking families in New York City."

"Ah, explains it that does. I have never been to New York and none of their relatives are criminals." *Why,* he wondered, *am I beginning to feel nervous?*

"Mr. Lepke, would you answer a personal question?"

"Perhaps," he said guardedly.

"Why aren't you married?"

"Please?" he said in confusion. "I don't understand."

Alaska State Library - Historical Collections

"You're a reasonably good-looking man, you have a profession, and you're very close to thirty years old, aren't you?"

"So why should I be married?"

"I'm not saying you should. I'm merely wondering why you aren't."

"I've been very busy in my profession, just as you have been in yours."

"Pardon?"

"You're not married, either. I assumed it was because of your commitment to photography and the suffrage movement."

"Well, women have the right to vote in the Territory of Alaska, so suffrage isn't one of my prime concerns at the moment. Oh, I advocate universal suffrage for women, but there's not much one can do from Alaska to change the nation, is there?"

"Probably not. Then why aren't you married?"

"I asked you first," she said firmly.

"Yes, so you did." He scratched his jaw and wondered how to approach this painful subject. Just tell her, he decided.

"You don't have to tell me about her if you don't want to," Florence said quietly.

"What? How did you—"

"Mr. Lepke, it's quite obvious to me you were hurt at some point in your life, and I doubt shabby treatment from a man would still be causing you pain."

He looked at her wonderingly. "How can you be sure it wasn't the other way around?"

"Because you aren't that kind of man."

Yes, that's true, he thought. "You're a very perceptive woman. Perhaps that's why you haven't married."

"Sir?"

"Women like you scare American men."

She nodded and gave him a small smile. "You're quite perceptive, for a man."

He laughed with her. The waiter returned with tea and coffee and left with their order. "At the beginning of my third year in college I met Alice," Lepke said. "She was starting her freshman year. We met in class, European History, 1815 to Present."

He drank some coffee and stared into space, seeing her again. "She wasn't especially gifted at scholarship, but she worked at it a great deal. I offered to help her with her history studies. We, I, any way, fell in love."

He focused on Florence. She watched him steadily.

"I called on her at her home. Her father was civil, but not welcoming. Alice and I saw a great deal of each other. She told me she loved me despite her father's attitude toward me. I believed her. I wanted to believe her." He sipped more coffee.

"He offered to send her to a different university, but she refused. Then, as summer approached, he made her another offer, a two year grand tour of European capitals."

"Where did he get that sort of money?" Florence asked abruptly.

"Sorry, I forgot to mention they were rich. Her grandfather was a partner in an early lumber combine. The transport I sailed in to the Philippines was smaller than their yacht."

"Oh, I see."

"I didn't at the time. It amazed me when she told me she was leaving the next day. That was part of it; she had to depart immediately. And she did." He paused for a long moment.

"I worked through the summer and tried to finish my final year of studies, but it was no use. Everywhere I went on campus, I saw her there in my memory. So to Portland I traveled to seek work. In two days only I found employment with the Pinkerton Agency. My military record impressed them."

"Mr. Lepke, she was a fool!" Florence blurted.

"Thank you for saying so. For the longest time I thought I was the fool. I thought I had missed an opportunity, said the wrong thing, misread a nuance, or committed some fatal *faux pas*. I thought about it so much it almost killed me."

"Killed you? Isn't that rather melodramatic?" A smirk played at the edges of her lips.

"Not really. I was on a work for the company, seeking a felon in a very poor neighborhood, when I began thinking about Alice. If the man hadn't stepped on broken glass, he would have successfully surprised, and killed, me."

"I guess you lead a melodramatic life," she said soberly.

"Mostly it's just tedious routine. Every now and then there are moments of abject terror or exhilaration, but mostly routine."

"So how did you stop thinking about her?"

"I trained myself to mentally review photographs of criminals every time I thought of her."

"How appropriate!" Florence said with a chuckle. "Did you ever see her again?"

"Yes. I happened to run across her and her new husband at a social event in Seattle."

"Husband! Oh, I'm sorry."

"So was he, actually. He was some sort of Italian nobleman, long on nobility and short on money. He was about fifty-five, had bad teeth, and an incredible garlic odor. She didn't seem very happy at that point."

"But still you pine for her."

"I often wonder what might have been." *Enough*, he decided. She knew the meat of it now. He could change the subject.

"So you've been afraid of women since then?"

"Not afraid. Just wary."

"But wary enough to misread the slightest touch of indecision, I'll wager."

He grinned in spite of himself. She had hit the target again.

"Very good, Miss Malone. The two times since then I have encountered eligible women socially, I retreated at the first sign of boredom or disinterest. Both times I congratulated myself on my narrow escape."

Their food arrived and they concentrated on their meal for a time. August finished first and sipped his second cup of coffee when Florence laid down her fork and looked up at him.

"It's a shame you became involved with a girl who would allow her father to come between you."

"One never knows what's going to happen between two people, Miss Malone."

"That's true," she said. "But sometimes you can get the odds on your side."

"Odds are for those who wager. I'm an investigator. I do my footwork first, then I make my deductions."

"Is that how you operate?" she said with a wry smile. "I've wondered at your reticence."

"But you do recognize it for what it is," he pointed out. He felt lightheaded. This woman affected him and he realized he enjoyed the feeling.

"Yes. I see it for what it is. But if it continues past a realistic point, I shall think you're a coward." She smiled, but he felt the steel in her words.

"Could we do this again next Monday?"

"That would be fine, Mr. Lepke."

"I think I'm going to enjoy our lunches, Miss Malone."

THE ALASKA DAILY EMPIRE
Juneau, Alaska, Tuesday, December 7, 1915

CONGRESS HEARS PRESIDENT WILSON'S ADDRESS

REAL CITIZENSHIP AND READINESS

FOR WAR WILSON'S THEME

EPIDEMIC OF FEVER IS FEARED

HILL LINE FREIGHTER WANTS AID

SERBIAN CAMPAIGN COST 7,000

HEARING IN KRAUSE CASE TOMORROW

Edward Krause will be given a preliminary hearing before United States Commissioner Marshall at 2 o'clock tomorrow afternoon, at the court house, on a charge of kidnapping William Christie of Treadwell on the afternoon of Oct. 30, by serving a fake subpoena on him. District Attorney James A. Smiser and Assistant Prosecutor J. J. Reagan will represent the government. Kazis Krauczunas will appear for the defendant

The star witness for the government will be Foreman Nick King, of the "700" stamp mill at Treadwell. King has identified Krause as the man who took Christie out of the mill, after seeing the prisoner at the United States jail.

30 —Juneau City, A.T., December 7, 1915—
Tuesday noon

Amanda couldn't take her eyes off the clock on the wall. Only six more minutes to go. She'd telephoned Williams two days after her final departure from his hotel room.

"I'm leaving you."

"I won't try to stop you, but I must speak to you privately as soon as possible." His words had been hesitant with a touch of urgency. She agreed to see him in the lobby of the Division Hotel.

She glanced over her shoulder for the third time to make sure Fiona still stood behind the desk. Fiona Malone and Maye Wattnem. What wonderful people these Alaskans were!

The door opened with a billow of cold air that vaporized as the lobby warmth enveloped it. Arnold Williams shut the door behind him and stood glancing about the room while pulling his gloves off, finger by finger. His eyes came to rest on Amanda. He nodded and moved across the room to her.

She stood and shook hands with him awkwardly. Her lip wanted to tremble, but she wouldn't allow it. She stared into his bright blue eyes.

"May we go somewhere a bit more private?" he asked lightly.

She shook her head. "No. This is private enough for anything I wish to do with you."

"I could kill you where you stand, if that's what you're worried about." A chill descended across his features.

"But you won't, of course. There's a witness here." Amanda smiled grimly.

"If I wanted to kill you, I would. I'd just have to kill her too."

Arrogant bastard! "Fiona," she called back over her shoulder without taking her eyes off Williams, "show him."

Williams frowned and looked back at Fiona. Amanda knew the moment he saw the shotgun— the skin around his eyes tightened. He looked at her again.

"We're getting off on the wrong foot here," he said in a low voice. "I mean you no harm. But if you tell anyone the slightest word about Mexico, I will kill you."

"What's it to me if you murder Mexicans? I just want to be free of you. You're no longer any fun."

His face softened. "Fun hasn't been one of my priorities since I was a stripling. You, on the other hand, have yet to attain adulthood. Once you've grown up I'm sure you'll be more interesting for a man."

Amanda felt her face burn. She had to concentrate on not slapping him. "Is there anything else you wish to say to me before you leave?"

"No. That's the lot. You'll be staying here then?"

"That's none of your business. But I do have something else to say to you. I have written a letter detailing everything I know about you and your actions. This letter is presently in the hands of a person whom I trust. If they do not see me every forty-eight hours, they will turn the letter over to the authorities. I didn't want you to think you would get off Scot-free if you murdered me some night."

The muscles in his jaw worked as he glared at her. "Just remember," he hissed. "If they come for me, I'll get you first, no matter where you're at or who you're with! It is upon your head."

"I won't tell a soul as long as you stay away from me," she said, fighting the quaver in her voice.

He turned and walked quickly to the door. He hesitated, looking back at her for a fleeting moment, before pushing out into the frigid daylight.

Amanda sat heavily in her chair feeling light-headed and unable to breathe. Fiona was instantly beside her.

"Amanda! Are you all right?"

"I, I would like a drink . . ."

"Certainly! Water?"

"No. I believe I would like some of your American whiskey." She smiled up at her new friend. "You see; I feel so very giddy. And I would like to celebrate."

Fiona smiled back at her. "I know where Maye keeps her bottle. I'll be right back."

"These Alaskans," she said to the empty room. "What wonderful people!"

31 —Auk Village, A.T., December 10, 1915—
Friday afternoon

"I thought you liked your job in the mine," George Mak-we said.

"It allows me to buy many things, Uncle," Jim Kisadis said earnestly. "But there is this part of me that wishes to go back to the village and live as we did in grandfather's time."

"There are those who do that. Most of them didn't stay near the white towns very long. But the ones who did stay have become accustomed to things your grandfather didn't have. It might be a hard thing for you to do."

"Do you think I can't do it?"

"That's not what I said. I know you can do anything you strongly believe in. I'm just asking how much you want to do this thing?"

Jim blinked and glanced down the snowy dock toward Juneau City. Dark, bruised clouds covered the sky and snowflakes randomly tumbled down. The oily smell of Treadwell's smoke hung around the edge of the nose. The rumbling of the stamps throbbed like a whisky headache.

"The thing becomes stronger every day. This Brotherhood some of our people are starting bothers me. They say we all must speak the white tongue and give up our ancient customs. That is why I had to speak to you, my mother's brother." He suddenly frowned. "Isn't that your brother-in-law?"

George had trouble changing direction mentally. It took him a moment to realize why Jim was pointing down the dock. When he finally looked behind him, Jee-nak was but a few feet away.

"Jee-nak, my brother. Why are you out on a day like this?"

"To have words with you, brother."

"This is my nephew, Jim Kisadis."

"You brought him to Tasnit John's house once, many years ago. He was a boy then," Jee-nak said as he nodded to the young man.

"I remember the visit," Jim said. "I was very impressed with the house, and was honored by your father-in-law's story."

"I will tell him of your good memory. George, I have talked to people about the green boat. Three remember seeing it; they thought it was a government boat."

George had his notebook in one hand and his pencil in the other. He licked the rounded tip of the lead. "What did they see?"

As Jee-nak spoke, George scribbled furiously. A gust of wind from the southeast forced them to turn away. The snow thickened to small, steady flakes. The temperature edged downward.

Jee-nak finished speaking. George put his notebook away.

"Tasnit John has aged so suddenly. Was it because of Amalie?" George asked.

"He is old. He was already a man when the Russians left. This is the first time you have seen him in three years."

"I cannot go back to that house. It brings me too much pain. Do you—"

"I understand, George, but I didn't until your last visit. I think differently about you now."

"And I, you, my brother." George grasped his hand. The two men smiled at each other as they slowly shook hands.

"If I hear anything more I will get word to you. Right now I'm going to get out of the weather. I'm too old for this." Jee-nak waved and walked into the wind.

George watched him for a moment. He glanced over at Jim. "You just saw something I thought could never happen."

"I'm honored," Jim said with a grin.

"He's right. It's too cold to be out here. Let's go see if your mother has some tea for us."

When they approached his sister's house, George noticed fresh footprints leading to the door. Store-bought boots, he thought, and small feet at that. They stamped their feet and entered the frame house.

Irene looked up from the table where she sat with her daughter, Ruth, and a white woman. George and Jim both saw the stranger at the same time and stopped.

Small in stature, the woman wore a conservative gray dress, and possessed the most lovely, no, lovely wasn't the right word, she had the most *feeling* face he had ever seen in his life.

"Here is my son, James, now, and my only brother, George," Irene said to the woman. She turned to the two men. "This is Julia Prescott. She is an anthropologist who wishes to know how much we've changed since we left Grandfather's village."

Julia looked up at the two men with quiet gray eyes. George felt his heart swell. He knew he stared at her impolitely, but couldn't remember how to stop.

"Pleased to meet you, Julia," Jim said politely.

"Thank you. I'm very happy to meet you."

George felt transfixed. Irene slowly lost her smile as she regarded her brother. "George? Are you ill?"

"No," he said absently, "I'm just fine." His wits began to return and he blinked. "Please forgive my boldness, Julia Prescott, but you are very beautiful to me," he said before he could control his mouth again.

Julia laughed.

Irene gasped and put her hand over her mouth. "George! Are you drinking again?"

"No!" he blurted. "I, I apologize. I usually don't say things like that to people I have just met." He stared at Julia for a long moment, and continued, "Especially white people."

"Well I'm not going to be upset because you think I'm beautiful." She owned a beautiful smile, too, he thought. Good, healthy teeth, firm jaw and pronounced laugh-lines. "You *are* a very direct man, but then, culturally that's the sign of a leader among the Tlingit."

"That's right. You're an anthropologist." His mind cleared then. He felt shaken. Not because he had seen a lovely woman, but because he had been smitten so abruptly and completely. She probably thought him a fool.

"Yes, I am. Does that make you uncomfortable?" She regarded him carefully.

"Well, I'm wondering why you're here asking questions about the old ways when you could be over in Hoonah or Angoon where they're still living that way."

"Because that's been documented. What hasn't been documented is the way one village's traditions have changed after thirty-five years next door to a white community. I find the possibilities just fascinating."

"Fascinating," George echoed. "This is sort of like collecting specimens for biology, isn't it?"

"You are upset. I'm sorry, you have an educated vocabulary and I thought I had stumbled on a fellow scientist. The thing I love most about cultural anthropology is that I get to closely study the human side of a people."

George squinted at her. "I'm not a scientist. Explain what you just said."

"I get to understand how another culture *feels* about things familiar to me." Her smile returned.

"You're gonna do all that in one visit?" Jim asked incredulously.

All three women erupted in laughter.

"Well I thought it was a good question," George muttered to his nephew.

"I didn't get the chance to tell you," Irene said, "Julia is going to stay here for a month or so. She rented the spare bedroom."

George felt very happy.

32 —Juneau City, A.T., December 13, 1915—
Monday noon

The bell on the shop door jangled. Florence looked up from the ledger to see August Lepke hurriedly shut the door against the cold, hard wind. Her heart quickened.

"Mr. Lepke, it's so nice to see you," she said as he approached.

He smiled down at her. Once again she felt thankful he practiced good dental hygiene. Many men of thirty-two had teeth that made one almost ill to look at.

"It's nice to see you," he said awkwardly. "Are you ready for lunch?"

"Yes. I'm famished. I thought you'd never get here."

He frowned and looked up at the clock on the wall. "But, I'm three minutes early."

"And I appreciate that. I'll only be a moment. I must get my coat." She felt good as she dashed into the back room.

He was such a fine man, she reflected. How could he think because some silly schoolgirl rejected him he was no longer worthy of a good woman? Perhaps he didn't believe there were any good women.

Florence slipped into her coat and pulled on her hat. The hat wasn't stylish, but it was very warm. Winter had snapped its jaws down hard on Gastineau Channel.

August and Mr. Winter were talking when she reentered the room and stood next to them.

"Sometimes the wind lasts for a couple days," Mr. Winter commented.

"The thermometer on the bank reads nine below zero," August said in disbelief. "And that's sheltered from the wind! We don't have weather like this down in Portland. It's a good thing I have this work almost wrapped up."

Florence felt her heart catch. Good humor deserted her and icy fingers squeezed her soul.

Mr. Winter frowned at August. "You're not going to let a little cold weather blow you out of Alaska, are you, Mr. Lepke?"

"I do work for the Pinkerton Detective Agency, sir. It's pretty much up to them." He looked down at Florence and smiled. "Ready to go?"

She forced a smile. "Yes. Let's be off."

They pushed out into the numbing wind. Snow flew thickly and drifted deep behind windbreaks. Merchants had ceased trying to keep their boardwalks clear. Very little moved on the street. The snow muffled the pounding of the stamp mills to a low rumble.

They dashed across the plank street and into the White Lunch Cafe. The warm, steamy atmosphere bolstered Florence's spirits. She felt grateful the room was nearly empty. They had things to talk about.

The waiter hurried up with menus as they took off their coats.

"My! You two are certainly brave to be out in this weather. Is our food that good?"

August grinned. "No. Just convenient."

They all laughed. August held Florence's chair as she sat down. He sat on the other side of the table and picked up his menu.

Florence watched him as he ordered. Didn't he feel the least bit of remorse about his imminent departure? Was she just being a silly goose in her belief a genuine attraction existed between them?

This was the third time they had taken lunch together. Hadn't he indicated with his attention she was more than a mere acquaintance to him? Perhaps he was just a very nice man who enjoyed her company, nothing more. Maybe she scared him last week. Maybe he *was* a coward.

She felt sad. With nothing more than 'feelings' for film she had developed a set of images on which she had never truly focused. And she thought herself a photographer!

"Miss Malone? Are you ill?" August asked.

"Ill?" She started. "Of course not."

"Well, you looked so downcast, and didn't respond to the waiter here."

She looked up at the waiter. "Sorry. Just woolgathering. I'll have the grilled ham with boiled potatoes. And a pot of hot tea."

Suddenly they sat alone in the middle of the room. The wind whistled and howled at the eaves, rattling the glass windowpanes. Florence was glad they weren't sitting by the windows.

"You know, I've been an investigator for over five years now," August said. "I'm very good at reading a person's face. You are upset about something. When I first came into the shop, you were in a more buoyant mood."

The waiter came bustling up with a pot of tea for Florence and coffee for August. As soon as the man departed, August continued.

"So it had to be the statement I made to Mr. Winter about the work being nearly finished. Is that correct?"

"Is what correct?" she asked, stalling, not knowing why.

"Is it correct that my statement to Mr. Winter, about being nearly finished here, upset you?" he asked slowly.

"Well, it did take me somewhat unawares, and . . . Yes. It upset me very much." She looked down and toyed with her tableware.

"Why? You knew I was here to build a case around this man. Once that task is finished why should I remain here?"

Her eyes locked onto his. She scowled. "Well when you put it that way, I have no trouble seeing why you will be leaving soon. Nor, I might add, do I think you will be missed as much as I once thought!"

"Florence, are you angry because I'm leaving?"

"Well, I just thought . . ." She hesitated, realized she was starting to cry, and decided with a toss of her head she was going to finish her statement before she left this thick-headed—

"Florence, do you care *that* much for me?"

He called her by her first name! Tears streaked down her cheeks. She knew she must look a sight, but she didn't care.

"Well, of course I care that much for you, you idiot! Why else would I spend time with you?"

"I had hoped," he said, "but I wasn't sure you cared. I, I don't know much about women . . ."

"Do you care for me, August?" she asked, sniffing.

"I started to fall in love with you the first day we met," he said with finality.

"Well then," she said, standing up, "show me!"

August stood so quickly his chair fell over behind him. He moved around the table and embraced her. Her heart pounded hard enough to burst.

"Florence," he said, staring down into her eyes. "I love you now and I always will!"

Before she could respond he kissed her with such intensity she barely heard the shocked waiter.

"Where do they think they are, Seattle?"

33 —Juneau City, A.T., December 14, 1915—
Tuesday afternoon

"Fiona, I must speak to you," Amanda said.
Fiona looked up from the bookkeeping. She wanted to finish the unpleasant task and felt annoyed at the interruption. She hesitated, tried to keep testiness from her voice when she answered.

"Yes?"

"Oh. I'm sorry. Were you busy? I can talk to you later."

"No." Fiona rubbed a hand over her forehead, and smiled wryly. "I mean; it's okay. I just hate doing ciphers. How may I help you?"

"It's, it's something I told Arnold," Amanda said, chewing her lower lip.

Fiona felt a wave of foreboding. Just as the night she arrived, Amanda seemed nervous and frightened.

"Well, what is it, Amanda?" she said, conscious of having made a decision.

"Well, I, there's just so *much* I really can't tell you . . ." She rubbed her hands together as if washing them, and frowned at Fiona.

"Well, don't be a goose about it! Tell me what you feel you can."

"I told him I wrote a letter, about, ah, that was in the hands of a friend." She stopped and licked her lips. Her hands were now clenched together so tightly they quivered.

"Yes?" Fiona said.

"That if the person didn't see me at least once every forty-eight hours, they would give the letter to the police," she said in a rush.

"Oh!" Fiona withdrew, or tried to. One thin, cold wedge of discomfort held open the door to this association— she *had* prompted Amanda to tell her. "You're saying he would harm you if the threat of the letter wasn't there to hold him back?"

"Perhaps," Amanda said guardedly.

"Perhaps you should go to the police anyway."

"No. He's far more convincing than I. They'd believe him and then he would harm me."

"Do you really have a letter?"

"Oh, yes. I had it when I told him about it. I just hadn't found the 'friend' yet." Amanda brightened; her hands unclenched, and fell away from each other. "But I think I have now."

Fiona had a sudden sense of being underwater and unable to grasp the safety line, mere inches beyond her fingers. She swallowed.

"I told you I would help, didn't I?" Fiona hesitated, fearful of what she would say next. She didn't think she was afraid of being harmed. But she knew if the letter were in her possession, she would probably open it.

The front door opened and August Lepke entered along with a gust of snow and arctic air. He leaned against the door to shut it. Fiona, feeling like a distressed maiden, identified him as a knight in shining armor.

"Oh, Mr. Lepke, you're just in time!" Fiona said, and in her peripheral vision saw Amanda start. "I'd like you to meet someone."

Not until the words were out of her mouth did she notice the shocked expression on Amanda wore. *Now what?* Fiona wondered. Amanda couldn't possibly know Mr. Lepke was a detective.

"I am?" Lepke asked. "In time for what?" He pulled off his heavy coat and shook snow from his hat.

"To meet," Fiona kept her eyes on Amanda's face, "Miss Amanda Landes Ganbor."

Amanda set her face and turned to him.

"Actually," Amanda said pleasantly, "it's 'Baroness,' but I'm not a stickler on titles. Good evening, Mr. Lepke. How nice to see you again."

Lepke had gone still, like a deer just spotting a human and watching carefully for the first hint of danger. Fiona felt if she clapped her hands sharply he would leap through the window.

"Good evening, Mrs. Williams. How are you?" he said neutrally.

"Mrs. Williams!" Fiona blurted. It finally dawned on her that these people already knew each other. For some odd reason, she felt piqued.

"This time it is Mr. Lepke who is incorrect," Amanda said, still staring at his face. "But he didn't know until now. I was never married to Mr. Williams. We were merely traveling companions."

Fiona became aware her mouth hung open, and shut it. Lepke's face proved a study of conflicting emotions. Neutrality won again.

"Why do you feel this knowledge should be of importance to me?" Lepke asked.

Fiona gave him an angry look. "Why, Mr. Lepke! How rude."

His face flushed and he looked down at his dripping hat and coat.

"It's an honest question, Fiona," Amanda said. She continued to look directly at him. "And I think he deserves an honest answer."

"That would be something new," he said in a low voice.

"I met Mr. Williams under very peculiar circumstances, in a life-or-death situation. He saved my life. I felt I owed him something." Fiona felt sure Amanda wasn't aware she lifted her chin when she stopped speaking.

Lepke stared at her intently. "And by the time you were on the *Humboldt*, you knew you had made a mistake."

"Y-yes," Amanda said. "You're very perceptive"

"But not intuitive I'm afraid, or I wouldn't have misinterpreted your actions at dinner on Thanksgiving. How may I be of assistance?"

Amanda gave Fiona a wide-eyed glance. "I need someone to hold a letter for me."

"A letter. How long am I to hold it, and whom do I surrender it to?"

"You sound so official, Mr. Lepke," Amanda said with a smile.

"That's because he's a detective!" Fiona chirped.

"What!" For an instant Amanda lost her self-possession. Fiona was impressed with how quickly she regained it.

Lepke shot a quick, unreadable look at Fiona. "Yes, Mrs.– ah, *Miss* Ganbor. I am an operative for the Pinkerton Detective Agency out of the Portland office. So I suppose one might say neither of us were completely candid before this."

"But then," Amanda said, "I never really asked, did I?"

"Nor did I." He gave her a professional smile. "Do you still wish me to hold the letter?"

"Well . . . wait, I have an idea. I will hire you to do a service for me. Is that agreeable?"

"If it does not interfere with my work. That is, if it doesn't take precedence over the task I'm already committed to." He looked at her and waited.

"Oh, I'm sure it won't. All I need you to do is hold a letter. If you do not see me for forty-eight hours, you are to open it and use the information however you wish. How much would you charge me for that service?"

"Sometimes I am out of town for two or three days," he said carefully. "I would not be able to vouch for your presence unless you were with me . . ."

Fiona saw Amanda's eyes flash.

". . . and that would not be possible," he continued. "So I am afraid I would not be able to keep that contract."

"Fiona!" Amanda exclaimed.

"Yes?" she answered.

At the same time Lepke echoed, "Fiona?"

"Fiona could send a wireless to you if the time passed and I was not present." Amanda turned to Fiona. "Couldn't you, dear?"

"Well, I could certainly try." She wanted to be in this contract, it was exciting.

"I'm sorry," Lepke said with a wave of his hand. "But I am not permitted to work with non-professionals in the field."

"What?" Fiona blazed. "You have an Indian assistant and you can't allow me to send you a blasted wireless message!" For the first time in her life she felt truly insulted. "I am not the night manager here because I am incompetent, Mr. Lepke!"

"Haw!" Amanda shouted, and popped her hands over her mouth for a moment. "You really *are* related to Florence."

Lepke flush deepened. "That's not what I meant, Miss Malone. Perhaps if Miss Malone and I joined forces as friends of yours, Miss Ganbor, I would not be compromising my position as I see it."

"Yes," Amanda said soberly. "I've noticed you're not much on compromising positions."

Lepke pulled back slightly. But before he could respond, Amanda contritely continued, "And I'm sorry for any I've put you in, sir."

Fiona saw Lepke relax for the first time since he'd confronted Amanda.

"You're forgiven. I apologize for not being more astute." He smiled. "I'd be honored to hold the letter. What am I to suppose has happened if I or Miss Malone don't see you for forty-eight hours?"

"You will think me murdered, no matter how natural my death appears."

Lepke stiffened. "Surely you're being a bit melodramatic?"

"No. Merely paranoid, as Dr. Freud would say."

He relaxed slightly. "Well, I never pay attention to philosophers."

"Frightened, then!" Amanda said sharply.

"Say what you mean. I have difficulty with English nuances, and I am tired of apologizing for the lack."

"If either of you don't see me for that length of time, I have probably been murdered."

"By Williams?" Lepke asked.

"I really can't say any more. Will you hold the letter? Please?"

He held out his open palm. "Certainly."

"It's, ah, it's up in my room," Amanda said carefully.

"I'll wait right here with your, my other friend, while you fetch it."

As Amanda hurried away, Fiona felt she had just witnessed the end of a moving picture but only seen the second reel.

34 —Juneau City, A.T., December 15, 1915—
Wednesday evening

Arnold Williams felt sure he'd found his man. He'd watched the swarthy, loud-mouthed poseur for over two hours. Men like this were made corporals as quickly as possible, before they ended up in a discipline battalion.

This one had been preaching anarchy. At home he would have been imprisoned. Or shot. But this wasn't Germany.

He let himself dwell for a moment on the loneliness surrounding his life. Before agreeing to the mission he hadn't thought about how it would feel to be in the middle of a foreign country, surrounded by potential enemies. Now it was the central element of his existence.

These Americans were a crude lot for the most part. But they possessed an energy he hadn't seen among the working class in Germany. Not that he had ever before considered the working class back in the Fatherland.

Over the past few days he came to realize why they picked him for this mission. His two years of penurious existence at Oxford made him unique among the *Junker* class. Had his father not punished him in such a manner, he would still be at the front.

Besides, he could do a great deal more damage here than in France. General Ludendorf was correct; this war had to be fought on a world-wide front if the *Entente* was to win, and he was also correct in his estimation of the American frame of mind.

It was only a matter of time before this raw monstrosity of a country came to the aid of England and France. And that would tip the scales. So Williams, and others like him, must cripple the American ability to wage or support a war.

Munitions plants in many of the American states had been blown up, electric dynamos sabotaged, and rail centers damaged. He suspected the existence of others like the late *Hauptmann* Heintzmann, carefully paving the way for an alliance with Mexico.

If the Americans knew what was good for them, they would think twice before entering the war. But the evidence here pointed to an impetuosity scarcely waiting for proper military training before rushing off to the trenches. If he could help cripple them before the fact, it might make a difference.

He needed confederates, however. He'd given up on the mysterious Mr. Moe ever contacting him. For the past two days he'd prowled the dives of Douglas and Juneau looking for malcontents. Anarchists or Irishmen would fill the bill nicely.

Williams edged down the scarred bar and stood beside the heavy, self-avowed anarchist. Catching the bartender's eye, he pointed to the man. A shot of whiskey appeared and Williams' dime disappeared.

The heavily bearded man swung around to behold his benefactor. "Thanks."

He took a sip and studied Williams carefully. "Have we met before?"

"No. I don't think so. I'm new in the territory."

"Sounds like you're new to America, too."

"You have a good ear, friend," he said, thickening his accent. "I heard you talking about how only the strong survive. It brought Europe to mind. Hard to tell who's going to survive over there."

"The smart ones, like us, who stay out of the rich man's war."

"M'name is Arnold Williams." He held out his hand.

"Pete Sommers." They shook.

"Is there some place we can talk privately? I'll bring a bottle."

"Well, sure," Sommers said, licking his lips. "C'mon."

The room was small, smelling of stale beer, grease, and unwashed bodies. The two worn tables and dozen chairs spoke mutely of innumerable poker hands. It was a perfect meeting place for desperate men testing the fabric of their destiny, Williams thought wryly.

Sommers pulled the chain on the lamp over their table and flooded the room with die-cut shadows. He refilled his glass and regarded his host.

"So what's your story? You over here to stay out of the war?"

"In a way. I'm over here to fight the war."

"Which war?"

"The one between the haves and the have-nots, between rich and poor, between the weak and the strong."

Sommers leaned back in his creaking chair and stared at Williams.

"You're a European *anarchist*?" he said in disbelief.

"Anarchy was born in Europe!"

"Well, sure. I know that, but I thought, I thought all you fellows were throwing bombs at arch-dukes and shootin' kings 'n stuff."

"Many of us have," Williams said in a low, confiding voice. "And many have not lived to boast of their success."

"Yeah, I suppose not." Sommers drank off the contents of a second glass, refilled it. "So what ya doin' here?"

"To strike the rich man where it will hurt him the most."

"Alaska Territory?"

"The Treadwell Mine, the Ground Hog, the Perseverance, the Little Treadwell, all of the big ones."

Comprehension slowly grew in Sommers' eyes. "By God, you might have something there!" He grinned. "That *would* twist their tails, wouldn't it?"

"One would hope," Williams said dryly.

"What do you have in mind?"

"I have envisioned a project that will shut down the mines forever and not endanger the agents at all."

"Agents," Sommers said.

"You are very astute. That's why I'm talking to you. I need a few brave men to assist me."

"Well, I'm here in Juneau City to help one of the men you need."

"Help him do what?" Williams asked.

"Either beat a charge of murder or break him out of the federal jail."

"One of the men. There are others?"

Sommers gave him a long, searching look. "Yeah, there are others. We're somewhat organized, but the others won't help you unless you help Ed."

Deep inside Arnold Williams' mind, a small voice cried out *cut your losses! Get away now!* "Tell me about him," he said, pouring another glass of whiskey, "and tell me why we need him."

35 —Juneau City, A.T., December 17th, 1915—
Friday morning

Heavy rain poured down in unrelenting profusion. Lepke pulled his collar up and struck out for the drug store through the snow cover now saturated to the point of watery mush. This didn't fit his idea of winter.

This whole work wasn't turning out the way he'd planned. Florence was so overwhelming! It nearly scared him to believe his good fortune.

The practical reality of all the emotion and love he had spent on Alice was akin to pouring water down a gopher hole. So with Florence he had held back, keeping her at arm's length, but his determination not to become romantically involved had proven to be thin ice.

He smiled to himself as he carefully picked his way down Front Street. She was quite a girl, ah, *woman*, certainly the most unusual woman he had ever met.

Which made him think of Amanda, who brought thoughts to his mind that belied the strict doctrines of Martin Luther with which he had been raised. True, he had strayed far from the religious path of his childhood, but she could even pull him past ethics, if he would allow it.

He wondered at himself, speculating about Amanda in the midst of thinking about Florence. He didn't feel contrite, only confused. His heart and mind waged war here in Alaska Territory.

Reason told him to finish the work quickly, get back to Portland, and report in for a new challenge. Heart wondered at his hesitation. Florence constituted a challenge worthy of any man. Why didn't he believe it?

When he got right down to it, that was the reason. He just didn't believe it. He would have to ask her again.

But what about his career? Seven years with the Pinkerton Detective Agency was nothing to drop casually next to cigar butts in the gutter. He felt sure that within two years they would offer him a much higher station.

Of course, if he accepted promotion he would be identified with strike breaking and oppression. First Jim Kisadis had brought up that view of the Agency, and then Florence had mentioned it at lunch a week ago.

"Have you ever had to harm a worker?" she had asked him.

"A worker? Do you mean a striker?"

"They're still workers. They're just tired of laboring for a pittance in order to make rich men richer." Her mouth lost its smile and iridescence flecked her eyes.

"I don't do that sort of thing," he answered. "They know I'm a detective, not a thug."

"Then you don't believe they're right, either! Do you?"

"There is no *right*. There is only *law*."

"You honestly believe there is no such thing as right and wrong?" she asked wonderingly.

"Of course there is such a thing as right and wrong. Nonetheless, there have to be laws to decide where one stops and the other begins. Great rights and great wrongs are easy to see. It is the small, the nuance, that needs definition in the modern world." He stared at her lovely hazel eyes. "Do you understand what I am saying?"

"Yes," she said crisply. "But you're wrong. The law says rich bosses can hire an army of mercenaries to come in and beat poor workers until they go back to their chains or die."

"You're spouting socialism!"

"I'm telling the truth!"

That stopped him. She was telling the truth. Why couldn't the Agency be more like the Texas Rangers he had read about as a youth?

Before leaving Germany he absorbed every western adventure novel he could get his hands on. Things changed too much before he got to America. Even the red Indians were broken, subdued, and relegated to contempt.

She was correct; it wasn't right. But was her truth his truth? If what they had started between them was to flourish, he had to change his life.

He savored the idea, let himself embrace it for a little while. Leave the Agency, and do what?

Although they hadn't discussed the question, it was quite obvious to him she didn't want to leave Alaska. This smug little outpost of civilization could offer a man a great deal, but he wasn't interested in mining, not even enough to clerk for it.

The local law enforcement was a bit of a joke. Juneau City boasted a police department as well as the U.S. Marshal. The federal job seemed a sinecure complete with heir apparent.

The Juneau Police Department existed to protect vested business interest. Lepke had glanced over the local laws after his arrival. He'd seen a good many of those laws being broken with impunity on Lower Front Street.

The police were obviously on the take. But they also kept the more earthy element localized and away from the lace-curtain part of town. Most of the miners were "young, single, and needed a relief valve," as one of them had put it.

Yet there were men like Krause in this north country. Eliminating cancers like him seemed very appealing. Thieves, murderers, anarchists —they ate into the vitals of society. He held a fierce certainty that men like him were the scalpels.

Right and wrong. Big right with a little wrong. Was that really the way of it? Was America all a careful hypocrisy? He considered Germany, realizing he was in danger of being hypocritical himself.

The hard fact of it was he had never before asked himself these questions because they hadn't occurred to him. He had accepted the every day *status quo* like a good German or American citizen.

Florence questioned everything. She would leave nothing alone. Since he had relaxed discipline, he would admit it —she scared him.

And he liked it.

The realization pulled him to a halt. He looked around at Juneau City with a new resident's perspective. Slushy snow and all, he decided, he just might like it here.

36 —Treadwell, A.T., December 20, 1915—
Saturday afternoon

"How do you know when to stop drilling, so you don't punch through into the channel?" Arnold Williams shouted in order to be heard over the rumbling from above. The miner's hat kept riding down to the bridge of his nose. He pushed it back in irritation.

"Aw, we got 'bout twenny foot o' greenstone t'ween us and salt water. We calls it the hanging wall," Mulrooney said. "When the powder men start hittin' it, they stop. 'Sides, you'd be surprised how easy it is to follow a vein of ore." The man, although shorter than Williams, possessed shoulders so wide they threatened the heavy fabric of his work clothing. Already in this tour through the mine, he had seen "Bulldozer" Mulrooney pick up pieces of ore in the eighty-pound range as if they were light but bulky objects.

"Hanging wall. That's the top of this, ah—"

"Adit," Mulrooney supplied. "Yeah, an' the bottom here is th' foot wall."

"What level are we on?" Williams asked carefully.

"Fifteen hunnert and sixty feet or so below the surface. They still got power run through here so they must be working this level somewheres." He pointed the lamp on his hat up at one of the dark light bulbs that seemingly erupted from heavy electrical cable every twenty feet.

"Doesn't it bother you the water is so close and the surface so far away? I mean, what if there was a cave-in, what would you do?"

Mulrooney flashed him a sarcastic smile. "I'd probably die."

"And you work here just the same?"

"Well, now. If I were t' quit here, I 'spose you'd be findin' me a job with that fancy paper o' yers?" Mulrooney bit off a piece of rope tobacco, offered the twist to Williams.

"No, thank you, I don't chew. As for the job, well, I'd be hard pressed to get you to London just to begin with."

"'Course ya would. An' the pay would probably be a whole lot less than I'm makin' here. Maybe they haven't told ya yet, but the Treadwell is the highest payin' mine in th' world. D'ya know I'm making' three-fifty a day! That's more 'n me old man is making a week back in Omaha workin' fer the fookin' Union Pacific."

"Uh, I had no idea," Williams admitted. "Then the working conditions here are better than most other mines?" The light from their lamps flashed over the sides of the adit and spilled across the footwall as they walked and talked.

He had told the superintendent he wanted a working man's viewpoint of the complex. They gave him an Irishman, which pleased him. Perhaps destroying this mine would be easier than he had anticipated. It wasn't hard to keep the man talking.

"Th' conditions have improved a great deal since the strike in '07."

"Strike? I didn't know there had been a strike here. What happened?" His eyes continually swept over the rock and machinery they passed. He didn't know what he was looking for, but hoped to recognize it on sight.

"Well, minin's a dangerous perfession at best, an' the workin' conditions weren't all that safe, ya understand. We was losing about one miner a month to one thing and another, mostly carelessness. But we all knew that was part o' the job when we hired on." He spat tobacco juice at the rock floor.

"A lot of these lads are fresh off th' boats from Europe. We bin gettin' Huns, Serbs, Slavs, 'n even Limeys by the score. They not wantin' ta fight in that useless war over there 'n all."

"Just a moment. Do not forget I am an Englishman! My country is upholding its honor—"

"Beggin' yer pardon, but that's a lot o' horse shit, 'n you know it! Yer obviously a smart man, college 'n' all. 'N' yer also here in America instead of fightin' at the front. Tell me this, Mr. Savin'-yer-Honor, jist what's the war all about?"

"Alliances. Honor. Duty. God and Kai, King," Williams snapped, nettled.

"I bet there ain't many privates 'n' sergeants who feel any alliance with any o' those Serbians 'n' Frogs. It's jist another rich man's war. Mark me words, somebody is gittin' rich outta this, an' it ain't you 'r me."

Williams hadn't looked at it in that light before. What patriot would? He let it pass. "You were telling me about a strike," he said firmly.

"Oh, yeah. Well the new lads 'r' usually th' ones what get hurt 'n' killed in these accidents, seein' as they don't know all the stuff ta watch out fer. Well, the company was burying these lads by jist wrappin' 'em in a blanket 'n' droppin' 'em in the ground!"

Mulrooney's glance swept over him again. Williams stared back, waiting for him to get on with the story.

"Well, why'd they strike?" he prodded, remembering the withered, rotting, claw-like hands and feet sticking out of the mud in the trenches.

"You find nothin' wrong wi' that?" Mulrooney asked in amazement.

"Once you're dead, what does it matter?"

"Ah, yer educated fer sure. No religion a'tall. Well, most of these lads 'r like me— no education past the third 'r' fourth grade." He clanked the iron bar he carried against the wall of the shaft.

"I know m' letters an' I kin write m' name. But I know that my most important possession is m' immortal soul. A goodly number of us 'r' Catholics. 'N' it matters to us that we're buried in consecrated ground, even if we are done wi' our bodies."

"I see. It was a religious strike."

"No, that's not the whole of it. It was a strike fer dacency. Most o' those boys didn't have a relative over here. Their families back in the old country had no way o' knowin' what ever become of 'em." Mulrooney was breathing heavily.

"So we jist stopped work 'til the company promised us a real funeral. One with a coffin, services, an' a man o' God there to put us away right. They also had ta contact the next o' kin, or at least try ta, an' tell 'em of their loved one."

"So the strike worked?"

"Well, first they brought in the army from Fort Chilkoot up there at Haines to keep order, but there wan't no disorder fer 'em t' sort out. We jist stopped workin' and that was that.

"So the supers all got together 'n' decided we wasn't askin' fer much. Besides, they heard there were some o' them wobblies tryin' to get us in the Western Federation of Mineworkers, an' that scared the bejasus outta 'em."

Williams had to concentrate to remember what wobblies were. Labor agitators, like the socialists back in Germany.

"Why didn't they just put the agitators in prison?" he asked.

"This isn't some monarchy, mister. We got rights in America."

"No offense intended, I assure you!"

"None taken. Anyways, they gave us what we asked for an' the Funeral Strike was over. Right after that they put together a company union an' started improving the workin' conditions." His posture changed, he straightened up and stuck his chin out.

"This is the best job I've ever had. The wife an' I live in a company house with running water, steam heat, and electricity. Me da back in Omaha only has electricity, a coal stove, 'n' an outdoor jakes; yet Alaska's called a frontier."

Williams chuckled with the man. Obviously this was no Fenian willing to strike at England any way possible. On the whole, Mulrooney had treated him with respect. He wondered what the Irishman's reaction would be if he found out his tourist's real purpose.

The burly man would probably kill him with his bare hands.

"Now here's one o' the problems wi' being down this far." Mulrooney pointed his bar and lamp at a pool of water against one side of the twelve-foot-wide tunnel. The water was draining off in a small stream down the slight slope ahead of them.

Williams felt his heart quicken with a lurch. "Has it sprung a leak?"

"Nothin' ta worry about. This rock has faults all through it. Water seeps in everywhere. Down at the twenny-five-hundred-foot level they got pumps goin' all the time. They pump about three hundred gallons a minute outta here."

"That certainly sounds like a great deal of seepage."

"This is nothing. You should see how much they get down in the Ready Bullion.
It's at least twice as much."

"That's the mine at the far end of this complex, correct?"

"Yeah. They all used to be interconnected by adits. But they was afraid the Ready Bullion would cave in an' flood everything. So in '12 they built a twelve-foot-thick concrete wall to isolate the weak sister, so to speak. But she's never flooded, yet."

"Which of the four has the richest ore?"

"Now how would I be knowin' that? D'ye think the Bradleys, Kinzies, an' their engineers tell the likes o' me what's goin' on down here? I just run the best mucking crew in the mine, that's all." He bit another chaw off his twist.

"Muckers are at the bottom of the shaft in more ways than one. But they couldn't run this mine without us. As far as I know the ore is holdin' up just jake, an' they're keepin' me on as long as I want th' job."

Williams eyed the seeping crack in the wall. Perhaps a good-sized dynamite charge would flood this shaft with salt water. Now he just had to find out how to use dynamite.

"Who are the blasters on your crew?"

"Ah, I keep fergittin' yer not a miner. We don't have blasters on our crews. The day shift and the night shift each work ten hours. They only blast between shifts, so there's no chance of killing a lot of men. That also gives the air enough time to clear. That's all we do, follow along behind where the powder men have been and clean up after them."

"Do you miss the fresh air?" Williams asked, surprising himself.

"Not if I don't think about it," Mulrooney said shortly.

"I'd like to talk to one of the blasters, if I might."

"They told me to let you talk to anybody ye wanted to, but I canna help wi' that request. You'll have to go through the office."

"Oh, of course."

A high whine edged in around the muffled thunder of the stamps above them.

"Is that the main lift I hear, that whining sound?" he asked loudly.

Mulrooney cocked his head for a moment, then nodded. "Right ye are. We've walked from th' Treadwell to th' Mexican lift. Do ye want to go further down or back to the top?"

"The top," Williams said quickly. He did not share the miner's confidence about the strength of the hanging wall.

They came to a wide bay where the shaft turned and went up. A frame of steel girders spanned the distance between roof and floor. Two heavy greased cables twitched lazily against each other in the middle of the connecting shaft nearly taut from great strain. A chain blocked the adit.

Mulrooney pulled a few times on a cord hanging down from a small metal frame, stopped, then pulled some more.

"This will tell the lift operator where we're at an' which way we want ta go," he said loudly over the rising noise level. The pounding of stamps, along with small streams of water, poured down the shaft into the depths.

"I see," Williams shouted back. He wondered if the ride up would be as disturbing as was the ride down. After hearing how dangerous mining could be, he planned to examine the cage closely.

The heavy shackle assembly on the cable suddenly surged from the depths into view, followed immediately by the cage. It groaned to a stop, cables slapping and dripping, then dropped a meter before plugging the shaft with its ponderous bulk. It was full of dark, wet ore.

"C'mon, we can ride on top," Mulrooney said as he hopped lightly onto the chunks of rock.

"But, what if they dump more ore on top of us?"

"It's already full, they ain't gonna ruin the lift just ta kill us! Now git on, quick!"

While Williams wondered what to do, his legs took over and he found himself crouching on the slippery, cold chunks of stone next to the stout miner. Mulrooney pulled on a cord. The cage dropped a meter and jerked to a quivering stop. The cables slapped again, splattering them with grit, water, and petrified bits of thick cable grease before the cage lurched and whined upward.

Williams stared at the massive metal sides of the cage. *It's more like a square bucket than a cage,* he thought. The raw, dark slabs of iron forming its walls creaked and groaned under the weight of the ore. Water constantly splattered over them. Their lamps gave objects knife-sharp edges and inky shadows while the rumbling of the stamps grew louder as they quickly moved upward.

Yawning passages would suddenly appear in the walls of the shaft above them, and offer a modest glance into their depths before flashing past. The power had been pulled out of those adits. The ore was depleted and the miners had no further use for the miles of laboriously hewn tunnels.

While passing the neglected openings, sighs seemed to issue forth and cool the cage with their dank breath. Williams shuddered. He felt reality slipping out of true.

"You get used to it," Mulrooney shouted amiably.

Williams frowned. The last man who shouted those words to him died a moment later when the French artillery shell hit their trench. He fingered the long shrapnel scar on his cheek.

The thunder of the stamps increased. Bits of debris and water showered down on him, and he became convinced the noise was cannon and the barrage was about to impact on them. Terror bent his mind for an instant before the cool, insulating detachment wrapped about him.

He looked at Mulrooney with death in his eyes.

One more accident, he thought. *They'll never know the difference. He's as much of an enemy as those Frenchmen.*

"Why ya lookin' at me so quare like?" Mulrooney demanded. "I told ya the noise took gettin' used to. Ya just gotta ignore it."

Williams carefully inched a hand and foot toward the man. The wet, slippery ore prevented an instant attack. *I've got to do this quickly,* he decided.

The cage suddenly erupted out of the close, dark shaft and into the bright, roomy chamber where men and supplies were loaded. The cage stopped. Williams shook his head to clear the bloodlust. A tic pulsed in his left eyelid.

"You okay there, Mr. Williams?" Mulrooney asked as they crawled down off the ore.

"Yes," he said shortly. "Yes, I'm fine. Thank you for the tour, Mr. Mulrooney. He held out his hand.

The miner squeezed it with an iron grip, holding the heavy bar in his other hand. "My pleasure. Y'know, fer a minute there I thought I was goin' to have ta cold cock ya. Ya were lookin' murderous."

The cage groaned into movement and went up through the roof to empty into the huge chutes that carried the rubble down to the ore trains for transport to the crushers and stamps.

"You're right," he shouted back. "This noise takes some getting used to, don't know if I could do it."

Mulrooney smiled as if accepting a compliment, and waved. "May ye be in heaven an hour before the devil knows yer dead." He turned and walked away.

If I don't do this right, Williams thought, pushing back his miner's hat, *we might get there together.*

THE ALASKA DAILY EMPIRE
Juneau, Alaska, Tuesday, December 21, 1915

British Premier to Increase Army; Hopeful of Future

ASQUITH ASKS FOR MILLIONS
TURKS CLAIM BIG VICTORY OVER BRITON
GERMANY HESITATES TO SETTLE
REICHSTAG VOTES LARGE WAR MEASURE
SURRENDER IS VICTORY SAYS VILLA
CHRISTIE SEARCHERS CONFIDENT

NATIVES ARE BELIEVED TO HAVE DROWNED

The gas boat "Portland" or "Yakutat," with three natives on board bound from Juneau to Yakutat has been missing since the 29th of October, and the natives of Sitka and Yakutat entertain grave fears for their safety. A telegram was received today by Governor Strong from Arthur Shoup of Sitka, telling of their disappearance. The cablegram reads:

Governor Strong. Juneau.

No one here has heard of George Martin and party since leaving Hoonah. They are reported to have obtained a supply of whiskey from Charley Moses of Tenakee. Were boarded after leaving Tenakee by Charles Smith. They had been on the rocks and had two holes in their boat. The keel was split and three ribs had been sprung. They had a good new boat 25 feet long by 9 feet wide with a new 10 h.p. Frisco Standard engine. They were poor engineers. The Indians here think they are lost. A. Shoup.

The natives at Yakutat are worried about the missing men and have written to T. A. Rasmussen of Juneau, asking him to get some trace of the men if possible. The natives, George Young and Tom Martin came down from Yakutat in October to get a boat which they had purchased from George Howard of Sitka. They secured a new engine from George Forrest of Juneau, and taking the Robert Fulton from Sitka started on their trip to Yakutat. They stopped at Tenakee where they are said to have secured a supply of whiskey, and again at Hoonah. They left there on October 29th and since that time nothing has been heard from them.

Mr. Rasmussen is trying to find someone recently returned from Lituya Bay who may have news of the men. Malcom Campbell arrived from there recently as well as Henry Roden, but neither man had news of the boat.

37 —Juneau City, A.T., December 22, 1915—
Wednesday afternoon

When Jack Malone entered the room, Charles Sulzer and his secretary stood. Sulzer crossed the room and shook hands warmly.

"Jack, you're looking fit."

"Of course, Senator. I get a lot of exercise keeping your interests under surveillance."

Both men laughed.

"Have a seat, Jack. Whiskey?"

"Sure, Senator. Do I ever let you drink alone?"

The male secretary handed Jack an amber-filled glass.

"Thanks, Whitney. How are you doing, lad?"

"As expected, Mr. Malone, as expected."

"Whitney," Sulzer said. "Would you please go get us some decent cigars? Pick up the latest Seattle paper, too."

"Certainly, Senator." Whitney put on his hat and coat and left the hotel room.

"Okay, Jack. What's going on up here? What noise are you hearing?"

"They need to be led, Senator. As usual, Wickersham is trying to walk on both sides of the fence at the same time. The word is out he has finally got a statehood bill ready for Congress and it will be introduced in the next session. The governor's not backing anybody until he sees how that fares."

"It'll never pass, of course, but it sure makes the judge look good here in the Territory," Sulzer mused. "So how can we beat him in November?"

"Well, Senator, if ye'll pardon me fer sayin' so-"

"You can dispense with the brogue, Jack. Just give me the facts."

"Okay, Charlie, I will. The first problem you have here in the capital is nailing down the nomination. There's some pretty tough competition out there. Especially from Nome."

"Oh, Jack," Sulzer said heavily. "How many times do I have to explain it to an old campaigner like yourself? They'll vote for whoever they think is going to do the most for each one of them. What the hell can an old buffalo from Nome do for the majority of the population?"

"Well, he's making all the correct anti-Wickersham noises, 'Statehood now, more roads,' that sort of thing. What you gotta do, Charlie, is make them understand the difference between you and Turner. Right now you're viewed as two peas in a pod."

"I'm a self-made man! Ben Turner is a hack who couldn't even make a living as a miner, for crissake."

"You're both territorial senators and new on the job. Outside of your copper-mining town nobody knows you."

"But I have a town named after me, surely that . . ."
"So does Bart Thane."
"Jesus, Jack. Don't bring up that glad-hander."
"I'm just being your devil's advocate, Charlie, not getting personal. I wish you had been able to get something passed in the first legislature."

"Well, I voted to give women the vote."
"Don't worry, everybody voted for that one. You won't have to bear all the blame."
Both men laughed. Jack drank off his whiskey. Sulzer brought the bottle over. "Here, let me top that off for you."

"Thanks. This prohibition thing, Charlie, how we gonna stop Chester gawddamned Kingsley Snow?"

"Get your customers on Lower Front Street to vote wet. Don't worry; it will never pass. It would be the most damn-fool thing the Territory could do. There's a lot of that kind of talk down in the states, too."

"When Wilson made Bryan his Secretary of State, I thought any damn thing was possible," Jack said with a laugh.

"That Bible-thumping flannel-mouth," Sulzer said. "He had his chance. Now that he's resigned, I don't think the president will have much trouble with this election."

"D'ya think Wilson will keep us out of the war?"

"Who cares?" Sulzer said. "We're as far from Europe as you can get and still be on the planet. A war in Europe isn't going to touch us. Why should it?"

"There might be some way to use it to our advantage . . ."

"Good point. Work on that aspect. Maybe we can come up with something, but if Wilson pushes the Triple Alliance any further, it will mean war. So I suppose we should start pounding the drum."

"Well, that won't be hard, not since the *Lusitania*. This country is itching to fight."

"Hell of a thing," Sulzer agreed. "Having a German name could be a real liability in this election."

"Not to worry. Like you said, we're as far from Europe as we can get. Up here you're just another proud member of the Pioneers of Alaska."

"I'm glad you're on my side, Jack. How are your girls by the way?"

"Great, just great. Fiona is working as night manager down at the Division Hotel, and Florence is still splashing chemicals for those photographers." Jack stopped and frowned.

"Something wrong?" Sulzer asked.

"Ah, it's Florence. She's taken up with a detective from the Pinkertons. Wanted me to have him over for dinner on Christmas Day. I told her absolutely not . . ."

"I'm fortunate in that respect. Both of my children are still young enough to handle with a switch."

The door opened and Whitney stepped in.

"Here are the cigars, Senator, and the Seattle paper."

"Thank you, Whitney. Was there anything else you wanted to add, Jack?"

"No, Senator." Jack was all smiles as he got to his feet. "I'll be askin' yer leave now."

Sulzer stood, handed him a cigar, and extended his hand. "Thanks, Jack. Keep up the good work."

They shook and Jack Malone left the suite. The whiskey gave him a rosy glow. Things looked good for November. It would be easy to subtly discredit the senator from Nome.

The temperature had dropped and snow once again fell lazily from the dark sky. On his way out, Jack glanced at the clock in the hotel lobby. Four o'clock in the afternoon and black as a banker's heart out there. Winter was taking more out of him than in the past. Perhaps he should buy a house in Washington City after Sulzer was elected delegate. One certainly couldn't find a more interesting place to live.

Thoughts of the future prompted optimism. He stopped in the doorway of the hotel and puffed his cigar into life. With the streets buried deep in snow, no more gas buggy traffic would be possible until spring break-up.

That's the way it should be, he thought. At least road apples smelled better than exhaust fumes. A man and woman walked past, completely oblivious to him.

Something about the woman tugged at his attention. He looked more carefully and recognized Florence. *That's the Pink*, he realized.

For a moment he was caught by indecision, then he moved down the steps and across the new snow.

"Florence!" he called. "Wait a moment."

38 —Juneau City, A.T., December 22, 1915—
Wednesday late afternoon

Reflexively, Lepke's right hand dropped into his coat pocket and rested on the butt of the .455 Bulldog revolver. Florence twisted around to see who called her name.

"Father? What are you doing here?"

"I was just leavin' the hotel. I saw you and the gentleman walkin' past so I thought I'd make me presence known." He smiled widely.

"Oh, of course," Florence said. "Ah, Father, this is August Lepke. August, this is my father, Jack Malone." Her eyes flashed an unreadable message at him.

"I'm very pleased to meet you, sir." Lepke extended his hand, still warm from the gun butt. "I've been looking forward to this moment."

"Have you now, Mr. Lepke," Jack said, taking his hand and shaking it once before dropping it. "I don't think I've witnessed anything that would be of help to you."

Lepke stared at the man, wondering what caused the malice in his tone. Was Jack agitated because Florence was here on the street with him? She hadn't mentioned him much at all, now that he thought about it. Only that he was in local politics.

"No, sir. You probably haven't," Lepke said, producing a polite smile, "but I have been looking forward to telling you what a bright, charming daughter you have here. I've enjoyed her company very much."

"Have you got the goods on Krause?"

"Uh, yes. Yes, I think I have. I really can't talk about it, however."

The air was getting colder. Their breath puffed out around their words.

"Then you'll be leavin' Juneau City soon?" Jack's eyes glittered in the dim radiance of the streetlight.

"Father!"

"Well, it's interesting you ask, Mr. Malone. Florence and I have just been discussing my future."

Jack's jaw seemed set in stone. The words scraped out one side of his mouth, "And what decisions have you come to, Mr. Lepke?"

"Father! You are being rude. What August and I say to each other is none of your business." Florence's voice carried a malice matching Jack's.

Lepke noticed her jaw line nearly duplicated her father's. He almost smiled at the likeness. *No, that wouldn't be the thing to do right now,* he decided.

"You're in the company of a *Pinkerton* detective, daughter. You know how I feel about *them*."

Lepke had heard the epithets "chink" and "nigger" spoken in the same tone of voice. He was beginning to understand why Florence had been evasive when he asked about her family. This man already had his mind made up. The wisest thing

August could do was leave.

"Florence, perhaps I should say good evening here and let you go on home with your father."

Her head snapped around and angry eyes blazed at him for an instant. "You stay right there!" Then she looked at her father again. "Father, there are many things you believe which I do not. If you want to let the past rule your future, that's your business, but it's not going to rule mine!"

Jack went livid. "That's the problem with givin' yer children a better life than yerself. They don't understand the true cost of it! This, this man," his finger stabbed through the breath cloud at Lepke, "works for one of the lowest concerns on th' face of the airth! They beat and kill honest workers for a few pieces of silver from the company bosses!" Jack was nearly shouting.

"That's why I'm quitting!" Lepke's voice cracked through the barrage of words.

Both Malones looked at him in surprise, and blurted simultaneously, "You are?"

"That's what I was going to tell you, Florence." He looked down into her eyes, completely ignoring Jack. "I think I can find employment here. If not what I've been doing," he glanced at Jack, "then a different pursuit. I've got three years of college behind me so that should count for something."

This wasn't quite how he had wanted to bring the subject up. He'd wanted a few answers from her first. He felt irritated. Jack wasn't exactly what he wanted in a father-in-law, either.

"Oh, August." She stared back at him, her mouth slightly open and her lower lip trembled. "Wh- What a big step!" She glanced at her father, and then asked earnestly, "Because of me?"

"Of course!" Now he let his smile free, and saw it mirrored by her lips. *Oh, hell, in for a penny,* he thought. "Florence, I love you. I want to marry you." He glanced over at Jack, whose eyes bugged above his quivering jowls, then continued, "But not until after I have found a new position. Okay?"

"Okay!" Jack screamed. People stopped to watch the commotion. Lepke felt tempted to hit the old man.

"Okay, he asks!" Jack's voice had a grinding to it that reminded Lepke of the gears in a motor-truck. "There's no work in this town for a professional assassin! An' ye'll be stayin' away from me daughter, 'r I'll have yer hide!"

Suddenly a policeman stood next to Jackand taking hold of his elbow. "What's the problem, mister?" He took a closer look. "Jack! What are you screaming about on a *city* street?"

Jack gave him a withering stare. "It's a family matter, laddie, so would ye be givin' me elbow back before I break yer arm?"

"Jack," the officer muttered in a low voice. "I'm gonna ask you real nice just once, then I'll haul you in like a gawddamned drunk. Would you take this discussion off the street, *please*?" He looked around at the small crowd. "Go about your business. This is all over."

The men and women moved away, self-consciously glancing in other directions. Lepke started to speak to the officer but was interrupted.

"Florence," Jack hissed. "If you don't come home with me right now, you'll be havin' ta find new lodgings."

"I said off the street, Jack." The policeman's voice rose.

"Officer," Lepke said.

"Father," Florence said, a tear popped from the edge of one eye, "if you cared about me at all, you wouldn't do this." She didn't sound cowed.

"I mean what I say!" Jack said quickly, barely keeping himself controlled.

"I'll move into Mrs. Bergman's tonight," she said evenly. "I'm sorry this has to be, but I am not your property. I'm just your daughter and I still love you."

"You'll burn in hell for this!" Jack shrieked.

"God damn it, Jack!" the policeman said. "That's it. You're under arrest!"

Florence pulled on Lepke's arm. "Take me away from here, August." She was crying.

Lepke turned stiffly and walked down the street with her wondering what to do now. He wanted a drink.

The noise behind them ceased. Lepke glanced back. A man in an expensive overcoat and fedora stood on the steps of the hotel talking to the policeman. Jack stood with eyes downcast, suddenly subdued.

Lepke gave the man a second look. He'd seen his picture somewhere . . .

"I'd like a cup of tea, August," Florence said with a tired sigh.

"Of course." He looked around the street. "There, the White Lunch. They're open."

At the door he looked back again. The policeman walked down the street alone. Jack Malone and his benefactor had disappeared.

Lepke carefully picked his way down the snowy boardwalk. Exhaustion weighed on him. He'd spent the remainder of the evening helping Florence carry suitcases and an electric lamp the three blocks to Mrs. Bergman's Hotel.

They had seen no further sign of Jack. After being introduced to Mrs. Bergman, who obviously liked Florence a great deal, they were pressed to stay for dinner at the restaurant on the bottom floor. The meal had been enjoyable.

He'd kept away from the subject closest to his heart. He didn't think it would be fair to burden her any further this night. He forced his attention back to the task at hand —getting safely down this slippery, snowy hill in the dark.

Suddenly he sensed movement ahead of him.

He stopped and peered through the swirling snow. Motion, dark against the shadowed buildings. Two men? He took another step and settled on the balls of his feet, rocking back and forth to get a firm stance in the snow.

"Who's there?" he called strongly.

One of the men snickered. The other mumbled inaudibly.

"Sorry. I didn't hear that."

The men moved toward Lepke. Now they were clearly silhouetted against the streetlights down the hill, a block behind them.

"Please don't come any closer," Lepke said formally.

"He's sure polite, ain't he?" the smaller one said with a sneer.

"Yeah, Si-" the big one began in a slow voice. The smaller man turned on him and pulled back his arm. He held a club.

"Shut yer gawddamned mouth, you stupid bastid! You say m' name an' they'll find you next to 'im in the mornin'!"

They returned their attention to Lepke and moved slowly forward. The small one panted, visibly excited. The big one shambled forward, watching Lepke closely. He also carried a club.

"One more time I tell you. Stop where you are," Lepke said firmly. The butt of the .455 felt slick under his damp palm. Adrenaline surged through him, making his knees twitch slightly.

"Or yew'll do what, fancy pants?" the excited one sneered. "Pee yer pants, 'r ask me 'please' again?" He sidled forward, presenting his left side. They were eight feet away.

Snow swirled around them. Lepke suddenly had the ludicrous notion that they were part of an unholy crèche scene. *No babies here*, he corrected himself.

The small man took the lead, picked up speed for a rush. He licked his lips and giggled as he pulled back his club.

August pulled out the revolver and pointed it at the small man's head. "You're under arrest!" he thundered.

The wild-eyed man hesitated for a moment, then shrieked, "Yew, shit-ass!" and swung the club at Lepke's head.

Lepke pulled the trigger and the heavy revolver bucked in his hand.

"The bullet entered above the left eye, blew the back of the head away and showered its contents over his accomplice. The impact snapped, ah, Silas' head back and knocked him into his companion. You fellows got here about five minutes later. By the way I'd like to commend you on your speed," Lepke finished, watching the two still-wheezing policemen.

Someone had telephoned the police when they heard the shot. Lepke no more than got the attacker's names out of a sobbing, frightened Ralph, when the police arrived at a run. The angular patrolman had out-distanced the heavier, mustached corporal by half a block.

"They," the corporal gasped, waved at the still body being attended to by the big, sobbing man huddling in the snow. ". . . attacked *you*?"

He doesn't believe me, Lepke thought. This is ridiculous. "Yes, damn it. *They* attacked *me!* Why is that so hard to grasp?"

"Well, sir," the other officer said. "We're just sort of surprised to see two men with a couple of sticks, attack an armed man."

"They didn't stop long enough to see if I was armed or not." Lepke's voice went low and angry. "They had clubs." He kicked at an axe handle on the ground, "and thought they had an unarmed victim."

"So you just shot him," the corporal said.

"We didn't vote on it, *Corporal.*"

The patrolman squinted at Lepke. "Hey. Ain't you the guy Jack Malone was pissed at earlier tonight? The detective from the states?"

"Yes. A. Lepke, Pinkerton Detective Agency," he said, "and a special deputy U.S. Marshal."

"Says who?" the corporal asked.

"Marshal Bishop. Do you want to see my badge?"

"That's him, Dan. Bishop pointed him out to me," the patrolman said.

"Well, why didn't ya say so when we got here?" The corporal's tone remained belligerent.

"Corporal, all I have been doing is answering your questions. You neither asked nor gave me the time to identify myself. I want to press charges against that man, Ralph Wikke. Assault and attempted robbery."

"We weren't tryin' to rob ya!" Ralph howled. "We was only gonna rough ya up some. Least that's what Silas told me." He sniffed and rubbed his sleeve under his nose.

"Why were you going to rough me up?" Lepke demanded.

"'Cause Silas **said** so." Ralph's tone made the statement obvious.

"Who told Silas to do it? Did someone give you money?"

"Nobody tells Silas what to do. You gotta ask him nice and then maybe he'll do what ya want."

"Did someone give you money?" Lepke pressed.

Ralph's forehead wrinkled in the dim light. The snow had ceased and the rumble of the rock crushers at Treadwell seemed very loud. The patrolman looked around them, started to speak.

"Wait, just one moment," Lepke said in his best law enforcement baritone. "Ralph, did someone give you money? Tell me, I want to know!"

"Yeah, Jack did 'bout a week ago. But that was fer helping him with Cullen..."

"Tonight, Ralph. Who gave you money *tonight?*"

"Silas. He gave me money tanight."

"Who gave it to Silas?"

"Maybe Jack Malone?"

"Why the 'maybe'?" the corporal asked.

"'Cause he gave us money last week, or two weeks, I forget. Maybe he gave Silas the money?"

"Never mind. Go ahead officers, take your man to jail."

"'Scuse me, deputy," the corporal said, "but I distinctly remember you telling us you arrested these men before the shooting. Wouldn't that make this a federal shindig?"

Damn, Lepke thought, *I'll never get to bed at this rate.*

"So I did, corporal. Would you gentlemen take care of the deceased while I escort this man to the U.S. jail?"

"Sure." The corporal grinned, then turned to the patrolman. "You stay here with Silas. I'll go get the undertaker."

"Sure, Dan."

"Damn it, Forsythe! That's *Corporal* Harrington."

"Sure, Corporal Harrington. Just hurry please. I'm already freezing my fanny off."

Lepke prodded a snuffling Ralph ahead of him. They took small, careful steps down Starr Hill, inching toward Telephone Hill where the U.S. courthouse and jail sat in silent domination. The clamor from the crushers and stamps at Treadwell beat on Lepke's tired ears.

39 —Juneau City, A.T., December 23, 1915—
Thursday early morning

Fiona yawned and glanced at the clock on the wall. Only 3:20am There was another three and a half hours yet before she could go home and fall blissfully into bed.

She turned another page of the November issue of *Pictorial Review* from New York. The pages were full of the latest fashions, fiction for women, and advertisements. She looked wistfully at an illustration of a woman holding her child.

What do I want? she wondered. Her position here at the hotel had a grand sounding name and all, but in reality she knew she was just a combined night clerk and accountant. However, the pay was handsome, especially for a young woman.

Still, it was boring. She always thought hotels were filled with exciting, intriguing men. Now she knew that for the most part the men who stayed here were either salesmen or gamblers.

Since the Division Hotel didn't have a saloon attached to it, there were very few of the latter. Some did defy description, which could be exciting. They could also be somewhat frightening.

She sighed. The only thing still to look forward to was Mr. Lepke's arrival. He was very late, which caused her some concern.

Of course, she felt sure he was a man who could take care of himself. She wasn't worried, just curious. Florence always said that curiosity killed the cat, which was just fine because Fiona knew she wasn't a cat.

Cold air brushed her skin and she looked up. Pete Sommers quietly shut the front door. *How strange,* she thought, *he's never quiet.*

He had been drinking. She could tell how much by his degree of squint. His leer reached maximum, which told her he'd enjoyed himself.

"Good evening, Miss Lovely Fiona." He pulled his hat off and parodied a flourishing bow.

She giggled. "Good evening Mr. Sommers."

He pushed his torso across the desk putting his face close enough to hers to smell hair oil, stale whiskey, and the stink of tobacco consumption. "Please tell me you'll go out with me some evening soon and trip the light fantastic!"

She pulled back more in response to his physical intensity than to his overwhelming scent. "It is strictly against the rules for me to be seen in public with a guest, Mr. Sommers. You wouldn't want me to lose my job, would you?" She smiled prettily at him, feeling safe.

"You work for Maye Wattnem, don'cha?" His grin looked feral.

"Yes." The smile slipped away as her face pulled down, not responding to the feeling she should smile politely at this man.

"Then if Maye says you can spend the evening with me, you'll do it?"

"Well," she said slowly, thinking furiously. "I don't think that's really a possibility, Mr. Sommers."

"But if she says it's okay, you'll allow me to take you dancing?"

"Only somewhere respectable," she said automatically.

"Wonderful!" he crowed.

"You have to be more quiet, Mr. Sommers. It's quite late." She was so angry at him and herself she felt like spitting. Maye would never give her blessing to this oaf. She'd see to that.

The front door opened and August Lepke slowly trudged in. Pete Sommers stared at him with an awed expression. Fiona wondered if Sommers might not be very drunk, and hoped he would forget their conversation. Then she gave her attention to the new arrival.

"Mr. Lepke! Good morning." She smiled at him and straightened her shoulders.

"Good morning, Miss Malone."

"You look all done in," Sommers said abruptly.

"Not quite, but close." Lepke moved past them toward the stairs.

"Well, what happened?" Sommers pressed.

Lepke stopped and looked at the man closely. "Why do you ask?"

"Well . . ." Sommers grinned, spread his hands and shrugged. "No reason. Just wondering, you know, why you're so tired. Musta been doing a lot of work?"

"Yes, quite a lot." Lepke turned and started up the stairs.

"Good night, Mr. Lepke," Fiona called, keeping her eyes on Sommers. The man seemed stricken.

"Good night . . ." The voice floated back down the steps. ". . . Miss Malone."

Sommers, chewing his lip, peered at the steps long after Lepke was lost from view.

"He got away from them," he muttered in a low voice.

"Pardon me, Mr. Sommers?" she said sharply.

"Oh, nothing, Miss Malone. Nothing." His eyes were out of focus and he scratched at one ear. He began walking back toward the door, then paused, and moved back toward the steps.

Maybe he's finally lost his mind, she thought.

He paused on the second step and looked back at her. "Good night, uh, Fiona." He went up without waiting for a reply.

40 —Auk Village, A.T., December 24, 1915—
Friday evening

"Welcome, Uncle, your presence honors us."

George smiled at the traditional greeting from his nephew. The small rooms swirled redolent with the rich aroma of salmon stew. Tomorrow would bring roast venison, fresh bread, potatoes from the market, and the warm company of family and friends. And Julia.

Although a white custom, Christmas resonated of the potlatch, George thought. Giving gifts to friends and family to celebrate a birth rather than a death was interesting without being too alien. But to celebrate the birth of a man born nineteen centuries ago took ancestor worship even further than the Tlingit people ever imagined.

Of course, Jesus was supposedly the Son of God, one god to deal with rather than the spirits of everything around them. However, with all the different churches who claimed to be the true religion of Jesus, how was one to know which spoke the truth?

Christmas, with few exceptions, made everyone feel good and George liked that. Life these days resembled a large table covered with many kinds of food. You couldn't eat everything, but you could certainly take the stuff that looked good to you.

He carefully put down the bag of presents he carried. A small tree stood in the corner where Irene's "extra" chair usually sat. The tree sported a garland of popcorn zigzagging around it, as well as a number of wood and glass ornaments.

Irene stepped in from the kitchen. "What did you say, James? Oh, George, welcome. Come in the kitchen and have tea with us."

He hung up his heavy coat and followed his sister. Julia sat at the table with Ruth, peeling a mound of potatoes. George felt warmth blossom inside him at the sight of her.

"Hello, George," she said, giving him a smile. "What's the weather doing out there?"

"More snow falling, even more on the way from the looks of the sky. Regular Christmas weather. How are you, Julia?"

"Fine as frog hair, like my daddy says."

"Do California frogs have hair?" he asked.

"No, they don't. I always assumed that expression meant their hair was so fine one couldn't see it at all."

"Oh." He wondered why their conversations always went like this, from the stilted to the absurd in mere moments. Near her he went awkward and cloddish. He felt sure he seemed a fool.

Yet he enjoyed being near her, talking to her, looking at her. In the past two weeks he found reasons to drop by the house at least once a day. Of course his duties as a policeman did require daily patrols through the village, and if the patrols ended here, what of it?

"Here, George." Irene handed him a cup of tea.

Grateful for something to do with his hands, he sipped it quickly. The tea bit at his tongue and warmed his belly. Julia finished peeling the last potato. Ruth put them in a large pot of water.

"There," Julia said, "one less thing to do tomorrow morning. You will be here for dinner, won't you, George?"

"Oh, Uncle George always has Christmas dinner with us," Ruth said, "and we have family and friends drop by all afternoon to visit."

He sat and stared at Julia, trying to think of something to say to her. Although never a garrulous man, after the fire he'd gotten quieter. All those lessons, all that reading, and he could think of nothing to say.

"George," Julia said. "Do you know anyone who would take me out to the old village at Auke Bay?"

"In this weather?"

"Well, no. In the spring, after the snow is gone."

"I never lived there, but our parents did," he said. "I wonder if the old house is still standing?"

"I'd love to see the village before it's gone completely."

"Sure, Julia, I'll take you. It used to be a pretty big village in the old days."

"That's what Irene was telling me. She also said there were just a couple of families living there now."

"I haven't been out there since grandfather died back in 1911!" he exclaimed. He hadn't even thought about the place for at least a year. Shame washed over him for letting his past go so easily.

"Do you know the area well?"

"Yeah. I spent a lot of time there when I was young. Our uncle lived there and I stayed with him."

"Is he the uncle who taught you about being a Tlingit man?"

"Yeah. He did all that. Then I went to work in the mines and never used any of it until I taught Jim, here. Funny how things happen like that."

"Sad, too," Julia said.

He swiftly looked up at her, wondering if he was being judged. He felt she constantly weighed, prodded, and evaluated him. She stared out the window, frowning. Such a strange woman!

"What do you mean, sad?" he asked.

"It's sad what the modern world has done to your beautiful culture. The Tlingit ruled this coast for hundreds of years. Now you can't even vote or go into some stores."

He narrowed his eyes. "There were some things we did that are far better ended. Just like there are things in the white culture that need changed."

"That's true." Now she stared at him. "Many people don't mention the negative aspects of their cultural past. You're a very unusual man, George."

"He's smarter than he gives himself credit for," Irene said. "He's come a long way since —" She looked up from her work. "I'm sorry, George. It was not polite of me to talk like that."

Julia gave him a questioning look. George thought she was going to ask. It was plain from her face she wanted to, but didn't. So he decided to tell her.

"When I was a young man—"

Someone pounded loudly on the door.

Jim went over and admitted an old man, Perry Goodhorse.

"I'm sorry to bother you. But I thought George might be here."

"I'm right here, Perry. What do you want?" George said, walking into the small front room.

"There's a couple of white men down at Barney's house. They got hooch and they're getting him drunk."

"Damn them! They know that's illegal," George said, reaching for his coat.

"That's not all," Perry said. "They want him to kill someone."

"Uncle, should I come with you?"

"No, Jim. You stay here. I'll be back soon."

Perry followed George through the door. Snow flew thickly from the south pushed by a sharp wind. Full darkness had fallen. The men walked as quickly as they could along the dock. The wind-driven incoming tide splashed and gurgled under the planks.

"Do you know who the men are?"

"I seen one of them before, 'bout a year ago, but I never seen the other one before tonight."

"Where did Barney meet them?"

"They come to his house. Him and me had just finished eating some deer stew when they knocked. They said they heard he was a strong man who could use some work. Barney asked what kinda work, an' they pulled out a bottle and said we all needed to drink on it."

"And you left?"

"I quit drinking, George, you know that. But I can't say no if everybody else is drinkin'. I told 'em I had to go home before going to work at the Ground Hog. Then I come and got you."

"You did the right thing, Perry. Thanks."

"You helped me get off the bottle, George. I can never repay that."

George flashed him a smile through the falling flakes. "You already have, my friend. What did they say about killing somebody?"

"When I went out, I went around to the window and listened for a minute. I wanted to know what kind of work they wanted him to do."

"Yeah?"

"One of 'em asked how much it would cost for Barney to kill a white man. Barney said he wouldn't kill nobody. They said this was a real bad white man that needed killing."

"Did they say any names?"

"I don't know. That's when I left."

They approached the house quietly even though the wind whistled around the eaves, rattled shingles, and sucked wood smoke from the stack. The house sat on pilings next to one of the long plank docks running out over the mud flats to deep water. George edged up to the window next to the door.

He could hear jovial voices. He pulled off his hat and used it to shield his face when he peeked through the window. Both white men had their backs to him. Barney sat by the stove, drinking from a large bottle.

Although legally empowered to arrest all three men, he didn't want to arrest Barney. The man had been sober for over a month, until tonight. The two white men were the guilty ones.

Barney had already been warned once and then fined once. *If the judge sees Barney again this soon, he'll put him jail,* George thought. *However this has to stop.*

He put his hand into his coat pocket where his pistol lay. The marshal hadn't said anything about carrying a pistol, but then George hadn't asked. He had yet to draw on anyone, but it made for wonderful reassurance.

George pushed open the door and stepped into the lamplight. Both white men looked at him curiously.

"Hi, ya, chief!" the black bearded one said.

"Want a drink, chief?" the brown-bearded, heavier man asked.

Barney focused on George, covered his mouth with one hand and started to giggle. "Oh, shit. Oh shit," he said through his fingers.

"What's wrong, Barney? Don't ya want to share the hooch?" the smaller man asked.

"Not with him!" Barney shouted in a gale of embarrassed drunken laughter. "He's the cop!"

Both men shot to their feet. George noticed they loomed over him. The heavier man dropped his hand into his pocket.

George pulled out his revolver, held it at waist level, covering them. "Put your hands in the air, right now!"

The smaller man did as he was told. The heavier man stepped behind his companion and pulled out a gun.

"Drop that or I'll—"

A shot cut George off. The lantern blew into pieces and the room went dark.

"God damn it!" someone shrieked.

Before George could decide what to do, a great force threw him against the cabin wall. It took him a moment to realize he had been hit with a chair.

"C'mon, dammit!" The fat one, George thought groggily.

"We can't just leave," the small man yelled. "We gotta take care of 'em."

George could smell kerosene very strongly now. His head hurt and he felt disoriented. He suddenly remembered the fire running over Amalie. The image drove him to his feet.

A match flared in the doorway and arced across the room toward the stove where the oil was warmest. The wall behind the stove whomped into flame. George dived through the door and pulled one of the men to the dock.

Before his quarry could react, George hit him on the side of the head with the pistol in his hand.

"Damned buck!" An explosion sounded next to George's head and he rolled away from it. A second shot rang out and then the other man ran down the dock toward Juneau City.

Flames, whipped by the wind, engulfed the cabin. Perry appeared in the doorway, dragging Barney. George jumped up and helped pull the man through the door.

Barney's face was blackened, his hair singed down to the scalp, and his clothes smoldered. The men hurriedly put snow on the places that smoked.

"Is he alive?" George asked.

"Yeah, I think so. How about the guy over there?"

George turned to the man he had knocked out. "Yeah, he's okay, I only hit him with the barrel of my gun."

He bent over and pushed the man's hat off to see which of the two he had collared. It was the younger one, but something was terribly wrong.

A bullet hole glistened darkly under the right eye and the hat was full of blood and brains. George felt relieved he hadn't fired his revolver tonight.

"Perry, go get the U.S. Marshal or one of his deputies. I'll wait here and do what I can for Barney."

The house was nearly gone. Embers danced capriciously in the air, streaming away to the north on the relentless cold wind. Barney moaned through a scorched face.

"Hell of a way to spend Christmas Eve, isn't it?" George asked the night.

41 —Treadwell, A.T., December 24, 1915—
Friday late night

"Caps are set!" shouted the powder monkey. The other three men on the blasting crew retreated around a bend in the stope. The powder monkey pushed the fuse into the last hole and braided it into the twist leading into the other nineteen charges.

"Ya got 'em all the right length?" the blaster asked.

Tightly packing dirt around the fuse, the powder monkey looked up and grinned, his teeth bright in his grimy face. "You know it, brother, I don't want no hang fire." He stepped back and took a final look at his handiwork. "Okay, Gus, light 'er off."

The blaster unwrapped a waxed pouch and selected a stick match. "Me da used ta call these 'lucifers.'" After replacing the pouch he struck the match on the rock wall and "spit" the fuses. "Fire in the hole!" Gus shouted.

Both men ran to where the other three men crouched. They waited, fingers jammed into ears.

A series of three stunning blasts erupted from the end of the stope. Three tons of rock wall mushroomed into instant rubble, chunks of rock the size of a man's head flew through the air with amazing velocity before crashing down onto the floor of the slowly forming bay.

"Okay, all clear. Let's get out of here," the powder man gasped. "They all blew." The men hurried away from the blast site, coughing on the fumes and dust. They moved quickly past the first electric lights in the hewn stone passageway on their way to the cage.

"By God," exclaimed one. "Tomorrow I get to sleep in for the day if I want."

"Yeah, a day off without making up an excuse. Quite a treat," said another.

"Yah, dot's fine fer you married guys, but I chust got a day of sittin' 'round d' bunk house vit' nuttin' ta do."

The quiet Irishman laughed at his friend.

"C'mon, Oley!" Gus challenged. "You'll have a great feed at th' chow hall and you can shoot snooker th' whole day. No wife and family to worry about. Just do whatever you please. You bachelors have th' life all right."

"Gus, you know how much yer family means ta ya! I chust vish I had married dot little gal over in Juneau when I had d' chance."

Suddenly a silence descended on the mine and their voices and footsteps made the only sounds.

"What the hell happened?" Gus exclaimed, craning his head and looking at the shaft around them.

The powder man laughed. "They just shut the stamps down for Christmas. You watch, there'll be a lot of babies made tonight because nobody will be able to sleep with it so quiet."

"Yah, dot's the udder ting about bein' married!" Oley said.

"Hell," shouted Gus happily. "That's the *only* thing about being married!"

They all laughed.

A slow grinding sound moved through the mine and reached their ears.

"Lissen!" hissed Oley.

The grinding rose to a higher pitch and the sharp reports of rock snapping and squealing assaulted their ears.

"It's a fookin' cave-in!" whispered the powder monkey.

"Jasus, Mary, 'n' Joseph!" prayed Gus.

The rumble grew to monstrous proportions. The men instinctively huddled against the wall of the stope. A blast of air pressure whisked past them.

"Please, Jasus, not yet!" Gus pleaded.

Nobody laughed at him.

The shaft became silent again.

"Let's go see if the hoist is still running," the powder man said in a low, urgent voice. They trotted down the long adit. Each man very aware of the amount of rock and water above them.

The Treadwell reached down to the 2,620-foot level and of late more leakage occurred than in the past. If the wrong piece caved in there would be no more mine. It was something they didn't talk about. None of them wanted to be in the mine when it happened.

The cast-iron cage sat at the bottom of the shaft waiting for them. They hurried inside and the powder man rang the bell. A collective sigh sounded as the lift lurched into life and bore them upward through the damp mineral darkness to fresh air, and life.

42 —Juneau City, A.T., Christmas, 1915—
Saturday morning

The pounding on his door woke Lepke. He held his pocket watch up in the shaft of light leaking between door and frame.

"Seven-thirty!" he mumbled.

The pounding resumed. "Mr. Lepke, are you in there?"

"What do you want?" he shouted.

"Urgent message!" came the answer.

"Damn," he muttered, sitting up and finding his robe in the darkness. "It had better be urgent."

He shuffled to the door and pulled it open. The light from the hallway made him wince. The morning clerk, a nervous thin man named Wheaton, stood there chewing his lip.

"I'm sorry, sir. The deputy said you were to be notified immediately."

"Deputy? Notified of what?"

"That a George Mak-we has been arrested and charged with murder."

Lepke's mind cleared instantly.

"By whom?"

"Ah, he didn't say, Mr. Lepke."

"Is the deputy still here?"

"He telephoned, sir. He said the accused wanted you to know."

"Damn right," Lepke muttered. "Thank you, Mr. Wheaton, I understand the message."

"Very good, sir. Sorry to wake you on Christmas morning like this."

"Quite all right. Merry Christmas, Wheaton."

"Thank you, sir. Merry Christmas to you too."

Lepke snapped on the light in his room and dressed hurriedly. Murder? George? There was either a mistake being made or else it wasn't murder.

He'd find out damn soon *that* was for sure. At five minutes of eight he strode into the Federal Jail.

"Well, if it ain't Pinkerton's finest!" Deputy U.S. Marshal Jim Clarke said with a sneer. He sat at a comfortable angle in his heavy office chair, feet propped up on the wide wooden desk.

"I want to see one of your prisoners," Lepke said.

"Which one? Mr. Krause? Mr. Miller? The felon Anderson? Or do you want to see our only Indian, Mak-we?" The deputy laughed, his belly and jowls shook in unison.

"You telephoned the hotel to wake me, so you know who I'm here to see."

"First tell me something. Why do you care what happens to this Indian?"

"He's a fellow law-enforcement officer, which is more than I can say for you."

Clarke dropped his feet to the floor, squared his shoulders and sucked in his gut. "You don't forget you're talkin' to a *U.S. Marshal*, mister!"

"So are you, *mister*. Now I want to see the prisoner."

"You're gittin' pretty damn uppity for a temporary deputy!" Clarke let his shoulders and belly sag into their usual positions. There was no further hint of movement.

Lepke quickly stepped around the desk. Grabbing the front of Clarke's shirt with both hands, he roughly pushed the man into the chair so it teetered back dangerously. If Lepke let loose, the chunky deputy would fall.

Clarke's face went red as he stiffened. He started to grab up at Lepke.

"If you touch me, I'll drop you on your fat butt," Lepke said calmly.

Clarke grabbed the chair arms instead, his eyes wide and hating.

"I'm going to tell you *one* more time," Lepke said carefully. "I want to see officer Mak-we. If you hinder me *one* more step I will personally arrest you and place you in that cage back there."

Clarke's eyes rounded completely into fear.

"How," Lepke continued, "do you think the prisoners would react to your unarmed presence?"

"Can't, do, that!" Clarke choked out.

"Can, and will, unless you stop ruining my Christmas further." Lepke pulled the man sharply forward and released the shirt. Clarke's face nearly hit the desk.

The deputy looked up, his expression wary, the eyes hooded. After pulling at his collar for a moment, he swallowed and said, "Listen, I got no beef with you. I don't want any trouble. Bishop thinks you're makin' us all look bad."

"What?" Lepke felt as if he had been struck. "Look bad, how?"

"You're nailin' Krause in a box that's damn near air-tight, an' you ain't even from around here. Bishop's takin' it personal. He told us to help you, but not to be in a rush about it. I'm only followin' orders."

"Do you realize how absurd this is?"

The deputy shrugged.

"I'm a trained *detective*, not a U.S. Marshal. My job isn't to uphold the law, it's to investigate criminal actions. Of course I'm boxing Krause up. It's the only reason I'm here."

Lepke stared down at the man for a moment. "If I have to, I'll go to the federal district attorney about this. If I do, you'll be subpoenaed. I'd better get professional treatment from this office or there'll be a new roster in here, no matter what Judge Wickersham says!"

"Don't go thinkin' I'll get up there alone and talk," Clarke said sullenly.

"You won't be alone, I guarantee it. Now I want to see Mr. Mak-we."

"Sure." He pulled himself to his feet with an unconscious groan. "Right this way."

Unlocked, the heavy plank door opened on a large, barred area with five cells at the back of the larger cage. Snores issued from behind locked cell doors. Somewhere a tap dripped monotonously. The odor of human methane and dirty socks assailed Lepke's nose.

The deputy moved quickly across the expanse of the larger "tank" and slipped his key quietly into the lock of cell five. Lepke squinted in the gloom and saw a figure standing by the narrow cot.

Deputy Clarke turned to Lepke. "Just come out when you're finished. Be sure to pull the door completely shut or I might have to shoot the prisoner as an attempted escapee." He strode away with his shoulders back.

Lepke entered the cell. "Merry Christmas, George," he said softly. "Tell me what happened."

"Merry Christmas to you, Mr. Lepke. Hope you've got awhile."

43 —Juneau City, A.T., Christmas, 1915—
Saturday morning

Arnold Williams concentrated on his breakfast. If he let himself think about how dangerously complicated his mission had become he'd lose his appetite again. He had to eat; he needed his strength.

Sommers failed to contact him last night about step two.

The first step, two nights ago, had also been the self-proclaimed anarchist's brainchild. Silas and Ralph not only failed to kill the detective, they eliminated themselves. Ralph now resided in the federal cooler and Silas lay in a cold shed eternally waiting for spring thaw.

Sommers had not been daunted yesterday morning. On to step two! He knew an Indian, he claimed, who would welcome the chance to shoot a white man. After all, weren't all Indians true anarchists at heart?

"That's what they were before the Americans beat them into submission," he exclaimed passionately. "Anarchists, fighting the strangling grip of Imperial Russia!"

"How many Indians have you discussed this with?"

"A couple. They agreed with me."

"Were they drinking?"

"We all were." Pete looked irritated. Williams thought that most of Pete's waking hours were spent with a drink in his hand. Yesterday afternoon the man produced a confederate, Bob Bennett, an old acquaintance from an unspecified past.

"Between me 'n' Bob, we'll get that Injun to take care of the Pink," Sommers had declared smugly.

The German hadn't known Lepke was a "Pink" until Sommers told him at their first meeting, ten days ago. The man also had to define "Pink" for him. The kaiser had military police, but nothing like this detective!

Pete also solved the non-appearance of Mr. Moe. From what Williams could deduce, Sommers had no idea Krause was working for Count von Papen. Krause did all the traveling for the "organization," Sommers said.

These men were no more anarchists than Williams was an Englishman. He had fallen in with cutthroats, thieves, and ruffians. But there did seem to be an organization that might be used to his ends.

It was obvious to Williams that the brains of the organization now sat behind bars. And to make any real use of this band of scattered rabble, he would have to help get Krause out of custody. Sommers easily became vocal about how the authorities could not prove their case against his leader.

Then there was that greasy Slav lawyer, Kazis whatever-his-name, all unctuous and prying. Insinuating he was the man Williams needed to talk with if "something wanted done." What cheek! But he wasn't fooled. The German was in jail, the rest were lackeys.

He realized his fork had stalled halfway to his mouth. The food on it looked gelid and repulsive. He dropped it all in the middle of his plate.

"Damn it!" he muttered furiously. Two tables away, another diner glanced up sharply and frowned at the oath.

He ignored him. If the man was of any importance he would be at his home on Christmas morning. Two years ago he had been home in Hesse for the ancient holiday.

It was Grandfather's last winter solstice before his death. The grand duke had led Bismarck's military police during the Franco-Prussian War. Williams smiled and wondered what the strait-laced old general would think of his grandson drinking coffee in a rude mining town at the edge of civilization.

Bismarck had been such a complete Lutheran he viewed coffee as a drug, a dangerous weakness his army could ill afford. To keep his men pure from the caffeine rage sweeping Europe, he had dogs trained to sniff out the aromatic beans. Possession of any amount was a military offense, punishable by flogging.

Grand Duke von Hesse had been zealous in searching out the "rotten apples" in the Prussian army. Just one withering raptor's glare from the old man could convince young Horst he was guilty of anything and everything—

Williams quickly glanced around the nearly empty cafe. He was almost surprised no one detected his mental slip. *I must stay in character,* he thought. *If I start thinking I am Horst von Hesse, Arnold Williams will make mistakes, and I could die.*

Sommers stepped in out of the dark morning, shut the outside door behind him and glanced around. Sighting Williams, he puffed across the room, very agitated.

"Arnold, old man," he said nervously in a low voice. "I think we might have a spot of trouble." He sat down at the table as if he belonged there.

"Do explain."

"The Indian didn't pan out."

"Why?"

"Well, 'bout the time we had him drunk enough to agree to the job, he had a visitor."

"The visitor is the spot of trouble, then?"

"Well, part of the trouble." Sommers frowned and glanced around.

The man was in a funk. All of Williams' instincts became alarmed. His patience snapped.

"Would you *tell* me what problem we have?" he whispered through clenched teeth.

"Bennett got shot. He, he's dead."

"How? The visitor?"

"It was the Indian cop, Make-do, or something like that, who came in and surprised us. It's against the law to give Indians liquor. He pulled a gun, had us cold."

"You killed him?" Williams said hopefully.

"I shot out the lamp and the place caught fire. Bennett hit him with a chair and we ran out the door. But the cop jumped Bennett and knocked him out." He hesitated.

Not good, Williams thought. *This is not good at all.*

"Well?"

"I shot at the cop, but I missed. I think I was the one who killed Bennett. I, I barely managed to escape." Sommers looked close to tears.

"You ran is what you mean. You killed your own comrade and then you fled from one inept red Indian policeman and a drunk. You're a damn coward!"

Sommers went red, instantly converting his shame to anger.

"Just a fukkin' minute, you bigmouth Limey," he hissed. "You can't sit on your ass and tell me how it should have been! You weren't there; you don't know."

"I know, because you just told me. I've seen enough action to know which parts were left out. You had better find the courage to get your detective out of the way soon. If you don't, I shall take my gold to men who aren't afraid to take risks for the cause."

My God, he thought. *If I get any more melodramatic, he'll start applauding.*

Sommers worked his jaw under the beard. Hate smoldered from his eyes. It would not be safe to be around this man any longer.

"Get us two more confederates, and we'll kill him. I have a plan," Williams said quickly.

"It might take a week or two to get them here, but I got just the boys for the job," Sommers said flatly.

"That's what you said about the first two."

"These boys are with the organization in Petersburg. They'll get the job done to specifications."

The waiter approached. "Would you like another place setting, gentlemen?"

"No," Williams said. "Thank you, but we were just leaving."

"Very well. Have a merry Christmas, sir."

"Yes. Thank you."

"It's *Christmas*?" Sommers asked.

"Yes. December twenty-fifth, the birthday of the Christ child. Big holiday in some places," he said dryly.

"No wonder the streets are deserted," Sommers said. "I thought it was a week off yet."

44 —Juneau City, A.T., Christmas, 1915—
Saturday morning

Lepke and Mak-we carefully walked down the icy steps of the federal building and into the bright blue light that precedes the rising sun. "I am in your debt, Mr. Lepke," Mak-we said.

"Think nothing of it. It was a false arrest. The deputy didn't really look at the matter and he was wrong. Even the judge agreed to that."

"But if I hadn't had you to call on, I would have spent Christmas behind bars. Thank you."

"You're quite welcome," Lepke said stiffly, beginning to feel embarrassed. "Please don't mention it again." Something out of place picked at Lepke's mind. "There's something amiss. What is it?"

"The crushers aren't working. They've shut them down for Christmas."

"That is it. It's too quiet," Lepke said wonderingly.

"Do you have plans for the day?" Mak-we asked.

"Ah, well, I am to go to an afternoon concert and then have dinner with Miss Malone at seven. Why do you ask?"

"It's a tradition of ours, my sister and me, to have friends and relatives drop by on Christmas Day for eats and tea. I wanted to invite you to come by, if you wished. That's all."

"May I bring Miss Malone?"

"Certainly!" Then George suddenly looked indecisive. "I really would like you to meet someone. A woman."

"Officer Mak-we, I'm not at all sure I understand you."

"Someone I am troubled about . . ." George's words drifted off uncertainly.

"Troubled, ah, George? In what way?"

"I, I think about her all the time."

Suddenly Lepke understood.

"Well, ask her to marry you, man!" he said, and grinned widely.

"It's not quite that simple," George said, looking at the ground. "She's white."

"She can't be from here."

"No. She's from the States. California. She's an anthropologist."

"Do you think she reciprocates your feelings?"

"I don't know. She, she always speaks pleasantly to me when I go over to Irene's, but she might just be very polite."

"Irene's?"

"My sister."

"Ah." Lepke's mind raced. "I don't think I could answer your question without meeting the woman, Miss . . ."

"Prescott. Julia Prescott."

"Yes. Miss Julia Prescott. With your sister she is staying?"

"Yeah, that's right."

"I will make it a point to drop by today. How do I find the house?"

George gave him directions and they parted. Hungry, Lepke headed for what was rapidly becoming his favorite restaurant, the White Lunch Cafe in the Alaskan Hotel. The temperature hovered around zero.

The slippery pathways through the great mounds of snow required careful negotiation. Over night the sky had cleared and the mercury dropped. A light breeze forced the chill even deeper into Lepke's bones.

He passed the community Christmas tree on the corner of Front and Seward Streets. The colored electric lights and dusting of snow gave it a festive appearance bringing a smile to all who looked at it. Florence took great pride in the tree as most Juneauites did.

There was something comforting and warm about this small town. Portland with its multitudes had more to offer in the way of commerce and entertainment. But Portland lacked the friendly, open personality that suffused the towns on Gastineau Channel.

As he pulled open the door of the cafe, two men walked out. Lepke recognized Arnold Williams and thought it curious for him to be with the new guest from the hotel. The two men glanced at Lepke.

"Well, Mr. Lepke," Williams said heartily. "Merry Christmas to you, sir."

"And Merry Christmas to you also, Mr. Williams." He looked at the other man. "And Merry Christmas to you, sir."

"Oh, yes. This is Mr. Sommers, from Petersburg," Williams said grandly. "We have just breakfasted together."

"Yes, we have met. Good to see you, Mr. Sommers," Lepke said, shaking the man's hand, noting his pale face and subdued mien.

"Yeah. Pleased to see you, Mr. Lepke."

"Well, I'm here for a late breakfast myself. Have a good day, gentlemen."

Lepke walked into the cafe but his mind worried at something.

He learned long ago not to cast about mentally for answers to these nagging little prods from his memory. All he had to do was wait long enough and the answer or solution would surface. The cafe was only a quarter filled with patrons.

In the middle of his second cup of coffee, the nagging ceased and his memory presented the fact that Sommers had been a name connected with Krause in Petersburg.

But why was he here, and what was he doing with Williams? For that matter, why had the man paled at the sight of me? And what about Sommers' strange comment the night Silas and Ralph had attacked Lepke.

Back to Williams. The fellow claimed to be a British journalist. What would a journalist want with a low type like Sommers?

Amanda's letter. It's about Williams, he realized. *I gave my word I would not open it unless she had disappeared from view for a full forty-eight hours.*

Every morning a note from her appeared in his box at the hotel, "I'm just fine, drop by for tea." He had prudently steered clear of her. For the first time in his life he really understood the portion of the *Odyssey* depicting the sirens.

He could not open the letter; he had given his word. There were other ways to find out what he wanted to know. After all, he was a detective.

He finished his meal and walked up Franklin to Third Street; it was time to meet Florence. Lepke felt thankful. that someone had cleared the snow off the wooden steps that climbed the steep hill to Mrs. Bergman's Hotel. The laughter of children echoed around the neighborhood as new sleds whizzed down the steep hills to plow into snow banks.

He found himself anticipating the stamp mills, as if they waited to break their silence with a thunderous crash and shatter everyone's eardrums. *Such fantasy*, he thought to himself with a smile. *This place is good for me.*

Florence sat in the lobby chatting with Mr. Staley, the desk clerk, when Lepke entered.

"Oh, there you are," she said brightly, rising to her feet and smiling at him.

"I'm not late, am I?"

"No, not a bit. I'm just happy to see you, that's all."

Relief surged through him unexpectedly. He felt suddenly disgruntled with himself. He wasn't some adolescent in the throes of his first romance to be moved by the whim of a pretty face.

Or was he? Did he not love this woman? Had anything before this really mattered?

I can't remember the last time I thought of Alice.

Once again he felt very good.

"Let's go to the concert early and get good seats," she said brightly.

On the front steps he again had the fleeting feeling of something amiss until the lack of noise from the stamps registered in his brain.

"Isn't it quiet?" he asked her.

"Yes. It's just wonderful. I get so tired of the noise."

They walked down the hill toward town. She received greetings from nearly every person they passed. The bright cobalt blue sky threw such radiance on the snow-covered mountains that the peaks shone.

It's all like a huge Christmas card, he decided.

"This is an impossibly beautiful place," he said casually.

"Yes, isn't it? When I was in college it amazed me how much I missed Juneau. But then I've lived here all my life. I'm sure everyone feels that way about their home."

"No. No, they don't. There are certain attachments one feels to their place of origin. But I remember no beauty about Hamburg. In fact, it was quite ugly."

"What about where you live now? I mean, where you lived before you came here for this work?"

"Portland? Oh it's a very pretty city for the most part. but it has nothing like this to offer." He swept his arm out toward Douglas Island across the sparkling waters of Gastineau Channel.

"We're very lucky, aren't we?"

"How do you mean?"

"We live here," she said simply.

"Yes," he said and grinned down at her. "We are."

People already sat in the Olympic Theatre when they arrived. By the time the concert started less than an hour later, every seat was filled and a throng of latecomers stood in the back of the hall. The Treadwell Band in their ornate uniforms dedicated the concert to the citizens of Juneau.

The concert began with the "Star Spangled Banner" and went through a variety of traditional and modern music, ending with "Alexander's Rag Time Band." The audience gave the band a standing ovation, which signaled yet another piece.

Dusk crept up the mountains when they left the theater.

"What would you like to do now?" Florence asked, as they walked briskly along the street.

"Let's go visit George Mak-we and his sister."

"Go to the Indian village?"

"I believe that's where they live."

"I'll go with you, but I want you to know that not too many white people go visiting in the village."

"I don't understand the prejudice against Indians in this place," Lepke said. "Down in the states there was killing on both sides before the red Indians were subdued. But up here there was no war I know about."

"I don't understand it eithe, but it's here, and it's a fact of life."

"Does it have to be?" he asked.

"Have you read Cervantes?" she asked with a smile.

"*Don Quixote?* Of course. I read it in college."

"You remind me of him."

The wind gusted and they both looked instantly at the sky. The most changeable element of southeast Alaska is the weather. Many had died because blue skies masked weather fronts moving across the islands of the Alexander Archipelago.

The weather could shift from a bright sunny day to gray clouds, forty to sixty knot winds and stinging rain or snow in an hour. Fishermen and mariners frequently and unconsciously ran an eye across the sky even when they were on land. The weather could mean life or death.

"It's going to storm, isn't it?" said Lepke.

"Yes. See that dark line down channel?" Florence pointed.

They quickened their steps. Lepke guided them unerringly to the house of Irene Kisadis. Lepke knocked.

The door opened and Jim Kisadis stood there, light streaming out around him. For a brief moment his face registered disbelief.

"Merry Christmas," he cried. "Please come in."

As they entered the house George stood and shook Lepke's hand. They all exchanged Christmas greetings.

"How nice to see both of you," George said. He turned and indicated the women who waited by the kitchen door.

"This is my sister, Irene Kisadis, her boarder, Julia Prescott, my niece, Ruth, and, of course, you've met Jim."

Lepke noticed Florence seemed to be experiencing some momentary inner turmoil. He spoke to each of the women. Irene was older than George, he guessed. Somewhat stout, dark hair and eyes, distinct laugh lines around the mouth, and he felt sure she had noticed Lepke's glance at Florence.

Ruth had her mother's heavy-boned figure. She hadn't said more than "hi" as they entered. A burn scar running along her right jaw line dominated her square face.

Julia Prescott seemed closer to Lepke's age than was Florence. He recognized her cool, gray-eyed look for what it was— assessment. The others in the house seemed slightly ill at ease, but not her. She just watched.

He realized an expectant silence had fallen, all looked at him. "This is Florence Malone," he said suddenly. "She is, ah, a photographer and works with the firm of Winter and Pond."

"I'm also rather fond of Mr. Lepke," she said with a laugh.

The comment broke the ice and everyone laughed with her.

"Come sit at the table, Florence," Irene said. "Will you both have tea with us?"

"Thank you, I will." Florence sat in the proffered chair and looked around, "You have a very comfortable home here, Irene."

Jim sat down in a chair by the door of the kitchen. George pulled two more chairs out of a back room, gave one to Lepke and sat in the other. The small kitchen became very crowded.

"You must be new to the community, Miss Prescott," Florence said.

"Yes, that's true." She smiled sweetly and glanced over at Lepke. "You are the Pinkerton detective I've heard so much about."

Lepke couldn't think of a response so he just nodded and didn't say anything.

"Where are you from, Julia?" Florence asked.

"California. San Francisco, to be exact." She sipped her tea and looked at Lepke again. "How soon do you think you will be finished with the Krause matter?"

"Next month. I will present all my evidence to the U.S. prosecuting attorney and make myself available for the first of the trials."

"How many trials will there be?" George asked.

"They have approximately thirty-seven indictments against him," Lepke answered. "I don't know, but they might try him on two or three counts at a time."

"Let's not speak of such grim things," Irene said firmly. "It's Christmas."

"Julia is an anthropologist," Jim said. "She is studying how the ways of our people have changed since the white men came."

"Then you'll be staying for some time?" Florence asked Julia, "or are you doing a complete study?"

"I'll be here for half a year at the very least. There is so much information to record." She smiled and gestured hopelessness with her hands.

"We have a number of views at the shop of the Auk and Taku people. Some are nearly thirty years old. You must stop by and I'll show them to you," Florence said warmly.

"Why, I'd like that very much. Thank you."

"Would you take my picture?" Irene asked.

"Of course. It would be an honor. No one has ever asked me to do their portrait before."

Lepke wished he had thought of that. He'd ask her later. There were so many little things he could do to please her, if they would only occur to him.

A gust of wind shook the house.

"I hope that's not a Taku Wind coming up," Jim said.

A firm knock sounded on the door. Jim opened it to reveal two short men.

"Begay, Frank! Come in, come in. Merry Christmas."

The Filipinos both wore stiff smiles that belied their ease. As Jim introduced everyone, Lepke noticed Ruth's eyes lost their remoteness and became energized. She moved away from the table and entered the living room.

"How nice of you to come all this way on Christmas," she said to the two.

"I wanted to give you this," Begay said, handing her a gaily wrapped package.

"We thought we'd go visiting in the daylight for a change," Frank said.

Everyone chuckled. Lepke noticed Julia closely watching the exchange between Ruth and Begay.

Florence looked around until her eyes came to rest on Lepke.

"Perhaps we should go soon. To be on the safe side, of course."

"Oh, a Taku will just ruin Christmas!" Irene said.

"This is the wind Mr. Winter was talking about?" Lepke asked.

Florence nodded.

"They can be very bad," George said.

"In that case I think we should leave. It's a long way to Mrs. Bergman's."

THE DOUGLAS ISLAND NEWS
Douglas, Alaska, Wednesday, December 29, 1915

Noted In Passing

"I am a sourdough," says Wm. Sulzer of New York. "I have made nine trips to Alaska."

The crop of bootleggers is still good at Anchorage. The government supports the town.

Attorney E. E. Ritchie, of Valdez, denies he is a candidate for delegate to congress.

The uncivil war between Seward papers has reached the point where one accuses the other of being a corner on d----d fools.

The sudden violent convulsions of Senator Sulzer over the stand of Delegate Wickersham on the matter of statehood for Alaska are taken by an exchange as indication that the Senator has an ambition of his own.

The Seward Post says: Pictures of Edward Krause, accused of doing away with several persons down at Juneau, have been received and posted on the bulletin board. Krause should shave off that mustache at once or his doom is sealed. If he escapes punishment he might let it grow again and apply at the movies for a job as "the villain." With pistols, saber, long sea boots and his head bound round with a blood red bandana, he'd make a peach of a pirate.

Juneau is becoming some city. It has sixty automobiles, a bank with deposits over a million dollars, and the Juneau-Douglas Telephone Company is putting in a new switchboard capable of serving 1700 phones.

45 —Juneau City, A.T., December 30, 1915—
Thursday late afternoon

Fiona hurried into the Division Hotel, and stood by the large pot-bellied stove while taking off her coat and muffler.

"Is the wind still bad out there, honey?" Maye asked from her small office.

"It's dreadful. I couldn't have walked another block if my life depended on it."

Maye chuckled. "I haven't had a chance to ask yet, how was your Christmas, dearie?"

"Oh, it was fine, I suppose. Father was glum all day. I think he misses Florence but is too stubborn to admit it. Sometimes I don't understand that man."

"Some men are like that, my dear. They want it all but won't give an inch."

"Speaking of men," Fiona said hesitantly.

"Yes?"

"That Sommers man. He's been pestering me something devilish to have dinner with him. Somehow it has come around to your allowing it or not, and—"

"Honey, if you want to go to dinner with Pete Sommers, you go right ahead," Maye said grandly.

"No. You don't understand. I don't care for the man at all. I think he is base and I really don't want to be alone with him."

"Then tell him that."

"He turns my words around on me. He means to get permission from you for me to be seen in public with a guest of the hotel. I, I don't want you to give him permission. Please."

"So that's what it was all about," Maye said thoughtfully.

"Pardon?"

"Well, I'm afraid it's a bit too late for that. He already asked me if there was a rule of the house pertaining to social engagements. I told him there was, but you were a good, level-headed girl and if you wanted to take in a dance with him that I had no objection."

"Oh, dear," Fiona said, feeling light-headed. She dropped her coat on the floor and abruptly sat down on one of the horsehair divans circling the stove.

"Are you all right, dearie?"

Fiona felt as though her stomach were falling a great distance. A dizzying detachment distanced her mind miles from her body. She thought she should answer Maye, but there really wasn't anything to say.

"Fiona? Are you ill?"

It would be up to her to stop him. She realized she feared Pete Sommers. He was *too* dangerous.

Maye stood in front of her with a small glass.

"Fiona! Drink this. It will make you feel better."

She numbly took the glass and swallowed the contents. The unexpected bite of the whiskey brought on a coughing fit and snapped her out of her foggy lassitude.

Maye patted her back. "There, now, that should help you."

Fiona stopped coughing and wiped tears from her eyes.

"He frightens me, Maye. I don't want to have anything to do with him," she said hoarsely.

"Well, tell him that."

"I," she cleared her throat, "I suppose I have no choice now. I know he'll be ugly about it."

"Just remember, honey, in some ways all men are alike, and there are a lot of them out there. If you don't like this fellow, tell him to be on his way."

"You're right. I just have to tell him to be on his way," Fiona said numbly. She rescued her coat and hung it up. Her hands were still shaking slightly.

"Look, honey, can you handle this place today? I've got to go down to the cafe for a couple of hours. Bones isn't well."

"Of course," Fiona said with an effort. "That's my job isn't it?"

"That's my girl," Maye said warmly. She puffed over to the clothes tree and pulled on her fur coat. "I'll be back before you know it."

After Maye left, Fiona added coal to the stove. She straightened up the small office and made sure the desk looked business-like. She still fussed behind the front desk when the front door opened in a howl of wind and a blast of icy air.

A person in overcoat, muffler, and fur hat pushed the door shut with a slam. Fiona's heart began to beat faster as the figure stood for a moment, regarding her. With a glance over the shoulder, the person took a few steps and stopped by the stove.

Fiona's heartbeat accelerated to a pounding in her head as she watched the coated figure slowly unwind the muffler from the face and push back the fur hat. Light and shadow played across the features for a moment, turning them into an African mask. She squinted, trying to recognize the mute figure as her hand closed over the shotgun under the edge of the desk.

She glanced down. In the shadows her whitened knuckles stood out clearly against the thick, wooden stock. Her knees felt weak so she moved her feet slightly to insure a solid stance. Her biceps tensed as she readied herself to raise the weapon.

The still-silent figure took a step toward her. She caught her breath and held it as the face came out of the shadows.

"Fiona, are you ill?" Amanda asked.

She felt the blood rush from her head. The floor flew up at her but disappeared in the darkness before it had time to arrive.

Something stung her face. Again. Insistent, nipping teeth wouldn't leave her be. She angrily opened her eyes, ready to lash out at the intrusion.

Amanda caught herself before she could lightly slap Fiona again.

"My God, Fiona. Are you all right? You had me so frightened."

Despite herself, Fiona laughed. She sat on the floor, legs splayed out. Behind her, the desk supported her weight.

"I, I had *you* frightened? You should have been in *my* shoes!"

"What caused that? Are you coming down with something?" Amanda rocked back on her haunches.

"No. I was just scared. I thought you were, ah, someone else."

"Who? Who can frighten you that much by just walking into the room?"

"It doesn't matter. I realize now how foolish I've been." She paused for a long moment. "I think I was more afraid of my own fear than I was of him."

Amanda's lip rose in a silent snarl that exposed her teeth. Her eyes flashed. "*Who*, damn it?"

"Pete Sommers," Fiona blurted. "He's been after me to go dancing with him. I just haven't refused him, yet."

"That fat, smelly man who's staying here? He's bothering you? Once I tell August, this Sommers person will quickly see the light."

"No. Please. I'm fine. Don't bother Mr. Lepke with it."

"I quite assure you, he won't mind at all."

"*Please*, Amanda! Just forget it."

The indigo eyes searched her face. Amanda pulled off her hat and tossed her head to shake loose the long, dark hair. Fiona saw something wild and dangerous in the woman's countenance.

"Fiona, you're my dearest friend in this place. If anyone tries to hurt you, I don't care who it is, I'll kill them."

THE ALASKA DAILY EMPIRE
Juneau, Alaska, Monday, January 3, 1916

FOUR BIG LINERS SUNK IN MEDITERRANEAN
Wilson Hurries Back To Capital;
Life Loss Includes U.S. Consul

ENGLAND AROUSED

PRESIDENT WILL WIN IN A WALK

WATER FAMINE CRITICAL; CITY COUNCIL MEETS

JUSTICE LAMAR, SUPREME COURT, DIES SUDDENLY

FRISCO AND SEATTLE HAVE SEVERE STORMS

BESSARABIA IS SCENE OF HUGE DRIVE

GOLD PRODUCTION NEARLY BILLION, ALASKA IS THIRD

46 —Juneau City, A.T., January 3, 1916—
Monday morning

For the first time since his arrival in North America, Arnold Williams received a visitor. The small, dark man with bad teeth glanced about nervously.

"You are Arnold Williams, correspondent for the *London Times*?" he asked after being admitted into Williams' room.

"Yes, that's correct."

"Where did you enter North America?"

"Why should I tell you anything?" Williams asked softly. He silently cursed himself for leaving the Luger in his coat pocket, across the room.

"I must ascertain you are the correct man."

"Correct? How do you mean correct?" The bitch had talked, he was sure of it. This was just a prelude to arrest.

The small man licked his lips and glanced around the room again. "I have a letter for a man with two names. The first name is Arnold Williams. Have you any idea what the other name is?"

Williams turned on the ball of his foot and strode across the room, pulled the pistol out of his coat pocket and leveled it at the man.

"How about Luger? Would that be the name?"

"N, *nein*, no." The man held his hands up in front of him. "I must know if you are Herr Horst . . ."

". . . von Hesse," Williams finished in a whisper.

The man nearly fainted with relief. "*Ja, das ist richtig!*"

"Speak English, you fool! Of course it's right. Who sent you?"

"Ludendorf, through the offices of many others," he whispered.

"What do you want?" Williams hissed.

"I am to give you this." He held out a long, gray envelope and a wallet.

Williams snatched them out of his hands.

"Tell me," the man said. "How can you stand the *Geräusch* in this place?"

"Speak English in this room! Noise?" Williams snapped. "The stamp mills? It becomes nothing after a time. I no longer hear it. Are you staying here in Alaska?"

"Ne— No. I return to Seattle tonight on the steamer." He pronounced it "Zeeadle." "I am to obtain an address where future correspondence will reach you."

"Send it here," he said offhandedly. "Americans never look at one's post. Did you just come from the Fatherland?"

"Yes. They insisted I come through Mexico. Such a country I have never seen!"

Williams broke into laughter. "Was your train attacked?"

"No. But I think that is the only thing that did not happen."

"You had it easy," Williams said, dismissing him. The wallet contained a hundred English sovereigns.

He tore open the letter. Heavy gray paper, nothing at the top of the page indicated origin.

You will do nothing until such time as the United States enters the war against the Entente. The possibility still exists the U.S. will side with the Triple Alliance rather than Britain and France. IF U.S. elects to make war on the Fatherland you will IMMEDIATELY destroy as many gold mines as possible before making your way back to Germany. MAKE NO MOVE UNTIL THAT TIME. The Kaiser is aware of your service to the Fatherland and sends his best wishes. God is with us!

The letter had no signature but Ludendorf's blocky hand was unmistakable.

Williams struck a match and lit the edge of the gray paper. The small man watched him silently.

"Exactly who gave you this letter?" he asked.

"The man who wrote it."

"Who told you where to find me in Alaska?"

"A captain whose name I am not permitted to repeat."

"Where?"

"The captain? In Seattle."

"He knew my name?"

"Ja, uh, yes."

"And how did you find me?"

"I asked for Williams at every hotel I came to. Finally I was told you were here. What else was I to do?"

"Did anyone ask why you sought me?"

"No."

"Good. You may leave."

Without another word the man left the room, shutting the door quietly behind him.

He felt trapped. Didn't they realize how difficult it was to be in this country? What was he to do with himself until the Americans decided which direction to take? What if they didn't enter the war at all, but continued supplying the English with munitions?

Journalists didn't stay in one place forever unless they found local employment. He had plenty of money. The hundred sovereigns would keep him quite handsomely for over a year if he became frugal with expenditures.

I should have asked when they would send more money, he thought. *I suppose I could always write to the consul in Seattle if need be.* The truth of the matter was that he still had funds left from his trip.

The two years at Oxford turned into much more of an education than his father supposed. He'd learned to live on almost nothing, picked up an English accent, and met Millie.

He allowed himself the luxury of thinking about how her hands felt on his body, how her mouth tasted, how she tasted. She was to have been a dalliance, a distraction. Never had he planned to fall in love with her.

She loved him immediately and completely. She supported him for over a year on her skimpy barmaid's wage while he played the wastrel university student. Then in late 1913, his father's message: *Kehrt zurück!* Return home.

He went. Of all the actions he had taken in his life, he most regretted not saying good-bye to her. He had never been as much a coward before or since as he was that day.

Perhaps when this is all over, he thought. *After victory is ours, I'll go back and she will understand I did what the Fatherland demanded of me. And because I have returned to her she will forgive me.*

THE ALASKA DAILY EMPIRE
Juneau, Alaska, Tuesday, January 4, 1916

Wilson at Helm During Crisis; Action Is Promised

ALASKAN CABLE IS SEVERED

FORDITES TO CROSS GERMANY IN SEALED CARS

CONSCRIPT PLAN NOW PROBABLE

PERSIA'S SINKING DESCRIBED

U. S. TO ACT WILSON'S PROMISE

MINER IS KILLED BY FALL OF ROCK IN ALASKA JUNEAU

AUTHORITIES SEEK EVIDENCE AGAINST KRAUSE

New evidence is being collected against Edward Krause, alleged wholesale murderer, whom the authorities believe did away with William Christie of Treadwell, James O. Plunkett of Juneau, Ole E. Moe of Seattle, Olaf Ekrem, a Duncan Canal prospector and ——— Yamamoto, the Japanese watchman for the Olympic mine in Wrangell Narrows. It will be two months before the grand jury goes into session and the authorities are leaving no stone unturned in building a case against the prisoner.

Posing as "Hartman"

It is said that Krause is getting mail in the same post office box here that he rented in the name Ole Moe, only the mail is addressed to him as E. Hartman. It is reported that a mortgage running to Hartman and given by Yamamoto is being foreclosed at Vancouver, and that Krause is posing as Hartman. It is said also that other papers belonging to Yamamoto and Ekrem have been found in Krause's possession and that Ekrem had $500 in money when he left Petersburg.

Ekrem and Yamamoto mysteriously disappeared from the Olympic mine, near Krause's cabin, in 1913. In this connection the Petersburg report says:

"It is claimed that at the time of these disappearances Krause was occupying the cabin on his claim, which is not far from the Olympic mine; also that Krause was seen in conversation with the men shortly before they disappeared," (continued on page three)

47 —Juneau City, A.T., January 7, 1916—
Friday afternoon

***I'm angry enough to hurt someone,* Pete Sommers reflected.** The damn Limey nagged at him constantly to get the boys here. Now Krause insisted on interrogating him. At least Ed didn't give him constant grief about the two bungled jobs.

"Tell me more about this Englishman," Krause said in his low voice.

"I don't know much about him, Ed. He just told me he was an anarchist come over here to help fight the bosses. Said he had money to help the cause and had definite ideas how to use the organization."

"Something here doesn't tally," Krause muttered. "Why isn't he in Europe doing something?"

"I dunno, Ed. You'd have to ask him."

"I will. Tell him I want to see him."

"He don't cotton much to orders."

"Tell him I asked to see him, you idiot. Don't give him any orders. Just a friendly request from one anarchist to another."

"Okay, soon as I leave here I'll go find him and tell him, uh, ask him."

"How much have you told him about the organization?"

"Oh, not much. Just that one exists and he's not the only anarchist in Alaska."

"You haven't killed the detective yet, have you?"

"No. Kazis said we should make it look like a robbery or something. I haven't been able to get the boys up here from Petersburg yet."

"Do it yourself."

"Not alone. That fellow is no pushover. He shot Silas deader 'n hell."

"He'd be dead in a day if I could get out of this damn place!" Krause paced around the tank, glaring at the guard in the corner.

"Maybe I should go, Ed."

"Yeah, go on. Get out of here. Tell him to come and see me. I want to talk to him."

"Sure. I'll ask him, Ed. Don't worry."

Pete was happy to leave the jail. There had been too many times in his past when he stayed and the visitor left. Hadn't been all that many visitors either.

He didn't relish telling Williams that Krause wanted to see him. The man was touchy. It was a toss-up which one of those men scared him most. All the same they were his only hope of an easier life. He might spout anarchist crap, but give him a chance to make some money off the class struggle, he'd grab it and be gone like a shot.

Fiona crossed his mind. He had played her long enough. It was time to reel her in. Maye told him to be careful with her; her old man had connections.

He didn't care about that. He didn't live here. As soon as the detective was dead he would get money out of the Limey one way or another and blow town anyway. Besides, the detective was going to be dead real soon.

A gust of mind-numbing wind hit him. The sky made a dark blue roof over the snow-covered mountains flanking each side of the channel. The temperature hovered around the zero mark.

He hurried down the street to the wireless office. After basking in the warm glow of the creaking coal stove for a few minutes, he went up to the window.

"Sendin' 'r receivin'?" the clerk asked.

"Sendin'."

"Who to?"

"Horace Powell in Petersburg."

"What'cha wanna say?"

"Ah, I need you both here right now. Come at once."

"How ya want it signed?"

"Pete. Will they deliver that?"

"Course they will. What's the address?"

"He'll most likely be in the Viking Tavern."

"That'll be half a dollar, Pete."

He dropped the coin on the counter. "When will he get it?"

"I'll send it right now. If he's at the tavern he'll have in within the hour."

"Thanks." Pete pulled his fur hat tight and went out into the icy wind. He hoped the Limey was in his room. It was just too damn cold to look all over town for him.

As he entered the Grand Hotel he remembered running into the detective on Christmas Day. Suddenly he saw the bullet hit Bennett in the face again, and he shuddered. He owed that detective and his trained Indian.

He walked purposely past the desk, heading for the stairs.

"Here now! Where do you think you're going?" the desk clerk asked.

Sommers stuck out his jaw so his beard quivered and let his coat fall open so the man could see his burly chest. "I'm going upstairs to see a friend if it's all the same to you."

"Who?" The clerk didn't seem to be impressed.

"Mr. Williams."

"He said he'd be over at the Louve if anybody came looking for him."

"Oh. Thanks," he said grudgingly, and reversed course. Well, at least he would get a drink out of this.

The Louve sat on the corner where the plank street bent to follow the shoreline. The building, like almost all of this part of town, was built on pilings over the tide flats. Sometimes the smell was almost more than a man could take.

As usual, Williams sat at a table in the back so he could see everybody who entered. Sommers briefly wondered who the man thought was going to come through the door. Then he spied the bottle on the table and all else left his mind.

"Mind if I sit with you?"

Williams looked up at him with disinterested eyes. "Sure, what the hell. Go get yourself a glass first."

Sommers moved over to the bar quickly and grabbed a glass off the top of a stack. He sat and stared at the bottle without touching it.

"Help yourself," Williams drawled.

"Thanks." He tossed back two shots and filled the glass a third time before speaking again.

"Ed Krause would like to talk to you."

"Why?"

"I told him how you were a European anarchist. He wants to meet you."

"I don't care much for jails."

"You think he does? Just remember, he's head of our organization. You want him on *your* side."

"From what I read in the paper, he can't even help himself, let alone me."

"It's up to you," Sommers said cagily. "I told him I'd pass along his request."

Williams eyed him sourly. "Y'know, Sommers, if you were twice as smart as you think you are; you still wouldn't be dangerous."

He felt hurt. "Now why you bein' such a piss-ant? You don't look like a man that wants for much."

Williams ignored the jibe and drank off his glass. "Okay, I'll go talk to the jailbird. I'll see you later."

For a moment, while staring at the quarter bottle of whiskey, Sommers couldn't believe his luck. Then Williams picked the bottle up, pushed in the stopper and handed it to the bartender. "Keep this for me, Harry. I'll be back."

Sommers sighed. He nursed his glass until even the smell of liquor was gone. He thought about Fiona again.

48 —Juneau City, A.T., January 7, 1916—
Friday afternoon

"He said he'd see you, mister. If you need me, just holler."

Williams concentrated on keeping his face free of the disdain he felt for the chubby deputy.

"Thank you, constable. I'm sure I'll be just fine." He followed the self-important man through a large barred cage reeking of urine, soiled clothing, and other unsavory odors.

"Krause, this is Mr. Williams from the *London Post*," deputy Clarke said importantly.

"That's the *London Times*, constable," Williams corrected.

"Oh, yeah." The deputy opened the cell door, allowed Williams to enter, and then locked the door behind him.

Williams smiled at the hulking dark man who remained seated on the narrow cot. "Good day. I wondered if you might agree to an interview?"

The heavy plank door to the office shut behind the deputy.

"You're no more a reporter than I am," Krause said softly. "Sit down." He pointed at the only chair in the cell.

"I'm sure you wouldn't have known if Sommers hadn't told you beforehand," Williams said quietly. "He said you wanted to meet me. Here I am."

"Why are you here?" Krause asked.

"Because you wanted to meet me."

"No. Why are you in Alaska? Why are you in North America?"

"To widen the war against ruling class. To hit them where it will hurt."

"You really a newspaper-man, or is that just a cover?"

"Does it matter?"

"It might. Most anarchists are a bit mad. You seem to be a pretty cool cucumber. I don't think you're an anarchist at all."

"What do you think I am?" Williams said lightly, subduing the tremor in his hand.

"I think you're crooked like the rest of us. It's quite a coincidence that you show up at the same time I land in the slammer."

Williams relaxed slightly. "Do you think I came all the way from England to fill the vacuum in your organization created by your absence?"

"No. I think you left England to stay out of the war. You just happened to be in Seattle when all this hot air about my alleged crimes hit the newspapers. Once I was arrested, you took the opportunity to cash in on another man's work." Krause leaned back against the bars of his cell and stared into Williams' eyes.

"Fascinating theory, old boy. As you say, it's all hot air."

"Convince me otherwise," Krause said shortly.

"I'm an anti-monarchist. Not quite the same as an anarchist."

"There are no kings in the United States," Krause pointed out.

"No, there aren't. However right now the United States is making noise about getting into the war. We don't want that."

"The war in Europe is being fought between kings, kaisers, and czars. You're an Englishman and yet you want England to lose the war? I don't buy that, mister."

"Germany and Austria cannot rule all of Europe. There would be revolution. With an English victory the revolution might not happen for another forty years," Williams said, using the last of his fabricated philosophy.

"I'm not sure I agree with your conclusions, but you have an interesting idea there. How are you going to keep the U.S. out of the war?"

"By breaking her will to fight, bankrupting her treasury, and destroying her ability to make munitions," Williams said automatically.

"You sound just like a German, do you know that?" Krause said blandly.

"No need to be insulting, old boy," Williams snapped.

Krause sat up quickly. "I wasn't insulting you, I was paying you a compliment. I was born in Germany, and have followed the war news with a great deal of interest."

"Well, I didn't mean to be insulting either. I'm so used to keeping up pro-British pretenses it has become a habit."

"What do you want from me?" Krause asked.

"Assistance in destroying the gold production capability of this area."

Krause laughed, and then lowered his voice again. "You got any idea how many gold mines there are around here? Over a hundred at last count."

"Perhaps 'destroy' is the wrong word. How about 'cripple' the mining industry?"

"That's still a pretty tall order, and you'd play hell getting out of here alive if the miners found out you were responsible for messing with their livelihood."

"I hadn't planned any advertisements," Williams said dryly. "If we could stop production at the Perseverance, Treadwell complex, Thane complex, Jualin, and the A-J, we'd pretty much have this area shut down. All the rest are minuscule by comparison."

"Shutting down nine mines without being caught is probably impossible. After you shut down the first one they'd put heavy security on all the rest."

"What if we hit them all at the same time, old boy?"

"Then the authorities would think it was a German plot and declare war the next day," Krause said. "Hell it would even look like a German plot to *me.*"

Williams leaned back in his chair. Two cells away a prisoner urinated into a heavy porcelain thunder mug. Krause was correct. Williams couldn't tell him the United States would already be at war if the mines were actually destroyed.

"Looks like you're damned if you do and damned if you don't," Krause said cheerfully. "Maybe you're going about it wrong."

"How should one go about it?" Williams asked stiffly.

"Pick out the biggest, the one that produces the most ore —"

"Treadwell," Williams interjected.

" —and make its destruction look like an accident," Krause finished.

Williams felt a swirl of affection for the dour murderer. "You've nailed it on the head!" he said with a smile.

Krause squinted at him. "In English it's either 'you've hit it on the head,' or 'you've nailed it.' Which are you, German or Austrian?"

"Excited, old boy. I'm merely excited," Williams said coldly.

"No matter. The results you are after would satisfy me to a tee. It's best we don't meet in here again. Until I beat this thing we'd better correspond through Sommers."

"He's a bit of an ass," Williams said.

"Yeah, but he's a malleable ass, and that's all that matters."

"Will he do as he's told?"

"If he doesn't, kill him."

49 —Juneau City, A.T., January 10, 1916—
Monday afternoon

Irene Kisadis and Julia Prescott hurried into the shop to escape the cold. Florence met them at the door, smiling nervously, wondering what to do with her hands.

"We're here," Irene announced, shifting the bundle she carried. "Are we on time?"

"Oh, yes," Florence said. "Won't you come back to the studio?"

She held the door as the women passed her. Julia smiled and quietly said, "Hello."

The studio had been ready for over an hour. The mottled "infinity" backdrop hung ready for Irene's portrait. Off to the side, a heavy wooden chair sat waiting for use.

"Have you thought about the composition, Irene?"

"I'm not sure what you mean."

"Do you wish to stand or sit? Do you like this background or would you like something different?"

Irene laid down her bundle and slowly took off her coat as Florence talked. She wore an immaculate white dress with two rows of ruffles around the bottom.

"What a lovely dress," Florence said softly.

"Thank you. I was married in this dress. I wish there had been a photographer present on my wedding day."

"The amazing thing is that it still fits you," Julia said.

"Twenty-two years can change a person, all right. My hair didn't have these gray streaks in those days, and my face wasn't lined," Irene said with a little laugh.

"Your face has so much character," Florence said. "You look so calm and wise."

"I would like to have this in the picture." Irene opened the bundle that proved to be a large Chilkat blanket wrapped in oilcloth.

"Oh, that will be wonderful in the background," Florence said.

"Not to mention an interesting meshing of two cultures," Julia said.

Irene laughed. "Always the scientist. You need to fall in love."

Julia smiled but said nothing. Florence nodded agreement, carefully took the blanket and hung it on the wall.

"There. Now if you'll stand right here. . ." She deftly positioned Irene between the blanket and the camera tripod. "Fine. I'll make a few exposures in each pose to make sure we have the correct aperture setting for the available light."

Florence moved behind the camera and put the hood over her head to shut out the light. She peered through the ground glass camera back and focused on Irene's eyes in the inverted image. If the eyes were in focus, so was the rest of the face.

She slipped a film case into the camera back. Moving out from under the hood, Florence put the lens cap on the camera. She studied Irene critically.

"How formal do you wish this photograph to be?"

"I want it to show a person who is someone with a life they are proud of. Do you know what I mean?"

"Yes. Yes, I think I do. Put you hands on your hips. Yes, that's it. Now look right at the lens, this part here."

Irene took her stance and gazed levelly at the lens cap.

Florence pulled the front slide out of the film case, exposing the sheet of film to any light passing through the lens. "Okay, when I take the lens cap off we will be taking the portrait. When I say 'now' I want you to take a deep breath and hold it, okay?"

Irene nodded.

Florence gripped the lens cap. "Now." She opened the small lens then after a moment she put the cap back on and said, "Okay, you can breathe now."

"That's all there is to it?"

"Yes." Florence smiled at her. "Now let's take another one just like it at a different f-stop."

Irene frowned at her.

"That's photographer talk for a different lens setting."

"Oh." Irene posed while Florence made nine more exposures.

"Okay, we're done. Give me two days to develop and print up some contacts, and you can come in and tell us how many of which pose you would like to purchase."

"I didn't know it would be this easy."

"She thought she would have to sit for hours," Julia explained.

"Not any more," Florence said with a laugh. "After all, it *is* 1916."

"Isn't it amazing how much easier life has become since we were girls?" Julia asked. "There's electricity and gas boats, automobiles and flying machines, telephones and typewriters, I could just go on and on."

"It's almost frightening," Florence said somberly. "It makes you wonder what else could be invented or improved."

"There's a lot of things that could be done for my people," Irene said flatly. "The white people could treat us like human beings instead of like dogs. That would be a good place to start."

Florence felt her face go red and could think of nothing to say.

"That's why there are anthropologists and ethnographers studying your people," Julia said. "We know everything is changing and we want to preserve a record of your old ways of life before the modern world swallows you like the rest of us. White attitudes about Indians and Eskimos are changing every day."

"It's hard to tell when you live here," Irene said.

"Not everybody agrees with the 'no Indians' signs, Irene," Florence said.

"But do you say that to the people who put them up? If white people don't say something about it, it will never stop. We will always be low as dogs in their eyes."

Once again Florence could think of nothing to say. She felt awful.

"Well, for many years that's how women, white women, were thought of in this country," Julia said. "Now we have the vote in Alaska and Wyoming, and are doing things that for many years only men could do."

"Like be a photographer," Florence said.

"How long did you work here before they let you take pictures of people?" Irene asked.

"Until today!"

The three women burst into laughter and hugged.

50 —Treadwell, A.T., January 10, 1916—
Monday morning

Begay Santo dumped the last twenty pounds of potatoes into the automatic peeler and shut the lid. The machine was a new and very welcome addition to the Treadwell kitchen. He opened the water valve and let the container fill half way. Then he flipped the power switch.

The heavy metal vat began spinning in its frame, rolling the potatoes against the rough inside walls, scraping the peelings from them. He smiled; he was so lucky to live in a modern age. Peeling potatoes by hand had been the worst part of his job.

Not that he wouldn't have done it gladly. After the grim hell of cannery work, Treadwell was like heaven. For the past week he had been thinking about the recent changes in his life.

Most of the boys would work for a few years, save all their money, then go back to the islands to marry the girls who waited for them, and start a small business or buy a farm. Florita Salamanca had been picked by his family to wait for him. So far she had waited three and a half years.

He must write soon and tell her she waited for nothing. Not only had he not saved money for their future, he didn't even want to go back. She was just a name and a faded memory.

Something deep inside said he should feel guilty for having that attitude, but he easily squelched the thought. *I'm different. They sent me away, and it no longer bothers me to be away from my family and my childhood home.*

And of course there was Ruth.

He felt fortunate to have met her. She was so wonderful, even though she thought herself ugly. He'd tried to tell her the scar was nothing, merely God's way of keeping her from perfection.

She was religious enough to consider his comment blasphemy. Which only made him treasure her more. Yes, he did love her.

Tonight he was going to first tell her that, and then ask her to marry him. His wages here were adequate to support a wife.

The door to the spud locker opened, breaking his reverie. Willie Ayamo stood there with a scowl on his face.

"Is there anything left in there?" he demanded, pointing to the spinning potato peeler.

Begay snapped the power switch off, and waited for the container to stop spinning. He refused to look at his uncle.

"I hear things about you, Begay."

The cylinder stopped and he opened the lid. The potatoes were about half the size they should have been. Begay took a deep breath.

"Please have the cost of the wasted potatoes taken from my pay envelope, Mr. Ayamo."

"Who shall pay for your wasted life? What shall I tell your mother who depends on you for her old age? And what about the aging woman who waits to be your wife?"

"I wasn't asked!" he snapped. "Nobody has ever asked me about the cost of their actions. You have worked in the canneries, you know how we are treated. They sent me off to earn and return, and they never once asked me if I *wanted* to go."

"We only send the best," Willie said in Tagalog. "You know that. It is a great honor to be chosen. You get to see so much more of the world, and you have the opportunity to bring back mental and physical wealth."

"I had to work like a coolie!" Begay shouted in English. "I was treated like a slave. Tricked and robbed of my money after working sixteen and eighteen hours a day to earn it."

"Slowly, it changes for us." Willie stubbornly stuck to Tagalog. "We only send those who can endure."

"I'm not going back, *Mr.* Ayamo. I will stay here in Alaska and raise a family which does not exile its sons for future wealth."

"This will kill your mother," Willie said softly. "Florita will be shamed, thus shaming her family . . ."

"Tell me this," Begay interrupted angrily, "is there still a Florita waiting for *you?*"

"You will be docked one dollar for the ruined potatoes," Willie said contemptuously in English. "Be very careful with your work. If I find fault with it, you will lose your job!" He turned and walked out the door.

Begay felt a swirl of emotions warring in his heart and mind. On one hand he felt liberated and free. On the other hand he felt completely alone in a very big world.

THE ALASKA DAILY EMPIRE
Juneau, Alaska, Monday January 10, 1916

English Battleship Is Mined:
All Troops Leave Gallipoli

100 LOST AS BRITON BOAT SUNK

ALL BRITISH FORCES LEAVE DARDANELLES

GERMANY'S PROPOSAL RECEIVED

SUFFRAGETTES SCORE A POINT

RICHNESS OF ALASKA IS SHOWN PRESENT AND FUTURE

Alaska's population is 44,000 today, (whites) an increase of 5,000 over the previous year. The prediction is made by Governor Strong that the next decennial census in 1920 will show a population of 100,000.

Fish products in Alaska during the past fiscal year were valued at $21,242,975, a gain of over $5,000,000.

Tourist travel the past summer was the greatest in Alaska's history.

Copper production in past calendar year was about $20,000,000 —an immense gain.

Alaska has 30,000 square miles of agricultural lands, besides large areas suitable for grazing.

Water power bids fair to be developed to a point where electric-chemical products will become an important industry.

Alaska is the home of healthy and happy children and epidemics among the white population are almost unknown.

Fur farming has become an important industry.

The value of the gold production of Alaska for the calendar year 1914 was $15,746,259. or about $140,000 over that of the previous year.

LAST INDIAN SLAVE DIES AT 110 YEARS

HOQUIAM, Wash., Jan. 10— "Humptulips Pete," said to be 110 years old and the last Indian slave on Gray's Harbor, died near Quinault last week, it was learned here today.

51 —Juneau City, A.T., January 14, 1916—
Friday morning

"**I've given your application a lot of thought, Mr. Lepke.** You're certainly well suited for the job, and this Krause thing proves we need a trained detective on the force. Even Mayor Valentine agrees with me on that." Chief of Police Ben Tinsley looked up from the papers in his hand and stared across his desk at August Lepke.

"Juneau City isn't Portland, Oregon and the police department isn't the Pinkerton Detective Agency, either. We are the protective part of a system that isn't always equal or just."

"Chief, can I interrupt you for just a moment?"

"Sure."

"I know what goes on down on Lower Front Street. I can tell you which officer picks up at which bar on which night. I also know Jack Malone is the unofficial mayor of that part of town, despite what Mr. Valentine says."

"You seem to know a lot, Mr. Lepke. Make your point," Chief Tinsley said softly.

"I want to stay here. I want to be a police officer, and I think I'd be a good one. But the system that operates Lower Front would tie my hands if I were part of it." He dropped his gaze from the Chief's face and stared at his hands for a moment.

"You want the job but you don't want to be in on the take? Is that what you're saying?"

"That says it pretty well," Lepke agreed, "is that possible in this police department?"

"You're not some Bible-thumpin' do-gooder are you?"

"I'm not a religious man, Chief, but I like to think I'm an honest one. If I'm being slightly dishonest in my job, I would have a tough time deciding how honest the citizens around me are. I don't want to have to stop and figure out who can do what every time I see a law being broken."

"It doesn't come up all that often," Tinsley said with a grin.

"Perhaps not, but I want to be able to follow my instincts and not worry about anything else. If I can't do that I don't think I would be a good officer for your force."

"Ain't you a deputy U.S. Marshal right now?"

Now Lepke grinned. "Yes, but I'd appreciate it if you didn't let the news get around. I want people to think I work for a living."

Ben Tinsley guffawed and slapped his desk. "You don't miss much at all, do you?"

"I try not to."

"Well let me explain our viewpoint. We have a community here that has laws and regulations. Some of the regulations are on the books to keep a few people happy. If they were strictly enforced it would make a lot of other people unhappy to the point we'd have more trouble than we could handle. Follow me so far?"

Lepke nodded.

"Okay, there are rules we follow to the letter down on Front and Main, but farther south, say in the cribs on Lower Front, we don't notice a lot of things as long as nobody is getting hurt that doesn't deserve it. The major industry here is gold mining, and most of those miners are young, single fellows who work their fannies off every day of the week. They need some place to let off steam. If we didn't have Lower Front for them, they'd be doing it in the middle of the shopping district."

"Why do you make the cat houses pay under the table if they're there for the good of the community?" Lepke asked flatly.

"Call it a tax on sin. There are things we have to do down there that don't fall under the descriptions in our books. We pass out a lot of blue tickets down in that part of town; they cost money."

"Blue tickets?"

"One-way tickets to Seattle or Skagway. If we can get certain types out of town we save money in the long run. You got any idea how much a prisoner can eat?"

"But what about the courts?"

"What about them? Our lawyers couldn't make a living if we didn't have the courts. But I'm of the opinion the courts keep too many people on the streets of Juneau who should have been given a blue ticket south long before."

"I can't argue with that, Chief. The way you explain it, your system makes a lot of sense, but there's one thing I have to ask if I'm to work here."

"What is it, Mr. Lepke?"

"I don't ever pick up 'special' money, pass it out, or get any in my pay packet. Is that too much to ask?"

"God, the boys are just going to *love* you! No, that's not too much to ask. Now, there's just one more understanding we need to discuss.

"Mayor Valentine isn't part of this arrangement. I'd be surprised if he didn't know about it, but he's never mentioned it to me nor I to him. So I hope it doesn't go against your grain to not bring the subject up in his presence."

"I don't think I ever met the man. I don't see a problem here."

"When can you start?"

"Anytime. But I have to be free to testify on the Krause work, and tie up any loose ends that are left over."

"That suits me, mister. As far as I'm concerned you're on the force as of tomorrow morning. I want to tell you up front this community needs you. The job you've done on Krause is just beautiful. We can hardly wait until it's all wrapped up and they hang that son-of-a-bitch."

THE ALASKA DAILY EMPIRE
Juneau, Alaska, Saturday January 15, 1916

Violation of Submarine Law Threatened By Germany

GERMANY PLANNING REPRISALS

FIFTY OF CREW THOUGHT TO BE LOST AT SEA

ROOSEVELT REDUCED ARMY 11,560 MEN

PEACE WORK TO WAIT ON FORD

EXPLOSION WRECKS SUB AND KILLS 3

U. S. CITIZENS QUIT MEXICO

BILLY SUNDAY INVITED TO VISIT JUNEAU

VON PAPEN ROASTED PRESIDENT

WASHINGTON, Jan. 15— Letters found in Captain Franz von Papen's effects and seized by British naval officers Thursday at Falmouth, while von Papen was proceeding home, reveal ugly reference to and criticism of President Wilson and his administration.

The disclosures involve several German consuls in the United States, some of whom may be required to hit the trail for home, as a result.

The state department this morning received cabled copies of the correspondence taken from the recalled German military attaché. Entries in von Papen's notes reveal that he paid money to persons now charged with conspiracy to dynamite munitions plants and cripple shipping in the United States. One notation showed the payment of $500 to the German counsel at Seattle just prior to the dynamite explosion there.

Ambassador von Bernstorff disclaimed any knowledge of von Papen's alleged acts in connection with the dynamite plot.

52 —Juneau City, A.T., January 15, 1916—
Saturday noon

"Are you Pete Sommers?"

He pushed himself away from the bar and looked around at the man standing behind him.

"Who wants to know?" he asked gruffly.

"I got a telegram for Pete Sommers. The bartender says that's you."

"Oh. That's different. Yeah, I'm Pete Sommers."

"Do you want me to read it to you?"

"No. I can read. Thanks anyway." He grabbed the envelope out of the man's hand.

The messenger stood there expectantly for a moment as Sommers tore open the envelope and unfolded the message sheet. With an audible sigh the man turned and walked out of the Louve.

Sommers reread the message to make sure he had missed nothing.

DEPARTING PETERSBURG 10AM ABD SOPHIA STOP MEET BOAT 8PM STOP PREPARE JOB STOP POWELL

"Finally!" he muttered to himself. Now he had to find the Englishman.

He left the bar and made his way to the Grand Hotel. As he walked in, the desk clerk looked up from a magazine.

"May I help you, sir?"

"Is Mr. Williams in?"

"Yes, sir. Room nineteen."

"Yeah, I know." He walked up the carpeted stairway and knocked softly on the door.

"Who's there?" came softly through the wood.

"Pete Sommers."

The door swung open to reveal Williams with a pistol in his hand.

"Come in."

Sommers felt his throat constrict when he saw the weapon.

"Pretty fancy gun y'got there. Can I have a look at it?"

"No. What do you want?"

"My boys will be in on the *Sophia* tonight. They want to get the job done on the detective first thing Monday."

"Excellent. Once we have Mr. Lepke out of the way perhaps we can get to work on our real task."

"You mean the mines?" Sommers asked.

"Of course, I mean the mines. Did you think it was whiskey talking?"

"Well, of course not!" Actually he had. The thought of sabotaging all the big mines in the Gold Belt frightened him. It would be very dangerous and it wouldn't make him wealthy if he succeeded.

"Why don't we rob a bank or two at the same time?" he asked hopefully.

"We don't need money, Mr. Sommers. We're anarchists, remember?"

"But how will we get away?"

Williams' blues eyes chilled to ice. "We'll steal a boat or take passage on a steamer. That's not our primary worry at this moment."

"Look, you and me might be real anarchists, but the boys ain't. They're gonna want money in advance for this." Sommers chewed his lower lip.

Williams laid the pistol down on the bureau, reached into his pocket and held his hand out to Sommers.

"Give each of them one of these. There's more where that came from."

Sommers stared down at the two heavy gold coins in his hand.

"What the hell are those?"

"Sovereigns. They're each worth a British pound, which is equal to about four American dollars."

"They ain't gonna kill anybody for four bucks each, I'll tell you that right now."

"Perhaps you will convince them our cause is just. And they will each receive four more when the job is finished."

"Uh, what about me? Don't I get anything for putting all this together?"

Williams flipped a coin into the air it glittered as it arced down to Sommers' hand.

"Same wage, same deal. But I'll give you an extra coin on one stipulation."

"What's that?"

"You help kill Lepke."

"Well, hell. Of course I'll help! I wouldn't miss putting that copper away for anything."

Williams flipped a fourth coin high in the air. Sommers caught it. "See that you don't miss. We have a lot to do, and perhaps very quickly."

"What do you mean?"

"If America gets into the war in Europe, we must be ready to destroy the mines."

"What's the war got to do with anything?"

Williams pursed his lips for a moment, his eyes narrowed slightly.

"It's all part of the big picture. We'll discuss it at length later. Now let's talk about the plan to kill the detective."

"Sure. How do you think we should do it? I thought we might break into his room and gun him down."

"No. That would guarantee witnesses; we don't want that. What you'll do is ambush him."

"There's too many people on the streets to do that. We can't take the chance."

"Not in town. Up on the road to the Perseverance Mine."

"How we gonna get him up there?"

"With this." Williams handed him a sheet of paper.

Sommers read the brief note and grinned. "Yeah, that'll get him where we want him!"

"By the way," Williams said in a lower tone, "who knows about our relationship besides you and Krause?"

"Nobody. Ain't that how you said you wanted it?"

"Oh, assuredly. I just wanted to know if you'd remembered," Williams said blandly. "Well, I know you've got things to do, and so do I." He walked to the door and opened it.

Sommers had no choice but to leave. He had hoped for a drink, but the gold in his pocket promised many drinks. He left with a smile on his face and a wave to his confederate.

Miss Fiona, he thought, it's high time we got together. As he made his way to the Louve he noticed the wind picking up.

Harry stood behind the long mahogany bar. "Hi ya, Pete. What'll it be?"

"Ya know what this is, Harry?" Sommers dropped a sovereign on the damp surface.

Harry caught the coin on the first bounce, peered at it. "Gold. Looks like Latin writing, and some old geezer. Where'd ya get it?"

"Don't matter where. Whattya think it's worth American?" Sommers said cagily.

"It ain't much bigger'n a two-and-a-half piece. I'll go that much."

"Two-and-a-half! That there's a Limey pound, worth four bucks American any day of the week!"

"If you knew what it was worth why'd you ask me?"

"To, uh, see if ya knew," Sommers said with a sniff.

"Yeah, I knew. I even know that's 'sposed to be King George." He dropped the coin and it rang on the bar. "What'll it be?"

"A dollar bottle of whiskey and a pitcher of beer." Sommers moved to the far end of the bar where sliced ham, roast beef and turkey lay on a tray. Bread, three kinds of mustard, butter and a pot of sauerkraut rounded off the free lunch.

"Hey, Harry, where's the horseradish?" he yelled as he piled a plate high with slabs of meat.

"Probably on one of the tables. Just look around. Where y'gonna sit?"

Sommers plopped down in a chair. "Right here. Let me know when it's almost eight, okay?"

"Sure, Pete. I'll tell Benny when he comes on at six."

Peter Sommers stuffed food into his mouth and washed it down with whiskey. This was the life! After he finished eating he ordered another pitcher of beer and thought about the good times to come after the detective was dead and Ed was out of jail.

He drank steadily as the day wore on. The patrons in the bar ebbed and flowed around him. Thoughts of Fiona Malone swirled through his mind and he was brooding about her indifference when Benny came over to his table.

"Gimme 'nother bottle," Sommers said.

"It's ten minutes to eight, Pete. You still want another bottle?"

Sommers thought hard. Why was eight important? He jammed his hand into his pocket to get the money for another bottle. He'd figure it out while he drank. "Here. 'Nother bottle." He pushed the paper across the table.

"Pete, this ain't money. It's a telegram."

That was it! He pushed back from the table. The abrupt motion caused his head to swim.

"Hey, Pete. This telegram says to meet the *Sophia* at eight. You'd better get going."

"Yeah," he agreed. He stood up and staggered past Benny. The bartender stuck the telegram into Sommers' shirt pocket as he passed.

"Walk careful now, 'cause that's a slippery street out there."

The cold air cleared his head. As he turned south down the frosty boardwalk, wind boiled down the street and numbed him to the bone.

"Shit!" he gasped. "'Nother goddamn Taku buildin' up!" He lowered his head into the wind and moved as fast as he could toward the P&O dock.

A boat whistle pierced the night sky, riding on the wickedly fierce wind. The *SS Sophia* edged up to the icy pier and lines sailed from her to the heavily dressed longshoremen as Sommers scuttled up. Snow whipped past the streetlights and the wind howling around the electric wires created an eerie keening.

He leaned up against a dray horse that kept trying to turn away from the wind. The gangplank swung up and cursing men fastened it to the boat with frigid linchpins. Bundled figures trudged down the plank with the wind at their backs hurrying toward town.

Two hesitated at the bottom of the gangplank. Sommers hurried out and peered at them.

"It's us, you stupid bastard! Now git us to a bar!" Powell bellowed over the wind.

The closest place was Armstrong's. As they hurried past the Division Hotel, Sommers tried to see through the frosted windows hoping to catch a glimpse of Fiona. The thought of her boiled in his brain and filled his groin.

They pushed into Armstrong's and crowded around the glowing coal stove.

"Jeezus, but she's cold out tanight!" Horace Powell exclaimed. He was a medium-to-skinny man sporting premature gray hair and matted beard. His breath smelled rank due to numerous rotten teeth that pained him constantly.

"Yah, dot she is," Bjorn Halvstaad agreed. "We by Gott better make gute wages on dis trip." The tall, sturdy Norwegian was a crack shot and cool-headed felon who would do anything for money. Both men lacked a sense of humor when it came to gold.

Sommers carefully felt around in his pockets. Thank goodness, there were three of the coins left. "Well, this is just a start, boys," he said grandly, dropping a sovereign in each man's hand.

"Whut the hell are these?" Powell asked, squinting at the gold.

Sommers told them. "You each get four more when the detective is taken care of," he added softly. "'N' here's how we're gonna go do it . . ." He outlined the plan swiftly.

"Who's payin' in Limey gold?" Powell rasped.

"Don't matter!" Halvstaad boomed. "Where's 'd' whiskey?"

"Yer treatin', ain'tcha?" Powell asked Sommers.

"Let's flip for it."

"Yah, dot's fair," Halvstaad said.

"Okay," Powell said. "Odd man out."

Sommers lost and bought the first round. His daylong intake of spirits had been numbed by the cold and the exertion of finding his friends. The glass of whiskey hit him like lightning. He instantly became drunk again.

"Jeezus, but yer a cheap date tanight!" Powell laughed.

"Yeah, 'n' I got a date, too," Sommers said solemnly. "Pretties' girl y' ever saw."

"Shit, Pete, yer not talkin' ta some rubes from the states here. We knows what kinda girls ya hang out with. Swedish steam baths, just like the rest of us."

"I'll show ya. I'm gonna go get 'er, righ' now! Bring 'er back 'n' innerduce ya!" Sommers spoke with all the dignity he could muster before staggering out the door without looking back.

Powell and Halvstaad laughed.

53 —Juneau City, A.T., January 15, 1916—
Saturday night

"Fiona, I'll be in my room if you need me," Amanda called to her friend.

Fiona looked up from her ciphers, smiled and waved. Amanda went up the stairs. Even this far into the building she could hear the Taku wind moaning around the walls.

The wind had come up an hour ago and relentlessly climbed in velocity to where it now keened. Before this Amanda hadn't realized how homey and comfortable the constant rumble of the crushers were. The howling wind pushed all other sounds before it.

She went into her room and closed the door. The curtain over her window billowed fitfully. A close check revealed the window shut as securely as possible —the wind came in through the minute cracks in the walls where the boards fit together.

"My God," she muttered to herself. "This is unbelievable."

She looked out the window. Gale driven white caps on Gastineau Channel threatened life and limb. Great clouds of spray cascaded over town. The ferryboats usually plying ceaselessly between Douglas Island and the mainland had disappeared into safe harbor.

Waves smashed at the boats tied to the docks stretching southward down the shoreline outside her window. Masts semaphored icy unrest, jerking back and forth in mad patterns as boats tied side-by-side scraped and crunched against each other and the wharves. The docks lay devoid of life as snow-laced spume whipped across the open planking, hitting the buildings with the force of sand.

A blast of wind stronger than its predecessors pressed against her window, causing the glass to bow slightly inward. Her imagination allowed it to burst in on her, and she winced at the phantom cuts and slices from shards. *I'd probably be blinded at the very least,* she thought.

One snowy-decked fishing boat rocked in wider arcs than its mates. The lines hadn't been snugged up as much as they should have been. Suddenly the spring line holding it to the dock parted with a crack like a pistol shot. The wind caught the boat, pushing it rapidly across the small dark lead of open water to the next dock.

She held her breath as the boat crunched into another vessel tied just below her window. The weather ground the boats together, like a spoiled child wrecking toys. Waves slapped both craft back and forth, adding to the destruction. As she watched, water crept across the snow-covered deck of each boat, bubbling up through mutually inflicted damage.

"Oh, no," she shouted, running to the door. She had to tell someone. Perhaps something could be done.

She hurried down the steps, her mind sorting out the words she needed to shout to Fiona. At the landing where the stairway turned, she slowed and saw her friend. At first her brain didn't register the sight of Fiona falling heavily to the floor, blood streaking from her nose.

For one long, erroneous moment, Amanda thought the boats had broken through the lower level of the building and hit Fiona. Then a hand shot down, grabbing the bodice of the fallen woman's dress, and ripped it loose. Fiona's right breast lay fully exposed.

Then two hands reached down and began fondling the exposed skin. Amanda could clearly hear a deep masculine panting overlaying the weak, nearly unconscious female moans.

Amanda's blood turned to ice as her mind burst with hate. Her feet carried her swiftly down the last steps and across the room to where Pete Sommers ripped at Fiona's skirt. Without even being aware of the act, Amanda whipped out the five-inch stiletto she always kept strapped to her leg; the same knife that had threatened Georg so long ago.

Just as she reached the animal, he sensed her presence and looked up. His besotted face leered bestial, his mouth salivating under wild eyes opened far enough to show white completely around the iris. The air snorting from his nostrils reeked heavily of alcohol.

She thrust the blade deep into his chest, sliding easily, like stabbing ice cream.

His eyes suddenly focused on her. "My God, woman, what have you done?" he said in a shocked tone.

"What was needed!" She spat on him while pulling the knife free.

Sommers clutched his chest, moaned, and lurched toward the door.

Amanda threw the knife behind her and bent over Fiona. "Why didn't you call me?" she asked. Tears blurred her vision.

"I . . . tried," Fiona said weakly. "H-he, hit me . . ."

"It's over now. Don't talk. We'll get some help." She lightly ran her hand over the purpling bruise on Fiona's left cheek. The eye had already swollen shut.

Wind howled through the foyer tugging at their clothing, the pages of Fiona's ledger flapped madly. Amanda looked up. The door stood open, Sommers was gone.

Suddenly a form lurched through the door, pushing it shut, and then stood there staring at them. Amanda's heart jumped. She'd just stabbed Sommers, had he come back to die in the lobby?

"What happened here?" Jack Malone howled. He rushed across the room and knelt next to his daughter. "Is, is she . . . ?"

"He only hit her. I came down just in time," Amanda said, suddenly wondering if she needed to explain the bloody knife behind her.

"Who?" Jack asked with a voice like thunder. His head snapped up and his burning eyes transfixed her.

She realized he had been drinking, and probably hadn't seen anything other than his daughter's injuries.

"Pete Sommers," she snapped. "He left just before you came in."

"Armstrong's! I just saw him go into Armstrong's."

"Under the counter, the shotgun . . ." Amanda urged.

Jack scrambled over to the desk and swept the weapon out into his hands. He bolted through the door, leaving it wildly swinging in the moaning wind.

Amanda hurriedly put the knife back in its sheath, then gathered Fiona into her arms and carried her into the back room. Out in the lobby, the door slammed shut and rapid footsteps hurried toward them.

"Hello? Is anybody here?" August Lepke shouted.

Amanda rushed to the door. "August! Sommers tried to rape Fiona!"

"My God," he said in a pained tone. "Is she," he paused for breath, "hurt?"

"I stopped him," Amanda said in a rush. "She's been punched around, but she'll be okay. Jack Malone just went after Sommers with a shotgun; he says he's in Armstrong's."

August left at a dead run.

54 —Juneau City, A.T., January 15, 1916—
Saturday night

Begay Santo decided to have just one beer and then he would go visit Ruth whether her family liked it or not. The criticism they received from both her family and the Filipino community astounded him. It seemed so unfair.

Why couldn't they leave them alone? He was twenty years old, Ruth was nineteen; they were both adults no matter how one looked at it. Each had been told they were bringing shame to their cultures by planning to marry the other.

Something had to change, and soon. It took all of his self-control to endure the rudeness he encountered at the Kisadis house. Jim was the worst with his continuous cant about tradition, ravens and eagles. Hard to believe he was the same man who had introduced Begay to his sister.

A man crashed through the door of the bar, holding his hands tight over his chest. He stumbled toward Begay at the back of the room and flopped into the chair on the other side of his table. Someone behind him said, "Sommers?" When Begay looked around none of the other men in the bar looked in his direction.

The man's eyes were wide and staring, his lips pulled back in a caricature of a grin. Through his heavy and labored breathing a slight froth of blood bubbled at the corner of his mouth. One hand fell away from his chest. Begay saw blood on the palm.

"Hey, are you okay, mister?" he asked. The man ignored him, staring back toward the door.

Suddenly a wild-looking man, hatless in a flapping coat, crashed through the door swinging a shotgun in a wide swath.

"Where is that sonuvabitch?" he roared. "I'm goin' ta kill the filthy pig!"

The room went completely still except for the wind whining through the open door. A dollar bill blew off the bar but nobody moved to retrieve it. About three-dozen men stood frozen, staring at him with thunder-struck expressions. Begay realized the man sought his new table partner.

"Wh-who ya looking fer, Jack?" John the bartender asked in a strangled whisper.

"Peter God-damned-to-hell Sommers! Where is the bastard?"

John pointed across the room to the table where Begay sat. "He, he just came in and sat down . . ."

Jack swung around. Men scattered out if the way of the double muzzles. Begay stumbled backward and his chair fell over. He rolled on the sawdust floor before regaining his feet to join the mass of men on the other side of the room. Nobody laughed at his clumsiness.

The man, Pete Sommers, sat leaning back in his chair, seemingly grinning, staring right at Jack. He didn't even blink. Begay was sure he was already dead, for he could detect no breathing motion in the chest. Just moments before the man had wheezed laboriously.

Jack held the shotgun at waist level and grated out, "Burn in hell!" Then he pulled both triggers.

Sommers' face and chest erupted in gore and his body flew back, smashing against the wall and sliding down into the shadows.

A man standing next to Begay vomited on the floor. They all stared at Jack, wondering if his mind had snapped and if he was going to kill more men. Begay thought the shotgun empty, but he wasn't about to inspect it at this point.

A well-dressed man quietly walked through the door, one hand in his pocket. He hesitated long enough to survey the scene before stepping over to the gunman.

"Mr. Malone, please give me the weapon," he said in a calm voice.

Every man in the room held his breath as Jack's hand tightened on the shotgun before turning and looking at the newcomer.

"Mr. Malone, you need to give me the gun right now." The man's voice was matter-of-fact. "Enough has happened here."

"He hurt my baby," Jack growled. "I'd kill him twice for that."

"Fiona is going to be fine, Mr. Malone, I just left the hotel. Now give me the gun. We have to go down to the station." Begay finally recognized Detective Lepke.

Jack looked into the shadowed corner again and visibly wilted. His head dropped and he stared down at the shotgun.

"Okay. Here." With shaking hands he pushed the gun into Lepke's hands. "Ben Tinsley is really gonna get a kick out o' this," Jack said as the two men walked toward the door. "He told me once if he'd been around when I first hit town, he'd 'a given me a blue ticket."

"Did you wound him before you came in the door, Mr. Malone?"

"No. He got here ahead of me. I shot him where he sat, grinnin' at me like it was the finest day of his life."

Lepke turned to one of the two policemen who'd arrived. "Corporal Harrington, get these men out of here and close the place immediately. Don't let anybody walk on this side of the room or remove anything. Okay?"

"Sure thing, detective."

Jack stared at the man in disbelief. "You're even givin' our boys orders now, are ye? You've got a lot of brass fer a Pink."

"I'm not a Pinkerton operative any more, Mr. Malone. Now I'm on the Juneau Police Department."

Then they went out into the fiercely blowing wind.

"Okay, everybody outta here, now," the corporal said. The men quickly grabbed hats and coats and rushed through the door. Begay approached the officer.

"Excuse me, Corporal?"

"Whattya want, sonny?" The man didn't even look at him; he stared at the body in the corner.

"That man was bleeding before," Begay said nervously.

"Yeah? Well it sure don't matter now, does it?"

"No. You misunderstand. The man was hurt before being shot."

"So what? He's dead now, ain't he?"

The man was so dense!

"He was dead *before* he got shot!" Begay yelled.

Finally the corporal looked at him. His face took on a professional sneer and he spoke through one side of his mouth.

"Git outta here before I run ya in!"

55 —Juneau City, A.T., January 16, 1916—
Sunday morning

"What did you say that made him stop?" Lepke asked.

"I, I threatened him with the shotgun," Amanda said. "Mr. Lepke, it's almost two o'clock of the morning, could we talk about this some other time?"

"We're almost finished. Where did you put the shotgun after Sommers ran out the door?"

"Oh, on the counter, I suppose. What difference does it make?"

"After you threatened Sommers with the shotgun, he ran out of the door. Then you turned around and put the shotgun on the counter before going to aid Fiona. Is that correct?"

Amanda shook her head and ran both hands through her hair. A tear escaped from the corner of one eye.

"I don't know! I was worried about Fiona. I wanted that animal to get away from her. I'm not sure what I did, August. She's going to be fine, not even a scar, so what does it matter?"

"It matters to her father. Jack Malone is charged with first-degree murder. If he's convicted, he could hang," Lepke said, closely watching her eyes.

"Hang, for killing that filthy beast? The man attacked his daughter, for Christ's sake! What's he supposed to do, give him a blessing?"

"He murdered a man in cold blood. The attack was over. Fiona was in no further danger at the moment Jack shot Sommers with both barrels."

"Please," she paled slightly, "must you be quite so graphic?"

"Miss Ganbor, I want you to think over what happened in here tonight, ah, last night. I want you to think it over very carefully because we're going to talk a lot about this before done with it we are. *Do* you understand what I'm saying?"

"Yes, August," she said looking into his eyes. "I understand completely."

"Are you staying with Fiona tonight?"

"Yes, Maye and I are going to take turns watching her. First I must get some sleep." She turned away from him. "Good night, August."

"Good night, Amanda."

She hurried up the stairs. His mind immediately went back to the tavern. There was something he had seen that didn't—

"Who the *hell* do you think you are?" Florence screamed as she came through the door. "Arresting my poor father like a common criminal just because he fought off that deranged trash?" She stopped in front of him, staring with wild eyes.

"Florence! How did you find out already?" he said bewilderedly.

"Oh, I have *some* friends in this town. But I guess none of them are on the police force!"

He wondered if she knew she was crying.

"Florence, your father shot an unarmed man to death last night. I *had* to take him in. It's my job."

"But he was only protecting Fio! Isn't that legal?"

"I don't know what you've heard. But Jack got here after Sommers escaped. Jack chased him to Armstrong's Tavern and shot him."

"Don't you mean 'executed' him?"

"Okay, call it what you will. Sommers was supposed to get a trial first."

"He would have been lynched before a trial ever took place," Florence said. "This town wouldn't have waited."

"We'll never know now, will we?"

"August, my father didn't do anything that any other red-blooded man wouldn't have done in his place, and you know it."

"I agree, Florence. Please, try to understand. We have to go through all the formalities no matter what the circumstances. I'm sure your father will be acquitted."

"Acquitted? You mean you're actually going to have him tried in court for this?"

"Hell, I don't know. That's up to the judge to decide at the inquest. I'm just doing my job by making sure all the rules are followed when the law is broken like this."

"They told me you were the arresting officer. Is that true?"

"Yes. I got there first and talked to him and we went down to the station together."

"You *arrested* my father."

"Well, in so many words. Actually I never formally arrested him. However at the station I did have to press charges against him. It's the law that —"

"To *hell* with your law!" she hissed. "And to hell with *you*. He was right. You're a viper I had taken to my, my bosom!"

"Florence, wait a minute!"

"No. I won't wait another second for you, August Lepke. In fact, I never want to see you again!"

Then she disappeared into the howling storm.

56 —Juneau City, A.T., January 17, 1916—
Monday morning

Jack, screaming obscenities, swung the shotgun around, pointed it at Lepke and fired oddly muted, rhythmic blasts. August Lepke jerked in his sleep and snapped out of the dream. Someone knocked on the door.

The dark room seemed to overflow with stifling heat. Still exhausted from his late hours of the day before he felt disoriented and not quite awake. His robe eluded him.

The pounding rose in volume.

Patience snapped. Wearing only his long johns, he went to the door and threw it open.

"What do you want?" he demanded brusquely.

The gangly teen-aged youth jumped in surprise. "Jeeze! You scared the crap outta me, mister."

"Well, you woke me, so we're even," he said in a normal tone. "What do you want?"

"Uh, are you August Lepke?"

"Yes."

"I'm 'sposed to give you this." He handed him an envelope.

"Oh. Thank you." Lepke closed the door and then opened it again. "Wait, don't leave yet!"

The boy had already started down the hallway. He stopped and looked back. "Why?"

"Just, just wait a minute." Even he wondered why he had the boy wait. He ripped open the sealed envelope and studied the laboriously penciled words.

I GOT INFERMASHUN YOU WILL FIND INTRESTIN. COME TO PERSAVERENCE MINE AT 2:30 TODAY. BARNEY SMITH

"The person who gave you this, what did he look like?"

"Old guy, gray beard and rotten teeth, real bad breath. Wore a derby dirtier 'n he was." The boy hesitated.

"Anything else?"

"He said, 'give this to that fuckin' cop. Tell him I can answer all his questions,' and then he gave me a quarter."

"Just a moment," Lepke went back to his bureau, pulled a dollar off the pile of coins, shuffled back to the door and gave it to the boy. "You have a good memory. What's your name?"

"Eddie Weber, Mr. Lepke."

"You're a good man, Eddie. Thank you."

"Thank you, Mr. Lepke."

As he dressed, he wondered what information Barney Smith could possibly have that was worth going all the way out to the Perseverance Mine. "Guess there's only one way to find out," he muttered to himself. He opened the shades and looked out.

The Taku had blown itself out. Smoke from Treadwell and the Alaska-Gastineau Mine down at Thane already stained the blue sky, but the mountains rose majestically from the water still bearing dark green trees and pristine peaks.

"My word. What a beautiful place." He pulled on his coat making sure the revolver rested securely in his pocket. He put on his hat and went down to the lobby.

"Mr. Lepke, did you get rested?" Maye Wattnem asked from behind the front desk.

"Yes, thank you. Is there a motor taxi that runs out to the Perseverance?"

"If the road is clear, Henry Jenkins would probably take you out in his Maxwell. Mark my words, he'll charge you good money for the trip."

"Does he have a telephone?"

"Oh, no. You need to walk down to Second and Seward, to the garage."

"How is Fiona?"

"She's just fine. She'll be back at work on Wednesday, she says."

"Thank you, Maye."

He walked out into the sunshine. His stomach growled and he realized he hadn't eaten for over twelve hours. He decided to make the White Spot his first stop.

While drinking his postprandial cup of coffee, his mind walked back over the events of the past two days. All through the meal he had been acutely aware of Florence's absence. He'd finally realized this cafe was where they had been together the most.

So he concentrated on the work at hand. Parts of the equation of Pete Sommers' last half hour seemed to be missing. Why had the fool accosted Fiona in a public building?

Why had he been bleeding *before* he was shot? Lepke had gone back to the bar and crawled through the sawdust and wood chips on the floor until he found what he searched for—a spot of dried blood on a curled wood shaving. The shaving lay at least ten feet from where Sommers sat down for the last time.

The shotgun blast had been directed away from this spot. But one had to remember this was not a quiet drinking establishment for gentlemen, it was a bar on Lower Front Street. The blood could have come from someone else entirely, and blood was blood; it didn't have fingerprints.

But Lepke distinctly remembered glancing down and seeing that spot of blood as he approached Jack Malone and his shotgun. The spot was fresh at that moment, shining wet and reflecting the electric light hanging from the ceiling, not ten feet away.

Sommers. Everything he knew about the man belied the way he grinned at his killer. Yet thirty-two witnesses claimed Sommers stared at Jack and smiled when he went to hell that night.

They found a gold English sovereign in his pocket, not a coin you saw every day in Alaska. It just didn't fit.

Jenkins Garage and Mechanical Repair sat on the corner in a weathered wooden building. Second Street had been cleaned and narrow tire tracks ran southeast from the closed double doors toward the Last Chance Basin.

Lepke entered through a smaller door built into one of the larger ones. The building smelled of coal dust, axle grease, and the sharp bite of gasoline. Two men strained liquid through a large white cloth.

"I'm looking for Mr. Jenkins," Lepke said.

"You found him," said the younger man. "Be with you in a minute."

Lepke looked around the open space. The building had no internal construction save for the post running from floor to roof in the center of the structure. Three automobiles filled part of the space.

Two sat in various states of repair and disconnectedness. The third looked complete. "Maxwell," painted in white script, ran across the bright green radiator. In one of the front corners of the building a coal bin squatted next to a large pot-bellied stove glowing with internal heat.

"What can I do for ya, mister?" Jenkins regarded him with interest as he scrubbed at his grimy hands with an equally grimy cloth.

"I'd like to hire you to drive me out to the Perseverance mine this afternoon."

"There's a motor taxi that goes out there first thing in the morning."

"I need to go this afternoon."

"Kinda short notice," he said laconically.

"For me, too. Will you do it?"

"I'm Henry Jenkins," he said with a grin and held out his hand.

Lepke took it without a moment's hesitation, shook and said, "Detective August Lepke, Juneau Police Department."

The grin disappeared. "Oh, you're the guy that nabbed Jack Malone."

"Actually I just talked him into walking down to the station with me. About the trip, will you do it?"

"Sure. Let me get something to eat and we'll be on our way."

The Maxwell's grumbling motor slowly gained independence from the racket of the fifty ore crushers after passing the Little Treadwell mine. Lepke felt tired. He longed to sleep, but this fruitless trip gnawed at him.

There had been no Barney Smith at the mine. Someone wanted him out of town for a few hours, why? He could find no reason for this wild goose chase.

The pounding roar began to fade in the distance and Lepke thought about the terrain. Returning from the Perseverance Mine, Silver Bow Basin Road wound across the Last Chance Basin and over Gold Creek just before the spot where the water carved down into the rock as it dropped toward sea level.

The road did not drop with the creek. It continued through the narrowing basin until it crossed a long bridge hugging the side of Mt. Roberts, curving around its granite flank, now hundreds of feet above the racing creek water. At that point all of Juneau came into view and the road angled steeply down into town.

Up this stream Harris and Juneau had followed a Tlingit guide to "discover" gold back in 1880, which put the town on the map. When Perseverance built the narrow road, they didn't bother with niceties like guardrails.

Lepke was glad he had paid attention on the way up to the mine since with darkness falling he wasn't going to see much on the way back. Trees on the slopes of Mt. Juneau became silhouettes against a darkening sky across the narrow valley. His mind idled; he wished it were possible to take a nap in the wildly bucking automobile.

The Maxwell's windshield suddenly shattered, the glass blew forward across the hood as the lightning-crack of a shot shattered the silence.

"What the hell?" Jenkins howled, twisting around to look behind them.

Lepke dropped to the floor between the seats, the .455 Bulldog in hand. Quickly he checked the loads, and then peered back down the rutted road.

Since their departure from the Perseverance, the afternoon light had faded quickly. Heavy dusk neared complete darkness. He couldn't see anything.

Jenkins kept the motorcar moving, but continued to glance over his shoulder.

"You watch the road in front of us, and I'll watch the road in back of us.

Agreed?" Lepke said tersely.

"Just as long as you watch real *good!*" Jenkins said forcefully.

Another motorcar followed them, its weak lamps glowing in the darkness like feral eyes. It was too far behind them to accurately hit with revolver fire. Maybe they could outrun it.

There was a flash from the rear motorcar; someone ripped a sheet in half over their heads. The boom of the rifle followed the round and echoed off into the hills.

"Gawddammit!" screamed Jenkins. "That was too damn close! Shoot back, man!"

"I can't hit them at this distance. How far are we from town?"

"Just under a mile, the plank bridge around the shoulder of Roberts is just ahead."

"Just as you get to it, pull up against the face of the rock and stop."

"Are you crazy, Mister Detective?"

"Stop shouting, I can hear you perfectly. No, I'm not crazy. If we don't get them here, they'll get us before we get to town."

Jenkins thought about that.

Another bullet whined past their heads. Abruptly Jenkins pulled up against the wall and put the engine in neutral.

"Put out the headlamps!" Lepke urged.

With the lamps out, they became part of the cliff face. Dust and grime coated the snow at road's edge. But Lepke could easily distinguish where the road ended, and a hundred feet of space began. Gold Creek murmured at the bottom.

"Turn off the motor."

"That's easy for *you* to say. You don't have to crank-start the God-damned thing!" Jenkins complained.

"Then leave it on and get shot."

The motor coughed and died.

He could hear them coming fast. They wanted to hurry and get around the curve. Then they could fire at the Maxwell as it geared down for the steep descent into Juneau City—or else they'd witness the wreck of a careening vehicle.

Sweat coated Lepke's palm. He worried the revolver would slip from his hand and be lost in the darkness. He tightened his grip.

The auto came sputtering and banging down the road and was upon them.

Just as the weak light approached, Lepke stepped out and fired twice at the driver. The rifleman sitting in the passenger seat jumped at the shots and tried to bring his weapon to bear.

Two things happened at the same time—the driver screamed and jerked with the impact of the bullets, still clutching the steering wheel—and Lepke shot the gunman twice.

The automobile veered sharply to the right, scattering gravel off the edge of the plank bridge as it disappeared into space.

For a long moment silence reigned. Then a crash, a faint afterthought of a noise compared to the shooting, echoed back up Gold Creek.

"Sounded just like a rock slide," Jenkins said wonderingly.

"I wonder who they were?" Lepke said.

"Well, you can find out in the morning. They sure as hell ain't goin' anywhere tonight."

57 —Juneau City, A.T., January 18, 1916—
Tuesday afternoon

Arnold Williams stepped out of the Grand Hotel and bumped into August Lepke. For an instant, Williams thought he beheld a ghost. The two thugs from Petersburg had left yesterday with boasts of how easy it would be to kill the detective, and yet here he stood.

"L-Lepke?"

"Mr. Williams, would you please come down to the station with me to answer some questions?"

"Station? What do you mean?"

"The police station, sir. Would you come along now?"

"Certainly." He fell into step along side Lepke as they walked down the frosty boardwalk.

The sun barely touched the peaks on Douglas Island and darkness would fall soon. The sky overhead remained a cold, bright blue. As the sun faded, the chill in the air intensified.

"Can you tell me what this is all about, old chap?"

"There's the station," Lepke replied. "Why don't we go on in first?"

"Very well," Williams said coolly. He didn't like this turn of events. How had they connected any of the others to him?

The desk sergeant looked up when they entered. "Good afternoon, Mr. Lepke."

"Good afternoon, Sergeant. We'll be back in the office."

The sergeant nodded and Lepke led the way through a door into a hall. He opened another door and stood back. "Right in here, Mr. Williams."

They entered a small office. A man sat off to one side at a small desk. Two chairs flanked a small table in the middle of the room. The day faded outside the barred window. The man switched on the overhead light.

"This is Mr. Morton. He is going to make a transcription of what is said in this room," Lepke said. Mr. Morton nodded but remained silent.

"Am I being charged with a crime?" Morton began scratching softly on his legal pad with a pencil.

"No. We are trying to shed light on events leading up to a series of shootings that have taken place over the past few weeks. We think you might have some information that could help us."

"I assure you, sir, that if I had information I thought pertinent to your community's well-being, I would volunteer it immediately!" Williams put as much muted outrage into his voice as he dared.

"Of course you would, Mr. Williams, but you may not realize you possess facts which might be relevant," Lepke said smoothly.

"Oh, I see." Williams realized there was no way out of this without incriminating himself. He sat down and crossed his legs. "Very well, carry on."

Lepke removed his hat and coat, pulled out a small leather notebook and sat down across from Williams.

"Do you know Silas Mason, Ralph Wikke, Robert Bennett, Peter Sommers, Horace Powell, or Bjorn Halvstaad?"

"Well, I knew the late Mr. Sommers, but none of the other names sound familiar. Who are they?"

"With the exception of Ralph Wikke who is in federal jail, they are all dead men. All died within the last month, and all died violently."

"I see," Williams kept his tone neutral.

"What was your relationship with Mr. Sommers?" Lepke asked, staring across at him.

Williams felt his heartbeat increase slightly. He willed it to slow, forced himself to be calm. "Mr. Sommers and I enjoyed playing poker with each other."

"You have also been seen on two occasions with him in public eating establishments," Lepke said flatly.

"Is that a question?" Williams asked blandly.

"As you didn't appear to be playing poker at the time, the facts suggest that perhaps your relationship covered more than games of chance."

"No," Williams smiled, "I assure you, it only covered games of chance. We did have Christmas breakfast together, and I believe, lunch at one other point. So what? Is it a crime to sup with acquaintances?"

"Of course not. What did you and Mr. Sommers speak about at these meals?"

"Oh, the war in Europe. Politics. Good food."

"What about the war in Europe? Which side did Mr. Sommers favor?"

"The Allies, of course. As do I."

"I see. What politics did Mr. Sommers espouse?"

Williams hesitated. He had heard Sommers blowing off his mouth about anarchy and his law of the jungle nonsense. If he had heard it, so had others.

"Well, actually he claimed to be a bit of an anarchist. Rather boring about it, in fact."

"Are you an anarchist, Mr. Williams?"

"Heavens, no! I'm a royalist first, last, and always," he said with a forced chuckle.

"What do you do for a living, Mr. Williams?"

"I'm a journalist for the *Times*."

"The *London Times*?" Lepke asked carefully.

"Yes, of course."

Lepke opened a small drawer and lifted out a piece of paper. Williams could see it was a cablegram. Lepke pushed it across the table to him.

"We received this in response to an inquiry about your background," Lepke said calmly.

Williams felt his heart slow. He forced himself to read the words.

LONDON, JANUARY 12, 1916

NO PERSON BY NAME OF ARNOLD WILLIAMS IS NOW OR HAS EVER BEEN ON STAFF OF LONDON TIMES STOP PHYSICAL DESCRIPTION OF SUBJECT DOES NOT MATCH THAT OF ANY PERSON CHARGED ON CRIMINAL WARRANTS AT THIS TIME STOP SCOTLAND YARD

He felt sweat break out on his brow. He cursed himself inwardly for not considering the possibility of this step. They must be suspicious of him or they wouldn't have bothered with the inquiry.

He looked up at Lepke and smiled. "So, you've discovered my little secret."

"What little secret is that, Mr. Williams? That you're a liar?"

"Come now, old man! That's a bit strong isn't it? You see, I *want* to be a journalist and work for the *Times*. So I am researching a story that will make them sit up and take notice of my skills, as it were." His heart raced now, and he knew he was visibly agitated.

"So you told everyone you already were a journalist in order to get the information you needed to write the story."

"Exactly!" Williams said, relief surging through him.

"Would you please put the contents of your pockets on the table?" Lepke asked.

"What for?"

"It would be best if you cooperated, Mr. Williams."

Morton scratched away on his notepad, occasionally glancing up from his work.

Williams stood and emptied his pockets on the desk.

Lepke pushed the items around with a pencil and listed them aloud for Morton's benefit. "Hotel key from the Grand, ticket stub from a production at the Orpheum, pocket knife of, ah, German manufacture, nine pennies, three nickels, two dimes, three quarters, and a gold two-and-a-half dollar piece in U. S. coin. Three other coins, gold, British." He looked up at Williams. "What kind of coins are these?"

"British sovereigns, my good man."

"You know, until the other day, I had never seen one of these," Lepke commented.

Williams suddenly realized how they had connected the other men to him. "Oh?"

"Yes, we found one on Peter Sommers' body. Any idea how he obtained it?"

"From me," Williams said, returning the detective's gaze. "I lost it in a game of cards. Are you sure he didn't have more than one? I had a bad run of luck last week."

"Perhaps that explains why we found them on the bodies of Powell and Halvstaad also," Lepke said dryly.

"Maybe Pete was unlucky at cards too," Williams said, trying to keep his smile lean.

"So where do you get your money if you're not really employed by the *London Times?*"

"I'm afraid I must admit to being a remittance man, old boy. My father can't abide the thought of me, let alone my presence."

"Do you still plan to impress the *Times* with your writing ability?"

"Of course. Just a matter of time, that's all."

"Would you mind," Lepke said slowly, "showing me your manuscript?"

"Well..." Williams was tiring of this oaf. Why should he have to prove anything? They had absolutely no proof to implicate him in their investigations. "I'm afraid not, old boy."

"Why, Mr. Williams?"

"Because, Mr. Lepke, it's all right here," he tapped his forehead with an index finger, "and has yet to be committed to paper."

Lepke leaned back in his chair and smiled at him. "You're very good, Mr. Williams. Very quick on your mental feet. What were you doing in Mexico?"

"Traveling," he said neutrally. *This is it,* he thought. *He knows about Mexico and he's just been baiting me!*

"Thank you for your time, Mr. Williams. You've been most helpful."

Morton rose and left the room with Lepke. Williams sat and stared at the contents of his pockets, aware of the German watch ticking in his waistcoat pocket, and wondering if they really had finished with him.

No, he decided, *not until one of us is dead.*

58 —Juneau City, A.T., January 24, 1916—
Tuesday morning

"He smelled of alcohol when he came into the lobby," Fiona testified. "He told me I had to go meet some of his friends right then. I said I had to finish my shift before I could call my time my own, but I wasn't going anywhere with him that night or any other."

She stopped talking and rubbed the slight faded bruise on her cheek. She looked up at the judge, who smiled sympathetically. She smiled back, and continued.

"He became abusive, started shouting I thought I was too good for him and I had led him to think that I, I would 'be his girl' while he was in Juneau." She wiped away a sudden tear. "I never led that man on. I was nice to him only because he was a guest of the Division Hotel."

"Was there anyone else in the lobby at the time, Miss Malone?" Judge Jennings asked.

"No, your honor. Amanda, Miss Ganbor, had been down earlier. I think she would have heard the noise if the Taku wind hadn't been blowing."

"I see," said the judge. "Please tell us what happened then."

"Well, he grabbed me by the arms and pulled me across the top of the front desk. He squeezed my arms very hard. It hurt a great deal, and I became very frightened." She swallowed with the intensity of the memory.

"Yes?" the judge said.

"I, I started to scream then, because I thought he was going to kill me. Then he hit me in the face and something clicked in the back of my head and everything went dark. When I opened my eyes again, Amanda was kneeling over me and bathing my face with water."

"Was anyone else in the lobby with Miss Ganbor?"

"Yes, Maye Wattnem was there also."

"But there was no sign of Mr. Sommers'?"

She shuddered. "No, your honor."

"Thank you, Miss Malone. You may step down."

Fiona walked over and sat down next to her father and sister. Jack looked worried. Florence was glacial. Jack patted her hand.

"You did jest fine, darlin'. Everything will be just skookum, ye'll see."

Florence ignored her and stared at the bailiff.

Amanda Ganbor was called to the witness box.

"State your name for the court."

"I am Amanda Beckwourth Landes Ganbor, Your Honor." She was beautiful, Fiona thought. Amanda's dress color matched her eyes and her hair could be used as a model for an advertisement. She didn't appear bruised or frightened.

"Would you please tell the court what you saw on the night in question?"

"Yes." She told of the boats and the wind, and running to tell someone of the wreck. She stopped talking and looked around the courtroom for a moment. Fiona thought she was looking at August Lepke when she continued.

"I saw Fiona fall to the floor like a sack of oats and just lay there. Her face was discolored over one cheek, and blood ran from her nose. When she fell I stopped moving, just stunned or something I suppose, so I started to move on down the steps. Then I saw this hand reach down and tear open her bodice."

Fiona heard sharp intakes of breath in the courtroom behind her, but she didn't turn. She kept her eyes on Amanda, her savior.

"Then I knew who it was and I raced down the steps. Just as I got into the lobby, he was taking liberties with Miss Malone's exposed state. I raced behind the counter and grabbed the shotgun that is always there."

"You had seen the weapon before this, Miss Ganbor?" the judge asked.

"Yes, your honor, I had. I told Sommers to get out or I would kill him on the spot. Then he ran out the door and I never saw him again."

"What happened then?"

"I tried to help Fiona. Then her father came in and saw us. He, he became very excited and angry."

"How soon after Sommers departure was this?"

"Mere moments. I told him she would be fine and Sommers was the guilty one. He jumped up and said something about seeing Sommers go into one of the pubs. Then he grabbed the shotgun off the desk and ran out the door. Directly after he left, August Lepke came in and I told him Jack had gone to Armstrong's with a shotgun after Sommers."

"Did you point out the weapon to Mr. Malone?"

"I can't honestly say if I did or not, your honor. I was quite beside myself."

"Thank you, Miss Ganbor. That will be all for now. Please keep yourself available in the event we need to clarify any points."

Amanda smiled at Fiona as she passed.

August Lepke took the stand.

Fiona sneaked a glance at Florence. Her sister's eyes focused on August, but her face remained totally devoid of expression. Fiona again felt the familiar sinking sensation in her stomach.

Somehow this was all her fault. She felt certain of that. Her whole family had been hurt by this awful thing. Her poor father could go to prison or the gallows, and her sister had rejected the only man she had ever loved because he had performed his duty.

August continued his testimony.

"When I entered Armstrong's Tavern, Sommers was obviously dead and Mr. Malone was standing in the middle of the room holding a smoking shotgun. I asked Mr. Malone for the weapon. He surrendered it after a moment and then walked down to the station with me as I requested."

"Was Mr. Malone completely rational when you got there?"

"No, Your Honor. When I first arrived he was upset to the point he snarled like a cornered animal. He stated he would have killed Sommers twice for hurting his child."

"Did he make any statement or action suggesting he considered his actions before killing Mr. Sommers?"

"No. From all I could deduce, he had immediately gone into a temporary dementia when he saw his daughter. I don't believe Mr. Malone had a rational thought from that moment until he agreed to surrender the weapon and accompany me to the police station."

"Thank you, Mr. Lepke."

Fiona saw a tear leak from the corner of Florence's eye before her sister quickly wiped it away.

"Would John Malone take the stand?"

He looked old up there. Fiona realized she hadn't really looked at her father for years. She knew what he looked like, had known all her life. Now he was suddenly old and appeared unsure of himself.

"Did you kill Peter Sommers on purpose, Mr. Malone?"

"Oh, yes. Y'see, he'd hurt me daughter, an' I couldn't be havin' that, Yer Honor."

"Did you think about what would happen after you killed him?"

"No, sir. It didn't matter."

"Did you realize you were killing an unarmed man? Did he tell you he was unarmed?"

"I didn't know he was unarmed. He didn't say damn all to me. He, he just grinned, so I put him down like I would any other mad dog."

"Grinned? Did you say grinned, Mr. Malone?"

"Aye. Like he'd just told the top story and won a liar's contest. He looked smug and bold and dangerous. And I killed him."

Judge Jennings sat and looked at Jack for a long moment. Then he rubbed the bridge of his nose and looked out at the crowded courtroom.

"This is not a trial as such, it is an arraignment of Mr. Malone. He freely admits he killed Mr. Sommers for harming the person of his daughter. There is no mystery to be solved here. No mysterious slayer to be sought out and brought to justice. All the court's questions have been answered in a forthright manner. It is now up to this court to pass judgment on the self-confessed killer of Peter Sommers."

The bailiff told Jack to stand in front of the judge's bench.

The judge sipped from a water glass and cleared his throat.

"It is the opinion of this court that although Mr. Sommers was stopped in the act of committing a heinous crime, and that he would have faced a long prison

term if brought before a court of law and convicted, it does not exonerate Mr. Malone from passing judgment without due process."

Judge Jennings looked down at Fiona's father and said, "Jack Malone, I hereby sentence you to one year in jail for the murder of Peter Sommers. Due to extenuating circumstances, I suspend nine months of that sentence. You will begin your sentence immediately in the U.S. jail. Have you anything to say?"

"Only thank you, Your Honor," Jack said.

"This arraignment is at an end, court is adjourned." The gavel banged down on the block of walnut.

Everyone got to their feet and waited for Judge Jennings to exit. Fiona felt tears running down her face as she dashed into the aisle to hug her father. Florence got to him at the same time.

The bailiff let them hug him for a moment, and then said gruffly, "I'm sorry, ladies, but I must remove the prisoner." He led Jack away.

"Only three months!" Florence said with great feeling.

"I'm so relieved, Flo. If they had hurt him or put him in prison for years and years, I just don't know what I would have done."

Florence put an arm around Fiona's shoulders. "It wasn't your fault. Father did what he thought he must."

Fiona looked into her sister's face. "So did August."

Florence closed up quick as a clam. "I don't want to talk about that man."

"I feel responsible for this turn of events," Fiona said. "He was the first man you ever—"

"I said I didn't want to talk about it, Fiona! Not now, not ever. Do you understand?"

"Y-, yes, Florence. I'm sorry."

"And stop being sorry. It wasn't your fault!"

Amanda came up to them. "I'm so glad he got off with a light sentence."

"Yes," Florence said. "Well, I must get back to work. I'll call on you later, Fio." She hurried out of the courtroom.

On the far side of the room Fiona saw August Lepke step from behind a partition and slowly walk away.

59 —Auk Village, A.T., January 25, 1916—
Wednesday evening.

"I think the man was dead, Mr. Mak-we!" Begay said fervently.

George was tired of this young man who continued to visit his niece despite her mother's wishes. He seemed intelligent but quite obtuse. That would never do.

"Even if he was already dead, what does it matter? Jack Malone would be doing three months for it anyway."

"But he said he didn't see Sommers until he was in the bar with the shotgun. If Sommers was *already* dead, someone *else* killed him!" Begay said carefully. "There. I have finally said it correctly."

The boy was right; he had finally made sense. Maybe George was the obtuse one here. He mentally went over the widely published events of Sommers' death. The last person to see him alive before he reached the bar was the Ganbor woman.

Maybe he should speak with Detective Lepke. George was pleased the police department had the good sense to hire the man. Finally there would be a police officer in Juneau who didn't immediately think Indians guilty of every non-witnessed crime committed.

Both Irene and Julia agreed with his assessment.

"Well? What do you think?" Begay asked.

George gave him a level look. "I think you might be right. I'll look into it. Now don't go shouting around about it, okay?"

"Sure, Mr. Mak-we, whatever you say." Begay grinned and turned to talk with Ruth at the table.

Irene edged up to her brother and turned her back to the young couple. Julia sat within earshot.

"Do you think he's right, George?" she said quietly.

"He saw what others didn't. I can think of no reason for him to really care one way or another. I think he may be telling the truth."

"It certainly shows him to be an honest man," Irene murmured.

George grinned at her. "Are you beginning to accept your de-facto son-in-law?" Julia laughed sharply and turned to look out the window.

"George! Don't you say that! Nothing is certain yet," Irene hissed.

He smiled and grabbed his coat. "I'm going to make my rounds. I'll be back for supper. Good day, ladies."

He walked around the Indian village in the dusk. Light shone softly out of windows, creating little pools of illumination along the otherwise dark plank street. The smell of burning coal reminded him he had forgotten to get more coal for his little cabin.

George had rebuilt a ten-by-sixteen boat cabin rescued from a decaying tug. He had winched it to a platform he built on the side of the hill, just up into the brush line. There he slept and went to be by himself. Most of the time he took his meals at Irene's house.

He spent many hours sitting at the front windows, looking out over the Auk village and Gastineau Channel. His little stove kept the place comfortable. But the coal supply neared exhaustion.

I need to do that tomorrow, he thought. The cloudless day eclipsed into starry night. As far as he could see, all was right with the village. His stomach grumbled about lack of food so he started back toward Irene's.

Fifty feet from her house, a shadow moved where a crude bench was nailed to the railing. A figure moved toward him.

"Hello?" he said, dropping his hand into his pocket to rest on the pistol.

"Hello, George," Julia said. "Isn't it a lovely night?"

"Yes," he said, his heart skipping a beat. "Yes, it is."

"Are you ready for dinner?" she asked.

"Yeah, I'm getting pretty hungry, but we probably have time for a walk."

"Oh, that would be grand. Why don't you show me your cabin?"

"Sure. It's not far. This way, please."

He saw her smile reflect light in the gloom. She moved to his side, put her arm through his and they moved along the planks together.

"So do you like it here?" he asked.

"Very much. I am so comfortable with your family. I know it's because they have gone out of their way to make me feel welcome, just as you have."

He was glad it was dark so she couldn't see his consternation. "Well, ah, I find it very easy to make you feel welcome."

"That's right," she said with a laugh, "you think I am beautiful."

"Well, you are!" he said defensively. "I am amazed you haven't had a husband."

"I have, George."

"You're married!" He abruptly stopped and stared down at her.

"No . . . not now. Does that shock you?"

"No," he said truthfully. "In fact it makes me feel easier about you."

"I'm glad," she said softly.

They began walking again.

"There's a stairway right up here. Be careful, there's no railing on the left side."

He let her move ahead of him. "Thirty steps to the top, then just go in the door."

Once in, she stood to one side as he crossed to the table and lit the oil lamp.

"Kinda cold in here, I'll start a fire," he said nervously, bending to the stove.

"What a beautiful little house! Irene didn't tell me it was paneled."

"Yeah, it was a nice boat to start with. Another season on the beach would have ruined it. I caught it just in time."

She walked around and looked at the shelves, the cupboards, the small library, and the built-in bed. Then she walked back over to the table and sat a bundle down.

"Where'd you get that?" he asked.

"I've had it all along. It's our dinner."

"Our dinner," he echoed inanely.

"Yes. Do you mind if we eat here together?"

"Oh, no. I, I would like that very much, Julia."

The boat stove began to radiate heat and he loosened his coat. She took hers off and began to prepare the food. He finally removed his coat and hung both of them on pegs near the door.

"How long were you married, Julia?"

"For a very short time. He left home and didn't come back."

"I can't imagine not wanting to come home to you."

"That's a very sweet thing to say, George. You don't really know me."

"I have studied you just as you have studied me and my family. I have seen you do work most white women would think beneath them, especially in the home of an Indian, and how many would come into the home of an Indian to begin with?"

"But I'm an anthropologist. I find other cultures fascinating."

"You are different from any other woman I have ever met or seen," he said flatly. "It's more than being fascinated. You are *accepting* of others and their ways."

"Come and eat."

The cabin became comfortably toasty. George felt an inner warmth long absent from his life. The food was simple but satisfying.

She talked about her college days in California, and he talked about going to the school conducted by the Sisters of St. Ann's.

"Do you have any idea how rare it is for an adult male Indian to go to school?" she asked.

"I know I was the only one at the time," he said with a chuckle.

"You're a very unique man, George. Most men would have been destroyed by the things you have endured."

"It wasn't easy," he admitted.

His small mantle clock chimed eight times.

"It's getting late, Julia."

"Yes, it is, isn't it?" She didn't move. Her gaze lingered on his face. "George, I want us to sleep here tonight. Is that all right with you?"

His heart swelled into his mouth, preventing speech. Her eyes glowed warm and inviting, tinged with anxiety as she waited for his answer. He opened and shut his mouth a few times, knowing he looked like a foolish fish but still unable to voice the emotions swirling through him.

After he hurriedly swallowed the last of his tea, he could finally speak.

"I, I'd like that very much, Julia. Are you sure about this?"

A slow smile pushed the anxiety from her eyes. "I've never been more sure of anything in my life." She pushed back from the table and stood to blow out the lamp. He also got to his feet, uncertain of what to do next.

In the darkness he heard the rustle of her clothing as it fell to the floor. Just as his fingers touched the buttons on his shirt, she moved in front of him. His eyes had adjusted to the incidental light limning the objects in the room.

She became a warm shape, fragrant and rounded. Her hands touched his, closing around them, pushing them down.

"Please, may I do it?"

He found it unnecessary to say anything. Her hands moved across him, unbuttoning, pulling garments off him, exposing his body and trembling erection. Finally they both stood unclothed. She took his hand and led him across the familiar cabin to his bed.

Dreamlike, he decided. This was all very dreamlike. *If this is only a dream* —she pulled him down to her —*I don't ever want to wake up.*

THE ALASKA DAILY EMPIRE
Juneau, Alaska, Friday, January 28, 1916

GERMAN FLAG TORN UP IN SWITZERLAND

BRANDEIS IS NAMED TO SUPREME COURT BY WILSON

COLD WEATHER HITS MONTANA; MANY PERISH

HARD CIDER MAY COME UNDER THE BAN AT SEATTLE

LIARS GAVE TIP

ALASKAN MINE OWNER CHARGED WITH SABOTAGE

NORTHERN MAN IS HEIR TO GOOD FORTUNE

ADMINISTRATION ARMY BILL BADLY ROASTED BY WOOD

CANADIAN WOMEN MAY BE GIVEN VOTE

BRITISH STEAMER HITS MINE; 300 LOST

WARNING SENT TO EUROPE

WASHINGTON, Jan. 28,— The State Department of the United States, through Secretary Lansing, has sent communications to all the European belligerents to make a general agreement to shape their submarine warfare in conformity with the principles of humanity and international law.

The government has taken the position that under the changed conditions of naval warfare, merchant ships should carry no armament whatever. All the powers were notified today that should they subscribe to such principles, armed merchantmen will be denied entry to American ports, except under conditions which apply to warships.

60 —Juneau City, A.T., February 14, 1916—
Tuesday afternoon

Florence Malone walked into the U.S. jail and stood in front of the guard's desk.

"Good afternoon, Miss Malone," Deputy Jim Clarke said. "Are you here to see your father?"

"Yes, if there's no problem," she said somberly.

"Certainly, right this way."

As he led her through the now familiar door and into the tank area, she reflected her soul seemed to be incarcerated along with her father. The joy had gone out of her life to the point her job had become a chore rather than a challenge.

Jack Malone saw her coming and walked across the tank to the visitor's table where they could talk separated only by a heavy wire screen. She sank into the visitor's chair and carefully searched his face as he sat down.

"How are you, Father?"

"I'm fine, Duchess, just fine. How are you?" He no longer had the stunned look he had carried with him the first two weeks after his arrest.

"Oh, things are just fine. Mrs. Milivich actually asked me if she should bring meals for you." She forced a chuckle and was rewarded with a tight grin from him.

"Florence, you needn't come up here and visit every day. They're treating me just fine. Only sixty days to go and I'm a free man again. I'm getting a lot of reading done."

"They shouldn't have locked you up at all," she said stubbornly.

"This may come as a shock to you, darlin', but Sommers wasn't the first man I've killed. He's just the only one they could ever pin on me."

He seemed jocular about the revelation. How odd, she thought, but *I don't really know my own father.*

"Why did you kill the others, Father?"

"Revenge, money, love, hate, honor. All those simple words have a different definition for every person what uses 'em. Sometimes your blood runs so hot that either they die or you do."

"I don't understand."

"That's good. How's Fiona?"

"She's back at the hotel, but working the day shift now. It's very strange, but this whole thing has brought her some very close friends."

"Who might they be?"

"Well, Amanda Ganbor and Maye Wattnem come immediately to mind."

"Maye Wattnem is Fiona's friend?" Doubt tinged his voice.

"Oh, yes. Maye paid for all of Fiona's doctor bills, gave her time off, a place to stay, and even hired Amanda to watch over her. At first Amanda refused to take money for caring for Fiona. Maye knew Amanda didn't have an income and insisted she accept a wage."

"How curious," Jack said absently. "Time has a way of twisting things back on you."

"What do you mean, Father?"

"Well," Jack said with a sigh, "when I first came to Juneau, Maye was with me. We'd met in Seattle and decided to try our luck up here."

"What do you mean, 'she was with you?' "

"You're a big girl. How do you think I mean it?" he said levelly.

"But you married Mother! What happened between you and Maye?"

"I left her. I met your mother and decided to change my life, become respectable. Your mother was my new life, Maye was the old."

"Your old life . . ."

"Was lawless. Why work for money when it was there to be taken? I've done my share of thieving an' swindling, darling, just you believe it."

"Why are you telling me all of this?"

"Well, it's hard to explain. You and me have had our differences in the past, and we both went our own ways. Now you've backtracked, so to speak, and to my way of thinking you're pretty much where you started."

"You don't want me to care about you? Is that what you're saying?" She suddenly felt close to tears. Her father was all she had left; nobody else needed her.

"I am rapturous you care about me, darlin' Duchess, but it pains me to see you turn from your own determined path for reasons that are nothing more than early morning fog on a summer day."

"Father, what the hell do you mean?" she said stiffly.

"Quiet now. We don't want these felons behind me to be a part of our conversation, do we?"

She glanced behind him. Edward Krause sat on his cot and stared at her with dead, black eyes. She felt her hackles rise.

"Please explain your self," she said quietly.

"I'm ready for me nap. You think for a bit an' you'll figure it out. One thing for certain, you've more than proved you're my daughter." He chuckled.

She realized he looked happier than she'd seen him in a long while. "All right, Father. I'll leave you to your nap and I shan't worry about your riddles. Is there anything you want me to bring you tomorrow?"

"Not a thing. Thank ye for comin', Duchess."

She watched him amble back to his cell and lie down on the cot before she made her way out. After a solid week of snow and cold, the weather hinted at spring. *It has been such a long winter,* she thought.

Mr. Pond, finally back from his most recent mining adventure, had given her half the day off. She walked slowly through town toward Starr Hill, enjoying the sunshine and listening to water draining off roofs and running under the plank street. Ahead of her, a couple walked arm-in-arm, chatting gaily.

Suddenly she realized it was Amanda Ganbor and August Lepke. A swirl of feelings rushed through her mind. She felt hurt Amanda was out walking in public with August. She was thrilled to see August and know he was well to the point she had to will herself to look elsewhere. None the less, she didn't wish to speak to them, for them to see her, or to even feel this way. So upsetting. She glanced behind her for a haven —nothing.

Her only escape was the entrance to a tobacco shop. She went in and carefully shut the door behind her.

"Miss Malone!" the proprietor said. "Whatever are you doing in here?"

"Hello, Mr. McCaul," she said brightly. "I just thought I'd pick up a few of those cigars my father likes so much."

"Oh, I see. How many did you want?"

"A dollar's worth," she said, watching the couple pass the shop.

"Ten Panatellas, it is. Is your father well?"

They hadn't noticed her; that much was obvious. Amanda said something that made August laugh. She was surprised at how much it hurt to see them together.

"Miss Malone?" McCaul said for the second time.

"Oh! I'm sorry. Just wool-gathering. What did you say?"

"Here's your cigars. That'll be a dollar. How is your father?"

"Oh, he's fine. You'd almost think jail agreed with him." She laughed.

McCaul didn't. "Isn't that a caution?" he said somberly.

"Yes. Well, thank you." She escaped through the door.

All the way up the hill to Fifth Street she pondered on the reasons behind her overwhelming gloom. It couldn't be August. Men always disappointed you if you gave them enough time.

What about . . . what's his name? The boy at the university . . . Yes, Eddie. Eddie certainly turned out to be a disappointment.

An unwelcome part of her mind countered with the fact Eddie had been just that— a boy. August was a man. *Same difference,* she thought with a frown. *Men just have more finesse when it comes to hurting you.*

Nobody understood. There had been a bond between them he had violated by attacking her father. He had violated her trust and wounded her to the quick.

She hadn't seen much of Amanda since that first day in the shop. The day she met August, and they had already met each other!

Her jaw dropped and she stopped walking. She never asked August about that. It had slipped her mind. Amanda had been passing herself off as a married woman, too.

She didn't want to consider Amanda much further in the direction her mind traveled. The woman was vivacious, pretty, intelligent, and a long way from her father's house.

Who am I to judge her actions?

She willed her mind blank and continued walking. Finally she turned off Seward onto Fifth. A man stood on their porch talking through the barely opened door to Mrs. Milivich.

She increased her pace and all but trotted up the shoveled walk to the porch. She heard Mrs. Milivich say, "There, behind you," before pulling the door shut and disappearing inside her refuge.

"You're Miss Florence Malone?" the young man asked.

"Yes?" she answered, looking at him closely. He was very young, in his teens but wearing a two-piece suit and wide-brimmed hat. One of the sort who hung out near billiard halls and smoked cigarettes until curfew.

"I'm supposed to give you this." He held out a paper-wrapped bundle with one hand. She took it uncertainly and felt relief when he turned and walked down the street.

"Oh! Wait," she called. "Thank you. Who, who told you to give this to me?"

He called back over his shoulder without stopping, "Read the card."

"Oh." She looked at the wrapping paper and it took her a moment to decide to go in the house before she opened it.

Indoors, she slowly took off her fox-trimmed coat and hung it up before returning to the bundle on the hall table. She stopped and stared at it, rubbing her hands on her hips absently, before pulling the string loose.

Flowers. Roses. *In February?* Their probable cost staggered her.

But why? It wasn't even, but it is! Valentines Day!

"My God," she said aloud. "I *have* been losing track of time."

She quickly picked up the small envelope and pulled out the message.

"My love for you is as strong as my sense of duty," it read.

She burst into tears.

"This is ridiculous. I need to talk to someone," she said aloud. She decided to go see Mary Bergmann.

On her way over to the Bergmann Hotel she reflected on how Mary was always there to listen. Florence's short residence at the hotel only deepened the bond with a good, life-long friend. Florence's mother and Mary had been friends.

Mary was in her fifties, but she remembered how it felt to be a young woman faced with life and its inherent problems. Florence had never met anyone who knew Mary and didn't regard her highly. Florence felt as if she had lost her way. Maybe Mary would be able to give her some direction.

Mr. Staley sat behind the desk when she arrived.

"Good afternoon, Miss Malone. How nice to see you."

"Thank you, sir. I feel good just being in the hotel. Is Mrs. Bergmann in?"

"She's up in her rooms. I'm glad you're here to cheer her up. She's been feeling poorly."

"Oh! Well I'll go right up then."

Mary Bergmann had her two rooms on the third floor. She once said if anyone had to walk up all those stairs it should be the owner, not the guests. Florence knocked gently at the door.

An unintelligible murmur was the response.

"Mary? This is Florence, may I come in?"

Murmur.

Florence pushed through the door. Mary sat in a huge horsehide chair, covered with blankets.

"Are you all right, dear?" Florence asked.

"I feel so bad," Mary said in a feathery voice. "I've never felt this bad before in my life."

"Who is your doctor?" Florence asked, moving over to the telephone.

"Parker," she whispered.

"Operator? Please get me Dr. Parker. This is an emergency."

Mary smiled weakly. "Oh, I don't think it's that bad!"

"I'll be the judge of that," Florence said primly.

"Hello. Yes, this is Florence Malone. I am at Mrs. Bergmann's. She needs to be seen by the doctor at once. She's in a bad way."

Florence listened for a moment. "Dr. Parker? Could you come up and see Mrs. Bergmann immediately? Yes, I do think it's necessary. Thank you."

"He's on his way, Mary," she said as she hung up the phone. "Is there anything I can get for you?"

"No. Please sit down. You look so worried!" she said breathlessly.

Florence spent five minutes chatting to her friend. The thought of laying her mental burdens on the sick woman had become repulsive.

A perfunctory rap sounded on the door and then Dr. Parker pushed in without further formality. He panted, completely out of breath.

"Excellent time, doctor! You have the swiftness of an athlete," Florence said.

"Th-, the three, flights of stairs," he gasped, "was the hardest part."

He ran a professional eye over Mary and opened his bag. He shook out a thermometer and popped it in her mouth. He took her pulse, and looked at the thermometer.

"103°. You are going to have a rest in St. Ann's Hospital, my good woman. Can you walk?"

"No, she can't," Florence said with finality.

"Very well. I'll call for some help."

While the doctor called the hospital, Florence held Mary's hand. Her skin felt papery and hot, her pulse had been replaced by the flutter of a small captured bird. Suddenly Florence felt afraid for her friend.

"You have a nice, quiet rest, Mary. There's a great deal I must talk to you about when you're better."

"You looked troubled when you came in, dear," she answered.

"I'm fine. Just being foolish. Don't you worry one second about anyone other than yourself."

Florence walked with the attendants as they carried Mary out on a stretcher. They put her gently in the horse-drawn ambulance and carefully moved up the hill to the hospital, less than a block away.

"Doctor," Florence said as he prepared to follow the ambulance. "What's wrong with her?"

"I don't know, but I mean to find out. I'll call you tomorrow."

"Thank you, doctor," she said to his retreating back.

61 —Treadwell, A.T., February 23, 1916—
Thursday morning

Begay Santo hurried into the spud locker, tied on his apron and looked around wildly. "What needs to be done next?" he asked Frank Bagio, who stared at him sullenly.

"Mr. Ayamo wants to see you," Frank said. "Right now."

"What's he want, Frankie? You gotta tell me!"

"Whattya think he wants? You think he's gonna pat you on the head for being late to work again? Go ask him. I don't know nothin'. I just work for a living."

Begay went into the huge kitchen that fed the miners. Shouts in Tagalog came from all directions. Men, mostly Filipinos, darted back and forth through the steam heavily laced with competing food odors. At the far end of the kitchen Mr. Finch reigned behind the large glass windows in the manager's office.

Mr. Finch rarely spoke to the men who worked the kitchen; that was the duty of his "right hand boy," fifty-six-year-old Willie Ayamo. Only Willie had free access to the office that signified his source of power and authority. Begay wandered into the swirling mass of steam and bodies, shouting, "Mr. Ayamo! Mr. Ayamo!"

Nobody stopped to give him directions or even to greet him. Begay Santo thought perhaps he consisted of steam and odor also. Men he had played cards with in the boarding house those first days, men with whom he had shared tobacco and talk, men who spoke his native Tagalog, all ignored him. They wouldn't even look at him.

Finally Begay let his shoulders slump and he turned to leave.

"Begay Santo!" The bellow cut through the organized chaos, stilling the chattering men and halting the frenzied movement.

Begay turned and found all eyes hard on him. Not one man broke the spell with a smile. Willie Ayamo stood on the far side of the kitchen, under the windows where Mr. Finch watched in bored distraction.

"Y- yes, Mr. Ayamo?" he said, hating his voice for quavering at this moment.

"Go to the payroll office and tell them you no longer work for the Treadwell Company. If they ask why, tell them you are not a good worker, that you are constantly late, that you make too many mistakes, and you have turned your back on your people. Now get out!" Willie turned his back and disappeared into the steam.

Instantly the kitchen became a hive of activity again, Begay seemingly forgotten. He pulled off his apron, dropping it on the floor, and started for the door.

Fred Beam, an energetic white boy fondly called "Sunbeam" by the staff, bumped up against him.

"Meet me after work, I know of a job you can get." Then he was swallowed by the darting, shrill mass of men in the cavernous kitchen.

Begay felt somewhat better. He had a friend here after all. Still, it depressed him that the friend wasn't a Filipino.

The clerk at the office didn't ask him why he no longer worked there. He already knew. He had Begay sign for the pay packet that was all prepared.

"The company's a real stickler for punctuality, boy. Mebbe you'll learn from this and keep a job at a different mine."

Begay stared down at the white clerk, a youth no more advanced in years than him.

"I'll keep that in mind, *boy*. Thanks for the advice," he snapped.

"Hey! Don't you go gettin' uppity on me!" The man's eyes were wide in sudden fear. They were alone in the office.

"What are you going to do, fire me?" Begay walked out, clutching his final pay envelope.

Sunbeam wouldn't be off work for another nine hours. He wouldn't tell Begay something he wasn't sure of. Somewhere a job waited for him. That was all he needed to know.

He hurried down to the Douglas dock and paid fifteen cents for the ferry to Juneau. On the way over he argued with himself about where to go first, Ruth's, or to see the Chinaman. The resolve burned strong in him to see the Chinaman first.

Ruth would understand and approve, he decided. He walked as fast as he could through the rain turning the snow underfoot to a sloppy soup. China Joe's Bakery had sat on the same corner since 1881.

China Joe was the only Chinese left in Juneau. In 1886 John Treadwell, the man who left his name on the mine he later sold for a pittance, had hired about eighty Chinese men from the Cassiar gold fields in British Columbia to work his mine.

The Chinese worked for significantly less money than would white miners. When the white miners asked him to get rid of the Chinese, Treadwell refused. The next day, August 7th, 1886, a mob of miners carrying clubs and torches went to the still-tiny town of Douglas and packed all the Chinese onto a sailing ship and sent them south to Wrangell.

China Joe was allowed to stay because he had grubstaked many miners in the early days, gave candy to the white children, and was altogether too popular to be included in this mass expulsion of his countrymen.

Now a very old man, he employed two Indians in his bakery and did a lively business with every ethnic group in Juneau.

Joe stood behind the counter when Begay walked in. The old man squinted up at the clock on the wall.

"You must be pretty big fella to get off so early in morning."

"I no longer have a job at Treadwell," Begay said shortly, "but I will have another job by tomorrow."

Joe nodded his agreement and kept his silence.

"The land you and I spoke of last week?"

"Yes?"

"I want to buy it. Here is my last pay packet from the mine. I offer it as down payment."

Joe took the envelope and expertly riffled the greenbacks inside. "Nineteen dollah not much down payment."

"It seems like a lot to me right now," Begay said with a smile.

Joe grinned. "You give me six more dollah by end of month. You give me fifteen dollah every month by the tenth for eight months and land is yours. You miss two months in row, all is mine again. Agreed?"

"Agreed!" The men shook hands.

Begay felt very good when he left the bakery. He had been saving his money since meeting Ruth. Sixty dollars sat in the bank to fall back on if need be.

Life was good, even in the rain. He went to find Ruth.

62 —Treadwell, A.T., March 4, 1916—
Saturday early morning

Arnold Williams pulled off his miner's hat and tightened the strap again. The powder crew insisted he wear the lamp-equipped hat or they wouldn't take him into the mine. In the past hour he had readjusted it six times.

At the face of the stope two men and their helpers drilled into the rock with three-and-a-quarter-inch Ingersoll-Sergeant pneumatic drills. The two machines were reminiscent of weapons from the Front. Very heavy, it took two men to set one up and an iron tripod to hold it in place while noisily boring holes into the rock.

The drill bits measured about eight feet long and wore down quickly. The driller would balance the rig while his helper changed bits. The grinding whine from the machine bounced off the close rock walls, putting Williams' teeth on edge. After his first close look he stayed back from the action.

He decided to "interview" the blaster.

"After you finish the drilling, how many holes will there be in the rock?"

"That all depends on exactly what we're doin' that day," Gus said.

"For instance," Williams said tersely.

"Well, if we're pushin' a drift, that's one thing. If we're blastin' out a stope, that's quite another."

"What's a drift?"

"A tunnel what runs along side or through the vein of ore yer workin'. Yer sittin' in a drift right now."

"So what's a stope?"

"A stope is where we actually work the vein."

"Oh. Where you blast it into manageable pieces and put it in the carts."

"Now yer catchin' on!" Gus said amiably.

"So how many holes are you drilling today?"

"We're cuttin' a drift today, so they'll be four along each side here . . ." With his finger he made a sketch in the dirt of a square box with a slightly domed top.

"Okay, these holes I numbered are the cut holes, an' they're angled so's they all point to the center of the rock face."

"They come to an apex, you mean?"

"In mining, the apex is where th' ore body comes closest to th' surface of th' ground. Them holes is seven feet deep. The next row of holes are the relievers, an' they're six feet deep an' angle in just a wee bit. 'N' finally, these outside holes are the trimmers, 'n' they're drilled five feet deep, but they angle outward toward the side walls."

"Then you just stuff dynamite into them and set them off?"

"Not quite, Mr. Journalist, not quite!" Gus said with a laugh. "We blow the cut holes first usin' No. 1 powder, which is seventy percent straight dynamite. Then we blow the relievers and trimmers with No. 2 powder, which is forty percent."

"Do you ever set a charge that doesn't go off?"

Gus made a quick sign of the cross. "It happens," he said shortly.

"What do you do in a case like that?"

"Nowadays we leave it for twelve hours an' nobody works that stope until the powder men come back and blow it proper."

"I get the impression the rule was come by the hard way."

"You ever seen a man blown to bits in front o' yer eyes?" Gus grated.

"No," Williams lied, "can't say that I have."

"It don't do much fer yer digestion."

"Where do you keep your blasting powder?"

"In a locked shed on the surface. In the old days they kept it inside the mine. They had a powder room on each level."

"Why did they move it to the surface?"

"Back in '11 they was havin' a shift change, 'n' somethin' touched off the powder. Thirty-eight men died in an instant."

After a moment's silence, Williams said, "I see."

"The odd thing was, something lived through it."

"Something?"

"Yeah. A mule. They had six mules down there to pull the ore carts between th' stope an' th' hoist like always. 'N' this one mule was standing between two other mules, an' nothin' happened to it. We never could figure that one out."

"Suppose I wanted to become a blaster in the mine, how would I go about it?"

"First ya get hired by the company ta work the powder crew. Then you'd start out bein' a powder monkey."

"What's that?"

"Powder monkeys carry all the powder and caps from the lift to the blasting site in heavy cotton bags. One trip fer powder an' one trip fer caps. Even then ya wanta be real careful an' not slip. Then ya stand there to help th' blaster while he sets th' charge. Usually he don't need no help, but ya stand there anyways."

"What if the blaster makes a mistake and it goes off?"

"Then ya go ta hell with him."

"Oh."

"Then th' blaster tamps down th' charge an' the powder monkey inserts th' fuse an' plugs the hole with dirt. Right before ya both git back from the site, ya 'spit' the fuse. That's all there be to it."

"Sounds like tense work."

Gus laughed. "That's good. 'Tense work' indeed!"

"Would you show me how to set a charge?"

Gus eyed in him disbelief. "With all yer education you wanna be a powder man?"

"Just once. I wish to really understand the process. Do we have to get special permission?"

"Hell, if we asked them about it, they'd throw you out right now. It's daft, man. They'd think yer crazy, 'n' they don't want crazy men down here."

"So I can't do it?"

"Who said that? We'll just set it up 'tween the two of us. No need to get the company involved."

"Thanks, Gus. I really appreciate it," Williams said warmly.

"Course you have ta pay fer the first three rounds at th' Douglas Tavern after the shift."

"Done! You've no idea how much I want to do this!"

"Well," Gus said, "I guess ye've got yer reasons."

THE DAILY ALASKA DISPATCH
Juneau, Alaska, Friday, March 10, 1916

PORTUGAL NOW AMONG THE ALLIES

HOW SOLDIERS ARE BLASTED BY SAPPERS

FOREIGNERS TO BE BARRED

INVASION OF MEXICO HAS NOW BEGUN
Col. Slocum Sends Troops to Pursue The Villa Forces

ACROSS BORDER ON MEXICAN SOIL

Carranza Is Notified of the Action.
Action in Washington Official—Circles on Slocum's Move.

Washington, March 10. The Administration is backing Colonel Slocum in sending cavalry troops into Mexico after Villa forces. Secretary Lansing has informed Carranza that the United States hopes there will be no objection on his part to the action of the American troops in crossing the border, owing to an emergency arising calling for such action.

The state department is prepared to meet any protests that might originate from Carranza or Mexican sources. There is undisguised satisfaction in official circles here over the action of Col. Slocum in dispatching troops against the invaders without waiting for permission from Washington.

COLUMBUS, New Mexico, March 10. The American cavalry, the New Mexico militia and cowboys and civilians were alert last night to guard against another surprise attack on the part of the Villa forces.

Heavy guards have been thrown out and are patrolling Columbus and vicinity. Military officials admit the possibility of a further attack. It was reported late last night that the Villa forces had appeared on the American side west of here, apparently intending to attack the Seventh U. S. cavalry stationed near Hachita, New Mexico.

63 —Auk Village, A.T., March 15, 1916—
Wednesday afternoon

George Mak-we walked into his sister's house and sat down at the table. Julia finished writing out the paragraph before looking up at him.

"George, how very nice to see you."

"Julia, I must talk to you."

"Well, you're here, I'm here. Go ahead and talk."

"Where's everybody else?" he asked nervously.

"Irene and Ruth went into town to get some groceries, and Jim went somewhere to look at a boat."

"We have to talk!" he said vehemently.

"George! What is it you wish to say?"

"This can't continue. It's making me crazy."

"You mean what you and I have been doing together?"

"Yes."

"Do you want to stop? Do you want me to stay here at night instead of coming up to see you?"

"No. I don't want to stop. I want to marry you."

She sat very still and looked at him, frowning slightly. "Why?"

"Don't you love me?" he asked.

"That's not fair, George. We had an agreement not to make this complicated."

"But it is complicated. I'm in love with you."

"I don't want to get married."

"You said you were married once. You mean you don't want to get married to me."

"I can't marry you, George. I can love you with my heart, mind, and body, but I can't marry you." Moisture gathered at the corners of her eyes.

"Can you tell me why not?"

"It just wouldn't be fair to you, you have to understand that."

"I'm afraid you're gonna have to be a little more specific," he said roughly, beginning to feel angry.

"I'm not going to stay here forever. When I finish my thesis I am going back to California and obtain my doctorate. I will probably teach in California."

"I can go with you."

"How far from here have you ever been?" she asked gently.

"I've been to Sitka, and Angoon, and even to Wrangell once. What's that got to do with anything?"

"If you took all the people in the Territory of Alaska and dropped them into San Francisco, they might fill a small neighborhood. There are many thousands of people there. None of them know what it is to be Tlingit."

"I can live with that."

"You can live with the stigma of being married to a white woman and being considered inferior at the same time?"

"You must think I'm stupid, Julia. Why would California be any different than Juneau when it comes to white ideas about Indians? You aren't scaring me with that. I've lived with it my whole life."

"But you haven't been married to a white woman before."

"Julia, I'm not frightened of living my life with you. But I think you're terrified at the thought of living your life with me." His heart ached, and his throat tightened. He needed to leave soon.

Tears ran freely down her face. "George, I haven't told you everything about me."

"What could make me stop loving you? I know you were married before. I don't care."

"What if I married you and you went to California with me, and, and my son hated you?"

"Son?"

"He's ten years old. He's staying with my mother right now. I didn't bring him with me because this trip was to be all business."

"That's who all those letters are from," George said slowly.

"Yes. They're from Jefferson Prescott, my son."

"Who is raising him? Who is teaching him the things a man must know?"

"My culture doesn't do that. I wish it did. We send our young to school to understand about the world and life."

"I've been to school. Three years of lessons the sisters gave me. But they didn't know nothin' about life. They only knew about books, numbers, and words."

"I cannot argue with that assessment, George. I am an only child; I have no brother to teach my son how to be a man."

"What about his father?"

"His father doesn't know the first thing about it either."

"Does his father live in California, too?"

"I don't know where that man lives any more," she said flatly.

"Doesn't he ever come to see his son?"

"No. Jefferson has never met his father."

"There's more you haven't told me."

She sighed. "I wasn't honest with you before. I was never married to his father. Prescott is my father's name." Fresh tears rolled down her cheeks, splashing on clenched hands in her lap. "He was my teacher in high school. He told me lies and I believed him. I trusted him."

"What happened when he found out you were with child?"

"I told him first. He told me not to worry. The next day he was gone and I never saw him again." She pulled a handkerchief from the sleeve of her dress and wiped her eyes and nose.

"You went to college anyway," George said admiringly. "You are a very strong person, Julia. I would be very proud to be your husband."

"Even with all that?"

He nodded slowly. "You told me a story about a brave woman who has not allowed bad fortune to stop her. Will you please marry me, Julia?"

She blinked a new tear away and smiled. "Oh, you silly man. Yes, I'll marry you!"

They were still embracing when Irene and Ruth walked in with a basket of groceries.

"No wonder she didn't want to go with us!" Ruth said with a cackle.

THE ALASKA DAILY DISPATCH
Juneau, Alaska, Sunday, March 19, 1916

ANOTHER BOAT IS TORPEDOED

LONDON SAYS WEST DRIVE IS A FAILURE

GOLD MINING AT TREADWELL IS A ROMANCE

SHOCK CAUSED BY DEATH OF JUNEAU WOMAN
ENTIRE COMMUNITY FEELS LOSS OF MRS. BERGMAN

Had Endeared Herself to Residents by Her
Many Kind and Unselfish Acts

Mrs. Mary E. Bergman died at 10 o'clock at St. Ann hospital yesterday morning. The news of her death caused a shock to the entire community, and the many expressions heard yesterday told in what high regard she was held by the people of Gastineau channel among whom she had resided for the past 19 years.

Death was due to a hemorrhage of the brain, following a complication of diseases from which she had been suffering for the past four weeks.

Mrs. Bergman was 53 years old. She was born in Hammell, Germany and moved to the United States and married Mr. Bergman in Seattle. After his death she came to Juneau in 1896.

For a time she was employed at the Franklin House. In two years time she returned to Germany to visit an aunt with whom she was raised. After the death of her aunt she returned to Juneau and worked for a time at the old Perseverance mine.

Later she was employed as a nurse at the Simpson hospital and then took charge of the old Circle Hotel for George Miller and ran it until 1906. In 1914 she opened the Bergman apartments, the first modern apartment house to be opened in Juneau.

Her life in Juneau had been filled with kind and unselfish deeds. No one was ever turned away from her doors hungry; she always had a kind word and consolation for those in trouble and she had staked numerous prospectors. In fact every old-timer on Gastineau channel and more recent residents who have enjoyed the pleasure of her acquaintance, can recall numerous kind deeds and unselfish acts. Many owe their lives to her careful nursing and a still larger number owe her devotion for comfort and kindness which are beyond price.

Surviving her are: Mrs. Goodman Jensen, of Yankee Cove, a niece, two brothers in Germany and a distant relative by marriage in Seattle. General Bergman, now in the German army, is a brother to her late husband. No funeral arrangements will be made until Mrs. Jensen arrives in Juneau and until the relatives are communicated with, if possible. It is estimated that Mrs. Bergman left an estate valued at $40,000.

64 —Treadwell, A.T., March 30, 1916—
Thursday afternoon

August Lepke tucked the paper bag under his arm and knocked on the door of the house. He noticed a dark rectangle where a sign had been removed from the wall near the door. The door eased open and a small boy peered out.

"May I help you, sir?" he said.

Lepke grinned. The boy couldn't be more than four years old.

"Yes, you could. I would like to speak to Mrs. Christie."

"That's my mother. Just a moment, please." The door eased shut again.

When it opened again a woman stood there. As tall as Lepke, her dark hair, slender build, and deep, haunted eyes made an arresting combination.

"May I help you?"

"Mrs. Christie, I am August Lepke. I am the Pinkerton operative hired by the consortium to investigate your husband's disappearance."

"I see." Her speech mirrored her manner: completely neutral.

Lepke felt uncomfortable. "In this bag a pair of trousers I have. The divers, they found them. It's all they found."

"Yes?"

"Would you be willing to look at them for possible identification?"

Her eyes dropped from his face to stare at the bag for a long moment. She chewed her lower lip with good, white teeth. After a deep breath she looked up at him again.

"I don't believe it will do any good, but I will look at them."

He opened the sack and pulled the ragged gray trousers out into the light, shook them once and held them up for her inspection. She stared at them silently. Her right hand twitched and then stilled.

"Please turn them around," she said softly.

He slowly moved his hands around the waistband so she could get a good look.

"They are the trousers he was wearing."

"You're sure?"

"Yes. I would recognize a hem I made," she faltered, "anywhere."

"I see. Thank you, ma'am. I'm sorry I had to bother you." He put the trousers back into the sack.

"That's quite all right. I want this to be over so I can go away from here. Anything I can do to hasten that day . . ."

He waited but she didn't continue.

"Yes. Well, thank you again. Good day." He tipped his hat and turned away. When he glanced back before turning the corner, the door was shut again.

Lepke slowly walked down to the Douglas boat dock.

The March sun slowly dropped behind the mountains on Douglas Island. The waning rays turned the snowy peaks of Mt. Juneau and Mt. Roberts a vivid pink under the still-bright blue sky. Juneau's lights sparkled distantly in the dusk at the foot of the mountains.

The *Gent* chugged across the channel and pulled up at the dock with no wasted motion. A dockworker caught the lines and tied them fast. Men hurried off the small ferry and walked purposely down the long wharf toward town. Lepke was one of the last of the small knot of waiting men to board.

He stood on deck in the nice weather, sheltered from the cold wind behind the cabin. Thoughts of the widow evaporated from his mind and he found himself thinking about Florence. He'd seen her at Mrs. Bergmann's funeral last week.

Most of the town attended. Lepke hadn't realized what a wonderful person she had been until he read the newspaper accounts and listened to her friends talk. He knew how to listen to people, how to hear what they didn't say as well as what they did. Mary Bergman had been one in a million. She would be sorely missed. The U.S. Marshal let Jack out to attend the funeral with his daughters.

Florence remained red-eyed and silent throughout the ceremony. Lepke stayed completely away from the family. Once he caught Fiona staring at him with an unreadable expression.

He glanced back at Douglas and Treadwell receding in the distance. Smoke from hundreds of stacks stained the sky off-white in front of the dark, shadowed mountains flanking the two towns. The rumble of the mills followed the small boat across the water.

Guess I'd best get used to the sound, he thought, *I'll hear it as long as I live here.* How long would that be? The reason he elected to settle here was to be with Florence.

She still wouldn't speak to him. He sent flowers on every conceivable occasion that could possibly warrant it. She wouldn't answer his notes. In order to not upset her he stayed away from the shop of Winter and Pond, going instead to the firm of Case and Draper with his minimal photographic needs.

Amanda had suddenly ceased her aggressive behavior and talked to him for hours on any subject he wished. They had become very good friends. She was one of the most intelligent women he had ever met. He wanted more than a confidant, however.

He had been ready to settle down and start a family with Florence. Amanda was a very handsome woman who would no doubt make some man a wonderful wife. Yet August still loved Florence.

So how long will you stay here? he asked himself. *How long will you go through the agony of seeing her on the street and not saying anything because you know she won't answer?* The anonymity of Portland began to look inviting again.

There weren't any noisy stamp mills on the Willamette or Columbia River, either. On the other hand he hadn't been invited to join a baseball team in Oregon like he had here. The City Hall Team asked him to try out next week. He told them he'd think about it.

He had played baseball in the army and found it amusing. It seemed he possessed a gift for pitching. Perhaps the gift still existed in his being.

The *Gent* pulled up to the Juneau City dock. The sun vanished completely behind the horizon and dusk advanced.

He tiredly pushed through the door at the hotel. A man in a tailored suit sat near the stove, glancing through the afternoon *Empire*. He looked up when August walked past.

"Excuse me, Mr. Lepke. Might I have a word with you?"

August turned and took a better look. He had seen this man before, but he couldn't place exactly when or where. "Happy to oblige, Mr. . . . ?"

The man stood up, offering his hand. He was balding, sturdily built, and obviously hadn't missed many meals. Slightly taller than Lepke, he possessed a ready smile.

"Sulzer, Senator Charles Sulzer of Sulzer, in the Sulzer Mining District. I have some questions for you."

"About what?"

"Your arrest of Jack Malone."

"Everything is in my report, Senator."

"Yes," he agreed. "Everything except your impressions of the event."

Lepke smiled grimly. "It was my impression he shot a man to death."

"I need to know how stable the man is, detective. He is one of my key people here in the capital and if he's not stable, he could be a serious political liability." Sulzer smiled professionally again. "You *do* understand my interest?"

"I'm not sure I can give you an answer. If someone harmed one of Jack Malone's daughters tomorrow, I'm certain the person would be dead by nightfall. However I don't believe him to be a casual murderer or common felon."

"Do you think he'd kill if provoked in some other way?"

"Senator, I believe Jack Malone will never harm another person as long as he lives. But by the same token, I certainly wouldn't provoke him just to find out."

"You're not convincing me, Mr. Lepke," Sulzer said with a forced chuckle.

"I'm not trying to convince you, I'm just answering your questions to the best of my ability."

"I want to know if the man is safe."

"Senator, if there's one thing I've learned in my years with the agency, it's that no man is safe. Not even you."

"Thank you, Mr. Lepke, I won't keep you from your evening any longer."

"You're welcome, senator."

Lepke watched the man leave, and then turned toward the stairs. Amanda stood by the dark, polished banister.

"August, I need to tell you about the letter."

THE DOUGLAS ISLAND NEWS
Published Every Wednesday
E. J. White, Editor and Proprietor
Wednesday, April 5, 1916

ANNOUNCEMENT

Having purchased the plant, business and good will of this paper, as per the announcement made in last week's issue by our predecessor, Mr. Chas. A. Hopp, we respectfully solicit a continuation of the patronage and support accorded the paper during the many years of his faithful and efficient stewardship of the same.

We realize the magnitude of our task in succeeding Mr. Hopp, who for the past eighteen years has not only given his patrons an able and reliable paper, but has also been a pillar of strength in the town of Douglas, standing for and advocating week after week that which has been for its betterment and advancement. He has been in the vanguard with those who have advanced Douglas from an unorganized mining camp to a city of all modern conveniences and improvements, and we but voice the heartfelt sentiment of those with whom he has made his home during all this time when we express the wish that for him and his family the future may contain all that tends to diffuse happiness, prosperity and success, no matter where their lot may be cast. The Hopps have it coming.

In assuming the ownership of the Douglas Island News we do so in the belief that there is a great future for "this side." We, with our good neighbor, Treadwell, possess not only the industry but also the natural locations and sites for a great city which has already blended from two into one and is still growing and sprawling in all directions. To further aid in this growth and development to the best of our ability is our intention and purpose. We do not believe that party politics should have any place in municipal governments, but that all, irrespective of party, should work together for the advancement of good government and the betterment of local conditions.

We are in hearty sympathy and accord with the present National administration, believing that President Woodrow Wilson is the right man in the right place at the right time. Not only, in our opinion, is he guiding the entire course of the nation aright, but his treatment of Alaska is all that Alaskans can desire.

Indications are that the temperance sentiment which is now sweeping like a tidal wave over both the United States and Canada, will engulf Alaska in the near future and, in our belief, the sooner it comes the better it will be from the standpoints of morality, healthfulness, economy, efficiency and the general public welfare. However, when Alaska goes "dry," it should be by desire and vote of Alaskans rather than by edict issued at Washington.

It is our intention to make a number of changes in the make up and appearance of this paper just as soon as they can be brought about. One will be that the paper will be all home-print in the near future and it will be enlarged to meet the rapidly growing demands of the community which it serves. We are in Douglas to make our home and a living for those dependent upon us and it is our intention to give our patrons the very best news service commensurate with the support extended.

In conclusion we wish to make it plain that we are the sole owner of this paper and that there are no strings, either visible or invisible, on us. Upward of thirty years experience in the newspaper business has convinced us that editorial management is as necessary to the success of a publication as is business management and, with malice toward none and charity for all, we will aim to make both managements of the Douglas Island News profitable to our patrons as well as to ourselves.

E. J. White

In Passing

Agitation for that bridge over the channel opposite Juneau should not be permitted to wane. It would advance the value of property on both sides fully twenty-five per cent, to say nothing of giving Juneau a chance to add several thousand to her population. A long, steady and unanimous pull will obtain the bridge, so pull.

The Germans are still hammering away at Verdun, France, but are not doing much other than making orphans at the rate of several hundred daily. Years after Europe's blood fest is over the question most frequently asked there will be, "Why did we do it?"

The cannery men of Alaska who are operating this season with white crews instead of Orientals, are deserving of credit other than what they might obtain at the stores. It might sound somewhat southern, but "Alaska fo' White Folks" would not be a bad slogan.

Already there is a heavy travel northward, every boat leaving lower coast points, especially Seattle, being crowded. It is predicted that Alaska will see the heaviest travel this summer she has witnessed since the year of 1898.

The Women's Roosevelt Club, of Seattle, has started a petition for his nomination. We had hoped to see Woodrow Wilson succeed himself, but it now looks bad for him.

65—Juneau, A.T., April 6, 1916—
Thursday morning

Amanda finished fluffing the pillows on the bed in the room and stepped back to admire her handiwork.

"Are *you* the maid?" a deep baritone asked behind her.

She gasped in surprise and jerked around to find a complete stranger in the doorway. What an enticing man, she decided. An impeccably tonsured auburn beard and mustache framed fine, white teeth. Auburn hair, neatly parted and combed, gave way to a broad forehead beneath which warm, intelligent blue eyes twinkled at her.

Aren't we the giddy one? she thought ruefully.

"Not really, sir. I am helping out the management today. The previous chambermaid eloped last night and a replacement has yet been to be found." She gave him her best smile. "But if there's something I can do for you . . ."

"Well," his smile broadened. "Actually I was just looking for another towel, but I seem to have found Astarte instead."

"You *are* a guest of the hotel?" she asked over her blush.

"Yes. I came in rather late last night on the *Sophia*. Barrington S. Wentworth, room nine, at your service." He bowed deeply.

She chuckled.

"Do you come to Juneau City often, Mr. Wentworth?"

"Please call me Barry, Miss . . ."

"Ganbor. Amanda Ganbor. I'm a widow."

"My condolences," he said gravely. "Did you recently lose your husband?"

"Last October." She wondered why she referred to herself as a widow, since she had never felt like one. Perhaps it was because of the bubbly feeling this man gave her and a determination to henceforth be honest with people from the very beginning, and she hoped this was a beginning.

"I *am* sorry. As there was no ring on your finger I automatically assumed you were still a maid. If I have been too forward I apologize."

"Nay, sir. I find you refreshing. You were telling me how often you travel to Juneau City?"

"This is my first trip. I'm up here to establish business relations with the druggists of Alaska."

"You are a salesman for a drug manufacturer, then?"

"Owlsly and Owings, purveyors of quality potions, pain killers, and panaceas. Home office, Portland, Oregon."

"And you have the Alaskan market?"

"Exclusively!" he said with a wink.

Amanda colored again. "If you'll excuse me, I'll fetch you another towel."

He stepped back and allowed her to leave the room first.

"And what do you do, Mrs. Ganbor, when you're not helping your hotel management friends?"

"Whatever I please," she said over her shoulder. He followed her closely.

"Would it please you to have dinner with a newcomer to Alaska?"

"I, ah, will consider it, Mr. Wentworth."

"*Please* do!"

They arrived at the linen closet at the end of the hallway and she gave him a fresh towel. He took the towel and pressed it to his chest, staring boldly into her eyes the whole time.

"Please don't think me impossibly forward, but you are, without a doubt, one of the loveliest women I have ever had the great fortune to meet."

She pushed past him. "I said I would consider your request, Mr. Wentworth. Now please don't press me any further."

"Where can I reach you?"

"Leave a message at the desk and I will be sure to receive it."

"Until then," he said breathlessly, and vanished into his room.

Amanda skipped down the stairs to the lobby. Fiona, hunched over the front desk reading a newspaper, glanced up at her.

"My, you certainly look the cat that swallowed the canary."

"Do I?" Amanda smiled, dance stepped twice and winked at her friend.

"Amanda! What on Earth . . ."

"Have you met Mr. Wentworth yet?"

"Who?"

Amanda pulled the register around so they both could read it and stabbed her finger down on his perfect copperplate signature.

"Him."

"I didn't even look at the register this morning. My, what lovely handwriting."

"What a lovely *man*. He's enough to make me swoon."

"You're not the swooning type, Baroness Ganbor," Fiona said with a smirk. "Unless it's to your advantage, of course."

"Why, Fiona! What sort of a woman do you think I am?"

They both laughed.

"Seriously," Amanda pressed.

"I think there's more to you than meets the eye," Fiona said slowly, "and you're easily the most unique person I have ever met."

"Is that good?"

"I believe so."

"I feel so very lucky to have a friend like you, Fiona." She smirked. "But wait until you *see* him!"

THE DAILY ALASKA DISPATCH
Juneau, Alaska, Sunday, April 9, 1916

TROOPS CLOSE ON THE TRAIL CHIEF VILLA

GERMANY DISCLAIMS SINKING BRITISH BOAT SUSSEX

GERMANS GAIN IN ADVANCE ON VERDUN

BOB BURMAN IS KILLED IN A RACE

REPUBLICANS REGARDED FAVORABLE TO HUGHES

ARMY BILL TO BE VOTED ON SOON

AN OPEN LETTER

Washington, D.C., March 30, 1916— To the Delegates to the Republican Territorial Convention, Seward, Alaska.

Gentlemen: The people of Alaska seem to have concluded that there ought to be an effective organization of the Republican as well as the Democratic party in the Territory and many of my most active friends and supporters have joined in the movement and are among your number. In view of their announced intention to present my name to your convention and because of many rumors tending to create misunderstanding and contention hereafter I feel impelled in fairness to my friends and to those who have long been my political opponents to make this public statement in advance of any action on your part.

I have not and will not enter into any combination or an agreement with or against any person or faction in or out of the Republican organization for control of the patronage, in whole or in part, or at all, or for the control of my action in any way whatever as the representative of all the people of Alaska or for any other purpose. I will not be bound by any pledge made for me without it is clearly stated in the platform or resolutions adopted by the convention. It seems to me there can be no successful unity of action or re-organization of the Republican party in Alaska without entire frankness with the men and women who do the voting, and because of that I address this communication to you in this public manner. I can better do without the nomination or the election to Congress than be placed in the attitude of having betrayed my associates or the people whom I have represented with freedom and confidence for eight years, and whom I must continue to represent with freedom and confidence, or not at all.

In the event of my election, I pledge myself to harmony and fair dealing with friends and past opponents alike, to the support of the bill which I have already introduced granting extended powers to the territorial government, to the support of the Statehood bill, to the creation of better transportation conditions and the control and reduction of burdensome freight rates, and generally in the upbuilding of the industries natural to our Territory and to the development of its great natural resources free from monopoly and unjust restraint. If you nominate me upon this understanding there will be but little chance for contention and disagreement hereafter.

>Respectfully,
>JAMES WICKERSHAM

KRAUSE CASE NEXT MONDAY

The case of the government against Edward Krause will be called for Monday in the district court. Kazis Krauczunas, the attorney for Krause, arrived early this morning on the *Princess Sophia* and it is presumed he will be ready for trial.

The charges against Krause in their order as follows: 1. Kidnapping. 2. Appeal from the commissioner's court. 3. Impersonating an officer. 4. Forgery. 5. Forgery 6. Forgery. 7. Forgery. 8. Robbery. 9. Forgery. The defendant has not pleaded to the last two charges.

66 —Juneau City, A.T., April 15, 1916—
Saturday night

Begay Santo walked tiredly through the door of Armstrong's and leaned on the bar. "Please, Mr. John, a beer." He dropped a quarter onto the wet surface.

"A beer it is, Mr. Begay." The tall schooner slid to a stop in front of the Filipino without spilling a drop of foam from its massive head. John picked up the quarter and replaced it with two dimes. "You seen these new dimes yet?"

Begay peered at the coins in front of him. "They put wings on her hat?"

"They tell me it stands for freedom of thought," John said. "That's about the only damned thing that's free in this country."

Begay smiled at him. "I'll drink to that!" He took a long, cool swallow of beer and wiped his mouth.

His feet hurt, he'd been on them all day down at the George Brother's Market. Sunshine had known where there was a job all right. The work was harder than at the Treadwell and only paid half his former wage. But it was better than nothing.

He looked around for a place to sit. The bar filled rapidly. Men crowded around the two pool tables in the rear, drowning out the click of colliding balls with comments and laughter.

The tables all had occupants. A few empty chairs sat at tables where others drank and played cards. All the occupants were white. He was the only Filipino in the place.

He resigned himself to standing while he finished his beer.

"Hey, you there at the bar!"

Begay turned to the voice. A dark mustached man gestured at him. Begay frowned in disbelief, pointing a thumb at his own chest.

"Yes, you. Would you like to sit down?" The man pointed to an empty chair at his table.

Begay glanced around. Nobody else seemed to notice or care. He shrugged elaborately and carried his glass of beer across the small distance and sat down.

The man stuck out his hand. "M'name's Arnold Williams, journalist for the *London Times*."

"Begay Santo, delivery boy for George Brothers Market," he said with a smile, shaking the hand.

"Ah, a sense of humor! I like that in a man." Williams sipped at his whiskey and stared hard at Begay. "You'll forgive me, but at first I thought you were an Indian."

"I was born in the Philippines. I came here to work at the Treadwell five months ago."

"Five months and you still haven't been able to get on?"

Begay gave him a measured look. "I got on the first day."

"Oh. Didn't like it there, I take it?"

"It is a long tale, Mr. Journalist Williams. One I am sure you would soon be bored of."

"Oh, ho! You don't know the nature of journalists, my friend. That's what we do for a living, listen to long tales and write stories about them. Tell me yours and I'll buy you a drink."

Begay thought about leaving. But what would it matter? This man would never write a story about a rebellious Filipino for a paper in London.

He took another drink of beer and began talking. Two beers later, Williams asked a question.

"So what does her family think of you now that you're a land owner and gainfully employed?"

"They think I'm still not a Tlingit, an' they're right. I'm just a Filipino in love with a Tlingit." His head felt slightly unwieldy and his tongue slurred words that rarely troubled him. "I also think I might be getting drunk," he said with an air of discovery.

Williams laughed and swung a hand casually, indicating the packed room. "You've plenty of company, my friend. Tell me, are you angry with the Treadwell for treating you so shabbily?"

"*Shouldn't* I be?" Begay demanded.

"Hell, yes, you should be!" Williams said and gave the table a glass-rattling slap. "You were unfairly singled out because you tried to be an individual. Swim against the stream and they'll get you every time."

Begay thought his new friend might be a little drunk, also. Williams tossed back whiskey like it was water. Now the man squinted at him and hunched over the table in a conspiratorial manner.

"You could take revenge, you know. Hit 'em where it really hurts."

What was this man talking about? Sure, the thought of revenge had crossed his mind. But what could just one man do, and what would be the result?

"I don't think I understand you, Mr. Williams," Begay said carefully. "How could I hit them?"

Suddenly Williams' intense eyes increased to a piercing blue that formed ice in Begay's belly.

"You'd have to want to hurt them, Begay. You'd have to need satisfaction so badly you'd risk your life for it."

Begay felt the beer boiling out of his brain. His hearing suddenly became especially acute. The journalist's words cut at his new-found security.

"I'm not sure I want to do that, Mr. Williams. What good would it do me to hurt the Treadwell?"

"Honor! You could regain your honor."

"I didn't lose honor, I lost faith. I don't think revenge could bring that back."

"That's pretty deep thinking for a grocery delivery boy," Williams said with a slight sneer.

Begay felt his temper rising. "Does my lowly position in commerce make my statement invalid?"

"You sound like a debating society member, Mr. Santo. I am growing bored with you."

"Thank you for the beer, Mr. Williams," he said as he got to his feet. "I hope you felt you got your dime's worth."

As he walked through the door into the crisp night air, Begay felt suddenly free of a trap. He wondered why the man had tried to inflame him to hurt the Treadwell. Why would Begay's troubles bring out that much venom in a complete stranger? Maybe he's one of those muckrakers.

He walked through town toward Ruth's house, wondering if she were still awake. The thought crossed his mind that perhaps he should tell someone of the journalist's words. But who would care what an Englishman said to a grocery boy? He let his thoughts go back to Ruth. Williams faded from his mind and he quickened his step.

THE DOUGLAS ISLAND NEWS
Douglas, Alaska, Wednesday, April 19, 1916

The Stroller
by E. J. White

Modesty being one of the Stroller's chief characteristics, it is with considerable temerity that he takes his typewriter (she also does plain sewing) on his knee to introduce himself to the readers of this paper, who are destined to know more of him as Time is laid away on the shelf of Eternity.

Some men are born great and others are born in Ohio. The Stroller was born in Ohio. Like many other boys born on a farm, he was of the earth earthy. About the first of April of each year he would burn his bed and engage in tilling the soil throughout the summer and fall, retiring again when the ides of November were iding. (Right here the Stroller will admit that the "Back-to-the-Soil" sentiment which is now spreading over our fair land has never appealed to him. He does not rave over the aroma of newly turned loam.) After demonstrating to the entire satisfaction of indulgent parents that he was a failure as an agriculturist, the Stroller was sent to a college from which he later escaped, taking with him a conviction that he had a mission to perform for the benefit of undone and sodden humanity.

At the early age of 22, that sap-rising period of youth which all men envy after passing 40, the Stroller went to Florida with the idea of reconstructing the unregenerate south. For a time he engaged in school keeping (the word "keeping" is used advisedly instead of "teaching") and even to this late day the palm of his right hand experiences a an itching sensation every time he sees a fine, long, lithe willow switch. Later he sank into the newspaper business as a means by which to reach more people in what he was then pleased to term his moral uplift. For six years he conducted a newspaper, drank moonshine whiskey, ate pie with a knife and in many other ways contributed to the gaiety of nations and endeared himself to the common people.

Looking back on his work in Florida the Stroller points with pride to two reforms worked by him. One was that the negroes on their way home from camp meetings in the early dawn would only steal chickens sufficient to last two days where formerly they had taken a week's supply, and the other was that the leading and most influential drunkards in the Stroller's community acted on his advice and put a squirt of lemon in it.

The expression "Southward the Star of the Empire takes its way" is now printed for the first time. "Westward" has always been the word employed whenever the Star of Empire decided on a move, and the Stroller realized this after harboring a case of chills and fever and investing most of his hard-earned increment in quinine for a period of several years, so he came to what the late Joaquin Miller was pleased to designate as the "Sunset shore of a Sundown Sea," the Pacific coast. Before the

Stroller had been six months in the Territory of Washington it had become a sister in the sisterhood of states and has been prospering ever since. While the Stroller does not take all the credit for making Washington a state, the fact remains that it had been a territory for a long time before he entered it.

Eighteen years ago the Stroller came to Alaska, settling in Skagway, where he and the late "Soapy" Smith held services in their separate and distinct professions. Later "Soapy" went to his reward and Stroller went to Dawson where he continued his missionary work, five years required to bring that town to a degree of sobriety that justified the force of the Royal Northwest Mounted Police being reduced more than one-half. For the past dozen years the Stroller has gone in and out before the people of Whitehorse, also in the Yukon, where his efforts along uplift lines, while slow in results, were finally crowned with success to such an extent that he deemed it his duty to move on to a larger field. He came to Douglas.

While in Dawson the Stroller inaugurated a Heart-to-Heart-Talks-with-Mothers department and, while it has never been popular with husbands, it is immensely so with the women—so much so that the Stroller has acquired the afternoon tea habit. He has since continued this department of his uplift work and will introduce it here during the coming fall when the long, dark nights come again. This precaution will be taken to prevent neighborhood talk among those who know not of the Stroller's mission—going about doing good.

There is one thing about the "Stroller's Column" which will commend it to readers in general: It never contains communications from "Veritas," "Taxpayer," "Old Resident," "Walking Delegate," or "Fond Mother." Our old friends may break into other parts of the paper every time they have an ache, but they are barred from this department.

In the meantime, no advance in the price of subscription to this paper will be made on account of this department, which assures a steadily increasing list, for while it is something he rarely ever mentions, the Stroller has not lost a subscriber to any paper with which he has been connected for the past fifteen years. Reading the Stroller is like the Castoria habit —once acquired, it is permanent.

67 —Juneau City, A.T., April 20, 1916—
Thursday morning

"Jasus, senator, Wick's tryin' ta go into the game with all the marbles in his pocket!" Jack Malone exclaimed.

"You must admit, it's a pretty neat piece of fiction on his part," Sulzer said. "You can tell he's been talking out both sides of his mouth for a good long time."

"Nobody believes this crap do they?"

"That's what you must find out, Jack. The Republicans might field a candidate who's firmly in their pocket. Our Eastern backers want to get rid of Wickersham. As long as I'm the only opposition, we've got it in the bag. But if there's a Republican in the woodpile . . . You've been back in circulation for almost two weeks but you don't seem to be getting about as much as before your, ah, incarceration."

Jack was quiet for a long moment. "Yes, well, I seem ta think it over a bit before I go rushin' through doors these days." He smiled at the senator. "Don't you worry, sir, I still know what's goin' on in this town. Such as the fact Mayor Valentine is backin' Wickersham."

Sulzer sighed. "Good man. That's exactly the kind of thing I need to know. Don't worry about Valentine. We'll beat Wickersham at his own game. I'm depending on you, Jack."

"I won't fail you, Senator."

"Excellent. Well, I've other matters to attend to now. I'll see you in the next few days?"

Jack sat his hat on his head, and picked up his coat. "You certainly will. In the meantime I'll make the rounds and talk to the boys. Good day to you, Senator."

The sun beat down as Jack walked out of the Grand Hotel. He stopped for a moment, savoring the warmth on his upturned face. After three months in jail he would never take sunshine for granted again— not that Juneau City had an overabundance to start with.

"Jack Malone! Good to see you."

Jack's eyes snapped open and focused on Ahab Driscoll. "Where the hell did you come from?"

"Now is that any way to greet an old chum?" Driscoll smiled, revealing gaps where teeth used to be. "I heard you might be looking for a bully boy or two. Word's out that all yours got used up."

"It wasn't none of my doing, I'll tell ye that!" Jack said quickly. "I'm not in the market, Driscoll. Sorry."

"But you know who is, right?" Driscoll's tone had an edge of supplication mixed with panic. "I really need to make some money, Jack."

"I got out of prison less than two weeks ago, Ahab. I've been out of touch, but the only place you'll find what you're looking for is down on Lower Front Street.

You're too far north here, go back the other way."

Driscoll started back down the street, glanced over his shoulder. "Thanks, Jack. I'll be seeing ya."

Jack watched him move swiftly away, easing through the men and women who filled the plank walks. The stamp mills muttered like loud old men in a bar. *That's a bad sign,* Jack thought. *I would have bet money Ahab Driscoll was in prison or hell, one of the two. You never think about your actions when you're young, but they have a way of sticking with you all your life.*

He continued slowly down the street toward Armstrong's. He didn't hurry for fear of overtaking his old associate. Besides, he had many things to think about. He worried about his daughters.

Fiona insisted not only on working for Maye, but also living in that damned hotel. Try as he might he couldn't talk her into moving back into the house. Of course it wasn't lonely with Florence at home again.

She worried him. She didn't argue. She didn't correct his behavior. She didn't do any of the things he had come to associate with the daughter he knew.

She went to work early and came home late. She cleaned the house constantly, offending Mrs. Milivich with her actions, who took them as a personal condemnation.

It took Jack three tries to explain to the old woman. He knew if there had been any other place for her to go, she would have left. *She's the only person in my life that's truly dependent on me,* he thought.

"Mr. Malone, may I speak to you, sir?"

Jack broke from his reverie and looked into the face of August Lepke.

"Wh-, what is it you want, detective?" he said.

"I have to ask you a question that, that if you don't answer, I will not ask again."

"Ask," Jack said, curiosity overriding his first inclinations.

"Did you try to have me killed because you thought I would hurt your daughter?"

"Do *what?*" Jack gasped. "I never tried to have you killed, sir! If I had, you'd damned well be dead!"

Lepke frowned at him. "You didn't set Silas and Ralph on me the night we met?"

"Hell, no. If I wanted someone to do a job for me, it wouldn't have been those two hammer-heads."

"That's not what Ralph told us. He said you hired him and Silas to beat up a guy. That you paid them for the job."

"Oh, that," Jack said with a grin. "I had them back me up, sure, but they never touched the victim. I kicked the man's arse meself! And that all happened way back in October or November."

"What about the two thugs from Petersburg?"

"Mr. Lepke, I have no idea what yer talkin' about. I know we're off to a bad start, but I do me own knuckle work. It's a point of honor, you might say."

The detective looked at him hard for a moment. "I believe you, Mr. Malone. Thank you for telling me."

"You're welcome. Was there anything else?" Jack made himself breathe.

"Ah, your daughter, Florence . . . is she well?"

"No. She's been totally unlike herself since the day you arrested me."

"I *had* to do that!" Lepke barked.

"Christ, man, I know that, but Florence took it personal. She's not quite as worldly as she'd like to believe. She doesn't understand the law, but I thought she understood duty."

"Mr. Malone, you've certainly changed your viewpoint since we first met."

"I'm a different man. It's taking me a bit of time to figure that out, but I'm getting there. A man's memories can be too strong, but some need to be let go."

"Sir?"

"Don't worry about it, and the name is Jack. Good day to you, Detective Lepke."

Jack walked off down the street feeling good. He felt free. He realized for the first time in his life he felt even with society.

68 —Juneau City, A.T., April 28, 1916—
Friday evening

Jack Malone sipped at his whiskey and reread the lead story for the tenth time. A curious elation seized him when word of the Irish revolt reached his ears. For the first time in twenty years he wished he were back in the old country.

He could still handle a rifle, by God! Here in Alaska what could he do? Perhaps raise food and money for the brave lads putting their lives on the line . . .

"After eight hundred years we're finally goin' ta throw the damned English out of Ireland!" he said to the dark, quiet kitchen. He finished the glass and poured another. Florence didn't understand his excitement when he showed her the article.

"But, Father, this is just another war in Europe. An ill-conceived one at that."

He disagreed on both points. This wasn't just another war, it was the *oldest* war in Europe, and the timing was perfect. The British had their hands full on the continent and would be hard pressed to bring enough force against the IRA to put down the revolt.

His heart brimmed. To be alive when Irish justice triumphed over the English invader was enough to make him drunk on emotion. Who needed whiskey? He tossed back the liquor and relished the warmth spreading outward from his stomach.

Half a century after leaving Dublin, he could still remember those dark, cobbled streets and swarms of children. The hunger of those days would always be with him. His father, Padriac, finally accepted alms from the church to put him, his wife, Maisie, and their three children in steerage to leave for America.

Jack could still taste the fear of that voyage in the dark, leaky hold of the ship. Nineteen days of cold, damp, rats, vomit, sickness, coughing adults, and crying babies. Six people died —three old people, two babies, and his little sister.

No amount of pleading from his mother would make the crew hold the small body for burial in America. Lillian was "buried at sea" after a quick ceremony performed by the captain. There being no priest on board, his mother felt sure the little soul would never attain heaven.

Jack filled his glass and took a pull from the bottle for good measure. As soon as the family stepped onto American soil Padriac had been drafted by the Union army. The American Civil War being in its final year. It took Jack's mother three months to learn her husband marched with General Sherman through the middle of the rebellious south.

Padriac never returned to his family. "Unaccounted for," read the official message. A new friend, knowledgeable in the ways of the United States, said that meant he had deserted and got away with it.

Maisie worked as a washerwoman to raise her two remaining children. Jack left home at fourteen and never looked back.

He shook his head and rubbed his misting eyes. How hard it had been in those days. If it hadn't been for the Fenians and the Order of St. Tammany, he wouldn't have had a chance. He wondered what happened to his sister.

After some mental arithmetic, he realized Kathleen Maisie Malone would have turned sixty-four years old last March 16th. *My God, she could be dead.* Being driven from their ancestral home by English taxes, and forced from the bosom of the family at an early age were the hallmarks of his generation of Irish.

He looked at the newspaper again. The words swam before his eyes and he realized he saw them through tears. He rested his head on his crossed arms and sobbed until he fell asleep.

THE DOUGLAS ISLAND NEWS
Douglas, Alaska, Wednesday, May 3, 1916

The Stroller
by E. J. White

The following is a private letter, which if it wasn't, might have been written by Juneau's retiring postmaster to his successor:

My Dear Z. M. B.:

Just a few hints that may be of benefit to you in your new position:

If you think handing out mail constitutes the principal duty of your office, you err exceedingly. Of this you will know more later. Some people who were never known to receive a letter, visit the post office regularly, sometimes oftener. People acquire the post office habit the same as they acquire the habit of going to the dock every time a steamer lands, or of going to funerals. We both know people who never miss a funeral even though they were not on nodding terms with the remains.

If, in canceling stamps, you remove a thumb, or finger nail, count ten or more before expressing your feelings.

The fellow who comes in and stands for an hour at a time before the money order window with his legs pointed to 28 minutes past 6 and insists on telling you stories, may annoy you at first, but by the time you assume a cold and clammy attitude toward him a few times, he will move on. If he don't, cancel one of his cheeks and date the other.

There was about a half a cake of soap in the washroom which I intended leaving but "Shack" sent up for it. He said it would probably be needed in the coming campaign.

In the event of a Taku wind blowing down the chimney, close the general delivery and open a bottle of old bourbon. The furnace poker has been missing since the cold spell in February and, if my memory is not at fault, either Governor Strong or Judge Jennings borrowed and forgot to return it. You might nose around Government house or the courthouse and perhaps you can locate it.

I found it wise not to carry the office money around in my raiment. It is sometimes a temptation to a man when he has his pockets full of money to drop in some place where four or five have just broken a new pack and are sitting in.

You will receive lots of letters about wandering Willies who came north in '97-8 and whose people back east have been expecting them ever since to bob up with a couple or three tons of gold. Most of them are holding down chairs in "paint stores" and think they are in luck if they eat four times a week. Consign such letters to the wastebasket, as answers to them would only give the old folks an ache.

You will also receive letters from sweet young things and frayed and frazzled old things who desire to annex themselves to something that wears pants—outwardly.

Turn such letters over to the cub reporters. They make good "copy."

Kowslphynistachwatsky is Bulgarian for "Is there a letter for me."

In addition to English and profane, you will be required to master eighteen or twenty other languages if you wish to be referred to by all the patrons of your office as "Our competent and efficient, genial and debonair postmaster." That word "debonair" always comes high.

Do not wear tight shoes as eight-hour shifts at the general delivery are conducive to corns, bunions, and in-growing toenails.

Any other suggestions I may be able to make from time to time will be cheerfully given. Any time you find yourself in deep water, call and I will throw you a line.

Respectfully,
E. L. H.

69 —Juneau City, A.T., May 10, 1916—
Wednesday morning

"Oh, Florence, how good to see you again."

She looked up from the pen scratches of her billing into the face of Julia Prescott.

"Julia! What are you doing here?" Then she caught herself and laughed. "What I mean of course is, what can I help you with?"

"Oh, I'm not here on business, I'm here to see you on a personal matter."

She glanced around the shop. Nobody there. She felt faintly annoyed she couldn't avoid this conversation. "Personal?"

"Well, yes. I wish to invite you to my wedding." Julia smiled at her.

For a short horrible moment, she thought Julia meant to marry August. "Oh! Wh-, who are you marrying?"

"George Mak-we. Oh, Florence, I love him so much!"

Florence abruptly forgot August. "George Mak-we! The Indian policeman?"

"Do you know any other George Mak-we? Yes. June 25th, a Sunday. Will you come?"

"Oh, Julia. Do you know what you're doing?"

Julia's smile faded and she stared into Florence's eyes. "I think so. I know I'm marrying what many would consider a social and racial inferior."

"But . . . Well, why?"

"Florence, why do you think?"

"Well, Julia," she felt tears running down her cheeks, "I suppose because you love him." She sniffed loudly and wiped her nose with her sleeve. "But do you know how people here will treat you? What they'll say about you because you married an Indian?" She wept openly.

"Why are you so upset about me marrying George?" Julia's hands came up for a moment then dropped to her side. "What's the matter?" She put her arms around Florence and hugged her. "I can live with the ignorant attitudes around me. Women have been doing it for centuries. I've even been adopted into the Eagle phraety because George is a Raven"

"But even the women will treat you shabbily," she sniffed.

"The circles I frequent won't mind a bit. In fact they're all coming to the wedding."

"Of course I'll come, Julia, but, I'd rather not see August Lepke. Is he attending?"

"No, I believe he will have left town by that time," Julia said flatly.

"Left town? He's leaving town?"

"That's what George told me. It's not common knowledge yet, so I'd appreciate it if you kept that to yourself."

"Oh. Of course. Thank you for, ah, letting me know I won't see him." A void suddenly opened inside her chest. It took all of her concentration to stay on her feet.

"Florence, you don't look well. Have you been getting enough to eat?"

"Of course, it's just been a long winter."

"Well, it's spring now. Why don't you come for a little trip with us this Sunday?"

"Little trip to where?"

"We're going out to the village at Auke Bay. I've wanted to see it since I arrived. It's been so nice that George agreed to get a boat if the weather holds."

"Weather like this hold for another four days?" Florence said with a laugh. "This is Juneau. It will rain twice before then."

"Well, if it doesn't, will you come with us? I really think you need the air and the distraction."

"Distraction from my work, you mean?"

"From whatever it is that's putting those lines in your face and those purple spots under your eyes. You're too young to carry baggage like that. Say you'll come with us, please?"

"If the weather holds," she said wanly, "I'll come with you."

"Thank you. I'll send word on Saturday as to where we'll meet. I'll see you then."

"Fine," Florence said with a forced smile. She felt relief when Julia left the shop. On one hand she envied her, but on the other, all that bustle and preparation was more than she could deal with these days.

Besides, I'm not going to marry anyone. There's not one man in the world I can trust, and I refuse to marry anyone I can't trust!

Her headache returned. It would be hard to concentrate on her work. Dr. Parker told her there was nothing wrong with her other than a "case of the nerves." She smiled despite the pain. In her mind's eye she pictured a wooden crate of tiny, hair-like wires, writhing fiercely.

She still liked her job, but it had taken on the aspect of a refuge rather than a challenge. She hadn't taken any views with her camera for months. It just didn't matter any more.

Perhaps I'll take a month and go visit Aunt Martha in Seattle, she thought. *It would do me good to get away from Juneau for a time. I wonder if August will go back to Portland?*

She froze her thoughts. *Where did that come from? I don't care where he goes, just as long as he can't harm my father any more.*

70 —Ground Hog Mine, A.T., May 14, 1916—
Sunday morning

For the second day in a row, the rain came down in sheets, making Williams grateful for the waterproofs he wore. The sun actually rose before he did this morning. To wake at 4am and find daylight was positively unnerving.

The Thane complex ran a late day shift on Sundays so the miners could worship their God before work. A large rock out-crop shielded the bunkhouse from the main adit.

He wasn't sure there was anybody on the property at all. Better to do what he came for and then quickly fade into the wet afternoon. He surreptitiously peeked around corners before moving between buildings. This was no time to be explaining his presence this far from Juneau City.

A large padlock secured the powder shed. Rain poured from the taller mill building behind it onto the sheet metal roof, creating a maddening din. Williams pulled out the hammer and struck one mighty blow to the padlock. It popped open instantly.

Inside the dry shed he moved swiftly, selecting a case of No. 1 powder, a detonator, and a small coil of fuse. He pushed the door shut and jammed the lock back together, wedging a small stone into it in order to make it look convincingly secure.

Hefting the case onto his left shoulder, he moved quickly to the mouth of the mine. The silence seemed strange as he entered the main adit. That's good, he noted. I'll hear anyone who might come in.

The hammer would serve a variety of uses. At the finger chute he stopped, eased the case of explosives to the floor, and pried the top boards off. Every stick of dynamite displayed the words "DUPONT No. 1" down its length.

He spent a feverish half hour wiring batches of four sticks to various supports and crossbeams on the finger chute. Then he carefully capped the detonator onto one stick in the middle of the structure. He knew sympathetic detonation would set the rest off. He measured off ten minutes worth of fuse and inserted it into the detonator.

Carefully he backed away from the chute, playing out the fuse from around the handle of the hammer.

"Hey! Who're you? What you doin' there?"

Williams froze. He twisted his head and looked at the man in wet oilskins. A big man, very suspicious, and about ten feet behind him, he decided.

"Hell, I'm doin' what they told me to do, what do you think?"

"You're settin' off a charge in the main adit on a Sunday morning?" The man took a step closer. "That don't make no sense."

Williams slid the fuse off the handle and scratched at the front of his slicker.

"Well, come here and look at this if you don't believe me."

The man stepped forward without hesitation. "What you got there?"

"This." He swung around, the hammer lashed out and caught the man on the side of the temple with a solid thunk. Blood spurted out around the steel head and the man fell without a sound.

He dragged the body over to the finger chute and dropped it on the rock floor between the tracks. He ran back to the hammer and coil of fuse and hurriedly moved backward to the entrance. The hammer was slippery.

He looked down at his hand and saw the man's blood mixing with the water still dripping off his slicker. Carefully he pulled a book of matches from his pocket and struck one. Instead of the dry zip of an igniting lucifer he was rewarded with a crumbly scritch as the match head disintegrated into pulpy grains.

Wet matches! He snarled a curse and went back to his victim. In the third pocket he found a small glass vial containing three stick matches. He grinned and glanced at the wound. The blood had trickled to a stop; it was coagulating. The sod wasn't dead!

"Well, friend, you will be in a moment," he muttered. He went back to the fuse and with a shaking hand struck one of the matches on the rock wall. The stick snapped and the flaming head fizzed into a puddle to hiss out of existence.

Damn it! Why is all of this happening?

He felt his heart pounding, and realized he was on a battlefield. It was quiet and damp, but it could be as deadly as France if he were discovered now. Who knew why the man had come in here?

Maybe there were others who waited for him. Others who might investigate at any moment. If more than one came he would be forced to use the Luger strapped at his side, and he didn't want that. It would create far too much noise.

This had to look like an accident. If he couldn't take care of a small part of an operation like this, how could he ever destroy the Treadwell or the Perseverance? He gripped the second match and slowly pulled it across the rock.

It flared into life and he pulled his thumb away, held the flame to the end of the fuse. It fizzed into life and began eating toward its doom, throwing off sparks in promise of a hotter instant hell. Williams dropped the fuse and headed for the entrance at a fast pace.

He followed the steel tracks around the curve in the tunnel and glanced ahead. The gray, rain-filled sky outside clearly silhouetted the two men lounging at the entrance. His heart fluttered in panic.

He glanced around the adit. He had to find a place that would protect him from the blast as well as from their sight. The wall was uniform in its hewn surface. There were no niches to provide seclusion.

He stood frozen by indecision. How much longer would the fuse last? Would he have time to go back and pull it free of the dynamite?

No! It would only be a matter of minutes before the two men investigated the absence of their companion. He had to do something. For an instant he considered the Luger again.

Suddenly the distance between he and them lengthened and he felt the old, familiar detachment settle over his mind. They are expecting someone to walk back out of this mineshaft. They will see their friend returning if they bother to look up, because that is who they saw enter.

Williams pushed the hammer up into the sleeve of his coat and began trudging stolidly toward the talking men. One chatted around a cigarette, boring the other one. The listener glanced up and saw Williams.

It took all of his resolve to continue walking. The man looked back at his chatting companion and then down at his feet again. At fifteen feet, Williams could hear the one-sided conversation.

"So dis little woman, she looks up at me, an' she says, 'My but yer a big boy!'"

Ten feet.

"An' I look down at her 'n' say, 'You ain't seed nutting yet!'" The man broke into a loud guffaw and slapped his slickered knee.

Five feet.

"You hear dat, Jim?" the man pronounced it "Chim." The two grinning faces swung toward him.

Williams brought his left boot up into the crotch of the listener, and swung the hammer over-handed at the joker, catching him in the top of the head. The booted man shrieked a painful "Oh!" and the joker's eyes rolled back in his head and he dropped like a sack of potatoes. Williams brought the hammer down on the back of the listener's head when he rolled forward heavily onto his face.

He glanced around. The rain clattered down on the surrounding metal roofs, creating a wall of white noise. He was sure nobody had heard anything.

But how many were about? Would anybody else come along looking for these three? He didn't have time for mental debate.

Grabbing the first man, he pulled him down the tunnel until he was out of the light from the mouth of the mine, laying him between the tracks. Then he raced back, grabbed the other one and pulled him clear back to the bay where the fuse sputtered busily within two feet of the dynamite.

He dropped the man and raced for the entrance. This wasn't enough time! He sprinted out into the open without slowing or looking for witnesses. Rain poured out of the sky as if nature protested his intentions.

Williams dashed around the mill and adjoining powder shed. He slipped on wet rock, nearly falling, but kept his feet. He pounded down the puddled track to where his horse stood dejectedly in the downpour.

He grabbed the reins and jerked them free from the budding limb. The horse moved away from him, snorting in uneasiness picked up from the man.

"Hold still, you stupid—"

The blast shattered the afternoon.

The pressure wave whipped down the brush-lined path to them and threw Williams against the horse. The animal shrilled in fear and panic, turned with a lunge and pulled the reins from Williams' hands before racing off down the muddy road.

The result of Arnold Williams' work.

Williams fell heavily to the ground and his left hand hit a rock the size of a man's head. He heard the little finger snap before he felt the pain. The agony flashed through him like electric current and he had to throttle his scream down to a smothered groan.

He jerked himself to his feet. Cradling his left hand with his right, he ran down the rain-filled road. Shouts and bells filled the soggy afternoon behind him.

71 —Juneau City, A.T., May 17, 1916—
Wednesday night

"More champagne, my dear?"

Amanda smiled into Barrington Wentworth's gaze, nodding her head. "This should be my last glass, or there's no telling what I will do."

"Now that sounds promising– very promising indeed."

The waiter materialized at their side. "Are madam and sir finished with the main course?"

"Yes," Barry said without taking his eyes off Amanda.

"Very good, sir." He collected the stack of plates and silverware, and departed.

"How often will you find yourself in Alaska?" Amanda asked.

"Not often enough. Probably every six weeks or so. If we don't keep the pressure up, the other pharmaceutical companies will run us out of the Territory."

"But aren't you intruding on their territory, as they see it?"

"It's everyone's territory in that respect. You must move quickly or lose it. It's a great deal like wooing a woman."

They chuckled together.

"Well, Mr. Wentworth, at this time you're the only purveyor of drugs in my life."

"I want to keep it that way. You promised to tell me over dinner how you came to be Alaska, and I haven't heard the story yet."

She maintained her smile but her mind went cold. She didn't want this man to be frightened off by the threat of Williams; therefore she wouldn't mention him at all. But how to explain her presence otherwise?

"From your silence am I to assume you don't wish to tell me?"

"My husband was killed by bandits in Mexico," she said briskly. "At that point I wanted to get as far from that place as possible. Someone had mentioned Alaska earlier in the day, so I decided to travel to that distant and romantic sounding land. And here I am."

"You're moved by whim, Baroness. I like that in a woman."

"How many women have you liked it in?"

"I *never* kiss and tell."

"Well," her smile returned. "I certainly like *that* in a man!"

He glanced around the Alaskan Grill. "Would you care for desert."

"Yes. I would enjoy desert."

He stared into her eyes. "Here, or at the hotel?"

She held his gaze, savoring the hunger evident there. "Oh, most definitely at the hotel."

His head snapped around, "Waiter, our check!"

The window in the hiotel room was opened a few inches to allow fresh air, and facilitated closeness.

"My God, but you're an incredible woman," Barry said with a sigh. Amanda snuggled at his side and smiled, feeling fulfilled and happy.

"You're an accomplished lover, Barry. I am very fortunate," she ran her hand down his hairy, muscular chest. "I'm so glad your employer gave you the Alaskan account."

"Yes." He rolled over to face her, cupped her breast in his hand and kissed the nipple. She felt herself quicken to him again.

"If you keep doing that . . ."

"Yes?" he asked lazily, stroking her.

"You're going to have me all excited again, and you know what happens then."

"You're insatiable!"

"It's been such a long time, you see, since I had a decent desert." Her hand moved down his body to resuscitate his ardor.

"Well," he said, his voice growing husky, "I think I can serve another course."

She laughed and rolled over onto him.

72 —Juneau City, A.T., May 19, 1916—
Friday morning

"Chief Tinsley, could I have a word with you?"

The chief glanced up at Lepke in surprise. "Sure, August. I didn't even know you were in the office."

Lepke sat down in the visitor's chair. "Chief, I think we have had an organized plot on our hands."

"All these killings and attempted killings?"

"Yes. I've gone over the records for the past five years. In the last six months we've had more people die violently than in the previous two years combined. With the exception of Silas Mason, all of them can be traced back to one man."

Tinsley's eyebrows shot up. "Then arrest him, detective!"

Lepke allowed himself a tight grin. "We can't arrest him. He's already in jail."

"What?"

"Peter Sommers was a close friend to Edward Krause. I suspect their relationship was a partnership in crime. Sommers killed Robert Bennett by mistake. Horace Powell and Bjorn Halvstaad both came to Juneau from Petersburg at the behest of Sommers. The three were seen together in Armstrong's Tavern less than an hour before Sommers died."

"So you think Krause put Sommers and his cronies up to getting you out of the picture?"

"Yes, that's exactly what I believe. For awhile I thought Jack Malone might be behind these attempts on my life, but I no longer think that is the case."

"If Jack Malone wanted you dead . . ." Tinsley began.

". . . I would already be dead," Lepke finished. "Yes, I know. He told me."

Tinsley grinned. "Jack's a scoundrel, make no mistake of that, but he's no back-shooter. He does have a code of ethics."

"I realize that, sir."

"So do you think this rash of killings has come to an end?"

"I sent a wireless to Marshal Wick in Petersburg asking about Krause's known associates there. From what he says, we may have eliminated the majority of them."

"Then it's all over. We'll approach the U.S. district attorney with our findings. He might want to add them to the list Krause already has to answer for."

"For awhile I thought Arnold Williams might also be in Krause's organization, but I've had him watched and he's kept his distance from Krause as well as his lawyer."

"Why on earth would a English remittance man want to kill you?"

"He's killed before, in Mexico."

"There's a war on down there, Lepke. Remember?"

"That's true. Even so, this man killed two non-combatants in cold blood for no discernable reason."

"How do you know?"

"An eye witness told me."

Tinsley curled his white mustache absently, staring into space. "Not our jurisdiction," he said finally. "If we arrested every man in this town who has committed a crime some place else, we'd have this jail stuffed like a sausage."

"Whatever you say. You're the chief."

"But keep an eye on him. If he pulls any fancy stuff here we'll at least give him a blue ticket."

"Okay, chief."

"Who was the witness?"

"Miss Ganbor. She was on the same train."

"Didn't they arrive here together?"

"Yes."

"Then we can't rule out a lover's quarrel as her motivation in bringing this information out. In fact we might take the whole thing with a grain of salt."

"I don't believe she's lying."

"If he murdered two people in Mexico, why didn't the Mexican authorities arrest him?"

"As you said, there's a war being fought down there. This happened at the end of an ambush. Many people were killed."

"Ah, well, there you have it," Tinsley said with a note of dismissal. "He probably thought he was being threatened and didn't wait to ask questions before shooting. Wasn't it like that in the Philippines when you were there?"

"I never knowingly killed a non-combatant," Lepke said flatly.

"And Williams is no soldier. Like I said, keep an eye on him."

August knew his time was up. "Thanks for listening, chief," he said as he left the small office.

"My door is always open, detective."

Lepke walked slowly back to his desk, rolled the top down, locked it, and dropped the key in his pocket. With the Krause trials moving along at their rapid pace, he wouldn't have as much time to shadow the Englishman as he would like. He wasn't ready to shrug off the man's actions in Mexico.

Amanda had clearly stated she thought Williams a murderer. She also said she felt frightened of him.

"But why are you telling me this now?" he had asked.

"Because Fiona didn't tell anyone other than me about her fear of Sommers. I don't want to make the same mistake."

Was it antipathy for an ex-lover? Women certainly seemed capable of condemning a man for reasons that wouldn't hold up in court. He shook his head and walked out into the misty day, trying not to think about Florence.

73 —Juneau City, A.T., May 24, 1916—
Wednesday afternoon

With a heavy heart Jack Malone walked into Armstrong's tavern and leaned on the bar.

"Jack?" the bartender said. "Is something wrong?"

"A double whiskey, if you please, John."

John turned and selected a bottle of Bushmills off the back bar, sat a glass in front of Jack and filled it to the brim. He set the bottle down and stared at the shorter man.

"Ya wanna talk about it, Jack?"

"Leave the bottle." Jack knocked back the glass, sat it down and nodded. "Do it again."

John filled the glass. "Jack, I, uh," he lowered his voice, "I know you're the boss, but if you keep doing that you're not gonna be able to walk."

"You're a good man, John. That's why I hired ya." He drained the glass. "Pour me another."

The bartender complied. At the other end of the bar a miner rapped his mug twice. "What I must do to beer get?"

"Take care o' yer customer," Jack ordered.

John moved away. Jack sighed. The whiskey wasn't warming him nor making his heart any lighter than when he came in.

"Well, if it ain't me old pal, Jack Malone."

Jack raised his eyes without raising his head. Ahab Driscoll stood there exhibiting what few teeth he still owned.

"I ain't in the mood to be jawin' with an Englishman, Ahab. Now move. Yer blockin' me light."

Driscoll's mouth flattened into a grim line.

"Yer gittin' kinda long in th' tooth ta be giving me orders like that, ya fat ol' mick. You think yer better'n me 'cause ya stayed in this one-horse town long enough ta bullshit ever' body inta thinkin' ya wuz somethin'!"

"I won't ask ya a third time, Driscoll. Now get outta me light!"

Out of the corner of his eye, Jack saw John reach under the bar for his bung starter. He raised his hand. "Leave it be, I'll handle this."

John nodded and moved back away from the men.

"Ya didn't *ast* me anything. Ya *tol'* me! You allus wuz—"

Jack's right uppercut caught Driscoll under the jaw hard enough to lift both his feet off the floor. The spindly man flew backward in a small arc and crashed heavily onto the floor. The buzz of conversation died and heads turned to watch.

Driscoll lay motionless for a moment, and then started working his jaw, fish-like. He rolled over, spit out a bloody tooth, and slowly pushed himself up to his knees.

"I, ugh, I fergot how hard—," He rubbed his jaw carefully. "—yer punch wuz, Jack." Driscoll reached out and held onto the bar for support as he regained his feet. He stayed back away from Jack, and scratched his belly with a distracted air.

"Get yer Sassenach ass out of this bar, Driscoll," Jack said flatly.

"An' you fergot," Ahab said conversationally, "that I allus carry *this!* A blur at the end of his hand clicked into an evil-looking stiletto.

Driscoll blinked and stared at the revolver that magically appeared in Jack's hand. The bore centered on Driscoll's face, the barrel didn't waver a millimeter.

Jack stared down the barrel at the man. "You shouldn't have come north again, Ahab. Ya shoulda stayed down south with the other cockroaches. I could blow yer brains out this instant and every man in this establishment would swear I did it in self-defense. I've only been outta jail fer a few weeks. I was there because I killed a man."

Driscoll let his hand slowly drop to his side. His eyes wide with fear, his mouth worked silently as it leaked blood and spittle.

"I ain't gonna kill ya this time, Ahab. I don't want ta bother w' the authorities over somethin' as worthless as you. If you was wearing a British uniform it would be another matter . . . Now get *out!*" he screamed.

Driscoll scrambled out the door. Jack put the weapon back in the holster under his arm. He leaned on the bar again.

"Jack?" the bartender said.

"The son of a bitch got me almost sober, John. Get me a new glass." As John moved away, Jack sensed a presence at his side.

Arnold Williams stood beside him with a bottle in one hand and a glass in the other.

"Must be my day fer worthless Englishmen!" Jack said with a snort.

Williams stared at him somberly. "Mr. Malone, I am as saddened by the Irish defeat as you are. Maybe even more so."

Jack squinted up at him. "Them's mighty strange words ta be comin' from a Limey journalist."

Williams produced a tight grin and his eyes caught the light. "I have many strange words, sir, if you'd care to listen in a less public location."

John sat a clean glass on the bar. Jack picked bottle and glass up and nodded toward the dark door marked "Office." "Let's be havin' some privacy and I'll hear what y' have ta say."

Williams sat down in the visitor's chair and Jack flopped into his creaky chair behind the cluttered desk dominating the middle of the room. Williams slowly took in the small office. On one side sat three heavy, wooden filing cases and a squat combination-lock safe. The wall behind the desk was covered with photographs and certificates. A large oil painting of an attractive woman dominated the wall to the right of the desk.

Williams stared at the painting for a long moment. "That's a very beautiful woman, Mr. Malone. Did you know her?"

"Me late wife," Jack said gruffly. "Let's be hearin' them strange words y' got."

"First I must ascertain a few points, sir. Is it true that you are angered, more than angered, over the execution of the Irish rebels?"

"Them boys was patriots, an' don't you ever be forgettin' it!"

"Quite so, quite so. Is it also true you would like to strike back at England for her brutal suppression of the Irish patriots?" Williams asked gently.

"With all me heart!" Jack said.

"Did it occur to you that keeping America out of the war in Europe would harm England? I realize the United States has kept out of actual combat even though she has been sending munitions and equipment to England by the ship load."

"An' where would ya be gettin' that kind of information, Mr. Williams?"

"From secret manifests, from shipping offices the length of the Atlantic coast, from men who think America should stay out of European affairs, and from good Americans who don't want their sons to die at the front." Williams pulled at his left cuff.

"Munitions, ya say," Jack mused. "An' how would I be stoppin' any of that business up here in the Territory?"

"If you could stop part of America's entry into the war, would you?"

"Well, Mr. Wilson is tellin' folks we won't be getting into the war. How can ya be so sure we are?"

"Because Germany will not stop submarine warfare, and America will not stop carrying war materials to England. Perhaps if America didn't have the wealth to support the Allies, that would change."

"Wealth," Jack repeated. "Y'want me ta rob banks?" He began to push articles around on the top of his desk.

"Nothing that chancy." Williams smiled. "Would you consider interrupting gold production from, say, the Treadwell complex?"

Jack's eyes went wide for a moment. "Now there's an idea! Who exactly do you work for, Mr. Williams?"

"The country that sold the Irish patriots their weapons and ammunition. The country that faces the English and French armies across 'no man's land' at the front. I killed Englishmen when I was still in uniform."

"You're a German spy with a Limey accent!"

"Agent," Williams said crisply. "I'm here to do my duty, not ferret out information and take it back." He breathed more quickly and his left eyelid began to twitch. "I need a confederate. Our causes amount to the same thing. Are you with me, Mr. Malone, or against me?"

"Jasus, this ain't a'tall simple, is it?" Jack picked up a pewter-framed photograph of Fiona and Florence and looked at it thoughtfully.

"No." Williams breathed heavily; his nostrils flaring and relaxing as if he had just ran for a mile. "It's quite complex. I must have an answer, sir."

"We won't have to kill any Americans will we?"

"No. We're only going to kill mines."

"Kill mines," Jack said thoughtfully. "You didn't have anything to do with the explosion out at the Ground Hog, did ya?"

"Yes. And I made the mistake of not working fast enough. Those men came in as I was leaving."

"You killed three miners all by yerself?"

"Yes. It won't happen again."

"Yer quite the surprise package, Mr. Williams, and I'll bet yer name ain't Williams, is it?"

"No. But if you don't know my real name, you can't slip and call me by it."

"True. By God, but yer one cool customer."

"I'll accept that as a compliment. I insist on an answer now."

"Well, I'm in, of course. You'd have ta try 'n' kill me if I said not, correct?"

Williams smiled in relief. "Yes, I would have had to kill you. I'm glad that's not necessary."

"Me, too," Jack said, mirroring his grin. "But it mighta been a bit more difficult than you think." He dropped the photograph flat on the desk, revealing the .32 revolver held tight in his right hand, pointing at the German's chest.

Williams went white and cleared his throat. "It appears I have finally found the right man."

"Just don't ever underestimate me, laddie," Jack whispered.

THE ALASKA DAILY EMPIRE
Juneau, Alaska, Friday, May 26, 1916

CHAS. A. SULZER UNANIMOUSLY NOMINATED

GRIGSBY; DONOHOE ARE ALSO ELECTED

PLATFORM OF DEMOCRATS AS ADOPTED TODAY

TWO AMERICAN SOLDIERS KILLED IN ATTACK

PRESIDENT MAY MAKE MOVE FOR EUROPEAN PEACE

PARIS IS WORRYING ON ATTACK

GERMAN EAST AFRICA FORCES ARE MOVING AGAINST BRITISH

FRENCH AEROPLANES BOMBARD TROOP TRAIN

GERMAN U. BOAT STRIKES GERMAN MINE

HUNDREDS OF CANNON PLACED ON FRONT LINE

WILL ABOLISH OFFICE OF VICEROY OF IRELAND

SENTENCES ON KRAUSE SET OFF UNTIL TOMORROW

Edward Krause was taken into court this morning to receive his sentence for the crimes for which he has been convicted, and the matter was set over until tomorrow morning while Judge Jennings investigates certain points.

When Krause was asked if he had anything to say why sentence should not be pronounced at this time, he stated that personally there was nothing to say, but that his attorney had a statement to make.

Kazis Krauczunas then made a motion asking that the imposing of the sentences be postponed until the next term of court on account of the effect they might have on the minds of the people of this district and the prospective jurors who will be called upon to hear the evidence in the murder charges. Assistant District Attorney James J. Reagan resisted the motion and it was taken under advisement by Judge Jennings.

74 —Douglas, A.T., May 29, 1916—
Monday afternoon

"I don't know why anyone would sabotage a mine and kill three men, detective. But I think that's exactly what happened."

August stared at the stocky man with deep-set eyes seeing only anxiety in his face.

"Well, Mr. Thane, this is an interesting hypothesis, but even you admit that the blast could have been accidental."

"Yes. It could have. I know it wasn't." Thane's eyes could bore holes in rock. "That crew was one of the best in the business. Do you have any idea what that means around here?"

"I can appreciate your point," Lepke said. "Even the best make mistakes."

"Not on a Sunday! They had the morning off. Happner was responsible for security, that's why he went into the mine. Boyle and Fennersen went with him for company. They had been playing cards with Dave Fowler. Happner interrupted their card game to do his rounds."

Thane licked his lips and continued staring intently at Lepke. "They didn't have time to rig a charge. They had no reason to rig a charge. Boyle was a powder man. He wouldn't have touched off the charge accidentally."

"They were gambling before the blast?" Lepke asked mildly.

"They were playing poker."

"Did those three men play a lot of poker?"

"How should I know? What are you getting at?"

"Men in debt do strange things, Mr. Thane."

"Are you suggesting one of those men sabotaged the mine?" Thane asked carefully.

"No. But the possibility exists someone who owed one of them money might have."

"Mr. Lepke, I think you're missing something very important here."

"What's that?"

"In the past six months there has been an incredible increase in violent deaths in this area. You have been intimately involved in three of them. Isn't there a larger pattern at work here that could account for this upswing in homicides?"

Lepke hesitated. Thane obviously wasn't superintendent of the operation because he married the boss' daughter.

"We believe there was a plot on my life, Mr. Thane. We also believe all of the possible assassins are behind bars or deceased. I don't see how the deaths of these men could be part of the picture, so to speak."

Thane scratched at his head and paced over to the window in agitation. "Frankly, I don't either. Even so, I know, I *know* this was no accident. I do not believe any of those three men set off the blast that killed them."

"Back to your question we are," Lepke said, surprised at the vehement manner of the other. "Why would anyone sabotage the mine? Who would gain by such an action?"

"Nobody I can think of at this late date," Thane muttered angrily. "I almost believe we have a madman on our hands."

"Perhaps a disgruntled employee? An ex-employee?" Lepke suggested. "Can you get me a list of all the men who have been fired from your mining company in the past, oh, six months?"

"Yes!" Thane said with a look of triumph. "I think you might have something there." He pushed a button on his desk and a young man in a suit opened the office door.

"Yes, Mr. Thane?"

"Adams, get Mr. Lepke the names of every man who has been fired from any company holding in the past six months."

"Do you want me to include Perseverance and the Ground Hog, too?"

"Absolutely!"

"We have the 'look out' list from Treadwell . . ."

"Good thinking, Adams."

Yes, sir." The door closed again.

"Who was trying to kill you, detective?"

"We're not certain. But we strongly suspect it was the Treadwell's ex-employee, Edward Krause."

"You've done an admirable job on casing up that batch of damaged goods."

"Thank you, Mr. Thane. I'm glad I was given the work to accomplish. After all, it brought me to Juneau."

"I imagine the police department isn't nearly as exciting as working for the Pinkertons."

"You're wrong, sir. The entire time I was a Pinkerton operative my life was only threatened once. That doesn't count my work here on Gastineau Channel."

Thane laughed. "Well, you've certainly cleared away some of the rougher elements in Southeast Alaska."

The office door opened again. Adams held three sheets of paper in his hand.

"Here you are, Mr. Lepke. On this top sheet are the names of men who left us or Treadwell holdings in a surly manner or made actual threats."

"Thank you, Adams." Lepke ran an eye down the column of names. "Davis, Gresham, Santo, Tudwell, and Wallace. It looks like I have my work cut out for me."

"If there's anything else the company can do to assist the police department, just let me know and you'll have it," Thane said earnestly. "Can't have people blowing up the mines that still have decent ore in them."

Lepke thought about the remark as he left the office. *There were mines here that didn't have "decent ore" any longer?*

THE ALASKA DAILY EMPIRE
Juneau, Alaska, Tuesday, May 30, 1916

ATTEMPT MADE TO ASSASSINATE ROOSEVELT
RAZOR KNIFE HURLED FROM STREET CROWD

GERMANS ARE BOMBING FRENCH LINES

MOOSE IN PLAN FOR REAL BOLT

JAMES J. HILL WILL BE LAID TO REST TOMORROW

VETERAN DROPS DEAD MAKING A MEMORIAL TALK

WILSON MADE MEMORIAL ADDRESS TODAY

VILLA CACHE OF GUNS FOUND BY MEXICAN PEOPLE

BALL PLAYER IS KILLED WHEN HIT OVER HEART

JUNEAU BOWS HEAD IN HONOR OF WAR VETERANS

COLONEL MOSBY OF CIVIL WAR FAME IS DEAD

75 —Juneau City, A.T., May 30, 1916—
Tuesday morning

Rain misted out of a grey sky as the *S.S. Jefferson* disembarked her passengers at the Juneau City dock. Driscoll eyed the crowd professionally, noting the marks whose pockets he would pick under different circumstances. A shabbily dressed man moved down the gangway and tripped, falling against a well dressed man of middle years.

Driscoll grinned as the stumbling man neatly lifted the mark's wallet, making it disappear, and then apologized to the mark for his clumsiness. The Soda Water Kid hadn't lost his touch. Keeping out of the Kid's sight, Driscoll hurried around and came up on his blind side.

"I saw that smart move, mister!" he said heavily, grabbing the man's arm.

"Move! What move? I ain't—" the Kid finally took in Driscoll's leering face. "Gawddamn you, Ahab. You near skeered th' shit outta me!"

"Sure did!" he laughed, dancing a little jig. He noticed people glancing at them and immediately stopped his foolishness. "Hey, where's Gump? I sent fer both o' ya."

"Wouldn't come. Said you got him two years in McNeil th' last time he listened to ya."

"Well, that sonuvabitch!" He wasn't really surprised at Gump's action since the bastard never had any balls anyway. "C'mon, let's go git a drink. We got lots to talk about."

The Louve Bar was home territory again. Two blocks from Armstrong's seemed a safe distance. He didn't want to see Jack Malone on his own turf ever again.

As it turned out he was gonna see a lot of Jack just the same. What a strange world. Who'd a thought he'd get paid to spy on his old confederate? And by a Limey at that.

After his run-in with Jack he sat in the Louve exploring his damaged mouth with a finger when the swell came up behind him.

"Didn't give you much warning, did he?"

Ahab pulled his finger out of his mouth and looked at the man carefully. Good clothes, ate well, and the fellow still had all his teeth. It all boiled down to money in Driscoll's book.

"No, he didn't," he allowed, "but what's it to you?"

"Think of me as a small piece of destiny, Mr. Driscoll."

"What's destiny, an' how'd ya know m' name?"

"Destiny is the way things end up– the finish."

"Ya mean, dead?"

"Not quite that far south. Your destiny, sir, is to have your revenge on Jack Malone."

"How'd ya know my name?"

"I witnessed Mr. Malone's mishandling of your person."

"You was in Armstrong's, ya mean."

"Exactly."

"An' jist how'm I 'sposed to get this here destiny on Jack?"

"I'm willing to help you. *If* you're willing to do it *my* way."

"Help me how?"

"With funds. Operating capital as it were."

"Money? Yer willin' ta give me money?"

"*My* way," he repeated.

"Who th' hell are you, 'n' why do you give a damn about me or Jack Malone?"

"Part of my way is you don't ask a lot of questions. It also means ten dollars a month to you, in gold."

Ahab licked his lips. That was pretty good money for a little destiny work. "Well, whut'm I 'sposed to do fer the money?"

"I want you to shadow Jack Malone without him knowing about it. Hire other men if you need to, but he mustn't know he's being watched."

"You sure 'spect a lot fer ten bucks a week!"

"I'll pay the other men the same amount. You hire them, you give them their instructions, and you tell them you're the boss. I pay the bills."

Driscoll thought himself dreaming. This was almost too good to be true.

"Uh, how 'bout I hire two more mugs?"

"Fine. That's a good round number. Are they here in town?"

"No. They're in Seattle . . ."

"I suppose you want me to pay their way north?"

"Well, Mister . . . say, what's yer name anyways?"

"Smith."

"Well, Mr. Smith, I know these here boys personal, an' they do good work 'n' don't ast a buncha questions. They kin do rough work, too, if ya catch m' drift."

"Give me their names and I'll go down to the Pacific Steamship Company and pay their passage."

"Uh, ya could jist give me the money, 'n' I could—"

"Skip the country," Smith said. "Understand one thing Mr. Driscoll; I am no damn fool. All things being unequal, this arrangement will benefit you far more than it will me. I can find men in your position more easily than you can find men in mine."

Driscoll held his hands up.

"Whoa. You do it any way you likes, Mr. Smith. Yer the boss."

"Damned right I am. What are the names of your friends?"

"Th' Soda Water Kid 'n' Gump Bailey," Driscoll said, smiling at this turn of events.

Smith stared at him with a frown.

"The *Soda Water Kid?* Are you attempting to pull my leg, Mr. Driscoll?"

"Yes! I mean no! I ain't tryin' ta pull yer leg. That's really his name. Ain't nobody 'cept him what knows his real name. He won't drink whiskey without soda water in it. That's how he got his name down on Skid Road."

"My God, you Americans! The other one's name is *Gump* Bailey?"

"Yeah, like th' folks in the funny papers. He jist loves them picture stories."

"Can you send them a wireless today?"

"Sure."

"Here's five dollars to send the message. Tell them to catch the first boat north. These tickets will only be good for one week, then they've lost their chance to visit this fair country."

"Yes, sir. I'll tell 'em." Driscoll grabbed the gold piece out of Smith's hand. "I'll go send th' message right now."

"I'll come back here in one week. Have your men where I can see them. I'll make sure you see me, and then I'll leave. You meet me five minutes later in the Germania dancehall. Understand?"

"You bet!"

A day before the deadline and he already had the Kid here. He smiled to himself as they walked along. They entered the Louve and Driscoll led his friend to a quiet corner and sat down at an empty table.

"What'll it be, fellas?" The beefy bartender scowled down at them.

"Whiskey," said Driscoll. "'N' m' friend here takes his with sody water."

"That'll be twenty-five cents, in advance."

Driscoll pulled a handful of change from his pocket, selected a quarter and handed it to the man.

The bartender lost his scowl. "Nuthin' personal. We get all kinds in here."

"I'm sure yew do," the Kid said grandly.

"Okay," Driscoll said as the bartender hurried away. "Here's th' deal. There's this feller I need ta have watched all th' time."

"What th' hell fer?"

"Fer the hell of it! You want a job 'r' not?" Driscoll snapped.

"I'm here, ain't I?"

"Then shut up 'n' lissen!" He told the Soda Water Kid how it was to be, going quiet only when the bartender brought their drinks.

"Ahab, yer hidin' somethin' from me about this here job."

"I got m' orders, an' I give you yers. Thet's all you need ta know."

The Kid looked at his empty glass. Driscoll waved at the bartender and he brought another round.

"Well, Ahab, whut 'r' yer orders?"

"Have a good time. We don't git to it 'til tomorrow."

The Kid grinned and tipped his glass. Driscoll felt smug. He hadn't wasted the time while waiting for his friends.

Mr. Smith's real name was Williams and he was a reporter from England. Some of the boys said he used to hang out with a guy named Sommers who got killed last winter. Sommers tried to rape Jack Malone's daughter.

Was that why Williams wanted Malone shadowed? Did he want to get revenge for the death of his friend? His friend had to be pure crazy to try something like that with Malone's daughter. Jack never forgot or forgave; everyone knew that.

There had been a time when he and Jack pulled strong-arm stuff together down in Seattle. *Been a long time,* he mused. *Jack was with Maye back then. Now there had been a fine sashay. I wonder what ever happened to her?*

His glass was empty again. He waved at the bartender.

76 —Auk Village, A.T., June 2, 1916—
Friday morning

George Mak-we shut the cabin door behind him and whistled as he skipped down the steps to the plank street. Bird song rose above the stamps in the sun-filled air. He was getting married to a wonderful woman in less than a month. He started whistling the ragtime tune a second time, but let it drift away when he saw Jee-nak striding purposely toward him.

The Taku Tlingit wore a clean suit that had to be twenty years old. A white dress shirt and scuffed brown shoes also attested to the seriousness of his visit.

"Jee-nak, my brother. What brings you this far from home?"

"Tasnit John went to his ancestors in the night. The wailing has begun. I thought I should tell you myself."

George felt a twinge of guilt at his light-heartedness, but it passed quickly. Tasnit John had led a full life for over seventy years. Even though custom would demand a public outcry of grief, George felt Tasnit had not gone to his ancestors early.

"The ceremony will begin tonight, then?" George asked.

"Yes. The women are preparing the house. Would you pass the word among your people?"

"Of course, my brother. My heart grieves for your loss."

"It would be a good thing if you made a speech for him," Jee-nak said softly.

"I-, I'll try. I am not good with words, but I will try."

Jee-nak nodded, turned and left.

"Well, there goes next week," George muttered, walking toward Irene's house. Along the way he stopped and told two families the news. Tlingits would come to the funeral ceremony from all the local villages and from as far away as Klukwan, Hoonah, Kake, Sitka, Angoon, and Wrangell.

Tasnit had been a leader from youth through his vigorous years. His death also represented a break with the past for the Taku kwáan. He had been the oldest male in the village and "hit saati," or speaker of his house. Great honor would be his as the people bid him farewell.

George knocked on Irene's door and Ruth answered. The girl stared at him with a neutral expression as he passed her. George wondered at her sullenness but said nothing.

Julia stepped out of the kitchen. "Who was it, Ruth? Oh, George!" she said with a smile. "How good to see you."

George took her hands in his and squeezed them gently. "It is good to see you, beautiful woman. Is Irene here?"

"Yes. She's upstairs putting away winter things. You look serious. Is something wrong?"

"Tasnit John died last night. He was my, ah, father-in-law."

"Oh. Were you close to him?"

"Not in the way you think. He was a leader among the Taku Tlingits and respected throughout the Tlingit nation. I'll go to his funeral ceremony for four evenings, starting in two days."

"May I go with you?" Julia's eyes gleamed with interest.

At first George felt annoyed with her. Then he realized this might be her only chance to see an old fashioned Tlingit funeral. The Alaska Native Brotherhood slowly gained success where the missionaries had failed—abolishing the potlatch as "pagan." This might be the last one *he* would ever see.

"You'd have to be, ah . . ."

"Circumspect?"

"Yeah, circumspect. In fact, you'd have to go with Irene rather than me. She could sit with you in the women's section."

"That's right. They divide the men and women inside the house, don't they?"

"Yeah," he said with a grunt. "You already know what to expect?"

"Pretty much, but I still want to see it for myself."

"Just don't take any notes while you're there, okay?"

"Would you rather I didn't go?" she asked earnestly.

"I think you should go. How else you gonna draw conclusions about the changes in our culture?" He smiled at her.

"George," she said uncertainly. "Sometimes I'm not sure if you mean what you say."

"I love you, and I mean that."

Irene thumped down the small stairwell. "Hello, George, how are you today?"

"I am fine, but Tasnit John is dead."

"Oh!" Irene stopped in the middle of the living room. "I'd better go get out my mourning dress and make some black paint."

"Julia wants to go with us," George said.

Irene looked at the woman for a moment. "Do you have a black dress? Or a very dark one we can rub ashes into?"

"Either. I have both."

"Let me see what you have."

The women left the room and George went into the kitchen to find something to eat. Ruth sat somberly at the table with a cup of tea in front of her.

"Is the long face for Tasnit John, Ruth?"

"They didn't want you to marry Amalie, did they?"

"Who?"

"Her family. Tasnit John and Rebecca."

He thought for a moment, sorting out his answer.

"Just answer the question, uncle," she said sharply.

"If you become rude I will not only stay quiet, I will also leave this house until you apologize," he said.

"I'm sorry," she said contritely. "I don't mean to be rude. I do want to hear the truth."

"No, they didn't want me to marry her. They said I wasn't good husband material, that I was too wild, and, and I drank too much." He lowered his voice. "They were right."

"But you married her anyway."

"Yes. I married her anyway."

"Begay isn't wild. He hardly drinks at all. He works very hard and I think he is good husband material," Ruth said, ticking off the points on her fingers.

"I think your mother and brother find it difficult to accept him because he isn't a Tlingit," George said gently.

"You're getting married, and Julia isn't a Tlingit."

George could find no words for her.

Irene and Julia walked into the kitchen. From the expressions on their faces, George surmised they had overheard the conversation.

"Your uncle is a man of thirty-five years," Irene said flatly. "You are a girl of nineteen who has not experienced life."

"I want to experience life! I want to marry the man I love. Why is that a bad thing?" Tears bloomed in Ruth's eyes.

"It's not a bad thing . . ." Irene began.

Ruth held her gaze. "Yes? Please continue."

"It's just . . . it's just not acceptable," Irene said, throwing up her hands.

"To who?"

"To *me!*"

"Did you and father choose each other to marry?"

"Of course."

"Did your families both agree?"

Irene stared silently at her daughter for a long moment. Finally she said, "Sometimes I forget what it was to be young. I think I haven't changed, but I have."

"May I ask something?" Julia said quietly.

"Certainly," Irene said.

"Perhaps you are worried your cultural heritage will be weakened by Ruth marrying a Filipino?"

"That's certainly part of my thoughts," Irene said.

"Would you feel different about him if he were to study the ways of your people?"

"I-, I don't know. I guess I had hoped she would marry a Tlingit, but this Oriental . . ."

"Mother, no Tlingit man has ever looked at me with anything other than pain or disgust in his eyes. All they see is *this*!" Ruth held her scarred jaw line up so all could see the knotted flesh stretching from her lower neck and up the side of her face.

"How did that happen?" Julia asked quietly.

"When she was just beginning to walk, she fell into a bed of coals at fish camp. All her hair on the side and back was singed off. We didn't know if she was going to live.

"We kept her burns wrapped in seaweed and moss. The pain went away but there was nothing we could do for the scar." Irene stared at her daughter with lustrous eyes. "Summon Begay, I would like to talk with him."

"To tell him what, Mother?" Ruth asked.

"To tell him what is expected of him as a member of this family," she said flatly.

"Oh, Mother!" Ruth stood and the two women embraced. Both cried.

George noticed tears running down Julia's face. His throat felt somewhat constricted.

"I must go tell the people about Tasnit John," he said gruffly. He escaped quickly. Then, at a leisurely pace, made his way the length of the village, telling the Auk people of Tasnit John's death.

Wailing erupted as he left homes of relatives of the deceased. Finally he made his way to his cabin. He opened bentwood boxes adorned with totemic devices. Some of the berry stain decoration on the boxes had faded, but remained visible.

Carefully, reverently, he lifted out the hat that had belonged to his uncle and great uncle. The Bear Clan hat was carved from a piece of yellow cedar painted with black, green, and red designs surrounding a growling bear at the crown. The bear appeared to be eating a salmon with two carefully formed paws whose claws curled up over the simplified fish. Mother-of-pearl formed fine, square-cut teeth in the bear's mouth; beaten copper discs became the eyes.

Hooked above the top of the bear's head were four flat, woven spruce-root cones. The cones represented potlatches given by his grandfather. Only very rich men could afford to give a potlatch.

There would be a potlatch on the third or fourth night of Tasnit's funeral. It was an old thing to do. Most modern Tlingits could not afford such an extravagance, and of course there was the ANB. Tasnit had hoarded his wealth to celebrate his own death. Once again George had the strong feeling this might be the last potlatch he would see in his lifetime.

"So much has changed," he muttered to the bear hat. He stripped off his white-man clothes and began to dress as a Tlingit warrior who would attend a solemn occasion.

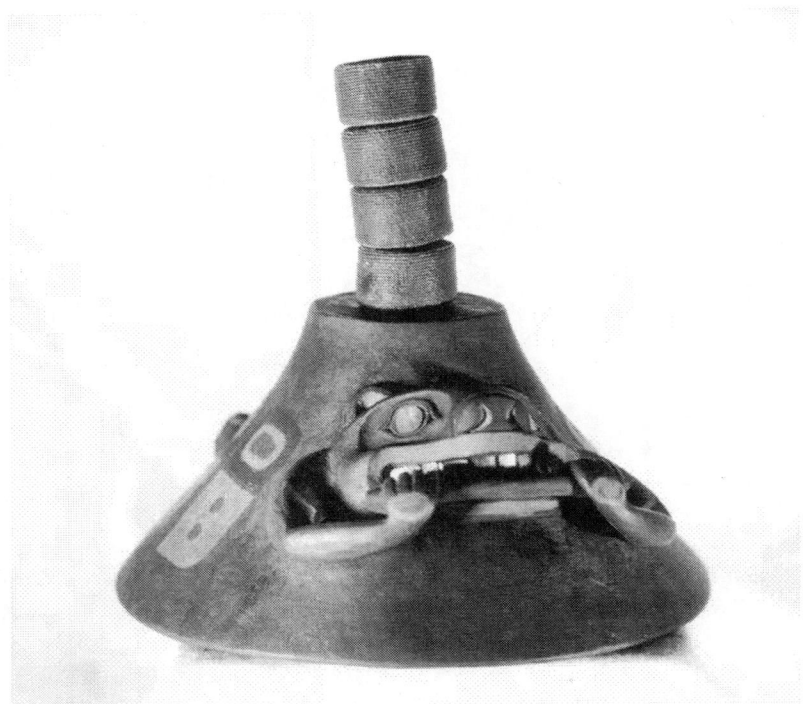

77 —Taku Village, June 8, 1916—
Thursday night

The emotional ceremony witnessed over the past three days completely entranced Julia. Like all of the other women at the funeral, a combination of grease and soot blackened her face. With the rest of the unrelated females, she sat at the far corner of Tasnit John's house, on the highest platform.

She realized they were farthest from the fire, a sign of little or no social standing. In the winter she might have lamented her position, but not now. She could see *everything*.

The corpse of Tasnit John, dressed in his finest clothing and wrapped in a beautiful button blanket, reclined at the back of the house. He seemed to be taking in the entire spectacle from under his carved Killer Whale Clan hat. Hanging on the wall behind and beside him were two American flags and a stunning Chilkat blanket.

Julia was as far from him as she could get and still be inside the house. Almost all the mourners, and spectators, sat between her and the deceased.

She wished she had a motion-picture camera. Enough had already transpired to fill a monograph. Each night after returning to Irene's house, she wrote a narrative of everything she had seen while it remained fresh in her mind. The first two nights had yielded twenty-six pages of careful notes.

She thought she just might double that number tonight. George looked so magnificent in his traditional clothing. The hard masculinity of his costume pulled at her.

He had never shown her the spruce-wood armor, deer hide shirt and pants, intricately carved war club, and that bear hat! She'd almost swooned when he walked into Irene's to accompany them to the Taku village. All the men wore their finest regalia.

The women all looked much like her —blackened face, dark clothes, mostly dresses, ashes rubbed carefully into hair, clothing and skin. *A man designed this ritual,* she decided. She focused on the platform in front of Tasnit John's body. George stood up to speak.

"Unlike many we have heard here in the past three days and tonight, I cannot speak well in the old tongue. I ask your forbearance." He turned and looked at Tasnit John as he continued.

"You were a great man for our people. You welcomed me into your house and made me your son. When the daughter you gave me for wife died, your heart was not heavy against me."

One of the soot-streaked women near the platform began to moan and chant, the widow, according to Irene.

"You have brought your people from the time of my grandfather into the world we now know. Much has changed, but peace still rules in our villages thanks to you and your brothers. Your labor is finished. We are here. We are healthy. We are grateful. Good-bye, my father."

Another now-familiar mourning song started in the group of close relatives and spread across the packed house. Two of the women, Tasnit's daughters, stood and moved their bodies in time with the singing. They rocked, bending at the knees, their upper torsos weaving back and forth beautifully, looking for all the world like willows in a high wind.

When the singing and keening stopped, an old man rose from the honored place between door and fire. He spoke for a moment in Tlingit and Julia thought this was yet another eulogy for the departed, but movement started on two sides of the house when he pointed in those directions.

Bentwood boxes were opened and bolts of bright red cloth brought out and passed hand over hand to where the old man stood. The bolts unrolled as they crossed the room. In Julia's imagination two wide wounds opened across the people. The old man sliced the cloth into irregular lengths while singing a dirge-like song. As each piece was sliced off, he called out a name and the cloth would be passed or tossed to them.

The distribution did not prove democratic by any means. Large piles began to grow in front of three older men. Many received a single piece, usually much shorter than the gifts distributed to the old men.

"Who are those men who are getting all the cloth?" Julia asked in a whisper.

"They are eldest in the clans," Irene whispered back. "They are very old men who will soon join Tasnit John."

Small tins of tobacco disappeared into the crowd. A long wooden bowl, carved and painted in a Raven motif made its way around the room, each person ate a spoonful of its contents, then passed it along. Although nearly empty when it arrived at the top tier, both Irene and Julia received a mouthful of berries mixed with sugar.

Julia normally didn't care for sweets of any sort. But the berries and sugar gave her a surge of energy, allowing her to rise above the lethargy that had crept over her.

Suddenly the wall behind Tasnit John's corpse moved to the side as men carried it out of the way. Until the mist-filled night air washed in across the crowd, she hadn't been aware of how warm and close the room had become. Abruptly she could smell the salt-tang of the sea as it edged in through the wood smoke and odors of cured leather, cedar, and wool.

Four men picked up the remains of Tasnit John and placed him on a stack of logs some forty feet behind the house. The crowd flowed through the new opening and surrounded the pyre. The four men added wood around and above Tasnit John, almost completely hiding the body from view. Julia stood just inside the house so she could see everything.

The entire crowd spontaneously broke into a mournful song. Men closest to the pyre squatted and beat poles on lengths of wood, which created a pulsating rhythm resembling a heartbeat. The bright costumes of the men, the somber dress of the women and the all-enveloping mist gave the scene a touch of animism, magic, and mystery, lifting the hair on the back of her neck as a shiver ran down her spine.

Fire appeared simultaneously at all four corners of the pyre. Julia wondered if the wood might be too wet to burn. In moments fire engulfed the entire construction, flames shot ten to twenty feet into the air. The sudden heat cleared the air around the crowd and forced them to step back.

People began to leave quietly. Julia glanced around and saw Irene beckoning to her. She took one last look at the funeral pyre.

"Go with God," she whispered. Then she followed Irene down the beach into the night.

THE DOUGLAS ISLAND NEWS
Douglas, Alaska, Wednesday, June 14, 1916

The Stroller
by E. J. White

The usually serene and light running domestic life led by the Stroller has been somewhat disorganized during the past few months, owing to change in location and other unforeseen contingencies and the result is that he is far behind with his correspondence, much of which has been yearning for answers for weeks and much of which much continue to yearn as it is not possible for the Stroller to clear his correspondence hook at one sitting, much as he would rejoice to do so. As it is, only the most urgent of the accumulated correspondence can be answered at this time. The remainder will be disposed of at a more convenient season.

To Student, University of Washington, Seattle: Cincinnatus was not a Greek but a Roman. You are evidently thinking of Socrates, "Old Socs" the Athens school children used to call him. Cincinnatus was a plain farmer until chosen by his fellow Romans to lead their army. He was plowing for spring wheat at the time a delegation called on him to take charge of the army and he left his oxen stand in the furrow for twelve years while he fought Rome's enemies. Later when he came home and found that his family had become somewhat disorganized during his absence (his sons ate pie with a knife and his daughters chewed gum), he loaded a scow with macaroni and sailed for America, where he founded Cincinnati, Ohio. The last time the Stroller was in Cincinnati he met a descendent of Cincinnatus. He was selling hot tamales. He said it was not a noble calling but that, as he had a large and rapidly increasing family, he was obliged to engage in any honest work that would enable him to catcha da mon.

Jefferson Davis Scott, Jacksonville, Florida: In the first place you were premature in shooting the nigger. The fact that he was merely walking along the road adjacent to your watermelon field every day was not conclusive evidence that he had designs on your melons when they matured. However, you were lucky that the charge against you was that of discharging a firearm within a half-mile of the church instead of the more serious one of murder. The further fact that you were fined $7.50 and costs when the regular schedule in your locality for shooting niggers is only $5 is evidence to the Stroller that you are not very popular. You say you never paid more than $5 before and that in several instances you were let off with $3. While $7.50 does look rather steep, the Stroller would not advise you to appeal the case. Better allow the judgment to stand and pay the fine. The judge evidently "has it in" for you and perhaps it will be well for you not to take a further chance before him. Unless you have extraordinary provocation, the Stroller suggests that you do not kill any more niggers for a matter of four or five months, by which time any sentiment which may have been engendered by your recent action will have been forgotten.

Clifford Sifton MacDougall, Red River, Manitoba: If you firmly believe the widow reciprocates your affections, go to it. The fact that her four sons are all older and larger than yourself, may result in some friction at times when picking out socks in the morning and on similar occasions, but if you are willing to risk it, the neighbors will not likely interfere.

Olga Nethersole Swansson, Enumclaw, Washington: Da not baen no yob open in your line hare, but the Stroller, who is Scandinavian faller hisself, will kape eye peeled an' let you know first ting when yob show up.

Grover Cleveland Smith, Glen Mary, Tennessee: You have grave cause for worry for, if this present temperance wave continues to gather strength, the old wildcat still which you say has been handed down from father to son for five generations and now your sole means of support, may fail you. But the Stroller cannot believe the temperance wave will have anything in common with your locality, for the last time he was there he noted two things: First—Everybody appeared to be possessed of an unquenchable thirst. Second—Moonshine was selling at 5 cents per drink or three for ten cents. What more could any man ask—a thirst and the privilege of tickling it for five cents—or bright red jags guaranteed to last 24 hours for twenty cents? The Stroller cannot harmonize temperance waves and the sentiment of your locality as he last knew it. Continue to plug along. Keep the old still dripping and don't worry about the bridge until you come to it. Suppose you still manage to pick off one of those "pestering revenuers" occasionally? Killing is too good for them. They ought to be given fifty years by a judge or Three Weeks by Elinor Glyn.

78 —Juneau City, A.T., June 15, 1916—
Thursday afternoon

"Mr. Santo, could I have a word with you?"

Begay looked up from stocking a shelf to see the sandy-haired detective he had met at Christmas. He stood up and brushed off his knees, straightened his apron.

"Of course, Mr. Lepke. How may I assist you?"

Lepke glanced around the George Brothers Grocery. "Is there some place we can speak privately?"

Begay looked at the clock on the wall. "It's only 4:30, I get off work at six. If you could wait until then?"

"This will only take a moment, but it's rather personal."

Begay's employer had been watching them from behind his cash register near the door. He quickly moved back through the store.

"Is there some problem here?"

"Good day, sir," the detective said. "My name is Lepke and I'm—"

"I know who you are, Mr. Lepke. Is Mr. Santo in trouble with the authorities?"

"I really don't think so, but I need to speak privately with him for a few minutes. Is there some place we—"

"Use my office," the stocky man urged, pointing. "Right back there."

"Thank you, sir. After you, Mr. Santo."

Begay led the way back to the small office. There was barely room for both the men to fit around the desk overflowing with paper.

"What is it?" Begay asked, feeling nervous.

"When you left your job with the Treadwell Mining Company, how did you feel?"

"Angry. Relieved. Why?"

"Relieved? Why were you relieved at getting dismissed?"

"It was the final step in becoming my own person, Mr. Lepke. I got my job at the Treadwell through my mother's brother. No other way. All of my life I have been danced about by my family like a puppet on a string."

"But you were angry when you left. The clerk made note of it."

Begay laughed. "The clerk. He spoke to me as if I were a child and he an old man. I resented his attitude because he didn't understand the circumstances of my dismissal, yet he saw fit to pass judgment."

"Exactly why were you dismissed, Mr. Santo?"

"I was late for work many times," he said with a sigh, "but the real reason was I had turned my back on my family and was courting a non-Filipina. You see, I was supposed to work hard, finish my college degree, and then go back to the Philippines and marry the woman my family had selected for me when I was a child."

"You decided you didn't want to do that?"

"I am living my life now, not waiting until I can afford it. The United States will not allow us to bring our women into the country. My family tells me not to return until I have accomplished all they wish. It's all too intolerable."

"You were heard making remarks about 'getting back' at the Treadwell."

"I was angry for about two weeks. Then I realized my dismissal was a blessing in disguise. With this job I am closer to Ruth and can live in Juneau. I have even purchased property to build a house."

"I see. Then you haven't done anything to gain revenge on the Treadwell Company?"

"No. But it's curious you ask."

"Why's that?" Lepke asked.

"A man in a bar asked me if I wanted to take revenge on the Treadwell. He said my honor was at stake."

"What kind of revenge?"

"He said I could really hurt it if I was willing to take the chance."

"What did you say?"

"I told him I hadn't lost honor. I had lost faith."

Lepke laughed. "Good answer! Do you know that man's name?"

"Oh, yes. It was Arnold Williams, the British journalist."

Lepke's eyes suddenly glowed with an inner fire.

"I think he was somewhat drunk at the time, so —"

"So he finally made a mistake!" Lepke's mouth twisted into a wry grin.

Begay wondered what was humorous about the situation.

"Thank you for your time, Mr. Santo. Please don't mention this conversation to anyone."

"Whatever you say, Mr. Lepke."

Lepke reached out and shook his hand. "You'll hear from me again. By the way, I think you've made an excellent choice for a wife, if you don't mind me saying so."

Begay grinned. "No. I don't mind at all. Thank you."

Lepke grinned back and then quickly left the office.

Begay walked slowly back into the store, wondering what the visit had been all about.

Mr. George appeared at his side.

"What was all that about, Begay?"

"I don't really know, but I think I'll invite him to my wedding."

79 —Juneau City, A.T., June 25, 1916—
Sunday afternoon

The crowd filled St. Nicholas Russian Orthodox Church. Florence found herself standing in the back of the small octagonal house of worship. She had walked past the building many times during her life but this was her first time inside.

Ikons adorned the walls. Gold leaf glinted redly from all of them. The church reminded her of a small Catholic chapel without pews.

Tlingits composed the majority of the congregation with a scattering of Russians. Begay Santo stood with his fiancé near the front. Irene Kisadis wore a striking blue dress. Visibly nervous, she constantly wrung her hands.

Florence thought she looked beautiful. More people crowded into the church to stand along the wall behind the early arrivals. She glanced around but didn't see the groom. She wondered who the best man would be.

Suddenly George Mak-we stepped through the door, hesitated for a moment as he took in the crowded room, then with a wide grin he completed his entrance.

Florence felt the blood rush from her head as August Lepke entered behind him. Both men wore snappy three-piece suits. August ignored the congregation as he urged George to the front of the church.

She lied to me! Florence thought. *Julia actually lied to me.* Briefly she considered leaving, but realized she would only draw unwanted attention. She vowed to escape as soon as the ceremony ended.

Then a bell rang and Julia Prescott walked regally through the door, her head held high. At her side, holding her arm and dressed in a suit duplicating those of the groom and best man, marched a boy of about ten or eleven.

The boy strongly resembled Julia. Florence didn't know her friend had a little brother. The priest came in from the vestry with two altar boys. She thought he looked even more ornately dressed than a Catholic priest.

Slowly Julia and the boy walked up the narrow aisle left by the congregation where there was barely enough room for them to proceed side by side. They stopped in front of the priest and total silence reigned. The boy stepped aside to stand next to August.

Florence let her gaze rest on August, examining him as carefully as she could from a distance of thirty feet. He had yet to look at the congregation. She suddenly realized he felt shy in front of this many people.

His eyes remained fastened on Julia. Finally Florence looked at George. His eyes were also on Julia. Even from the back of the church she easily saw the love the man felt for his bride.

Something splashed on her hand and Florence realized she was crying, again. The priest began the wedding ceremony. Bells rang and everyone knelt.

She followed the ceremony vaguely while her mind swirled with conflicting emotions. Once she thought she and August would stand in front of a group of friends like this.

The flowers had stopped. He never came into the shop. Only rarely did she see him walking on the street. Fiona ceased speaking of him in Florence's presence.

Everyone had done as she demanded and now she heard nothing of him. The part of her mind that always remained rational asked, why did she even think about him now? And she realized she still loved him.

Now it was too late. One too many times she turned away and now he no longer tried to catch her eye. Seeing him in discomfort, at a loss up there in front of all, had done it. She knew now he wasn't always in command. There were moments when he too doubted his abilities. There were moments when he entertained fears.

A pain blossomed between her breasts, so intense she nearly cried out, but she bit her lip instead and clenched her fists to her chest. Soon it passed and she felt her heart beating again. Her head seemed clearer than it had for months.

The priest wrapped his surplice around the joined hands of George and Julia while he blessed them in Russian. He dipped his hand in a small bowl held by an altar boy and sprinkled holy water on the couple. Then they stood in front of him again and the congregation relaxed.

"Do you, George Mak-we, before God and man, take this woman, Julia, to be your lawfully wedded wife, to cleave only unto her, to have and to hold, in sickness and in health, from this day forward until death do you part?"

"Oh, yes. I do!" George said with a smile.

"Do you, Julia Prescott, before God and man, take this man, George, to be your lawfully wedded husband, to honor and obey, to cleave only unto him, to have and to hold, in sickness and in health, from this day forward until death do you part?"

"I most certainly do!" She mirrored George's smile.

"Then by the power vested in me by the Holy and Universal Church, I pronounce you husband and wife."

George pushed back his wife's veil and they kissed ardently. Bells rang from above and the church emptied as people rushed for the door. Florence looked for August, but he had disappeared.

She was one of the last to approach the door.

"Florence!" Julia called. "Please wait a moment." She hurried over to Florence as George trailed behind.

"Congratulations to both of you!" Florence said. "You make such a lovely couple. I'm so happy for you."

Julia took Florence's hand in hers. "Thank you so much for coming, and I'm sorry I didn't have a chance to tell you about August changing his plans . . ."

"That's fine, Julia. Really it is. Now I must get out there to see if I can catch the bouquet."

"Good luck!" Julia called after her.

Florence stepped into the sunshine. The day reigned cloudless, beautiful, and warm. People lined both sides of the steps and the walk leading down to Sixth Street.

Someone handed her a small bag of rice and she took her place at the end of the line. As she expectantly watched the church door, a hand settled on her left forearm. She looked around to find August staring at her with eyes that reminded her of a Basset hound.

"Florence, I want to apologize—"

"Never apologize for doing what you believe is right, August. I was so very wrong in my treatment of you. Can you ever forgive me?"

Stunned, his mouth opened but nothing came out. Then he glanced away abruptly.

"Look out!"

She turned and saw something flying at her face. Instinctively she reached up and grabbed the bridal bouquet out of the air. The crowd applauded and she laughed and hugged August who hugged her back.

Happy tears, she thought. Happy tears.

80 —Juneau City, A.T., July 4, 1916—
Tuesday afternoon

A cherry bomb exploded next to Williams on the sunny street. Jack Malone laughed as the man jerked horribly, and glared about the crowded street in vain for the perpetrator.

"This ain't exactly yer cup of tea is it, Mr. Williams?" He noticed the man had developed a tic in his left eyelid.

"No. If you had ever fought in a war you would understand my reactions to these sharp reports."

"Well, here we are safe 'n' sound at Armstrong's. C'mon, I'll treat ya to a drink."

"Bloody American holidays!"

They entered the dim establishment. Miners off work for the 4th packed the place elbow to elbow, laughing, drinking and talking. Jack stepped to the end of the bar and signaled to one of the three feverishly working bartenders.

"What'cha need, Jack?"

"Michael, me lad, get me a bottle of Bushmills and two glasses, if ya please."

With bottle and glassware in hand, Jack nodded toward his office door. "After you, Mr. Williams."

Williams threw back the first drink as soon as Jack finished pouring.

"A few firecrackers and yer wind is up that bad?"

"Just last year, as I sat in a train compartment, the man next to me had his brains blown out. Completely ruined my new suit." He tossed back his second drink.

Jack sat the bottle down and sipped at his whiskey. "God, but that's good." He looked over at Williams. "What happened to the killer?"

"Bandit raid on a train." He shrugged. "Who knows? We shot a lot of them and they shot a lot of us. Added to my experiences on the front and it boils down to the fact I don't like those damn little bombs you people give your children to play with."

Jack grinned. "They rarely hurt themselves, or anyone else for that matter."

"We need dynamite." Williams poured more liquor into his glass.

"Oh, you want *big* bombs!"

"Not for your stupid holiday," Williams said with a growl.

"What for?"

"We're going to destroy the Treadwell complex, aren't we?"

"With dynamite? You have to know what yer about if ya go messin' with that stuff."

Williams inhaled the aroma from his glass and gave Jack a ghastly grin. "Let me worry about that part. You just get the explosives."

"An' where d'ya think I could get dynamite? Jist go down ta Young's Hardware and, by the way, I'll be needin' a case o' dynamite along with those nails?"

Williams laughed. "That would be rich. Hell, Jack, I don't care how you do it, just do it."

"When do you, we, need it?"

"Best get it as soon as you can. We can store it here somewhere." He looked around the room, pointed to a shadowed corner next to the file case. "Hell, we can put it right over there."

"I'll work on it." Jack felt uneasiness in his stomach. Then the thought boiled into his mind of Irishmen being hung on their own soil by the damned British and the uneasiness vanished like a gold piece on Lower Front. "I'll work on it," he said with conviction.

"Good man. Thanks for the whiskey." Williams left.

As soon as the German left, Jack jumped up and went to the bar.

"Michael, have ya seen Sean Clancy?"

"Yeah. 'Bout an hour ago him and that string bean what works for him was in for a few. But I think they went back down to th' warehouse."

"Thanks, Michael. Give me a new bottle o' Bushmills."

The streets ran dense with humanity on a jag. Jack pushed his way good-humoredly through the crowds of men. Every now and then a woman's shriek cut the air. *Probably a drunk whore tying to drum up a bit of business,* he thought.

His mind burned with the image of an Irish patriot lunging and strangling at the end of a rope, or jerking from the impact of a firing squad's bullets, dropping to the ground, kicking his way into eternity. *Jasus!* He shook his head.

Clancy sat sharing a bottle with Rankin just inside the open door of the warehouse. Jack stepped into the shade and dropped his butt on a nail keg beside them.

"By Christ, but she's a hot one taday!"

"Hap'y 'Pendence Day, Jack," Rankin mumbled through a sodden grin.

"An' th' same to ya, Bobby Rankin."

"Jack," Sean said. "Have a drink." He handed his bottle over solemnly.

"Thanks. I will." He took a long pull at the bottle and wiped his mouth appreciatively. "That's good whiskey."

"I got a letter from me brother."

"Didja now?"

"He says you run him outta town, Jack."

"That's true, Sean. I told him not to come back 'r I'd cut his nuts off."

A fat tear ran down Sean's face. "Why'd ya do that?"

Jack took another long pull from the bottle. "'Cause you couldn't. 'Cause it needed done. 'Cause yer my friend and I couldn't let yer worthless brother put you in an early grave. That's why."

Sean looked at him with eyes that refused to focus. "I don't know whether to hit ya or hug ya!"

Jack drank the last of Sean's liquor and threw the bottle over his shoulder. He opened the Bushmills and thrust the bottle out. "Why don' ya just have a drink instead?"

Rankin weaved back and forth on his keg, eyes glazed and mouth hanging open. "Thas a g'idea, Jack." Then he toppled over backward onto the plank floor and began snoring.

"'Kay," Sean said, taking the bottle.

"Sean Clancy, I need yer help."

"Wha'cha need thish time?"

"A couple cases of dynamite."

Sean looked at him owlishly. "Say what?"

"I need a couple cases of dynamite."

"Wha' th' fook fer?"

"Where were ya born, Sean?"

"Born? County Cork in God's own Ireland, an' y' know it."

"Ya know what's happenin' in the old country these days, Sean?"

"Yes." He looked down at the wood planking. "Good men 'r' dying 'cause they're Irish."

"We can hit the English, Sean, from right here on Gastineau Channel," Jack said earnestly.

"How?"

Jack smiled and began talking.

81 —Treadwell, A.T., July 4th, 1916—
Tuesday afternoon

The pitcher hurled the ball at the catcher but the batter caught it with a resounding "crack," sending it soaring into left field. August Lepke sat in the dugout and watched the batter race around the diamond as his teammates cheered and whistled. With two outs and the score 4 to 2 against them in the bottom of the seventh inning, the Juneau City Hall team seemed to fight a losing battle.

The Treadwell team wore snappy uniforms and worked like a well-oiled machine. They also hit wondrously well. August knew he needed to keep his mind on the game, but he found himself thinking about Florence rather than pitches and hits.

Since coming to Juneau his thinking had changed about a great many things, not the least of which was religion. Ambiguous best described his lifelong attitudes about the Lutheran Church and its doctrines.

Since leaving Germany, serving in the American Army, and his long career with the Pinkerton Agency, his ambiguity had slowly evolved into a benign indifference. One of life's biggest mysteries was how some people could become completely obsessed with religious philosophy to the point of structuring their lives around it.

Sure, he believed in law, justice, and basic rights for all people. Past that he retained no convictions. Right and wrong didn't hinge on a religious rationale, but rather on the obvious effect that actions had on the population as a whole.

That's why he quit the Pinkerton Agency. It specialized in justice for those who could afford it. He grinned. *My word, I'm becoming a progressive!*

"Yer out!"

The City Hall team emerged from the dugout and trotted to their positions.

"Lepke!" Cam Byrnes, their manager, waved him over.

"Yah, Cam?"

"Lepke, didn't you tell me you could throw pretty good?"

"I do okay from right field, don't I?"

"You do great. That's why I think you're wasted out there."

"Oh. Where do you want me then?"

"I want you to pitch the rest of the game. Brown is tired and his arm is going."

"What's he think about that?"

"He told me to try you."

"Sure, Cam, I'll try it."

An uncharacteristic nervousness settled over him as he approached the pitcher's mound. He enjoyed this wild game, but he didn't like being the center of attention all that much. So very much depended on the pitcher's skill and it had been a long time since he played this position.

The first batter stepped up to the plate and the catcher threw August the ball.

"Lookie here!" someone shouted from the Treadwell dugout. "It's their team copper. Don't hit the ball or he's liable to pinch ya."

The catcalls picked up in volume and he blanked them out. Concentrating on the area directly in front of the catcher, he wound up and threw the ball as hard as he could.

The batter swung, meeting only air.

"Strike one!"

The catcalls increased from both sides until they blended into noise as meaningless as the sound of a waterfall or the crushers. The Treadwell batter was one of their poorer hitters but August knew better than to lower his performance level. He burned the ball at the catcher.

The batter swung.

"Strike two!"

Angry now, the batter rapped the plate with the bat and exaggerated his stance. August didn't give him time to change his mind. He threw the ball a bit slower this time, hoping to catch the man off guard.

The batter began his swing too early, tried to check it slightly and missed completely.

"Strike three, yer out!"

"Hey, Lepke," the first baseman yelled. "You can let them hit a few, that's why we're here!"

"Stick around, I might need you," he yelled back, feeling good.

The next Treadwell batter had hit the ball every time he came to bat. Only luck and a decent outfield had kept the score as close as it was. Burton, the batter, possessed more than his share of self confidence.

August felt his stomach muscles clench and sweat dripped down the side of his ribcage. This had to be the hottest day he'd yet experienced in Juneau. Burton tapped the bat on the plate and took his stance.

August threw higher than usual on purpose.

Burton swung. Halfway through the swing he realized he'd been suckered and pulled the bat back.

"Strike one!"

Burton wasn't smiling now. He glared across the sixty feet between them, silently promising legal mayhem. He waited, no bat-tapping or limbering swings this time.

August knew Burton possessed lightening reflexes, perhaps that could be used to advantage here. Carefully he folded his right hand into position to throw a knuckle ball. He pulled back and with great exaggeration of strength, threw the ball.

The ball wobbled across the distance and Burton swung furiously before it got to him.

"Strike two!"

The two teams and the crowd had fallen silent. August could feel all eyes on him and his mouth went dry. His knees quivered and his right hand trembled slightly.

He pulled back and fired his fastest ball at Burton.

The man swung but the ball was in the catcher's mitt before the bat left his shoulder. The crowd broke into cheers and Burton threw the bat down and stomped off to his dugout. August waved to the water boy and he jogged out with

the bucket and dipper.

"Gee, Mr. Lepke, you're a pretty keen pitcher!"

August smiled at him and kept drinking. Nothing tasted as wonderful as water! Applause broke out from the Treadwell bleachers.

Buck Higgins, Treadwell's all around star player, swaggered up to the plate. Higgins was the Treadwell pitcher and also a good hitter. Rumor had it he once played professionally down in the States.

"Well this isn't the States," August muttered. He tried to keep his anxiety confined to his brain. Higgins easily topped 220 pounds, standing 6'4" in his stocking feet. No fat showed anywhere on the man, as appropriate for an underground shift foreman.

"Give me yer best, copper!" Higgins grated.

August threw a fast one. Higgins slashed viciously at it, missing.

"Strike one!"

Everyone in the Treadwell bleachers gasped in unison as the Juneau bleachers erupted in applause.

Higgins grew dark in the face and held the bat as if it weighed no more than a toothpick. He seemed to be ready for anything. August squinted in the bright July sun and threw another fast one, even harder than the first.

Higgins swung smoothly and the bat ever-so-slightly touched the edge of the ball as they passed in their separate trajectories.

"Strike two!"

Now Higgins became nervous. He licked his lips and rubbed his nose. After adjusting his cap three different ways and wiping his hands on his pants legs, he took his stance.

August threw wide. Four like that would walk any man to first base. Higgins swung anyway.

"Strike three, yer out!"

Suddenly the team surrounded August, patting him on the back, lightly hitting his arm, everyone grinning.

"Good going, August."

"By God, boys, I think we got us a ringer here."

"You just want to let us sit in the bleachers next time we've got the field?"

"Now if you could just bat . . ."

August felt a degree of elation unlike anything he'd ever felt before. Not even war produced this kind of emotion. To know he held a team to three outs without them ever touching the ball . . . well, they *did* touch it, but barely.

He went into the dugout and collapsed on the bench. Cam Byrnes sat down beside him.

"August, you're damn good with that ball! How about being the regular pitcher?"

"Let's see if I can through this game get, then we'll talk."

They grinned at each other.

THE DOUGLAS ISLAND NEWS
Entered at Douglas Post Office as Second-Class Mail Matter
PUBLISHED EVERY FRIDAY
Subscription Prices, $3.00 per Year in Advance
E.J. WHITE
Editor and Proprietor
Friday, July 7, 1916

THE CELEBRATION

Pioneers on the island, those who have participated in the first and all subsequent Fourth of July celebrations, agree that the celebration of this year and this week was the best in the history of island civilization from the standpoints of unity of purpose on the part of all the people, enthusiasm and high-class, clean, manly sport.

In the first place the people decided to build a celebration and they worked together for that purpose, each and every one doing his share to make the undertaking a success. That it was a glowing success due to the combined efforts of the people, not of Douglas alone, not of Treadwell alone, but of both towns.

The weather was all that could be desired—regular made-to-order weather—and holiday attire was visible everywhere. But best of all was the holiday spirit that pervaded the island. Everybody had it and was of true Americanism.

It is doubted that anywhere on the American continent a better or more interesting game of baseball was witnessed than that between the crack rival teams of the island Tuesday morning. Eleven innings without a score has a few, but only a few, parallels in the history of the great game. The contests which went before the baseball were clean and manly and those which followed were of the same order. The children won and lost with the demeanor of old sports and of true Americans. On the whole, the islanders have occasion for feeling a pride in themselves, their firemen, their baseball players, their children—in fact, their populace collectively and as a unit—over the wholesome, sober, high-class and successful manner in which the 140th anniversary of the nation was observed by them. The Fourth of July, 1916, will ever be remembered as a red-letter page in Douglas history.

With Roosevelt supporting Hughes and Parker, named as candidate for vice-president at the late B. Moose conclave at Chicago, supporting Wilson, it is fifty-fifty. The question is, how many of the former "Moosers" can the colonel bring with him back to the fold of the G.O.P.? The next question is, can a really good "Mooser" return to the old party without sacrificing the principles for which he yelled himself hoarse four years ago while accusing those still in the old ranks of being corrupt and everything else that was evil.

While there will be more tourists in Alaska during the next 60 days than were ever seen here during any former "open season" for tourists, the benefits derived by ordinary business interests from such visitors are small in proportion to that which results from strangers who come north with a view of locating and establishing themselves in some legitimate business. It is an old, and partially true, saying that the average tourist leaves the east with a clean shirt and a twenty-dollar bill and sees half of Alaska before changing either. This may be somewhat overdrawn, but the fact remains that the tourist who come this way are not profligate with their money. It is the man who comes north and travels around with the idea of selecting a future home that helps the communities he visits.

Jessie Pomeroy, a lifer in the Massachusetts state prison, had been in solitary confinement since 1876, forty years. Every Sunday evening he is permitted to sit in an obscure corner and listen to the prison chaplain for an hour but is not permitted to hold converse with any of his fellows. Pomeroy was sentenced when he was sixteen years of age for the murder of two playmates. During his confinement he has read all the eight thousand volumes of the prison library and has mastered six languages. He was ignorant and uneducated when committed to prison, but is now reckoned to be one of the best-read men in the state. Only recently he witnessed a moving picture, shown by the chaplain to illustrate his Sunday talk. Pomeroy enjoys excellent health and has no difficulty in whiling away the time. And we have heard people complain of lonesomeness and loneliness in Alaska. The most isolated light-keeper on the Alaska coast or any old coast—well, he can see the sun occasionally and that is what the Pomeroy person never does.

In Fairbanks a hotel man and his wife engaged in a family fight. The man went to jail and the woman went to the hospital. She got out first and her first act was to go to the jail and get her husband out. There is no accounting for the vagaries of the female of the species.

82 —Auke Bay, A.T., July 9, 1916—
Sunday afternoon—

Florence's heart ached at the sight of the dilapidated Indian houses. Beyond the clean, sandy beach, nestling in the tree line, the long row of buildings sat facing the Inside Passage. Surrounded by thickets of willow and devil's club, towering Sitka spruce, yellow cedar, and western hemlock kept the abandoned dwellings in deep shadow. Behind the natural shelf where the village sat, mountains angled steeply upward, ultimately touching the clouds.

Julia chatted with her husband and son as they moved away from the buggy. The horse stood in its traces, munching at roadside grass. A weathered but still magnificent totem pole dominated the knoll.

August and Florence hung back, not quite as eager to invade the all but silent village site. Ravens racketed in the dense foliage and an eagle screamed from the top of a spruce on the forested mountain before launching out and lazily circling above them. Sun sparkled off the water and the heat of the day saw shirtsleeves slowly undone and rolled up.

"It looks so, so sad," Florence said.

August nodded, his eyes working carefully over the visible length of the village.

"Florence, August!" Julia called. "Come on. George is going to show us where his grandfather lived."

August glanced at Florence. "Well? Want to go?"

"I suppose."

She twined her arm around his and held on as they trudged up the beach. Her sensible low-heeled shoes were not designed for walking in sand. More than anything she wished she could take them off and go barefoot.

The thought made her smile and she glanced up at August, wondering if he would be scandalized. He looked down at her.

"I have trouble still believing we are together again."

She squeezed his arm fondly. "Well we are, despite my silliness."

"We all do what we feel we must," he said. "You weren't being silly. You were doing what you honestly thought right."

"You're a strange man, August Lepke."

They stepped into the shade where a large plank house slowly succumbed to the elements.

"My grandfather lived here," George said as he ran his eyes over the walls. "I can remember when this paint was new and dark."

Florence squinted. Smudges translated into totemic designs. The faded, chipped paint looked tired. The side of the house leaned drunkenly inward, pulling the roofline down with it.

When he spoke, George's voice carried pain. "Twenty-seven people once lived in this house. Three generations. Not one of them could read or speak English, solve a mathematical equation, or owned a pair of shoes. Yet every one of them knew who they were, where they fit into their world, and had a good idea of what they could achieve during their life. Times have changed."

"For better or for worse?" Julia asked her husband.

"I don't know. What do you think?"

She sighed. "Frankly, I don't know either."

"Can we go inside, George?" Jeff asked.

Florence watched the mixed wariness and pride in George's face as he gave assent to his new son. How odd for him, she mused, to suddenly have a family from a completely different culture after so many years alone.

Knowing August had changed the way she looked at people. Before she met him she never would have considered spending the day with an Indian who married a white woman. Just putting it in those terms caused her reserve to surface.

Thinking about George and Julia became something totally different. Familiarity with them deepened every day. She liked them. They were people, not labels on different colored bottles. The knowledge gave her a sense of freedom as well as a tinge of fear.

Her life consisted of boundaries, some she fought, some she agreed to, and the rest she ignored. The ignored category remained unexamined. If they didn't affect her, why bother?

Since childhood she heard adults speak deprecatingly about Indians, Filipinos and Negroes as if those races had no more substance than that of trained beasts. Her own father, easily one of the touchiest men on earth and prone to violence if someone slighted the Irish, tossed off racial epithets as naturally as breathing. "Stroller" White, the editor of the Douglas paper personified the official attitude toward non-whites.

Knowing Irene, Jim, and Ruth Kisadis, as well as George Mak-we, made her re-examine how she thought, and felt, about those of another race. But Julia's marriage made her choose; she could not sit off to one side of the issue and blissfully ignore it any longer. The most frightening aspect of understanding your ignorance was realizing how many others hadn't even begun to question theirs and, in fact, did not want to think about it.

For the first time in her life, Florence felt shame for her race.

"Florence? Are you coming with us?" Julia asked.

Florence felt her face warm and silently blessed the shady trees. She didn't want to explain away a blush just now.

"Yes. Of course I'm coming."

The mold-covered wooden steps held their weight but proved slippery. The heavy plank door hung at an angle, the upper leather hinge, green and foul with fungus, had parted long ago. The dank, dim interior smelled of rotting wood.

George swallowed and pointed. "I used to sleep over there. Often I would wake before the others and go down to the beach to see what the sea had left in the night. Sometimes I would run out to Guard Island and pretend I was one of the young men who were always there in the old days."

"They lived there?" Julia asked.

"No. They guarded the village. From out there one can see for miles. If boats were sighted they would be able to tell the village if the visitors were friends or enemies so the people could prepare."

August peered back through the door at the small island. "Is the little neck of land connecting it to the shore ever covered with water?"

"Only at very high tides. If they needed to communicate during those times, they would beat on a drum."

"How many people lived here?" Florence asked.

"As many as three hundred once. After the white men came to Juneau the people began moving there. Now only two houses are occupied by old people."

"It's so sad!" Florence said.

George looked at her with soft eyes. "Yes, it is, isn't it?"

"But it's fascinating, too." Julia said from across the room. She had not stopped moving since entering the structure. She bent to study something on the floor.

"My wife the scientist," George said with a smile.

"Does your family still own the land?" August asked.

"The Auk people own it together. We don't have deeds or anything. That's not how we do things."

"What's to keep someone, a white person, from coming here and building a house?" Florence asked.

"They wouldn't be happy here unless they had asked permission from the Auk people. Besides, who would want to live this far from Juneau?"

"We came less than twenty miles," August said. "It's really not all that far."

"I don't think it's something we need to worry about yet," George said.

"You said there were still people living here?" Florence asked.

"Yes. Two couples, very old, still lived here last year."

"Would it be impolite to visit them?" Julia asked.

"We should pay our respects, as you white people say," George said with a smile.

They left the house and Jeff skipped down the beach ahead of them. He skidded to a halt and pointed out toward the water.

"Hey, everybody! Look!"

Out in the sparkling water a great mound of glistening black moved easily, fluidly, breaking out of the water, dipping below the surface, then rising again. A second, smaller body moved beside the first.

"Oh. A whale, two whales!" Florence said, a thrill running through her. Sometimes the great leviathans came up Gastineau Channel and sported about in front of town before moving down channel again. It had been a long time since she had seen any.

"Humpbacks," Julia said. "They sing, you know."

August chuckled. "What sort of songs?"

"Well, definitely not rag time," Julia said.

"My father heard them sing once when he was out with some other men," George said. "They were afraid they were calling to the men to join them. They left that place very quickly."

"I wish I could hear them sing," Florence said.

"That would be interesting," August said.

"Our teacher told us Eskimos eat whales," Jeff said. "Is that true?"

"Yes," Julia said. "They take bowhead and humpback whales and they eat every part of them and use their bones to build their houses."

"I don't think I could kill them," Florence said.

"Then it's a good thing you're not an Eskimo," Julia said with a laugh.

"In the old days my people would hunt the whale," George said. "I cannot remember the last time that happened."

"Someone's coming down the beach," Jeff said, dropping back to walk with the adults.

An old man limped down the sand toward them, using a staff to take weight off his left foot. His hair and beard were completely white and wild, as though he had just walked through a windstorm.

Florence thought him savage-looking in his long deer hide shirt and bare feet. His intricately carved staff had mother-of-pearl inlays that flashed as he moved. He scowled horribly at them. Ten feet in front of them he stopped and said something in Tlingit.

They all stopped and looked at George, who ventured a few words in return. The man spoke again.

"Do you have English, uncle?" George asked.

"Some, not many."

"My grandfather lived back there when I was a boy," George said, pointing.

"You Genx-akaa," the old man said. "I hark when you no larger than that." He pointed at Jeff. "What do you want here?"

"I wished to show my friends the village. This is my wife, Julia, my son, Jeff, my friends August and Florence."

"I am Jax-seh." He smiled, showing very few teeth. "I go now." He turned and limped away from them.

"Perhaps we should go the other way?" August said.

George stared after the old man. "I don't remember him at all."

Julia pulled him around and they began walking back toward the skiff in silence.

Florence realized she didn't know who her grandparents were. Not even their names. "George, how long has your family lived here?"

"Gosh, I don't know, a long time though. My grandfather told me his grandfather's grandfather came here as a young man to live with the people of this village. How long do you think that would be?"

"Close to the beginning of the eighteenth century," Julia said in a hushed tone. "Before the American Revolution!"

"This is an old village," George said, nodding his head.

I don't even know my grandmother's name, Florence thought, *and I always thought we were the civilized ones in this country.*

"Come walk with me." August tugged at her arm and she followed him up a game path winding through the trees before crossing the small ridge behind the mute houses. Once into the tree line the ground vegetation thinned and many trails crossed back and forth under the vast canopy.

"It's like a church. A cathedral," Florence said.

"This is my kind of church," he said. "Full of life and living things, animals and nature, not ikons and crosses."

"Are you a pantheist?"

"Probably."

"Why, August! That's, that's paganism!"

"I did not mean to upset you, but how I feel it is."

"I must be married in the Catholic Church. My children must be raised Catholic, like I was."

He stopped walking and sat in a sun-warmed grassy spot near a wind-fallen tree. He patted the grass beside him.

"Here. Sit please."

She thought they should settle this standing, but the grass did look inviting and her feet were sore. She sank down beside him.

"Not until today did I realize why this Alaska place I like so much." He waved his hand outward. "The trees. Trees are very important to Germans, especially old trees like these."

"August . . ."

"That's where your Christmas tree came from, you know. Old Germany. My ancestors worshipped trees and your ancestors made them part of a ceremony honoring the birth of a Jew who was born in a desert."

"Stop it, August," Florence said firmly. "Don't make me dislike trees because you wish to be sacrilegious."

"Florence, I can't make you do anything. You do whatever you wish. As for me, I will not tell my children they must worship thus and so, they will decide for themselves."

"How can they know if they are not shown?" she cried. Pain cut through her chest and she pressed both hands to herself until it passed.

He didn't notice. "I have no objection to explaining religions to them, but they will not be forced to participate. If they decide to become a Christian, or a Muslim, or a Hindu, that is their right, but forced they will not be."

Why this? she wondered. *Was there always going to be something pushing them away from each other? Didn't he understand the church was in her blood as much as the trees seemed to be in his?*

"Oh, August," she said with a small moan. "You are pulling me apart. Every time I turn around you are doing something I not only don't understand, but seems hurtful and hateful." Hot tears ran from her eyes.

"I couldn't hurt you if I wanted to," he replied, "but there are things I feel deeply about and I had to tell you of them. If we cannot compromise on this I fear we will not be able to compromise on anything."

"You want me to surrender my religion for you?"

"No. I just do not wish it forced on me or my children."

"Our children! They will be our children, August, and you wish to condemn them to a life of paganism and darkness, never to have their souls redeemed . . ."

"Is that how you see me, dark and pagan? I was raised in a strict Lutheran family until I left home to join the army." He gestured wildly. Somehow he lost letters in the middle of "Lutheran." "Church never felt right to me. It always seemed like an affectation, a role we all assumed one day a week and had nothing to do with the rest of our lives. I felt so unclean about my small part I stopped having anything to do with it."

"You are missing so much!" Florence said, wiping her eyes.

"What do I miss? Being a hypocrite? I am an honest man. I became a citizen of the United States by bearing arms in her defense—" He broke off and stared down at the ground. "But there was hypocrisy in that, also."

"How?"

"We fought Filipinos who only wanted us to get out of their country like the Spanish before us. The officers told us we were liberating the Philippines. Once the Spanish were gone, we stayed. We protected them by killing them!" He spat on the ground.

"I don't know anything about that," she said softly, "but I do know my religion is important to me. My mother is in heaven with God; I know that. I don't want my children thinking she just died like a flame in the night and is lost in darkness. I can't live with that, August."

"Maybe you can't live with me, Florence."

THE DOUGLAS ISLAND NEWS
Douglas, Alaska, Friday, July 14, 1916

It does not look right in this period of the so-called Christian Era for a ship to be compelled to travel under the water to get a cargo of baby food to a country to save its infants.

Measles have developed in Juneau and it is sincerely hoped the epidemic will not reach this side of the channel, where, to quote from Abe Potash, "Der family vat ain't got ash many ash six, ish considered ash practically childless."

The divisional Democratic convention for the purpose of placing in nomination candidates for the territorial legislature will be held in Juneau on August 1st. Douglas Island is entitled to seven delegates in the convention.

The landing of a merchant submarine at an American port with a cargo valued at one million dollars is a triumph for Germany that the entire world must admire. Also it will somewhat relieve the dye-stuff stringency in this country.

Chas. A. Sulzer, democratic nominee for delegate to congress, was a visitor on the channel last Saturday and Sunday, leaving here for the interior via Skagway and the Yukon River. People who know Sulzer best are his best friends and warmest admirers. Than that no man can have a better reputation. He will make a clean campaign and will make friends wherever he goes.

After practically walking through life to save car fare, Mrs. Hetty Green, America's richest woman, is dead. She left her money behind the same as Harriet Beecher Stowe, Julia Ward Howe, Victoria Woodhull and other noted American women left behind record of their good works—noted American women whose great praises will be sung generations after Hetty Green and her millions are forgotten.

So far as we are concerned, we hope Colonel Roosevelt will be granted his request to raise a division of volunteers for fighting purposes and be given a commission to command them. He is a good fighter and is much safer in the army than as pater familias in the White House.

All over Alaska a sentiment is growing against candidates for Alaska offices who make their homes in Seattle and who do not spend an average of three months in the country they expect to honor them by voting them into prominent positions. In a business way it is very nice and proper for Seattle to manifest a lively interest in Alaska. It helps all around. But in politics—well, carpetbaggers are just as unpopular in Alaska as they were in Dixieland forty years ago. There was cause for their unpopularity in the land of cotton and there is cause for their unpopularity in the land of gold and one-streak bacon, Charley Sulzer's campaign button says "Alaska for Alaskans," and it is a good motto to stick up on the wall alongside of "God Bless Our Home."

Throughout the East, people are now dying from excessive heat, while here in Alaska it is just warm enough to make a dish of ice cream enjoyable about 2 o'clock in the afternoon. Before or after that something hot is preferable.

The greatest need of Douglas is a hotel at which visitors can be accommodated the same as they are accommodated in other towns, many of which are not one-forth as large as Douglas. Nearly every day sees some person come here who has interests on the island and every evening sees that person or persons going to Juneau to spend the night for the reason they cannot be accommodated here as well as across the channel. It is admitted by persons interested that a good hotel in Douglas would pay a fair dividend on the money such hostelry would cost, yet no one appears to back his expressed judgment with sufficient capital to relieve the pressure. And it certainly is a pressure for any town the size of Douglas to be as poorly supplied with hotels as she is. As long as Douglas is content to entertain her visitors only in daylight, she will never be in a better position to hold them here than she is at present.

Delegate Wickersham had filed charges at Washington against a number of transportation companies operating in the north, including the White Pass railroad, the charges setting forth that certain of the companies are operating mines in connection with their other business. If there is a law against operating mines in connection with railroads or steamboats, the question naturally arises: Why such a law? Many mining properties are so situated as to be valueless without means of transporting ore from them and in order the property may be realized on, it is necessary that transportation lines be built and maintained. Anyhow, if a corporation hauls its own ore over its own railroad or steamship line, it is a poor law that says it nay. If the resources of this great northland are to be developed, freak legislation must be dispensed with. The plain truth of the matter is that somebody is taking a sideswipe at the Guggenheims, and to reach them, other concerns and corporations are implicated.

83 —Juneau City, A.T., July 20, 1916—
Thursday afternoon

Fiona sat alone in Maye's darkened office, holding both hands to her aching head as the pain throbbed in harmony with her heartbeat. She opened the small chest where Maye kept her medicines, there had to be something . . .

She picked up bottles, peering at labels in the dim light leaking in from the lobby, dropping the rejects and picking up others. Jenkins Bitters. Wimple's Woman's Restorer. Palmolive lotion. Carmen powder. Ingram's Milkweed Cream. Was there nothing but vanities in this chest?

Two bottles left, Magnolia Balm, and Leonard's Liquefied Laudanum.

"Thank God!" she said quietly to herself. In moments she uncorked the laudanum and took a tentative swallow. The taste twisted her face and she quickly washed down the drug with a glass of water from the pitcher on the bar.

She dropped into the large Morris chair, took a deep breath and waited for the pain to cease. The throbbing eased and a lassitude crept over her. The desk bell rang out in the lobby.

Before she could rise, she heard Amanda.

"Oh, sir, you have no idea how energetically I have been watching for your return."

"Why, Baroness! How very pleasant to see you. Ah, are we alone here?"

Fiona smiled. In her mind's eye she could see the man glance about. The voice sounded familiar, but she couldn't place it.

"I believe we are. Fiona was here half an hour ago, but she complained of a headache."

"Amanda, thoughts of you have plagued me every moment I was away from you!" the man said urgently. "I have arranged to be here in Juneau City for five whole days and I want to spend every night with you!"

Fiona's eyes popped open and she jerked to attention.

My word, that is rather forward! The remnants of her headache vanished.

"Oh, Barry, you have been in my thoughts ceaselessly. I was so afraid you weren't returning to Alaska, but now you're here, and I know you'll do the correct thing."

Fiona leaned forward quietly in preparation to rise for a peek, but the chair creaked alarmingly, and she froze.

"My, how ardent you are, darling. Ah, 'do the correct thing?'"

"Barry, I am with child."

Fiona covered her mouth with a hand to keep from gasping aloud. That's why she's been acting so strangely, Fiona thought.

"Are you quite sure?" His voice suddenly turned brusque. "We only had the one night."

"Why, I'm absolutely certain, Barry."

"Are you sure it's mine?"

The solid crack of a slap sounded loudly.

"Despite your experience of my seemingly easy virtue, I assure you you're the only man I've slept with since my husband died in October of last year! If you don't want to own up to your responsibility in this matter just simply say so. But don't you insult me with your tawdry attempts to belittle my actions or imply what is not!"

"I-, I'm sorry. I'm so sorry." Fiona could hear the pain in his voice. "I'd do the right thing. I'd marry you if I could, but I can't."

"Why ever not, Barry?"

"I have a wife and three kids in Portland."

Fiona sprang out of the chair and hurried quietly to the door. Amanda stood staring at the handsome drummer about whom she had waxed so eloquent a few weeks ago. Her face appeared totally bloodless and her mouth hung open.

Fiona grasped the doorframe, debating whether or not to rush to Amanda's side.

"Wife?" Amanda said brokenly.

"Yes. Listen. You do what you must, but, well, I have an elixir which . . ." He licked his lip. ". . . which can cause you to abort if you administer it correctly."

Amanda backed away from him. Her mouth clamped into a firm line. Her body drew in on itself and her hands came up in a defensive stance.

"You're all alike! Italian, Austrian, or American. You bloody men think it's like popping a pustule or combing your hair!"

She spat at his feet. "I require but one thing from you, sir, and that is to never again set eyes on you. Now get out of here before you lose blood."

"Amanda . . ." his hands rose in supplication.

"Get out!" she shouted, tears streaking down her face.

He snatched his bulky grip off the floor and hurried out the door.

Fiona flew to her friend's side and hugged her tightly. Amanda's body shook with silent sobs and she laid her head on Fiona's shoulder.

"'E has a wife," she said with a moan. "He told me he was single, constant, and discreet." She sniffed loudly. "He said he didn't kiss and tell."

"Oh, Amanda. What do you want to do?"

The dark woman pulled a hanky from her sleeve and blew her nose loudly. "I want to get drunk."

"I'll get you a drink if you like, but I don't think getting drunk will be of much benefit."

"I know," she said tiredly. "I would like a drink, but I promise not to get drunk."

"Why don't we go into Maye's office," Fiona said.

Amanda shuffled toward the door. "Is that where you were?"

"Yes."

"So you heard everything."

"I'm afraid so."

"Good. Now I have someone to talk with about it." She sniffed loudly.

"You always did."

"I know. It's such a devilish subject to bring up in polite conversation. Lovely weather we're having isn't it? Oh, by the by, I'm in the family way."

Both women broke into laughter.

Amanda dropped into the chair recently vacated by Fiona.

"What am I going to do, Fio? What am I bloody going to do?"

Fiona handed her a glass of whiskey. "What do you want to do?"

Amanda sipped and leaned back, her eyes staring into space. "I know what I don't want to do. I don't want to abort this one."

"This one?"

"This is the third time I've been pregnant. The first time I was fifteen and horrified my Italian lover because I chose abortion over marrying him. By his standards I was from a rich family and he saw me as beddable and bankable income." She sipped again.

"You don't have to tell me all this . . ."

"I need to say it, Fio, but you needn't listen if you wish not."

Fiona sat on the footstool and put her hand on Amanda's knee. "If you want me to hear it, I'll listen."

"The second was my husband's. He didn't even know about it. What a bloody lout he was. I wasn't about to give him a child the very first thing. I'd never have gotten out of Austria again."

"But you want to keep this one."

"Yes. At first it was because I was in love with Barry, and having a family with him appealed to me so very much." She sniffed again and wiped her nose. "As soon as he told me, I knew he didn't matter any more, but this child did."

"What will you do, Amanda?" Fiona asked softly. "How can you support yourself and a child?"

"I don't know," she said, draining her glass. "I'm not going to worry until I have to. May I have some more whiskey?"

"No. If you are with child you need to be drinking milk and eating three decent meals every day."

"Well listen to you, Auntie Fiona. This is me we're talking about here. I'll do as I bloody well please."

"Obviously."

Amanda laughed until tears came. "Damn me, but I'm glad you're on my side."

"I'm on that baby's side first," she said quietly. "You're going to take care of yourself if I have to hog-tie you." A rush of emotion flowed through her. "Oh, Amanda. It will have to be a beautiful baby with such a lovely mama!"

84 —Juneau City, A.T., July 21, 1916—
Friday morning

"Mr. Lepke, would you come in here a moment?" Chief Tinsley asked.

"Certainly, Chief." August entered the office and Tinsley shut the door behind him. On the other side of the room stood a middle-aged man wearing the uniform of a U.S. Army major.

August stopped and took a closer look. He had seen this man before, right here on the streets of Juneau, and not in uniform, either. Tinsley began to pace around in the small office: a sign of agitation.

"Detective Lepke served in the army for one enlistment and rose to the rank of sergeant," Tinsley said to the major. "He fought in Cuba and the Philippines. He earned his stripes on the battlefield, and was recommended for the Medal of Honor."

"Very impressive," the man said.

Tinsley swung around and fixed August with a long, level look. "Major Anderson went to military school, graduated, joined the army and was commissioned a second lieutenant. He served at the War Department in Washington during the unpleasantness in Cuba and the Philippines. While there he went up through the ranks to brevet major. He resigned his commission and came to Juneau where he operates a dry goods business on Seward Street."

"I see," August said, wondering what this was all about.

"Did you receive it, Mr. Lepke?" Anderson asked.

"Sir?"

"The Medal of Honor?"

"No. They gave me the Silver Star and another stripe instead."

"I see," the major said, twisting his mustache and permitting himself to exhibit a slight smile.

"You are a brevet major. May I ask your permanent rank?" Lepke asked.

"Yes, well." The major stood up straight, lifting his jaw slightly. "First lieutenant, actually." Something outside the window caught his attention.

"Well, nice meeting you, Major. "I'll be in my office, Chief." August turned to leave.

"It's not that simple, detective," Tinsley said. "I wish it were. Major Anderson has been appointed as the head of the civilian militia for Juneau, and he needs someone with experience to drill the men."

"Appointed by whom?"

"Governor Strong, Mr. Lepke," Anderson said. "I'm sure you're aware of his authority here in the Territory?"

"What has this to do with me then?" Lepke asked Tinsley.

"The governor has asked if you would serve as a master sergeant in the militia."

"Is this a thing I can refuse?"

"Not if you wish to retain your honor!" Anderson said.

August stared at the man, doing his best to rein in his anger. "Have you ever heard a shot fired in anger, Lieutenant?"

"It's Major to you! And, ah, I didn't have the good fortune to serve on the battlefield for our country. I have, however, been trained to lead men in battle and plan to do so if we get into this thing in Europe." Anderson cleared his throat and gazed out the window again.

"Chief, I put four years in the army and seven with the Pinkertons, I'm tired of following the directions of others."

"You follow my orders, Detective Lepke. What's the difference?"

"Yours have a rationale to them that is obvious to me. We serve the community. I want nothing to do with this civilian militia."

"My God, Tinsley. The man's a coward!" Anderson said.

August started across the room to throttle the man, but the chief's voice stopped him.

"He most certainly is not!" Tinsley snapped. "This man has faced death right here in Juneau and not shown the slightest bit of yellow. I believe you owe Mr. Lepke an apology."

"You want an officer to apologize to an enlisted man? Surely you're joking, Chief Tinsley."

"Mr. Lepke is not a sergeant, he's a lieutenant of detectives. Nor is he in the army, Mr. Anderson. I'm not joking in the slightest. You owe this officer an apology."

Anderson's face twitched and his mouth worked silently as his emotions battled within. "Why, I, ah, that is, uh, I didn't realize you were now an officer, Mr. Lepke. Surely you can understand my misunderstanding?"

"I understand quite a lot. Exactly why did you resign from the army and move north?"

"My health," he said quickly.

"You came to Alaska for your health?" Tinsley said.

"Clean air. Washington has such foul air most of the time."

"Then you must stay indoors on the days when Treadwell's smoke is drifting over town?" Lepke asked.

"I'm not here to be questioned like a common criminal!" Anderson said, looking at Tinsley. "Is this . . . officer . . . going to be my regimental sergeant major or not?"

"Regiment! How many kids do you think you're going to get into this little gun club?" Lepke asked. He debated with himself whether he would quit his job or not if ordered to serve under this martinet.

"We will accept as many able-bodied men from the area as possible. The War Department is advocating the formation of local militias so the task of mobilization will be easier in the event the United States enters the war. Any student of the European War can tell you the war would have been over by now if any of the belligerents had been able to instantly field an army."

"May I have some time to think this over, major?" Lepke asked.

"Certainly. How much time do you think you'll need?"

"A week?"

Tinsley stared at August keenly.

"Certainly," Anderson said magnanimously. "A week will pose no hardship at all."

"What are the requirements for entry into the militia?" Lepke asked, trying to sound off-hand.

"Why, the desire to serve one's country. What other possible requirement could there be?"

"Good point, Major Anderson," Tinsley said smoothly. "You'll be hearing from us by the end of the week."

"Excellent. Well then, I'll be off."

Tinsley waited for a long moment after the door closed behind the major, then turned to Lepke. "You got more than your arm up your sleeve, Detective. What are you planning?"

August wrote furiously on a notepad. "I need to send a wireless to the War Department." He finished writing, ripped off the page and jammed it into his pocket. "I want to find out what Brevet Major Anderson's exact affliction was that prompted his retirement from the service. The man obviously loves being a soldier."

Tinsley grinned widely, showing his horse-like teeth. "You don't much like the major, do ya?"

"It was people like the major who drove me from the army. I don't think I can work with that man, especially if I must be a sergeant. He's wrong about the European war. They all had standing armies and mobilized immediately; if they had to put an army together from scratch they might have thought more about it and found some other way to handle their differences."

"The thing is, you are probably the best sergeant material on Gastineau Channel."

"Thank you, chief, but I will not be subordinate to an ass like that."

"Go send your message. And be sure to let me know when you get an answer."

"You'll be the first person I tell, chief. I promise." August left the office whistling a popular rag.

85 —Juneau City, A.T., July 25, 1916—
Tuesday afternoon

"All thet gawddamned Irishman does is go to Armstrong's and then goes home," the Soda Water Kid said.

"So what's wrong with thet?" Driscoll asked. "Sounds like easy money to me."

"I'm bored! It's damn near as bad as following a Baptist."

Driscoll waved at the bartender who immediately brought more whiskey. Over the past few weeks the crowd in the Germania seemed to be thinning. Ahab heard men darkly muttering about things German, and he liked that; the bartender passed out more generous portions.

"Guess that's part of havin' a steady job, being bored and all," Driscoll said.

"Y'know, I'm thinking about gettin' me some one-eyed eel snapper." The Kid scratched at his scrawny beard.

Driscoll gazed at the Kid for a long moment. "You'd have to take a bath first. Ain't no woman in her right mind would let you get close for less'n five dollars the way you stink."

"Well, piss on you, too! If'n I stink, you smell dead!"

"Maybe so, but I ain't out to plug pastries like you are."

"Sometimes, Driscoll, I think I should just do you a favor and blow your fucking brains out."

"Better men than you've tried, and I'm still here."

"Piss on it. You comin' or not?"

"Where?"

"You drunk? I just said I was goin' down to the Row."

"I ain't drunk, but I thought you were. Yeah, I'll come and watch."

"The hell!" the Soda Water Kid said as he staggered out of the bar.

Sunlight blinded Driscoll for the first block of their journey. The Kid kept bumping into marks. He managed to lift two wallets despite his condition.

Driscoll smiled in admiration. Nobody else on this earth had hands like the Kid! Something nagged at the back of his mind but he found it easy to ignore everything right now.

Eternal summer daylight glowed all about them as they wandered up to the first small house with an unnaturally large front window. On the other side of the glass sat a woman wearing only a thin chemise. If one looked closely enough, the material proved transparent.

Driscoll squinted hard. The Kid stood beside him with his tongue hanging out. The woman shut the red curtains.

"Well, gawd-damn!" the Kid said. "Ain't our money good enough for her ladyship?"

"'Spect not," Driscoll mumbled. He'd never seen a cigar girl do that before. He looked at the Kid carefully. He appeared quite the specimen all right.

The Kid's ragged wool jacket would fall apart if washed, and shiny knees and seat highlighted his grimy pants. His left boot sole hung open mouth-like at the toe. Above the scraggly beard, greasy hair hung over his worn, dirty collar. He looked crusty enough to powder.

"I got an idea, Kid," he said slowly. "At the next window, just hold your money up so's the gal kin see it 'steada you."

The Kid nodded sagely. At the next house he held up a five dollar gold piece. The woman inside looked at the coin, then at the Kid, then back at the coin. She motioned him in.

Driscoll laughed and settled down on the doorstep to wait for his friend. The warmth of the sun almost had him asleep when someone shook his shoulder.

"Stand up, you."

Driscoll looked up into the face of a city patrolman, a man in a suit stood behind the officer.

He scrambled to his feet and pulled his hat off his head, clenching the brim in both hands.

"Yeah? Is there some problem, officer?"

"I want you to stand right here by this nice gentleman," the cop said.

"Sure!" Driscoll surreptitiously glanced at the man in the suit. Another cop for sure with a jaw set like that! He knew he was in no condition to successfully run away.

Don't take no fortune-teller to see bars in my future, he thought glumly.

"Lieutenant," the cop called from inside the crib. "Would you come in here, please?"

The lieutenant motioned to the door. Driscoll turned and went into the cool, shaded room. The cigar girl stood dressed in a housecoat smoking a cheroot. The cop had two wallets in his hand.

The Soda Water Kid sat on the floor with his pants around his ankles, looking more dazed than drunk. All three of them looked at the lieutenant when he came through the door behind Driscoll.

"Are you the Miss Adams that called?" the lieutenant asked.

"Yes. Soon as I saw those," she pointed at the wallets, "I went in the back and phoned. I'm not going to be no receiver of stolen goods!"

"Says he found both of them on the street," the cop said.

"Found two lost wallets in one short walk?" the lieutenant said cheerfully. "You're a pretty lucky man, mister. What is your name, anyway?"

"They calls me the Soda Water Kid."

"What did your mother call you?"

"Fer dinner!" he said, throwing his head back and cackling like an old woman.

The cop deftly kicked him in the kidney and he gasped and fell over.

"You're not in some theatrical act here. Tell the lieutenant your real name."

The Kid lay moaning on the floor. The lieutenant's eyes moved to Driscoll. "Who are you?"

"Ahup, uh, Ahab Driscoll, Mr. Lieutenant, sir."

"What's his real name?" he pointed at the moaning Kid.

"I never heard him called anything but what he said, the Soda Water Kid."

"How long have you known him?"

Driscoll licked his lips and thought fast. Jesus, how was a man to know what was safe to say?

The beefy cop moved next to him. "The lieutenant asked you a question."

"Yeah, I know. I'm just tryin' ta recollect when I first met th' Kid, here. Musta been about, oh gosh, as far back as '07, or '08."

"Here in Juneau?" the lieutenant prodded.

"Naw. Portland, Oregon. Nice town, Portland."

The lieutenant stared at him hard enough to scorch skin. Hard eyes. Cop eyes. He'd seen them many times before. He suddenly felt more afraid of this lieutenant than of the beefy knuckles in uniform.

"Honest, mister!" he said, trying to keep his hands from shaking.

"Driscoll, yes. I remember you now. You got two years for stealing an old lady's purse."

He felt his insides go hollow. *How the hell did he know that? That was years ago!*

"Uh, yeah." He tried to keep the awe out of his voice. "That's right. I did."

The Soda Water Kid moaned and pushed himself off the floor. "I need to piss!"

"Get him out back, Forysthe," the lieutenant said.

Forysthe grabbed the Kid's arm and drug him through the small kitchen and out the back door.

"Aw, hell. He pissed on my floor," the cigar girl said.

Driscoll glanced down. A trail of water ran across the floor to the door. He snickered.

"Since you find it so amusing," the lieutenant said, "why don't you clean it up?"

"What?"

"Clean it up."

"With whut? I don't see no mop."

"Use your coat."

"Yew can't make me clean up another man's piss with my own coat!" He was suddenly angrier than he'd been in months. Since Jack Malone knocked some of his teeth out, in fact.

The lieutenant stared at him.

"Either you do it with your coat or we'll use your coat with you in it!" The brown eyes went hard and shiny as buttons. The bastard meant it.

Driscoll dropped his gaze to the floor and pulled off his coat, completely forgetting about the sap tucked in his waistband at the small of his back. The lieutenant snatched it out.

"Well, what have we here? A sap, and well used at that. I suppose you boys found this on the sidewalk also?"

He wanted to cry. Everything that could go wrong, had. It just wasn't fair!

"No, I didn't find it on the fuckin' sidewalk!" The white anger, the killing rage that could sweep over him in seconds, boiled from his narrow chest into his brain; obliterating thought and common sense.

Driscoll snapped his head back to glare at the bastard and gauge the distance. He heard the growl roll from his throat just before he leaped, and the world went black.

86 —Juneau City, A.T., July 28, 1916—
Friday morning

Tourists crowded Winter and Pond's curio shop. Two tiny ladies vied for Florence's attention, both demanding to know whether the small wooden totem poles they held were of Alaskan origin or inferior copies executed by "southern Indians."

"Those are carved by young Tlingit men over in the village of Angoon, ladies. They make them especially for visitors."

"How nice," one said, bright eyes dancing behind the lenses of her spectacles. "But why do they demand such a high price?"

"Those take many hours to carve and paint. At fifty cents they are a bargain," she said firmly.

"Well . . . What do you think, Ruth? Should we spend that much on the boys?"

The other woman, even more bird-like than the first, peered closely at the carving in her hand. "I wish the workmanship was better. I'm just not convinced they're worth that much."

Florence bit her lip to keep from shooing them out of the shop. This part of her job could be so vexing!

"Well, you ladies think it over." She turned from them and ran full into Fiona. "Oh! Fio. Where ever did you come from?"

"I was right behind you, obviously, waiting for you to finish with those—"

"Yes, well, I'm sorry I ran into you that way." She grabbed Fiona's arm, turned her around, and steered her toward the back room.

"—dear little ladies, so I could speak with you."

They entered the back of the shop.

"My God, Florence. How do you ever put up with them?"

"I think of it as my penance for living in paradise. I must get back out there. What was it you wanted?"

"Have dinner with Amanda and me tonight, okay?"

"That would be fun. What time and where?"

"The Line Cafe at seven o'clock."

"The Line . . ."

The service bell on the counter tinkled.

"All right. It's against my better judgment to go into that place, but I'll do it."

The ringing became continuous. Florence hurried out.

"We'll take these," the bright-eyed lady said, "if you'll drop the price a quarter dollar each."

"Miss, could I get a better look at that mask up there?" a man asked.

"I can't do that," Florence said to the lady.

"Pardon me?" the man said.

"Oh, yes, sir. One moment, please." She pulled the small stepladder over and retrieved the Indian mask off the wall. "That's very old and delicate, sir," she said, handing it to him.

"These can't possibly be worth fifty cents!" the lady said waspishly.

"Well then, don't buy them," Florence said, instantly regretting her words.

"Well, I never!" the lady said. "What rudeness!" She slammed the totem down blindly toward the counter just as the man lay the mask down. The totem landed squarely on the brow of the carved, concave mask.

With a hollow "thwock" the mask split down the middle.

"I ain't payin' for that!" the man said instantly.

"If you were watching what you were doing, that never would have happened!" the woman shrilled, glancing about rapidly, searching for allies. "No wonder nobody lives up here except for Indians and poor white trash!"

Florence went light-headed with anger. She forced herself not to slap the woman. August suddenly appeared beside the trio.

"An unfortunate accident," he said calmly. "Perhaps you folks could split the cost of the artifact for the management?"

"Who are you?" the lady bristled.

"Just a white trash police lieutenant."

Florence snorted but managed not to laugh outright.

The woman visibly reigned in her indignation. "How much is it?"

Florence turned the pieces over and pointed to the penciled "$30" on the back.

"That's pretty dear!" the man said.

"It's almost fifty years old and unique," Florence said. "That's why we kept it up on the wall."

"Ya coulda said something!" the man said.

"She told you it was very fragile," August said curtly.

"Oh, I didn't think you heard that." The man pulled out his wallet.

"Well, I don't think it's worth that much!" The bright bird-eyes blazed at them.

"That's why I'm suggesting you split half the cost with this gentleman, here."

The woman looked up at August and blinked. "Well, since you put it that way."

As money changed hands, a ship's whistle cut through the morning. The shop cleared in moments. Florence looked down at the money on the mask halves.

"They didn't even demand the pieces."

"How much do you want for that damaged merchandise?" he asked.

She chuckled.

"Well, since the company broke even on it, so to speak . . ." They both laughed.

"You could probably purchase this damaged artifact for a mere five dollars."

"Five dollars! How about I take you to lunch instead?"

"You still don't get the mask."

"That's not what I came in for any way," he said with a grin.

"What did you come in for, August?"

His grin faded slowly.

"I would like you to have lunch with me and dinner tonight."

"I have a previous engagement tonight," she said lightly. "Sorry." His face dropped and she felt sinfully pleased at his discomposure.

"A prev—! Ah, how about lunch?"

"Today?" She admitted to herself her conduct bordered on awful. Of course he had been awful on the trip to Auke Bay and still hadn't apologized for it. Was that it? Was she punishing him?

"Yes," he said quietly. "Today. If you don't have other plans."

"I'd love to have lunch with you." She glanced at the clock. "I don't get off for another half hour."

"I'll wait." He moved away and found something interesting in a glass case.

"What happened to this?" Percy Pond said from behind Florence.

She turned to see her employer gently holding the pieces of the mask together. Florence quickly explained the accident.

"Then Mr. Lepke suggested they share half the cost of the piece, and they agreed."

Pond stared at August as if the police officer had suddenly sprouted wings.

"Thank you very much, Mr. Lepke. That was most kind of you."

"Well, to tell you the truth, Mr. Pond, I rather enjoyed doing it. They weren't being polite to Miss Malone and I thought the situation needed a touch of justice."

"Haw, that's good. A touch of justice. If this had happened in Douglas, Stroller would probably write it up."

"I'd just as soon not be in the newspaper."

"Unless it's on the sports page, right?"

"Right."

"Mr. Pond, if it's all right with you, I'd like to leave a bit early for lunch," Florence said.

"Certainly. Bon appétit!"

Moments later she strolled down the plank sidewalk arm in arm with August.

"Where would you like to have lunch?" he asked.

"You choose. You know the town now. I only decide for cheechakos who are lost without friendly advice."

"Hmm. And do you assist all cheechakos who come to you for advice?"

"Only the ones I find intriguing."

"Are you having dinner tonight with someone intriguing?"

Her eyes flashed to his face for an instant and then she continued her casual observation of the busy street. He was actually worried! For some reason that surprised her.

"Well, yes. I'd say they were at least that, perhaps even fascinating."

"They?"

"August, if you want to know who I'm having dinner with, why don't you just come right out and ask me?" She laid the joviality on heavily.

"Because it's none of my business and I don't want to pry." He sounded almost prim.

"Ho, ho! What are you doing right now? I'd certainly call it prying."

His face creased into a smile and he regained control of himself. "Miss Malone, how could you say such a thing? I'm merely making polite conversation."

"Oh, I see. Are they putting up another concrete building?"

"What? Where?"

"Up there on Franklin Street. See? Where are we eating? I'm starved."

He pulled out his watch, opened the cover and stared at it, then snapped it shut.

"We're just in time for our reservations," he said, opening the door to the Alaska Grill.

"August! This place is far too expensive."

"Not to worry. The meal is a reward from the owner."

"You're wasting it on lunch? A reward for what?"

"Dear Miss Florence, I'm not wasting lunch if I'm having it with you. One of the patrolmen and I apprehended a couple of ne'er-do-wells who had filched the owner's wallet. He didn't even miss it until we returned it to him."

The maitre' d'hotel hurried over to them and bowed from the waist with a flourish.

"Lieutenant Lepke, how good to see you, sir. Miss Malone, you grace us with your presence. Right this way, please." He pranced off through the room ahead of them.

"How much was in that wallet?" Florence whispered.

"Three hundred and seventy dollars," August whispered back. "The monthly payroll for his staff."

Florence sipped her tea while August finished his meal.

"You sure didn't eat much," he said.

"You sure eat a lot! You didn't used to eat that much."

"Usually I have to pay for it."

"Oh, that's right," she said with a laugh. "I'm honored that you asked me to share your hero's meal."

He laid down his napkin and picked up his coffee.

"I asked you because I want you to marry me." He finished off the coffee.

Florence felt stunned. She had anticipated this for some time, but he had been so disagreeable and distant the last few times they'd been together, and . . .

"Florence, do you know your mouth is hanging open?"

"August, I don't understand you. When we were with George and Julia that day at Auke Bay, you were downright disagreeable. The two times I've seen you since then you were at best friendly, but much closer to civil. Now you say you want to marry me!"

His somber face held no trace of humor now. The brown eyes probed her, as if penetrating her skull and examining her thoughts, seeking answers of his own. He shrugged.

"I'm not good at this. There was no way to practice—," He waved his hand vaguely in her direction. "—this intensity that happens between us. I have never been smooth and suave with women. I'm sorry."

"Oh, don't be! That's one of the things I find most endearing about you. You don't do everything behind a mask or a façade. You're abrupt and immediate, but that's because you're honest. And I love you for it."

"I thought you didn't understand me," he said slowly.

"Well, I didn't understand your actions over the past few weeks, as it is, you just explained it." She sipped her tea, gathering her thoughts. "Do you really want to marry me?" she asked from behind the cup.

"Yes. There are things we must work out between us that won't be easy, but I now realize life without you would not be bearable, no matter what compromises

I must make."

"You're going to give it all away if you don't watch it."

"Give what away?"

"The compromises. Oh, I don't know what I mean." Her mind whirled. He stared at her.

"What?" she asked.

"Well, what do you say?"

"About what?"

"Marrying me!"

"You haven't asked me yet, August," she said gently.

"I just did!"

"No. You said you wanted to marry me. You didn't ask me to marry you. That's an important distinction."

He puffed his cheeks out in exasperation and blew toward the ceiling. The waiter hurried over.

"May I get you something else, sir?"

"Yes. Give me the ring now."

Florence felt a sense of unreality as the waiter took a small box from his vest pocket and handed it to August.

"Thank you, Spencer."

"You're most welcome, Mr. Lepke." He nodded to Florence and then vanished into the kitchen.

"May I have your hand . . ." August asked.

She extended her left hand and he slipped a ring on her finger. It fit perfectly.

". . . in marriage?" he finished.

She burst into tears.

"Florence?"

"How did you do that? How did the waiter have a ring in his pocket that fits my finger perfectly?" She sniffed.

"I gave it to him to hold until I was ready for it. I took one of your gloves down to Mayor Valentine. He measured the diameter of the ring finger and then I picked out a ring."

"Oh." Her chest felt hollow and full at the same time. Her mind, however, began to shake off the numbness threatening to engulf her. He stared at her.

"August, I . . . I have never been so overwhelmed in my life. This is such a surprise. I don't feel equal to the moment." She sniffed again and wiped her eyes.

"Does that mean you won't marry me?"

"I wish I could stop crying! Yes, I'll marry you!" Her heart felt as if it were ready to burst. She held up her hand to admire the small glittering stone on the gold band.

"I'll marry you tomorrow if you wish!" she said happily.

He rose to his feet and moved around the table, took her hand, pulled her to her feet and kissed her.

The waiters, kitchen staff, and other diners all applauded.

As August walked her back to work, he asked in an offhand tone, "Whom are you having dinner with tonight?"

"Fiona and Amanda."

He experienced a sudden coughing fit.

The afternoon sped by in a haze. She finally understood what people meant when they said they were walking on clouds. Life had a way of twisting on you just when you thought the puzzle became obvious.

Mrs. Milivich poked her head into the parlor as Florence entered the house.

"Vill you be ta home for dinner?"

"No, Mrs. Milivich, I won't. I've been invited to dine with Fiona and Amanda."

"Yah." She started to pull back into the kitchen.

"Mrs. Milivich!"

"Yah?"

"Look," she held up her hand, "Mr. Lepke asked me to marry him."

The old woman stared at her, and slowly emerged from the kitchen. She ghosted across the floor toward Florence, never losing eye contact, until she stood in front of her. Old hands reached out and took young ones, holding them tenderly.

"How I vish your mother could be here to share your happiness. You look so much like her. Sometimes I tink she has come back . . ." Mrs. Milivich dropped Florence's hands and embraced her.

"You vill be happy. He is a goot man, I hear." Then she went back to her kitchen.

"My God," Florence said to herself. "What an unbelievable day." She went upstairs to change.

"I'll certainly be doing all the talking tonight," she said to her mirror. "Won't they be surprised with what I have to tell them!"

87 —Juneau City, A.T., August 2, 1916—
Wednesday afternoon

George Mak-we hurried toward the police station. Detective Lepke wanted to see him, the note said. Perhaps he had some news about the trials of the killer Krause.

George carried news of his own. He smiled to himself, feeling content. Such a wonderful wife he had.

Every morning when we awoke next to her, his great fortune overwhelmed him all over again. Julia understood him like no other person he had ever met. Now she was going to give him a child.

He stepped into the police station and stopped. Chief Tinsley looked on as Lepke spoke to a man in army uniform.

". . . didn't quite tell us everything about your military career, did you Major Anderson?"

"I don't know what you mean, detective."

The sandy haired detective pulled a cablegram from his pocket.

"Allow me to read you something, War Department, Washington, D.C., Lieutenant, Brevet Major, Arnold Oscar Anderson resigned his commission for the good of the Army July 7, 1914."

All eyes in the room fastened on Anderson. Dark red spots appeared high on his cheeks.

"His court martial conviction for embezzlement considered lenient in that he was not obliged to serve time in federal penitentiary. Under no circumstances should this man be allowed to head the militia of any state, territory, or possession of the United States. Signed, Colonel W. H. Bascomb, U.S. Army.'"

Anderson's jaw muscles worked silently beneath the skin. Twice he opened his mouth but issued no sound. Finally he said, "Does the governor know?"

"Yes," Tinsley said. "I told him yesterday when this arrived."

"Why did you do this to me?"

"You didn't offer your services," Lepke said. "You arrogantly demanded to be put in charge of the lives of other men. No sane man would do that unless he was trying to prove something."

"I would have done an excellent job! All the training I've had is just going to waste." Tears coursed down his cheeks. "I'm completely wasted as a storekeeper."

Anderson walked slump-shouldered past George and into the street.

"By God, Lepke. How did you know?" Tinsley asked.

"Like I told him, no sane man relishes having the lives of others under his direction in a war." He waved at George. "Officer Mak-we, how good of you to come over right away."

They shook hands.

"What can I do for you, my friend?" George asked.

Lepke pulled him into a small office and shut the door.

"I would like you to be best man at my wedding."

"Florence?" George felt elated. "I am so happy for you! Now you can enjoy the same kind of happy married life I have."

"How is Julia?" Lepke asked.

"With child."

"George! What wonderful news. How does Jeff like the idea of a new brother or sister?"

"He's not sure about it all yet. He and I talk a lot about what it means to be a man, both white and Tlingit. The hunting and fishing part of being a Tlingit fascinates him, but the more family-oriented traditions either elude him or he just doesn't care."

"Have you adopted him yet?"

"No. We're waiting to see if he really wants to be adopted. He has to accept the whole culture or nothing at all."

"A child," Lepke said. "It's all rather miraculous isn't it?"

George shrugged. "It's a part of life I don't really understand, so, yeah, I guess it is miraculous. I have trouble with that word. The Sisters of St. Ann used it a lot."

"In a very different way, I'm sure," Lepke said with a chuckle.

"It didn't have anything to do with what happens between women and men, that's for sure. When are you and Florence going to have the ceremony?"

"Late April. She wants a spring wedding, says it's a time of birth and renewal."

"What day?"

"The twenty-third. It's a Monday, I think. Two o'clock in the afternoon at the Cathedral of the Nativity of the Blessed Virgin Mary. Quite a mouthful, isn't it?"

"Yeah." George felt a shiver run up his back and into his hair, and immediately felt troubled. The sensation had only happened twice in his life; just before Amalie died, and when an old friend said he'd see George in a few days. The man drowned the next day when his boat sank in a storm. George never talked about it to anyone.

"George, is something troubling you?"

"No. I was just hunting for goats."

"Hunting for goats?"

"Irene says when I start thinking about things, my eyes focus on something far away, like I'm hunting for mountain goats."

"Oh. Well, will you be my best man?"

"If I can be. Julia is talking about leaving for California right after the baby comes."

"When is the child due?"

"Late March or early April."

"That's going to be a busy time, isn't it?"

"Without question," George said, wondering what would happen between now and then.

"Is Begay still wooing Ruth?"

"Yes. Irene has resigned herself to the fact her grandchildren are going to have two cultures to draw from."

"Have they set a date yet?"

"No. Begay is obsessed with having a home to move into before they get married. He's building a house way up on Gold Street, behind the business district." George pointed up toward Mt. Roberts.

"Well, you can't say he's lazy."

"No. He's an industrious young man, and I think he's going to make Ruth a fine husband."

"Well, I have to go out now. Where are you headed next?"

"Oh, nowhere in particular. Just walking around."

"Good. You can go with me to the Division Hotel."

"Are you still living there?"

"Yes," Lepke said ruefully. "I suppose I should rent a house or an apartment, but I rather enjoy living in a hotel because I don't have to worry about laundry."

George laughed. "There's another excellent reason to get married."

"Don't let Florence hear you say that. She has her own notions about division of labor in the home."

They left the police department and sauntered down the sidewalk. The town buzzed with tourists, miners, and deliverymen. A Ford rolled past, popping and shuddering as the driver manipulated the throttle.

"Think those will ever replace horses?" George asked.

"Down in the States they're all over the place. People are going from one end of the country to the other in them. At first I thought they were just a rather expensive toy, but I'm not so sure any more."

"I don't see how they would be of a lot of use here."

A Dodge Brothers truck rumbled past loaded with supplies.

"Make a count some time," Lepke advised. "There're more of those things around here than you think."

As they neared the Division Hotel, Jack Malone emerged.

"This should be interesting," Lepke said softly.

George didn't have time to ask why before Jack was upon them.

"Well, well, well, if it ain't Mr. Lepke. Top o' the day to ya, sir."

Lepke halted. "Good afternoon, Mr. Malone. I wonder if I might have a word with you?"

"I've always got time ta speak to me prospective son-in-law," he said with a grin. "What's on yer mind?"

"I didn't realize you already knew, sir."

"I wouldn't have if Mrs. Milivich hadn't told me."

"Mrs. Milivich?"

"Me housekeeper of twenty years. Florence told her."

"I see. Well, I know it's customary for the man to ask the woman's father for permission first. But, Florence isn't like most other women, is she? I mean, she has her own opinion about everything and I thought it best to ask her first."

Jack grinned at him. "And?"

"And, well, now I'm asking you if you have any objections?"

Jack's grin faded. His suddenwrinkled eyelids put George in mind of a tortoise he had once seen.

"As ya know, there was a time in the not so distant past when I would just as soon shot ya as look at ya, but you helped me in a court of law because you saw the truth of a situation and not just the black and white of it. You're a damned decent man, August Lepke, even if ye ain't an Irishman, an' I'd be proud ta have ya fer a son-in-law."

Lepke's face colored and then heightened when Jack stepped forward and hugged him. As soon as Jack released him, he stepped back.

"I'd like you meet Officer George Mak-we. He is going to be my best man. George, this is Florence's father, Jack Malone"

George shook the man's hand. "I'm honored to meet you, sir."

"Honored?"

"Yes. It isn't every day one meets a legend."

Jack threw back his head and laughed. "By God, Mr. Mak-we, you should be selling soap or swampland real estate. You've got the gift o' blarney, you do!"

George glanced at Lepke. "That was a compliment, wasn't it, sir?"

"One o' my best. Could I offer you gentlemen a drink?"

"Thank you, Mr. Malone," Lepke said, "but I am trying to stop our officers from drinking while on duty, so I must set an example."

"And I don't drink any more, Mr. Malone. But I am touched by the offer," George said.

Jack's eyes widened. "By God, an honest cop and a sober Indian. What's the world coming to?"

"Maturity?" Lepke said with a slight smile.

"That'll be the day! Good day to you, gentlemen. Mr. Mak-we, I'm proud to have made your acquaintance." He walked off down the street whistling.

"Didn't you once tell me he hated you?" George asked.

"Yes, and he did, just because I was a Pinkerton operative."

"This must be very strange for you."

"George, my life keeps getting stranger and stranger. C'mon up to the room with me."

They entered the lobby. George hadn't been in the Division Hotel in some months. Very little had changed.

"Good day, officers," Fiona said from behind the front desk.

"How are you today, Miss Malone?" Lepke asked.

"It's nice to see you again, Miss Malone," George said.

Fiona rolled her eyes. "What must I do to get you both to call me, Fiona?"

"It just doesn't sound right," Lepke said.

"Do you really want me to call you by your first name?" George asked.

"Yes, George, I do."

"Okay, Fiona. I will."

Lepke started up the stairs and George followed.

"Help me work on him now," she called to George.

"I will."

In his room, Lepke changed his shirt and rinsed his face in a basin. George sat, silently watching the man, wondering uncomfortably why Lepke wanted him here.

The police detective slipped on his vest and suit jacket, checked his appearance in the mirror, and turned to George.

"I need someone I can trust to back me up on something."

This is why I'm here, George thought. "Back you up on what?"

"I am convinced we have a saboteur on our hands."

"What? Why? I mean, why would someone sabotage anything in Alaska?" George felt astonished, wondering if Lepke spent too much time alone.

"That's exactly what I asked myself when the thought first occurred to me," Lepke said with a fierce grin.

"What answers did you come up with?" George asked.

"Look at the newspapers. Every day we are drawn closer and closer to the war in Europe. Down in the states the authorities have caught German agents who were intent on blowing up munitions plants or railway centers. Some weren't caught in time and succeeded in destroying vital industrial plants. Vital, that is, for a country at war."

"But we're not at war."

"Not yet. I firmly believe it's only a matter of time."

"We're so far from everything. The only thing we produce here is gold."

"Exactly!" Lepke, now seated on the bed next to George, stared with eyes almost glowing with intensity. "What does it take to run a war? To pay your army and navy? To buy arms, ammunition, uniforms, mules— to buy anything?"

The idea of it washed over George so suddenly he blinked. "Money. Gold!"

"Yes! Gold! How can we fight a war if we don't produce gold? It's ingenious. If they can stop our gold production, they can stop our entry into the war."

"But, who . . . ?"

"The Germans, of course."

"No," George said quickly. "I realize it's probably the Germans behind something like this, but who in Juneau is doing these things?"

"A very smart man. He has cloaked his actions from the very beginning. But the link I had been searching for was provided by your prospective nephew."

"Begay Santo?"

"Yes. He was approached by a man who urged him to damage the Treadwell mine as an act of revenge."

"He was?"

Lepke grinned.

"Who?"

"Have you met the journalist, Arnold Williams?"

"No. I have seen him, I know who he is. But I have never met him."

"Good. "Here's what I want you to do . . ."

THE ALASKA DAILY DISPATCH
Juneau, Alaska, Thursday, August 3, 1916

WHEAT PRICES ON THE JUMP

CIVILIANS BE TRAINED UNDER NAVY

ONE AIRSHIP IS WINGED BY SHORE CANNON

RUSSIANS ENCIRCLE TEUTONS

PROGRESSIVES MEET TODAY

WILSON WATCHES THE SITUATION

CASEMENT TO MEET DEATH AT DAWN TODAY
Be Executed at Nine O'Clock in Pentonville Prison on Charge of High Treason
WAR MINISTER SAYS WILL BE NO REPRIEVE

Appeals Have Been Received From Many Sources Asking That the Government Commute the Sentence to Life Imprisonment

LONDON, Aug. 3.—Sir Roger Casement, Irish patriot and former British government consular agent, will be executed at 9 o'clock in Pentonville Prison this morning.

Lord Robert Cecil, minister of war, made the announcement last night, that the British government was determined that no reprieve should be granted.

Appeals from many parts of the world have been received asking that the death sentence be commuted to life imprisonment. A large part of them are from the United States and even President Wilson has asked that clemency be exercised.

Sir Roger Casement will be executed on the charge of high treason, growing out of the attempt to land munitions on the coast of Ireland from a German vessel several months ago, preceding the so-called Irish rebellion. Born in Ireland, he was formerly employed by the British government as a consular agent in Africa.

88 —Dupont Dock, A.T., August 9, 1916—
Wednesday evening

"Be careful, O'Sullivan!" Sean Clancy hissed. "If ya drop one o' them we could both be blown to smithereens!"

"Calm down. This stuff is pretty stable. We toss it around all the time."

"An' may be that's so," Clancy said with a grunt as he took another case from the smaller man and sat it on the bottom of his small boat, "but we don't want any pryin' eyes about now, do we?"

O'Sullivan glanced around in the soft evening light. "No. For fact we don't at that."

"Okay," Clancy said and sat down on the boat seat with a thump. "That makes six. Christ, but that's hot work. Could I offer ya a nip 'r two?"

O'Sullivan licked his lips and smiled. "Just as soon as you cover up them boxes."

Sean pulled a tarp over the dynamite and produced a bottle of whiskey from beneath his bench. "Here ya go, Tommy, me lad."

O'Sullivan eased his light frame down into Clancy's boat and accepted the bottle. After a long pull he passed it back.

"Christ's blood, but that's decent whiskey!"

"Only th' best fer Irish patriots!" Clancy said before drinking deeply. He glanced around. "It was surely smart o' them ta build their dynamite dock so far from the towns. Too bad I can't catch the next train ta the Perseverance."

"What I don't understand," O'Sullivan said hesitantly, "is what you're gonna do with dynamite here in th' Territory?"

"It's much bigger than us," Clancy said with a wink. "Our part is ta provide the cause with the means to strike a blow for Irish independence." He patted the tarp beside him. "An' we've done just that, Tommy, me lad."

"Manifests are easy to change," O'Sullivan said with a shrug. "It's a damn sight easier than facing a firing squad in Dublin."

Clancy tipped the bottle again and handed it back to O'Sullivan. "I've got family in the old country. Don't hear from them all too often. The last letter said two of me cousins were joining the Fenians. For all I know, they've been put up against the wall . . ."

"We never hear from our folks back in Ireland," O'Sullivan said, corking the bottle and setting it down. "I'm sure they're doing their part. Who's your contact man on this?"

Clancy's stomach lurched with the implications of the casual, off-hand question.

"I can't be telling you that, Tommy. Y' know better than to ask."

"Sure. I understand. It's just that there are a few people on my end to keep happy, and they like to know who they're dealing with."

"Me. They're dealing with me. Sean Clancy."

"That's good enough for me," O'Sullivan said, standing and stretching. "Well, I've got to get back to my job before somebody notices my absence."

"Thanks fer yer help, Tommy, I won't be forgetting it."

O'Sullivan pulled himself onto the dock, looked down at the man in the boat. "Sure. Let me know if you need anything else."

Clancy wound the pull rope around the top of the Johnson outboard and jerked on it. The small motor burbled to life and he adjusted the throttle quickly as the boat moved through the water. He twisted around and waved to O'Sullivan, who waved back.

A weight lay in his gut. No true patriot would ask questions like that. What did he really know about the man? Where in Ireland did his people come from?

He hated the idea of telling Jack Malone about this, but he dared not ignore the incident. Besides, he could be wrong. O'Sullivan could have just been making conversation, merely wondering about the organization here in Alaska.

As he motored past Thane on his way to Juneau City, the weight in his gut grew heavier.

89 —Juneau City, A.T., August 16, 1916—
Wednesday afternoon

"Is there anything else you need besides nails?" Begay Santo asked.

"Maybe another carpenter?" Ponce Villanueva said with a laugh.

"Are you telling me you can't handle the job?" Begay said, immediately regretting the testiness in his voice.

"No, Begay," the short Filipino said heavily. "I was only making a joke. Don't worry we'll get your house done in no time at all. You understand?"

"Yeah," Begay said, unsuccessfully trying to make his mouth form a smile. "I'm just putting everything I own into this."

"I know. Don't worry. Just go get us another keg of nails and enjoy the walk on the way down. You'll work hard enough on the way back."

"Okay. I'll be back in about an hour."

Begay waited until Ponce and the two Indian helpers busied themselves before he pulled himself away and started down hill toward town. It will be a good house, he told himself. One worth the suffering.

All of Juneau, Gastineau Channel, and Douglas Island lay spread out before him. One more week and the house would be livable, but only for a determined bachelor– not for a new wife. Ruth settled gently on his mind and he smiled.

He glanced up. The gray sky held the promise of rain, prompting him to increase speed. The idea of carrying a keg of nails up a slippery mountain held little appeal.

So many tasks had to be accomplished before he went back to his job at George Brothers Market on Saturday. He liked his job, and his employers were very fair. Last month they gave him a 10-cent an hour raise in pay.

At times he felt angry with himself for not being more industrious while employed by Treadwell. He thought often about how much more money he had made across the channel. He also knew it was not good to dwell on what-might-have-been. It usually ruined his day.

"You don't laugh any more," Ruth had complained. Perhaps not as much? He desperately wanted to believe he had grasped happiness out of the mess of his life.

"I am living my life. What more could a man ask?" he said loudly to the steep path. Abruptly he glanced around to see if anyone heard his words. Except for him, the brush-covered slope lay empty.

He reached the rough plank walk, and finally the stability of a long stairway running down between houses. The bottom of the steps ended on Lower Front Street, sandwiched between a miner's bar and a cigar store with rooms to let above it. As Begay moved onto the busy street, a cigar girl leaning against the wall gave him a slow once-over before moving her gaze elsewhere.

She possessed a hard-edged beauty he associated with the working girls. More and more he encountered them in his dreams. Sometimes the dreams didn't let go of his mind for days.

He stared at her for a long moment as she peered down the street in the other direction. Her eyes moved back across his, and stopped. She smiled.

"Got a few minutes, big boy?" she said in a throaty voice, just loud enough for him to hear.

His face grew hot and he dropped his eyes to the walk, stepped past the appealing perfumed scent of her, mumbled, "Sorry," and walked quickly down the street.

Someday he would not have the strength to walk past. He needed very much to be married soon. How could Willie Ayamo and the others stand their womanless existence?

There must be a steamer in port, he thought, *the streets are teeming with strangers.* Men and women, for the most part older than him, and dressed in clothing far too heavy for the day, pressed into shop doors, staring, chattering and taking snaps of all the wrong things. Compared to them, Begay felt he belonged here.

He savored the weighty, substantial feeling. A few passing miners nodded to him but most looked through him, as did all the tourists. They were here to see remarkable sights, and a short Filipino in soiled work clothes didn't quite fill the bill.

He dodged into a grocery and bought some apples, feeling guilty about not buying them at George Brothers, but they were two blocks down the street in the opposite direction, and he had a house to build. He made himself hurry on to Juneau Hardware.

Pushing hastily through the door, he ran full into Detective Lepke. The apples flew out of their sack and spilled across the floor.

"Look out, there!" Lepke shouted, jumping back. "Mr. Santo? Excuse me, I didn't see you coming."

"The fault is all mine," Begay said, his face hot for the second time in ten minutes. "I am hurrying more than I need to be. Excuse me, please."

Lepke knelt at the same time Begay did and they both swiftly picked up apples. Men passed by, ignoring them. In moments the apples again filled the sack and the two rose together as if on cue.

"So, are you still working for George Brothers?"

"Yes. They have kindly given me a week off so I can work on my house."

"George said you were cutting a streak on that."

"Mr. Mak-we spoke to you of my house?"

"Sure. He said you were working hard to make enough money to build."

"Did, did he think that was a bad thing?"

"No!" Lepke grinned. "Truth of it told, I think he is impressed with your industry."

Begay felt light headed. This was almost too good to be true. Up to this very moment, George Mak-we had seemed a remote, humorless statue firmly dispensing white law in the Auk village. Long ago Begay abandoned his initial attempt to make a friend of the man. It was enough that he would eventually be a relative.

Now everything changed. His face barely contained his smile. "What wonderful news that is, Mr. Lepke! Thank you for telling me."

"Begay, I haven't given you anything. You've earned everything you have and I'm proud to know you." The detective took his hand and firmly shook it.

Emotion raged in his chest. He was closer to tears than when Ruth agreed to marry him. He felt vindicated in his choices, and very happy.

"Thank you, Mr. Lepke. I am proud to know you, too."

"Well, I must see to my keys." Lepke grinned once more and moved off to the counter where he began inspecting a small display of keys.

Begay found kegs of nails at the back of the long store and selected one. By the time he got to the counter his arms were already tired. The trip up the hill hung before him like a penance.

Still his steps would be light. He only had to think of Lepke's words, of being accepted. Distractedly, he watched the man in army uniform stride into the store.

At first he mistook him for the recruiting sergeant from the courthouse. Then he noticed the small gold oak leaves on the stiff uniform collar. Finally he noticed the revolver in the man's hand.

The major stared with bottomless eyes across the room. Begay followed the man's gaze to Lepke, who, still examining keys, faced away from the stranger. Begay snapped his eyes back to the man and felt his heart jerk in fear as the other raised the gun and pointed it at the detective's back.

Suddenly all of his senses came alive, inundating him— the smell of newly forged nails, the sack of apples, seasoned hickory axe and pick handles, the silage aroma of new rope— the easy drone of conversation, boot heels on the hardwood floor, the awful click as the soldier cocked the pistol— the lingering taste of sawdust from his own new house on his lips, the brassy bitterness of helplessness as the muzzle wavered toward Lepke's back, the acidic bile rising in his throat— the glitter in the man's eyes, the knuckle on the trigger finger whitening more and more—

"You are the enemy!" the major screamed hoarsely.

"No!" Begay shrieked, he dropped the apple sack and with astonishing strength hurled the nail keg.

The major pulled the trigger an instant before the keg hit him in the side of the head and snapped his neck. Very few of the many customers and clerks in the crowded hardware were aware of anything out of the ordinary until the gunshot blotted out sound and thought.

The impact of the bullet knocked Lepke against the counter, scattering keys and a display of dollar watches before his legs went loose and he fell to the floor, unmoving, blood pooling beneath him.

The major's body went sideways with the weight of the keg, and his head received the full shock of forty pounds of tightly packed nails. The skull shattered with a sound reminiscent of a breaking melon. Brains and blood spilled across the dusty floor, splattering the pant legs and boots of half a dozen men.

"What the hell!"

"My God. That man is shot dead!"

"Get the police! Get the police!"

"Get a doctor!" Begay screamed at them. "Detective Lepke has been shot!" He knelt and cradled Lepke's head. Someone behind him vomited.

The yelling and screaming faded around him as he held Lepke in the center of a white, hushed space. If he didn't hold Lepke, the man would die. Begay knew it. He stared down at the ashen face, the closed eyes, the rapidly moving chest. "Don't die," he said. "Please don't die." He continued repeated the words until they became timeless litany.

A hand squeezed his shoulder. "We'll take him now."

Begay snarled up into the face of the police corporal.

"It's okay. We'll get him to the hospital," the corporal said gently. Two men moved in beside the prone detective and lifted him carefully onto a stretcher.

Begay rocked back on his butt, crying. A ring of whispering men stood around him, staring.

"Did you see that? He threw a gawddamn keg of nails twelve feet!"

"Him 'n' th' cop were jist takin' right over there a minute ago."

"That army feller is deader'n hell, all right."

"Who'd think a man's haid hed thet much in it?"

"That detective feller ain't gonna make it, mark m'words."

Begay jerked to his feet. "You lie! He's going to live!"

The corporal returned, motioned the others out of the store, held a hand up in front of Begay. "It's Mr. Santo, isn't it?" he asked.

"Yes. Yes, I am Begay Santo." He had to force the words past the lump in his throat.

"That was a hell of a thing you did. I'm half again your size and I don't think I could throw a forty pound weight six feet, let alone twice that."

"I, I didn't think about it. I just wanted to stop him . . ."

"Sure. I understand. Would you come down to the station with me so we can write down everything that happened?"

"I am being arrested?"

"No. You most certainly are not. We just need to have everything recorded. It's

the law."

"Of course." Begay hesitated. He realized he didn't want to see the major or see what he'd done.

The corporal seemed to read his mind. "Here, let me guide you. You won't need to look down."

"Thank you." Begay followed the man to the door, and then hesitated. "I must look. I must know what I have done."

The policeman nodded.

Begay stared for a full minute before stepping outside to vomit on the boardwalk. The rain felt good.

90 —Juneau City, A.T., August 18, 1916—
Friday afternoon

August Lepke forced his eyes open. The light blinded him so he squeezed them shut again. He felt awful. Besides his throbbing head and parched mouth, his back and chest ached with every breath.

What happened to me? The last thing he remembered was talking to Begay Santo.

"I saw his eyes move, doctor." Florence's voice held restrained excitement.

"Water," August croaked.

Someone lifted his head and put glass to his lips. Water trickled into his mouth; nothing had ever tasted sweeter. He wanted more and tried to raise his hand to tip the glass farther.

His arm felt leaden, immovable, and his hand barely touched the sheet over him.

"No, August," Florence said breathlessly. "Don't try to move or you'll hurt yourself."

He drank more water and when the glass left his lips, felt exhausted. This time he forced his eyes to stay open. He smelled antiseptic alcohol and starched linen. *Is this a hospital?*

Florence stood on one side of the bed, eyes large with worry, face haggard with exhaustion. On the other side of the bed a nurse he didn't know flanked Dr. Parker who appeared more rested than Florence. Light poured through the window.

"Why am I in hospital? What happened to me?"

"Arnold Anderson shot you in the back with a .45 caliber revolver," Dr. Parker sounded as if he were giving a deposition.

"A forty-five!" August quailed at the thought. "How is it I'm not dead?"

"You came close enough!" Florence snapped.

"Steel-jacketed slug," the doctor said, "went right through you. If he had used a soft-nosed bullet we'd be burying you today."

"What damage?" August asked, trying unsuccessfully to assess ahead of the doctor's answer.

"Punctured a lung, nicked a rib going in —cracked it in the process —and exited your chest just below the rib cage. You are an incredibly lucky man, lieutenant. If his aim had altered in the slightest you would have suffered massive damage, steel-jacket or not."

"When, how long have I been here?"

"Two of the longest days of my life," Florence said.

"She's been by your side the entire time," the nurse said.

"Was Anderson apprehended?"

Dr. Parker snorted. "Always the policeman, huh? Anderson was killed when he shot you."

Florence leaned over and said in a low voice, "Begay Santo killed him and then held you until medical help arrived. He's a bit of a hero right now."

Exhaustion stole over August and he fought the need to sleep. "How long must I be in here?"

"That depends on you, detective," Dr. Parker said in an authoritative tone. "Your wounds are cauterized and sterile, but infection is always a possibility. If you rest quietly and do what we tell you, you might be out of here in six weeks."

"Six weeks..." August tried to say more but had to rest his eyes for a moment. When he opened them again, shadows filled the room, light reflected off the partly opened door. "Where did everyone go?" he said to himself.

A darker shadow in the corner moved and Florence came to his side. "August, how do you feel?"

"Weak. If I had more strength, I think I'd be angry."

Her smile flashed in the dim light. "I like the sound of that, Lieutenant."

"Could I have more water?" His throat felt raw from the few words he had uttered.

Florence carefully lifted his head and let him drink. This time he didn't try to move his hands. After hours of drinking he finally moved his face to the side and she took the glass away.

"Doctor Palmer said you would be thirsty." Her words seemed to float in the darkened air. August wondered if he were losing his mind.

"I can almost see the shape of your words," he said dreamily. "They're like clouds. How can that be?"

"You're heavily sedated on morphine. You've probably been having some pretty wild dreams."

He tried to remember if he had dreamt or not. Thoughts eluded him. *Like trying to catch bats,* he decided.

Something settled in the front of his mind and he let it out his mouth before it could fly away. "I didn't know Anderson was there. I wouldn't have turned my back on him."

"Two witnesses saw him outside the hardware store," Florence said. "He waited for you to turn your back before he entered. The man was a coward."

"I've never been shot before. I thought a horse kicked me."

"It was a Colt revolver." He heard her chuckle and the sounds became geometric forms in the air over his bed. The forms danced above him and they fascinated him for the longest time.

91 —Juneau City, A.T., August 26, 1916—
Saturday morning

George Mak-we knew the detective was about to wake up. Although still asleep, Lepke's breathing changed rhythm and the muscles in his face twitched. George turned and looked at Begay Santo. "He's waking up."

"How do you know?" Begay didn't take his gaze off the detective's face.

George smiled. "Professional secret."

August Lepke opened his eyes and peered at the two men.

"You look like you got a hangover," George said. "How do you feel?"

"Better," Lepke said with a wan smile, "than I did a week ago. It's good to see you, George." He shifted his eyes to Begay.

"Thank you for what you did, Begay. If you hadn't stopped him he probably would have fired again . . ." Lepke's eyes closed and George thought he had nodded off again.

Begay opened his mouth to answer, then hesitated.

Lepke opened his eyes wide, which emphasized the rich brown of them. "I didn't realize you were so strong. Throw a keg of nails like that."

"I'm not that strong," Begay said. "The doctor told me I was in an agitated state. He said people have performed miraculous feats when excited. An old woman once lifted a freight wagon off her son when the wheel slipped off and the thing fell on him." Begay shut his mouth with a snap and blushed.

George touched his arm. "You sound somewhat agitated now."

"I am glad I was there to help, Detective Lepke. I am honored to have you as a friend and would do anything I could for you." Begay sat on the edge of his chair.

"If in this room anyone feels honored, it is I," Lepke said with a heavy accent. His eyes closed.

"We're tiring you out," George said. "We'll come back another time." He pushed himself up out of the chair.

"Wait!" Lepke's eyes were wide open again. "Yes, I'm tired, but first I must hear what is happening out there."

"I've enlisted a few people, like you asked. We have Williams under constant surveillance. We've all noticed something you're not gonna like."

"I don't like anything about that man," Lepke said sleepily.

"He's getting real chummy with Jack Malone."

"What? How chummy?"

"They sit and drink together at Armstrong's. They go in the office and stay for hours. They keep their voices low most of the time. How does it sound to you?"

"Mein Gott!" Lepke said. "This can't happen. Would you get word to Jack I'd like to see him?"

"Of course, I'm not telling you how to handle a work, but if they are confederates, I—"

"Thank you for the advice. I promise to be careful. Thank you both for coming, it does me gut, now I must sleep." He closed his eyes and began to lightly snore.

George and Begay left quietly. In the hall Begay glanced up at George. "Is there some way I can help you on your work?"

George's estimation of the small man grew another notch. "I don't know yet. But there might be something you could do. I appreciate you asking."

"Anything," Begay said. "Just let me know."

92 —Juneau City, A.T., August 30, 1916—
Wednesday evening

When he heard the news about Lepke, right here in Armstrong's, Williams became ecstatic for all of five minutes. Now maybe there wouldn't be any more snooping into his business! The detective's nose had seemed to find every move he made.

How ironic were the circumstances of Lepke's shooting. After all the gold he had spent to achieve the same results, well, nearly the same results, an addled toy soldier does it for nothing. Word on the street had it that the German detective was still in a bad way. People also said Florence Malone's constant attention kept the man alive.

Williams knocked back another whiskey and let his mind wander to Driscoll. Both he and his unsavory assistant had vanished weeks ago much to Williams's chagrin. Now he didn't know what Jack Malone was up to when he wasn't actually with him.

The subject of his thoughts walked into the bar. Jack stopped and spoke to the bartender before moving through the smoke-filled room to where Williams sat in the rear.

"You're getting to be one of me best customers, Mr. Williams," Jack said as he sat down. In a softer voice he added, "Are you sure it's a good idea to be drinkin' this much?"

Williams stared at him. "That's a hell of a thing for an Irishman to be asking me!"

"Ah, but that's exactly it, you see. The Irish are weaned on whiskey, while the G—, while other races are not. I've only your best interests at heart."

"Have a drink, Jack." Williams pushed the bottle toward him.

Malone pulled a shot glass from his pocket and grinned. "I thought you'd never ask."

They drank in silence for a few minutes. Williams wondered what the other had to report. His ability at reading Jack Malone's moods and expressions had improved. There would be news from him this meeting. He would bet on it.

"We've got six cases of dynamite," Jack said in a whisper.

"What grade?"

"Seventy per cent. That's what you said to get, ain't it?"

"Yes. Very good." Williams felt electricity run through his veins. Something actually went according to plan. Hope brightened the horizon!

"Got some bad news, too."

"What?"

"The governor's startin' up a militia."

"A militia?" Williams said loudly. "What for?"

A few men looked over at them.

"Well," Jack said, consternation evident in his face, "I'm not sure exactly why."

"Who's in charge of it?" Williams asked, keeping his tone loud.

"Major Anderson was to have been in charge, but . . ."

"Don't they have a replacement?"

"I don't think so. Governor Strong's askin' the army to send someone from Chilkoot Barracks to take over."

"Do you know this man, the governor?"

"Why?" Jack's eyes glinted.

"I know something about military matters. I can certainly drill a gaggle of civilians and train them to perform a manual of arms."

"Christ, but you've got a lot of brass!"

"At least I won't shoot anybody in the back."

"You're sure of that, are you?"

"Of course. I'm like you, Mr. Malone. I hit them when they're looking."

"You'll never guess what I heard this morning." Foreboding darkened his words.

This is what he came to tell me, Williams realized. Ice formed in his belly as he gently rubbed his fingertips over the rough table, cognizant of the dip and whorl of wood grain.

"What did you hear, Jack?"

Jack smiled and rubbed his nose, took another drink of whiskey. Williams could feel his liquor now, heavy in his frame, solid in his mind. Chains of addiction.

"Remember that Sassenach son-of-a-bitch I laid out in here the day you and I first talked?"

"That ugly little skinny bloke?"

"The very same."

"Yeah, I kinda remember him. What about him?"

"He's in the slammer for fair."

"Oh? What for?"

Jack stared into Williams's eyes. "Somehow he got the wherewithal to bring a blackguard friend of his up from Seattle or Portland."

When he was angry, Jack's heavy brogue evaporated like mist on a hot day, Williams noted. The man did seem to be angry.

"So how did he end up in jail?"

"The Soda Water Kid is one of the best pickpockets on the Pacific coast. Even when he's drunk he can do it without the mark catching on. Last month he lifted two wallets when he was drunk, and then went down to the row to get his ashes hauled. As soon as the girl sees the wallets, she turned him in to the cops."

"Sounds stupid to me. How did Driscoll end up in jail?" As soon as the words were out of his mouth, Williams cringed and felt his face flush. He would have given his left hand not to have uttered that name, but now it lay beyond retrieval.

"Well," said Jack, his eyes glinting, "it seems your friend was waiting outside for the Kid to finish his manly chore and the police nabbed him as they advanced on the scene of the crime, as it were."

"What do you mean, 'my friend'?" Williams asked thickly.

"I'll get to that. Anyway, he was discovered to be the owner of a well-used sap by none other than Detective Lepke—"

"That son-of-a-bitch!" Williams blurted.

"... who relieved him of same. In the process, your friend, Driscoll, tried to subdue the detective with fisticuffs. We all know how good he is at that!" Jack grinned at him fiercely, eyes flashing.

"What's your point, Jack?"

"Being who he is, and what he is, Driscoll has been running off at the mouth in the slammer," Jack said, still grinning, "... and he said he was in the employ of a certain Mr. Williams, Limey journalist."

Williams couldn't breathe. How did Driscoll discover his name? Why would the *Schwein* tell everyone in prison about the arrangement?

"Which brings me to a couple of questions, Mr. Limey journalist Williams..."

"Surely you don't believe this man's ravings?"

"I've know Ahab Driscoll since he was a lad of sixteen. When he bludgeoned his first seaman on the Seattle docks, I was the one he passed the swag to. I know more about that worthless bastard than his mother, father, and the police, all put together. He'd give Jesus to the Romans for *five* pieces of silver!"

Williams concentrated on filling his glass with whiskey. If he didn't spill any, he'd be okay. Never before in his life had fear taken a grip on him like this.

The detached, calm ability to deal with it proved totally elusive. He suspected the whiskey had a lot to do with that. He sipped the pungent fluid and looked Jack in the eye.

"So you believe him, is that what you're saying, Jack?"

"Why?" Jack whispered. "Why is this man in your employ?"

"I'm by myself. I don't have friends or confederates who would do or die for me, as you do. The only ally I possess is a bag of gold sovereigns, so I use it."

"Why Driscoll?"

"I thought he would watch you and you'd never know about it."

"Watch me? I thought we were in this thing together!"

"If we'd arrived on the same boat, I wouldn't need that sort of insurance. But you've been here for years. You have a bloody army you could raise if you wanted. I'm alone."

Jack grinned again. This time he actually looked amused.

"You've got angles on yer angles, don'cha?" He poured another whiskey.

"At least that damned detective is out of our way," Williams said, relief spreading through him.

"I've been meanin' ta speak to you about him."

"About the fact our number one problem is going to marry your daughter?"

Jack nodded. "That, and a few other things."

"So, speak."

"We can't kill him."

"I can't promise you that, old boy. That man has been a thorn in my side for some time now. He already destroyed one organization I was hoping to rely on."

"Krause's organization?" Jack asked in a disbelieving tone.

Williams felt the tension bloom between them. Now what? "It doesn't really matter, does it? The bloke is behind bars and that's that."

"That son of a bitch killed a good friend of mine just because he wanted his boat! How can your cause use scum like that?"

"I had nothing to do with him, Jack. He was being paid by the German military attaché to help us any way he could. As far as I know we never received a return on all the gold we spent on him."

"Just as long as you don't try to break the bastard out of jail."

Williams felt his scalp prickle. Why hadn't he given that possibility more thought when Sommers suggested it? He had spent time and money searching for desperate men and here sat a perfect specimen right under his nose!

"The look on your face gives me pause, Mr. Journalist. I'm not at all certain I like that."

"Don't worry, Mr. Irishman," he said staring at Jack. "We completely understand one other."

93 —Juneau, A.T., September 4, 1916—
Monday afternoon

George Mak-we and Jim Kisadis leaned against the wall of a cigar store, waiting for Williams to leave Armstrong's. Both men loitered clear of the foot traffic wearing shabby clothes soiled enough to discourage closer inspection.

"How many people you got watching this man?" Jim asked quietly.

"Three, besides you. Perry Goodhorse, Jee-nak, and Begay Santo."

"Good men."

"I only pick people I can trust." George peered from beneath the wide brim of his hat at the passing crowd. "There are strange doings going on and Lieutenant Lepke is the only one who understands it. We gotta be his eyes while he's in the hospital."

"Why does he want to see me?" Jim tried to be nonchalant but George noticed a slight strain in his nephew's voice.

"He just wants to talk to you. He's already talked to the other three."

"Would you go with me?"

"Wouldn't miss it for all the tea in China." George flashed a smile.

"There he is, Uncle." Jim nodded toward the street and then looked away indifferently.

George smiled on the inside. Jim had a talent for this. He watched Arnold Williams glance up at the increasing clouds, light a thin cigar, and then amble off down the street.

The good thing about this, George thought, *is that it's almost impossible to lose track of somebody.* The town is just too small. Williams increased speed and nimbly pushed through the crowd.

"Where's he's going?" Jim voiced George's thoughts.

"I don't know. I'll stay on this side of the street, you cross over and stay on his heels."

"I won't let him see me," Jim said, reading George's mind again.

"Good. Now hurry." George moved purposefully down the street, keeping close watch on the journalist's stained Panama hat as it bobbed through the crowd on the opposite side of the plank street.

Williams passed the Division Hotel and crossed over to George's side of the street. Jim stopped at curbside and glanced at George who motioned for his nephew to stay. Now they were in the "decent" part of town where Williams tipped his hat to women and nodded to men.

George straightened out of his slouch and buttoned his jacket as he followed the journalist up Franklin Street. Williams turned and vanished through a doorway. George strode past the door without slowing but carefully read the words painted on the glass.

He circled the block and found Jim where he last saw him.

"You might as well go home," George said. "I'll wait for him to come out."

"Where'd he go, Uncle?"

"He's in the Territorial Militia recruiting office, talking to an officer." George scratched his jaw. "I don't know what he's up to."

94 —Juneau, A.T., September 8th, 1916—
Friday evening

Jack Malone mopped his steaming face with a handkerchief and grinned at the crowd. "Now, you boys know what short shrift we get from the likes of Wickersham and his fat-cat Republican friends!" he shouted. The Odd Fellows Hall bulged with the crowd.

Nothing like free beer and roast beef sandwiches to pack 'em in, he thought.

"But Wickersham says he ain't no Republican!" someone shouted from the thick press of humanity.

"Of course not!" Jack roared. "Why should he pick a side when he can have it both ways? But if you look closely at his record, see who contributes to his campaigns, you'll find yerselves with a handsome list of prominent Republicans from here in the Territory as well as Seattle and Portland.

"Mr. Mayor Emory Valentine is runnin' Wick's campaign here in Juneau. Ya know how good a Republican the mayor is! Wick's always on about the mining companies from the States operating up here. Says they should be owned by Alaskans.

"But you'll notice the mine he hates the most is the Treadwell, because they treat their workers well and pay 'em an honest wage fer an honest day's work. His Republican friends who have minin' interests here in the Territory pay a full dollar less a day and whine that high wages are breaking their backs!"

His words struck home and the hall shook with shouts and stamping feet. Jack let them continue until their anger abated.

We got an answer for those money-grubbin', fat-cat Republicans and their pet delegate. Mr. Delegate Wickersham can go back to being Judge Wickersham after the election, because we're gonna toss him out on his fancy-pants arse! Alaska for Alaskans!"

The hall filled with a roar of approval and cheers. A chant began in the back of the hall and more and more men took it up. "Sul-zer! Sul-zer! Sul-zer!"

Jack grinned widely. Sean Clancy had the gift of timing that was for sure. Jack waved his arms over his head. The chanting died down.

"All right, boys! It's my privilege to present a man who worked his way from the ground up. A man who treats the working man with the respect he deserves, and the man who is going to Washington City next March as the Delegate from Alaska —Territorial Senator Charles Sulzer!"

Jack stepped to the side as Sulzer jumped to his feet from his chair beside Jack. His pate glistened with perspiration and his once-starched collar hung slack. His tie and suit coat hung over the back of his vacant chair. Sulzer held his hands out as if about to embrace a large woman or lie about a fish.

The crowd in the stifling hall went wild. Jack stepped down off the podium and slipped behind the large U.S. flag hanging from the rafters, pulled out a flask and drained the last half. Someone touched his elbow and he jerked around to face Arnold Williams.

"You're in pretty thick with that fellow," Williams said.

Jack replaced his flask. "And what business is that of yours?"

"How many causes are you into? Or," he said hurriedly before Jack could reply, "how many causes are you into that work against each other?"

"How does this work against anything you're interested in?" Jack felt the whiskey hit his head and wished he had the convenience of enjoying it.

"How does electing this plutocrat to a non-voting position five thousand miles from here aid us in striking a blow against the English?"

Sulzer shouted something and the crowd cheered. The hall reeked of unwashed bodies, tobacco smoke, stale beer, and damp wool. Jack suddenly felt tired of Arnold Williams, or whatever his name was, and his cloak and dagger nonsense.

"The man has allies in Washington City, y'see," Jack said slowly, as if explaining something to a child or a halfwit, "and those allies either can voteor can influence votes that pertain to the direction this country goes.

"There's as many immigrants from the Entente countries as there are from the Allied countries in the United States. We can still go either way."

"Rot!" Williams said with a sneer. "The U.S. will never join the 'murderers of the *Lusitania*,' even though the ship flew a British flag and carried a cargo of munitions for the British army. You bloody Americans have already picked your side and are just waiting for the most politic moment to jump in and save the Allied cause!"

Jack blinked. The son-of-a-bitch was right. Until this very moment he had believed the coin still spun in the air —but it had come up tails some time ago. *I must be getting old,* he thought.

"So you don't think there's any benefit to getting Charlie elected to Congress?"t

"Not for Ireland, or Germany, or me." Williams narrowed his eyes.

Jack scowled back at him. "Life will go on after we strike our blow, Mr. Williams, and I don't have an unlimited supply of sovereigns to pay for my keep."

"I've secured a commission in the militia," Williams said, "which will work to our mutual benefit."

In quick succession the multiple ramifications of the action bloomed in Jack's mind. He admired the brass of the man on one hand and felt a chill of fear on the other. Someone tapped him on the shoulder.

Whitney, Sulzer's secretary, said, "He just gave me the high sign, Mr. Malone. The senator is about to finish."

"Just a moment, Whitney." Jack turned back to Williams, but the man had vanished in the crowd.

95 —Juneau, A.T., September 13th, 1916—
Wednesday morning

Fiona Malone felt happy with her promotion to daytime desk clerk for the Division Hotel. The modest raise in wages boosted her mood even further. Her life had struck a balance she enjoyed, even though there didn't seem to be a promising beau in the picture.

"Can't have everything," she said to herself.

Two whiskey drummers occupied the plush divan in the center of the lobby. One snored lightly and the other read the morning's *Alaska Daily Empire*. Both men had solicited her company for "an evening on the town." She had become adept at turning down advances even though most of them gave her more enjoyment than she would admit.

Amanda's last two choices in men gave one pause. On the face of it, Mr. Williams seemed quite the adventurer, and Mr. Barrington Wentworth quite the charming prince. *Did all men lie?* she wondered.

August Lepke came to mind and she smiled. No, she decided, not all of them. She envied Florence, but felt happy for her at the same time.

Fiona worried about Amanda. The woman spent most of her time alone in her room. Nothing other than the life growing inside her seemed to interest her any more.

A man came through the door carrying two large suitcases. Fiona thought they must be practically empty from the nonchalant way he hefted them. His knee-length coat dripped rain.

Over-weight, she thought, looking at the girth of his chest. *Sad, he owned a rather handsome face.* He dropped the suitcases in front of the desk and showed perfect, white teeth.

"Good morning," he glanced at her left hand, "Miss. Have you room at the inn?" He pulled off his hat and dropped it onto one of the suitcases then began unbuttoning his coat.

Fiona chuckled. "You don't have a wife out there on a donkey do you, sir?"

"No wife," he said, letting his coat swing open to reveal the reversed collar, "no donkey."

"Oh!" Fiona felt her composure flee. "I'm sorry, Father. I didn't realize—"

"Reverend James Thistle, Miss . . . ?"

"Ah, Malone, Fiona Malone," she said quickly. "Are you sure you're in the right hotel, Reverend Thistle?"

"Are you saying this is the wrong hotel, Miss Malone?" He pulled off his overcoat.

"Not at all." She felt warmth rising in her cheeks. What she assumed to be fat translated into the wide-shouldered, deep-chested physique of an athlete. "We don't get a lot of business from the clergy here."

"So I am told." His smile dazzled her again. "Judging from your name and your first assumption as to my faith, I'd say you were a Roman Catholic?"

"Yes. And my employer is a Unitarian. And you, Reverend?"

"Episcopalian, Church of England. Either will do."

"Oh. My friend, Amanda, is a member of your faith."

"I'd like to meet her some time. Now then, about the room?"

Fiona rattled off rates and felt more surprise when he paid for a month's lodgings in advance.

"May I ask why you chose the Division Hotel, Reverend Thistle? Not that we don't look forward to having you as a guest," she said quickly.

"I'm told it's aptly named. Living here until I locate other accommodations makes my work easier. When I walk out the front door I can turn left to find the righteous and the saved, or I can turn right and be exactly where I am needed."

"You're not here to take over a parish?"

"No." His smile all but disappeared and he picked up his key. "You might say I'm on a pilgrimage, Miss Malone, to find my faith."

Fiona watched him disappear up the stairs. *This is such an interesting place*, she thought.

96 —Juneau City, A.T., September 19th, 1916—
Tuesday afternoon

August Lepke carefully slipped his arms into the overcoat held by Doctor Parker. His wound no longer constantly ached, and things seemed normal unless he moved suddenly or tried to do too much by himself. Putting on an overcoat without aid fit in the latter category.

It felt as if a metal band circled his torso and therefore circumscribed his life. More than once over the past four weeks August came to the conclusion that if Begay hadn't done it already, with his bare hands he would have killed the bogus Major Anderson for his cowardly act.

The irony of the event had not escaped him. After four years in the army, three and a half of them in a combat situation, he received his first gunshot wound from an American brevet major!

"Now, we're agreed on this, aren't we?" Dr. Parker asked.

"Yes, doctor." Lepke gingerly lowered his arms as the coat settled on his shoulders. "Miss Malone will return me to the hospital after the ceremony."

"Immediately after the ceremony," Parker prompted.

Florence laughed. "We both promise, doctor. You would have made a wonderful Mother Superior!"

Lepke tried to laugh with them, but pain stopped him.

"Oh, I'm sorry, August. I didn't mean to hurt you."

He smiled through the pain. "You didn't, I did. It's nothing."

He eased down into a wicker wheel chair and Florence pushed him to the Otis elevator.

"Have fun," Dr. Parker called after them.

As soon as the elevator door shut, August looked up at Florence. "Kiss me, please. Right now!"

She bent and complied, stopping only when the elevator did. A motor taxi waited at the street. Henry Jenkins stepped out of his green Maxwell and smiled at them.

"Mr. Lepke, so good to see you up and about. Looks like you didn't have a good driver the last time somebody shot at you."

Lepke grinned. "I'll make sure you're with me next time."

"Do that," Jenkins said. "Here, let me give you a hand getting into the motor buggy. That's it."

August wilted back as Jenkins helped Florence into the rear seat. Jenkins took his place behind the wheel, released the hand brake and edged the throttle forward. They rattled less than a block before Jenkins pulled up in front of the Cathedral of the Nativity of the Blessed Virgin Mary.

George Mak-we and Jim Kisadis helped August out of the taxi.

"I think it would have been easier to walk," he muttered to Florence when she stepped down beside him.

"Shush," she whispered. "Henry wanted to do something nice for you."

"Thank you, Mr. Jenkins," August said.

"Any time, Lieutenant!" He putted away.

"Me and Jim are going to get on each side of you," George said, "and support you up the steps and to the pew. Okay?"

"Thanks, fellows. I don't think I could do it without you."

Jim laughed. "I don't think you could either."

Bows and flowers decorated the circular room. The bride's half of the church teemed with witnesses and well-wishers. The groom's half held a handful of people, only two of which were Filipinos.

"Friends of the bride or the groom?" a young Filipino asked.

"Both," August said. "But we'll stand on the groom's side."

"We won't take that personally," George said, smiling.

August grinned tightly. His body ached and he felt exhausted, but he wouldn't miss the wedding of Begay and Ruth for anything. Since he had agreed to marry Florence in this church, he tried to pay attention to events.

The Catholic Church contained rows of pews. All worshippers stood, knelt, and sat at signals from small bells. In Lepke's case the priest had agreed to allow the wounded officer to sit throughout the entire ceremony.

The pain-killing morphine won out and he drifted. Triumphant organ music pulled him out of his reverie and he opened his eyes to see Begay firmly kiss Ruth while the priest beamed down at them.

Ruth looked stunning in her gown, glowing with happiness. Sentimentality washed through August and he found himself on the verge of tears.

"Mein Gott!" he muttered. Florence, weeping openly, glanced over at him, instantly understood.

"It's okay, darling," she whispered. "It's the medicine. Wait here. I'm going to go throw rice."

Half of the cathedral emptied as Begay and Ruth spoke with the priest. They turned and walked hand-in-hand down the aisle. Begay stopped next to August.

"Mr. Lepke, we are so happy you could be here today," Begay said.

"How are you feeling?" Ruth asked.

"Fine," August lied with a smile. "My very best wishes for your happiness. You are both very lucky people."

Ruth bent over and kissed his cheek. "Thank you for being our friend," she whispered.

August shook Begay's hand before the couple moved toward the door where happy chatter waited. August listened to the cheers and applause, smiling to himself. He realized someone stood next to him.

"I'm Father Mulcahey," the priest said. "I think we need to chat in the near future, Mr. Lepke."

August noted the man's lack of a smile. "About what?"

"The immortal souls of your children and perhaps the condition of your own."

"Not today," August said. "I'm much to weak to fight with you."

Mulcahey smiled. "Perhaps I should strike while the iron is hot."

"The iron isn't hot, Father," Florence said, coming up to them. "It's very tired. We'll be by to see you after the new year."

"You look more and more like your mother every year, my child. God rest her soul." Mulcahey crossed himself. "So nice to see you both." He nodded and moved away toward the vestry.

"Thank you for the rescue," August whispered.

"I thought he might have a crack at you," Florence murmured as she helped him to his feet. "The word is out you're a heathen."

"Surprised he didn't kick me," August said and hurt him self with a laugh.

George and Jim appeared at each elbow and helped him down the steps to a waiting wheelchair. August could hardly wait to get back to the hospital.

THE DAILY ALASKA DISPATCH
Juneau, Alaska, Saturday, September 23, 1916

AN OVERFLOW CROWD HEARS WICKERSHAM
Reference to Republican House and Senate Brings Cheers

SULZER VISITS TANANA CREEKS WITH SELLERS

VILLA STILL PUZZLER FOR OUR OFFICERS

GUN FIGHT WITH I.W.W. MEN

KRAUSE CASE IS UNDER WAY BEFORE JURY
Government Reviews What It Is Prepared to Prove in Opening

DEFENSE PROBABLY NOT HAVE WITNESS
Court Room Well Crowded;
Indicates That Interest in the Case Is Not Waning Any.

The sensational case of the mysterious disappearance of James O. Plunkett from Juneau last October, and for whose disappearance, and alleged death Edward Krause has been indicted by a federal grand jury, got well under way yesterday in the district court.

The courtroom was well filled with interested spectators among whom were noted several women. The petit jurors who are to try the case were called. All witnesses who are to appear in the case were excluded from being present in the courtroom during the taking of testimony.

Kazis Krauczunas represents the defendant, and the government case is being handled by District Attorney Smiser and his assistant, John Reagan.

The opening statement on behalf of the government was made by Assistant Attorney Reagan who (continued on page 6)

97 —Juneau City, A.T., September 25th, 1916—
Monday afternoon

Following the color guard, the Treadwell Band stepped out smartly playing "Stars and Stripes Forever." Arnold Williams, natty in his new uniform, echoed the captain's command, "Fore-ward, harch!" The sixteen members of the Juneau Detachment of the Alaska Territorial Militia lurched off, quickly found their step, and marched importantly behind their sergeant.

Williams smirked at the irony of training men for an enemy army. Not that any of these dolts would ever see the front, let alone hear a shot fired in anger.

They are toy soldiers. Every one of them.

His contempt fit a sergeant's temperament perfectly.

They marched down Front Street to the wye and, rather than continue down Lower Front, made a sharp column left and marched up Franklin Street past their headquarters. The recruiting parade attracted a decent crowd for a Monday afternoon.

Williams neatly stepped out of ranks and marked time as his men swung past. A glance to their rear found ten young men, between sixteen and twenty from the look of them, following eagerly.

Some things transcend borders, Williams thought. The lure of the uniform netted young men in every country. *Well, that's what this is all about —more cannon fodder.*

Captain Crowley, a regular army officer from Chilkoot Barracks at Haines, pounded along, his paunch straining his uniform jacket to the breaking point. Convincing the old warhorse to bring him into the militia as a sergeant took less effort than Williams had anticipated.

"Show me the manual of arms," Crowley ordered after Williams lied about graduating from an English military boarding school. After his demonstration Williams passed a short quiz on close order drill commands and was awarded the triple chevrons now on his arms.

Williams knew sergeants bore the brunt of running armies. The stripes gave him access to weapons and explosives, as well as keys to federal locks. For the first time since his arrival in Alaska Territory, he felt confident of successfully completing his mission.

If an alarm should be raised about security, the militia would guard the mines. No one on Gastineau Channel worried about guarding the guards.

98 —Juneau City, A.T., September 29, 1916—
Friday afternoon

Amanda Ganbor shrugged into her loosest dress and peered at herself in the full-length mirror.

"Doesn't matter," she murmured, "it's still bloody obvious I'm with child."

For once she felt grateful for the rainy day— she could hide her condition with a raincoat. Fiona had assured her she would be able to wear a coat from now until the baby was born next February. *Not that it made any difference,* she reflected. After some magic day in February, she would have a child that couldn't be hidden under her coat.

Abruptly she fancied a pickle. The fancy quickly evolved into an urgent craving. Amanda slipped into her shoes and pulled on the raincoat. As she opened the door and hurried into the hall she glanced back into the room, an old habit left over from gaslights, and ran full into someone.

Amanda bounced as if she had hit a telephone pole and thumped down on her bottom. Stunned, she sat in the open doorway. Her eyes refused to focus, her mind whirled and she gasped for breath. Strong hands grabbed Amanda's arms firmly, lifted her gently to her feet and steadied her against the wall.

"I am so dreadfully sorry!" a baritone voice exclaimed. "I wasn't watching where I was going. I didn't think another soul shared the hallway with me."

"Two souls, actually," Amanda murmured, focusing on the striking owner of the voice.

"Excuse me?"

"Oh," Amanda collected her thoughts. "I was just saying you are not entirely at fault, sir. I wasn't watching where I was going either." She puzzled at his accent and allowed herself to appreciate his openly handsome features before wondering if she had found yet another salesman.

"Are you hurt? I did knock you down . . ."

His suit coat hung open revealing a massive chest covered by a once-white shirt frayed at the cuffs and open at the neck. "Nothing bruised but my dignity, I assure you, Mr. . . ."

"James Thistle, at your service, Miss . . ."

"Amanda Ganbor," she said, letting her voice cool. "What do you peddle, Mr. Thistle?"

"Salvation," he said with a smile. "It's actually Reverend Thistle. Amanda, you say? Then you're the resident Episcopalian?"

"You are Church of England?" she asked in astonishment. "Whatever are you doing in the Division Hotel? Have you been exiled?"

His smile lost its humor and his face darkened. "In a manner of speaking, but your accent suggests you might also be an exile, Miss Ganbor."

"It's *Baroness*." She put frost into her response. She didn't care if this cheeky man was a minister or not, her life was no business of his. "Pardon me for my clumsiness and thank you again for helping me up."

She whisked around him and hurried down the stairway. Mae and Fiona were huddled deep in whispered conversation behind the front desk.

"Will we be having choir practice in the lobby?" Amanda said sharply.

Maye and Fiona both gave her dumbfounded stares.

"Well, we've got bloody preachers running about the hallways, knocking people about—"

"Amanda!" Fiona said. "Why are you so upset?"

"Because I want a bloody pickle." Despite herself, she began to cry. "And, like a perfect cow, I get knocked down by a perfectly beautiful man in the hall and the only thing I can think of is to wonder if he's got a wife hidden somewhere . . ." She openly sobbed. ". . . and then I realized no decent man is ever going to look at me again anyway—"

Maye grabbed Amanda and held her tightly to her ample bosom. "It's all right, dearie. You're just feeling low. That happens when a woman is with child. Why when I was carrying—"

Even in her distraught state, amazement thrilled through Amanda at Maye's words. She pulled away to stare at her in shock. A glance at Fiona showed her equally dumbfounded.

"You have a child!" Amanda said. "Why have you never spoken of it before?" Her depression slid away like a silk sheet.

"Did you . . . lose it?" Fiona asked.

Maye's arms dropped to her side and a flush suffused her cheeks. She put Amanda in mind of a child who can conjure no defense for a prank. Maye dropped into her office chair and stared at the floor.

"Maye." Amanda felt quick guilt. What a prying clod she could be! "You don't have to tell us anything. It's we who owe you . . ."

"Nothing," Maye said. "You girls have put meaning back into my life. Sometimes I pretend you're my daughters."

Amanda held her silence, caught Fiona's glance and imperceptibly shook her head. They both waited.

"I had a daughter the first year I was in the Territory. My married sister agreed to raise her if I would help with expenses. My daughter grew up thinking I was her Aunt Maye instead of, her . . ." Maye's voice broke and she choked back a small sob, ". . . mother."

"Is she still with your sister?" Amanda asked.

"No. My daughter married a young lawyer in Olympia three years ago. My sister died last year, without ever telling her the truth."

"Did your sister have children of her own?" Fiona asked.

Maye shook her head. "Couldn't, even with all her praying and church-going. She saw Lillian as the wages of my sin and her reward."

"That's beastly!" Amanda snapped. "Do you correspond with Lillian?"

"I force myself not to answer her letters quickly. Always waited at least two weeks. She usually takes a month to answer."

"Why don't you tell her?" Fiona asked. Tears glistened on her face.

"My sister was a pillar of the community. Me, I own a barely respectable hotel and cafe. A peek into my past would make a friar faint, and Lillian's husband is entering politics. No, I would be an obstacle to their future."

Fiona brushed at her cheek. "But—"

"I got used to this a long time ago." Maye stared at each of them in turn. "Too much has happened to turn back the clock now."

"Did her father ever know?" Amanda asked.

"I don't want to talk about this any more. You still want that pickle?"

Amanda considered. "No, but I do want to know more about that minister down the hall from me."

"Give me a couple more days," Maye said with a wicked grin. "The word's not in yet."

99 —Juneau City, A.T., October 2, 1916—
Monday morning

August Lepke, supported by his cane, slowly limped into the Police Station. The four officers present stood and applauded. August grinned, wiping rain off his coat and easing onto a bench. "Thanks, fellers. It's good to be back."

Chief Tinsley hurried out of his office. "Lieutenant Lepke, you're on convalescent leave. What are you doing here?"

"Keeping my sanity. I can sit behind a desk, Chief. Please. I can't read another magazine or even look at a novel. I need my mind involved in something worthwhile and real."

Tinsley and the officers broke into laughter.

"If you could only see your face," Tinsley said. "Okay. You can work half a day. If I think you're over extending yourself, I'll have the boys take you home in the paddy wagon. Agreed?"

"Agreed. Thanks, Chief." He pushed himself to his feet, entered his office, and sat down at his desk.

This was more like it, he thought. A pile of paper filled his "IN" box and he picked up the top sheet, recognizing George Mak-we's careful hand. As his eyes ran down the page he learned of Arnold Williams' recent enlistment.

"What perfect cover," he muttered. Despite himself, he admired the man's gall.

A hearty knock pulled his attention to the door. Jack Malone's grin lit his face. "How's me prospective son-in-law this rainy day?"

"Jack! Please come in and sit down. Horrible day out there."

Jack dropped into the visitor's chair, his grin dimmed down to a tight smile. "It always rains the whole month of October here. Yer Indian policeman said you wanted to see me."

"Are you working with Arnold Williams?"

Jack blinked and the smile disappeared. "Well now, yer the detective. What do you think?"

August held the older man's gaze. "You own a bar. You drink with lots of people. This I understand, but what do you do when the two of you go into your office, lock the door behind you and stay for hours?"

Jack's eyes narrowed and his lower lip developed a pugnacious angle. "So yer spying on me now?"

"Actually we were keeping a murder suspect under observation and you came into the picture. He's not a reporter, you know."

Jack grinned. Secret knowledge danced in his eyes. "Don't you be worrying, August me boy. I have the man's measure."

"So you know he's a murderer." August stared, willing himself not to blink.

Jack blinked. "If you could prove that, he'd already be in the slammer."

"He murdered two Mexican nationals; we have an eyewitness. Unfortunately, Mexico is well out of our jurisdiction."

"Well, there ye have it. Other places, other times."

"Jack, this man is dangerous."

"He's also in the militia." August felt nettled at how much Jack was enjoying himself. "He's just a remittance man trying to find a life for himself."

August thought Jack's tone was off, the man didn't believe his own words. Why would Jack lie to him? For a moment he considered putting a tail on Jack, then common sense regained the upper hand.

Jack Malone was cagey enough to let people see what he wanted them to see. If he was into something illegal or secret, nobody August could muster would ever be able to catch the old fox at it. Jack blinked again.

"So that was the whole of it? You just wanted to tell me Williams ain't a reporter?"

"For the sake of your daughters, I implore you not to get mixed up with this person."

"I'm not wet behind the ears any more, lieutenant. Your concern is appreciated but uncalled for, I assure you."

"Thanks for coming in, Jack."

"How's the wound?"

"Sore, but knitting well. Dr. Parker did a good job of putting me back together and keeping me free of infection."

Jack nodded. "Parker's the best, no doubt of it." He got to his feet. "For the sake of me oldest daughter, take care of yourself, detective."

"You, too, Jack."

August paged through the pile of paper. Footsteps came into the office. He glanced up, wondering if Jack had experienced a change of heart and would tell him what he wanted to know.

George Mak-we stopped in front of the desk. Water ran off his coat and dripped off the hat he held in his hand. The planes in his face seemed hewn from wet stone and the dark eyes radiated great energy.

"George! How good to see—"

"My nephew, Jim Kisadis, has been helping me watch Williams. Begay and Jeenak have been helping, too, but now he's missing."

"Missing," August repeated, confused. "Who's missing, Williams?"

"Not Williams. Jim. You gotta help me find him, detective."

100 —Juneau City, A.T., October 2, 1916—
Monday afternoon

Jim Kisadis could barely see through his swollen eyes. The tall man sat smoking a cheroot, facing him from across the boat cabin. The boat rose and fell on agitated water inside a boathouse.

"You're a very stubborn man," Williams said. "I don't even know your name."

Rain, driven by the moaning wind, lashed the thin-walled boathouse. It seemed to be an ally for this tall, deadly man, but Jim had also been careless.

Cold and wet, he tried to remain unobtrusive while following Williams. The tall man had left the militia office at a fast pace, never looking back. He'd walked straight to the jumble of private docks and wharves edging Lower Front Street.

Jim hurried to keep up, feeling the full brunt of the storm beating against his body. White-capped waves covered Gastineau Channel and the wind lofted sheets of salt spray that stung unprotected skin like swarms of liquid hornets. Boats, moored the full length of the spidery dock system, danced and jerked like tethered sea stallions.

Wind whined and sang through ropes and hawsers, keened from the rigging. Jim's street shoes slid on the soaked planking, forcing him to slow his pursuit. He edged around a small warehouse and found the dock empty of all but the storm.

For the first time he questioned his own actions. What did the man's destination matter? Jim realized the vulnerability of his position.

He retreated back around the corner of the warehouse. A stunning blow smashed into his face. Pinwheels of light and pain exploded behind his eyes.

When his senses returned, he found himself tied to a chair inside a boat cabin. His face radiated such intense pain he felt sure it glowed.

"Who are you and why are you following me?" Williams sounded casual, almost disinterested.

Jim didn't respond. He carefully pulled with his hands to test the bonds. His hands remained immobile.

"You won't get free of those ropes unless I want you to," Williams said. "I'll ask you nicely one more time; who are you and why are you following me?"

Jim discovered his legs were held tight against the chair legs. The chair itself seemed heavy. Oak maybe. No other way to look at it —he was in a fix.

The rope end slashed fire across the side of his face and he screamed with the pain before he caught himself and bit it off. Never before in his life had he experienced pain like this. For a moment he considered telling the man what he wanted to know.

"Who are you?" Williams repeated, heat rising in his voice, "and why are you following me?" He swung the rope again.

Jim, ready this time, rolled his mind under the pain and let it wash over him.

He'd seen sea ducks do that in heavy surf. The pain lost intensity and when the rope hit him the third time it was if he watched from a distance, observing someone else's torment.

Williams screamed something in a language Jim didn't understand and threw the rope on the deck, sat down across the room and lit another cheroot.

Jim reflected on his heritage, the things his uncle taught him when he was a boy. He remembered how bereft he felt when his uncle married and moved away from the village.

For a time he pretended his uncle didn't exist, especially during the long years when he drank. That had changed and for the longest time now Jim felt honored that George Mak-we was his uncle. He would not dishonor the man or his family.

Williams dropped the smoking butt on the wooden deck and ground it out with his boot. "Did I do something to you without knowing it? Is someone paying you to keep tabs on me? Are you working for Jack Malone?"

Jim tried not to frown. Jack Malone? Why would this man's confederate have him followed? Jim wished he could tell his uncle this thing before he died.

He knew Williams had no intention of letting him live. The absolute fact of his own death didn't frighten him, but he needed to die well.

A push downward with his feet told him the chair was not attached to the deck. Although his wrists were pinioned to the chair legs, his elbows could swing out four, maybe six, inches.

His mother's face flashed through his mind and he said good-bye quickly, pushing her back into his memories. No more time existed for sentiment if he wished to die like a Tlingit warrior. Williams pulled a long, thin knife out of his coat pocket.

"I promise you a quick death if you answer just three questions: Who are you? Why are you following me? And who are you working for?" He ran his thumb back and forth along the side of the blade.

"If you don't answer my questions, I will skin you alive. Starting with your face." Williams walked slowly toward Jim.

Jim waited impassively. He saw the tall man's eyes flick back and forth over his face, searching for fear. The eyes pinched together slightly, the only outward sign of the mounting consternation within.

"You don't believe I'll really do it," Williams said through gritted teeth. "Well, let me show you!" He reached for Jim's hair.

Jim pushed down hard with his feet and threw all of his weight backward. The chair rocked back and slammed to the floor. Williams lunged forward to grab Jim, lost his balance and fell on top of the chair.

As Jim's feet swung up with the front of the chair, he snapped his left foot to the side, hitting Williams in the testicles. The chair crashed onto the floor and Jim's head bounced off the deck, intensifying his pain and fogging his mind at the same time.

Dimly he heard Williams scream in pain and roll away from him. The knife lay on the floor, shining in the lamplight. Jim willed himself out of the pain and threw his weight to the left, toward the knife.

The chair rolled and he fell on his side with all his and the chair's weight on his wrist and forearm. The pain in his wrist seemed worse than what he suffered from his face, but his fingers closed around the knife handle.

He heard Williams stagger to his feet. *"Scheisskopf Indianer!"*

Pain slammed into the back of his head and jammed his jaw against his chest. Jim rolled with the blow and again threw his body to the left so he rolled over on his face and knees.

The grinding weight on his face made him scream. The chair finished its momentum, thudding down on his right arm. He clung to the knife with his left hand, the blade hidden by his arm.

Williams stood awkwardly, hunched over and holding himself with both hands. His eyes gleamed in the lamplight and his face twisted with pain and hate. "You will die slowly for that, I promise you."

Jim's damaged face throbbed in cadence with his rapidly beating heart. Fog edged in and blurred his peripheral vision. It wouldn't take much more to make him lose consciousness.

He couldn't give up. He was a warrior and wanted to see his enemy's blood before he died. "You can't even defeat a man that's tied up, let alone in a fair fight."

"This is war, you fool. If you have the initiative, you keep it. You don't give it away." Williams' voice carried a parade ground ring and the hint of an accent that wasn't British.

"Where you from, white man? You sure ain't no Englishman, no matter how hard you pretend."

"What's the difference?" Williams grinned, snapped to attention and clicked his heels together. "Leutnant Horst von Hesse, Imperial Hussars, at your service."

"Don't know about where you come from," Jim said through a painful grin, "but if I'm gonna get serviced by a hussy, she has to look a damn sight better than you!"

The German's face paled and his lips thinned into a sneer as he closed the distance between them. "I'll teach you to besmirch an officer's name!" He stopped at Jim's feet and bent over him, reaching for the chair back.

I hoped he'd want to sit me up, Jim thought. He waited until Williams had his hands around the chair back, and then he whipped the knife up and into the man's body as far as he could reach.

"Gott im Himmel!" Williams shrieked, jerking away from the bloody blade and grabbing his wounded side. His eyes went wide with shock and he stared wordlessly

at Jim for a long moment before reaching inside his coat and pulling out a pistol.

"Coward!" Jim hissed.

The crack of the Luger knocked him back and he again hit the deck. His mind clouded and he did what he could before total inkiness lifted him out of his pain.

101 —Juneau City, A.T., October 2, 1916—
Monday late afternoon

August Lepke clucked loudly to the horse and lightly snapped the reins along the soaked hide. Obediently, the horse pulled the mariah farther down Lower Front Street. The wind whistled between the buildings as the entire Juneau Police Department and the Territorial Militia continued their house-to-house search.

Jack Malone, sitting next to August, took another pull off his flask and dropped it into his coat pocket. "I don't know how the hell you expect these men to keep warm if you don't let 'em take a nip now and then."

"I want them to have all their wits about them." August peered grimly into the storm. "Some of these men have their hands full trying to walk and talk at the same time, let alone carry a load under their belts too."

"Y'got a point there, Lieutenant." Jack grinned wryly and pulled the flask out again. "Besides, it looks like I didn't bring enough to go around anyway."

"I appreciate you helping me on this, Jack. This young man wouldn't be out here if it weren't for me."

"Ah, but it's one of them 'line of duty' affairs, ain't it?"

"Above and beyond." August nodded.

"Still 'n' all," Jack pressed, "you can't blame yourself if this turns out rum."

A whistle pierced the storm.

"They've found something," August said. "Over there, by the dock."

Lepke carefully climbed out of the mariah into the teeth of the storm. He caned down slippery ramps as fast as safety allowed to where an officer stood waving outside a boathouse. The corporal glanced down as Lepke neared.

"We found him, sir." His grim tone conveyed more than his words.

Lepke hurried in out of the storm. He hadn't taken time to look at the boathouse, didn't realize it belonged to the government until he saw the *Celia* rocking gently in the dim interior. The corporal helped Lepke aboard.

Jim, tied to a heavy chair, lay on his side, staring unseeingly at his right hand. Welts on his face testified to physical abuse, but it was the bullet in his chest that killed him.

Lepke forced himself to see a crime scene and not someone he knew and liked. He must keep emotion out of it so nothing would be missed.

The door to the boathouse slammed open and everyone looked up as George wailed, "Jiiiimm!"

Lepke glanced up at the four police officers in the small cabin, said swiftly, "Don't let him touch the body until I say it's okay!"

They nodded and poised themselves. The *Celia* rocked as George rushed aboard. He burst through the door, stopped and stared at his nephew.

"Oh, Jim, have I led you to this?" Tears ran down his face and he stepped toward the body. One of the officers edged in front of him.

"George," Lepke said softly, "give us a moment to look for clues so to catch the criminal. I am so sorry for your loss."

George didn't look up. "Look for your clues. I know he was following Williams."

"We have to be sure." Lepke nodded at one of the officers, "Get some more light in here." He bent and studied the wooden deck around the corpse.

Lepke motioned to the remaining two officers. "Forsythe, Harrington. Very gently move him over about a foot."

When the officers moved the corpse, a long-bladed knife covered with blood came into view. Jim's last message to them became visible to all.

Three streaks of blood ended where Jim's right hand had lain. All three streaks bent at an angle, and even though they ran together at one end, every man in the room recognized the three chevrons of a sergeant.

"Williams!" George said in a hard voice.

"He's wounded, too." Lepke pointed at the bloody knife and the line of blood leading to the door. He reached down and touched a blood drop. "Still sticky. This happened in the last hour."

He pushed himself to his feet, ignoring the ache from his wound. "Keep looking. We've covered most of the town already. He can't have gone too far with a knife wound."

The police officers hurried back into the storm. George gave Lepke a beseeching look. "Now?"

August nodded and stepped back, bumping into Jack. The man's face looked ashen.

"D'you really think Williams did it?" Jack whispered.

August pointed toward the door and they moved out onto the small deck.

"Yes, I think Williams did it. How many sergeants are there in the area? We know Jim was following Williams. Had been for some time."

"On the soul of my mother, I got nothing to do with this."

"But you know more about the man than you're telling me, Jack. That looks damned suspicious."

"Politics. All we talked about was politics."

"He never mentioned anything about murder?"

Jack's mouth opened but he remained silent. His eyes roamed around but focused on nothing. He licked his lips and opened his mouth again.

"Don't lie to me, Jack. That would make you an accessory to murder."

Jack sighed, seemed to deflate. "He's a damned spy."

"Williams? A spy? For England?"

Jack's mouth made a quick, mirthless smile before going flat again. "He's a German spy. Saboteur. He killed them three boys out at the Ground Hog Mine when he blew the main shaft."

"Were you in on that?"

"I haven't killed anybody here in years," Jack said with a snort, "and never was it murder!" He pulled out his flask, shook it. "Damn. I'm out of whiskey. This is thirsty work. Come on down to Armstrong's and I'll tell you the whole of it."

August felt dazed, even foolish. A spy and saboteur! "Yah, sure. Let's go."

Maybe I'll even have a drink myself, he thought.

102 —Juneau City, A.T., October 2, 1916—
Monday evening

Williams gingerly moved through the forest, cursing the rain and wind. The knife wound burned with each step, but the sphagnum moss he'd stuffed into the cut kept it from bleeding.

How could he have made such a stupid mistake? He should have located the knife immediately after dropping it. The Indian was tied so tightly...

Williams stumbled over a huge root hidden by the weeds, nearly falling. He caught himself against a huge tree trunk and felt stabbed all over again. This time he allowed himself to scream with the pain.

As if in response, the rain fell harder and the roaring wind increased. Soaked to the skin, Williams knew he would die from exposure if he didn't find shelter soon. Dusk sank rapidly into darkness and he decided to try his luck farther up the mountainside.

The involuntary shivering transferred to his jaw and his teeth began to chatter. A hopeless fear spread through him, reminding him of night barrages on the front. Only now it was water falling through the air, trying to kill him.

He laughed at the image and realized he wandered close to hysteria. *What an ignoble way to die,* he thought.

A flicker in the gloom caught his eye. He squinted, wiping rain from his eyes, hoping he wasn't hallucinating. There, through the rain, a glow of red. A fire!

Williams crawled uphill so he wouldn't stumble and fall. From somewhere in his frenzied mind came the notion if he fell down the fire would go out. He bit his shivering lip to keep from laughing.

Now he could clearly see the flames leaping, illuminating the interior of a small cave. There was some sort of protocol Americans used when approaching the fire of strangers. As a boy he'd read about it in Red Indian novels.

"Hello, the fire." His voice barely rose above a croak and the wind and rain effectively tore it off his lips. He slid his right hand into the sopping overcoat pocket and gripped the Luger.

No matter what the fire's owner felt, Williams would not leave this miracle of salvation. He edged into the circle of light. A bundle of rags and furs lay against the wall.

He twisted his head about, wondering at the location of the person who had saved his life. Peering into the gloom at the back of the cave he realized his mistake. This wasn't a cave; it was a tunnel. A mine.

The irony of the situation boiled laughter from him and he sank onto the pile of dry, warm furs and rags. For the first time in twelve hours he allowed himself to relax and close his eyes.

"Y'got ennything ta drink?"

Williams' Luger pointed at the person before his eyes opened.

"Hey, you!" the old Indian woman yelled, backing away from him. "Don't hurt me!"

Williams lowered the pistol, let it lay across his knee. "Who are you? Are you alone here?"

"Nobuddy here 'cept me." She examined him with her eyes. "You got ennything ta drink?"

"No, but I have money. What's your name?"

"Ain't no place ta buy hooch up here!" She spat into the fire and flopped down next to Williams.

He moved the pistol slightly, catching her interest. "I asked you for your name."

"Stella. M'name's Stella. What my momma called me."

"Christ, that's rich," Williams said with a laugh. "You're stellar all right. A rare piece of the firmament indeed." He threw back his head to laugh and winced at the sudden pain in his side.

"You drunk?" Stella asked.

"Wish to God I was!" He looked at her more closely. She reeked of smoke, fish, and cheap whiskey. However she didn't have the years he first thought. He decided she wasn't older than twenty-five.

"Why are you up here, Stella? Have you committed some crime against your people?"

"None of your business," she said crisply. "What you doin' up here, hidin' from the guy who knifed you?"

Williams smiled in spite of himself. "You don't miss much, do you?"

"I see lots of things," she whispered. "Then I get drunk and tell people what I seen 'em do." She shook her head. "I shouldn't do that. They don't like it at all."

"So you live here alone?"

"Sometimes men come to visit," she said slyly, "but they bring me hooch to get me happy."

"I'll make you a deal," he said, watching her eyes. "I'll give you a gold piece if you'll let me stay here."

"Gold!" Her eyes rounded and for a moment she looked like the girl she had been before her social decline.

"But! You must not tell any one I am here. You must not let any of your visitors see me. Do you understand?"

She nodded. "I'll even fix your wound, if ya want."

"I'd like that, but first I want you to wash your hands."

"Sure. Whatever you say . . . Uh, what's your name?"

"You may call me Horst," he said with a smile.

"Horse. That's a funny name for a man."

THE DAILY ALASKA DISPATCH
Juneau, Alaska, Saturday, October 3, 1916

VARNA LIKELY TO BE TAKEN BY RUMANIANS

GREECE STILL PUZZLE WITH POWERS

HINDENBERG GETTING OLD

SWEDEN MAY BE DRAWN INTO THE FIGHT

HUSBAND WANTS WIFE TO GO TO CHURCH

JUNEAU NIGHT SCHOOL FORMALLY ORGANIZED

SAYS WICKERSHAM WILL WIN THREE TO ONE

LOCAL INDIAN FOUND MURDERED

Authorities say James Kisadis, of the Auk Village, was found murdered late Monday night. One of the investigating officers said the man was bound to a chair and shot. Rumors that Kisadis was working for the Juneau Police Department at the time of his death could not be confirmed.

A grisly turn of events had the crime take place on the boat Celia, owned by condemned murderer Edward Krause. Krause is in custody at the federal jail awaiting execution on May 11th for the murder of James O. Plunkett.

102 —Juneau City, A.T., October 17, 1916—
Tuesday afternoon

George Mak-we watched as miners hurried from one place of business to another on the mud-splattered boardwalk. Two weeks and not a glimpse of his quarry. Williams had not kept an appointment with the militia captain, or turned up at his hotel, or at Armstrong's, or the Germania.

The bastard had vanished from the face of the earth. Every steamer departing Juneau, Thane, Douglas, or Treadwell was searched from bilge to weather deck, bow to stern. He had to still be here. Due to the Juneau Ice Field, only birds could go overland to another area.

After a careful search, they found no evidence of missing skiffs, gas boats, or canoes. Although George felt Williams was as malevolent as a demon from hell, the man was not a wraith who could vanish into thin air.

Williams had skillfully gone to ground. George vowed to find and kill him. As revenge burned in George's brain, his objectivity evaporated.

Jee-nak and Begay helped comb the regular spots where Williams was so well known. All three of the hunters had overheard others remarking on the strange disappearance of the Englishman.

Whatever Jack Malone told August about Williams had not been repeated to others. George made a mental note to question the police lieutenant on the subject.

Although still early, light faded from the rainy sky and George decided to go home for food. As he walked, he tried to think of where else a fugitive might hide in the area. Perhaps an abandoned mining building up the Perseverance Trail, or out the road to Auke Bay.

Once snow fell, it would be easier to tell which buildings people used and which were truly abandoned. By the time he reached home he had thought of three possibilities within a half mile of where he stood. Those would be next, he decided.

George opened the door and walked into a dark kitchen. He wondered where Julia could be. She must have been gone for hours or she would have left a light on for him.

"I'm over here, George." Her voice startled him and his hand moved halfway to his revolver before he regained control.

"Jesus, woman! You scared hell out of me!"

"Guess that makes us even," she said with a sniff. He realized she was crying. "'Cause you're scaring the hell out of me."

He clicked on a wall switch. Julia sat in the corner by the window, staring out into the night. Her face glistened from tears and the redness of her eyes bespoke hours of upset.

"What are you talking about, Julia?" He tried to keep his voice concerned and caring, but even he heard the edge to his words.

"You're a completely different person than the man I married. You are obsessed with finding this Williams animal —"

"That's my job!" he snapped. "I'm hunting for a murderer who —"

"You're hunting for absolution! You are so mired in guilt you can't even see past your pain."

"That son of a bitch murdered my nephew! Am I supposed to treat this work as if I'm keeping an eye out for a bootlegger or a fishtrap robber? That animal attacked and killed a member of my family who I helped raise —" George's voice broke and he fought back a sob, unable to continue.

Julia stood and moved across the room toward him, her stomach large with child. "What about Jeff? You've shut him out completely. My– our son is grieving for his uncle and all he gets from you is a hollow-eyed absence of emotion. Have you cried for Jim yet? You didn't at the funeral."

"I cried when I found him," George said, looking around the room. "Where is Jeff?"

"At Irene's house. It makes them both feel better."

George felt another dimension of guilt swirl about him. This was getting worse all the time. "I didn't come home to argue with you."

"No. You came home to eat so you can continue to hunt. What will you do when you catch him and don't have this pursuit to hide behind?"

"I'll kill him!"

"And then what? Mutilate the body? Revenge is an empty meal, George. It won't change anything. It won't bring Jim back. He's gone forever."

"He's dead because I sent him out to die!"

"Road apples!" she snapped. "He's dead because he was ambushed in the line of duty. If anyone is to blame it's Jim himself for getting too far out on a limb."

"Shut up!" George felt angry enough to strike this razor-tongued harpy. Where was her sense of propriety? "I'll hear no more of this!"

The red spots high on her cheeks testified to her anger, but Julia kept her voice level and deceptively soft. "I'll put up with this for one more month. If you can't get past this horrible event for the sake of your family, I have no hope of sharing anything else with you. You are not responsible for Jim's death, but you are responsible for a number of lives." She put both hands on her swollen abdomen.

George wanted to shout. He wanted to cry. His thoughts flew away half formed as more roiled into his brain. Where to start, how to explain?

He couldn't, so he turned and stumbled out into the night.

104 —Juneau City, A.T., November 8, 1916—
Wednesday evening

"**Whaddya think, Jack?**" Sean Clancy weaved in place, too drunk to walk but too excited to sit. "We got 'em out ta vote in record nummers . . ." He paused to belch. ". . . An' I think Wick's gonna need hisself a new way ta make a livin'."

Jack smiled at his friend. He smiled at everyone tonight. "After tonight the honorable James Wickersham can go back to sentencing drunk Indians to a month in the slammer!"

Jack felt grand. To all indications Sulzer was ahead in Fairbanks, Ketchikan, Sitka, and Douglas. Here in Juneau and up in the little construction town of Anchorage, the race was neck and neck. "Of course, nothing will be official for at least a month." Jack tossed back another shot of whiskey. "The Bush vote will make or break our man, like always, but he's from the Bush himself!"

"Does that worry ya, Jack?" Sean tried to convey concern but only succeeded in resembling a bewildered owl.

Jack laughed. "Hell no. We got it in the bag! Wilson's gonna win in a walk and take a Democratic majority with him."

Somebody across the crowded Alaskan Bar shouted angrily above the band music and someone else punched him cold. Jack felt the old tension in his gut, waiting to see if that would spark off a general melee. When the normal hum of the throng resumed, Jack felt relief.

"Jasus, I must be getting old," he mumbled. Wasn't that long ago he would have started the melee himself. Fifty-nine wasn't old. He didn't feel old inside. Thought he hadn't changed much since thirty.

When he shaved every morning he could still see the once firm jaw line and clear, dark eyes. If prodded, he would admit to the webbed lines around those eyes and the slight but unmistakable jowls softening a once jutting chin. His hair not only thinned on a regular basis, but the survivors steadily marched toward gray.

Well, dammit, he thought, I've not had an easy life, but I will now, by God.

A cigar-smoking, portly man, tricked out in a seventy-dollar suit and wearing a hundred-dollar overcoat, sidled up to Jack. "Mr. Malone, may I offer you a prime Havana?" He held out a cigar, which in poorer light could have passed for a small club.

Jack smiled and accepted the cigar, began preparing it for consumption. "And what, Mr. Watkins, brings a staunch Republican into a Democratic bar during an election party?"

"The direction of the wind, you might say." Watkins replaced his own cigar and made the end glow brightly, blew smoke toward the cloud nearly obscuring the pressed tin ceiling. "Seems to be a Democratic wind in the Territory tonight."

Jack grinned around his cigar and puffed it into life. He took it out of his mouth and regarded it like a grandchild. "That's a fine smoke, Mr. Watkins. I thank you."

"I'm told you have Senator Sulzer's ear."

"Your informer is correct. What of it?"

"One of the problems we've had with Dele-, ah, Judge Wickersham . . ." Both men grinned. ". . . is his adamant attack on corporate investments from the states. Especially the San Francisco mining companies. Why, we wouldn't even be on the map if it weren't for outside investors."

Jack's grin remained fixed. For years this man had snubbed him, referring to him as an "upstart Irish bartender." Now here he was, trying to keep his place at the trough. Jack appreciated irony.

"I'm guessing you're wanting to know if Delegate Sulzer will see the matter a wee bit differently. Correct?"

"Succinct, and on target," Watkins said.

"Well, I'm sure you remember Delegate Sulzer came to the Territory, invested his own money, and became wealthy as a result."

"Of course I remember that. You lads made it a prime theme in your campaign prop-, ah, your campaign."

"The senator paid for his own campaign, accepting no corporate donations from stateside concerns."

Watkins' smile finished evaporating. "Your point being, Mr. Malone?"

"We don't owe anything to anybody. It's a new ball game, as the boys say."

"Do you think I'd be in here if I didn't know that?"

Jack laughed, felt the old edge glisten in his brain. "Ah, Mr. Watkins, you're a heathen Republican, but I never took you for a fool. I appreciate a practical man." He glanced around the room.

Sean Clancy lay passed out on the floor. "Hey, you two, pick him up and put him someplace he won't get stepped on."

As two men, barely able to move them selves, struggled to lift the sodden Clancy, Jack turned back to Watkins. "Why don't we go somewhere a bit more private and discuss this at length?"

Watkins smiled and led the way to the door.

The band played on.

THE DAILY ALASKA DISPATCH
Juneau, Alaska, Saturday, November 14, 1916

NOTE GIVEN TO GERMANY BY NORWAY

BAYONET CHARGE AGAINST TEUTONS

SULZER LEAD IS REDUCED SOME MORE

WILSON NOW WORKING TO THE FUTURE

BRITISH TAKE MANY POSITIONS

NATION-WIDE STRIKE OF RAILWAY MEN

MINE OWNERS AND EXPERTS ARE MEETING

WAS SUNK WITHOUT WARNING BE GIVEN

STARCH TRUST TO BE DESOLVED

FIRE SWEEPS MAIN PART OF DAVIS CITY

105 —Juneau City, A.T., November 14, 1916—
Tuesday afternoon

"Oh, Amanda, this is such a sad day." Fiona Malone studied the hem of her black dress in the mirror as she turned from side to side.

"I didn't realize Bones was so important to Maye," Amanda said from her chair. Her pregnancy not only had become obvious to anyone who cared to look, but it also left her continuously sapped of energy. She wasn't worried about how her black dress fit; she really didn't care.

Bones, Maye Wattnem's cadaverous right hand man, had collapsed at the Line Cafe during the dinner hour on Sunday last. By the time a doctor could be fetched, Bones had released his divine spark. When Maye heard the news she became utterly prostrate with grief, leaving the operation of both the Line Cafe and the Division Hotel to Fiona and Amanda.

After a day and a half operating the cafe, Amanda felt ready to pitch it all, but she owed these women her very life. Never again would she find friends as fast and true as these. She knew that with a certainty.

"Do Americans always inter their dead instantly?" Amanda asked. "The man is barely cold . . ."

"Maye wanted it done quickly." Fiona added a small amount of powder to her nose. "She and Bones depended on each other more than I realized. Maye's a bit of a soft touch once you get past her gruffness."

"She certainly took a liking to me," Amanda said. "Thank God."

"I'm going to bring her down now. It's nearly time for the funeral." Fiona cast an appraising glance at Amanda. "Are you ready?"

"As ready as I'll ever be in this condition."

By the time Fiona supported Maye step-by-step down the stairway, Amanda had donned her long coat and stood near the door holding a coat for Maye. The large woman already wore a severe black hat with a thick veil that obscured her face but couldn't muffle her small sniffs and choked sobs.

Wordlessly, Amanda helped Maye into her coat. At that moment the motor taxi pulled up in front of the hotel. Henry Jenkins had draped his green Maxwell with black crepe.

With the light covering of snow from the night before, the car and crepe appeared darkly ominous against the street. The women emerged and Henry helped Maye into the back seat of the taxi. Amanda pulled her increased bulk up by herself and tried not to think about how tired she felt and how her bladder always seemed full.

The First Presbyterian Church sat a block downhill from the Cathedral of the Nativity of the Blessed Virgin Mary, which Amanda thought was an awfully big name for such a small Catholic church. As they helped Maye from the taxi and entered the First Presbyterian Church, Amanda realized Bones' funeral wasn't going to draw a large crowd.

Four people sat in the pews. Fiona's sister and August Lepke were two of them. The other two worked at the Line Cafe.

Christ, she thought, *I hope more people than this come to see me off.* It suddenly occurred to her she would be hard pressed to draw this large a crowd. The thought chilled her far more than did the weather.

Amanda had no more than gratefully settled in her seat when the minister entered from the vestry. They all stood. Maye leaned heavily on the back of the pew in front of them.

"Please be seated," the minister said. "I have been instructed to ask God's indulgence on this man and let it go at that. This I cannot do.

"Mr. William Allen Stout was not known to me during his life, but it has befallen me to usher his soul to God's promise. This I will do. I have been made aware Mr. Stout ended his mortal coil laboring among the less fortunate and economically deprived of our community.

"This is laudable and honest. We need more like him and I know he shall be sorely missed among his friends and fellow workers. If any among you would like to say a few words, please stand."

Maye grunted and pulled herself up, the knuckles on her hands gleamed pale against the back of the dark pew. She pushed aside her veil and stared at the casket in front of the pulpit.

"Bones worked every day of his life," she said with a rasp. "He was a faithful and honest man, and God don't make enough of that sort." She stopped and wheezed for a moment. Amanda wondered if she could think of nothing more to say. "He was more than an employee to me. He was more like a son, and at the very least he was one of my few, true friends. I will miss him more than I can say."

Maye dropped heavily into the pew, wheezed twice and leaned gently against Fiona, mumbling something. Amanda wondered how she could suddenly stop wheezing after doing it all day.

"Maye?" Fiona said in a small voice, pushing the woman upright. "Maye!" She looked up at the minister. "Please help her, I think she stopped breathing!"

Suddenly August stood at Amanda's side. "Please, Miss Ganbor, would you move into the aisle?"

Amanda stood and watched August lower Maye to the pew seat and undo the throat buttons on her dress. Maye's eyes rolled whitely back in her head and her mouth hung open slack and rubbery. August put his ear to her mouth and listened intently.

He sat up and looked at Fiona. "I'm sorry, Fiona. She's gone."

Amanda thought it odd the whole scene could evaporate so quickly, and then she fell into a faint.

106 —Juneau City, A.T., November 23, 1916—
Thanksgiving Evening

"**I want to thank you all for coming,**" **Fiona said, looking at each of her guests in turn.** "This is the most somber Thanksgiving in my memory." Her eyes lingered on her father for a moment. "Save for the first one after the death of my mother."

Florence watched her father stare through Fiona and into a distance only he could fathom. Under the table, August's grip on her hand tightened. This was certainly the strangest Thanksgiving she had ever experienced.

The Line Cafe displayed a CLOSED sign in the front window, but the small establishment bulged with invited guests and the remains of a splendid meal. Every employee of the Line Cafe and the Division Hotel who had no family in the Territory had come. George and Julia Mak-we and Jeff Prescott sat together.

George stared uncomprehendingly at Fiona as she spoke. He seemed to be in his own private hell these days. Julia, radiant in pregnancy, looked his exact opposite. Irene Kisadis sat between Julia and her daughter, Ruth, whose husband, Begay Santo, sat to his wife's left.

We even have a minister, Florence mused. Reverend James Thistle sat close to a very pregnant Amanda Ganbor. It seemed obvious the reverend and Amanda were interested in each other, but Florence knew Amanda was now gun shy when it came to men, and the reverend seemed strangely inept with women.

Everyone in the room stiffened and Florence gave her attention back to Fiona.

". . . lost several friends and loved ones in the recent past," Fiona said. "We must be thankful for the time we had with them and know they now sit at the side of God and look down on us." Her eyes glistened at the corners and Florence fought a lump in her own throat.

"I have such confused thoughts about Maye's final requests. When her lawyer, Tim McDaniel, told me she had left the hotel and cafe to me, I nearly fainted." Fiona held a small sheaf of rolled paper she twisted nervously in her hands.

Florence noticed Fiona seemed to be staring at their father, and Jack, in return, avoided her gaze. Did he feel guilty about once having been involved with Maye? That had been long ago, and besides, Florence had not shared her father's revelation with Fiona.

"Life is strange." Fiona glanced around at the rest of her guests and smiled, "and I am thankful for Maye's gift to me, but I think it only fitting I also share. So I would like to announce that as of today the Line Cafe belongs to Amanda Ganbor."

A gasp of surprise ran around the table and then everyone but Amanda broke into applause.

"Why, Fiona!" Amanda exclaimed. "You needn't do that. I. I mean, thank you, but this is too much!"

"It's too late," Fiona said with a smile. She tossed the roll of paper that landed perfectly in front of Amanda and slowly uncurled. "There's the deed, made out in your name, already signed by me and notarized by Mr. McDaniel. Congratulations, Amanda. You're now an Alaskan businesswoman."

Amanda shook her head slowly, looking first at the deed and then at Fiona. "I haven't the words to describe what this means to me, other than to be thankful for the friends I have found in this place." She ran her brimming eyes over everyone at the table.

Reverend Thistle held up a goblet of wine. "To our friend and hostess, Fiona Malone!" Everyone stood and raised their glasses except Amanda, who remained sitting, dabbing at her eyes with a handkerchief.

When the group sat down again, Julia Mak-we remained standing. "I also have a bittersweet announcement to make." She tried to smile but Florence could see her heart was neither light nor happy. "Jeff and I are leaving for Seattle on the *Princess Sophia* tomorrow afternoon."

Nearly everyone in the group gasped or murmured something to them selves. Julia gave George a wistful glance, then continued. "I'm not sure when, or if, we'll be back, but, like Amanda, I wanted to thank all of you for your warmth and friendship."

Julia stared at Irene and tears ran down the cheeks of both women. "Some of you have become family as well as friends and I know I will always find refuge here in Juneau."

"Please don't go!" Irene said and choked back a sob. "I can't bear to lose you, too."

George abruptly stood and walked wordlessly out into the wintry night, slamming the door behind him. A hush fell over the room.

"I'm sorry, Irene," Julia said softly, "but you see how it is."

Ruth put an arm around her mother's shoulders. "I was going to wait and tell you when we were alone, but you're going to be a grandma next summer."

"Oh, how wonderful!" Julia cried. "Congratulations to you both."

Florence watched Julia as the others focused on a suddenly embarrassed Ruth. Julia sank down into her chair, staring past the CLOSED sign in the front window while hugging her son to her side.

Florence felt she'd had enough emotional twists for one night. She leaned close to her fiancé. "August, would you please take me home now?"

"Certainly. I'll get our coats."

The dinner party had run its course. Three of the employees left. The others sought their wraps.

Fiona sat down next to Florence, whispered, "Maye's last words to me were very peculiar."

"Peculiar? What did she say?"

"She said, 'you look just like your sister.' and then she died."

"You don't look that much like me," Florence said. "Was she delirious?"

"That's what I thought at the time, but I have been going through her papers and I found this photograph . . ."

Florence professionally inspected the workmanship of the photograph before she examined the subjects. An excellent piece of work, good finish, quality linen paper, and the image evidenced the full range of possible tonality. A modern wedding portrait: the man with his hair parted fashionably in the middle and his hands nonchalantly in his pockets.

At his side stood the bride, her hair in a somewhat severe style and looking sober but serene. The woman in the photograph was Fiona.

"How?" Florence stared into her sister's eyes. "This can't be you!" she whispered in a hiss. "I mean, who is this woman?"

"There were other papers." Fiona chewed her lower lip for a moment before continuing, "I also found a diary. This is Maye's illegitimate daughter, Lillian, our half-sister."

Both women looked up as their father walked out into the night.

THE DAILY ALASKA DISPATCH
Juneau, Alaska, Saturday, November 24, 1916

VILLA ATTACK ON CHIHUAHUA IS A FAILURE

RAILROAD PROBLEM ONE THAT PRESSES IN CONGRESS

DREADNAUGHT OF RUSSIANS BEEN SUNK

HEARINGS BY COMMISSIONS ON RAILROADS

TWO MASKED MEN HOLD UP A TRAIN

MANY SIGNERS FOR PEACE MOVE

SAN FRANCISCO. Nov. 24-(Associated Press)- Over 40,000 signatures of California residents have been secured for the nation-wide peace movement to have America represented in the neutral conference committees.

Thus far those taking the petitions about claim there have been very few who have refused to sign while the majority of people have shown an eagerness to be among the signers.

EDITOR IS KILLED

Chicago, Nov. 24- Maj. John R. Lewis, editor of the Montreal Star, was killed in action at the front.

106 —Juneau City, A.T., December 1, 1916—
Friday night

Jack Malone beamed at his daughters. It seemed a long time since they had sat at their proper places around his table. Mrs. Milivich looked ten years younger tonight as she bustled about the kitchen.

"I don't know why this room seems smaller," Fiona said, "but it does."

"Looks the right size to me," Jack said.

"Your horizons have expanded, Fio," Florence said, "and that changes everything."

"Wait until we get to Washington City!" Jack said. "Then your horizons will really change."

"Father . . ." Florence looked him square in the eyes with an expression he knew so well; he wasn't going to like what she had to say. ". . . I am getting married in four months. As much as I'd like to see Washington, I'm afraid it'll have to wait for a visit from me and my husband."

"That doesn't surprise me, Duchess. In fact I anticipated your decision." Taking Florence to Washington City would be a full time job for any man, Jack mused, and he was going to have his hands full with running Delegate Sulzer's office anyway.

"Did you anticipate me not going either, Father?" Fiona asked.

Jack felt like he'd been kidney punched; found it difficult to breathe for a long moment. "What!" he said in a strained voice. "I thought you wanted to go—"

"I did, a few months ago, but now I'm a business owner and have obligations—"

"Business?" Jack said with a snort. "You mean that flea trap hotel that Maye Wattnem—"

"How dare you call the Division a flea trap! We work ourselves faint every day to keep that place clean, comfortable, and above reproach! At least we don't take food out of children's mouths by selling their fathers intoxicants!"

"Jasus, girl, don't get your back up! You sound like you voted for Snow and his Prohibition ticket."

"For what it's worth, I did!" Fiona's nostrils flared and color charged her cheeks from hair to jaw line.

Christ, they both came away with their mother's temper and sharp tongue.

"Princess," he said in a placating tone. "I'm sorry. You're right, the Division is a good, clean hotel, but can't you hire a manager for a year or so and come to Washington City with me? Me and Mrs. Milivich can't set up a whole house by ourselves."

"Me, to Vashinton go?" Mrs. Milivich said. "I sorry am, but I tink not, Mr. Malone."

Jack thought he might drown in this sea of contrary women. "Why ever not?

Are ye not my housekeeper? I'm moving my household to the nation's capitol city."

"I take care of this house," the old woman said firmly. "I vish to see Florence marry." She gave Fiona an appraising glance, "and Fiona too, some day. I stay here, I tink."

"What if I sell this house?" Jack said, wondering if he might have gone too far.

"Then I keep house for Florence and her husband, no?"

Florence blurted out a laugh before she could stop herself.

"Father," Fiona said with a smile. "We all know Washington City is a man's world. Juneau City is more comfortable. You'll have no trouble finding some nice lady to keep house for you."

Florence gave Fiona an odd look. Jack thought they had something more he wouldn't like. What could be worse than everyone abandoning him in his moment of victory?

"Father . . ." Florence hesitated and foreboding washed over Jack. ". . . I can't think of any way to put this delicately. So . . . how many children do you have?"

Bewilderment usurped his foreboding. "What the hell sort of a question is that? "Yer both sitting right in front of me. I have no other children!"

"You told me once," Florence swallowed and her face grew rosy, "that you had been with Maye, before Mother."

"Well, that was different, y'see." Jack had to swallow to clear his throat. "Me and Maye, well, we was young back then and I was at my wildest. Sure, we, ah, were together for awhile, but we didn't start no family."

Jack felt a calm descend on him. His wild oats days with Maye were something he didn't think about much. He had loved her madly for a time, but her domineering personality had quickly burned away the fog of lust from his vision.

"Jasus," he said. "The fights we used to have. We coulda sold tickets." He looked at each daughter. "We wasn't together long, me and Maye. We was too much like each other."

Fiona sighed and, with her elbows straddling her plate, rested her face in her palms. "Thank God, you really didn't know."

"Daddy," Florence said with a smile. She hadn't called him that in over a decade. "I'm not your first child. Maye bore you a daughter after you married Mother."

"The hell!" he shouted. "Did she tell you that? Why on Earth would she make up something like that?" He felt doubly angry. Angry that Maye would lie to his daughters about something so significant, and angry she wasn't here so he could confront her.

"You were both alike." Florence's smile infuriated him, looking like a cat with a mouthful of canary. "She was so stubborn she went south and had her baby and never told you about her."

"So where is this mythical child? What's her name? Maye didn't raise no kid here in Juneau, I'd have known about it."

Fiona handed him a photograph. Wedding picture. He had his own somewhere in the attic. He peered hard at the bride.

"Fiona! Who is this man? Is this some sort of practical joke?"

"Look carefully, Daddy," Fiona said, a little too sharply to suit him. "The resemblance is remarkable, but there are differences. Her jaw looks more like Maye than it does you."

Going from disbelief to fully convinced in the blink of an eye was an entirely new experience for Jack. The truth of it hit him like a five-pound sledge. He felt faint.

"Father!" Florence said. "Take a breath."

Now he understood the little digs Maye had sent his way over the years. A vast melancholy filled him as he looked at the photo of his daughter. "What's her name?"

"Lillian," Fiona said. "Maye gave her to her sister to raise. She thinks Maye was her aunt. It was part of the agreement."

"But Maye named her, didn't she?"

"How did you know, Father?"

"Because she named her after my youngest sister who died as a small child on the trip over from Ireland. What a perfect name for the daughter lost to me."

108 —Thane, A.T., December 6, 1916—
Wednesday afternoon

Arnold Williams felt impressed by Stella's suggestion. "You really think a disguise would work?" he asked her.

"As long as nobody sees you who knows you," she said with a toss of her head. "You're so tall and got that big nose and scar."

"Thank you, but I think I was very aware of all that."

"Naw. Folks forget what they really look like to other people and keep seeing themselves the way they want to." Stella vigorously scratched her leg and stirred the foul-smelling pot of roots and bark. He thought she possessed very shapely legs.

The stab wound gave him pain only when he over-exerted himself. In the belief it would make him stronger, he always ignored the ache for a few minutes.

"If you stain your skin with this stuff, we can pass you off as an Indian from somewheres south. It gets so smoky down in them village houses nobody will be able to tell the difference."

"There's some Auk Tlingits know me." Williams watched her face wrinkle as if she smelled something worse than the contents of her kettle.

"We pretty much stay away from them. They think they own everything that touches salt water. We tell 'em they're fulla shit." She emitted an evil-sounding cackle and continued stirring.

Williams remembered a Shakespeare play with a scene reminiscent of this one. Millie insisted they attend and, despite his misgivings, he enjoyed the performance. The thought occurred to him he would be no farther from Millie right now if he were on the moon.

The practical military officer in him knew the chances of completing his mission hovered near zero, let alone escaping this monstrous wilderness alive, but this woods maiden possessed a brain under all that smoke and soil she wore. Passing as someone far down on the social scale might prove easy.

Who ever looked at Indians? If he hadn't noticed the same one over and over in his travels about Juneau, he would not have realized one followed him. He wished he knew who had put the man up to it, and why.

Jack Malone? No. Jack didn't need to do that. He always knew where Williams was and whom he spoke to. Jack had ears everywhere.

"I think this stuff's done," Stella announced. "We'll let it cool off some and then we'll put some on ya, see how it works." Her leg gleamed in the firelight.

"Good. Now, what say we see how you work?"

"You give me another gold coin?"

"That's the agreement." Williams smiled as she stood and dropped her soiled dress around her ankles.

THE DAILY ALASKA DISPATCH
Juneau, Alaska, Saturday, December 16, 1916

HUSBAND OF "BABE" BROWN UNDER ARREST

LOS ANGELES DYNAMITER CONVICTED

NATIONAL PROHIBITION IS DEFEATED

NATIVE TOWN TO ORGANIZE MUNICIPALITY

GOVERNOR TELLS ABOUT THE NATIVES
Slowly Learning to Prepare Gardens and
Raise Vegetables Says Report of Governor

JUNEAU HOSPITAL PROVED BOON TO SICK NATIVES
Introduction of Reindeer Among the Northern Natives
Has Been Means of Saving Them From Starvation
and Promoting Their Prosperity

Touching upon the Native population the annual report of Governor Strong says: "According to the United States census report of 1910, there were in Alaska 25,331 persons classified as Indians. This included those of mixed blood, of whom there is a considerable number.

The natives of southeastern Alaska are by far the most prosperous in the Territory. Health conditions among them are undoubtedly better than elsewhere. Civilizing influences are apparent in many of the native towns and villages, due to the work among these natives of the teachers of the United States Bureau of Education, under whose direction schools are maintained, and the influence of the missionaries who labor among them. The gospel of cleanliness and sanitation is preached and practiced by many of the teachers and preachers, as well as the doctrine of godliness, and the results of their combined work is seen in the village streets, in the homes, and in the personal appearance of these people.

Some of these native towns have a measure of local (Continued on page 3)

109 —Juneau City, A.T., December 17, 1916—
Sunday evening

Amanda Ganbor watched the last customer leave the Line Cafe. She glared at Reverend Thistle. "You're ruining my business, you know."

"Madame?" He smiled with all the affectation of an overacting thespian. "Pray tell, how could I be ruining your business?"

"You're doing too bloody much proselytizing in here, that's how."

He instantly became serious. "I'm sorry, Amanda, I had no idea that—"

"I know, I know." She waved him down. "It isn't like you do it on purpose. It just happens, but it's running my clientele out the door faster than I'd like. As much as I hate to, I'm going to have to ask you not to come in unless you're having a meal, James."

His dejection tugged at her heart, but she felt resolute. It would besmirch Maye's memory if Amanda let this place go under in the first year she owned it. This man interested her, but so had Barry.

The fact he seemed interested in her said something about his intentions. She just wasn't sure what. He either felt strongly about her despite the fact she would give birth to another man's child, or else he thought her loose and an easy sexual target.

Her first instinct was to assume the second scenario, but her heart hoped for the first. When she let herself go she thought James one of the most handsome men she'd ever met.

His physique aroused her to the point of weak knees. He always treated her like a lady, and he seemed to always be in close proximity.

"Amanda, if I don't talk about God on the premises, can I be here when I'm not eating?"

"But why would you want to be here if you couldn't spread your almighty word?"

"To be near you, of course."

Amanda's heart raced. She willed her voice steady. "Why, James?"

"Well what do you think?"

"I think it could one of two reasons . . ." and she told him her conclusions.

"I would never take advantage of you," he said in a quiet, sincere voice.

"That's music to my ears, James, but I heard the same song seven months ago." She placed her hands on her stomach.

"There's much I don't know about you," she said. "You're the most close-mouthed man I ever met when it comes to your past. This town thinks I'm outrageous for appearing in public when I'm pregnant, let alone operate a cafe, and you're here buzzing about me like a bloody bee around nectar. You tell me you care about me, yet you don't care enough about me to tell me where you were four months ago, not to mention what you were doing."

Amanda felt she had said far too much. The poor bloke would probably take to his heels now and she couldn't blame him. She was tired of his evasiveness. It was time to think about her future and not waste it on fairy tales about any Prince-bloody-Charming.

"You're absolutely correct." He glanced around the empty cafe. "May I put up the closed sign and lock the door? I want to tell you some things about myself that might color your view."

Amanda nodded. "I am all ears."

She made fresh tea while he locked up and drew the blinds. They sat at one of the tables in the dining area. He sipped his tea, staring into her eyes as he talked.

"For seven years I ministered to an affluent congregation in Massachusetts. If you want the name of the town, I'll tell you, but it really doesn't matter."

Amanda shook her head and he continued.

"One of my wealthiest parishioners was a banker in his late sixties. He had worked hard to get where he was in the world and hadn't married until his middle fifties. On their wedding day his wife was two months past her nineteenth birthday."

Amanda frowned. "That sort of thing is very common in England, although I think it must be ghastly for the poor girl."

James smiled wryly. "Mrs. Ge—, ah, the wife approached me and told me she was very unhappy, and as her minister, what should she do? When I mentioned prayer, she laughed."

Amanda held up her hand. "How old was she when she approached you?"

"Thirty-two."

"And how old were you?" she asked.

"Twenty-eight."

"Do continue!"

"This isn't meant to be salacious." His eyes smiled at her but his mouth remained modestly prim. "She told me she wanted a man who could perform husbandly duties. She was tired of ministering to herself."

"My word!" Amanda knew she blushed. *What a fascinating woman*, she thought. *How I would love to meet her.*

"I told her the town was far too small for a woman of her social stature to go around looking for a bohemian lover. She looked me straight in the eye and said, 'I know. That's why I came to you.' I told her I didn't know of anyone . . ."

Amanda smiled. "Were you leading her on or were you actually that naïve?"

"I honestly believe it started as naïveté, but toward the end I knew she wanted me. But, she had to say it— I wouldn't."

"Why not? Didn't you want her?"

"Absolutely. Very much. As near as I can estimate, that was when my hypocrisy began."

"So you ministered to her in the flesh as well as the spirit."

"Precisely how I was going to put it," he said. His face reddened as he spoke and now he looked as uncomfortable as a man could get without squirming.

"So what happened, James? You're here, she's not." Amanda had a shocking thought. "Is she?"

"No. We, ah, saw each other as often as possible. I appointed her choir director when the previous lady surrendered the position due to her advanced years. We managed to stay very discreet."

"You fell in love with her, didn't you?"

"Of course. I even planned to marry her when her husband passed on, but he yet breathes, the last I heard."

Amanda saw pain etched deep in his face. She decided here sat a man who didn't lightly give himself to anyone. That he revisited this awkward and anguishing episode purely to placate her warmed her heart immeasurably.

"After two years, we grew careless. She became pregnant."

Amanda's heart cooled slightly.

"Her husband knew it wasn't, couldn't be, his. He threatened to divorce her and cut her off without a penny unless she told him who the man was. So she told him."

Amanda nodded, feeling grim. "Then he threatened you with public exposure unless you left town."

"Exactly," James Thistle said, surprise in his face.

Amanda shrugged. "You're here, not dead. It was the only logical conclusion."

"Yes. So here I am, less than what I seem."

"Are you in the Line Cafe because I am also with child, and you saw possible redemption?"

He started in shock. "My God, no!" He caught himself and glanced at the ceiling before staring into her eyes again. "You are a brave woman whom I at first pitied."

"Pitied! Why you sanctimon-"

He held up his hand. "At first. That didn't last past our second meeting. You are in charge of yourself. You seem so strong and definite."

She smiled inside. This wandering clergyman had obviously never met a diplomat's daughter before. She wished she had the strengths he attributed to her. All she said was, "I see."

"You awe me, Amanda. I am attracted by your intelligence, your bearing, your strength, and your beauty. We all make mistakes. Some of us are luckier than others because it doesn't show."

She laughed. "James, you sound like a man in love."

"Haven't you been listening? I am in love. With you."

His eyes reminded her of a Bassett hound but she held herself to a smile.

"You're smiling. I hope that's a sign that you're happy with how I feel."

More than anything she wanted to take this earnest man into her arms and not let go, but she had to be without-a-doubt sure of him. "James, I'm going to have a child."

He opened his mouth to speak but she held her hand up. "Allow me to finish. The child's father is a salesman who told me things I wanted to believe— as you just have.

"I would like nothing more than to believe you, but any future incaution on my part would be borne by my child as well as myself, and I can't take any more chances. You be my good friend for now, and we'll see what transpires."

"You'll not find a more resolute friend than James Madison Thistle." His chest swelled and she saw the boy in him. "I'll help you in any way I can."

"Stop running off my customers with discourses on sin and redemption. I know you feel deeply about all that. The only thing my customers are going to get inside this cafe is food."

"Very well. When I'm in here I won't even wear my collar."

"I hope to see a lot of you," she said, blushing.

110 —Juneau City, A.T., December 24, 1916—
Sunday afternoon

George Mak-we followed the footprints into the forest. Snow steadily fell out of the sky, muffling sound and blanketing the earth ever deeper. The cold nipped at George's nostrils. Flakes caught in his unkempt beard and he absently brushed them away.

The tracks wound up slope between trees, around clumps of brittle, winter killed, impotent devil's club, and disappeared between two ancient glacial boulders. Either of the rocks could more than hide a man. George thumbed off the safety on the .30-.30 and crept forward, wondering if this was a trap like the one that killed his nephew.

He stopped moving as the wave of pain and hate washed over him. People had stopped talking to him, not that he bothered answering. Now when they saw him approach they crossed the street or went into their homes.

When Julia and Jeff went south, George returned to his old boat cabin on the ridge over the Auk village. He only used the cabin for sleeping and storing food. Irene visited once and told him he looked like a madman, his house was filthy, and not to let Jim's murderer kill two people. George ignored her until she left.

Now the anger ebbed and he felt the hunter take control again. He eased into the trees, skirting both boulders. After a moment he saw the tracks receding farther into the woods and he stepped onto the trail again.

Even in the falling snow, the prints remained sharp, well defined. Whoever made them was inside the range of his rifle if it came to that. *I hope it's Williams,* he thought.

His mind smoldered, a damped bank of coals created by hot, white hate. How good it would feel to end that animal's life! Unbidden, unwelcome; Lepke crossed George's mind.

"Officer Mak-we, your professionalism has vanished," the lieutenant told him during a chance meeting on Lower Front. "You've allowed emotion rather than reason to direct your efforts. That won't work."

George had pulled off his badge and tossed it on the planks at Lepke's feet. "I don't need this no more. Ain't much left here worth protecting, the way I see it."

"George, it wasn't your fault. If anybody's, mine it was!"

George walked away from him. He thought he was getting pretty good at that: walking away. The shame ate at him.

Something moved in the gray forest ahead of him. He froze, slowly brought the rifle up to his shoulder and peered down the barrel. Something moved again. A man. George squinted a little more. He was tall, definitely tall enough to be Williams.

George held his position, waiting for his quarry to move out into the open. The man moved again, stretched and moved something with his arm. George's arms began to ache.

He brought the rifle down to port arms and inched ahead, never taking his eyes off his prey. The trail curved and suddenly the figure stood in full view, totally unaware anyone watched him.

George brought the rifle up and aimed at the center of the chest, shouted, "Williams, you can't run from me now!"

The man jerked his head up in surprise. A heavy beard covered the lower half of his face.

Pretty poor disguise, George thought.

The man raised one arm in front of his face as if George were the sun breaking though clouds. His other hand dropped to the holstered revolver on his hip.

George hadn't spotted the weapon until that instant. He decided Williams wanted to make a fight of it. He pulled the trigger on the .30-.30 and shot him in the chest.

The heart-stopping loud boom and the authoritative recoil of the weapon brought George out of his funk. He realized he didn't know for sure who his target was, but he had hit him.

The man threw his arms wide when the bullet struck and his body jerked backward, sprawling against something which immediately collapsed with the weight. One booted foot lifted off the ground and shook. George hurried up and crouched next to his victim as the foot fell into the snow with a soft thud.

The man lay on an old army tent and tattered belongings lay tumbled in the snow. His bright blue eyes tried to focus on George. "Why?" made its way through the bubbling blood and past his red-smeared lips.

Before George could say anything, the man died. He stared down at the dead face and felt his heart chill with sober realization.

It wasn't Williams.

George rocked back on his haunches and sat on the cold ground. His eyes filled with tears and he sobbed in anguish. He screamed into the darkening sky and allowed grief for Jim, for this innocent derelict, for his vanished life, for himself, to pour out.

For over an hour he sat silent next to his victim before the cold forced him to move again.

111 —Juneau City, A.T., December 30, 1916—
Saturday night

Police Lieutenant August Lepke strolled down the boardwalk with Corporal Harrington. Holiday cheer echoed from every bar and dance hall. Out-of-tune piano music and the laughter of excited women sometimes pierced the constant pulse of the stamp mills.

"One of the quietest New Year's weekends I can remember." Harrington nodded to a passer-by and continued, "Of course I've only been a policeman for seven years."

Lepke smiled but remained silent. Williams walked through his mind, smirking and winking like the villain in a two-reel. *Where was the man?*

Many residents thought the murderer had successfully escaped Alaska Territory. August knew better. That is, he knew his quarry well enough he felt sure of his conviction.

From what Jack said, Williams was an officer in the Imperial German Army. No, he would not retreat, not yet. Not before he managed to bring victory, no matter how Pyrrhic, out of this situation.

Vigilance would collar his quarry. Harrington said something in a warning tone. "I'm sorry, corporal, what did you say?"

"There's some sorta row going on over there." He pointed across the slush-filled street to where a throng of people shouted and waved fists.

"I wanted to keep my feet dry for at least an hour," Lepke muttered. "Come on, corporal. Let's stop this before it begins."

They moved apart and approached the shouting men from different quarters. Both officers held their nightsticks in full view.

"He's a yellow-dog murderer 'an the rest o' youse is just like him!" The speaker, August decided, was a bachelor miner out on the town who had eaten dinner off the free bar lunch between steins of beer. Most of the nine men looked to be miners and they had three men in militia uniforms surrounded.

"You can't smear a man for what someone else did!" yelled the smallest militiaman. "We ain't standing up for that skunk anyways. Hell, he was only there for less 'n' two months!"

Lepke pushed into the middle of the group. "What's all the ruckus here?" He put himself between the two talkers.

Some in the group recognized him and pulled back. Others, seeing Harrington's uniform, melted quietly into the night.

The miner raised his head and tried to focus on Lepke. "Havin' us a little discussion, mister. What's it to you?"

Lepke pulled his jacket aside, allowing his badge to reflect ambient light. "You're making a lot of angry noise and I'm interested in keeping the peace."

The miner's eyes focused instantly. "Oh. Sorry officer. I didn't mean to be cheeky. Just kinda fired up over that militia sergeant what killed them boys out at the Groundhog."

"He wasn't really in the militia," Lepke said. "He is a German saboteur who lied to the authorities."

"That's what I was tryin' to tell ya!" the militiaman said.

Lepke held up his hand. "The other thing is this," he said to the miner, "don't use one man to measure another. I too was born in Germany. Do you think I'm a saboteur also?"

More miners drifted off. The miner scuffed at the slush. "You're right, officer." He looked up at the militiaman. "No hard feelings, soldier. Can I buy you and your buddies a drink?"

Lepke scowled at the militiaman.

The man hurriedly shifted his attention from Lepke to the miner. "Yeah. No hard feelings. Whattya say, boys. You up for a beer?"

The men streamed toward music and light. Harrington grinned. "You're pretty good, lieutenant. Didn't knock a single head."

"I agreed with him. Why should I hit him? Williams has me also fired up. My friend, George Mak-we has become obsessed about hunting him down."

"Speak of the devil—" Harrington blurted.

George Mak-we, gaunt and disheveled, staggered down the street toward them. Lepke nearly recoiled at his appearance. George stopped and squinted at them.

"'S that you, Lepke?"

"George, my friend, what happened to you?"

George looked away into the night. "I killed the wrong man. You better arrest me."

"What man did you kill, George?" Lepke closed the distance between them. George reeked of whiskey. "Is that why you started drinking again?"

"You knew I used to drink?"

"You've come a long way since those days, George. I'm proud to know you, but I must know, did you kill someone?"

"Yeah. I thought I was trackin' Williams. Big feet, size tens, just like his. Way off in the woods, like an animal hiding . . ."

"Who did you kill?"

"Dunno his name. Seen him around here." George waved loosely at the street. "Rummy, didn't have a real job. Didn't have no place to live, 'cept in the woods." Tears ran down George's face.

"You need some sleep, George. I'm going to put you in a cell so you can get some rest. Tomorrow I want you to show me the man, okay?"

"Okay. I don't know if I really thought he was Williams or I just wanted him to be Williams."

"Come on, George. We'll talk about it tomorrow."

The three men started moving toward the jail.

"Corporal Harrington, would you please run ahead and make sure the isolation cell is free? I want him to be able to sleep good tonight."

"Sure, lieutenant. Happy to oblige." Harrington tossed a salute and hurried away.

Lepke kept his arm around George, more for moral support than physical.

"I'm so ashamed," George said brokenly. "I really liked bein' a cop, even if I couldn't arrest white people."

"Do you want to arrest white people?"

"I want to arrest people who hurt others, steal from 'em, 'n' things like that. Whites do that more 'n' Indians. Simple as that."

"I can't argue with your attitude or your mathematics."

"But, you don't know what it's like, killing' the wrong man!"

"Every man who makes his living by carrying a weapon lives constantly with the likelihood of doing just that." Lepke glanced around. Nobody paid them any attention. "And I, too, once killed the wrong man."

George stopped and stared at Lepke, his eyes round and white in the ambient light. "You what?"

"When I was a soldier in the Philippines. I thought the man breaking into the storehouse was a saboteur and I shot him." Lepke shrugged. "He turned out to be a hungry man who needed food for his family."

"What happened?"

"Happened? They gave me another stripe for doing my duty! That was the day I decided not to be a soldier any longer. It did nothing to alleviate my guilt and shame."

"Maybe you do understand how I feel," George said.

The two men shuffled on toward morning.

112 —Taku Village, A.T., December 30, 1916— Saturday night

Williams followed Stella through the village. Moonlight reflecting off snow provided nearly enough light to read by. Although Williams felt nervous about this foray, he eagerly looked forward to talking and mixing with other people. Even if the people were mere savages.

"One 'a them Taku people told me about this party," Stella said.

"Yes, you mentioned that earlier," Williams said just loud enough to be heard.

"Don't talk to no one, though," she said quickly. "You don't sound like no Indian, from here or no wheres else."

A light breeze off the water cut at his ears and face like an icy razor. The humidity seemed to magnify the incessant growl of the stamp mills.

"We discussed that earlier, also." He decided if her fears grew any worse, he would return to their mine by himself. What if she became drunk and spoke of him to others?

"Maybe this isn't a good idea," he said. "I could give you money for another bottle and we could go back . . ."

"No! I wanna see somebody besides you. Don't worry. Everything's gonna be fine."

"You're sure there's no Auk Tlingits here?" he pressed. His hand wrapped around the knife in his pocket. It wasn't as good as the one he left on the boat, but it was the best Stella could come up with. The Luger lay hidden in the mine.

"Shouldn't be. They don't like each other too much." She stopped and peered ahead of them. "There it is."

A huge fire threw contorting shadows against the walls of what once had been three surrounding houses. The village had seen better days and what was left could only be described as dilapidated. A crowd of people milled about, talking, eating, drinking. Williams wondered if it was excitement or fear that made his heart beat faster. "Not much difference between them," he muttered.

"That's cause you're not an Indian!" Stella snapped.

He gave her a startled look. Her hearing obviously was more acute than she had let on. He filed the information away.

"Who's that?" a deep male voice challenged from the shadows.

Two huge Tlingits moved next to Williams, both carried clubs. Never before had he seen such large specimens of this race. This time when his heartbeat accelerated he knew it to be fear.

"He's with me!" Stella yelled, pushing herself between the Williams and the men. "Can't I bring a friend to this party?"

Both men peered down at her in the flickering light. "Oh, Stella," said one.

"Good to see you," said the other. "We're just making sure no white men get in here and arrest us for drinkin', you know?"

"Who's your friend?" the first man asked. Both men scrutinized Williams.

"He ain't from around here," she said quickly. "He's from down in the states. One a them Outside Indians."

"Where you from?" the first man asked.

Williams had researched American Red Indians before he left Prussia. "Oklahoma." He held out his hand. "Cherokee."

Both men gravely shook hands.

"Why'd you come up here?" the second man asked. "They can't treat you worse than they do here."

"Too much talk!" Stella shrilled. "Go guard. We want a drink."

Both men laughed and moved back into the shadows. Stella glanced up at Williams. "Pretty fast thinking for a Cherokee."

"Fast enough."

They moved closer to the fire. People called Stella's name and bottles were thrust into their hands. Stella immediately began talking to two women.

Williams sniffed at the bottle and found no odor. He took a sip and felt fire course down his throat and explode in his gullet. *"Gott sei Dank!"* he cried.

Stella honed in on him. "What's the matter? You're talking strange again."

"What is this stuff?" he hissed. "I think I've poisoned myself!"

She cackled. "First time you ever had hoochinoo? It's good stuff!" She took a long pull off her bottle and leered at him. "Try it again, 'Cherokee.'"

Williams watched her fall back into the discussion she had just left. He tasted the hoochinoo again. Until now he thought schnapps stood head and shoulders above other liquors in its ability to take away one's breath. This stuff approached suffocation!

He found himself chuckling and realized he felt at ease for the first time in months. *I needed this,* he thought.

A tall, lanky Indian wearing an out-of-fashion, but neat and clean, suit approached him. "Excuse me, but haven't we met some where before?"

Williams' euphoria vanished as he shook his head. "Cherokee," he said roughly. He glanced around but Stella had vanished in the growing throng.

"It's just that I know your face from somewhere. My name is Jee-nak, I live in Tasnit John's old house. Did you know Tasnit John?"

Williams realized the man was tipsy and probably wouldn't remember this conversation. His heart slowed back toward normal. "Don't know this village," he said, mimicking the diction he once heard a stage actor use when portraying a Red Indian. He glanced around for Stella again.

Jee-nak frowned. "Oh. I'm sorry if I bothered you." He turned and wandered away.

Williams tossed back some hoochinoo, gasped as the liquid lit off his gut. The euphoria washed back over him and he gazed about, smiling and enjoying this novel experience.

A sharp motion caught his eye and he focused on Jee-nak. The man stared hard at him. Williams watched recognition bloom in the man's face, followed quickly by something else, fear, or hate. He couldn't be sure. Jee-nak disappeared into the shadows.

Williams glanced around but could not see Stella or Jee-nak. Cursing, he pushed his way through the boisterous crowd. The stamp mills grumbled, predicting doom as he hurried back to the mine.

113 —Juneau City, A.T., New Year's Eve, 1916—
Sunday afternoon

"... then I shouted for him to surrender, or something." George rubbed his face with both hands looking up again. "I'm not sure what I said, but he went for the revolver on his hip, and I thought it was Williams, and he was going to try and kill me."

"And you fired," Lepke said.

"Yeah. I fired."

Harrington walked into the office and Lepke shifted his attention to the corporal. "What did you find out?"

"The coroner says the man has been dead for about a week. Killed by a single .30-.30 shot in the heart. The revolver was loaded and had a round in the chamber."

"Do we know his name?"

"Sven Halvorson, an out-of-work miner. Folks said he lost his job when he started hearing voices in the noise from the stamps."

"Voices? What did he think they said to him?"

Harrington pursed his lips and stared at George before he spoke. "That someone was trying to kill him."

"Mein Gott," Lepke said.

"The spirits were talking to him," George said. "That happens sometimes."

"Do they talk to you?" Lepke asked.

"No. I wish they would."

"You really thought he was going to shoot you?"

"Yeah, I really did."

Lepke chewed his lower lip, glanced at Harrington. "Is Chief Tinsley here?"

"No. He took the weekend off. I could ring him up if you want."

"Perhaps I should do the ringing." Lepke gripped George's shoulder. "You're not the first officer to go through this sort of thing. I'll be back in a few minutes."

George nodded and Lepke left the office. Harrington sat down and pushed some paper around on the desk. George felt used up. Empty.

The hate that drove him to kill an innocent man had been fueled by his energy. Now he felt limp and drained. Lepke was trying to keep him from being charged with murder.

Part of George found Lepke's attempt repellent, trying to stretch the law. The other part of George fervently hoped the man would pull it off. He thought about Irene.

His sister had been right about Jim's murderer killing two men. George shook his head. What to do now? How could he atone for the death of a troubled, innocent man?

Footsteps sounded outside the office. George and Harrington looked up, wondering what Lepke had to say, but it wasn't Lepke.

"Carson?" Harrington said to the first man.

"Jee-nak!" George blurted at sight of the second man. "What are you doing here?" Jee-nak looked exhausted and drawn his bleary eyes blinking quickly as he focused on George.

Carson spoke first, "This guy says he's got important information for Officer Mak-we. Said it couldn't wait—"

"Yes!" Jee-nak burst out. "I saw him last night! I came looking for you. Everyone said you had become sick in the mind over your nephew's death."

"You saw who?" George asked sharply.

"The killer. The one you hunt!"

Harrington raised his hand as if slowing traffic. "You saw Williams?"

"Yes!" Jee-nak grinned wildly and George realized the man teetered on the edge of collapse.

"Where?" George felt his heart quicken as energy flared though him.

"Wait a minute," Harrington said. "Let me get the lieutenant so we can all hear it from the beginning." He rushed out of the room. Carson shrugged and walked back to the front desk.

"Where?" George hissed.

"He was with Stella. The strange one who lives up the mountain there." Jee-nak pointed. "They came to a celebration in my village last night. He has changed his color."

George shot to his feet, shouldered past Jee-nak— and ran full into Lepke.

Lepke held his ground as George tried to push past. "George, you've already made one mistake. Don't make it two."

George stared at the lieutenant's face, recognizing stubborn resolution. He felt his energy dampen back to a smoldering core. "Sorry, August. You're right."

They sat in the small office and listened as Jee-nak told of the party, and of the uninvited guest. George stared through a window at Mt. Roberts. Somewhere up there . . .

". . . is where Stella lives." Jee-nak's unease revealed itself in the stiffness of his speech. "I asked some friends and they looked at me strangely, said I shouldn't mess with her because I was married. I told them I wasn't interested in her, but needed to know where she lived. They didn't believe me, they laughed and made rude jokes, but they told me how to find her place."

"Is it a cave or a mine shaft?" Lepke asked.

"They didn't say, but there aren't many caves around here, so it's probably a mine shaft."

Lepke pursed his lips and followed George's gaze. "Can you show us?"

"Could I have some water?" Jee-nak swallowed. "I'm pretty dry."

Lepke caught Harrington's attention and nodded. In moments the corporal returned with a glass. Jee-nak took his time drinking.

George watched his brother-in-law's tired eyes and knew when he made his decision.

"Yeah, I guess I could do that."

Although it was only early afternoon, dusk lay deep on the shadowed mountainside. The heavy rumble of the stamps roiled over them, a constant cauldron of noise. The heavy smell of moisture suffused the air; snow was imminent.

George carried his rifle, muzzle down, and watched where he put his feet. *Don't want to fall on my face.*

Jee-nak, unarmed and visibly uneasy, led the other four men up the forested slope. The men stretched across the steep flank like a slow-moving wave, each within sight of the man on either side of him. George, to Jee-nak's left, had Patrolman Smith to his own left.

Lepke and Corporal Harrington struggled uphill on Jee-nak's right. George wondered if Lepke should be doing this much work, what with his wound and all. George felt more clear-headed and sane than he had in weeks.

I hope we finish this today.

Jee-nak swiveled his head to the right, hesitating for a moment. Then he glanced over at George, speaking just loud enough to be heard, "The detective says he and the corporal smell smoke."

Despite the increasing cold, George's hands became sweaty inside his gloves. His thumb caressed the hammer on the .30-.30 but he resisted the urge to cock it.

In front of them the forest thickened and he realized they approached a barely concealed rock face. They were close to the mine. Close to Williams.

A trail wound through the trees. Boot prints, one set large, the other smaller, ran in both directions through the three-day-old snow. *Finally*, George thought, *the right trail.*

"There." Jee-nak's voice carried relief.

As George and the policemen peered through the gaunt brush at a large dark opening in the mountain, Jee-nak turned downhill and disappeared into the growing night.

The opening seeped inky black. Nothing could be discerned in the vast blot. George glanced at Lepke who motioned him forward. The two policemen already approached the lieutenant.

"Okay," Lepke said staring at each man in turn, his eyes nearly luminous in the darkening woods, "here's what we're gonna do . . ."

Moments later George eased through the brush back to his earlier position. Patrolman Smith brushed George's elbow as he passed. Movement ceased.

"Williams!" Lepke's shout startled George even though he anticipated. "It's over. Time for you to come out!"

A breeze moved through the trees, causing branches to stab and scrape at each other.

"You're badly out-numbered, Williams." Lepke's voice edged back toward conversational. "You'll never get past us."

The breeze freshened, blowing snow off the branches onto them. After a moment's hesitation the breeze increased into a light wind and the snow thickened. George realized they stood in the beginning of a snowstorm.

"Harrington," Lepke said in the darkness. A battery lamp clicked on and a stream of brilliance bathed the mouth of the cave. Stark shadows spilled across the ceiling and one wall of the professionally cut mine shaft.

"Williams! In one minute we're going to fill that opening with a hail of bullets. Do you, a soldier of the kaiser, want to be wounded or killed by a ricochet? That's much less heroic than surrendering."

The thought suddenly struck George they had been suckered again. That nobody was in there. Or else it was another trap.

"Cut the bloody light!" The mine amplified Williams' voice, lending it the resonance of a deity.

"Jesus," Smith said. "He's really in there!"

George's sliver of guilt over his doubt evaporated.

The lamp winked off, leaving a blackness so profound it threatened to absorb them. Snow sped past George's face. He cocked his rifle and heard three metallic echoes.

"I'm going to light a cheroot, Lepke. Okay? I want to have one last smoke as a free man." The voice easily drowned out the stamp mills.

"Go ahead, Williams." Lepke sounded official. "But if you try anything, we'll kill you dead."

"Oh, I've no doubt about that." A match flared and they clearly saw Williams puff a cheroot into life. George also glimpsed a low wall of loose rock spanning the mine entrance before the match died.

Patrolman Smith shifted his feet and George glanced at the noise, saw the man crouch over, quivering like a cat, ready to sprint into the cave.

The end of the cheroot glowed in the blackness. George couldn't help but think how easy it would be to aim just behind that gleaming coal and blow Williams' head into mush.

"Talk to me, Williams," Lepke ordered.

Silence.

Only George heard Patrolman Smith's whisper, "That son-of-a-bitch is gonna get away."

The red gleam moved slowly downward.

"Williams, I mean it!" Lepke thundered.

A gust of wind swirled snow round them and the gleam brightened momentarily. George suddenly understood.

Patrolman Smith sprayed snow and grit behind him as he charged toward the opening. "He's trying to escape! I'll get him!"

"No! Get away!" George screamed. "That's a fuse!" He turned and ran back through the trees and clinging brush. He heard oaths and grunts around him as the others followed.

A slam of bright air so loud it lacked sound threw him through the trees into deeper blackness.

114 —Juneau City, A.T., New Year's Day, 1917—
Monday morning —

Florence Malone bent into the wind, struggling through the deepening snow as she made her way up the hill to St. Ann's Hospital. Walking into the warm interior felt like a dream come true. A nun ghosted up to her.

"Good morning, Miss Malone. Are you here to see Lieutenant Lepke?"

"Good morning, Sister Alphonse Marie." Florence removed her headscarf and shook bits of ice and snow off onto the floor. "Yes, I am. Which room is he in, please?"

"Two fourteen. Why don't you take the elevator?"

Florence smiled her thanks and took the advice. As she walked into August's room, she heard Dr. Parker say, "If you'd hit that tree any harder, it would have killed you."

She quietly stopped just inside the door. Dr. Parker continued unwrapping the bandage around August's head. He carefully examined the scraped and bruised part that had partially stopped Lepke's flight through winter air. His chest had taken the rest of the impact.

"How does it look, doctor?" she asked.

Dr. Parker glanced over his shoulder at her, flashing a grin. "Ah, you can't hurt a Dutchman by hitting his head. He took a blow that would have probably killed you or me and it barely gave him a concussion."

"Did it traumatize his gunshot wound?"

"No. I don't think so, but I want him to stay here for a couple of days just to make sure."

Lepke laughed. "I feel like a prize hog or something. Does anybody talk to me yet?"

Florence thinly echoed his laugh. "How are you, August?"

"Dr. Parker says I'll live. To be honest, I feel pretty good considering what happened."

"There's a rumor going about that Patrolman Smith is dead. That he was . . ." she hesitated, not sure of how much to ask at this point.

"Patrolman Smith had the misfortune to be charging when he should have been retreating," August said slowly. "Our rescuers believe they found all of him."

Florence squeezed her eyes shut and shuddered. "Any sign of that Williams animal?"

"No."

Dr. Parker efficiently finished rewrapping August's head. "There we are. You're doing fine, Mr. Lepke. If the pain seems to increase or if you suddenly feel pressure inside your head, have the nurse fetch me at once. Frankly, I think you're out of the woods in more ways than one."

He nodded to Florence as he went out into the hall. She pulled the door shut behind him. "So how are you really?"

"Sick at heart, if know you must."

"Why? Williams fooled everyone there."

"I was in charge. I gave him leave to smoke a last cheroot. I allowed him to kill a good man and maim two others as well as myself."

"How's George?"

"Dr. Parker says he's going to lose his left leg from the knee down."

"Jesus, Mary, and Joseph," Florence said in a low tone.

"I think I feel worse about it than he does," August said.

"What do you mean?"

"He feels losing his leg is penance for . . ." August stared through the window blinds at the thick snow flying sideways.

"For what?"

"For his sins, I guess. He's done nothing the rest of us haven't done on occasion."

"August, you're not making sense."

"Must be the stuff Dr. Parker gave me for pain. I'm talking too much."

How can he talk too much to me? Florence wondered, feeling a pang of emotional pain. *He's being evasive, hiding something from me about George. Perhaps he's protecting George?*

"Should I leave and allow you to rest, darling?"

"I am grateful for your visit, please understand, but I feel so very, how to say, emptied out?"

"Drained?" she supplied with a forced smile.

"*Ja*, drained is it."

Florence moved to him. She rubbed his brow as his eyes fluttered and closed. "Go ahead and sleep, my love."

He fell asleep at once. She examined him critically. *Far too thin,* she decided, *and all the new bandages with him barely over being shot last year!*

She felt hot tears collect in the corners of her eyes.

Would he always be like this? Constantly courting death and suffering injury to deal with people who in the long run didn't possess as much goodness in their whole body as he did in his little finger?

She pulled the covers up around his neck and left the room.

115 —Juneau City, A.T., January 2, 1917—
Tuesday afternoon

Jack Malone hurried along Lower Front Street, cursing. What with the election and all, he had completely forgotten about the purloined explosives he held in trust for the German agent. Since 1917 started the temperature hovered in the low 20s and Jack wore his heaviest overcoat and warmest wool muffler with his trademark fedora.

Carefully, he turned the corner and stepped into the shadowed alley leading to the warehouse. The tang of salt air became more pronounced and for some reason the gloomy alley felt colder than the well-lit street.

Jack owned the small warehouse, one of his many, but didn't advertise the fact. A man never knew when he might need a good amount of space out of the public eye. "Or give 'im enough rope ta hang himself," he muttered.

When he saw the door, he fumbled in his pocket for his key chain. By the time he sorted through the keys by feel and hurriedly put his gloves back on, he stood in front of the door. He reached down to grasp the lock, and it wasn't there.

"Sweet Jesus!" he said as his mind filled with foreboding. He pushed the door open and stood in the frosty interior while his hand patted the wall seeking the light switch. Once found, he snapped it up.

Various boxes and crates sat around the space. The tarp, which once covered the dynamite, lay crumpled on the floor. Sean Clancy's six cases of dynamite were gone.

Jack's knees went weak and he abruptly plopped down on a wooden crate. He felt his heart thumping in his chest as he ignored the bitter cold seeping though his pants and into his ample hindquarters. A multitude of ramifications cascaded through his mind.

Where could that damn German have hidden the stuff? he wondered. *How did he move six cases out of here without someone seeing him? Did he have other confederates? Were there more crazed, desperate men bent on destruction here in Juneau City?*

"I'm an accessory," Jack moaned. "I'm responsible for that policeman's death, for George Mak-we's leg . . ."

Not used to situations where he didn't have at least a modicum of control, Jack felt deflated and betrayed. His mind raced as he examined his options, rejecting one after another. Finally he arrived at the truth of the matter: There was absolutely no way he could fix this, change it, or make it right.

Jack sat watching his breath fog and dissipate, feeling defeat and the weight of his years.

THE DAILY ALASKA DISPATCH
Juneau, Alaska, Wednesday, January 10, 1917

JUNEAU MAY BE ALASKA OFFICE FOR 450 MILLION SYNDICATE

PROHIBITION FOR ALASKA TO BE HEARD

ODESSA IS GOAL OF TEUTONS

WOMEN ARE AFTER WILSON FOR SUFFRAGE

WHAT MAY BE EXPRECTED FROM AUSTRIAN RULER

CODY FIGHTS HIS LAST FIGHT WITH BRAVERY
FAMOUS OLD PIONEER MAKING A GAME FIGHT

Denver, Jan. 9—Buffalo Bill is resting easy, says his physician at midnight. Although in a comatose condition, he may live several days. His physician declares that he will survive at least twelve more hours.

116 —Juneau City, A.T., January 15, 1917—
Monday morning

Amanda Ganbor, ignoring her aching back, forced herself to smile at the two miners who staggered up to the lunch counter. "What will it be, gentlemen?"

"We'll hev th' beer, 'n' whar's the free lunch?" said one.

"Yeah," muttered the other. "Where's the free lunch?"

"I'm sorry. This isn't a saloon, it's a cafe. We don't serve beer or give away food."

The first peered down at her ample belly under the stained white apron. "Look's like ya gave sumpthin' away, honey!"

Before she could respond, Rev. James Thistle grasped both men by their collars and lifted them off the floor. "If you've nothing better to do than plague this hard-working woman," he said, slamming them together like a pair of cymbals, their heads connecting with a melon-like *thonk*, ". . . you can do it somewhere else!"

He smacked their heads together a second time, pushing the front door open with the larger of the two, and threw them in a moaning heap on the icy boardwalk.

Amanda smiled tiredly at him as he walked back into the room still muttering. "A couple of months ago I could have managed them myself," she said. "Thanks for the assistance."

"You should be getting more rest, Amanda. That child is due in little more than a month."

"Do I shock you by not hiding my condition, Reverend Thistle?"

"You worry me because you're not taking care of yourself."

"I own a cafe. It makes a very slim profit. I need to be here."

"Money isn't everything. There's your health—"

"Through the generosity of two fine women, I have something," she said, her tone fierce, "and that something isn't just a cafe, it's security. I didn't have to marry some tottering old fool, or some young horse's ass to attain it.

"This child," she grabbed her burgeoning stomach, ". . . and the Line Cafe are all I have in the world. I'm going to do right by both of them."

"Of course you are," he said. His jaw tightened and his eyes seemed to glint and sparkle. "That's exactly why you're going to hire me as manager, effective immediately."

"James, this isn't theology. What do you know about running a cafe?"

"It's nearly as difficult as running a large restaurant. Like the one my parents own in Pittsburg. The one I worked in full time from the time I was eight years old until I entered seminary, and worked there every summer until I graduated."

Amanda tried not to show her amazement. "Pittsburgh; that's a rather large city, isn't it?"

"Quite. The Thistledown Restaurant can hold one hundred twenty diners indoors and another eighty outdoors, weather permitting. I've been everything from dishwasher to cook's assistant to cashier to maitre 'd. I could run this place with one arm tied behind my back."

"I couldn't pay you much . . ."

"Three squares a day and I sleep on the cot in the back, plus seven dollars a week."

"You drive a hard bargain. You also have to take off the reversed collar while you're on duty."

He stared at her for a moment and then looked up at the ceiling. It's just for awhile," he said to the lights.

"Your parents truly own a large restaurant in a large city. You're not just making this up?"

His electric eyes held hers. "I'll never lie to you. Not now, not ever. Yes, my parents own a large, prosperous restaurant in Pittsburg, Pennsylvania, USA. In fact, I want to make some changes in here I believe will improve business."

Amanda grinned at him. "You are rather amazing, James. Do as you will. You're the manager."

"You won't regret this."

"I'm sure I won't. Now take over. I'm going upstairs and take a nap."

"Bully." He unhooked his collar and pulled off his jacket. "Charlie Payne," he shouted to the cook. "Please get two cups of coffee and come in here. We have much to discuss."

117 —Juneau City, A.T., January 19, 1917—
Friday morning

George Mak-we drifted in and out of consciousness. Each time he woke, he wished the pain in his damaged leg would go away. Every time he drifted into sleep he saw the burning fuse, felt the panic well up in his chest, felt his body flying through the darkness until his leg hit the tree.

At least I'm not dead, he thought. He remembered being shocked awake when the rescue team put him on the stretcher. He also remembered one of the men vomiting when he found a piece of Patrolman Smith.

George knew his pain would be much worse if not for the laudanum. Still, it felt like sharp-toothed animals constantly chewed on his left leg. No amount of opiate could completely suppress the pain.

The only thing that hurt worse was the pain in his heart when he thought about Julia and Jeff. and the child he and Julia had made together. Late March, he remembered, was when he would become a father.

A tear slipped from his left eye. He didn't even know where they had gone. Ketchikan to the south and Klukwan to the north encompassed the entirety of his known world.

San Francisco was as remote to him as China, or the Moon.

Dr. Parker's voice cut through his reverie. "George, how are you feeling today?"

"My leg hurts a lot, doctor. Other than that, I feel pretty good."

Dr. Parker pulled up the blanket and felt the bandage tightly wrapped around the injured limb. "It's hot, George. I think I know what I'm going to find when I take the bandage off."

"It isn't going to be good news, is it?"

"From here," Parker touched his leg just below the knee, " . . . on down, has to come off."

"Or I'll die," George said.

"Or you'll die."

"How soon do you want to do it?"

"I have the surgery being prepared right now. All I need is your approval."

"You're one of two white men I trust. If you say that leg's gotta come off, you take it."

"I feel honored, Officer Mak-we." He began unwrapping the bandage.

118 —Juneau City, A.T., January 17, 1917—
Wednesday afternoon

Weak and famished, Arnold Williams stumbled down the mineshaft toward the growing light. The clear sky and sun edging behind the mountains on Douglas Island nearly blinded him when he finally emerged into cold open air. He wondered what day it was.

How long ago had it been since he ambushed the verdammte police with his dynamite bomb? How many of them he had killed? Everybody, he hoped. Especially Lepke.

Hunger painfully enveloped him like a cloud of mosquitoes. He peered about in the fading snowy afternoon, wondering exactly where he was in relationship to Juneau City. Long before he killed her, Stella had told him about the small portal that offered a back way out of the mineshaft.

If it had not been for her insistence on attending the drunken bacchanal in the Taku Village, they would both still be safe in the mineshaft.

By the time she returned to the camp, his anger had escalated beyond reason. He waited silently in the dark for her.

When she finally stumbled into the shaft opening, calling his name and giggling, he said nothing. She mumbled and sang incessantly. Once she slipped and fell, where she lay laughing for minutes.

He waited. His smoldering anger fanned by her excesses, her foolishness, her total disregard for his safety. Finally she found the oil lamp and put fire to it. As soon as she sat the lamp down on its ledge, he seized her by the throat.

"You have endangered my being and my mission for the last time!" he said in German as he throttled the life out of her. She feebly grasped at his hands, trying to pull them away from her throat. Her brain lacked sufficient oxygen to carry out complicated actions and she sagged in his grip as he crushed her larynx.

His hands clenched, remembering her throat, and he slowly moved downhill through the woods. A name burned in his brain. He must find the man, Jee-nak.

This Jee-nak person has directed the police to me, and has threatened my mission. Somehow the man knows who I am, despite the dark stain covering my skin. First food, then Jee-nak.

Wood smoke wafted across his nose, accompanied by a hint of cooking food. Saliva flooded Williams' mouth and his stomach clenched painfully in response. Trying to hurry, he tripped on a snow-covered root and fell flat on his face.

Quietly, he pulled himself to his feet and carefully threaded down through the trees, following the smoke. A small shack sat at the edge of a modest clearing. A path led down slope. At the bottom he could see the waters of Gastineau Channel reflecting the steel blue of the darkening sky.

Williams eased up to the shack, his soldier's eyes gathering information as he moved. Footprints in the snow led in two directions, down the path, and over to the simple privy. A thump sounded inside the shack and Williams flattened against the wall.

The door banged open and a man lurched down the three steps into the yard and shambled toward the privy. Williams glanced about and spied a snow-covered woodpile, disturbed only at the end closest to the door. He bent and found a section of tree limb about two feet long.

The smell of cooking food encompassed him, pulling at his attention. His stomach grumbled so loudly he feared the man in the privy might hear. He edged around the back of the shack and waited.

In moments the man emerged and grabbed a handful of snow as the privy door swung shut behind him. He scrubbed his hands absently with the snow as he slogged back to the shack.

Williams decided the man had a few more years than him, was maybe a few centimeters taller, but somewhat thinner. No matter. As the man crossed in front of the shack, Williams ran swiftly up behind him.

The man grasped the door handle. With the thick piece of branch, Williams hit him in the back of the head where the neck joins the skull. Without a sound the man crumpled and fell beside the steps.

Williams went through the door without a second look at his victim. His peripheral vision noted the unkempt mess, which served as a bed, and the general clutter of a man who lives alone and doesn't care about order. His attention fixed on the small wood stove with the cast iron skillet that popped and crackled with cooking food.

The skillet contained eggs mixed with small pieces of potatoes and meat. It smelled heavenly. Williams grabbed the handle in his left hand and screamed when the metal burned his skin.

He looked wildly about for a rag, something, anything. He found a wad of soiled cloth on the stained table and used it as a hot pad. He set the pan on the dirty oilcloth covering the table and searched until he found a fork.

The food was absolutely the best meal he had ever eaten. After a few mouthfuls he noticed the bubbling coffee pot on the back of the stove. Within a half hour he felt completely restored.

After dragging the corpse behind the shack he took stock of his situation. He found a trunk of clothes and selected a wool shirt and wool trousers, both clean, *Gott sei dank*. A heavy coat smelling of fish and a checkered wool hat with earflaps fit better than the shirt and trousers.

Elation rushed through him when he found the nine-inch fish knife. Between that and his Luger, once again, he felt formidable.

Williams hadn't shaved since the night of the *Indianer* party and his beard approached derelict proportions. He examined himself in a fragment of mirror nailed to the wall. The reflection didn't resemble the journalist, Arnold Williams, in the slightest.

In fact, he looked quite mad.

Descending the trail proved much easier than going through the forest. The closer he came to the channel, the louder the stamp mills became. Having been inside the mountain and away from the constant noise, it now irritated him more than ever.

Across the channel the Treadwell complex and Douglas gleamed with hundreds of lights. He realized he was south of Juneau City, nearly to Thane. Excellent! He was less than a half-mile from his hidden dynamite.

He slowed as he neared Gastineau Channel. Somewhere along here he would encounter Thane Road and possible traffic.

In moments he stood in the middle of the frozen, rutted road. Nothing moved along it in either direction as far as he could see. Still, he reasoned, it would be better to go on down to the beach and walk on the tide flats. He needed to think out his next move, as well as plan the death of Jee-nak.

The beach seemed easier walking than the road had offered, and Williams made good time. In less than a half hour he could see the first weathered plank houses of the Taku Village at the edge of the high tide line. He eased into the trees.

How to find where this Jee-nak lived? He ran his right hand lovingly over the Luger in his coat pocket. The fish knife and its sheath fit quite nicely next to the pistol.

Keeping to the edge of the trees and brush, Williams moved quietly toward the village. Perhaps luck would favor him and he would locate his quarry without speaking to anyone else. The thought hadn't completely cleared his mind when the first dog barked sharply.

Suddenly a pack of half-wild dogs burst out of the trees at him, yapping and growling. He bent and grabbed a piece of driftwood, swung it at the animals who danced back out of range, barking even harder.

No good, this is no good, he thought. One of the larger curs made a lunge for his leg and Williams smashed the wood down on the dog's head, dropping it instantly. For a moment the other six retreated before renewing their assault.

Williams swung at another dog, but missed. *They learn quickly,* he thought. For a moment he played with the idea of shooting them, but quickly dismissed the thought. *Only if it comes to my survival,* he decided.

"What's going on over there?" a voice shouted.

Williams looked up into the face of Jee-nak, a mere ten meters away. Jee-nak frowned at Williams. "Who are you? What are you doing there?"

He doesn't recognize me! Williams fought to keep from smiling. He released the club and waved for Jee-nak to come over as he grasped the Luger still in the coat pocket.

The dogs, recognizing a familiar voice, dropped back into the trees. Williams followed the animals with a glance. They waited three meters back in the woods and brush. No easy retreat there.

"What do you want?" Jee-nak shouted. "Why don't you speak?"

Williams waved again and Jee-nak took a step toward him. Williams waited and Jee-nak stopped, staring hard. "By the Raven!" he blurted. "It's you!"

Williams jerked the Luger clear of his pocket as Jee-nak turned and ran toward the house. Williams took careful aim and squeezed the trigger. Jee-nak abruptly turned to the right as the weapon fired. A chunk of wood flew from the side of the house.

Jee-nak disappeared. The dogs also disappeared into the trees as soon as the gun fired. Cursing, Williams turned and ran back down the beach toward his dynamite cache.

THE DAILY ALASKA DISPATCH
Juneau, Alaska, Wednesday, January 31, 1917

WORLD PEACE DEBATE IS ON IN U.S. SENATE

$402,000,000 REVENUE BILL UP IN HOUSE

BLIZZARD RAGING OVER NORTHWEST

CRUISER SUNK MINE EXPLOSION

YOUNG FIGHTER KILLED WITH HEART BLOW

SCANDAL IS COMING SURE OVER LEAK
**At Last House Rules Committee Lays
Hands-on Evidence Involving
President's Brother-in-Law in Leak**

IRENE SHERMAN PROGRESSING NICELY
The grafting of skin from the body of her father to that of Irene Sherman, the little girl who was so badly burned recently at Fairbanks, was successfully undertaken at St. Joseph's Hospital at that place and the child is progressing nicely.

119 —Juneau City, A.T., February 5, 1917—
Monday afternoon

Fiona Malone added the column of figures a second time and smiled when the tally mirrored the first. *The secret to running a successful business was mathematics,* she decided. In addition to honest help.

The second part was the more difficult of the two. Last week Fiona had discovered that Carol, the housekeeping maid who had worked for Maye for over five years, was stealing from the hotel. Anger burned through her all over again at the thought of it.

The door opened and a figure bundled against the cold came in. For a moment Fiona remembered the day, over a year ago already, that she met August, Amanda, and that horrible Pete Sommers— all in the space of an hour. She refocused on the person approaching the desk.

A woman, Fiona decided, somewhat smaller than herself. The woman unwrapped a scarf from around her neck and face, an Indian. Fiona caught a glimpse of scar tissue on the neck and chin.

"May I help you?" Fiona realized she was hardly more than a girl.

"Are you Miss Malone?"

"Yes. I am Fiona Malone."

The girl smiled and held out her hand. "I am pleased to meet you. I am Ruth Kisadis Santos. Your sister attended my wedding."

"Oh, of course. I'm so pleased to meet you. It must be thrilling to be the wife of a hero."

Ruth shrugged. "I am proud of Begay, but most people have already forgotten his actions."

"I haven't, nor has my sister, I assure you."

"I heard you were looking for a housekeeper."

"That's true, but I didn't realize it was common knowledge."

"There are no secrets in this town," Ruth said, shrugging again. "I would like to apply for the position."

"You don't even know what it pays."

"It's also no secret the Malones are straight people. I'm sure you pay a fair wage. I am a good worker, and I'm also honest. I won't steal from you."

"The position includes making beds, washing and hanging laundry, pressing sheets, folding laundry, emptying chamber pots, and sweeping and scrubbing floors. The wage is a dollar fifty a day. This is hard work, Ruth, and I know you're pregnant."

"I can do the work, Miss Malone, and I'd like the position."

Fiona smiled. "I know you can do the work. The job is yours with one proviso."

"What's that?"

"You call me 'Fiona.'"

Ruth smiled, showing beautiful, white teeth. "Thank you, Mi- I mean, Fiona."

"Do you want to start today or tomorrow?"

Ruth pulled off her coat. "What needs to be done?"

Fiona gave Ruth a tour of the building, outlining each task. "I think that covers the immediate situation, Ruth. If you have any questions, just ask."

"Okay, Fiona."

Fiona heard the front door open and hurried out to the desk. Rev. James Thistle stood there.

"Is there something I can do for you, Rev. Thistle?" Fiona asked.

"Yes, there is. Pardon me for leaping into the middle of this without the usual amenities, but I need to get back to the cafe and haven't much time."

"Go right ahead, is something wrong?"

"She won't marry me. Why not?"

"You are referring to Amanda?"

"Of course! Please don't make light of this."

"I'm sorry. I don't mean to be cruel. I'm sure Amanda will marry you— if she marries anybody."

"I love her. I want to give that child a name. Why is she treating me this way?"

Fiona wanted to hug him and assure him everything would work out, but she felt as much at sea about this as he did.

"She's had some bad luck with men. Give her a little more time and I'm sure she'll—"

"More time? She's almost out of time before she becomes a mother." With visible effort he stopped and took a deep breath. "Pardon me for being so emphatic, Fiona. I'm at wit's end. I just don't know what else to do."

"James, all you can do is be there. When the moment arrives and she realizes your worth, you just sweep her off to the altar."

James Thistle stared at her, shook his head and went back to work, muttering under his breath.

120 —Juneau City, A.T., February 10, 1917—
Saturday afternoon

Edward Krause, deep into the philosophy book, jerked in surprise at the jailer's voice, "You got a visitor, Krause." He glanced up, wondering who the old man was. He looked like a bum.

"What do you want of me? Do you think I killed somebody you cared about?"

The old man glanced over his shoulder at the retreating turnkey and sat down on the bench on the other side of the bars. He leaned forward, reducing the distance between their faces to less than half a meter, said in German, "You do not recognize me. That is good."

Krause took in the foul smelling overcoat, the woodsman's dog-eared cap, the frayed trousers and shirt. He shrugged. "You somebody I know from Petersburg? Maybe I bought you a beer once?"

"I need you out here with me. I need you to earn the money the Fatherland has spent on you."

Krause stared at the face, delving behind the scruffy beard, the spotty complexion, putting one name after another to the face— none of which fit. "Maybe you better tell me who the hell you are so we can get on with this conversation."

"The last time I was here, you thought I was an English journalist."

Krause blinked in surprise. "That's a hell of a disguise you got there, Mr.—"

"*Don't* say my name," the man said quickly.

"Tell ya the truth," Krause said. "I'm not real sure I know it."

"You don't. As long as you are a prisoner you will remain ignorant of my true identity. But we are going to change that."

"Change what?"

"Your status. Do you want to be free?"

Krause leaned forward so his forehead touched the bars. He whispered harshly, "You have no idea how badly I want to be out of here. These fools have already sentenced me to fifty-eight years and the murder trial will be finished soon. It doesn't take a genius to guess what they will give me for that."

"Then you are willing to help me in return for your freedom?"

"You bet your whiskers I am. What do you want done?"

"I have over five cases of dynamite. We are going to blow a hole in the Treadwell Mine so the ocean pours in and destroys it. I need the help of a dedicated son of Germany to help me."

"Blow the Treadwell?" Krause said. He started to add "Are you crazy?" when he noticed the man's eyes. They burned with more zealotry than he had ever seen before in his life. Wrong question.

"Blow the Treadwell," Krause said again in a studied manner. "You got this thing all planned out?"

"Yes, but I need you out here. Take this, quickly."

Krause swiftly grabbed the small, cloth-wrapped bundle thrust through the bars. He made it disappear.

"Thanks, friend. Do we have a time table for this break out?"

"Begin working on the bars. I will visit again to tell you when the time is right. It shall be soon. Very soon."

Krause stared into the man's face, desperately trying to remember everything he knew about him, wondering how difficult it was going to be to get clear of him once he was outside this damn jail.

"I'll be waiting right here. You say the word and I'm all action."

"After we blow the mine, we kill Lepke."

Krause felt a surge of hate rush through him. "Now that will be an unmitigated pleasure!"

"Gut! Gott mit uns!" The man stood and shambled away.

Whatever you say, mister, Krause thought. *Whatever you say.*

121 —Juneau City, A.T., February 15, 1917—
Thursday afternoon

Amanda Ganbor hovered on the edge of exhaustion. Her feet hurt, her back ached, and her baby kept kicking her bladder. The regular waitress had slipped on an icy walk and sprained her ankle.

Amanda already knew a pregnant waitress would drive off more custom than not. So she took over dish washing while the nineteen-year-old Filipino, Ponce Bagio, waited tables. She watched him move quickly and efficiently among the customers deciding his talents were wasted back here in the deep sink. But then, whose wasn't?

James bustled in the back door with two sacks of groceries from George Brothers Market. "Begay sends his best."

"How very sweet of him," Amanda said, trying to get a burned spot off a kettle. "Remind me to talk to Eric about the benefits of stirring more often."

"I'm not sure he would hear you. He seems to march to a different drummer."

Amanda smiled. What James said was true. Eric, their scarecrow-of-a-man cook created magic in the kitchen, but he seemed to be in his own world, rarely hearing advice or instruction, let alone heeding it.

Amanda balanced the kettle on the edge of the sink and began to really lay into the spot. The pot slipped, her arm hit a ladle sticking out of the soapy water. The container hit the floor and the ladle splashed water over her.

She squatted to pick up the kettle and felt pressure abruptly shift in her abdomen. Her undergarments became sodden and for a moment she believed the water had come from the sink.

"Oh! James! My water broke!"

"You broke what?" he said, hurrying to her side.

"The baby is coming," she said, still squatting.

"Oh. Here, let me help you upstairs."

Amanda stood, felt things shifting, moving inside her. The urge to push overwhelmed her and the corresponding contraction staggered her. "I need to sit, or lie down, at once," she gasped.

James pushed open the door to the storeroom where his cot and belongings occupied one wall. He carried her in and laid her on the cot. "Be still, I'll get help."

"Call Dr. Parker," she said through a groan.

He ran to the telephone, jamming the earpiece against his ear, and cranking the handle twice. "Operator?" he shouted into the mouthpiece. "Get me Dr. Parker immediately. This is an emergency!"

Contractions rippled through Amanda like the waves of a rapidly incoming tide. Every contraction violently wrenched her muscles and she grimly suppressed the urge to scream. Sweat poured down her face and arms as she panted with the exertion.

"James, I thi— aaahh!" The contractions seemed far too close for this early in the birth. Dr. Parker told her the contractions would be many minutes apart in the beginning.

"The doctor is on his way, Amanda," James said in a quavering voice. "What can I do for you?"

"Get Fiona! She— aaahh!"

James ran out the door. Ponce filled the door. "Miss Ganbor, can I be of help?"

"Shut the cafe," she gasped. "Then, uuhnn, go home."

"I can't leave you like this!"

"Out!" she screamed.

Another contraction wrenched through her and she heard a high, thin keening. She realized it was her own voice.

Cool hands on her forehead. "I'm here, Amanda!" Fiona snapped orders to people Amanda couldn't see or didn't care about. "Clean, hot water, lots of it. Now!"

"Amanda, listen to me," James said with full baritone authority. "You must marry me, now."

The thought bounced above the next two waves of pain. *Why have I hesitated this long?* she wondered. For some reason she couldn't object further.

"Yesss!" she said, riding the pain.

She felt her drawers stripped away, hearing the slap as they wetly hit the floor. Her outer clothing vanished and clean sheets magically appeared over her. She stared down at her thinly veiled belly and watched in amazement as muscles in her upper torso suddenly rose up and rolled smoothly downward into a wave of pain.

"That's amazing!" she gasped.

Fiona appeared above her. "Dr. Parker is here."

"Miss Ganbor, you seem to be quite far along," Dr. Parker said in a chiding tone. "Why didn't you call for me an hour ago?"

"Only been minutes," she said, panting.

James pushed into the small room. "Make way there. I've got a minister!"

Amanda laughed, feeling dreamy and disconnected. Ministers bearing ministers. What next? Another contraction twisted the mirth out of her.

"Damn it, I want this to stop," she screamed.

"Amanda, do you know who I am?"

She peered into the worried face of the Salvation Army man who worked with the poor on Lower Front Street. "Of course I do, Captain Van Zee. How are you?"

He smiled. "James wants me to marry the two of you. Do you agree?"

Amanda moved her eyes over to James, who stared down at her with a look closer to horror than love. "Sure. Why not?"

"We are gathered here in the sight of God and those present to join this man and this woman in holy matrimony . . ."

Amanda panted through the next contraction and fought the urge to push.

"I do," James said, beaming at Amanda with tear-filled eyes.

She smiled at him, finally allowing herself to believe this good man. *Such a handsome man.*

"Amanda?" Capt. Van Zee said.

"What?"

"Do you take James to be your lawfully wedded husband, to have and to hold, in sickness and in health, from this day forward for as long as you both shall live?"

She opened her mouth to respond and the contraction seemed to tear her in half. "I, aaaahhhh! Do!"

Capt. Van Zee said something else but Amanda missed it while fighting for her sanity. James kissed her fervently, surprising her. She returned the kiss and smiled as he pulled back.

"Now that child's name is Thistle," he said.

"Amanda," Dr. Parker said in an urgent voice. "I want you to push, now."

She pushed, feeling as if she were blocked with concrete.

"Again, harder!" Dr. Parker ordered.

"It's crowning," Fiona said.

Amanda moaned, entering the pain, letting it wash around and over her. She pushed with all of her strength despite the ripping, tearing sensation in her lower extremities blossoming into a white-hot sear of agony.

Release!

"Look at the hair!" Fiona exclaimed. "Oh, Amanda," she said laying an impossibly small, wrapped form on Amanda's chest, "it's a beautiful baby girl."

Amanda pushed the blanket away from the tiny, wizened face. "She's all slimy and red underneath. Will that change?"

Dr. Parker laughed. "Once we get her cleaned up, she'll be so beautiful she'll take your breath away."

The newborn clenched her perfect, miniature hands, opened her blue eyes, and stared at her mother.

"Hello, Fiona Maye Thistle," Amanda whispered. "Welcome to the world."

122 —Juneau City, A.T., February 17, 1917—
Saturday afternoon

Edward Krause, dressed in a blue suit, and feeling oddly naked without his mustache, stood in front of Judge Robert W. Jennings.

He had seen a lot of the judge over the past year. Far more than he wished. Yesterday the foreman of the jury had announced a verdict of guilty in the murder of James O. Plunkett. How this band of rabble could have detected his actions and motives without understanding the obvious philosophy of the situation was beneath contempt. Kazis Krauczunas, his lawyer, had tried every legal maneuver in his repertoire to stall the sentencing, including asking for a retrial and a postponement until Monday. All had failed.

Have you anything to say before I pass sentence?" Judge Jennings asked.

They weren't going to sleep unquestioning, he decided, *I'll make them wonder until their dying days.*

"Just a few words. I am about to be sentenced to death upon the verdict of a prejudiced jury and the false testimony of Kohn, Garfield, and McCaul. Garfield was mistaken in his evidence about the letter and I have never been in McCaul's.

"My request for a change of venue was denied. If Plunkett is dead I had nothing whatsoever to do with it." He stopped himself, knowing that he would shriek and curse at them if he continued. It didn't matter; the crazy saboteur was going to spring him.

Judge Jennings spoke in a soft, modulated tone that carried an expression of pathos. "It is the judgment of the court that on the eleventh day of May, 1917, you be taken by the United States Marshal for the first District of Alaska and be hanged by the neck until you are dead. May God have mercy on your soul."

123 —Juneau City, A.T., February 20, 1917—
Tuesday afternoon

August Lepke and Florence Malone felt grateful for the warmth inside St. Ann's Hospital. Sister Alphonse Marie walked up to them.

"It's nice to see you in here as a visitor rather than as a patient, Lieutenant Lepke."

"Thank you, Sister. It does seem rather strange."

"Good evening, Sister," Florence said. "Could we see George Mak-we?"

"Of course. He's in one twenty, just down the hall there."

George lay staring out the frosty window. He rolled his head over, regarding them quietly as they entered the room. "All right, are you really there or is this a medicine dream?"

"If you're talking to us," Lepke said with a wide grin, "...we're very much real."

"How are you, George?" Florence asked.

"Pretty good, considering." He offered a weak smile but let it slide away. "I think I'm finally sane again."

"You saved our lives, you know," August said. "Harrington and I would have followed Smith in another instant. You figured it out and yelled."

"Was Smith married?" George asked.

"Next June," August said.

"I didn't think he acted like a married man."

"No," August said. "Williams was seen down in the Taku Village again."

"Was the witness sure it was him?"

"Yah. It was Jee-nak who saw him. Williams took a shot at him, but missed. By the time Jee-nak came back with a rifle, Williams was gone."

"I'm glad Jee-nak is okay. Took me a while to warm up to him, but he's a good man. Your boys find any sign when they went looking for him?"

"No, but Jee-nak said he's disguised as an old fisherman, even got a scruffy beard. The militia is searching all the cabins and sheds between here and Thane."

"Have you heard from Julia?" Florence asked.

George stared out the frosted window again. "No. I don't even know where she and Jeff went. I think she's probably done with me, and I don't blame her."

"Oh, George, there's always hope." Florence glanced up at August. "You still love her, don't you?"

"More than anything in the world," he said. "She is so beautiful to me."

August cleared his throat. "Did you know that woman, Stella?"

"No. Heard of her, but I never met her."

"Williams killed her. Left her body close to the dynamite bomb . . ."

"You gotta kill him, August. Don't ever give him another chance."

"I won't," August whispered. "I feel responsible for Smith, the loss of your leg, Harrington's broken leg—"

"That's enough!" George glared at him. "That's the same kinda thinking that killed that poor man in the forest and damn near killed all of us up there on the mountain. I've had a lot of time to think this out.

"We're professionals in a profession where people get hurt if they aren't careful, or lucky." He slapped his left thigh. "This is part of the job. Ain't your fault we're hunting a vicious animal."

"You still have your job, you know," August said. "No white man on Gastineau Channel will look down on you ever again."

George grinned. "There'll be new people."

"They'll get told." August's voice carried a grim edge. "Not only that, the boys took up a collection. As soon as you're up and about, and the doc says it's okay, they're buying you a new leg."

George's eyes glistened and he swallowed. "The Juneau Police Department did that?"

August nodded. "You betcha. I think they even have enough for a spare."

The three friends laughed together as new snow peppered against the window.

124 —Juneau City, A.T., February 23, 1917—
Friday evening

Arnold Williams hummed a Teutonic marching song as he wired sticks of dynamite together. He had it all planned in detail. Once he had Krause out of jail, they would both pose as militiamen.

Both would carry backpacks stuffed with explosives, and each would have a rifle. A check on the mine, they would say to the lift operator at the Treadwell. Then they would plant the dynamite and light an hour fuse.

By the time the bomb went off and blew a hole under the water line, they would be back on the Juneau side. A simple boarding of a fishing boat and away they would go across the channel and kill police lieutenant Lepke.

Williams finished wiring the six sticks together. He eased them down in the open case with the others, and picked up six more loose sticks.

Getting back to Germany would be difficult, but not impossible. He wondered if they could impersonate soldiers long enough to go over on a troop ship. Probably not.

Wind rattled the windows of the small shack and his head snapped up at the noise. This was such a raw, pitiless land. The mineshaft had remained livable only as long as a large fire burned.

As soon as the fire went out, the cold swept in. Stella had been useful in that way. Warmth.

The fisherman's shack served his needs quite well. The man must have been mentally deficient, because nobody came near the place.

"Couldn't have planned it better, myself," he muttered in German. Every night he sneaked into town and stole food and at least one newspaper. The fools who lived along the channel proved to be very trusting. So many doors left unlocked.

Even so, he only stole small amounts wherever he went, nothing big, expensive, or noticeable. Not to kill the golden goose was his motto.

The Americans argued daily on whether to enter the war or not. He had to act soon. But he wasn't quite ready yet.

It wouldn't matter in the long run. Even if America joined the Entente, once the Treadwell died, they would run out of gold. Then a victorious Germany could extract concessions and territory from the Americans as well as the British and the French.

He laughed in the cluttered cabin and wondered how the walls could throw the sound back as cackling. Arnold Williams set the wrapped dynamite down and picked up another six loose sticks.

Footsteps crunched up his snowy path. He pushed the dynamite against the wall and dropped an armload of dirty laundry over it. His sour overcoat hung near the door and the Luger waited in the closest pocket.

A loud knocking rattled the door. He opened the door a crack and saw two men in militia uniforms. Both carried military-issue Springfield rifles.

"Yah?" Williams called. "Vot is it you vant?"

"I'm Corporal Harris, Territorial Militia. Who are you?"

"Olaf Knudson," Williams said, thickening his accent.

"We're looking for a fugitive. We need to take a look around your cabin. Okay?"

"Yah, sure." He opened the door and the two men stepped inside. The corporal wrinkled his nose and the private coughed.

"Kinda close in here," the corporal said. The militiamen glanced around the room and looked at each other.

"Well, thanks, Mr. Knudson. Sorry to have bothered you."

Williams watched them slip and slide down the hill and turn toward Thane before he lowered his curtain.

These people are such fools.

He pulled the box of dynamite out and went back to work.

THE DAILY ALASKA DISPATCH
Juneau, Alaska, Wednesday, February 24, 1917

PARTIAL CONSCRIPTION BILL ENTERS CONGRESS OF THE UNITED STATES OF AMERICA

TORNADOES KILL MANY IN SOUTH

WILSON CALLS SENATORS TO MEET MARCH 5

SEEK REMEDY FOR SOARING FOOD PRICES

VILLA TROOPS NEAR JUAREZ

THIRTEEN SHIPS TORPEDOED; HADEN LOST GETTING AWAY

CALL RESERVES FOR FOOD RIOT

THREE MILLION RUSSIANS FLED

A MILLION MEN DOOMED TO DIE

FUNSTON FUNERAL 10 THIS MORNING

NEW METHOD TO CURE FISH HERE
$300,000 Company Incorporated in Juneau Yesterday to Preserve Fish In New Way

The Baconized Alaska Salmon Company is the name of a new corporation which filed its papers with the clerk of the court in Juneau yesterday and whose capital is three hundred thousand dollars. The incorporators are Floyd Hampton, F. M. German and Albert Martin and the capital is made up of three hundred thousand shares of a par value of one dollar each. None of the stock is for sale here.

"We ask nothing here," said Mr. Hampton and all the stock to be disposed of locally has been subscribed. The company has a new process of preserving salmon which is very interesting. It will be sugar-cured, dried and baconized. It will be wrapped in paper to (Continued on page three)

125 —Juneau City, A.T., March 1, 1917—
Thursday evening

Moving carefully down the gangplank of the *S.S. Jefferson*, Julia Prescott Mak-we took hold of her son's hand.

"Now you take good care of your mama," the purser called to Jeff, "... and we'll take good care of your ship, Jefferson."

"Bye," Jeff called, waving and smiling. "Thanks for showing me the bridge, Mr. Chase."

Even though darkness hid most of the town, Julia felt relieved to be back in Juneau. She hoped her trip was not in vain. A waving handkerchief semaphored from the crowd at the bottom of the plank.

"Julia! Jeff!" Florence called.

"Mama! There's Miss Malone!" Jeff said. "Is she going to take us to where George is?"

"Yes, I'm sure she is."

Once off the angled ramp, the women embraced and Julia felt another surge of emotion. "Oh, it's so good to see you again, Florence. I was of no use whatsoever in San Francisco. All I could think about was Juneau, and Alaska, and all my wonderful friends."

"And your husband," Florence said with a smirk.

"How is he? Does he know?"

"He's a changed man, Julia. He's a very contrite man. He knows he made mistakes and owns up to them, and no, he doesn't know you are coming back. I mean, that you are back." She laughed.

"I need to get off my feet soon," Julia said. "Could we go down to Amanda's cafe? How are she and little Fiona doing?"

"I've only seen the baby once, but she's as beautiful as her mama." Florence looked around them in the busy darkness. "Oh, there's Harry Jenkins!"

"Harry Jenkins?" Julia murmured to Jeff. The boy shrugged.

"Come quickly," Florence said, darting ahead. "He has a motor taxi."

"A motor taxi!" Jeff exclaimed. "Neat!"

Florence spoke to the man as Julia and Jeff made their way along the slippery street. The man nimbly dashed around the automobile and held the door for Julia. "Right this way, ma'am."

In moments they putted along, the streetlights throwing their shadow before them again and again, like phantom steps. Jeff sat in the front seat next to Jenkins and chatted about the vehicle.

"Is he well?" Julia asked. "Has his leg healed?"

Florence told her about the police department's collection. "Dr. Parker says it will be completely healed in a few more weeks, and that it will take George time to get used to the artificial limb."

"But is he well mentally? Is he still obsessed with Jim's death?"

"He's past that," Florence said. A shadow passed over the younger woman's face, and Julia intuited something wasn't being said.

"What aren't you telling me?" Julia whispered.

"Am I that transparent?"

"Tell me."

In a whisper Florence told her about the man George mistakenly killed in the forest. "You can't ever tell him you know about this. I'm not even supposed to know. He's been through a great deal and feels guilty."

"The police said nothing?"

Florence shrugged. "August says this sort of thing happens now and then. It isn't something they are proud of, but it's something they face every time they arrest a suspected felon."

"The poor man," Julia said. "Killed because he was afraid."

Florence gazed out at the passing buildings. The Maxwell pulled up to the boardwalk in front of the Line Cafe.

"Here we are, folks," Harry Jenkins said jovially.

As they exited, Florence handed the man a coin. "Keep the change, Harry."

"Thank you, Miss Malone."

Julia pushed through the cafe door. Rev. James Thistle, without his reversed collar, hurried forward. "Julia, Jeff! How wonderful to see you both again."

Julia returned his hug. He looked down at her swollen belly, then back to her face. "How soon?"

"This month. I can hardly wait."

"Wait until you see little Fiona Maye." He grinned inanely. "She is the most beautiful, the most perfect—"

"Julia!" Amanda emerged from the kitchen.

Soon they all sat around two tables pushed together, chatting. Julia glanced at the Regulator clock on the wall. "How late may George have visitors?" she asked Florence in an aside.

"Until eight." She checked the time. "I'll call Mr. Jenkins. He'll have you up there in no time at all."

Julia and Jeff watched the motor taxi clatter off and then walked into the hospital. A nun gave directions. Julia hesitated outside the door to room 120.

"It's okay, Mother," Jeff said.

"How do you know so much?" she asked with a smile, and pushed into the room.

George looked up from the book he was reading. He blinked, "I thought they reduced the amount of medicine they were giving me."

"Hello, George," Julia said.

The book slid out of his hands and fell on the floor. His eyes went round. "Are you really here?" he whispered.

She went to the bedside and took his hand in hers. "Yes, we're here, and if you want, we'll stay."

George burst into tears.

126 —Juneau City, A.T., March 5, 1917—
Monday evening

"It's Wilson for four more years!" Jack shouted. "Everyone drink to the President!" He threw back the whiskey and laughed.

"Jack, 'tis a fine party yer having," Sean Clancy said.

"It's a great day for the Democrats and all other freedom-loving people." Jack felt wonderful. "Delegate Sulzer took his oath so it's a great day for Alaska Territory ta boot!"

"I wonder what Wickersham will do now?" Clancy mused.

"Go earn an honest living," Jack shouted. "If he can remember how!"

The group of men around them roared in laughter. Armstrong's teemed with men, smoke, and droning talk. More men, hearing of the free beer, tried to enter the crowded building.

"When do you travel down to Washington City?" Clancy asked.

"April second, on the Princess Sophia to Seattle, and from there by Great Northern Railway to points east."

"Does yer reward fer that journalist still stand after yer gone?"

"'Deed it does," Jack said with a snort. "$500 in gold to any man who brings the brigand in, dead or alive."

"Jack, I must be askin'..."

Jack watched the indecision on his friend's face. "So ask, Sean Clancy. What is it?"

Clancy glanced at the chaos around them, leaning forward he whispered, "Wuz it our dynamite then, that the feller used on the coppers?"

Jack felt heaviness well up in his chest and the shroud of guilt increase its weight across his shoulders. "I'm not for certain, but I suspect that to be the case. We was taken in by that son-of-a-bitch, with him pretending to be a patriot and all."

"You and I did it for the cause o' Irish independence, Jack. Nuthin more, nuthin less."

"We were taken down the garden path like we was still wet behind the ears!" Jack smacked his glass down on the bar and John stepped up and filled it with premium whiskey. "Make's me feel young, it does!" he said with a growl.

Clancy laughed. "Then it's good for something, you old dog."

Jack's good humor instantly returned and he laughed with his old friend.

"So who d'ya thank will win the presidency in '20?" Clancy asked.

"Nineteen and twenty," Jack said. Suddenly a cold hand touched his neck and he twisted to see who was being so free with his person. No one stood close enough to have touched him and pulled away.

The cold seemed to crawl down his back. Jack felt himself abruptly sober.

"What the hell?" he said softly.

"Who did you say, Jack?" Clancy asked.

"I don't even know who's running, Sean. No way to predict."

"Maybe Bryan will try again. He's got the habit."

"I always felt Bryan was more Republican than Democrat," Jack said, still wondering at the phantom cold. "Cheap money, indeed."

A portly man wearing a cashmere overcoat pushed through the crowd, the huge cigar in his mouth jutting upward like the mast on a battleship.

"Well, well, well," Jack said. "If it isn't Mr. Watkins, late of the Republican Party."

"Good evening to you, Mr. Malone." Watkins shook his hand and accepted the glass of whiskey that John magically produced. "I bring news which you may not welcome."

"And what might that be?"

"Wickersham is going to contest the election. He claims the winner was declared before all the ballots were counted."

"Come along, Watkins. The man is crying in his beer. After all, he has to go out and find a real job now, and he's out of practice!"

"I think he's got a case," Watkins said with a frosty grin. "I wanted to let you know first thing. We do have an understanding."

"I appreciate your forthrightness, sir, but if you don't mind, I'm going to wait a bit before I get worried."

"That's your call, Mr. Malone. I just didn't want you to get blind-sided on this."

"I'll remember this courtesy, Mr. Watkins."

Watkins drained his glass and sat it on the bar. "Thanks for the drink." He smiled and disappeared through the door.

"What's this mean, Jack?" Clancy asked.

"Trouble we didn't see coming, that's what."

127 —Juneau City, A.T., March 9, 1917—
Friday night

Begay Santo's feet throbbed and his back twitched with pain as he walked home from work. Still he felt good. These days he experienced a continuous feeling of satisfaction.

His wonderful Ruth carried their child. She also had a job with Fiona Malone where she made a good wage and enjoyed her work. They neared completion of the addition to their new home where Irene would live. With her daughter married and her son deceased, Irene led a lonely life down in the Auk Village.

When the child arrived Begay knew the extra pair of loving hands would be welcome. Julia's return has taken the edge off the pain of George's handicap. As Begay neared the turnoff to his house, his mind moved to the murderer, Williams.

The grinding, mindless din of the crushers pulsed through the darkness. Not until Independence Day would they again fall silent.

Begay remembered the encounter in Armstrong's, when Williams tried to enlist him in his mad scheme. A few days ago, August Lepke told Begay to carry a weapon until Williams was brought to justice. "He seems to be after people who know him," Lepke had said.

Running his hand into the overcoat pocket and feeling the comfortable, oiled solidity of the revolver made Begay smile. Although the hour was early for the drinking crowd, the cold kept most people off the streets. The crash of a breaking bottle startled Begay and he peered ahead at the die-cut shadows lining Lower Front Street.

Feeling suddenly nervous, he spied a man going through the trash bin outside the White Spot Cafe. Begay felt a sardonic pleasure the proprietor of the White Spot would have a mess to clean up in the morning. Under the White Spot's name on its long wall sign, were the words: WHITE HELP ONLY.

The nervousness returned when the man heard Begay's footsteps and turned to face him. The inky, cloud-covered sky leached the brightness from the few electric streetlights. Begay couldn't make out the man's features.

Even so something about the figure gave him pause. Begay realized he did not want to close the distance between them. Something warned him to cross the street, or go into one of the bars. This impulse made him feel foolish, and he suppressed his uneasiness, forcing himself to continue.

The man in the shadows straightened up, watching Begay's approach. What was it Lepke said about Williams? Begay thought hard, trying to remember. Then he had it.

"He wears shabby clothes, overcoat, and hat with ear flaps. He has grown an unkempt beard. He is armed and dangerous." Lepke's voice faded in Begay's mind as his steps again slowed and he stared at the man.

The problem with the description was it fit so many men this time of year,. just as it did the man standing before him. Abruptly Begay turned and crossed the snow-covered street, not caring how the derelict would perceive his actions.

Begay felt comforted by his choice, yet he kept a keen eye on the man at the garbage can. Just as Begay stepped into the cone of light projected by a street lamp, the man shouted, "I thought it was you!"

Begay's bones turned to water as he recognized Williams' voice. He pawed at his overcoat pocket while watching Williams thrust a hand deep into the pocket of his own overcoat. Begay felt an icy hand clutch at his heart when Williams pulled a weapon out. Light reflected off the barrel of a pistol.

For a long, airless moment, Begay thought this all might be a dream, something frightening conjured up by his imagination. The first shot zipped past his head and the flat crack of the weapon merged with the breaking glass of the store window next to him.

Frantically, Begay dived to the icy boardwalk behind the false security of a small pile of snow. He scrabbled at his revolver, finally freed it and cocked the hammer. Another bullet whizzed past his face and he rolled to one side and came up in a crouch, aiming toward the trash can.

Nobody stood there. Bottle fragments gleamed on the frosty boardwalk. Begay stared into the shadows until his own mind created flickers of movement.

A deep voice boomed off to his side, "Hey! You put that gun down right now or I'll shoot!"

Begay turned his head and saw a city patrolman aiming at him. Begay dropped his revolver on the walk and raised his hands. "I didn't do the shooting! It was Arnold Williams. He tried to kill me!" He pointed toward the abandoned garbage can.

The officer closed the distance between them. "Mr. Santo? Is that you?"

"Yes! Detective Lepke told me to carry a weapon. I thought I wouldn't need it. But he was right . . ."

"Calm down. We'll get to the bottom of this."

THE DAILY ALASKA DISPATCH
Juneau, Alaska, Saturday, March 10, 1917

ARMED AMERICAN SHIPS GET READY TO SAIL TO DEFY THE SUBMARINE THREAT OF WAR

GERMANS GUILTY OF SINKING SHIP

WITNESS SAYS I.W.W.'S FIRED FIRST SHOTS

DEADLOCK IN SENATE STILL HOLDING FAST

WOMAN AVIATOR OFFERS HER SERVICES TO THE UNITED STATES

GERMANS TAKE THE OFFENSIVE

SANTIAGO STILL HELD BY REBELS

GERMANY TO DEFY U.S. AND WAGE SUB WARFARE TO THE END

CONGRESS ALSO FEARS BIG FIGHT OVER ORGANIZATION

TERRITORY HAS ABOUT $217,000
Contrary to General Opinion the Fish Tax Cases
Have Not Been Finally Settled by Supreme Court

The report of the territorial treasurer has not yet been presented to the legislature but it is known that on the first of January this year the territory had to its credit the sum of two hundred and seventeen thousand dollars. Since that time some changes have taken place, which may alter the figures slightly.

Another fact which has been learned from official sources, but which is not generally known, is that the fish tax cases have not yet been fully decided. They are up again now before the United States Supreme Court on a writ of error and it is quite possible that months may be required to finally dispose of them.

128 —Juneau City, A.T., March 12, 1917—
Monday evening

August Lepke knocked on the front door of a miner's boarding house. A middle-aged woman opened the door.

"Yah? For you what can I do?"

Lepke glanced down, saw the ring on her finger. "Good evening, missus. We're looking for a man—"

The door opened wider and a large, burly man wearing an undershirt and trousers held up with galluses glowered out at him. "Why are you bothering us with your search? You think we have him under the bed, heh?"

Lepke had seen this man in the drunk tank more than once. He was one of the few miners who lived in town and worked out in Gold Creek Basin. There would be no help from this house.

"The man we seek is a murderer. He is armed and dangerous. His name is—"

"Williams, yah?" the man said with a sneer. "The way I hear it, he only kills coppers and friends of coppers. Is that right?"

"No," Lepke said, turning to walk away, " . . . he has also killed at least three miners out at the Groundhog. Sorry to bother you." He joined Patrolman Buhrman, a new hire, on the boardwalk.

"Any luck, lieutenant?" Buhrman asked.

"No, quite the opposite. Antagonistic they were."

"Yeah, I've been running into the same thing." They walked down the dark street together. "It's the war," Buhrman said. "Everyone thinks we're going to get into it."

"What has that to do with apprehending a murderer?"

"Lots of these people are Germans and Austrians. They're worried we're going to look at them as enemies."

"Only if they break the law," Lepke said firmly. "Only if they break the law."

Corporal Forsythe walked up. "We went through every building on Lower Front, lieutenant. No sign of him. He's gotta be hiding outside the city limits."

Lepke ground his teeth, something he was doing too often these days. "Then he's on this end of town. He's been spotted at the Taku Village and on Lower Front Street. Never anywhere else."

"Maybe that's because there's more people down here," Buhrman said.

"He's got a point, Lieutenant," Forsythe said. "Whatever else Williams is, he ain't stupid."

"No. He's very cunning. I am amazed at how he avoids us."

"Maybe tomorrow we should start searching the houses between here and Thane," Buhrman suggested.

"The militia has already done that," Lepke said. "They said they found nothing suspicious."

"How would they know?" Buhrman asked.

"We gave them a description," Forsythe explained. "They said about half the people they talked to fit it."

"Did they make a list of where those people were?"

"Not to my knowledge," Forsythe said, glancing meaningfully at Lepke.

"Come along," Lepke urged. "We have a few more doors to knock on."

At the next house a man answered and, as soon as he saw the police, said, "I ain't done nothing. Whattya want here?"

Corporal Forsythe explained and as Lepke watched the man's face, knew he didn't hear the officer's words.

"You sure this ain't got something to do with me not joining the militia?" the man asked.

"The militia? Clean out your ears, fellow!" Forsythe's patience showed at the seams, Lepke thought. "We're looking for a murderer who isn't too particular about who he shoots."

"Ain't seen no murderer, I'll let you know if'n I do," the man said, pushing the door shut in their faces.

The three officers shared a bewildered look.

"Okay." Lepke glared about in the darkness. "To hell with it. I can't keep paying you boys overtime if we don't come up with some results. I feel like we're tying to grab air."

"We're doing the best we can, Lieutenant," Forsythe said.

"Yeah," Buhrman added.

"I know that. But our best isn't enough good. I'll see you both tomorrow."

August trudged through the crisp night. He suspected the two officers whispered about him as they made their way home. But he didn't care.

He rode a tiger in this place, and everyone knew it. It was one thing to be eaten by the tiger, but quite another to have it happen in front of an audience.

Is that it? he asked himself. You only fear failure if it is to be witnessed? Nein, he answered himself.

I cannot fail in this thing. Williams has made this personal, a slap in the face. I will bring him down if it kills me even!

Tomorrow he would go speak to the militia captain again. Perhaps his men did make a list.

THE DAILY ALASKA DISPATCH
Juneau, Alaska, Saturday, March 17, 1917

RUSSIA BECOMES A REPUBLIC!

DYNASTY OF THE ROMANOFFS END AND PEOPLE RULE

GERMANY THREATENS MOST CRITICAL SPOT IN U.S. DEFENSE
MEXICO MAY HAVE A NEW REVOLUTION

BRITISH LOSE A DESTROYER

BILL TO LIMIT JURISDICTION OF COMMISSIONERS

PREPARING TO MOBILIZE THE GUARD FORCES
War Department Sends Plans to State Adjutants General How to Prepare If War Comes

(Associated Press) Washington, March 16—Preparatory to any demand that might be made on the army by developments in the German affair the war department today sent instructions to the stated adjutants general outlining a plan for mobilizing the national guard in event of war. The mobilization will be under regular army officers and the guardsmen will take the oath of federal service. Every unit will be required to muster in full war strength.

129 —Juneau City, A.T., March 20, 1917—
Tuesday afternoon

Arnold Williams practiced his shuffling limp as he climbed Telephone Hill to the federal jail. Not one person had given him a second glance on his slow trip through town. He had discovered if he chewed his beard and muttered to himself, people tended to avoid even looking at him.

While he reveled in his successful deception, his mind burned with a plan of action. The hard part would be freeing Krause. After that, victory lay in his palm. With two Germans working together, these serfs had no chance.

"What can I do for you, fellow?" the fat man behind the desk asked without interest. The man leaned back in his chair and Williams knew his body odor probably opened doors faster than words.

"I need this Krause man to see," he said in his heavy Scandinavian accent.

"Krause? Why do you want to see a murderer?"

"He used to boats build, yah? He build my boat, I t'ink."

"He built your boat? So you want to see him about that?"

"Yah?"

"Ah, hell." The man pushed his chair back and hoisted himself to his feet. "Why do I always get the half-wits? C'mon. I'll give you ten minutes with Krause and then out you go, okay?"

"Yah?" Williams said, following closely.

Krause stared at Williams silently until the deputy closed the door between the office and the cell area. "They've got a bigger manhunt going for you than they did for me. You must be crazy to be here."

"You build boat for me, yah?" Williams said loudly, glancing at the closed door. He lowered his voice, "This is the last place they would look, so keep your voice down."

"How is they didn't recognize you in there?" Krause nodded toward the door.

"Those schwein would have to be introduced before they recognized me. Then they would have doubts. I walk among them with impunity. The militia have even come to my door and not recognized me."

Krause chuckled. "You've got ballocks, *mein Herr*. So when do I get out here?"

Williams raised his voice. "You did gut job on my boat! But there is problem with motor, yah?" Quickly he whispered, "April 12th, late. Right before they shut the doors for the night."

"What do you want me to do?"

"I want you to slip out when I create a diversion. You meet me on the south end of the Taku Village, on the beach."

"Then what?"

"I'll tell you on the beach. We are going to carry the war to the heart of this place. They are going to learn to fear the Imperial German Army."

"You're in the German Army?"

Williams glared at him. "Shut up! I've already told you everything you need to know. I'll see you on the beach in two and a half weeks."

Williams turned and walked out the door. Other matters now pressed in on his mind. He had a score to settle which could wait no longer.

130 —Juneau City, A.T., March 28, 1917—
Wednesday afternoon

Jack Malone left his lawyer's office and made his way down Seward toward Front Street. A one-legged man on crutches accompanied by a boy moved slowly uphill toward him. Something about the man caught his eye and Jack looked closer.

As the three pedestrians came together, Jack recognizing George Mak-we, felt a quick jab of guilt. "Good afternoon, Officer Mak-we. How are you this fine day?"

George stopped, smiling widely. "Good day to you, Mr. Malone. May I introduce you to my stepson, Jefferson Prescott."

The boy stepped forward and extended his hand. "Pleased to meet you, Mr. Malone."

"The pleasure is all mine, Jefferson." Jack warmly shook his hand. "That's a fine name you have there. Thomas Jefferson was the first Democrat president."

George laughed. "Jeff, Mr. Malone here is probably the most prominent Democrat in Juneau, or at least the most outspoken. Jeff and I would like to tell you he has a new brother and I have a son as of yesterday."

Jack grabbed Mak-we's hand and pumped it. "My congratulations, sir! What wonderful news. Do you still wait to name newborns or have you decided?"

"That was the old ways. His name is George, his mama insisted on it."

"I haven't had the pleasure of meeting your wife, but both of my daughters speak very highly of her. Please extend my warmest wishes to her and your new son."

Father and son moved on up the street. Jack continued toward Lower Front Street.

I should have said something about his leg, Jack thought. *But why, to ease my own guilt? George knows nothing about my stupid gullibility in the matter. Why confuse the issue?*

"Because someday he might find out!" Jack snapped out loud. He glanced around to make sure nobody saw him talking to himself.

A son, he thought. *How I envy him. I've got two, no, three, of the loveliest daughters possible, but I always wanted a son.*

"Well," he said to himself. "That makes two things we can't do anything about." He quickened his pace toward Armstrong's.

A great thirst settled on him and the idea of a neat whiskey warmed his soul. The sun dipped behind the mountains on Douglas Island, plunging Juneau into twilight under a deep blue sky.

"I'm glad I stayed here," he murmured. When he and Maye arrived in the ten-year-old rough gold camp all those years ago, it had been with the idea of making a quick killing and moving on. He smiled ruefully. "And we both stayed," he whispered to the gathering dusk.

He thought about Emily, about how proud she would be of their daughters. They were as independent and intelligent as their mother. They had her fire and her fine looks.

My God, she was so beautiful, even on her deathbed. The cancer attacked so swiftly, she went so fast . . . Jack swallowed around the familiar lump in his throat.

He spied Garnet, a prostitute working out of one of his cribs, lounging on the corner ahead. She gave him her best smile until she recognized him and her eyes went wide with fear. "Hi, Jack. How ya doing?"

He slowed, smiling back at her. "I'm just fine, Miss Garnet, and what are you doing on the street?"

"It's a slow night, Jack. I'm just taking some air."

He stared at her, saying nothing.

"Look, I wasn't being outrageous or nothing. Just friendly."

Jack smiled. "Have a good evening, Miss Garnet."

"You too, Jack. Thanks."

They both knew the rules. If the cops found her soliciting on the street, they would make things tough for Jack. And it would cost him $50 to keep her from getting a blue ticket on the next boat south.

He saw a miner wander into the front door of Armstrong's, half a block ahead. He smiled.

"Mr. Malone." The voice slid out of the deepening shadows in an alley. "A word with you, sir."

Jack stopped, shading his eyes from the relative glare of a street lamp. "Who's there? Come out where I can see you."

"If you'll step in here, you'll understand why I don't wish to be seen on the street."

Trying to place the voice, Jack glanced around. The boardwalk in front of Armstrong's waited, bereft of pedestrians. In the other direction he saw Garnet, who in turn watched him in idle curiosity.

Jack felt nettled. He wanted to be having a drink, not skulking about in an alley. Despite his misgivings curiosity won out. He stepped into the shadows. "Who the hell are you?"

The man wore a derelict's clothing, but stood tall, like a gentleman. "I know the disguise is good, so I won't take offence if you don't recognize me."

Jack suddenly knew the voice. "Williams! By God, man, you've got some brass. The police department is searching high and low for you."

"The police, to borrow one of your quaint phrases, couldn't find their arse with both hands."

"You'd better hope so. So what are you doing here? Don't you already have the dynamite?"

"Yes, no thanks to you."

"The hell! Who do you think arranged for it in the first place?"

"The same man," Williams grinned, "who put five hundred dollars on my head, dead or alive."

Jack felt his stomach knot, considered running. Williams wouldn't dare follow. "So you know about that, do you?"

"It's the talk of Lower Front Street." Williams' tone weathered quickly from congenial to menacing. "Not that any of the denizens have bothered to leave their cozy seats in taverns to search for the 'murderer' Williams."

"You murdered that Indian lad in cold blood," Jack snapped. "You tortured him, and then you shot him like a dog."

"He wouldn't tell me why he followed me, or who put him up to it. I'm not a man to be taken lightly."

"You've gone crazy, Williams. That was the work of a madman."

"He was nothing!" Williams hissed. "Just another dead enemy of Imperial Germany. We have a greater mission. One that must be executed soon."

"Blowing the Treadwell?" Jack said with a laugh.

"You're in this, Jack, at your own doing. Here's your chance to strike a blow for Irish independence against the hated English."

"I live here. Any sabotage done to the economy here only hurts my friends and neighbors, not the English, nor does it help Imperial Germany. You've got to give this thing up and get away while you can."

"If you had any discipline, you would know orders are not to be disputed, or changed at whim. I am a soldier of the kaiser. Ludendorf himself issued the orders to me personally. You have no concept of the honor—"

"Honor! To murder a boy tied to a chair carries no honor. This mission of yours has twisted you into something despicable."

"You have agreed to help me carry out this mission. To desert in the face of the enemy is punishable by death."

When he saw the pistol in Williams' hand, Jack felt a chill on his cheeks that worked its way down his back. The madman still held the weapon at arm's length, pointed down. Jack was fast at drawing his concealed revolver, except when his overcoat was buttoned snugly over his suit coat.

Jack casually took hold of his coat front with his right hand, edging his fingers between the folds. "Don't be daft, man. I'll help you escape. There's no way you can pull this off and get away."

"Get away? A soldier does not escape the battlefield or the battle. The soldier does his duty, serves his country. Are you with me, Mr. Malone?"

Jack turned slightly, pushing his hand a little further into the coat. "What do you want me to do?"

Williams turned his head to look behind him. Jack's gloved hand slid inside his coat and touched the handle of his revolver. Williams' hand came up and pointed the pistol at Jack before the murderer turned his head to stare with pitiless eyes.

"You had your chance. Lepke's next." The pistol fired twice.

Jack felt the searing burn of the bullets and shock instantly enveloped his being. He staggered back, staring wonderingly at the retreating Williams. Despite himself his legs gave way and he fell against the wall, collapsing on the ground. He heard Garnet's shriek.

She held his head and he stared at her, needing to say so much before…

"Jack, Jack!" Garnet's voice echoed, as if coming from a deep well.

Jack tried to reply but a great silence enveloped him and he heard his beloved Emily say, "John Malone, come and take my hand." So he did.

131 —Juneau City, A.T., March 29, 1917—
Thursday afternoon

August Lepke ran a hand through his hair and checked his desk a final time. Everything seemed to be in order. Chief Tinsley had stepped into his office ten minutes earlier.

"Lieutenant, I know you were as close as family to Jack Malone. So why don't you go be with your fiancée. She needs you more than the city does today."

Lepke thought through the options faced by the JPD, decided everything possible was already underway. Two 9mm shell casings were found in the alley where Jack Malone was murdered. They matched the single shell casing found aboard the Celia next to Jim Kisadis.

Williams had struck again. Through the police department, August petitioned the Governor's office for militia assistance in searching for Williams. Finally he allowed himself to leave his desk.

He walked through the outer office where the duty sergeant stopped him.

"Lieutenant, this man would like to speak to you."

Lepke tried to remember where he had seen the man before.

"You probably don't remember me, Lieutenant Lepke. M'name's Clancy, Sean Clancy. Jack Malone was me best friend."

Tears suddenly ran down the man's face. "And I think I helped kill 'im."

"Come in and sit down, Mr. Clancy. Tell me why you believe that."

Clancy sat down and wiped his face with a handkerchief. "We got sold a bill o' goods, we did, me 'n' Jack."

"What bill of goods was that, Mr. Clancy?"

"He told us we was strikin' a blow fer Irish independence."

"Who did?"

"That Williams fellow, of course."

"How did you help him?"

Clancy buried his face in his hands and his shoulders shook. Lepke used the time to take in the man's sturdy work clothes, the muscles evident in his arms and shoulders. "Would you like some water?"

Clancy wiped his face again and then loudly blew his nose. "Naw. What I need is a good stiff drink o' whiskey with me friend, Jack, but that ain't never gonna happen again, is it now?"

"No."

"All right then, here's th' truth of it."

Lepke listened to the story of the stolen dynamite, noting the parts obviously left out. "Who helped you steal it at the dock?"

"I'm not sayin'," Clancy said. "It was me and Jack what were the responsible parties. I'm here to take me share of the blame and tell you about Williams havin' dynamite."

"He's already used some of it, you know."

"I know," Clancy said hoarsely. "That's why Jack put a price on the man's head."

"He did what? Do you mean a reward?"

Clancy nodded.

"How much?"

"Five hundred dollars. Dead or alive."

"Why didn't he tell the police department, or the mayor, about this civic donation?"

"Because you'da asked him why he was doing it. He was trying to fix what he broke, don't ya see?"

"No wonder Williams murdered him." Lepke rubbed his forehead. "Where did you store the explosives?"

"One a Jack's blind warehouses. He had 'em all over Juneau and Douglas."

"Blind warehouses. What do you mean?"

"Look around at all the buildings sittin' quiet with nice big padlocks on the doors. Nobody ever goes near 'em in the daytime, but at night sometimes, wagons make deliveries or haul somethin' away.

"There's always somethin' to get past the customs man, 'r the tax fellows. Everybody does it a wee bit, but with Jack it was a full time occupation."

"He seemed to have a lot of occupations."

"Don't ya know it. He was good at all of 'em, he was." Clancy smiled with pride. "There'll never be another like him."

"Jack told me about Williams being a German saboteur, but he didn't tell me about the dynamite. He may have saved one life if he had."

Clancy shook his head. "He always thought he had a firm grip on everything. He let his heart get in the way of his head this time."

"You realize that you have just confessed to grand larceny, accessory to murder, accessory assault on a police officer, and intent to commit sabotage."

"That's a lot of trouble, isn't it?" Clancy said, swallowing hard.

"Yes. However, you have come forward of your own volition, given evidence which hopefully will help us apprehend a murderer, and you show great contrition. That should help your case."

"I don't care what they do ta me, 's long as they get that bastard, Williams," Clancy said bitterly.

"I will release you on your own recognizance if you promise not to leave town."

"And where would I be going except ta hell?"

August walked with Clancy out of the building. Clancy turned south on Lower Front, August went north toward the home of the late Jack Malone.

132 —Treadwell, A.T., April 2, 1917—
Monday afternoon

"Well, Superintendent Smizer, I think we've got this pretty well under control," August Lepke said.

"Pretty much, lieutenant," Smizer said, watching the militia stopping and questioning men on their way to work. "This might slow up the shift changes, but I think it will be worth it."

"Of course," August said, " . . . there's nothing to stop him from landing along the beach in a skiff. We don't have enough militia to guard the whole water front."

"I'll alert the men," Smizer said. "There isn't much goes on around here what doesn't attract attention."

"Williams is a trained saboteur. He's also a soldier with combat experience. All this makes him a very dangerous man."

Smizer squinted at August. "I'm very grateful for your lead in this, Lieutenant. We could have had a calamity of major proportions here without your warning."

"Until this man is in custody or dead, the danger is constant. The fact he has eluded both the Juneau Police Department and the Territorial Militia proves he is very cunning."

"Well, fore warned is fore armed. Now, if you'll excuse me, I have other duties that call." Smizer shook Lepke's hand and strode away down the busy street.

August glanced around the huge complex. He decided trying to protect something this big bordered on the ridiculous. The militia uniforms at each dock and on both streets connecting Douglas and Treadwell pacified the fears of most residents and workers.

Some felt very different. As August passed one of the check points, he heard a miner complaining.

"You think I don't know what's doing here? You looking for Germans, *ja?* Well, you found one. Now what?"

"Hey, we're looking for a murderer. That's all," said the militiaman.

"Since when they got the army looking for murderers? Since war talk started, that's when!"

August walked quickly toward the Douglas boat dock where the gas boat *Gent* was arriving. "The only way the militia will capture Williams is if he introduces himself," he muttered under his breath.

Six other men waited on the dock for the *Gent* to finish unloading. Lepke stopped at the back of the group and watched the disembarking men go past.

"Juneau City passengers!" the deck hand shouted.

August felt grateful there were so few passengers. Everyone could fit comfortably inside the cabin and avoid the intense cold crossing Gastineau Channel. He spied a bench and slid onto it with a sigh.

"It's Mr. Lepke, if I'm not mistaken," a cheerful voice boomed out.

August looked up into the horsy face of Mr. Melton. "Yes, Mr. Melton, you're quite correct. Are you still with Ingersoll-Rand?"

"Quite a memory you have there," Melton said, sitting down beside him. "If my memory serves, we met at Thanksgiving dinner in '15, right?"

"Once again correct you are," Lepke said.

"Y'know, I never did catch what it is you do for a living."

"Well, when we met I was a Pinkerton agent."

"Is that a fact?" Melton seemed genuinely impressed. "You weren't the detective that got the goods on Krause, were you?"

"Yes, I handled that work."

Melton sat up straight. "Well done, Mr. Lepke! Most impressive to say the least. I even saw a piece in the Portland Oregonian praising your professionalism."

August felt his cheeks warm. "Thank you, but I just did my job."

"And refreshingly modest, to boot," Melton said with a huge smile. "Are you still with the Pinkertons?"

"Oh, no. I am now with the Juneau Police Department."

"Is that right? Y'know, I've thought about that Thanksgiving quite a bit over the last sixteen months."

"Ja?"

"Yeah. Remember that reporter, Williams? Well he said he was going to mention the company when he did his story on the Treadwell complex, and—"

"Excuse me, Mr. Melton, but Arnold Williams, which isn't his real name, is not, nor ever was, a reporter."

"You don't say?"

"He is an agent of Imperial Germany sent here to sabotage gold mines. He has murdered seven people including a prominent citizen and a police officer. He is responsible for injuries to three others including myself."

Melton worked his mouth but nothing came out. His eyes bugged slightly as they remained fixed on Lepke's face. His mouth snapped shut and he tried again. "What about that beautiful wife of his?"

August grinned. "Actually they weren't married."

Melton audibly gasped.

"Amanda Ganbor needed a traveling companion after her husband was murdered in Mexico. She knew nothing of Williams' past, and, from what I have seen, I suspect that is all they were."

"Do say! Is she still in the area?"

"Yes. She operates the Line Cafe with her husband, Reverend James Thistle."

Melton seemed to deflate. "Is that a fact? Well, you folks have certainly have had some excitement around here, haven't you?"

August gave him a hard look and bit off his reply. Yelling at this insensitive fool wouldn't help anything. "How long will you be in Juneau?"

"I have another meeting with the Treadwell folks tomorrow and then I'm off to Seattle on the *Jefferson* in the evening."

"You must travel a great deal. Do you have a family?"

"Heavens no. I suppose I may have been tempted to indulge in matrimony, but ... Well, let's be realistic, Mr. Lepke, I'm not exactly Douglas Fairbanks, am I?"

August, taken aback, could make no reply.

"Perhaps someday, Mr. Lepke, I'll meet a member of the fair sex who sees past my lack of beauty and finds something compelling. Nobody, sir, I assure you, will be more astonished than myself."

"Mr. Melton, you can be a very surprising man. I'm sure some day you will find yourself astonished."

To August's surprise, Melton went red. "Very kind of you to say so, sir. Very kind."

133 —Juneau City, A.T., April 4, 1917—
Wednesday afternoon

"Jack Malone was an institution in this community," Father Mulcahey said to the packed cathedral. "He would have made light of a statement like that. That was his way, but he never sent a charity-seeker away empty-handed, he remained an honest man in his dealings, and he never lied unless he thought you needed to hear it."

Despite herself, Fiona laughed along with the majority of the other mourners.

"There's no doubt in my mind that right now Jack is making a deal with St. Peter. Not about getting into heaven, but about which part he'll get to run." Mulcahey let the laughter ebb before continuing.

"I knew Jack Malone for over twenty years. When I first met him, for reasons unimportant now, I thought him an evil man. What I didn't realize at the time was Jack took care of his own.

"He viewed personal responsibility as the supreme measure of a person. He never lacked in that respect. It got to the point I regarded it as another one of the graces."

A tear ran down Fiona's cheek, surprising her. She thought she had cried herself out days ago. Beside her, Florence quietly blew her nose in an already sodden handkerchief.

Fiona thought the last time her father had been in this church was for her mother's funeral. He would have enjoyed Father Mulcahey's eulogy, and probably would have tried to top it.

"When I look out over the mourners here today, I see every part of this community," Mulcahey said, "and on every face I see true sadness. There are no idle curious among us. This packed house of God testifies to what a good man Jack Malone was.

"Our only condolence is that he now sits at God's side, probably betting on the odds of the rest of us getting there. I am going miss him very much."

Father Mulcahey crossed himself slowly so the congregation could finish crossing themselves with him. Incense fogged the air and Fiona felt somewhat faint. Mrs. Milivich, sitting on Fiona's left, sobbed quietly and Fiona put her arm around the old woman and hugged her.

Florence nudged her and Fiona rose along with her and August, helping Mrs. Milivich rise to her feet. As they walked down the aisle, Fiona saw every pew filled to capacity and standing mourners filled the back and a portion of the aisle.

Amanda and James Thistle sat in the second row with the Mak-we's, the Santo's, and Irene Kisadis. The more Fiona looked, the more she saw her life here in Juneau. People she had attended school with, the nuns who had taught them, the shopkeepers and merchants. Even bartenders and questionable women.

Walking down the aisle with her sister brought home to Fiona who her father had been and who she was. *How, I wonder,* she thought, *can I feel so rich and so bereft at the same time?*

A string of automobiles filled Fifth Street. A Cadillac hearse headed the group. The four of them entered a second Cadillac, and then waited while the other mourners poured out of the church and either entered automobiles or started the seven-block walk to Evergreen Cemetery.

"I'll be back in a moment," August said, getting out of the auto. He disappeared back into the church.

"I knew this day would come," Florence said, "but I didn't think it would be this soon."

"It shouldn't have been," Fiona said.

"Your mama vill be happy to see him," Mrs. Milivich said with a sniff. "Und I know he vill be happy to see her."

Fiona found herself weeping again.

"They come now," Mrs. Milivich said.

Six men carried the polished mahogany coffin. Sean Clancy and John Price, the long time bartender at Armstrong's, had the front. Chief of Police Tinsley and Michael Christenson, the nominal head of the Democrat Party in Juneau, carried the middle. August Lepke and Keith Busch, a union organizer and close friend, brought up the rear.

Each of them knew her father in a completely different way, Fiona realized. There was overlap, of course, but each of those men carried the remains of a Jack Malone only they knew.

"I wonder if any of us really knew him," she said out loud.

"It looks as if a lot of people did, Fio," Florence said. "But I don't think any of them will miss him as much as we will."

The rear door of the hearse latched and moments later the procession moved through the lovely spring day toward Evergreen Cemetery.

THE DAILY ALASKA DISPATCH
Juneau, Alaska, Friday, April 6, 1917

WAR BEGINS THIS MORNING

SENATE PASSED RESOLUTION FOR WAR LAST NIGHT; HOUSE WILL HAVE IT AT 10 A.M.

CHURCHILL SAYS AMERICA'S HELP IS GOD GIVEN

BOTH SIDES NOW CLAIM SUCCESS ON WEST FRONT

PEACE ADVOCATES LABORING STILL

GERMANS HAVE MORE MEN THAN EVER BEFORE

EXORBITANT WAR PROFITS NOT TO BE TOLERATED

SINK OVER FOUR SHIPS EACH DAY

HOUSE PASSES THE TWO BILLS CARRYING MONEY FOR ALASKA

ARMY OFFICERS OPPOSED TO SENDING UNTRAINED FORCES ABROAD; CALL MEN UNDER 30

JUNEAU ELKS ARE WITH COUNTRY AND PRESIDENT

WICKERSHAM CONTEST ABOUT READY TO FILE

James Wickersham Has Received All Alaska Papers In Connection With His Contest for Seat In Congress

Washington, D.C., April 4—(Special)—The contest papers of James Wickersham for a seat in Congress as the delegate from Alaska will probably be filed today. The papers from Juneau which included certified copies of the proceedings and count of the canvassing board, oral and written opinions of Attorney General Grigsby and copies of the court proceedings before Judge Jennings are included in the papers.

The contest as soon as filed will be turned over to the proper committee. Judge Wickersham under the rules has 30 days in which to file. Chas. A. Sulzer is then allowed 30 in which to answer. The Alaska contest will probably be the last heard and may take 3 months (Cont.)

134 —Juneau City, A.T., April 6, 1917—
Friday morning

"Lieutenant, we got every cell filled with suspected saboteurs and pro-Germans," the desk sergeant said. "How am I supposed to run a police department if we're turning the place into a flop house?"

August grudgingly looked up from his desk. The paperwork he had ignored for the last six weeks threatened to bury him. Now he was trying to make a sizable dent in the stuff.

"Who says they're saboteurs?"

"Well, some of 'em fit the description we put out. Some of 'em have made comments against the President, or the army, or the war in general. Some of 'em just have German names and other people think they're spies."

"Every one in the last category you will release. What Dummköpfe we have in this town! The rest I will come and inspect."

As August got to his feet he wondered how long it would be before someone accused him of being a spy because he was originally from Germany. He quickly went through the lock-up, peering at men, questioning some, ignoring most. He stormed back to the duty sergeant's desk.

"Release them all. We will closely question any others who fit Williams' description. As for sabotage, I want proof! If there is a law against being a German or having a German last name, also I should be in jail!"

"Yes, sir." The sergeant picked up the ring of cell keys and went towards the lock-up.

August forced himself back to his own littered desk and sat down. Immediately, a knock at the door interrupted him.

"Vas?" he thundered, looking up.

Corporal Harrington, wearing civilian clothes, stood hat-in-hand in the doorway.

"Corporal, you're off your crutches. Excellent."

"Lieutenant, I'd like a minute of your time. I know you're busy—"

"Not at all. Come in, sit down. What can I do for you?"

"Well, I wanted to tell you, personal. I'm resigning today."

"Because of your injuries?"

"Oh, no," Harrington said with a laugh. "I've enlisted in the army. They're going to give me sergeant stripes first thing."

Lepke stood and shook Harrington's hand. "Good luck, cor- uh, sergeant. You'll find the army much different than police work."

Harrington grinned wryly. "I sure hope so. I'm pretty tired of being a nursemaid to drunks. The next time I see an enemy German, I want to be able to shoot him."

"I made a mistake up there, Harrington. I'm sorry."

"That wasn't a cut at you, lieutenant. I've always known I could question you within reason. I thought you were being a real gent up there. Really, sir, no hard feelings. That's why I wanted to tell you first. It's been an honor and a privilege working with you."

"Thank you, Harrington. That means much to me. You always wonder what the men think of you . . ."

"You're doing fine, Mr. Lepke. Keep up the good work." Harrington stood and saluted. August returned the salute and Harrington left the office.

August sat down and stared blindly at the door. The thought of putting on an army uniform and shooting at strangers held no appeal for him. Even less did he wish to subject himself to the orders of men he held in low esteem, or worse, loathed.

Suddenly, at the age of thirty-four, he felt like an old man, but, he reasoned, he'd already been through a lot. He had scars to prove it. "War is a young man's business," he said to the door.

War. Now that the United States was officially an enemy of Imperial Germany, August felt certain Williams would strike. On the day Jim Kisadis died, Jack told August that Williams had a grand scheme to destroy the Treadwell Mine.

Since that day, August constantly thought about how it could be done, and how it could be stopped. With all of the gold-bearing shafts below Gastineau Channel, the how became obvious.

Flood the shafts. How could he do that? Easily. Place a charge near the hanging wall of green rock and light the fuse.

With Treadwell Superintendent Smizer, August had gone over a plan of the mine. The place was beyond huge. It stretched for four-and-a-half miles along Douglas Island.

All of the extraction process took place above ground, but the actual mining, where stopes bit into the ore bearing veins, took place far below the surface of the channel. The working adits were now at the 2,700 ft. level below ground.

August rubbed his face. The thing turned into a security nightmare. The only way to save the Treadwell complex was to get Williams before he acted.

Paperwork suddenly seemed frivolous. He put on his hat and coat and left the office.

THE DAILY ALASKA DISPATCH
Juneau, Alaska, Thursday, April 12, 1917

GERMAN SUBS IN THE PACIFIC!

ENEMY U BOATS OPERATE NEARBY; VESSELS WARNED

VOLUNTEERS WELCOME BUT MEN MUST GO

REPORT ANOTHER MUNITIONS VESSEL HEADED FOR MEXICO; AGENT KILLED BY SMUGGLERS

7 BILLIONS AS REVENUE PROPOSED

BRITISH AND FRENCH COME

DECLARE TRAITORS CAUSED EXPLOSIONS

WOMEN WILL FORM PATRIOTIC LEAGUE

FEAR RACER TEAMS TAKEN OUT BY ICE
Mail Carrier Sends Serious Reports To Nome About All-Alaska Sweepstakes Men
RACE IS ABANDONED AT LEAST FOR THE PRESENT

(Associated Press) NOME (Via Seattle), April 11—Paul Kjegstad, one of the drivers of teams taking part in the All-Alaska Sweepstakes race has been found without his team seven miles from Soloman by the Council mail carrier. The team was later found scattered all over the tundra, except one which was dead. The most serious circumstance connected with the matter, though, is that the mail carrier saw none of the other three teams or their drivers and he fears they may have been taken out by the ice while crossing Golovin Bay. The public declines to accept this opinion, however, and hopes to see all the men return as the race has been called off and will be started again in ten days, directions having been sent ahead for the drivers to return to Nome. Ayer and Stephenson, the former one of the most skilled and prominent dog racers in the country, have started out to search for the missing racers. There is quite a lot of uneasiness felt as the wind was blowing strong, the temperature was at zero, and the blizzard was terrific. (Continued on page 3)

135 —Juneau City, A.T., April 12, 1917—
Thursday night

Waiting outside the Juneau courthouse, Arnold Williams checked his watch. The basement served as the federal jail. From his visits and careful conversations with Ed Krause, he knew the layout of the jail as well as the schedule of activities within. The time to act neared.

He recalled the cage of steel bars reaching from floor to ceiling. A large open area containing tables, chairs, toilets and washbasins sat inside the cage. Five cells formed the north side of the cage. The entire cage was set in from the walls of the jail so jailers could walk around the whole thing for inspection purposes.

Krause occupied cell number five. Rather, Williams corrected himself, Krause at this moment should be hiding in the walk way, with the toilets screening him from the two jailers who should be at the wheel gang lock securing all five cells at once.

"They no longer pay attention to me," Krause told him. "I offer no resistance to the rules, I read all the time, and I am very quiet. After dark, my cell is the least illuminated."

Their plan received aid by virtue of the incarceration of two men being held for trial on separate murder charges. One of the men had given the jailers trouble in the past and they paid close attention to him at lock down.

A steel door secured the cell area from the office. The office opened to the outside by a second heavy steel door. A third jailer always sat in the office during lock down.

Williams was to distract the third man so the office would be clear. He glanced at his watch again. Fifteen minutes until nine.

He straightened his coat and started to move out of the shadows toward the jail. The outer door opened and a portly man called back over his shoulder, "I'll be right back, fellows. I almost forgot to bank the fire in the courthouse."

Williams watched in elation as the man ambled around the corner of the building. In moments he heard his footsteps slowly going up the wide, wooden stairs in front of the building.

Creeping up and peeking in, Williams saw the door to the cell area. It stood open and he clearly heard an authoritative voice call, "Everybody into your cell."

Williams felt his pulse pounding in his temple. Inside, the same voice called out, "Are you all in?"

Ed Krause's voice called out, "Not yet."

At that moment Williams saw Krause slip through the first door and slam it, flipped the hasp over and wedged a peg in it. Seconds later he hurried through the outer door and stopped short when he saw Williams.

"My God, you gave me a start! I thought it was the other jailer."

Inside they heard one of the jailers yell, "C'mon, Pete, quit fooling around."

"They'll figure it out in less than a minute," Krause snapped. "Let's get out of here."

They circled behind the courthouse and descended a path to the Auke village.

"Okay, what's your plan?" Krause asked as they hurried through the night.

"Well," Williams began. Behind them two shots shattered the still night.

"The fat's in the fire now," Krause said, speeding up as they neared the docks and board walks.

"What I have planned," Williams said, puffing to keep up, "is for us to go to the cabin where I've been hiding. I have militia uniforms for both of us. Tomorrow, we will take the explosives to Treadwell by skiff, and set the charges."

"Sounds good." Krause said. "Listen. I'm worried two of us will attract attention tonight. How about we split up and I'll meet you at your cabin?"

Williams peered at his comrade, catching his profile against distant lights. The man did have a point. They had to get through town without being discovered, and the alarm had been sounded.

"Do you know the area between Juneau and Thane?"

"I know all of Southeast Alaska," Krause said with a snort. "You couldn't lose me if you wanted to."

Williams felt his misgivings abate, somewhat. "Very well." He quickly described the cabin and how to find the path.

"Yeah, I know that place. A crazy fisherman used to live there. Talked to himself all the time."

"Was he a friend of yours?"

"No. I have no use for mental deficients."

"Gut. You will not see him again." Williams felt Krause's appraising glance.

"We are a great deal alike," Krause said. "The Treadwell doesn't stand a chance against the two of us."

THE DAILY ALASKA DISPATCH
Juneau, Alaska, Friday, April 13, 1917

EDWARD KRAUSE, UNDER SENTENCE OF DEATH FOR MURDER OF CAPTAIN PLUNKETT, ESCAPES FROM PRISON
REWARD OF $1000 FOR HIS CAPTURE
Boats and Armed Men Out In All
Directions In Search of Doomed Murderer

THINK SUBS OFF MEXICO

LLOYD GEORGE WELCOMES U.S.

WICKERSHAM PROTEST HAS BEEN FILED
Gives Several Reasons Why He Should Be
Given His Seat In This Congress

BRITISH ARE WINNING YET

DOG RACERS ON HOME RUN
Seppala Leading At Candle But
Anderson Is Only Two Minutes Behind Him

WANTS WOMEN TO RAISE VEGETABLES

BLOCKADE OF U.S. PORTS EXPECTED

NORTHWEST MAY BUILD 500 SHIPS

HOUSE TALKS WAR REVENUE

CAUSE OF FACTORY EXPLOSION HIDDEN

PROGRESSIVES FAVOR DRAFT

RECRUITING CAMPS BLOOM ON PENNSYLVANIA AVENUE

136 —Doty Cove, Admiralty Island, A.T., April 13, 1917— Friday afternoon

Edward Krause's hands ached from rowing. His stomach sorely missed breakfast and lunch, but bars no longer caged him; he roamed free.

Through the night he had rowed completely around Douglas Island in the skiff he stole at Norway Point. The plans of Williams kept him entertained through the long, dark hours.

Let the fool try and blow the Treadwell, he thought. *I've already got enough on my plate.*

The thought of a plate increased his hunger. The labor of rowing all night coupled with missing two meals began to tell on him. He felt weak and a little faint.

He peered about, recognizing Doty Cove on Admiralty Island to starboard. Directly ahead lay Grand Island. Smoke drifted out of Doty Cove, so there must be a cabin there.

Unless his luck had completely run out, word couldn't have traveled this far. He pulled for the cove, wondering what the occupant of the cabin might be having for lunch.

He wished he could have gotten a revolver from Williams last night. but he didn't want to alert the man to his impending defection, and asking for a weapon might have done just that. It unsettled him to be unarmed.

The unsuspecting homesteader in the cove would have a weapon, perhaps money. The law of the jungle held out here. Only the strong would survive.

In all of his years in Alaska, he had never stopped at this particular cove. The odds for the homesteader being a stranger were better than even.

He would ask to warm himself by the fire, he decided. Every fireplace, every stove, had a cast iron poker close by. Krause saw the homesteader turn away in his imagination, saw himself strike. Saw himself win yet again.

He grinned with anticipation as the skiff ran up on the beach. Krause stretched and surveyed the field. A small river ran out of the mountains, past the now visible cabin three-quarters of a mile away, and emptied into the ocean next to where he stood in his skiff.

He saw it was possible to row up the river nearly to the cabin. A skiff lay on the shore there, well above the high tide line.

No, he thought. If anything goes awry at the cabin, he would have a better chance running to the beach than trying to row away quickly. A well thought out plan insures success.

He stepped out onto the beach and pulled his skiff out of the water. This might take awhile and he didn't want the tide taking his boat. Slowly he advanced toward the cabin.

A woman stepped out on the porch and began sweeping. Krause squinted at the windows in the house, trying to see if anyone lurked inside. She made the only movement he could see.

Better and better, he thought. Women were easier to intimidate than men. They were easier to kill, too.

He stepped out of the scanty shoreline brush and walked toward the cabin. The woman looked up, showing no surprise, he noted.

"Good morning," she said, watching him carefully.

An alarm went off in Krause's brain. This was not the friendly greeting he'd anticipated. She—

A man stepped out of the door behind the woman. He carried a rifle leveled at Krause. "Are you Ed Krause?"

They knew! How could they already know? Anger flooded through him, clenching his jaw so tight it became hard to speak.

Denial wouldn't work, because Krause recognized the man and knew by this time the man recognized him. *What was the name? Franz?* He realized he needed to answer, get out of this some way.

"Yes." Krause measured the distance between them, about ten feet. He then glanced at the corner of the cabin, no more than six feet. He realized flight was his only course of action.

He turned to run and the man shot him in the side. The pain staggered him, overtaking his entire universe of reason and bringing him down to his most elemental. He grabbed for where his revolver used to be.

"Arvid!" screamed the woman. "He's got a gun!"

That was the name, Krause thought, fighting pain and shock, *Arvid Fransen.* The second shot blew the thought away along with the rest of his life.

137 —Juneau City, A.T., April 16, 1917—
Monday morning

"Lieutenant, the new marshal is here to see you," Sergeant Courtney called.

"Send him in." August signed the report he had just finished reading and looked up as a well-built man entered the office. August stood and offered his hand.

"I'm August Lepke, detective lieutenant. Pleased to meet you."

The man grinned and returned a firm handshake. "Josias Tanner. Newly appointed U.S. Marshal."

"Please sit down." August nodded to an empty chair and sat back in his. "I've heard of you. Didn't you help round up the Soapy Smith gang in Skagway about twenty years ago?"

"Now, they told me you hadn't been in the Territory very long, Mr. Lepke. That's ancient history."

"I think maybe 'legend' is a better term."

Both men laughed.

"We've just held a major house cleaning up at the jail," Tanner said. "I've come across some information I think might help you."

"And that would be?"

"First, on behalf of the United States Government, I would like to apologize for the way Marshal Bishop treated you. It was unprofessional and uncalled for."

"The man was ill, I understand."

"He had a stroke last year. Maybe we can blame it on that. Anyway, when he resigned and Judge Jennings offered me the job, I accepted on one condition; I could clean house."

Lepke smiled. "That must have been interesting."

"Well, you've no doubt heard the three jailers all got the sack. So did Deputy Clarke." Tanner leaned back in his chair and regarded Lepke thoughtfully.

"They, being Bishop and Clarke, withheld information and evidence which could have helped you in this murder work you've got underway."

"Anything that's still relevant?"

"I'm not sure. When the FBI interned the German Counsel in Seattle they did it before word of our declaration of war got out. As a result they confiscated records that would have otherwise been destroyed.

"One of the papers they retrieved was a list of saboteurs and provocateurs. Their locations were also included. One is listed as being here in the Gastineau Channel area."

"Williams," August said. "It has to be."

"Well, according to the list his real name is Horst von Hesse. He's an officer in the Hussars and has seen action on the Western Front. He may have ordered the machine-gunning of unarmed French prisoners of war."

"How long has the marshal's office this information possessed?"

Tanner gave him an appraising look. "Ten days. The FBI was Johnnie-on-the-spot getting this stuff out. I want you to know my office will share all information about criminals in this area with you as soon as we get it."

"You're a real breath of fresh air, Marshal Tanner. Thank you for coming over to tell me this."

"We owed you this, Lieutenant Lepke, at the very least."

"I heard it was a homesteader who got Krause?"

"Shot him dead. Thought Krause had a gun."

"He didn't?"

"Nope."

"It is my contention," Lepke said, "that Williams, or von Hesse, helped Krause break out of jail to help him sabotage local mines."

Tanner smiled. "That's a federal crime. Now my office is in this thing with you."

"I can't prove it."

"You don't have to."

"Well then, let me share all the information I have on this man." August turned to his file cabinet and pulled out a large folder. He opened it and pointed to the top sheet. "First, he was observed killing two Mexican nationals . . ."

138 —Treadwell, A.T., April 20, 1917—
Friday early evening

Arnold Williams ghosted along the shoreline, keeping the skiff less than two yards off Douglas Island. Clamor filled the night. Freshly mucked ore rumbled from the lifts into train cars; steel wheels screeched on steel rails as the cars rolled toward the crushers; dumped ore crashed and thudded into the batteries of crushers. Finally, the slamming and banging of the iron balls smashing ore inside the monstrous, ever-turning, steel vats of the crushers themselves all combined to overwhelm mere mortals.

Beneath this harsh pandemonium lurked the attendant mechanical sounds; electric motors humming, belts whispering and slapping on pulleys and wheels of various sizes. Water coursed through pipes large and small, washing across the banks of wide, flat, side-to-side shaking belts of the frue vanning machines where lesser minerals sluiced away, leaving only their heavier cousins as the ore progresses toward pure gold.

All of this telegraphed down to Arnold Williams as he rowed silently, staying in the shadows of the vast system of docks and wharfs along the massive face of the Treadwell complex. Finally he spied his target, the tower of the 700 Mill main hoist.

Skillfully he beached the boat under a long wharf, and clambered out. He dragged it up on the sand. He picked up the uniform jacket with sergeant's chevrons and pulled it on. With a final look around under the wharf he lifted the case of dynamite to his shoulder and trudged up the beach toward the hoist.

The huge oil-fired donkey engine brought a ton of ore to the surface and automatically dumped it into the giant hopper where it would be parceled out to rows of waiting train cars. While the process of dumping kept the few men present occupied, Williams moved briskly to the hoist operator's shack.

"What'cha want, soldier?" the man bellowed over the din.

"A moment of your time," Williams said, pulling out a sheet of paper. "Here's an order from Judge Jennings, countersigned by Superintendent Kinzie, authorizing me to set up an ammo dump in some of your empty stopes."

The man peered uncertainly at the typewritten letter. "It could be Andrew Carnegie hisself givin' me a million dollars for all I know. I can read numbers and sign my name, that's it." He grinned. "So where down there do you want to take that case of explosives?"

"The highest level will be fine, that way we don't take up more of your time than necessary."

"Don't matter to me, soldier. It all goes on the time sheet. There's just you? Not much of an ammo dump."

"More will follow." Williams patted the case. "This is more symbolic than practical."

"Oh, yeah. Symbolic. Go ahead and step onto the lift, I'll have O'Meara, the cageman, put you off at the first level. You do whatever he tells ya. Got it?"

"Got it. Thanks."

The din nearly drove him mad as he stepped into the grimy, dented, steel lift. The bright lights and inky shadows cast O'Meara as a troll from a wood engraving.

"Who the hell are you and where do ya think yer goin'?" O'Meara growled.

Williams pointed to the lift shack and the operator flashed O'Meara a thumbs up.

"Git over here away from the edge," O'Meara said in a less threatening growl. "Don't wanna get that fancy uniform all smeared with rock and blood."

"You're right about that," Williams agreed.

O'Meara pulled on a chain. With a lurch the lift dropped into blackness. Abruptly the lift stopped and O'Meara unhooked the chain across the entrance to the first level.

Williams stepped over the eight inches of space and into the adit. O'Meara re-attached the guard chain and gave the signal chain a solid jerk. The lift dropped away and all Williams could see was the great maw of the shaft, heavy steel cables popping each other, and a steady, small stream of water and light debris falling into the depths.

With an effort he pulled himself away from the shaft, already seeing it as the gate to hell. The barrage of noise seemed far less down here. The adit stretched out ahead of him. To one side lay a set of rails where ore carts once ran, paralleled by a well-worn path, the result of muckers trudging back and forth all the days and nights it took to empty this level of gold-bearing ore.

Through a curtain of detachment from reality, Williams felt a fierce sense of elation building within him. Finally he stood at the culmination of his mission. He could do it by himself after all.

Krause deserved his bullets, he thought. *After all, he was a deserter. Lepke will be the next to die.*

He followed the tracks to the second stope and entered the vast, dark space. Williams sat the dynamite case on the hewn rock floor and located the hand torch. As he flashed the beam around, examining the empty stope, he noticed the voices.

Perhaps it was merely the acoustics in the dome of rock, but he distinctly heard whispers. He stopped moving, straining to hear what they said. It reminded him of the frustration of trying to listen to a conversation through a hotel wall.

The words themselves eluded him, but the rise and fall of conversation swooped and soared through the stope, audible bats constantly darting out of reach. Williams elected to ignore the voices and concentrated on finding the perfect location to place the dynamite. He played the torch light over the hanging wall separating him and the miles of shafts from the saltwater of Gastineau Channel.

The top of the stope loomed about sixty meters over him. He decided the channel hugged the entire rear wall of the chamber. Therefore, he could firmly place the charge at the juncture of wall and floor.

"I really haven't much other choice," he said to himself, listening to his words echo through the whispers. He thought back to Bulldozer Mulrooney's explanation of the mining process and its inherent dangers.

Suddenly he heard the steady drip of water through the whispers and background rumbling of the mining operations. He followed the sound to its source, very near the back wall. Water seeped out of the wall about three meters above the floor, staining the rock for the space of a meter before disappearing through the floor.

Williams examined the floor and found where the water seeped back into the rock, presumably to leak farther down into the mine.

This must be the weakest portion of the wall, he thought. *The very spot to place the charge.*

He carried the case over and carefully lifted the pre-wired explosives out and pressed them against the wall. Methodically he braided an hour's worth of fuse onto the bundle and unrolled the rest across the floor. In moments he found enough rubble to completely bury the charge, hoping it would help direct the force of the blast into the wall.

He closed the empty case and carried it across the chamber, setting it near the entrance. He knelt and struck a match, held it to the end of the fuse. The vibrant fizz quickly became lost in the general growling, whispering ambiance of the stope. Williams hurried toward the lift.

139 —Treadwell, A.T., April 20, 1917—
Friday late afternoon

David Keith watched the sergeant wave and hurry off toward the waterfront. He'd put in four years as a soldier, getting out in '10. Try as he might, he could never recollect a sergeant doing manual labor when there was a private or a corporal in the area.

"Well, maybe they were all diggin' ditches somewheres else," he said to the levers as he dropped O'Meara and the lift down to the 2,500 foot level. The intricate demands of his job kept his attention for the next half hour. The door opened and he glanced over to see Mr. King, the shift foreman.

"Thought it was that sergeant coming back," Keith said with a grin.

"Sergeant? What sergeant is that?"

"The one settin' up the ammo dump on the first level."

"Ammo dump!"

Quickly Keith explained. "He had a piece o' paper signed by Judge Jennings and Mr. Kinzie hisself, Mr. King."

"How well do you read?"

"Not much," Keith admitted.

"Have you ever seen Superintendent Kinzie's signature before?"

"Once or twice."

"Judge Jennings' signature?"

"Uh, never."

"So it could have been a forgery, couldn't it?"

Keith nodded unhappily, responding to another request from below he started the lift toward the surface. "But why would he want to do something like that if the army wasn't behind it?"

"We're at war. He could be a saboteur."

"Here, at the Treadwell?" Keith grinned with the idea of it. "We're a hell of a long way from France."

"Just the same, I'm going down and look around. First level, you said?"

"Yes, sir."

King opened the door and a heavy tremor shook the shack. Suddenly a cloud of smoke boiled out of the main shaft and dissipated into the dark sky.

"That was a charge going off!" King yelled. "A damn big one."

"Should I finish the dump before you go down?" Keith asked, feeling his stomach clench. Getting fired from the Treadwell was almost as bad as getting a blue ticket from the cops— you were finished in the community.

"No, hold it at the surface." King darted into the shack and grabbed the telephone. "Kirby, get a couple of good men and meet me at the main lift as soon as you can get here."

"Mr. King, I—"

"Save it, Keith. This is as much my fault as anyone's. I should have issued instructions covering this sort of thing. Nobody else goes down that shaft unless you know them or they're with a foreman."

"Yes, sir."

"Even if they have a note from President Wilson."

"Yes, sir."

"There's Kirby." King darted out of the door and with the other three men clambered onto the load of ore already in the lift. When he waved, Keith sent them down to the first level and held the lift there in readiness while they investigated.

Minutes creaked by as he watched the clock on the wall above the window. *This ain't gonna look good on my record,* he thought. *I'm gonna find that damn sergeant and break his*— The bell rang. First level. Wants to go to second level. Keith dropped the lift to the second level, held it there. *—break his gawddamned head for him. Then I'll take what's left down to the channel and find myself a crab trap, and—*

The bell rang again. Second level to surface. He pulled one lever toward him and eased the clutch lever off so the lift wouldn't jerk the men all over the place.

Once at the surface, King hurried back into the shack. "It could be worse. There's an eight-square-foot chunk blown out of the hanging wall, and it's leaking, but there was a leak there before and this didn't seem to make it any worse."

"Thank God," Keith said, feeling faint from relief.

"I'll send some engineers down tomorrow to take another look at it. I'll need you to stop at the office after your shift and dictate what you told me to Morgan, so we can get a report out immediately."

"I'll be there, Mr. King. I'm real sorry this happened—"

King cut him off with a wave. "Me too." He hurried off toward his office.

On the first level, three hundred feet below the surface, the rock in the wounded stope slowly adjusted to the lack of support. With creaks and ticks, the rock settled in tiny, minute movements. The blast had microscopically widened the crack in the hanging wall through which seawater leaked.

The crack now widened in such a way that water ran farther down inside the wall, eroding portions just inches from the blasted face of the stope. The explosion had hurled the debris that covered the charge into the roof and walls of the cavern like quartz bullets. Some of the roof areas hit by the debris fractured, tiny granules of rock trickled down, creating space between larger pieces.

The rock surface between the main lift and the beach had rested on a large block of gold-bearing quartz for eons. The same block of quartz that had been weakened first by the sinking of the main shaft, and then weakened more by the drifts, adits, and stopes blasted out of it. Now it settled even more.

The surface, the beach, sagged a few inches. The smallest amount of pressure would overload the depleted block of quartz. The thick rock surface weighed thousands of tons.

The tide in Gastineau Channel neared its ebb. The next tide would reach higher on the massive slab. The tide after that was the spring tide, the highest of the year, and it would push seawater to within thirty feet of the mouth of the main shaft.

In twenty-eight hours the weight on the crumbling quartz would be increased by multiple tons of salt water.

140 —Juneau City, A.T., April 20, 1917—
Friday late night

Horst von Hesse peered through binoculars at the area around the Treadwell main lift. He expected chaos, mass consternation, and emergency actions. But— nothing!

"Perhaps the charge didn't go off. Maybe the dripping water extinguished the fuse . . ." he spoke aloud to the night, standing on the beach, flanked by the dark forest.

The voices murmured something he didn't quite catch.

What had gone wrong? Perhaps someone found the sputtering fuse and put it out? Had it detonated to no effect?

That meant he would have to go back, use everything he had left. He had four more cases of dynamite, but how would he regain entry to the mine? With four cases to move he could not do it alone.

Who? All his confederates were dead. There wasn't time to search out another Sommers or Krause. "They were all incompetent anyway," he said with a hiss, lowering the binoculars.

Hesse pulled the skiff up into the brush and covered it with deadfall. He trudged back to the cabin concocting one plan after another, rejecting all of them. Finally he realized he wouldn't be able to get back into the Treadwell. He had failed to complete his mission. Bitter frustration welled up, eating at his mind.

"Lepke. That *verdammter* Lepke!" he screamed. "Once and for all, I will deal with him."

As Hesse mulled his options he felt the old familiar sense of heightened awareness, sharper senses of smell and hearing. Over the last few years— since he started killing men— his interest in women had abated. To be sure, if one was at hand and willing, he enjoyed sexual victory.

He much preferred taking the life of a man, especially men who were in their physical prime, constituted a challenge, and, preferably, were armed. He realized his heart pounded at a furious rate.

How to kill Lepke? He knew the officer was always armed. The previous attempts on his life probably made Lepke extremely aware of his surroundings.

A trap, Hesse decided, was the answer, but what should he use as bait? Himself? Surely Lepke would bring a squad of officers and overwhelm him with sheer numbers.

Simple assassination wouldn't do in this case. Jack Malone had been different; Jack had broken faith and become a traitor. Lepke represented the most challenging sport to date.

At the cabin, Hesse stripped off the uniform, threw it on the floor. He wistfully thought about the luggage left in his small hotel room, but knew the police had probably confiscated all of his belongings by now.

Belongings. Lepke and Florence Malone had become engaged. If anything would cause Lepke to lose perspective and do something rash, it would be a threat to Miss Malone.

Hesse grinned wolfishly. Killing a woman held no abhorrence for him. In fact, the thought of killing Amanda Ganbor nearly made him giddy.

"No," he said to the cabin. "Lepke first, and Florence Malone if need be." Anyone else, he decided, would be icing on the confection.

141 —Juneau City, A.T., April 21, 1917—
Saturday morning

As Florence Malone unlocked the shop door at Winter & Pond, she remembered her employers were away. The men owned a cabin on the Taku River, some twenty-five miles from Juneau, where they took fishing holidays. Mrs. Winter and the children often joined them.

Mr. Pond had no family, being one of those set-in-his-ways bachelors who seemed to proliferate the territory. At any rate, Florence realized, she would be on her own today.

The brief tourist season wouldn't begin until late May or early June. She didn't expect many customers, since the day dawned sunny and warm even though snow still lurked in shaded areas. She immediately fell into her daily routine of sweeping, dusting, and arranging items to conform to her sense of balance.

In two more days she would become Mrs. August Lepke. Try as she might, she couldn't resist smiling. *How odd,* she thought. *I always thought Fiona would be the first to marry, the only one of us to marry, and now...*

Fiona and Amanda had arranged for her wedding dress, which they presented to her last night. She looked beautiful in it, and she had never felt that way about herself before. Other matters she had avoided contemplating also came to mind lately.

August knew she wasn't a virgin and he admitted he wasn't either, but there had only been one person for each before this. It doesn't signify, she decided.

The prospect of having a sexual life thrilled her more than she would ever admit. She wondered how he looked naked, and giggled. She felt she walked on air.

She finished the chores and went into the back shop to check the chemical inventory. Halfway down the list she heard the bell on the front door ring as someone entered. She dusted off her hands and hurried out.

"Oh, it's you, Trevor."

"Hi, Miss Malone," said the thirteen-year-old. "I need a quart of fixer and twelve sheets of printing paper."

"Taken any good views lately?" she asked as she gathered his supplies.

"I carried my big camera up Mt. Roberts the other day," he said breathlessly. "Got some nifty views of Juneau and Treadwell."

"You certainly have more energy than I do." By touch, Florence transferred the dozen sheets of light-sensitive paper from one box to another in the dark bag. She closed both boxes and then pulled them out into the light.

She tied a sturdy cord around the box for Trevor. "Do you want me to put that on your bill?"

"Yes, please. Father said he'd settle with Mr. Winter at the end of the month."

"That's fine." She handed him the dark brown bottle and the box. "Are you coming to my wedding?"

"Mother and Father are," he said, coloring slightly. "I haven't decided yet."

"I'd be ever so grateful if you could take some candid views of the ceremony and reception."

He brightened. "I hadn't thought of that. Mostly I take scenics, but I could try. I can't promise what the results will be."

"I'm not asking for guarantees. I know you're a good photographer. I would be proud to have 'Trevor Davis, Photographer' on the corner of my wedding views."

"Thanks, Miss Malone. I'll be there."

Florence went into the back to finish her inventory as Trevor left the shop. She realized she left her list and pencil on the counter in the front. She turned and took one step, running full into a man.

"Ohmigawd!" she blurted, stepping back, her heart pounding. "I didn't hear you come in. You startled me so."

He stood in the small shadowed hall, his features obscured. She took in his rough clothing, the faint miasma of body odor mixed with old fish. His complete stillness unnerved her.

"Wh-what can I do for you, sir?"

"Call Mr. Lepke. Tell him your life is in danger and he is to come at once."

Florence blinked, not placing the voice, and not sure she really heard him correctly. "Is, is this a practical joke of some sort? Who are you?"

He stepped forward. She immediately stepped back, maintaining the distance between them. When he took the second step, light washed over his features.

She automatically stepped back again, staring at the dark eyes, the close-shaven face, the scarred cheek. "Arnold Williams?" she said unbelievingly.

"Not any longer. My name is Horst von Hesse. I am here on a mission for General Ludendorf and the Imperial German Army."

"Did he tell you to murder my father?" she spat, rage lifting up out of her soul like lava from the volcanoes she had read about in college. She stepped toward him and he stepped back into the shadow. "Did he tell you to murder poor Jim Kisadis?"

She took another step forward and he automatically retreated. "Did your general tell you to murder people who couldn't fight back?" she screamed. "You filthy bastard!"

Light exploded in her brain and she slowly realized she lay on the shop floor. Her face felt numb, strange, and she touched it. Her fingers came away bloody.

Arnold, no, von something German, stood above her staring down. He held a gun in his hand. "Can you hear me?" he asked, his voice echoed.

"Yes?" she said. Her voice sounded weak to her.

"I'm sorry I had to strike you, but you didn't do as I asked. Now, I want you to get up and call Lieutenant Lepke."

"So you can kill him, too?"

His eyes grew colder, something she hadn't believed possible.

"You're going to kill both of us, aren't you? That's why you told me who you really are."

"If you don't call him I will shoot you right now."

Florence's heart beat so hard she thought it would burst from her chest. She didn't want to die, but this madman was going to kill her whether she called August or not. She shook her head.

"*Vas?* You refuse!" He leveled the weapon at her head and his thumb clicked something on its side.

142 —Juneau City, A.T. April 21, 1917—
Saturday afternoon

"Lieutenant, there's a kid here wants to see you."

Lepke looked up from his paper work. A skinny boy stood fidgeting in the doorway. "I'm Lepke. What can I do for you?"

"I know who you are, lieutenant. You're Miss Malone's fiancé. She asked me to take some views of your wedding."

"Who are you?"

"Trevor Davis, I'm a photographer, but that's not why I stopped."

August nodded.

"I stopped in to the shop to buy some stuff, and when I opened the door to go out, a man pushed by me and went in."

"So?"

"I heard a click, a loud one. So I looked back and the man had turned the sign over."

"What sign?"

"The sign that says whether they're open or closed. He turned it so it said closed."

Lepke stood up, reaching for his coat. "What did he look like?"

"A fisherman. Smelled like fish, too."

August left the office at a run. The streets and boardwalks were crowded and he knocked down at least three men, perhaps more, he didn't keep count. Twenty feet from Winter & Pond's, he slid to a stop.

Walking at a normal pace he passed in front of the shop. He didn't turn his head to peer into the business, but scanned the window with his peripheral vision. No movement he could discern.

August walked around the corner to the back door. The door would be locked. As a lieutenant in the JPD, he had a passkey which could open any business in the down town area.

Pressing his ear against the back door, he listened intently for noise. Nothing. Are they even in there?

Carefully, quietly, he eased the key into the lock and pulled the door tight against the jamb as he gently turned it. A faint click told him the door could be opened. He pulled his .455 Bulldog revolver from his shoulder holster, cocked it, and opened the door.

The door swung inward and he slid through the smallest opening possible. He pushed the door shut but not enough to latch. Stacks of boxes on either side made for a sound-muffling, high-walled passageway.

August slowly moved toward the turn at the far wall, approximately twelve feet away. As he neared the turn, he heard a low voice but couldn't make out the words.

A man's voice, he decided.

Suddenly Florence's voice, clear and sharp, "You're going to kill both of us, aren't you? That's why you told me who you really are."

The other voice mumbled again and August pressed himself into the darkest part of the passageway as he turned the corner. The storeroom joined the lab and back shop area through an open door. Light streamed through the opening; once he entered he would be visible to anyone in the next room.

"*Vas?* You refuse!" August instantly recognized the voice of Arnold Williams. He also heard the sound of a safety clicking off.

August crouched down and leaned into the doorway, revolver clutched in both hands. Florence lay on the floor six feet away. Williams stood over her, pointing a Luger at her head.

Williams caught August's movement out of the corner of his eye. Without a word he brought the pistol up and, as fast as he could pull the trigger, fired three rounds at August.

The first bullet sliced across August's right bicep. The burning pain of the wound made him jerk the Bulldog up and to the right. He fired a shot and bobbed back out of the door way. He knew he had missed.

The ringing boom of the .455 made hearing difficult for a few moments. He heard Williams shout something. Didn't catch it.

"What?" he shouted.

"You have obstructed me for the last time, Lepke! Today you die."

"Florence!" August yelled. "Are you all right?" He shrugged out of his suit jacket and glanced at his wounded arm.

"Yes, my love." He could hear the fear in her voice.

"This is between you and me, Williams. Get her out of the line of fire!" Although the wound created a great deal of pain, he observed it wasn't very deep, even though it bled profusely.

"Why should I? She means nothing to me, and everything to you. Dispatching her would put you at an emotional disadvantage."

"Is this what they taught you in Berlin, *Hauptmann* Horst von Hesse? That killing unarmed civilians was the duty of an Imperial Hussar?" August ripped his shirtsleeve off and tied it around his arm above the wound.

Silence stretched for what seemed hours.

"How did you know that?" Hesse said in a conversational tone.

"Your consul in Seattle kept excellent records which he neglected to destroy before he was interned. The FBI has a complete list of every German agent in North America. You cannot escape." The blood flow slowed to a trickle.

"If you think I'm going to surrender to be hung at a later date, you're even thicker than I thought."

"So you're going to murder more innocent people and pretend you're a real soldier?"

"You are the enemy!" Hesse screamed. "You are all the enemy!"

"Not everyone is a soldier, *Herr Hauptmann*. Since when did an honorable soldier make war on non-combatants?"

"This is my battlefield. I am striking a blow for the Fatherland!"

"I thought you were going to blow up the Treadwell. What happened? Couldn't manage that?"

"I didn't use enough dynamite yesterday," Hesse said bitterly.

"So that was you down on the first level?"

"*Ja.* The rock wall is thicker than your head."

August examined everything in the storeroom, seeking an advantage. Nothing here but photographic supplies. Chemicals, paper, various cast iron stands, magnesium powder and potassium chlorate— flash powder!

August silently crept over to the heavy cardboard canister, slowly removing the lid.

"If you come through the door," Hesse called, ". . . I will only shoot you and not Miss Malone."

"Do I have your word on that?" August picked up the five-pound canister and positioned it under his left arm. To dump the contents all he had to do was tilt it downward.

"Yes. You have my word."

"Then have her move out of the line of fire. I don't want her getting hit with a ricochet."

August felt the man hesitate, looking for tricks, trying to decide how this could be turned against him. August tried to remember what he knew about flash powder. Could he use too much?

"Move over there, against that wall," Hesse said.

August heard Florence get to her feet and move to his left, away from the small passageway leading to the show room. *At least she's not between us,* he thought.

"I've done as you asked, *Herr* Lepke. Now please come and keep your part of the bargain."

"Very well," August said, dumping a small pile of flash powder in the middle of the doorway.

"What— " Hesse blurted.

August stepped back away from the pile, aimed his revolver at it, and squeezed his eyes shut before he pulled the trigger. The boom deafened him in the small room and the sudden "whoof" of flash powder scorched his pants leg and brightly illuminated the blood in his eyelids.

Hesse bellowed in confusion. August dropped the canister and plunged through the door, immediately dodging to the right. Hesse, momentarily blinded, fired three shots through the empty doorway.

With an overhand swing, August brought his revolver down on Hesse's gun hand. At the last instant Hesse pulled back and August's revolver landed squarely on the barrel of the Luger, snapping it out of the man's hand.

Hesse instantly plunged through the passageway into the show room.

August hesitated long enough to ask Florence, "Are you hurt?"

"Nothing serious. Be careful!"

Her words followed him through the passageway. He burst into the show room and stopped himself by grabbing the doorframe. His gaze moved over the crowded showcases, artifacts, and curios.

Hesse was nowhere to be seen. August could see the front door was still locked. Masks, ladles, bows, spears, and other Tlingit implements and weapons covered the walls. A rank of totem poles of various sizes stood against the wall between showcases. This shop had always reminded him of a small, crowded museum.

The rectangular room held twelve display cases, two, against the far wall, stretched from floor to ceiling, as did two to his left. Between that wall and where he stood the remaining display cases were waist high and arranged in two hollow squares allowing a clerk to work from behind four of them at once. Each set of four cases had enough room between them for a person to move freely through each corner of the square.

August couldn't tell if anything was missing or not, how Hesse may have armed himself, or where he hid.

"Captain, if you don't surrender, I will be forced to shoot you." Nothing moved; the shop sank back into a brick of silence. "I carry a .455 Bulldog revolver. It makes a very large wound."

Silence.

August took another step, which allowed him to see into the middle of the closest square of cases. Nothing. He felt his pulse throbbing in his wound. He constantly ran his gaze back and forth over the entire room, searching for movement or some portion of a human.

He felt his senses sharpen, heard the rattle of a passing gas buggy, almost felt rather than heard the floor beneath him creak as he shifted his weight. The burned residue of the magnesium stung his nostrils, masking other odors. His Bulldog revolver seemed heavier than he remembered.

The constant pain in his arm tried to dominate his mind. He took another step, sweeping his eyes across new space. His nose itched and he wanted to wipe his brow. He realized sweat inched down out of his hairline. August opened his mouth to breathe as breathing through his nostrils seemed far too loud. His tongue tasted brassy.

Where was Hesse?

He glanced at the cases to his left. Nothing. *Where would I hide?*

He thought back at how much time had elapsed between knocking the Luger out of Hesse's hand and August arriving in this room. Five seconds? Ten seconds?

That ruled out the far bank of display. Not enough time. The quarry was much closer. August took another step.

From between the wall cases to his left, motion blurred in his peripheral vision. He swung his weapon to bear and a numbing blow broke his left forearm. In reflex he squeezed the Bulldog's trigger and fired a bullet into the ceiling.

Hesse swung the Tlingit war club again. Gasping in pain, August ducked and the blow missed his head, but it hit his revolver, knocking it out of his hand to smash through a glass showcase. Hesse immediately pulled the club back for another swing.

August threw himself forward onto the floor as the club cut the air over his head. His left arm felt molten with pain and his right hand still stung from his weapon being knocked away. The wound on his right bicep throbbed in cadence with his hammering heart. He rolled over and the war club crashed down in the space just vacated.

August kicked out and hit Hesse a glancing blow on the knee. The agent pulled back with a gasp of pain. August rolled over and scuttled between two display cases.

He searched for a weapon while watching for Hesse. A long wooden rod tipped with a two-pronged hook hung in a clamp behind the case. August remembered seeing Florence lift out-of-reach items off the wall with it.

He grabbed the rod and tried to hold it in both hands. His left arm radiated more agony and he rested the staff in his left hand for balance. He quickly stood with the staff in front of him. Hesse instantly swung the war club, hitting the rod in the middle, shearing it in half.

August dropped the left half of the rod and jerked back as Hesse swung downward, smashing the glass top of the display case, destroying a row of Native-made dolls in traditional dress. For the first time, August got a good look at the club. Brutal, with three stone blades set into the heavy wood handle. A wrist loop swung unused at the butt of the weapon.

Breathing heavily, Hesse maneuvered between the cases and swung again. August parried the blow, knocking the club to the side. Immediately he followed through with a swing at Hesse's head, which the man easily dodged.

Hesse brought the club up and caught the rod squarely, knocking it up out of August's hand to crash against the wall. August knew he couldn't move fast enough to get out of range of the next blow. He futilely crossed his arms over his face as Hesse pulled the club back in perfect batter's stance, a rictus grin smearing his face.

He completed the back swing and the club began its forward surge when Hesse jerked, his body locked up, and a surprised expression flooded over his face.

August watched as the man let the club drop from still-curled fingers and twisted to look behind him. Florence stood in the passageway, an Indian bow in her right hand. An arrow stuck out of Hesse's back, buried between his shoulder blades.

Florence already had a second arrow nocked on the string. Her eyes seemed to burn across the room at them, blood smeared from her nose across part of her face, staining the bodice of her dress. "*That's* for my father," she said, pulling back the second arrow.

She aimed and released the string. "*This* is for Jim Kisadis!"

The arrow thudded into Hesse's right side just under his arm. "Millie!" he said in a croaking voice, and fell to the floor.

August knelt beside him, touched the arrow piercing the chest, felt the heart at the other end of the shaft quiver and cease. August clutched the showcase and pulled himself up. He stared at the woman he loved with new eyes.

"Do I need to shoot him again?" she asked.

"No. He's dead. Where did you learn to shoot like that?"

"Archery class at college. At the time I felt it a wasted effort." She chewed at her lower lip, tears glinted in her shadowed eyes.

August moved past Hesse's corpse, between the cases, to stand in front of Florence. "Are you all right?"

"I killed a man," she said with a sniff. "Must you arrest me now?"

He put his right arm around her and hugged her to him, ignoring the pain and laughing. "Never, you fantastic, surprising creature."

He heard the bow fall to the floor and she embraced him, crying. "Oh, thank God, he's dead."

August patted her back, whispered in her ear, "Thank you for saving my life."

"Any time," she said with a sniff. "Now will you marry me?"

"Right on schedule."

Pounding on the front door broke the embrace. Patrolman Buhrman peered through the glass as August unlocked and opened the door.

"We got reports of a gunshot, lieutenant."

"Williams is dead," August said. "My left arm is broken, my right arm has a flesh wound. I'll be up at the hospital."

"Have you considered just renting a room up there?" Buhrman asked with a grin.

Florence, following August out the door, looked over her shoulder and said, "No, that won't do, Officer Buhrman. He's moving in with me."

143 —Treadwell, A.T., April 22, 1917—
1:00 AM Sunday morning

The tide inched up the beach on Douglas Island. The great slab of rock under the sand settled lower, easing down into space recently vacated by the steady trickle of quartz pebbles, greenstone shards, and assorted fractured debris. The crack in the wall on the first level had widened to the point that a steady stream of water now poured into the abandoned stope.

The engorged stream further eroded the fissure, strengthening the flow, which accelerated the rate of erosion. The wound had escalated into a hemorrhage. Water filled the floor of the stope, ran out into the passageway, and poured down the shaft of the main lift.

On the surface the tide continued inward. Tons of seawater pressed down on the rock slab. In the depths of the mine, at the 2,300-foot level, the blasting crews detonated their explosives, creating loose ore for the day shift to muck.

When the powder men ascended on the main lift, they endured the heavy volume of water pouring down from the first level. Once they reached the surface, the shift foreman was called.

At 1:30 AM, the rock surface shifted and dropped three feet.
The men grouped around the main shaft felt what they believed to be a light earthquake. Seawater commenced pouring into the main lift shaft from the surface.

Livingston Wernecke held the title of chief geologist for the Treadwell. Due to a massive cave-in of stopes in 1913, F.W. Bradley, president of the Alaska Treadwell Gold Mining Company hired him in 1915 to study the subsidence problem and make recommendations. In October 1916, he submitted a plan to the Board of Directors.

He had surveyed all surface buildings for cracks, finding many. Every level of the mine underwent inspection. He found glacial boulders at the 700-foot level that had fallen from the surface.

The pumps of the Treadwell, Mexican, and 700 Mines pumped a total of 379 gallons of water a minute to keep the water level down. Wernecke told the Board if they continued existing practices, the mines would flood. He told them how to save the complex: bulkhead all levels above the 1,550-foot level joining the three mines; fill all open stopes with tailings to prevent further cave-ins; search for the fault allowing salt water into the mines and build a coffer dam around it; and fill 300 feet of Gastineau Channel along the beach with tailings from the mines.

The Board agreed to his plan. The schedule would be completed by December 1919.

"Let's get out of here. The whole mine is caving in!" Wernecke shouted to the cageman, Enrico Vienono.

Vienono tugged the bell cord three times and the lift ascended through a growing stream of water, sand, and rock. Wernecke had spent the last six hours in the depths of the Treadwell, trying to assess damage and figure out a way to stop the sudden calamity.

One thing he hadn't planned on was somebody trying to blow the mine up. The blast on the first level had become the linchpin of disaster. The cage stopped at the 900-foot level.

Cold water fell in a four-inch sheet from the surface. Suddenly two men dove through the sheet and into the cage.

"Just us," shouted stope boss Jack Conley.

"Yah!" Lars Nielson, pump man, yelled, his large frame shivering. "Git us outta here, by golly."

The carbide lamp illuminating the cage flickered under the deluge of water and sand. Vienono reached for the bell chain as a cascade of water and rock sprayed over the cage, knocking him to his knees.

"I'll get it!" Conley yelled. The increasing din of the collapsing mine thundered around them. Wernecke thought the noise was worse than walking through the main bank of crushers.

The lift lurched and started upward, picking up speed quickly.

"Is the night shift all out?" Conley shouted.

"Brought the last load up fifteen minutes ago," Vienono yelled. "We're the tail on the dog."

Wernecke felt exhausted, filthy, and useless. At least he felt safe now that the lift neared the surface.

The lift stopped with a bounce and fell.

All four men shouted in fear. The lift dropped about twenty feet and ground to a halt as the emergency dogs grabbed on the heavy cables. The carbide light guttered and went out, leaving them in total dark and din.

"What happened?" Conley bellowed.

"I dunno!" Vienono yelled back. "This don't never happen before." Icy water and grit splashed off the framework of the cage, soaking them. The noise continued to mount in volume.

"Maybe the lift works caved in!" Conley shouted. "Maybe it's gonna come down on top of us."

"Shut up!" Wernecke shouted into the dark. "Things are bad enough without us getting panicked!"

"What is that stink?" Vienono asked.

Wernecke sniffed, recoiled from the heavy odor of feces.

"I think I shit myself," Nielson muttered.

Wernecke wished himself out of here. He knew himself at twenty-eight to be the youngest man in the cage, thought fleetingly about his wife and daughter at home. *What a worthless way to die.*

Vienono mumbled in Italian and Wernecke thought it sounded like praying.

"Wonder how long it will take for the water to rise," Conley said in the darkness.

Wernecke didn't say anything, even though he just had the same thought. Bits of sand and rock stung his face and the cold from the wet walls seemed to seep into his marrow. He shivered.

The lift jerked and again the men all cried out. The cage moved and for a moment Wernecke thought they were falling.

"We're going up!" Conley said, wonder in his voice. "That's the first time in my life I ever had a prayer answered!"

Wernecke squinted up into the darkness, seeking light but only getting grit in his eyes. The cage seemed to increase speed. Abruptly they broke into clear air and electric light.

The cage shuddered to a stop and all four men rushed out onto the surface. A hand fell on Wernecke's shoulder.

"Thought we lost you down there," Tom Wayland, an engineer, said.

"You weren't the only one!" Wernecke said, shivering in the raw air. "Any blankets around here?"

Wayland shouted to someone and in moments Wernecke wrapped himself in heavy wool.

"We've lost her, Tom," he said, staring at the constantly widening mouth of the main shaft. Seawater poured in through a growing breach to the channel.

"Yeah, I know," Wayland said. "Me and Charlie Horner spent half the night down there trying to figure out how to save her."

"Get back!" someone shouted and the crowd of men hurriedly moved away from the edge.

A geyser of seawater shot into the air from the center of the shaft. The spout topped out 200 feet above the shaft head frame and dropped back into the hole. A slice of embankment between the shaft and the beach suddenly caved in.

The Natatorium, a fully equipped gymnasium complete with a swimming pool, creaked and groaned on the lip of newly lost ground. Boards popped and snapped around the base of the building.

Suddenly the structure lost definition, and instantly turning into a pile of debris, slid into the hole. On the other side of the streaming maw, the firehouse went into the water and disappeared. More of the surface gave way and sank under the roaring current.

"I once saw the Yukon at White Horse rapids," Wayland said. "This is just as big and just as fast."

Another piece of ground vanished and raw earth gleamed under the concrete foundation of a huge oil tank. The side of the tank bulged and dipped, suddenly splitting open and releasing thousands of gallons of raw crude oil once destined for boilers.

The stink of the crude smothered the tang of salt air, adding yet another dimension of tragedy to the scene.

Wernecke heard Conley somewhere in the crowd. "That fookin' hole is swallowing our whole lives!"

A fitting epitaph, Wernecke thought.

144 —Juneau City, A.T., April 23, 1917—
Monday afternoon

"Ain't that just the damnedest thing?" George Mak-we said. "That stinking Hun did it after all."

August said nothing, intent on fixing his boutonniere with one hand.

"Here, let me help you with that," George said. He hooked his cane over his forearm and quickly pinned the flower on August's suit coat.

August let his free hand fall to his side. His left arm throbbed inside its heavy cast. August had refused all pain-killers for fear he would become even more tongue-tied than usual. The two men stood next to the Cathedral of the Nativity of the Blessed Virgin Mary under a clear sky in warm sunshine.

Juneau approached a record high temperature for the date.

August thought George looked quite the gent in his matching three-piece suit. "The rings you have?"

George squinted at him. "How many times you gonna ask me that?"

"Sorry. I wish this to end. I mean start."

Begay Santo stepped out of the side door; his usher's sash giving him added authority. "Father Mulcahey says he's ready for the victim, I mean, groom."

George laughed and the men stepped through the door. August glanced around. People packed every pew, and he knew them all by sight.

In front of the altar stood Father Mulcahey and Fiona Malone, the maid of honor. She looked stunning in a frilly gown of spun blue. August was surprised that Fiona didn't have men falling at her feet in droves.

Father Mulcahey wore a tight smile. "Do you still want to take the leap, Mr. Lepke?"

"I do," August said firmly.

The priest laughed. "Well, you have your lines memorized."

"Wait till you see her, August," Fiona said. "And, for that matter, wait until she sees *you*."

August glanced over the congregation. In the front pew Rev. James Thistle sat beside his wife, Amanda and Julia Mak-we. Both women held babies.

An omen, August thought. Next to them sat Irene Kisadis with her daughter, Ruth Santo, large with child. August rolled his eyes.

He let his gaze wander over the other pews. Chief Tinsley; Sergeant Harrington in his army uniform; Patrolman Delmar Buhrman; Max and Edna Hastain; John Price; Michael and Marla Christenson; Dr. Parker; Keith Busch with his wife, Kimberly; Jee-nak; India Spartz, the Territorial Librarian; Tim McDaniel, Jack Malone's lawyer; Sean Clancy; Harry Jenkins; Colette Herring, the—

The organist launched into the "Wedding March" and every head turned to watch Florence enter. She wore a white, many-layered gown, which made August

think of an angel wrapped in clouds. He noticed the bruise on her cheek had vanished or else hid behind expert use of cosmetics.

He felt like the luckiest man in the world. To either side of her walked her escorts, Lloyd Winter and Percy Pond. Trevor Davis stood, looked through the finder on his box camera, tripped the shutter and sat down next to his parents.

When Florence neared August, Mr. Winter and Mr. Pond stopped, bowed from the waist and hurried to their pews. At this distance August could see that over her face Florence wore the sheerest veil he had ever seen. She gave him a dazzling smile.

She leaned over and whispered, "It's all going to be wonderful, isn't it?"

"Of course," August said.

Father Mulcahey made the sign of the cross. The wedding mass began.

THE DAILY ALASKA DISPATCH
Juneau, Alaska, Tuesday, April 24, 1917

EFFECT OF DISASTER TEMPORARY

MINES LOST BUT MEN WILL WORK ON JUNEAU SIDE

SAYS DEPUTY FIRED FIRST

GERMAN AGENT KILLED IN JUNEAU

PLAN TAXES FOR RAISING WAR REVENUE

FIRST LOAN FOR BRITISH

THE BRITISH RESUME DASH IN THE WEST

REPORT BELGIANS IN SERIOUS STATE

GREAT ARMY IS CERTAIN

BIG DINNER FOR BALFOUR

DANISH SHIPS MAKE MONEY

MILLION BOYS FOR FARMING

COLORADO DRY

(Associated Press) DENVER, April 23—Governor Gunter today signed the Prohibition bill, which was passed by the last legislature.

Author's Note

That the Treadwell Gold Mining Company operated from 1883 to 1917 is fact. Edward Krause lived and died as depicted in these pages, with a few embellishments on my part. He was brought to justice through the efforts of a Pinkerton agent whose name I have changed since I fictionalized the rest of his life. With few notable exceptions, the other characters in this novel are the product of my imagination aided by the archives of the Alaska State Historical Library.

With two exceptions, the headlines and articles of the period media are exact quotes. After the cave-in, Stroller White (whom I accurately quote) lived the rest of his life in Juneau. Mining moved across the channel to Juneau and Douglas Island languished.

Today one can walk through Sandy Beach on the south end of Douglas, Alaska and into the heavy brush covering the remains of the Treadwell complex. The walk is worth the effort, for the ghosts still linger.

In the years it took me to write *Treadwell*, I realized the story wasn't complete, that August and Florence, not to mention all the others, still had more of their lives to share. I have outlined three additional novels.

Thane: The Assassination of President Warren G. Harding (1921-1923); *Douglas: The Great Fire* (1935-1937), and; *Juneau: The Plot to Kill FDR* (1942-1945). I call this the *Gastineau Channel Quartet* and hope to have the next novel finished within the next few years.

I would like to express my appreciation to the librarians at the Alaska State Historical Library, who maintain an incredible collection of photographs of the Treadwell in its prime as well as extensive records; to the late Mr. Robert N. DeArmond, "Mr. History" as far as Juneauites are concerned, for the invaluable gift of his extensive files on the Krause case; to the overworked librarians at the University of Washington, Special Colections; to the "can do" librarians at the University of Alaska Fairbanks Archives; and, finally, to David and Brenda Stone for writing their excellent book on mining in Juneau, *Hard Rock Gold*, in which pages I mined the genesis of this novel.

Juneau, Alaska-October 1989 — Las Vegas, Nevada-September 2011

Addendum

In preparing this volume for publication I had help from Walt Boyes, Colette Herring Compton, and my editor, Paula Goodlett. They have my eternal gratitude.

LWC, September 2011

Photo by Delmar Buhrman

Leonard Wayne (Stoney) Compton has had novelettes and short stories published in *Universe 1, Tomorrow, Speculative Fiction, Writers of the Future, Vol. IX* and *Jim Baen's Universe.*

His novel, *Russian Amerika* (Baen Books) was published in 2007 and its sequel, *Alaska Republik*, in February 2011.

He is an Illustrator for the US Navy at NAS Corpus Christi, Texas.

During his 31 years in Alaska he worked as a produce apprentice; shipping & receiving clerk; gandy dancer for the USAF/Alaska Railroad; emergency firefighter for BLM; school bus driver; cameraman and film editor for KTVF-TV in Fairbanks; media specialist for Tanana Chiefs Health Authority; art director for *Tundra Times*, an Alaska Native weekly newspaper; freelance artist in Fairbanks and Juneau; art director for KTOO-FM&TV public broadcasting for Juneau; operated Ptarmigan Ptransport & Ptours in Juneau; was a Motorcoach Commander for Princess Tours; and worked for the Alaska Departments of Fish & Game, and Health & Social Services. For a year and a half he worked for the National Oceanic & Atmospheric Administration at the Alaska Fisheries Science Center in Seattle. For two years he was a Visual Information Specialist for the 6th Combat Training Squadron at Nellis AFB, Nevada where he developed a great appreciation for JTACs.

He is a native of Grand Island, Nebraska. He served an enlistment in the U.S. Navy where he had the honor of being a crewmember on *USS Yorktown, CVS-10*, as well as in VR-24 Detachment in Naples, Italy.

He is the proud father of Sarah Maisie and Danford Gordon.

His fine art has been included in juried shows from New York to Hawai'i, and Alaska to California.

He now lives near Corpus Christi, Texas with his dancer wife Colette, their fluctuating number of cats, and Pullo, their Queensland Blue Heeler.

Photo Credits

ASL: Alaska State Library, Juneau. Alaska
UAF: University of Alaska Archives, Fairbanks, Alaska
UWLSC: University of Washington Libraries, Special Collections, Seattle, Washington
LOC: Library of Congress

Page	Collection	Description	Negative /Locator Number
2	UWLSC	Poppy Dreams/Fran Kunishige	UW 29028z
4	LOC	Pancho Villa and Staff	
6	LOC	The Mexican Rebel Army	
18	ASL	Treadwell General Office, Case & Draper	P39-0968
20	UWLSC	Douglas, Alaska	UW 29022z
22	ASL	Amalgamation Room, Case & Draper	P225-322
30	UWLSC	View down steep street in Juneau	Thwaites 247.426
32	UWLSC	Salmon on cannery floor	UW 29802z
36	ASL	St Ann's Hospital, Douglas	P39-1021
38	ASL	Revilla Hotel	
39	ASL	Steamer Jefferson, Case & Draper	P39-0088
40	UWLSC	N Main looking south	Thwaites 247.429
41	LOC	Alaska Governor's Mansion	
43	UWLSC	View of Juneau from the water	Thwaites 247.521
46	UWLSC	Seattle Police Patrol paddy wagon	SEA 0607
49	LOC	Steamer Humboldt	
50	UWLSC	AK Gastineau housing at Thane	UW 29804z
51	UWLSC	AK Gastineau Mining Co. mill	UW 29805z
54	ASL	1500' level Ready Bullion C&D	P39-0872
56	ASL	Working men's quarters	P75-423
58	ASL	Winter & Pond Store	P87-0995
64	ASL	Auk Village, Juneau – D. Waggoner	P492-11-067
70	UWLSC	Front Street, Juneau	UW 29806z
73	UWLSC	Dock scene, Seward AK	UW 29809z
76	UWLSC	View of street in Juneau 1916	Thwaites 247.643
82	UWLSC	Treadwell dock with railroad tracks	UW 29805z
84	UWLSC	Vanner room	Klondike 29031z
85	ASL	Superintendents residence, Treadwell	P01-0731
86	ASL	Treadwell Office – Louis Pederson	P75-416
88	ASL	Treadwell Club – Case & Draper	P39-0888
97	ASL	Treadwell Store – Louis Pederson	P75-409
99	ASL	Hotel Cain – Case & Draper	P39-0569
107	ASL	Men in gambling hall – Winter & Pond	P87-2565
111	ASL	Valentine Building, 1912	Juneau-Buildings-03
124	ASL	Interior of house of Haida chief	Kasaan-08
138	ASL	Alaskan Hotel	Juneau-Hotels-12
145	ASL	Auke Village – Case & Draper	P39-1172

Page	Collection	Description	Negative/Locator Number
163	UWLSC	Drillers in the Treadwell	Klondike 29028z
166	ASL	Ready Bullion bulkhead – H.F. Snyder	P38-041
167	ASL	Treadwell hoisting engine – C&D	P39-0912
171	LOC	Charles Sulzer	
197	ASL	Front Street, Juneau AK	Juneau-Snow Scenes-35
213	ASL	Interior of Louve Saloon, Juneau	P44-03-178
217	ASL	Winter & Pond Photographic Studio	P87-0991
221	ASL	Treadwell peeling machine – C&D	P39-0907
243	ASL	Rocky Point on Silverbow Basin Rd	P45-0154
245	UWLSC	Perseverance Mine mill	UW 24740z
253	ASL	Juneau Courthouse	Juneau-Courthouse-14
265		Mary Bergmann	
271	ASL	Stope mining – Harry F. Snyder	P38-045
315	ASL	Bartlett Thane – Winter & Pond	P87-2356
318	UWLSC	Gov Strong arriving by boat	Klondike 29036z
325	ASL	Bear Clan hat	P243-3-010
327	LOC	Chief Ano-Tlosh – Winter & Pond	
329	ASL	Taku chief lying in state – W&P	P87-0268
335	UWLSC	St Nicholas Russian Orthodox Church	UW 29800z
342	UWLSC	Baseball game at Treadwell	UW 29557z
505	UWLSC	Night view of Juneau	UW 29803z
544	ASL	Natatorium at Treadwell – W&P	P117-118
544	ASL	Treadwell Natatorium 4/21/17 – Snyder	P38-070
546	UAF	Woman in wedding dress- Albert Johnson	1989-166-410
545	ASL	Treadwell cave-in April 23, 1917	

Over the course of many years I mined many archives for images pertinent to this novel. In the beginning I thoughtlessly copied the image without thought of noting location or ownership. The few images listed here with no collection information are the ones I could not relocate when formatting this manuscript. Any help in this direction would be appreciated.

Made in the USA
Charleston, SC
17 April 2012